NANA

By

EMILE ZOLA

With an Introduction by

JOHN C. LAPP

New York

HARPER & BROTHERS, PUBLISHERS

Library of Congress catalog card number: 56-12648

20208

Introduction

I

During his career Zola frequently felt obliged to deny vigorously that his life had any connection with his novels. He would protest that he was only a journeyman of letters, conscientiously and methodically fulfilling his quota of work each day. "Ah, if you only knew," he wrote to a hostile critic, "how amused my friends are by the stupefying legend the crowd is regaled with every time my name appears in a newspaper! If you only knew that this blood-drinker, this ferocious novelist, is merely a good bourgeois, a studious and painstaking fellow, living quietly in his corner, wrapped up in his convictions!" Behind defensive statements of this kind there also lay a life-long abhorrence for the Romantic theory that the writer and his work are somehow identical. Yet despite his constant struggle for scientific detachment, a knowledge of Zola's life can help us to an understanding of his work.

He was born in Paris in 1840, the son of an Italian father and a French mother. His father died in Aix when Emile was six years old, leaving the boy to be brought up by his mother and grandmother. Without completing school, although he had been a bright student, he returned to Paris with his mother in 1858. Years of genuine privation followed; orphanhood and poverty were to be themes of his novels for which he needed little documentation. Finally, in 1862, he found a position as assistant to the publisher Hachette, and this gave him some time to write. Some of his short stories were published, and finally his first novel, the autobiographical *Confession de*

Claude, appeared in 1866. But royalties were slim, and he yearned to devote himself exclusively to letters: the obvious solution was the press, and by sheer audacity and force of purpose he obtained a post as literary critic on *L'Evénement,* thus beginning a career of journalism that ended only in 1881, when accumulated successes had made him financially independent.

It was after publishing three more minor novels that he had begun laying plans for his life work, the *Rougon-Macquart.* In 1870 he married, setting up the comfortable bourgeois household he was to maintain until his death. The first in the series, *La Fortune des Rougon,* appeared in 1871, and from that time onward, he turned out novels almost yearly until the twentieth and last, *Le Docteur Pascal.*

But the new project went unnoticed, save by admiring colleagues, until the seventh volume, *L'Assommoir,* appeared. This great proletarian novel, which is also a perfect work of art, was an instant success, bringing its author wealth and fame. Although it is seventh in line, *L'Assommoir* is Zola's first truly naturalist novel. Naturalism, a novelistic method Zola invented, is realism with scientific pretensions. The naturalist writer sees man as completely subject to the laws, conditions, and forces of nature. His characters are of necessity victims rather than heroes, slaves not masters of their fate.

Despite earlier Romantic tendencies, encouraged by his omnivorous reading of Musset and Hugo, and it may be, his unhappy adolescence at Aix, Zola had come very early under the influence of the new scientific and social movements of his time. The works of Michelet and Taine had helped to confirm his growing belief in determinism, and more specialized studies such as Prosper Lucas' *Treatise on Natural Heredity,* a now outmoded study, helped to crystallize in Zola's mind his concept of the novel.

Zola's life work, the twenty novels comprising the *Rougon-*

Macquart, clearly reflects its author's scientific goal. The family provides an overall unity, which he later emphasized by including in two of the volumes an elaborate family tree with a tag on every branch explaining, in Lucas' terminology, the various elements of the original stock each character had inherited. At the same time, Zola never neglects the second major influence on man in Taine's famous triad: race, environment, and stage of development, and indeed environment frequently crowds out heredity altogether. In *L'Assommoir,* for instance, Gervaise's fate seems almost entirely due to her miserable life and her husband's inebriety. Her occasional allusions to her parent's drunkenness actually impress the reader only as ignorant superstition.

The last of the series, *Le Docteur Pascal,* appeared in 1893. His next project—*The Three Cities: Lourdes, Rome,* and *Paris* —carried out his idea of the role of the city in modern life already sketched in *Une Page d'Amour.* Henry James, after meeting Zola, said that the only thing that had happened to him was to write the *Rougon-Macquart.* But there were two other events of signal importance: his liaison with Jeanne Rozerot, who bore him two sons and gave him, in his fifties, a new optimism, and the Dreyfus Affair, which coincided with the last volume in *The Three Cities.* There exists much conflicting testimony on his role in this cause célèbre, and recent critics have tended to deprecate it as mere self-aggrandizement. But to the unprejudiced, the record still shows that Zola, at great personal hardship, defended an innocent man against overwhelming odds, and that his stand was consistent with the principles expressed in his work. Indeed, there is something solemnly stirring in the spectacle of this myopic little novelist, emerging from the quiet corner of his study to pit the resources of his writer's craft against bigotry and ignorance, and in the end, to win.

His last novels, in the uncompleted *Four Gospels,* mark a

distinct decline in his powers: besides their abuse of didacticism, they suffer extensively from a defect present in his work from the beginning, but which he had long been able to control, a tendency toward repetition and self-plagiarism. Death interrupted this new project in 1902. It was a death rather typical of those in realistic and naturalist novels—sudden, almost capricious; unattended, unspectacular: death from carbon-monoxide poisoning, caused by a faulty chimney flue.

II

Although since his death Zola's works have continued to be read by a vast public, until recent years he has been neglected or belittled by critics. This lack of critical esteem derived from a number of factors: the inevitable down-grading of reputation that follows the death of important writers, the rise of symbolism, the antipathies aroused by his defense of Dreyfus. Yet novelists have continued to be influenced by Naturalism, both in France and abroad. The works of Jules Romains, Martin du Gard, and more recently, Sartre, unmistakably bear its imprint. Zola is of course the direct ancestor of two generations of American writers: that of Frank Norris and Theodore Dreiser, as well as that represented by Ernest Hemingway and James T. Farrell. And in a recent article on the American novel since the Second World War, Malcolm Cowley has remarked that the Naturalistic method is still that of most modern American novelists. Today, a renewal of interest in Zola as an artist is effectively refuting Martin Turnell's comment in his book on the French novel that "for the most part Zola's novels belong to the study of political and sociological propaganda rather than to the study of fiction."

What elements combined to produce the method which left its mark on so many major novelists, French and foreign? Hippolyte Taine's *Introduction to English Literature* was perhaps the strongest single influence on the young Zola. The works of

Balzac and Flaubert had turned him toward contemporary subjects and the real world; Taine's scientific determinism provided him with the explanation for human character and actions by social forces. Lucas' theories on heredity suggested the unifying element—characteristics transmitted through a family—for the *Rougon-Macquart,* subtitled "The Social and Natural History of a Family under the Second Empire." This epic—which opens with a novel on the Coup d'État of Napoleon the Third, and whose actual climax is the disaster of Sedan, was, Zola announced, to be based on "the clash of ambitions and appetites," those of a family "thrown into the modern world, making superhuman efforts which, because of its own nature and influences which it undergoes, remain unsuccessful." It may approach success, only to fall back again, and in the end produces what Zola calls "moral monstrosities": the priest, the murderer, the artist.

Despite these scientific pretensions, despite the painstaking documentation that preceded each novel as the series progressed, Zola's Romantic, visionary and poetic style persisted, nor did it always remain subservient to his realistic aim. This, perhaps more than any other fact, explains why, of his Naturalist colleagues, and those who became his disciples, Zola alone is eminently readable today. Although his science is dated, his psychology almost nonexistent, he somehow unerringly chose subjects of universal interest, investing them with a special portentousness that made them live. The chief clues to this lasting power as a novelist lie, not in his scientific realism, but in two elements of his art that one may call lyricism and fatalism. The former endows the most drab and mediocre contemporary characters and scenes with an extra dimension, often an archetypal quality. Through the latter, his novels rise above mere scientific determinism to the level of tragedy.

The tragic in literature is of course inseparably linked with the dramatic, and it is not surprising that from the first, Zola conceived of the *Rougon-Macquart* as a drama. In the first publicity notices (which he wrote himself, in 1868), he called it "a series of dramatic episodes, in the form of novels." It was perhaps inevitable then, that in his writing he should lean heavily toward the dramatic or scenic method, which presents the characters directly, reproducing their conversation and gestures at given moments. Of the various results that this method produces one of the most important in Zola is a uniquely personal style which consists of his using the vocabulary of the characters, not only in indirect discourse, but even in passages of narrative or description. Shunning the role of the omniscient author, Zola presents directly not only his characters' actions, but their inner thoughts, and through their "point of view" scenes and events that acquire thereby a special perspective.

One outcome of this method is that it builds a close relationship between character and reader. In Zola, however, this intimacy differs from the one which exists between, say, the reader and Julien Sorel in *The Red and the Black,* although Stendhal also makes us privy to his hero's thoughts. Yet not only does Stendhal himself intervene constantly, but Julien's subtle thought processes keep us forever weighing and interpreting, so that we remain close to the method of the omniscient author because we are constantly learning future plans or actions. Zola's characters never have subtle or far-reaching thoughts, but simply reactions to circumstances as they arise. The inner thoughts of Gervaise in *L'Assommoir* convey little but the hopelessness of her situation. This is no active mind, at grips with a hostile world, but a mere receptacle, moved by the simplest desires, whose only ambition is "to have a decent place to live, not to be beaten, and to die in her own bed." She yields passively to circumstances: "People were wrong to think her strong willed; on the contrary she was quite weak; she let herself be pushed, for fear of troubling anyone," and fearing the future, compares herself to "a penny tossed in the air, that may come down heads or tails."

Very often a novelist's treatment of time can be most significant, and this is true, in a negative way, for Zola. Though on occasion a character like Gervaise may express dread of what is to come, the fatalism in Zola's plots prevents any real feeling of progression in time; one never has, for instance, the Proustian feeling that "time's winged chariot" is bearing the characters on to doom or decay. Zola largely neglects even such a superficial aspect as the historical dating of events. Each novel, though it supposedly portrays some facet of the Second Empire, is actually contemporary to the author's time; each chapter within a novel has a present all its own. Noticing this anachronological quality in *L'Oeuvre,* the novelist and librettist Ludovic Halévy complained to Zola that dates were lacking: "One never knows exactly when you begin, when you end; this produces in the reader an uneasiness, a hindrance, an everlasting question-mark." Zola's reply that circumstances in the novel were dated by events "well-known to the world of artists," is not altogether convincing, and his concluding sentence is significant: "The main truth is, that for reasons too lengthy to explain, I was obliged, as in almost every novel of the series, alas, to crowd events together and heap them one upon the other."

Zola subjects the characters who participate in these events to a treatment equally arbitrary. Frequently they exist independently of their relationship to their various relatives and even of their own earlier incarnations in previous novels. His working notes, in the National Library in Paris, reveal how, when characters recurred, he had to alter ages, dates and even characteristics he had assigned earlier. But this is not necessarily a fault, for too close an insistence on family ties would quite probably have resulted in a mechanical quality that Zola avoids by stressing environment. Probably for this reason certain of the characters, despite the fact that, as Zola wrote, he "submitted people to things," sometimes break loose from the mechanism of fatality he imposed upon them. Nevertheless, the Zola character does not achieve the special uniqueness that makes an Emma Bovary, a Micawber, a Julien Sorel, or a Charlus exist in our imaginations long after we have laid the novel aside. Critics have suggested that this is because they lack "inner life," because they do not develop from one end of a novel to the other. It should be remembered that it is also a natural result of Zola's method: his reliance on "big scenes," his disregard of time, his preference for what he called "massive constructions" over analysis. Thus, a character seldom dominates the action, and tends to lose prominence whenever the action becomes complex. As an example, during the riveting contest in *L'Assommoir,* when Goujet and Mes Bottes compete for Gervaise's favor, her reactions are not unique in themselves, not those of a particular individual, but rather those of any woman coyly aware that she is the motive for a duel.

Zola's primary characters may also lack uniqueness because they are surrounded by so many secondary figures. Despite his early statement that he would need "few characters, two or three principal figures, deeply drawn, then two or three secondary figures, as closely related as possible to the heroes, serving as complements and contrasts," he came to create, in a single novel, as many as sixty characters, twice as many as in the average novel of Scott. Yet how restricted is their world, even if they inhabit the metropolis! Wherever they go, they encounter one another. In *L'Assommoir,* the Street of the Drop of Gold is all the universe for Gervaise and her compeers; on such rare excursions as the tour of the wedding party, they seem to cling together taking their cramped life with them. As they climb the Vendôme column, the author describes no panoramic view, but only the men pinching the women's ankles as they go up the stairway, or the women clutching at

x

one another, afraid to look out. Unlike Stendhal, whose characters in their moments of exaltation gaze upon wide vistas, Zola confines his people spatially.

But in this crowded world, Zola seeks perspective in another way, by carefully determining each character's degree of prominence. He once told a friend, "I am decidedly in favor of more intricately composed machines, in which the characters are not crushed together in the background for want of perspective." According to this formula, Zola groups his secondary figures in an infinite number of degrees of importance. Apart from the large number whose prominence we may determine by the frequency of their appearances, or by the length of their dialogue, Zola makes remarkable use of what one might call "shadow characters." These are sometimes "familiars," characters who haunt given places, and appear only when those places become scenes of action. On other occasions, they may serve as portents of disaster, like the undertaker Bazouge, in *L'Assommoir,* or the ragpicker Queen Pomaré in *Nana,* but even more frequently they serve to hint at a complexity of background, suggesting that the immediate action of the novel is only part of variegated mysterious events. At the vanishing end of the scale is the unnamed character, who drifts as if by accident through a scene and out again, never to return, foreshadowing the style of modern cinematists like René Clair. And indeed, much as on the motion picture screen, Zola, through his character composition, attains perspective within a narrow frame.

These questions of time, space, characterization, are matters of art, matters of style. With regard to more conventional aspects of style, such as the novelist's language itself, critics have traditionally condemned Zola. It is true that his writing is not subtle, and that one is seldom conscious of any polish, any seeking for the original or the evocative term, the startling simile or metaphor. Most of his effects are rhythmic, deriving from shifting accents, repetition, or imitative harmony, and while frequently successful, tend at times to become labored. Yet in general his style admirably suits his purpose. For instance, frequently in descriptive sentences an adjectival phrase brings out the lack of uniqueness we noted earlier in many of the characters. He writes of Mme. Hennebeau in *Germinal* that she possesses "the sensuality of a greedy blond," thereby placing the character in a class. Often he generalizes by stressing plastic quality or immobility, especially in women, who frequently resemble statues or goddesses. Mme. Hennebeau looks like "a Ceres gilded by autumn"; Hélène of *Une Page d'Amour* appears "with her hands crossed, in her tranquil attitude of mother and widow," or again, she is "a brown-haired Juno with golden glints."

But it is within a broader range than the phrase or sentence that Zola's style is most memorable. In passages such as this description of a sun-baked Provençal village he reveals a power of composition and a skill with color worthy of an Impressionist painting:

The country stretched out for two leagues, closed in by a wall of yellow hills, which pine woods dotted with black. It was a terrible region of dried moors and spiny ridges tearing up through the earth. The few patches of tillable soil spread out in blood-colored ponds: red fields, with lines of sickly almond-trees, the gray crests of olive-trees, rows of vines, striping the countryside with their brown trunks. It looked as if an immense fire had passed over everything, strewing the heights with the ashes of forests, burning the fields, leaving its brightness and its furnace heat in the hollows. At rare intervals the pale green square of a wheatfield added a gentler tone.

III

Nana belongs with *La Débâcle, La Terre,* and *L'Assommoir* as one of Zola's greatest works. In the list of ten novels he had already planned when he submitted his project to the publisher Leroux appears the entry: "Anna Ledoux: le demi-monde." This brief note suggests that the novel was to deal mainly with the world of vice and prostitution, and that it was to treat a universal subject rather than one typical of a particular political regime: the dominance of the flesh. That this theme remained uppermost in his mind is borne out by the working notes written years later: *Nana* was to be first of all "the poem of male desire"—the crumbling of every standard, marital and familial love, religion, political loyalty, cultural and artistic integrity, before the power of sex.

A primary function of the heroine is therefore symbolic: Zola imagined her as an idol adored by a grovelling multitude of males. But to create merely a symbol would have been to ignore the first requirement of the novel: that it reproduce life. Nana is also a flesh-and-blood woman; her lineage is clear, for she is the daughter of Gervaise Coupeau of *L'Assommoir*, whom society had destroyed. This relationship, rather closer than is customary between novels in the series, provides the direction of Nana's destructive force: her triumph is a vengeance of the underprivileged. A metaphor, perhaps inspired by *King Lear*, drives the point home: "The wren goes to it, and the small gilded fly/Does lecher in my sight." Zola presents his Nana, whose destructive beauty is the product of a tainted race, as the "golden fly, sprung from a dunghill to corrupt palaces."

If Zola seems earlier to have chosen as his setting the world of vice—"the demi-monde"—fortunately he decided to make his immoral heroine an actress (though of mediocre talents) and the theatrical setting with its color and variety helps to distinguish the novel from the stories of prostitutes that were a frequent subject of contemporary realism. Zola knew nothing of the theatrical world, and little of the other, but it was his good fortune to have excellent informants. Chief of these were Ludovic Halévy, a successful novelist and the collaborator of Meilhac and Offenbach, whose amusing stories of famous coquettes Zola found invaluable, and a close friend, Henri Céard, who provided verbatim records of light ladies' conversation and detailed descriptions of their parties that Zola gratefully incorporated. On his own account the novelist made frequent visits to the Théâtre des Variétés, where much of the action takes place, acquiring a knowledge of the architecture of the theatre, and—a significant source of his book's originality—information on the technical side of costuming, staging, make-up, and the vocabulary of actors and stage hands.

But it required great skill in construction to combine all these elements: the theme of the eternal courtesan, the story of the girl of the streets, the saga of upper-class debauchery in the garish world of the boulevard theatre. Going one step beyond the dramatic method, which, as we have seen, best suited his talent and design, Zola has built the whole novel along theatrical lines. The very first chapter transports us to the Théâtre des Variétés, so that the reader becomes a second audience, watching in turn the spectacle of the audience of characters and finally the spectacle itself, *La Blonde Vénus* (imitated from Offenbach's *La Belle Hélène*). Yet the novel resembles rather the Palais Royal farce than the well-made play: plot in the sense of a sequence of cause and effect scarcely exists; instead we witness a series of scenes. Zola expressly resolved, in his working notes, that Nana's career should consist of "ups and downs" (*des hauts et des bas*), and the fourteen chapters that begin with her triumph on the stage and end with her death from smallpox closely follow this prescription. Moments of success are interspersed with periods of degradation; there is no directly ascending or descending line or no key moment, as in *L'Assommoir*, which determines the heroine's eventual downfall.

The chapters themselves are essentially "scenic," in that

they do not flow from preceding chapters but present the characters in different settings. Each follows a highly theatrical rhythm, the movement being that of the entrance on stage. Zola will present a scene, whereupon an ever-increasing number of characters appear, frequently in order of importance, until the novelistic stage, usually a room, is crowded. This rhythm helps to stress a central element in the theme: the fatal attraction between the high and low levels of society, which Zola underlines by a series of parallel scenes. Thus, the remarkable chapter on Nana's dinner party follows immediately upon Countess Muffat's reception; not only do many of the same guests appear at both, but even the conversation follows similar lines. As he reminded himself in his working notes, there should be a "continuous parallel between Nana's party and the Countess'." The setting itself has a certain architectural complexity; Nana's apartment contains a number of rooms and hallways leading to her boudoir which gradually fill up with her suitors. A favorite device is the dramatic "curtain." This may consist of the bedroom door dramatically flung open by Nana herself to reveal to an audience of rejected suitors the favorite of the moment, or it may take other forms: at Countess Muffat's dinner party, for example, the guests themselves act as a curtain, suddenly moving aside to reveal "at the end of a chaise longue, a little man of sixty, with bad teeth and a cunning smile." On another occasion Muffat watches from the street below the silhouettes of his wife and her lover in a lighted window. Suddenly the light goes out—again the curtain is drawn.

The dramatic use of light extends beyond the curtain device. It may function as a spotlight, as when Nana and Satin watch the old ragpicker in the circle of light cast by a street lamp, or it may help to lend visual depth to a metaphor, that of the Golden Fly, when firelight or lamplight flicker goldenly over Nana's naked body. Other dramatic devices are the eavesdropping scene, the stage direction—"[Nana's apartment] looked as if a party were to be thrown hastily, amid a wave of good fortune, when nothing was yet in its place"—rapid fire dialogue, and offstage sound.

The star of the drama is far more prominent than the central characters in other Zola novels. She possesses a temperament that distinguishes her even in the crowds that assemble again and again. Just as, on the Variétés stage, she is the focus of every gaze, so by some act of caprice, some sudden violence or exuberance, she retains our attention in the mass. These "characteristic" fits of passion, which take a number of forms, nevertheless present the reader with something of a dilemma. As we have pointed out, Zola tended to create uncomplicated characters. Yet the definitely recognizable traits of the famous coquettes such as those Halévy and Céard furnished him, were essential to his portrait. No less essential, however, was the fact that Nana, though a rapacious destroyer of men, must remain unconscious of her role, an unwitting instrument of fate, or, as Zola preferred it, of her tainted heritage. The *femme fatale* of earlier Romantic literature was almost always a sadist taking pleasure in the torment her ascendancy enabled her to inflict, and fully aware of her destructive powers. Zola, reacting against Romanticism, conceived of Nana rather as a capricious beauty, who, when her whims bring death or disaster, is genuinely shocked and surprised. As he stressed in his working notes, repeating the phrase several times: "as to moral character, *a good-hearted soul,* that is what dominates . . . She becomes a force of nature, but without wanting to be."

Unfortunately, on occasion Nana's good-natured unconsciousness seems incompatible with her destructive proclivities. When, for example, she humiliates Muffat, forcing him to romp about on all fours like a dog, or to trample and spit upon his uniform, as she kicks him, Zola's assurance that there is really nothing sadistic in all this is rather unconvincing; it is hard to believe him when he writes, "It was not cruelty on her part, for she remained a good natured girl; it was like an ever-rising wind of madness that blew into the closed room."

There is also the problem of Nana's Lesbianism. The subject of inversion, which has been treated openly in the twentieth-century novel, notably by Proust and Gide, deeply interested Zola, but he dared approach it only obliquely. Nevertheless, Nana's and Satin's illicit passion forms a definite episode in the novel, and the Lesbian café of Laure Piedefer is the setting of a remarkable and original scene of Saphic jealousy. Undoubtedly Zola introduced the topic chiefly as one more aspect of what he called "vice from below," rather than as a character trait. But to the modern reader inversion is closely linked to personality. The Lesbian makes a choice, often because of disgust for the male, or out of rebellion against her lot; once again, Nana's basic "involuntariness" seems ill-adapted to this aspect of her career.

The characters surrounding Nana fall into two chief groups: those representing society and those representing the theatrical world. The first is divided in two: Count and Countess Muffat and their circle on the one hand, and the ideal family, Mme. Hugon and her sons, on the other. Of these, the more important is the Muffats, whose ruin symbolizes the engulfment of the ruling class. Muffat himself is almost too pliant to be real, but certain secondary characters are drawn with particularly incisive strokes: Steiner, the wealthy Jewish industrialist who competes with Muffat for Nana's favors, Bordenave, the boisterous impresario who insists on calling his theatre a brothel, Fontan the satyr-faced comedian, La Faloise, the fop.

Once again Zola marshals an imposing number of "shadow" characters, who, appearing briefly and dimly in the background, help to suggest social forces at work beyond the immediate action of the novel. Among these are the enigmatic Venot, mysterious representative of the Church, and the procuress La Tricon, who resembles an impoverished aristocrat, and whose occasional appearances backstage impose awed silence upon the actresses. Helping by contrast to bring out Nana's opulent sexuality are the asexual Mme. Jules, the theatre dresser, her bodice bristling with pins, or the epicene coiffeur, François. Two figures, briefly glimpsed, each suggest a possible outcome of Nana's career: the wealthy retired prostitute Irma D'Anglars, and "Queen Pomaré," the famous courtesan turned ragpicker. A number of actresses, in their dialogue and omnipresence, have almost a choric function. Zola's listing of their names whenever there is a gathering reminds one of the refrain of *Widdicombe Fair*. He characterized them usually by a single distinguishing trait (Lucy Stewart: "consumptive, but never dying") and in the case of one of their number, Tatan Néné, suggested in Rabelaisian fashion her private attributes by her name.

At the death of the fallen idol, these figures that had crowded around her pedestal have disappeared: Nana lies dead of smallpox in a room at the Grand Hotel, while the crowd in the streets below shouts "To Berlin!" Zola seems to be slighting Nana's death scene, since she dies so suddenly after her triumphs abroad. But the naturalist heroine cannot die, like Hugo's Jean Valjean, in a tender apotheosis; her career has been "ups and downs," and its final hour is only a final irrevocable descent. Yet Flaubert was not wrong when he called her death "Michelangesque." For although there is now no link between the dead woman and the reader, she retains her stature through the skillful orchestration of the dénouement; in her final moment she symbolizes France herself on the eve of defeat and degradation, an omen and preparation of the true climax of the *Rougon-Macquart, La Débâcle*.

JOHN C. LAPP
University of California at Los Angeles

xviii

BIBLIOGRAPHY

By far the best book on Zola in English is F. W. J. Hemmings' *Emile Zola* (1953), which skillfully combines biography with an appraisal of the novels, and contains a most useful bibliography. The same author has carefully assessed Zola criticism of the past thirty years in "The Present Position in Zola Studies," an article in *French Studies* (1956). Angus Wilson's *Zola* (1952), offers a lively treatment, chiefly from the psychoanalytic point of view.

Henry James' essay in *Notes on Novelists* (1914), is still of considerable value. More recently two brief but penetrating articles by Jared Wenger have appeared in PMLA: "Character—Types of Scott, Balzac, Dickens, Zola" (1940), and "The Art of the Flashlight: Violent Techniques in Les Rougon-Macquart" (1947).

For the convenience of the reader, there follows a list of the *Rougon-Macquart* novels with their dates and English titles: *La Fortune des Rougon*, 1871 (*The Fortune of the Rougons*); *La Curée*, 1872 (*The Rush for the Spoil*); *Le Ventre de Paris*, 1873 (*Fat and Thin*); *La Conquête de Plassans*, 1874 (*The Conquest of Plassans*); *La Faute de l'Abbé Mouret*, 1875 (*Abbe Mouret's Transgression*); *Son Excellence Eugène Rougon*, 1876 (*His Excellency*); *L'Assommoir*, 1877 (*The Dram Shop*); *Une Page d'Amour*, 1878 (*A Love Episode*); *Nana*, 1880 (*Nana*); *Pot-Bouille*, 1882 (*Piping Hot*); *Au Bonheur des Dames*, 1883 (*The Shop Girls of Paris*); *La Joie de Vivre*, 1884 (*The Joy of Life*); *Germinal*, 1885 (*Master and Man*); *L'Œuvre*, 1886 (*His Masterpiece*); *La Terre*, 1887 (*The Soil*); *Le Rêve*, 1888 (*The Dream*); *La Bête humaine*, 1890 (*The Human Animal*); *L'Argent*, 1891 (*Money*); *La Débâcle*, 1892 (*The Downfall*); *Le Docteur Pascal*, 1893 (*Doctor Pascal*).

CHAPTER I

AT nine o'clock in the evening the body of the house at the Théâtre des Variétés was still all but empty. A few individuals, it is true, were sitting quietly waiting in the balcony and stalls, but these were lost, as it were, among the ranges of seats whose coverings of cardinal velvet loomed in the subdued light of the dimly-burning luster. A shadow enveloped the great red splash of the curtain, and not a sound came from the stage, the unlit footlights, the scattered desks of the orchestra. It was only high overhead, in the third gallery, round the domed ceiling, where nude females and children flew in heavens which had turned green in the gas-light, that calls and laughter were audible above a continuous hubbub of voices, and heads in women's and workmen's caps were ranged, row above row, under the wide-vaulted bays with their gilt-surrounding adornments. Every few seconds an attendant would make her appearance, bustling along with tickets in her hand, and piloting in front of her a gentleman and a lady, who took their seats, he in his evening dress, she sitting slim and undulant beside him whilst her eyes wandered slowly round the house.

Two young men appeared in the stalls; they kept standing, and looked about them.

"Didn't I say so, Hector?" cried the elder of the two, a tall fellow with little black mustaches, "we're too early! You might quite well have allowed me to finish my cigar."

An attendant was passing.

"Oh, Monsieur Faucherey," she said, familiarly, "it won't begin for half an hour yet!"

"Then why do they advertise for nine o'clock?" muttered

1

Hector, whose long thin face assumed an expression of vexation. "Only this morning, Clarisse, who's in the piece, swore that they'd begin at nine o'clock punctually."

For a moment they remained silent, and looking upwards scanned the shadowy boxes. But the green paper with which these were hung rendered them more shadowy still. Down below, under the dress circle, the lower boxes were buried in utter night. In those on the second tier there was only one stout lady, who was stranded, as it were, on the velvet-covered balustrade in front of her. On the right hand and on the left, between lofty pilasters, the stage-boxes, bedraped with long-fringed scalloped hangings, remained untenanted. The house with its white and gold, relieved by soft green tones, lay only half disclosed to view, as though full of a fine dust shed from the little jets of flame in the great glass luster.

"Did you get your stage-box for Lucy?" asked Hector.

"Yes," replied his companion; "but I had some trouble to get it. Oh, there's no danger of Lucy coming too early!"

He stifled a slight yawn; then, after a pause,—

"You're in luck's way, you are, since you haven't been at a first night before. The *Blonde Venus* will be the event of the year. People have been talking about it for six months. Oh, such music, my dear boy! Such a sly dog, Bordenave! He knows his business, and has kept this for the Exhibition season."

Hector was religiously attentive. He asked a question.

"And Nana, the new star, who's going to play Venus, d'you know her?"

"There you are, you're beginning again!" cried Fauchery, casting up his arms. "Ever since this morning people have been dreeing me with Nana. I've met more than twenty people, and it's Nana here and Nana there! What do *I* know? Am I acquainted with all the light ladies in Paris? Nana is an invention of Bordenave's! It must be a fine one!"

He calmed himself, but the emptiness of the house, the

dim light of the luster, the church-like sense of self-absorption, which the place inspired, full as it was of whispering voices and the sound of doors banging—all these got on his nerves.

"No, by Jove," said he, all of a sudden, "one's hair turns gray here. I—I'm going out. Perhaps we shall find Bordenave downstairs. He'll give us information about things."

Downstairs, in the great marble-paved entrance-hall, where the box office was, the public were beginning to shew themselves. Through the three open gates might have been observed, passing in, the ardent life of the boulevards, which were all astir and aflare under the fine April night. The sound of carriage wheels kept stopping suddenly, carriage doors were noisily shut again, and people began entering in small groups, taking their stand before the ticket bureau, and climbing the double flight of stairs at the end of the hall, up which the women loitered with swaying hips. Under the crude gas-light, round the pale, naked walls of the entrance-hall, which with its scanty First Empire decorations suggested the peristyle of a toy temple, there was a flaring display of lofty yellow posters, bearing the name of "Nana" in great black letters. Gentlemen, who seemed to be glued to the entry, were reading them; others, standing about, were engaged in talk, barring the doors of the house in so doing, while, hard by the box office, a thick-set man with an extensive, close-shaven visage was giving rough answers to such as pressed to engage seats.

"There's Bordenave," said Fauchery, as he came down the stairs. But the manager had already seen him.

"Ah, ah! you're a nice fellow!" he shouted at him from a distance. "That's the way you give me a notice, is it? Why, I opened my *Figaro* this morning—never a word!"

"Wait a bit," replied Fauchery. "I certainly must make the acquaintance of your Nana before talking about her. Besides, I've made no promises."

Then, to put an end to the discussion, he introduced his cousin, M. Hector de la Faloise, a young man who had come to finish his education in Paris. The manager took the young man's measure at a glance. But Hector returned his scrutiny with deep interest. This, then, was that Bordenave, that showman of the sex, who treated women like a convict-overseer, that clever fellow who was always at full steam over some advertising dodge, that shouting, spitting, thigh-slapping fellow, that cynic with the soul of a policeman! Hector was under the impression that he ought to discover some amiable observation for the occasion.

"Your theater—" he began, in dulcet tones.

Bordenave interrupted him with a savage phrase, as becomes a man who dotes on frank situations.

"Call it my brothel!"

At this Fauchery laughed approvingly, while la Faloise stopped with his pretty speech strangled in his throat, feeling very much shocked, and striving to appear as though he enjoyed the phrase. The manager had dashed off to shake hands with a dramatic critic, whose column had considerable influence. When he returned, la Faloise was recovering. He was afraid of being treated as a provincial if he shewed himself too much nonplussed.

"I have been told," he began again, longing, positively, to find something to say, "that Nana has a delicious voice."

"Nana!" cried the manager, shrugging his shoulders, "the voice of a squirt!"

The young man made haste to add,—

"Besides being a first-rate comedian!"

"She! Why she's a lump! She has no notion what to do with her hands and feet."

La Faloise blushed a little. He had lost his bearings. He stammered,—

"I wouldn't have missed this first representation to-night for the world. I was aware that your theater—"

"Call it my brothel," Bordenave again interpolated, with the frigid obstinacy of a man convinced.

Meanwhile, Fauchery, with extreme calmness, was looking at the women as they came in. He went to his cousin's rescue when he saw him all at sea, and doubtful whether to laugh or to be angry.

"Do be pleasant to Bordenave—call his theater what he wishes you to, since it amuses him. And you, my dear fellow, don't keep us waiting about for nothing. If your Nana neither sings nor acts, you'll find you've made a blunder, that's all. It's what I'm afraid of, an the truth be told."

"A blunder! A blunder!" shouted the manager, and his face grew purple. "Must a woman know how to act and sing? Oh, my chicken, you're too *stoopid*: Nana has other good points, by Heaven!—something which is as good as all the other things put together. I've smelt it out; it's deuced pronounced with her, or I've got the scent of an idiot. You'll see, you'll see! She's only got to come on, and all the house will be gaping at her."

He had held up his big hands which were trembling under the influence of his eager enthusiasm, and now, having relieved his feelings, he lowered his voice and grumbled to himself,—

"Yes, she'll go far! Oh, yes, s'elp me, she'll go far! A skin, oh, what a skin she's got!"

Then, as Fauchery began questioning him, he consented to enter into a detailed explanation, couched in phraseology so crude that Hector de la Faloise felt slightly disgusted. He had been thick with Nana, and he was anxious to start her on the stage. Well, just about that time, he was in search of a Venus. He—he never let a woman encumber him for any length of time; he preferred to let the public enjoy the benefit of her forthwith. But there was a deuce of a row going on in his shop, which had been turned topsy-turvy by that big damsel's advent. Rose Mignon, his star, a comic actress of much subtlety and an adorable singer, was daily threatening to leave him in the lurch, for she was furious, and guessed the presence of a rival. And as for the bill, good God! what a noise there had been about it all! It had ended by his deciding to print the names of the two actresses in the same sized type. But it wouldn't do to bother him. Whenever any of his little women, as he called them— Simonne or Clarisse, for instance—wouldn't go the way he wanted her to, he just up with his foot and caught her one in the rear. Otherwise, life was impossible. Oh, yes, he sold 'em; *he* knew what they fetched, the wenches!

"Tut!" he cried, breaking off short; "Mignon and Steiner. Always together. You known Steiner's getting sick of Rose; that's why the husband dogs his steps now for fear of his slipping away."

On the pavement outside, the row of gas-jets, flaring on the cornice of the theater, cast a patch of brilliant light. Two small trees, violently green, stood sharply out against it, and a column gleamed in such vivid illumination that one could read the notices thereon at a distance, as though in broad daylight, while the dense night of the boulevard beyond was dotted with lights above the vague outline of an ever-moving crowd. Many men did not enter the theater at once, but stayed outside to talk while finishing their cigars under the rays of the line of gas-jets, which shed a sallow pallor on their faces and silhouetted their short black shadows on the asphalt. Mignon, a very tall, very broad fellow, with the square-shaped head of a strong man at a fair, was forcing a passage through the midst of the groups, and dragging on his arm the banker Steiner, an exceedingly small man with a corporation already in evidence, and a round face framed in a setting of beard which was already growing gray.

"Well," said Bordenave to the banker, "you met her yesterday in my office."

"Ah! it was she, was it?" ejaculated Steiner. "I suspected as much. Only I was coming out as she was going in, and I scarcely caught a glimpse of her."

Mignon was listening with half-closed eyelids, and nervously twisting a great diamond ring round his finger. He had quite understood that Nana was in question. Then as Bordenave was drawing a portrait of his new star which lit a flame in the eyes of the banker, he ended by joining in the conversation.

"Oh, let her alone, my dear fellow: she's a low lot! The public will shew her the door in quick time. Steiner, my laddie, you know that my wife is waiting for you in her box."

He wanted to take possession of him again. But Steiner would not quit Bordenave. In front of them, a stream of people was crowding and crushing against the ticket office, and there was a din of voices, in the midst of which the name of Nana sounded with all the melodious vivacity of its two syllables. The men who stood planted in front of the notices kept spelling it out loudly; others, in an interrogative tone, uttered it as they passed; while the women, at once restless and smiling, repeated it softly with an air of surprise. Nobody knew Nana. Whence had Nana fallen? And stories and jokes, whispered from ear to ear, went the round of the crowd. The name was a caress in itself; it was a pet name, the very familiarity of which suited every lip. Merely through enunciating it thus, the throng worked itself into a state of gayety and became highly good-natured. A fever of curiosity urged it forward, that kind of Parisian curiosity which is as violent as an access of positive unreason. Everybody wanted to see Nana. A lady had the flounce of her dress torn off; a man lost his hat.

"Oh, you're asking me too many questions about it!" cried Bordenave, whom a score of men were besieging with their queries. "You're going to see her, and I'm off; they want me."

He disappeared, enchanted at having fired his public. Mignon shrugged his shoulders, reminding Steiner that Rose was awaiting him, in order to shew him the costume she was about to wear in the first act.

"By Jove! there's Lucy out there, getting down from her carriage," said la Faloise to Fauchery.

It was in fact Lucy Stewart, a plain little woman, some forty years old, with a disproportionately long neck, a thin, drawn face, a heavy mouth, but withal of such brightness, such graciousness of manner, that she was really very charming. She was bringing with her Caroline Héquet and her mother—Caroline a woman of a cold type of beauty, the mother a person of a most worthy demeanor, who looked as if she were stuffed with straw.

"You're coming with us? I've kept a place for you," said she to Fauchery.

"Oh, decidedly not! to see nothing!" he made answer. "I've a stall; I prefer being in the stalls."

Lucy grew nettled. Did he not dare shew himself in her company? Then suddenly restraining herself, and skipping to another topic,—

"Why haven't you told me that you knew Nana?"

"Nana! I've never set eyes on her."

"Honor bright? I've been told that you've been to bed with her."

But Mignon, coming in front of them, his finger to his lips, made them a sign to be silent. And, when Lucy questioned him, he pointed out a young man who was passing, and murmured,—

"Nana's fancy man."

Everybody looked at him. He was a pretty fellow. Fauchery recognized him; it was Daguenet, a young man who had run through three hundred thousand francs in the pursuit of women, and who now was dabbling in stocks, in order from time to time to treat them to bouquets and dinners. Lucy made the discovery that he had fine eyes.

"Ah, there's Blanche!" she cried. "It's she who told me that you had been to bed with Nana."

Blanche de Sivry, a great fair girl, whose good-looking face shewed signs of growing fat, made her appearance in the company of a spare, sedulously well-groomed, and extremely distinguished man.

"The Count Xavier de Vandeuvres," Fauchery whispered in his companion's ear.

The Count and the journalist shook hands, while Blanche and Lucy entered into a brisk mutual explanation. One of them in blue, the other in rose-pink, they stood blocking the way with their deeply-flounced skirts, and Nana's name kept repeating itself so shrilly in their conversation that people began to listen to them. The Count de Vandeuvres carried Blanche off. But by this time Nana's name was echoing more loudly than ever round the four walls of the entrance-hall amid yearnings sharpened by delay. Why didn't the play begin? The men pulled out their watches, late-comers sprang from their conveyances before these had fairly drawn up, the groups left the sidewalk, where the passers-by were crossing the now vacant space of gas-lit pavement, craning their necks, as they did so, in order to get a peep into the theater. A street-boy came up whistling, and planted himself before a notice at the door, then cried out, "Woa, Nana!" in the voice of a tipsy man, and hied on his way with a rolling gait and a shuffling of his old boots. A laugh had arisen at this. Gentlemen of unimpeachable appearance repeated, "Nana, woa, Nana!" People were crushing, a dispute arose at the ticket office, and there was a growing clamor caused by the hum of voices calling on Nana, demanding Nana in one of those accesses of silly facetiousness and sheer animalism which pass over mobs.

But, above all the din, the bell that precedes the rise of the
curtain became audible. "They've rung, they've rung!"
The rumor reached the boulevard; and thereupon followed a
stampede, every one wanting to pass in, while the servants
of the theater increased their forces. Mignon, with an
anxious air, at last got hold of Steiner again, the latter not
having been to see Rose's costume. At the very first tinkle of
the bell, la Faloise had cloven a way through the crowd,
pulling Fauchery with him, so as not to miss the opening
scene. But all this eagerness on the part of the public irritated Lucy Stewart. What brutes were these people to be
pushing women like that! She stayed in the rear of them
all, with Caroline Héquet and her mother. The entrance-
hall was now empty, while beyond it was still heard the
long-drawn rumble of the boulevard.

"As though they were always funny, those pieces of
theirs!" Lucy kept repeating as she climbed the stair.

In the house, Fauchery and la Faloise, in front of their
stalls, were gazing about them anew. By this time the
house was resplendent. High jets of gas illumined the great
glass chandelier with a rustling of yellow and rosy flames,
which rained down a stream of brilliant light from dome to
floor. The cardinal velvets of the seats were shot with hues
of lake, while all the gilding shone again, the soft green
decorations chastening its effect beneath the too-decided
paintings of the ceiling. The footlights were turned up, and
with a vivid flood of brilliance lit up the curtain, the heavy
purple drapery of which had all the richness befitting a palace
in a fairy tale, and contrasted with the meanness of the pro-
scenium, where cracks shewed the plaster under the gilding.
The place was already warm. At their music-stands the orchestra were tuning their instruments amid a delicate trilling
of flutes, a stifled tooting of horns, a singing of violin notes,
which floated forth amid the increasing uproar of voices.
All the spectators were talking, jostling, settling themselves

in a general assault upon seats; and the hustling rush in the
side-passages was now so violent that every door into the
house was laboriously admitting an inexhaustible flood of
people. There were signals, rustlings of fabrics, a continual
march-past of skirts and head-dresses, accentuated by the
black hue of a dress-coat or a surtout. Notwithstanding
this, the rows of seats were little by little getting filled up,
while here and there a light toilette stood out from its surroundings, a head with a delicate profile bent forward under
its chignon, where flashed the lightning of a jewel. In one
of the boxes the tip of a bare shoulder glimmered like snowy
silk. Other ladies, sitting at ease, languidly fanned themselves, following with their gaze the pushing movements of
the crowd, while young gentlemen, standing up in the stalls,
their waistcoats cut very low, gardenias in their button-holes,
pointed their opera-glasses with gloved finger-tips.

It was now that the two cousins began searching for the
faces of those they knew. Mignon and Steiner were together
in a lower box, sitting side by side with their arms leaning
for support on the velvet balustrade. Blanche de Sivry
seemed to be in sole possession of a stage-box on the level of
the stalls. But la Faloise examined Daguenet before any one
else, he being in occupation of a stall two rows in front of
his own. Close to him, a very young man, seventeen years
old at the outside, some truant from college, it may be, was
straining wide a pair of fine eyes such as a cherub might
have owned. Fauchery smiled when he looked at him.

"Who is that lady in the balcony?" la Faloise asked suddenly; "the lady with a young girl in blue beside her."

He pointed out a large woman, who was excessively tight-
laced, a woman who had been a blonde and had now become
white and yellow of tint, her broad face, reddened with paint,
looking puffy under a rain of little childish curls.

"It's Gaga," was Fauchery's simple reply, and as this name
seemed to astound his cousin, he added,—

"You don't know Gaga? She was the delight of the early years of Louis-Philippe. Nowadays, she drags her daughter about with her wherever she goes."

La Faloise never once glanced at the young girl. The sight of Gaga moved him; his eyes did not leave her again. He still found her very good-looking, but he dared not say so.

Meanwhile the conductor lifted his violin bow and the orchestra attacked the overture. People still kept coming in; the stir and noise were on the increase. Among that public, peculiar to first nights and never subject to change, there were little subsections composed of intimate friends, who smilingly foregathered again. Old first-nighters, hat on head, seemed familiar and quite at ease, and kept exchanging salutations. All Paris was there, the Paris of literature, of finance, and of pleasure. There were many journalists, several authors, a number of stock exchange people, and more courtesans than honest women. It was a singularly mixed world, composed, as it was, of all the talents, and tarnished by all the vices, a world where the same fatigue and the same fever played over every face. Fauchery, whom his cousin was questioning, shewed him the boxes devoted to the newspapers and to the clubs, and then named the dramatic critics —a lean, dried-up individual, with thin spiteful lips, and, chief of all, a big fellow, with a good-natured expression, lolling on the shoulder of his neighbor, a young miss over whom he brooded with tender and paternal eye.

But he interrupted himself on seeing la Faloise in the act of bowing to some persons who occupied the box opposite. He appeared surprised.

"What!" he queried, "you know the Count Muffat de Beuville?"

"Oh, for a long time back," replied Hector. "The Muffats had a property near us. I often go to their house. The Count's with his wife and his father-in-law, the Marquis de Chouard."

And, with some vanity—for he was happy in his cousin's astonishment—he entered into particulars. The Marquis was a Councillor of State, the Count had recently been appointed Chamberlain of the Empress. Fauchery, who had caught up his opera-glass, looked at the Countess, a plump brunette with a white skin and fine dark eyes.

"You shall present me to them between the acts," he ended by saying. "I have already met the Count, but I should like to go to them on their Tuesdays."

Energetic cries of "Hush" came from the upper galleries. The overture had begun, but people were still coming in. Late arrivals were obliging whole rows of spectators to rise, the doors of boxes were banging, loud voices were heard disputing in the passages. And there was no cessation of the sound of many conversations, a sound similar to the loud twittering of talkative sparrows at close of day. All was in confusion; the house was a medley of heads and arms which moved to and fro, their owners seating themselves or trying to make themselves comfortable, or, on the other hand, excitedly endeavoring to remain standing so as to take a final look-round. The cry of "Sit down, sit down!" came fiercely from the obscure depths of the pit. A shiver of expectation traversed the house: at last people were going to make the acquaintance of this famous Nana, with whom Paris had been occupying itself for a whole week!

Little by little, however, the buzz of talk dwindled softly down among occasional fresh outbursts of rough speech. And, amid this swooning murmur, these perishing sighs of sound, the orchestra struck up the small lively notes of a waltz with a vagabond rhythm bubbling with roguish laughter. The public were titillated; they were already on the grin. But the gang of clappers, in the foremost rows of the pit, applauded furiously. The curtain rose.

"By George!" exclaimed la Faloise, still talking away, "there's a man with Lucy."

He was looking at the stage-box, on the second tier to his right, the front of which Caroline and Lucy were occupying. At the back of this box were observable the worthy countenance of Caroline's mother, and the side face of a tall young man, with a noble head of light hair and an irreproachable get-up.

"Do look!" la Faloise again insisted, "there's a man there."

Fauchery decided to level his opera-glass at the stage-box. But he turned round again directly.

"Oh! it's Labordette," he muttered, in a careless voice, as though that gentleman's presence ought to strike all the world as both natural and immaterial.

Behind the cousins people shouted "Silence!" They had to cease talking. A motionless fit now seized the house, and great stretches of heads, all erect and attentive, sloped away from stalls to topmost gallery. The first act of the *Blonde Venus* took place in Olympus, a paste-board Olympus, with clouds in the wings and the throne of Jupiter on the right of the stage. First of all Iris and Ganymede, aided by a troupe of celestial attendants, sang a chorus while they arranged the seats of the gods for the council. Once again the prearranged applause of the clappers alone burst forth; the public, a little out of their depth, sat waiting. Nevertheless, la Faloise had clapped Clarisse Besnus, one of Bordenave's little women, who played Iris in a soft blue dress with a great scarf of the seven colors of the rainbow looped round her waist.

"You know she draws up her chemise to put that on," said he to Fauchery, loud enough to be heard by those around him. "We tried the trick this morning. It was all up under her arms and round the small of her back."

But a slight rustling movement ran through the house. Rose Mignon had just come on the stage as Diana. Now, though she had neither the face nor the figure for the part, being thin and dark, and of the adorable type of ugliness peculiar to a Parsian street child, she none the less appeared charming, and as though she were a satire on the personage she represented. Her song, at her entrance on the stage, was full of lines quaint enough to make you cry with laughter, and of complaints about Mars, who was getting ready to desert her for the companionship of Venus. She sang it with a chaste reserve so full of sprightly suggestiveness that the public warmed amain. The husband and Steiner, sitting side by side, were laughing complaisantly, and the whole house broke out in a roar when Prullière, that great favorite, appeared as a general, a masquerade Mars, decked with an enormous plume, and dragging along a sword the hilt of which reached to his shoulder. As for him, he had had enough of Diana; she had been a great deal too coy with him, he averred. Thereupon Diana promised to keep a sharp eye on him and to be revenged. The duet ended with a comic yodel which Prullière delivered very amusingly with the yell of an angry tomcat. He had about him all the entertaining fatuity of a young leading gentleman whose love affairs prosper, and he rolled around the most swaggering glances, which excited shrill feminine laughter in the boxes.

Then the public cooled again, for the ensuing scenes were found tiresome. Old Bosc, an imbecile Jupiter, with head crushed beneath the weight of an immense crown, only just succeeded in raising a smile among his audience, when he had a domestic altercation with Juno on the subject of the cook's accounts. The march-past of the gods, Neptune, Pluto, Minerva and the rest, was well-nigh spoiling everything. People grew impatient, there was a restless, slowly-growing murmur, the audience ceased to take an interest in the performance, and looked round at the house. Lucy began laughing with Labordette; the Count de Vandeuvres was craning his neck in conversation behind Blanche's sturdy shoulders, while Fauchery, out of the corners of his eyes, took stock of the Muffats, of whom the Count appeared very

serious, as though he had not understood the allusions, and
the Countess smiled vaguely, her eyes lost in reverie. But, on
a sudden, in this uncomfortable state of things, the applause
of the clapping contingent rattled out with the regularity of
platoon-firing. People turned towards the stage. Was it
Nana at last? This Nana made one wait with a vengeance.

It was a deputation of mortals whom Ganymede and Iris
had introduced, respectable middle-class persons, deceived
husbands all of them, and they came before the master of
the gods to proffer a complaint against Venus, who was assuredly inflaming their good ladies with an excess of ardor.
The chorus, in quaint dolorous tones, broken by silences full
of pantomimic admissions, caused great amusement. A neat
phrase went the round of the house: "The Cuckold's Chorus,
the Cuckold's Chorus," and it "caught on," for there was an
encore. The singers' heads were droll; their faces were discovered to be in keeping with the phrase, especially that of a
fat man which was as round as the moon. Meanwhile Vulcan arrived in a towering rage, demanding back his wife, who
had slipped away three days ago. The chorus resumed their
plaint, calling on Vulcan, the God of the Cuckolds. Vulcan's
part was played by Fontan, a comic actor of talent, at once
vulgar and original, and he had a *rôle* of the wildest whim-
sicality, and was got up as a village blacksmith, fiery red wig,
bare arms tattooed with arrow-pierced hearts, and all the rest
of it. A woman's voice cried in a very high key, "Oh, isn't
he ugly?" and all the ladies laughed and applauded.

Then followed a scene which seemed interminable. Jupiter
in the course of it seemed never to be going to finish assem-
bling the Council of Gods, in order to submit thereto the
deceived husband's requests. And still no Nana! Was the
management keeping Nana for the fall of the curtain then?
So long a period of expectancy had ended by annoying the
public. Their murmurings began again.

"It's going badly," said Mignon radiantly to Steiner. "She'll get a pretty reception, you'll see!"

At that very moment the clouds at the back of the stage were cloven apart, and Venus appeared. Exceedingly tall, exceedingly strong for her eighteen years, Nana, in her goddess's white tunic, and with her light hair simply flowing unfastened over her shoulders, came down to the footlights, with a quiet certainty of movement, and a laugh of greeting for the public, and struck up her grand ditty,—

"When Venus roams at eventide."

From the second verse onward, people looked at each other all over the house. Was this some jest, some wager on Bordenave's part? Never had a more tuneless voice been heard, or one managed with less art. Her manager judged of her excellently; she certainly sang like a squirt. Nay, more, she didn't even know how to deport herself on the stage: she thrust her arms in front of her, while she swayed her whole body to and fro in a manner which struck the audience as unbecoming and disagreeable. Cries of "Oh, oh!" were already rising in the pit and the cheap places. There was a sound of whistling too, when a voice in the stalls, suggestive of a molting cockerel, cried out with great conviction,—

"That's very smart!"

All the house looked round. It was the cherub, the truant from the boarding-school, who sat with his fine eyes very wide open, and his fair face glowing very hotly at sight of Nana. When he saw everybody turning towards him, he grew extremely red at the thought of having thus unconsciously spoken aloud. Daguenet, his neighbor, smilingly examined him; the public laughed, as though disarmed, and no longer anxious to hiss; while the young gentlemen in white gloves, fascinated in their turn by Nana's gracious contours, lolled back in their seats and applauded.

"That's it! well done! Bravo!"

Nana, in the mean time, seeing the house laughing, began to laugh herself. The gayety of all redoubled itself. She was an amusing creature, all the same, was that fine girl! Her laughter made a love of a little dimple appear in her chin. She stood there waiting, not bored in the least, familiar with her audience, falling into step with them at once, as though she herself were admitting, with a wink, that she had not two farthings' worth of talent, but that it did not matter at all, that in fact she had other good points. And then, after having made a sign to the conductor which plainly signified, "Go ahead, old boy!" she began her second verse:—

"'Tis Venus who at midnight passes—"

Still the same acidulated voice, only that now it tickled the public in the right quarter so deftly that momentarily it caused them to give a little shiver of pleasure. Nana still smiled her smile: it lit up her little red mouth, and shone in her great eyes, which were of the clearest blue. When she came to certain rather lively verses, a delicate sense of enjoyment made her tilt her nose, the rosy nostrils of which lifted and fell, while a bright flush suffused her cheeks. She still swung herself up and down, for she only knew how to do that. And the trick was no longer voted ugly; on the contrary, the men raised their opera-glasses. When she came to the end of a verse, her voice completely failed her, and she was well aware that she never would get through with it. Thereupon, rather than fret herself, she kicked up her leg, which forthwith was roundly outlined under her diaphanous tunic, bent sharply backwards, so that her bosom was thrown upward and forward, and stretched her arms out. Applause burst forth on all sides. In the twinkling of an eye she had turned on her heel, and was going up the stage, presenting the nape of her neck to the spectators' gaze, a neck where the

red-gold hair shewed like some animal's fell. Then the plau-
dits became frantic.

The close of the act was not so exciting. Vulcan wanted
to slap Venus. The gods held a consultation, and decided to
go and hold an enquiry on earth before granting the deceived
husband satisfaction. It was then that Diana surprised a
tender conversation between Venus and Mars, and vowed that
she would not take her eyes off them during the whole of the
voyage. There was also a scene where Love, played by a little
twelve-year-old chit, answered every ˙question put to her
with—"Yes, mamma! No, mamma!" in a winey-piney tone,
her fingers in her nose. At last Jupiter, with the severity of
a master who is growing cross, shut Love up in a dark closet,
bidding her conjugate the verb "I love" twenty times. The
finale was more appreciated: it was a chorus which both
troupe and orchestra performed with great brilliancy. But,
the curtain once down, the clappers tried in vain to obtain
a call, while the whole house was already up and making for
the doors.

The crowd trampled and jostled, jammed, as it was, between the rows of seats, and in so doing exchanged expressions. One phrase only went round—"It's idiotic." A critic
was saying that it would be one's duty to do a pretty bit of
slashing. The piece, however, mattered very little; for people were talking about Nana before everything else. Fauchery and la Faloise, being among the earliest to emerge, met
Steiner and Mignon in the passage outside the stalls. In this
gas-lit gut of a place, which was as narrow and circum-
scribed as a gallery in a mine, one was well-nigh suffocated.
They stopped a moment at the foot of the stairs on the right
of the house, protected by the final curve of the balusters.
The audience from the cheap places were coming down the
steps with a continuous tramp of heavy boots, a stream of
black dress-coats was passing, whilst an attendant was making every possible effort to protect a chair, on which she had

piled up coats and cloaks, from the onward pushing of the crowd.

"Surely I know her," cried Steiner, the moment he perceived Fauchery. "I'm certain I've seen her somewhere— at the Casino, I imagine, and she got herself taken up there— she was so drunk."

"As for me," said the journalist, "I don't quite know where it was; I am like you, I certainly have come across her."

He lowered his voice, and asked laughing,—

"At the Tricon's, perhaps."

"Egad, it was in a dirty place," Mignon declared. He seemed exasperated. "It's disgusting that the public give such a reception to the first trollop that comes by. There'll soon be no more decent women on the stage. Yes, I shall end by forbidding Rose to play."

Fauchery could not restrain a smile. Meanwhile the downward shuffle of the heavy shoes on the steps did not cease, and a little man in a workman's cap was heard crying, in a drawling voice,—

"Oh, my, she ain't no wopper! There's some pickings there!"

In the passage, two young men, delicately curled and formally resplendent in turn-down collars and the rest, were disputing together. One of them was repeating the words, "Beastly, beastly!" without stating any reasons; the other was replying with the words, "Stunning, stunning!" as though he too disdained all argument.

La Faloise declared her to be quite the thing; only he ventured to opine that she would be better still if she were to cultivate her voice. Steiner, who was no longer listening, seemed to awake with a start. Whatever happens, one must wait, he thought. Perhaps everything will be spoilt in the following acts. The public had shewn complaisance, but it was certainly not yet taken by storm. Mignon swore that the piece would never finish, and when Fauchery and la

Faloise left them in order to go up to the foyer, he took Steiner's arm, and leaning hard against his shoulder, whispered in his ear,—

"You're going to see my wife's costume for the second act, old fellow. It *is* just blackguardly."

Upstairs, in the foyer, three glass chandeliers burnt with a brilliant light. The two cousins hesitated an instant before entering, for the widely-opened glazed doors afforded a view right through the gallery—a view of a surging sea of heads, which two currents, as it were, kept in a continuous eddying movement. But they entered after all. Five or six groups of men, talking very loud and gesticulating, were obstinately discussing the play amid these violent interruptions; others were filing round, their heels, as they turned, sounding sharply on the waxed floor. To right and left, between columns of variegated imitation marble, women were sitting on benches covered with red velvet, and viewing the passing movement of the crowd with an air of fatigue as though the heat had rendered them languid. In the lofty mirrors behind them one saw the reflection of their chignons. At the end of the room, in front of the bar, a man with a huge corporation was drinking a glass of fruit-syrup.

But Fauchery, in order to breathe more freely, had gone to the balcony. La Faloise, who was studying the photographs of actresses hung in frames alternating with the mirrors between the columns, ended by following him. They had extinguished the line of gas-jets on the façade of the theater, and it was dark and very cool on the balcony, which seemed to them unoccupied. Solitary and enveloped in shadow, a young man was standing, leaning his arms on the stone balustrade, in the recess to the right. He was smoking a cigarette, of which the burning end shone redly. Fauchery recognized Daguenet. They shook hands warmly.

"What are you after there, my dear fellow?" asked the

journalist. "You're hiding yourself in holes and crannies—
you, a man who never leaves the stalls on a first night!"

"But I'm smoking, you see," replied Daguenet.

Then Fauchery, to put him out of countenance,—

"Well, well! what's your opinion of the new actress?
She's being roughly handled enough in the passages."

"Bah!" muttered Daguenet, "they're people whom she'll
have had nothing to do with!"

That was the sum of his criticism of Nana's talent. La
Faloise leant forward, and looked down at the boulevard.
Over against them the windows of a hotel and of a club
were brightly lit up, whilst, on the pavement below, a dark
mass of customers occupied the tables of the "Café de
Madrid." Despite the lateness of the hour, the crowd were
still crushing and being crushed; people were advancing
with shortened step; a throng was constantly emerging from
the Passage Jouffroy; individuals stood waiting five or six
minutes before they could cross the roadway, to such a distance did the string of carriages extend.

"What a moving mass! And what a noise!" la Faloise
kept reiterating, for Paris still astonished him.

The bell rang for some time, the foyer emptied. There
was a hurrying of people in the passages. The curtain was
already up when whole bands of spectators reëntered the
house amid the irritated expressions of those who were once
more in their places. Every one took his seat again with an
animated look and renewed attention. La Faloise directed
his first glance in Gaga's direction, but he was dumbfounded
at seeing by her side the tall fair man, who but recently had
been in Lucy's stage-box.

"What *is* that man's name?" he asked.

Fauchery failed to observe him.

"Ah, yes, it's Labordette," he said at last, with the same
careless movement.

The scenery of the second act came as a surprise. It

represented a suburban Shrove Tuesday dance at the "Boule Noire." Masqueraders were trolling a catch, the chorus of which was accompanied with a tapping of their heels. This 'Arryish departure, which nobody had in the least expected, caused so much amusement that the house encored the catch. And it was to this entertainment that the divine band, led astray by Iris, who falsely bragged that he knew the Earth well, were now come in order to proceed with their inquiry. They had put on disguises so as to preserve their *incognito*. Jupiter came on the stage as King Dagobert, with his breeches inside out, and a huge tin crown on his head. Phœbus appeared as the Postillion of Lonjumeau, and Minerva as a Norman nurse-maid. Loud bursts of merriment greeted Mars, who wore an outrageous uniform suggestive of an Alpine Admiral. But the shouts of laughter became uproarious when Neptune came in view, clad in a blouse, a high, bulging workman's cap on his head, love-locks glued to his temples. Shuffling along in slippers, he cried in a thick brogue,—

"Well, I'm blessed! when ye're a masher, it'll never do not to let 'em love yer!"

There were some shouts of "Oh! Oh!" while the ladies held their fans one degree higher. Lucy in her stage-box laughed so obstreperously that Caroline Héquet silenced her with a tap of her fan.

From that moment forth the piece was saved—nay more, promised a great success. This carnival of the gods, this dragging in the mud of their Olympus, this mock at a whole religion, a whole world of poetry, appeared in the light of a royal entertainment. The fever of irreverence gained the literary first-night world: legend was trampled under foot, ancient images were shattered. Jupiter's make-up was capital. Mars was a success. Royalty became a farce, and the Army a thing of folly. When Jupiter, grown suddenly amorous of a little laundress, began to knock off a mad cancan, Simonne, who was playing the part of the laundress, launched a kick at the master of the immortals' nose, and addressed him so drolly as, "My big daddy!" that an immoderate fit of laughter shook the whole house. While they were dancing, Phœbus treated Minerva to salad-bowls of negus, and Neptune sat in state among seven or eight women, who regaled him with cakes. Allusions were eagerly caught, indecent meanings were attached to them, harmless phrases were diverted from their proper significations in the light of exclamations issuing from the stalls. For a long time past the theatrical public had not wallowed in folly more irreverent. It rested them.

Nevertheless the action of the piece advanced amid these fooleries. Vulcan, as an elegant young man, clad, down to his gloves, entirely in yellow, and with an eye-glass stuck in his eye, was for ever running after Venus, who at last made her appearance as a fish-wife, a kerchief on her head,, and her bosom, covered with big gold trinkets, in great evidence. Nana was so white and plump, and looked so natural in a part demanding wide hips and a voluptuous mouth, that she straightway won the whole house. On her account Rose Mignon was forgotten, though she was made up as a delicious baby, with a wickerwork burlet on her head and a short muslin frock, and had just sighed forth Diana's plaints in a sweetly pretty voice. The other one, the big wench who slapped her thighs and clucked like a hen, shed round her an odor of life, a sovran feminine charm, with which the public grew intoxicated. From the second act onwards everything was permitted her. She might hold herself awkwardly, she might fail to sing some note in tune, she might forget her words—it mattered not: she had only to turn and laugh to raise shouts of applause. When she gave her famous kick from the hip, the stalls were fired, and a glow of passion rose upward, upward, from gallery to gallery, till it reached the gods. It was a triumph too when she led the dance. She was at home in that: hand on hip, she enthroned Venus in the gutter by the pavement-side. And the music, seemed made for her plebeian voice—shrill piping music, with reminiscences of Saint-Cloud Fair, wheezings of clarinets, and playful trills on the part of the little flutes.

Two numbers were again encored. The opening waltz, that waltz with the naughty rhythmic beat, had returned, and swept the gods with it. Juno, as a peasant woman, caught Jupiter and his little laundress cleverly, and boxed his ears. Diana, surprising Venus in the act of making an assignation with Mars, made haste to indicate hour and place to Vulcan, who cried, "I've hit on a plan!" The rest of the act did not seem very clear. The inquiry ended in a final gallop, after which Jupiter, breathless, streaming with perspiration, and minus his crown, declared that the little women of Earth were delicious, and that the men were all to blame.

The curtain was falling, when certain voices, rising above the storm of bravos, cried uproariously,—

"All! All!"

Thereupon the curtain rose again, the artistes reappeared hand in hand. In the middle of the line Nana and Rose Mignon stood side by side, bowing and curtseying. The audience applauded, the clappers shouted acclamations. Then, little by little, the house emptied.

"I must go and pay my respects to the Countess Muffat," said la Faloise.

"Exactly so; you'll present me," replied Fauchery; "we'll go down afterwards."

But it was not easy to get to the first-tier boxes. In the passage, at the top of the stairs, there was a crush. In order to get forward at all, among the various groups, you had to make yourself small and to slide along, using your elbows in so doing. Leaning under a copper lamp, where a jet of gas was burning, the bulky critic was sitting in judgment on the piece, in presence of an attentive circle. People in passing mentioned his name to each other in muttered tones. He had laughed the whole act through—that was the humor going the round of the passages: nevertheless he was now very severe, and spoke of taste and morals. Further off, the thin-lipped critic was brimming over with a benevolence which had an unpleasant after-taste, as of milk turned sour.

Fauchery glanced along, scrutinizing the boxes through the round openings in each door. But the Count de Vandeuvres stopped him with a question, and when he was informed that the two cousins were going to pay their respects to the Muffats, he pointed out to them Box Seven, from which he had just emerged. Then, bending down and whispering in the journalist's ear,—

"Tell me, my dear fellow," said he, "this Nana—surely she's the girl we saw one evening at the corner of the Rue de Provençe?"

"By Jove, you're right!" cried Fauchery. "I was saying that I had come across her!"

La Faloise presented his cousin to Count Muffat de Beuville, who appeared very frigid. But, on hearing the name "Fauchery," the Countess raised her head, and with a certain reserve complimented the paragraphist on his articles in the *Figaro*. Leaning on the velvet-covered support in front of her, she turned half round with a pretty movement of the shoulders. They talked for a short time, and the Universal Exhibition was mentioned.

"It will be very fine," said the Count, whose square-cut, regular-featured face retained a certain gravity.

"I visited the Champ-de-Mars to-day, and returned thence truly astonished."

"They say that things won't be ready in time," la Faloise ventured to remark. "There's infinite confusion there—"

But the Count interrupted him in his severe voice,—

"Things will be ready. The Emperor desires it."

Fauchery gayly recounted how, one day, when he had gone

down thither in search of a subject for an article, he had come near spending all his time in the aquarium, which was then in course of construction. The Countess smiled. Now and again she glanced down at the body of the house, raising an arm which a white glove covered to the elbow, and fanning herself with languid hand. The house dozed, almost deserted. Some gentlemen in the stalls had opened out newspapers, and ladies received visits quite comfortably, as though they were at their own homes. Only a well-bred whispering was audible under the great chandelier, the light of which was softened in the fine cloud of dust raised by the confused movements of the interval. At the different entrances men were crowding in order to talk to ladies who remained seated. They stood there motionless for a few seconds, craning forward somewhat and displaying the great white bosoms of their shirt-fronts.

"We count on you next Tuesday," said the Countess to la Faloise, and she invited Fauchery, who bowed.

Not a word was said of the play; Nana's name was not once mentioned. The Count was so glacially dignified that he might have been supposed to be taking part at a sitting of the Legislature. In order to explain their presence that evening, he remarked simply that his father-in-law was fond of the theater. The door of the box must have remained open, for the Marquis de Chouard, who had gone out in order to leave his seat to the visitors, was back again. He was straightening up his tall, old figure. His face looked soft and white under a broad-brimmed hat, and with his restless eyes he followed the movements of the women who passed.

The moment the Countess had given her invitation, Fauchery took his leave, feeling that to talk about the play would not be quite the thing. La Faloise was the last to quit the box. He had just noticed the fair-haired Labordette, comfortably installed in the Count de Vandeuvres's stage-box and, chatting at very close quarters with Blanche de Sivry.

"Gad," said he, after rejoining his cousin, "that Labordette knows all the girls, then! He's with Blanche now."

"Doubtless, he knows them all," replied Fauchery, quietly. "What d'you want to be taken for, my friend?"

The passage was somewhat cleared of people, and Fauchery was just about to go downstairs when Lucy Stewart called him. She was quite at the other end of the corridor, at the door of her stage-box. They were getting cooked in there, she said, and she took up the whole corridor in company with Caroline Héquet and her mother, all three nibbling burnt almonds. A box-opener was chatting maternally with them. Lucy fell out with the journalist. He was a pretty fellow, to be sure! He went up to see other women, and didn't even come and ask if they were thirsty! Then, changing the subject,—

"You know, dear boy, I think Nana very nice."

She wanted him to stay in the stage-box for the last act, but he made his escape, promising to catch them at the door afterwards. Downstairs, in front of the theater, Fauchery and la Faloise lit cigarettes. A great gathering blocked the sidewalk, a stream of men who had come down from the theater steps, and were inhaling the fresh night air in the boulevards, where the roar and battle had diminished.

Meanwhile, Mignon had drawn Steiner away to the "Café des Variétés." Seeing Nana's success, he had set to work to talk enthusiastically about her, all the while observing the banker out of the corners of his eyes. He knew him well; twice he had helped him to deceive Rose, and then, the caprice being over, had brought him back to her, faithful and repentant. In the café the too-numerous crowd of customers were squeezing themselves round the marble-topped tables. Several were standing up, drinking in a great hurry. The tall mirrors reflected this thronging world of heads to infinity, and magnified the narrow room beyond measure, with its three chandeliers, its moleskin-covered seats, and its winding staircase draped with red. Steiner went and seated himself at a table in the first saloon, which opened full on the boulevard, its doors having been removed rather early for the time of year. As Fauchery and la Faloise were passing, the banker stopped them.

"Come and take a *bock* with us, eh?" they said.

But he was too preoccupied by an idea, he wanted to have a bouquet thrown to Nana. At last he called a waiter belonging to the café, whom he familiarly addressed as Auguste. Mignon, who was listening, looked at him so sharply that he lost countenance, and stammered out:

"Two bouquets, Auguste, and deliver them to the attendant. A bouquet for each of these ladies! Happy thought, eh?"

At the other end of the saloon, her shoulders resting against the frame of a mirror, a girl some eighteen years of age at the outside, was leaning motionless in front of her empty glass, as though she had been benumbed by long and fruitless waiting. Under the natural curls of her beautiful gray-gold hair, a virginal face looked out at you with velvety eyes, which were at once soft and candid.

She wore a dress of faded green silk, and a round hat which blows had dinted. The cool air of the night made her look very pale.

"Egad, there's Satin," murmured Fauchery when his eye lit upon her.

La Faloise questioned him. Oh, dear, yes, she was a street-walker—she didn't count. But she was such a scandalous sort, that people amused themselves by making her talk. And the journalist, raising his voice,—

"What are you doing there, Satin?"

"I'm bogging," replied Satin quietly, without changing position.

The four men were charmed, and fell a-laughing. Mignon assured them that there was no need to hurry; it would take twenty minutes to set up the scenery for the third act. But the two cousins, having drunk their beer, wanted to go up into the theater again; the cold was making itself felt. Then Mignon remained alone with Steiner, put his elbows on the table, and spoke to him at close quarters.

"It's an understood thing, eh? We are to go to her house, and I'm to introduce you. You know the thing's quite between ourselves—my wife needn't know."

Once more in their places, Fauchery and la Faloise noticed a pretty, quietly-dressed woman in the second tier of boxes. She was with a serious-looking gentleman, a chief clerk at the Office of the Ministry of the Interior, whom la Faloise knew, having met him at the Muffats. As to Fauchery, he was under the impression that her name was Madame Robert, a lady of honorable repute, who had a lover, only one, and that always a person of respectability.

But they had to turn round, for Daguenet was smiling at them. Now that Nana had had a success, he no longer hid himself: indeed, he had just been scoring triumphs in the passages. By his side was the young truant schoolboy, who had not quitted his seat, so stupefying was the state of admiration into which Nana had plunged him. That was it, he thought; that was the woman! And he blushed as he thought so, and dragged his gloves on and off mechanically. Then, since his neighbor had spoken of Nana, he ventured to question him.

"Will you pardon me for asking you, sir, but that lady who is acting—do you know her?"

"Yes, I do a little," murmured Daguenet, with some surprise and hesitation.

"Then you know her address?"

The question, addressed as it was to him, came so abruptly that he felt inclined to respond with a box on the ear.

"No," said he, in a dry tone of voice.

And with that he turned his back. The fair lad knew that he had just been guilty of some breach of good manners. He blushed more hotly than ever and looked scared.

The traditional three knocks were given, and among the returning throng, attendants, laden with pelisses and over-coats, bustled about at a great rate in order to put away people's things. The clappers applauded the scenery, which represented a grotto on Mount Etna, hollowed out in a silver mine and with sides glittering like new money. In the back-ground Vulcan's forge glowed like a setting star. Diana, since the second act, had come to a good understanding with the god, who was to pretend that he was on a journey, so as to leave the way clear for Venus and Mars. Then, scarcely was Diana alone, than Venus made her appearance. A shiver of delight ran round the house. Nana was nude. With quiet audacity, she appeared in her nakedness, certain of the sovran power of her flesh. Some gauze enveloped her, but her rounded shoulders, her Amazonian bosom, her wide hips, which swayed to and fro voluptuously, her whole body, in fact, could be divined, nay, discerned, in all its foamlike whiteness of tint, beneath the slight fabric she wore. It was Venus rising from the waves, with no veil save her tresses. And when Nana lifted her arms, the golden hairs in her arm-pits were observable in the glare of the footlights. There was no applause. Nobody laughed any more. The men strained forward with serious faces, sharp features, mouths irritated and parched. A wind seemed to have passed, a soft, soft wind, laden with a secret menace. Suddenly in the bouncing child the woman stood discovered, a woman full of restless suggestion, who brought with her the delirium of sex, and opened the gates of the unknown world of desire. Nana was smiling still, but her smile was now bitter, as of a devourer of men.

"By God," said Fauchery, quite simply, to la Faloise.

Mars in the mean time, with his plume of feathers, came
hurrying to the trysting-place, and found himself between
the two goddesses. Then ensued a passage which Prullière
played with great delicacy. Petted by Diana, who wanted
to make a final attack upon his feelings before delivering
him up to Vulcan, wheedled by Venus, whom the presence
of her rival excited, he gave himself up to these tender delights with the beatified expression of a man in clover.
Finally, a grand trio brought the scene to a close, and it
was then that an attendant appeared in Lucy Stewart's box
and threw on the stage two immense bouquets of white lilac.
There was applause, Nana and Rose Mignon bowed, while
Prullière picked up the bouquets. Many of the occupants
of the stalls turned smilingly towards the ground-floor occupied by Steiner and Mignon. The banker, his face blood-
red, was suffering from little convulsive twitchings of the
chin, as though he had a stoppage in his throat.

What followed took the house by storm completely.
Diana had gone off in a rage, and directly afterwards, Venus,
sitting on a moss-clad seat, called Mars to her. Never yet
had a more glowing scene of seduction been ventured on.
Nana, her arms round Prullière's neck, was drawing him towards her, when Fontan, with comically-furious mimicry
and an exaggerated imitation of the face of an outraged husband, who surprises his wife in *flagrante delicto,* appeared
at the back of the grotto. He was holding the famous net
with iron meshes. For an instant he poised and swung it,
as a fisherman does when he is going to make a cast, and,
by an ingenious twist, Venus and Mars were caught in the
snare, the net wrapped itself round them, and held them
motionless in the attitude of happy lovers.

A murmur of applause swelled and swelled, like a growing
sigh. There was some hand-clapping, and every opera-glass
was fixed on Venus. Little by little Nana had taken possession of the public, and now every man was her slave.

A wave of lust had flowed from her as from an excited
animal, and its influence had spread, and spread, and spread
till the whole house was possessed by it. At that moment
her slightest movements blew the flame of desire: with her
little finger she ruled men's flesh. Backs were arched and
quivered as though unseen violin-bows had been drawn across
their muscles; upon men's shoulders appeared fugitive hairs,
which flew in air, blown by warm and wandering breaths,
breathed one knew not from what feminine mouth. In front
of him Fauchery saw the truant schoolboy half lifted from
his seat by passion. Curiosity led him to look at the Count
de Vandeuvres—he was extremely pale, and his lips looked
pinched—at fat Steiner, whose face was purple to the verge
of apoplexy—at Labordette, ogling away with the highly-
astonished air of a horse-dealer admiring a perfectly-shaped
mare—at Daguenet, whose ears were blood-red and twitching with enjoyment. Then, a sudden idea made him glance
behind, and he marveled at what he saw in the Muffats' box.
Behind the Countess, who was white and serious as usual, the
Count was sitting straight upright, with mouth agape and
face mottled with red, while close by him, in the shadow,
the restless eyes of the Marquis de Chouard had become cat-
like, phosphorescent, full of golden sparkles. The house was
suffocating, people's very hair grew heavy on their perspiring
heads. For three hours back, the breath of the multitude
had filled and heated the atmosphere with a scent of crowded
humanity. Under the swaying glare of the gas, the dust-
clouds, in mid-air, had grown constantly denser as they hung
motionless beneath the chandelier. The whole house seemed
to be oscillating, to be lapsing towards dizziness, in its fatigue
and excitement, full, as it was, of those drowsy midnight
desires which flutter in the recesses of the bed of passion.
And Nana, in front of this languorous public, these fifteen
hundred human beings thronged and smothered in the exhaustion and nervous exasperation which belong to the close

of a spectacle, Nana still triumphed by right of her marble
flesh, and that sexual nature of hers, which was strong enough
to destroy the whole crowd of her adorers and yet sustain no
injury.

The piece drew to a close. In answer to Vulcan's triumphant summons, all the Olympians defiled before the
lovers, with ohs! and ahs! of stupefaction and gayety.
Jupiter said, "I think it is light conduct on your part, my
son, to summon us to see such a sight as this." Then a re-
action took place in favor of Venus. The Chorus of Cuckolds
was again ushered in by Iris, and besought the master of the
gods not to give effect to its petition, for since women had
lived at home, domestic life had been becoming impossible
for the men; the latter preferred being deceived and happy.
That was the moral of the play. Then Venus was set at
liberty, and Vulcan obtained a partial divorce from her.
Mars was reconciled with Diana, and Jove, for the sake of
domestic peace, packed his little laundress off into a constella-
tion. And finally they extricated Love from his black hole,
where, instead of conjugating the verb *amo*, he had been
busy in the manufacture of "dollies." The curtain fell on an
apotheosis, wherein the Cuckold's Chorus knelt and sang a
hymn of gratitude to Venus, who stood there with smiling
lips, her stature enhanced by her sovran nudity.

The audience, already on the feet, were making for the
exists. The authors were mentioned, and, amid a thunder of
applause there were two calls before the curtain. The shout
of "Nana! Nana!" rang wildly forth. Then, no sooner was
the house empty, than it grew dark: the footlights went out,
the chandelier was turned down, long strips of gray canvas
slipped from the stage-boxes and swathed the gilt ornamentation of the galleries, and the house, lately so full of heat and
noise, lapsed suddenly into a heavy sleep, while a musty, dusty
odor began to pervade it. In the front of her box stood the
Countess Muffat. Very erect and closely wrapped up in her

furs, she stared at the gathering shadows and waited for the crowd to pass away.

In the passages the people were jostling the attendants, who hardly knew what to do among the tumbled heaps of out-door raiment. Fauchery and la Faloise had hurried in order to see the crowd pass out. All along the entrance-hall men formed a living hedge, while down the double staircase came slowly, and in regular complete formation, two interminable throngs of human beings. Steiner, in tow of Mignon, had left the house among the foremost. The Count de Vandeuvres took his departure with Blanche de Sivry on his arm. For a moment or two Gaga and her daughter seemed doubtful how to proceed, but Labordette made haste to go and fetch them a conveyance, the door whereof he gallantly shut after them. Nobody saw Daguenet go by. As the truant schoolboy, registering a mental vow to wait at the stage-door, was running with burning cheeks towards the Passage des Panoramas, of which he found the gate closed, Satin, standing on the edge of the pavement, moved forward and brushed him with her skirts, but he in his despair gave her a savage refusal, and vanished amid the crowd, tears of impotent desire in his eyes. Members of the audience were lighting their cigars, and walking off, humming—

"When Venus roams at eventide."

Satin had gone back in front of the "Café des Variétés," where Auguste let her eat the sugar that remained over from the customers' orders. A stout man, who came out in a very heated condition, finally carried her off in the shadow of the boulevard, which was now gradually going to sleep.

Still people kept coming downstairs. La Faloise was waiting for Clarisse; Fauchery had promised to catch up Lucy Stewart with Caroline Héquet and her mother. They came; they took up a whole corner of the entrance-hall, and were laughing very loud when the Muffats passed by them with an icy expression. Bordenave had just then opened a little door, and, peeping out, had obtained from Fauchery the formal promise of an article. He was dripping with perspiration, his face blazed, as though he were drunk with success.

"You're good for two hundred nights," said la Faloise to him with civility. "The whole of Paris will visit your theater."

But Bordenave grew annoyed, and indicating with a jerk of his chin the public who filled the entrance-hall—a herd of men with parched lips and ardent eyes, still burning with the enjoyment of Nana, he cried out violently,—

"Say, 'my brothel,' you obstinate devil!"

CHAPTER II

AT ten o'clock the next morning, Nana was still asleep. She occupied the second floor of a large new house in the Boulevard Haussmann, the landlord of which let flats to single ladies in order by their means to dry the paint. A rich merchant from Moscow, who had come to pass a winter in Paris, had installed her there, after paying six months' rent in advance. The rooms were too big for her, and had never been completely furnished. The vulgar sumptuosity of gilded consoles and gilded chairs formed a crude contrast therein to the *bric-à-brac* of a second-hand furniture shop— to mahogany round tables, that is to say, and zinc candelabras, which sought to imitate Florentine bronze. All of which smacked of the courtesan, too early deserted by her first serious protector, and fallen back on shabby lovers, of a precarious first appearance, of a bad start, handicapped by refusals of credit and threats of eviction.

Nana was sleeping on her face, hugging in her bare arms a pillow, in which she was burying cheeks grown pale in sleep. The bedroom and the dressing-room were the only two apartments which had been properly furnished by a neighboring upholsterer. A ray of light, gliding in under a curtain, rendered visible rose-wood furniture, and hangings and chairbacks of figured damask with a pattern of big blue flowers on a gray ground. But in the soft atmosphere of that slumbering chamber, Nana suddenly awoke with a start, as though surprised to find an empty place at her side. She looked at the other pillow, lying next to hers: there was the dent of a human head among its flounces: it was still warm. And groping with one hand, she pressed the knob of an electric bell by her bed's-head.

"He's gone, then?" she asked the maid who presented herself.

"Yes, *Madame*, Monsieur Paul went away, not ten minutes back. As *Madame* was tired, he did not wish to wake her. But he ordered me to tell *Madame* that he would come to-morrow."

As she spoke, Zoé, the lady's maid, opened the outer shutters. A flood of daylight entered. Zoé, a dark brunette, with hair in little plaits, had a long canine face, at once livid and full of seams, a snub nose, thick lips, and two black eyes in continual movement.

"To-morrow, to-morrow," repeated Nana, who was not yet wide awake, "is to-morrow the day?"

"Yes, *Madame*, Monsieur Paul has always come on the Wednesday."

"No, now I remember," said the young woman, sitting up. "It's all changed. I wanted to tell him so this morning. He would run against the nigger! We should have a nice to-do!"

"*Madame* did not warn me; I couldn't be aware of it," murmured Zoé. "When *Madame* changes her days, she will do well to tell me, so that I may know. Then the old miser is no longer due on the Tuesday?"

Between themselves they were wont thus gravely to nickname as "old miser" and "nigger" their two paying visitors, one of whom was a tradesman of economical tendencies from the Faubourg Saint-Denis, whilst the other was a Wallachian, a mock count, whose money, paid always at the most irregular intervals, never looked as though it had been honestly come by. Daguenet had made Nana give him the days subsequent to the old miser's visits, and as the trader had to be at home by eight o'clock in the morning, the young man would watch for his departure from Zoé's kitchen, and would take his place, which was still quite warm, till ten o'clock. Then he too would go about his business. Nana and he were wont to think it a very comfortable arrangement.

"So much the worse," said Nana; "I'll write to him this afternoon. And, if he doesn't receive my letter, then to-morrow you will stop him coming in."

In the meantime Zoé was walking softly about the room. She spoke of yesterday's great hit. *Madame* had shewn such talent, she sang so well! Ah! *Madame* need not fret at all now!

Nana, her elbow dug into her pillow, only tossed her head in reply. Her night-dress had slipped down on her shoulders, and her hair, unfastened and entangled, flowed over them in masses.

"Without doubt," she murmured, becoming thoughtful; "but what's to be done to gain time? I'm going to have all sorts of bothers to-day. Now let's see, has the porter come upstairs yet this morning?"

Then both the women talked together seriously. Nana owed three quarters' rent; the landlord was talking of seizing the furniture. Then, too, there was a perfect downpour of creditors; there was a livery-stableman, a needlewoman, a ladies' tailor, a charcoal-dealer, and others besides, who came every day and settled themselves on a bench in the little hall. The charcoal-dealer especially was a dreadful fellow—he shouted on the staircase. But Nana's greatest cause of distress was her little Louis, a child she had given birth to when she was sixteen, and now left in charge of a nurse in a village in the neighborhood of Rambouillet. This woman was clamoring for the sum of three hundred francs before she would consent to give the little Louis back to her. Nana, since her last visit to the child, had been seized with a fit of maternal love, and was desperate at the thought that she could not realize a project, which had now become a hobby with her. This was to pay off the nurse and to place the little man with his aunt, Madame Lerat, at the Batignolles, whither she could go and see him as often as she liked.

Meanwhile, the lady's maid kept hinting that her mistress ought to have confided her necessities to the "old miser."

"To be sure, I told him everything," cried Nana, "and he told me in answer that he had too many big liabilities. He won't go beyond his thousand francs a month. The nigger's beggared just at present; I expect he's lost at play. As to that poor Mimi, he stands in great need of a loan himself; a fall in stocks has cleaned him out—he can't even bring me flowers now."

She was speaking of Daguenet. In the self-abandonment of her awakening she had no secrets from Zoé, and the latter, inured to such confidences, received them with respectful sympathy. Since *Madame* condescended to speak to her of her affairs, she would permit herself to say what she thought. Besides, she was very fond of *Madame;* she had left Madame Blanche for the express purpose of taking service with her, and, Heaven knew, Madame Blanche was straining every nerve to have her again! Situations weren't lacking—she was pretty well known, but she would have stayed with *Madame,* even in narrow circumstances, because she believed in *Madame's* future. And she concluded by stating her advice with precision. When one was young, one often did silly things. But this time it was one's duty to look alive, for the men only thought of having their fun. Oh, dear, yes! things would right themselves. *Madame* had only to say one word in order to quiet her creditors and find the money she stood in need of.

"All that doesn't help me to three hundred francs," Nana kept repeating, as she plunged her fingers into the vagrant convolutions of her back hair. "I must have three hundred francs to-day, at once! It's stupid not to know any one who'll give you three hundred francs."

She racked her brains. She would have sent Madame Lerat, whom she was expecting that very morning, to Rambouillet. The counteraction of her sudden fancy spoiled for her the triumph of last night. Among all those men who had cheered her, to think that there wasn't one to bring her fifteen louis! And then one couldn't accept money in that way! Dear Heaven! how unfortunate she was! And she kept harking back again to the subject of her baby—he had blue eyes like a cherub's, he could lisp "Mamma" in such a funny voice that you were ready to die of laughing!

But, at this moment, the electric bell at the outer door was heard to ring with its quick and tremulous vibration. Zoé returned, murmuring with a confidential air,—

"It's a woman."

She had seen this woman a score of times, only she made believe never to recognize her, and to be quite ignorant of the nature of her relations with ladies in difficulties.

"She has told me her name—Madame Tricon."

"The Tricon," cried Nana. "Dear me! that's true. I'd forgotten her. Shew her in."

Zoé ushered in a tall old lady, who wore ringlets, and looked like a countess who haunts lawyers' offices. Then she effaced herself, disappearing noiselessly with the lithe serpentine movement, wherewith she was wont to withdraw from a room on the arrival of a gentleman. However, she might have stayed. The Tricon did not even sit down. Only a brief exchange of words took place.

"I have some one for you to-day. Do you care about it?"

"Yes. How much?"

"Twenty louis."

"At what o'clock?"

"At three. It's settled, then?"

"It's settled."

Straightway the Tricon talked of the state of the weather. It was dry weather, pleasant for walking. She had still four or five persons to see. And she took her departure, after consulting a small memorandum book. When she was once more alone, Nana appeared comforted. A slight shiver agitated her shoulders, and she wrapped herself softly up again in her warm bed-clothes, with the lazy movements of a cat who is susceptible to cold. Little by little her eyes closed, and she lay smiling at the thought of dressing Louiset prettily on the following day, while, in the slumber into which she once more sank, last night's long feverish dream of endlessly rolling applause returned like a sustained accompaniment to music, and gently soothed her lassitude.

At eleven o'clock, when Zoé shewed Madame Lerat into the room, Nana was still asleep. But she woke at the noise, and cried out at once,—

"It's you. You'll go to Rambouillet to-day."

"That's what I've come for," said the aunt. "There's a train at twenty past twelve. I've got time to catch it."

"No, I shall only have the money by-and-by," replied the young woman, stretching herself and throwing out her bosom. "You'll have lunch, and then we'll see."

Zoé brought a dressing-jacket.

"The hairdresser's here, Madame," she murmured.

But Nana did not wish to go into the dressing-room. And she herself cried out,—

"Come in, Francis."

A well-dressed man pushed open the door and bowed. Just at that moment Nana was getting out of bed, her bare legs in full view. But she did not hurry, and stretched her hands out so as to let Zoé draw on the sleeves of the dressing-jacket. Francis, on his part, was quite at his ease, and without turning away waited with a sober expression on his face.

"Perhaps *Madame* has not seen the papers. There's a very nice article in the *Figaro*."

He had brought the journal. Madame Lerat put on her spectacles, and read the article aloud, standing in front of the window as she did so. She had the build of a policeman, and she drew herself up to her full height, while her nostrils seemed to compress themselves whenever she uttered a gallant epithet. It was a notice by Fauchery, written just after the performance, and it consisted of a couple of very glowing columns, full of witty sarcasm about the artist and of broad admiration for the woman.

"Excellent!" Francis kept repeating.

Nana laughed good-humoredly at his chaffing her about her voice! He was a nice fellow was that Fauchery, and she would repay him for his charming style of writing. Madame Lerat, after having re-read the notice, roundly declared that the men all had the devil in their shanks; and she refused to explain herself further, being fully satisfied with a brisk allusion which she alone knew the meaning of. Francis finished turning up and fastening Nana's hair. He bowed, and said,—

"I'll keep my eye on the evening papers. At half-past five as usual, eh?"

"Bring me a pot of pomade, and a pound of burnt almonds from Boissier's," Nana cried to him across the drawing-room just as he was shutting the door after him.

Then the two women, once more alone, recollected that they had not embraced, and they planted big kisses on each other's cheeks. The notice warmed their hearts. Nana, who up till now had been half asleep, was again seized with the fever of her triumph. Dear, dear, 'twas Rose Mignon that would be spending a pleasant morning! Her aunt having been unwilling to go to the theater, because, as she averred, sudden emotions ruined her stomach, Nana set herself to describe the events of the evening, and grew intoxicated at her own recital, as though all Paris had been shaken to the ground by the applause. Then, suddenly interrupting herself, she asked with a laugh if one would ever have imagined it all when she used to go trapesing about the Rue de la Goutte-d'Or. Madame Lerat shook her head. No, no, one never could have foreseen it! And she began talking in her turn, assuming a serious air as she did so, and calling Nana "daughter." Wasn't she a second mother to her, since the first had gone to rejoin papa and grandmamma? Nana was greatly softened, and on the verge of tears. But Madame Lerat declared that the past was the past—oh, yes, to be sure, a dirty past with things in it which it was as well not to stir up every day. She had left off seeing her niece for a long time, because, among the family, she was accused of ruining herself along with the little thing. Good God, as though that were possible! She didn't ask for confidences, she believed that Nana had always lived decently, and now it was enough for her to have found her again in a fine position, and to observe her kind feelings towards her son. Virtue and hard work were still the only things worth anything in this world.

"Who is the baby's father?" she said, interrupting herself, her eyes lit up with an expression of acute curiosity.

Nana was taken by surprise, and hesitated a moment.

"A gentleman," she replied.

"There now!" rejoined the aunt. "They declared that you had him by a stonemason who was in the habit of beating you. Indeed, you shall tell me all about it some day; you know I'm discreet! Tut, tut, I'll look after him as though he were a prince's son."

She had retired from business as a florist, and was living on her savings, which she had got together sou by sou, till now they brought her in an income of six hundred francs a year. Nana promised to rent some pretty little lodgings for her, and to give her a hundred francs a month besides. At the mention of this sum, the aunt forgot herself, and shrieked to her niece, bidding her squeeze their throats, since she had them in her grasp. She was meaning the men, of course. Then they both embraced again, but, in the midst of her rejoicing, Nana's face, as she led the talk back to the subject of Louiset, seemed to be overshadowed by a sudden recollection.

"Isn't it a bore I've got to go out at three o'clock?" she muttered. "It *is* a nuisance!"

Just then Zoé came in to say that lunch was on the table. They went into the dining-room, where an old lady was already seated at table. She had not taken her hat off, and she wore a dark dress of an indecisive color midway between puce and goose dripping. Nana did not seem surprised at sight of her. She simply asked her why she hadn't come into the bedroom.

"I heard voices," replied the old lady. "I thought you had company."

Madame Maloir, a respectable-looking and mannerly woman, was Nana's old friend, chaperon, and companion. Madame Lerat's presence seemed to fidget her at first. After-wards, when she became aware that it was Nana's aunt, she looked at her with a sweet expression and a die-away smile. In the meantime, Nana, who averred that she was as hungry as a wolf, threw herself on the radishes, and gobbled them up without bread. Madame Lerat had become ceremonious; she refused the radishes as provocative of phlegm. By-and-by when Zoé had brought in the cutlets, Nana just chipped the meat, and contented herself with sucking the bones. Now and again she scrutinized her old friend's hat out of the corners of her eyes.

"It's the new hat I gave you?" she ended by saying.

"Yes, I made it up," murmured Madame Maloir, her mouth full of meat.

The hat was smart to distraction. In front it was greatly exaggerated, and it was adorned with a lofty feather. Madame Maloir had a mania for doing up all her hats afresh; she alone knew what really became her, and with a few stitches she could manufacture a toque out of the most elegant head-gear. Nana, who had brought her this very hat in order not to be ashamed of her when in her company out of doors, was very near being vexed.

"Push it up, at any rate," she cried.

"No, thank you," replied the old lady with dignity. "It doesn't get in my way: I can eat very comfortably as it is."

After the cutlets came cauliflowers and the remains of a cold chicken. But at the arrival of each successive dish Nana made a little face, hesitated, sniffed, and left her plateful untouched. She finished her lunch with the help of preserve.

Dessert took a long time. Zoé did not remove the cloth before serving the coffee. Indeed the ladies simply pushed back their plates before taking it. They talked continually of yesterday's charming evening. Nana kept rolling cigarettes, which she smoked, swinging up and down on her backward-tilted chair. And as Zoé had remained behind and was lounging idly against the sideboard, it came about that the company were favored with her history. She said she was the daughter of a midwife at Bercy who had failed in business. First of all she had taken service with a dentist, and after that with an insurance agent, but neither place suited her; and she thereupon enumerated, not without a certain amount of pride, the names of the ladies with whom she had served as lady's maid. Zoé spoke of these ladies as one who had had the making of their fortunes. It was very certain that, without her, more than one would have had some queer tales to tell. Thus, one day, when Madame Blanche is with Monsieur Octave, in comes the old gentleman. What does Zoé do? She makes believe to tumble as she crosses the drawing-room; the old boy rushes up to her assistance, flies to the kitchen to fetch her a glass of water, and Monsieur Octave slips away.

"Oh, she's a good girl, you bet!" said Nana, who was listening to her with tender interest, and a sort of submissive admiration.

"Now, I've had my troubles," began Madame Lerat. And edging up to Madame Maloir, she imparted to her certain confidential confessions. Both ladies took lumps of sugar dipped in cognac, and sucked them. But Madame Maloir was wont to listen to other people's secrets without ever confessing anything concerning herself. People said that she lived on a mysterious allowance in a room whither no one ever penetrated.

All of a sudden, Nana grew excited.

"Don't play with the knives, aunt. You know it gives me a turn!"

Without thinking about it, Madame Lerat had crossed two knives on the table in front of her. Notwithstanding this, the young woman defended herself from the charge of superstition. Thus, if the salt were upset, it meant nothing, even on a Friday; but when it came to knives, that was too much of a good thing: that had never proved fallacious. There could be no doubt that something unpleasant was going to happen to her. She yawned, and then with an air of profound boredom,—

"Two o'clock already. I must go out. What a nuisance!"

The two old ladies looked at one another. The three women shook their heads without speaking. To be sure, life was not always amusing. Nana had tilted her chair back anew and lit a cigarette, while the others sat pursing up their lips discreetly, thinking deeply philosophic thoughts.

"While waiting for you to return, we'll play a game of bézique," said Madame Maloir, after a short silence. "Does *Madame* play bézique?"

Certainly, Madame Lerat played it, and that to perfection. It was no good troubling Zoé, who had vanished—a corner of the table would do quite well. And they pushed back the tablecloth over the dirty plates. But as Madame Maloir was herself going to take the cards out of a drawer in the sideboard, Nana remarked that, before she sat down to her game, it would be very nice of her if she would write her a letter. It bored Nana to write letters; besides she was not sure of her spelling, whilst her old friend could turn out the most feeling epistles. She ran to fetch some good note paper in her bedroom. An inkstand consisting of a bottle of ink worth about three sous stood untidily on one of the pieces of furniture, with a pen deep in rust beside it. The letter was for Daguenet. Madame Maloir herself wrote in her bold English hand, "My darling little man," and then she told him not to come to-morrow, because "that could not be," but hastened to add that "she was with him in thought at every moment of the day, whether she were near or far away."

"And I end with 'a thousand kisses,'" she murmured.

Madame Lerat had shewn her approval of each phrase with an emphatic nod. Her eyes were sparkling; she loved to find herself in the midst of love affairs. Nay, she was seized with a desire to add some words of her own, and assuming a tender look, and cooing like a dove, she suggested,—

"A thousand kisses on thy beautiful eyes."

"That's the thing: 'a thousand kisses on thy beautiful eyes!'" Nana repeated, while the two old ladies assumed a beatified expression.

Zoé was rung for, and told to take the letter down to a commissionaire. She had just been talking with the theater messenger, who had brought her mistress the day's playbill and rehearsal arrangements, which he had forgotten in the morning. Nana had this individual ushered in, and got him to take the letter to Daguenet on his return. Then she put questions to him. Oh, yes! Monsieur Bordenave was very pleased; people had already taken seats for a week to come; *Madame* had no idea of the number of people who had been asking her address since morning. When the man had taken his departure, Nana announced that at most she would only be out half an hour. If there were any visitors, Zoé would make them wait. As she spoke, the electric bell sounded. It was a creditor in the shape of the man of whom she jobbed her carriages. He had settled himself on the bench in the ante-room, and the fellow was free to twiddle his thumbs till night—there wasn't the least hurry now.

"Come, buck up!" said Nana, still torpid with laziness, and yawning and stretching afresh. "I ought to be there now!"

Yet she did not budge, but kept watching the play of her aunt, who had just announced "four aces." Chin on hand, she grew quite engrossed in it, but gave a violent start on hearing three o'clock strike.

"Good God!" she cried roughly.

Then Madame Maloir, who was counting the tricks she had won with her tens and aces, said cheeringly to her in her soft voice,—

"It would be better, dearie, to give up your expedition at once."

"No, be quick about it," said Madame Lerat, shuffling the cards. "I shall take the half-past four o'clock train, if you're back here with the money before four o'clock."

"Oh! there'll be no time lost," she murmured.

Ten minutes after, Zoé helped her on with a dress and a

hat. It didn't matter much if she were badly turned out. Just as she was about to go downstairs there was a new ring at the bell. This time it was the charcoal-dealer. Very well, he might keep the livery-stable keeper company—it would amuse the fellows. Only, as she dreaded a scene, she crossed the kitchen, and made her escape by the back stairs. She often went that way, and in return had only to lift up her flounces.

"When one is a good mother, anything's excusable," said Madame Maloir sententiously, when left alone with Madame Lerat.

"Four kings," replied this lady, whom the play greatly excited.

And they both plunged into an interminable game.

The table had not been cleared. The smell of lunch and the cigarette smoke filled the room with an ambient steamy vapor. The two ladies had again set to work dipping lumps of sugar in brandy and sucking the same. For twenty minutes at least they played and sucked simultaneously when, the electric bell having rung a third time, Zoé bustled into the room, and roughly disturbed them, just as if they had been her own friends.

"Look here, that's another ring. You can't stay where you are. If many folks call I must have the whole flat. Now, off you go, off you go!"

Madame Maloir was for finishing the game; but Zoé looked as if she was going to pounce down on the cards, and so she decided to carry them off without in any way altering their positions, whilst Madame Lerat undertook the removal of the brandy bottle, the glasses, and the sugar. Then they both scudded to the kitchen, where they installed themselves at the table in an empty space between the dish-clouts, which were spread out to dry, and the bowl still full of dish-water.

"We said it was three hundred and forty. It's your turn."

"I play hearts."

When Zoé returned she found them once again absorbed.
After a silence, as Madame Lerat was shuffling, Madame
Maloir asked who it was.

"Oh! nobody to speak of," replied the servant carelessly;
"a slip of a lad! I wanted to send him away again, but he's
such a pretty boy with never a hair on his chin, and blue
eyes, and a girl's face! So I told him to wait after all. He's
got an enormous bouquet in his hand, which he never once
consented to put down. One would like to catch him one—
a brat like that who ought to be at school still!"

Madame Lerat went to fetch a water bottle to mix herself
some brandy and water, the lumps of sugar having rendered
her thirsty. Zoé muttered something to the effect that she
really didn't mind if she drank something too. Her mouth,
she averred, was as bitter as gall.

"So you put him?—" continued Madame Maloir.

"Oh, yes, I put him in the closet at the end of the room,
the little unfurnished one. There's only one of my lady's
trunks there and a table. It's there I stow the lubbers."

And she was putting plenty of sugar in her grog, when
the electric bell made her jump. Oh, drat it all! wouldn't
they let her have a drink in peace? If they were to have a
peal of bells things promised well. Nevertheless, she ran off
to open the door. Returning presently she saw Madame
Maloir questioning her with a glance.

"It's nothing," she said, "only a bouquet."

All three refreshed themselves, nodding to each other in
token of salutation. Then, whilst Zoé was at length busy
clearing the table, bringing the plates out one by one and
putting them in the sink, two other rings followed close upon
one another. But they weren't serious, for, whilst keeping
the kitchen informed of what was going on, she twice repeated her disdainful expression.

"Nothing; only a bouquet."

Notwithstanding which, the old ladies laughed between

two of their tricks, when they heard her describe the looks
of the creditors in the ante-room after the flowers had arrived. *Madame* would find her bouquets on her toilet-table.
What a pity it was they cost such a lot, and that you could
only get ten sous for them! Oh, dear, yes, plenty of money
was wasted!

"For my part," said Madame Maloir, "I should be quite
content if every day of my life I got what the men in Paris
had spent on flowers for the women."

"Now, you know, you're not hard to please," murmured
Madame Lerat. "Why, one would have only just enough to
buy thread with. Four queens, my dear."

It was ten minutes to four. Zoé was astonished—could
not understand why her mistress was out so long. Ordinarily, when *Madame* found herself obliged to go out in the
afternoons, she got it over in double-quick time. But Madame Maloir declared that one didn't always manage things
as one wished. Truly, life was beset with obstacles, averred
Madame Lerat. The best course was to wait. If her niece
was long in coming, it was because her occupations detained
her, wasn't it so? Besides, they weren't overworked—it was
comfortable in the kitchen. And, as hearts were out, Madame Lerat threw down diamonds.

The bell began again, and when Zoé reappeared she was
burning with excitement.

"My children, it's fat Steiner!" said she, in the doorway,
lowering her voice as she spoke. "I've put *him* in the little
sitting-room."

Thereupon Madame Maloir spoke about the banker to
Madame Lerat, who knew no such gentleman. Was he getting ready to give Rose Mignon the go-by? Zoé shook her
head; she knew a thing or two. But, once more, she had
to go and open the door.

"Here's bothers!" she murmured, when she came back.
"It's the nigger! 'Twasn't any good telling him that my

lady's gone out, and so he's settled himself in the bedroom. We only expected him this evening."

At a quarter past four Nana was not in yet. What could she be after? It was silly of her! Two other bouquets were brought round, and Zoé, growing bored, looked to see if there were any coffee left. Yes, the ladies would willingly finish off the coffee; it would waken them up. Sitting hunched up on their chairs, they were beginning to fall asleep through dint of constantly taking their cards between their fingers with the accustomed movement. The half-hour sounded. Something must decidedly have happened to *Madame*. And they began whispering to each other.

Suddenly Madame Maloir forgot herself, and in a ringing voice announced,—

"I've the five hundred! Trumps, Major Quint!"

"Oh, do be quiet!" said Zoé, angrily. "What will all those gentlemen think?"

And in the silence which ensued, and amid the whispered muttering of the two old women at strife over their game, the sound of rapid footsteps ascended from the back stairs. It was Nana at last. Before she had opened the door, her breathlessness became audible. She bounced abruptly in, looking very red in the face. Her skirt, the string of which must have been broken, was trailing over the stairs, and her flounces had just been dipped in a puddle of something unpleasant, which had oozed out on the landing of the first floor, where the servant girl was a regular slut.

"Here you are! It's lucky!" said Madame Lerat, pursing up her lips, for she was still vexed at Madame Maloir's "five hundred." "You may flatter yourself at the way you keep folks waiting."

"*Madame* isn't reasonable, indeed she isn't!" added Zoé.

Nana was already harassed, and these reproaches exasperated her. Was that the way people received her after the worry she had gone through?

"Will you blooming well leave me alone, eh?" she cried.

"Hush, ma'am, there are people in there," said the maid.

Then, in lower tones, the young woman stuttered breathlessly,—

"D'you suppose I've been having a good time? Why, there was no end to it. I should have liked to see you there! I was boiling with rage; I felt inclined to smack somebody. And never a cab to come home in! Luckily it's only a step from here, but never mind that, I did just run home."

"You have the money?" asked the aunt.

"Dear, dear! that question!" rejoined Nana.

She had sat herself down on a chair close up against the stove, for her legs had failed her after so much running; and without stopping to take breath, she drew from behind her stays an envelope in which there were four hundred-franc notes. They were visible through a large rent she had torn with savage fingers in order to be sure of the contents. The three women round about her stared fixedly at the envelope, a big, crumpled, dirty receptacle, as it lay clasped in her small gloved hands.

It was too late now—Madame Lerat would not go to Rambouillet till to-morrow, and Nana entered into long explanations.

"There's company waiting for you," the lady's maid repeated.

But Nana grew excited again. The company might wait: she'd go to them all in good time when she'd finished. And, as her aunt began putting her hand out for the money,—

"Ah, no! not all of it," said she. "Three hundred francs for the nurse, fifty for your journey and expenses, that's three hundred and fifty. Fifty francs I keep."

The big difficulty was how to find change. There were not ten francs in the house. But they did not even address themselves to Madame Maloir who, never having more than a six-sou omnibus fare upon her, was listening in quite a disinterested manner. At length Zoé went out of the room, remarking that she would go and look in her box, and she brought back a hundred francs in hundred-sou pieces. They were counted out on a corner of the table, and Madame Lerat took her departure at once, after having promised to bring Louiset back with her the following day.

"You say there's company there?" continued Nana, still sitting on the chair and resting herself.

"Yes, *Madame*, three people."

And Zoé mentioned the banker first. Nana made a face. Did that man Steiner think she was going to let herself be bored because he had thrown her a bouquet yesterday evening?

"Besides, I've had enough of it," she declared. "I shan't receive to-day. Go and say you don't expect me now."

"*Madame* will think the matter over; *Madame* will receive Monsieur Steiner," murmured Zoé, gravely, without budging from her place. She was annoyed to see her mistress on the verge of committing another foolish mistake.

Then she mentioned the Wallachian, who ought by now to find time hanging heavy on his hands in the bedroom. Whereupon Nana grew furious, and more obstinate than ever. No, she would see nobody, nobody! Who'd sent her such a blooming leech of a man?

"Chuck 'em all out! I—I'm going to play a game of bézique with Madame Maloir. I prefer doing that."

The bell interrupted her remarks. That was the last straw. Another of the beggars yet! She forbade Zoé to go and open the door, but the latter had left the kitchen without listening to her, and when she reappeared she brought back a couple of cards, and said authoritatively,—

"I told them that *Madame* was receiving visitors. The gentlemen are in the drawing-room."

Nana had sprung up raging, but the names of the Marquis de Chouard and of Count Muffat de Beuville, which were inscribed on the cards, calmed her down. For a moment or two she remained silent.

"Who are they?" she asked at last. "You know them?"

"I know the old fellow," replied Zoé, discreetly pursing up her lips.

And, her mistress continuing to question her with her eyes, she added simply,—

"I've seen him somewhere."

This remark seemed to decide the young woman. Regretfully she left the kitchen, that asylum of steaming warmth, where you could talk and take your ease amid the pleasant fumes of the coffee-pot, which was being kept warm over a handful of glowing embers. She left Madame Maloir behind her. That lady was now busy reading her fortune by the cards: she had never yet taken her hat off, but now in order to be more at her ease she undid the strings and threw them back over her shoulders.

In the dressing-room, where Zoé rapidly helped her on with a tea-gown, Nana revenged herself for the way in which they were all boring her, by muttering quiet curses upon the male sex. These big words caused the lady's maid not a little distress, for she saw with pain that her mistress was not rising superior to her origin as quickly as she could have desired. She even made bold to beg *Madame* to calm herself.

"You bet," was Nana's crude answer; "they're swine, they glory in that sort of thing."

Nevertheless, she assumed her princess-like manner, as she was wont to call it. But just when she was turning to go into the drawing-room, Zoé held her back, and herself introduced the Marquis de Chouard and the Count Muffat into the dressing-room. It was much better so.

"I regret having kept you waiting, gentlemen," said the young woman, with studied politeness.

The two men bowed and seated themselves. A blind of embroidered tulle kept the little room in twilight. It was

the most elegant chamber in the flat, for it was hung with
some light-colored fabric and contained a cheval-glass
framed in inlaid wood, a lounge chair, and some others with
arms and blue satin upholsteries. On the toilet-table, the
bouquets—roses, lilacs, and hyacinths—appeared like a very
ruin of flowers. Their perfume was strong and penetrating,
while through the dampish air of the place, which was full of
the spoilt exhalations of the washstand, came occasional whiffs
of a more pungent scent, the scent of some grains of dry
patchouli ground to fine powder at the bottom of a cup.
And as she gathered herself together, and drew up her dressing-jacket, which had been ill-fastened, Nana had all the appearance of having been surprised at her toilet: her skin was
still damp, she smiled, and looked quite startled amid her frills
and laces.

"Madam, you will pardon our insistence," said the Count
Muffat, gravely. "We come on a quest. Monsieur and I
are members of the Benevolent Organization of the district."

The Marquis de Chouard hastened, gallantly, to add,—

"When we learnt that a great artiste lived in this house,
we promised ourselves that we would put the claims of our
poor people before her in a very special manner. Talent is
never without a heart."

Nana pretended to be modest. She answered them with
little assenting movements of her head, making rapid reflections at the same time. It must be the old man that had
brought the other one: he had such wicked eyes. And yet
the other was not to be trusted either: the veins near his
temples were so queerly puffed up. He might quite well have
come by himself. Ah, now that she thought of it, it was this
way: the porter had given them her name, and they had
egged one another on, each with his own ends in view.

"Most certainly, gentlemen, you were quite right to come
up," said she, with a very good grace.

But the electric bell made her tremble again. Another call, and that Zoé always opening the door! She went on,—
"One is only too happy to be able to give."

At bottom she was flattered.

"Ah, *Madame*," rejoined the Marquis, "if only you knew about it! There's such misery! Our district has more than three thousand poor people in it, and yet it's one of the richest. You cannot picture to yourself anything like the present distress—children with no bread, women ill, utterly without assistance, perishing of the cold—!"

"The poor souls!" cried Nana, very much moved.

Such was her feeling of compassion that tears flooded her fine eyes. No longer studying deportment, she leant forward with a quick movement, and under her open dressing-jacket her neck became visible, while the bent position of her knees served to outline the rounded contour of the thigh under the thin fabric of her skirt. A little flush of blood appeared in the Marquis's cadaverous cheeks. Count Muffat, who was on the point of speaking, lowered his eyes. The air of that little room was too hot: it had the close heavy warmth of a greenhouse. The roses were withering, and intoxicating odors floated up from the patchouli in the cup.

"One would like to be very rich on occasions like this," added Nana. "Well, well, we each do what we can. Believe me, gentlemen, if I had known—"

She was on the point of being guilty of a silly speech, so melted was she at heart. But she did not end her sentence, and for a moment was worried at not being able to remember where she had put her fifty francs on changing her dress. But she recollected at last: they must be on the corner of her toilet table under an inverted pomatum-pot. As she was in the act of rising, the bell sounded for quite a long time. Capital! Another of them still! It would never end. The Count and the Marquis had both risen too, and the ears of the latter seemed to be pricked up, and, as it were, pointing towards the door: doubtless he knew that kind of ring. Muffat looked at him; then they averted their gaze mutually. They felt awkward, and once more assumed their frigid bearing, the one looking square-set and solid with his thick head of hair, the other drawing back his lean shoulders, over which fell his fringe of thin white locks.

"My faith," said Nana, bringing the ten big silver pieces, and quite determined to laugh about it, "I am going to entrust you with this, gentlemen. It is for the poor."

And the adorable little dimple in her chin became apparent. She assumed her favorite pose, her amiable baby expression, as she held the pile of five-franc pieces on her open palm and offered it to the men, as though she were saying to them,— "Now then, who wants some?" The Count was the sharper of the two. He took the fifty francs, but left one piece behind, and, in order to gain possession of it, had to pick it off the young woman's very skin, a moist supple skin, the touch of which sent a thrill through him. She was thoroughly merry, and did not cease laughing.

"Come, gentlemen," she continued. "Another time I hope to give more."

The gentlemen no longer had any pretext for staying, and they bowed, and went towards the door. But just as they were about to go out, the bell rang anew. The Marquis could not conceal a faint smile, while a frown made the Count look more grave than before. Nana detained them some seconds so as to give Zoé time to find yet another corner for the new-comers. She did not relish meetings at her house. Only, this time, the whole place must be packed! She was therefore much relieved when she saw the drawing-room empty, and asked herself whether Zoé had really stuffed them into the cupboards.

"*Au revoir*, gentlemen," said she, pausing on the threshold of the drawing-room.

It was as though she lapped them in her laughing smile

and clear unclouded glance. The Count Muffat bowed
slightly. Despite his great social experience, he felt that he
had lost his equilibrium. He needed air, he was overcome
with the dizzy feeling engendered in that dressing-room, with
a scent of flowers, with a feminine essence which choked him.
And, behind his back, the Marquis de Chouard, who was sure
that he could not be seen, made so bold as to wink at Nana,
his whole face suddenly altering its expression, as he did so,
and his tongue nigh lolling from his mouth.

When the young woman reëntered the little room, where
Zoé was awaiting her with letters and visiting cards, she
cried out, laughing more heartily than ever,—

"There are a pair of beggars for you! Why, they've got
away with my fifty francs!"

She wasn't vexed. It struck her as a joke that *men* should
have got money out of her. All the same they were swine,
for she hadn't a sou left. But at sight of the cards and the
letters her bad temper returned. As to the letters, why, she
said "pass" to them. They were from fellows who, after
applauding her last night, were now making their declarations. And as to the callers, they might go about their business!

Zoé had stowed them all over the place, and she called attention to the great capabilities of the flat, every room in
which opened on the corridor. That wasn't the case at Madame Blanche's, where people had all to go through the
drawing-room. Oh, yes, Madame Blanche had had plenty of
bothers over it!

"You will send them all away," continued Nana, in pur-
suance of her idea. "Begin with the 'nigger.'"

"Oh, as to him, *Madame*, I gave him his marching orders
a while ago," said Zoé, with a grin. "He only wanted to tell
Madame that he couldn't come to-night."

There was vast joy at this announcement, and Nana
clapped her hands. He wasn't coming, what good luck! She

would be free then! And she emitted sighs of relief, as though she had been let off the most abominable of tortures. Her first thought was for Daguenet. Poor duck, why she had just written to tell him to wait till Thursday! Quick, quick, Madame Maloir should write a second letter! But Zoé announced that Madame Maloir had slipped away unnoticed, according to her wont. Whereupon Nana, after talking of sending some one to him, began to hesitate. She was very tired. A long night's sleep—oh, it would be so jolly! The thought of such a treat overcame her at last. For once in a way, she could allow herself that!

"I shall go to bed when I come back from the theater," she murmured greedily, "and you won't wake me before noon."

Then raising her voice,—

"Now then, gee up! Shove the others downstairs!"

Zoé did not move. She would never have dreamt of giving her mistress overt advice, only now she made shift to give *Madame* the benefit of her experience, when *Madame* seemed to be running her hot head against a wall.

"Monsieur Steiner as well?" she queried curtly.

"Why, certainly!" replied Nana. "Before all the rest."

The maid still waited, in order to give her mistress time for reflection. *Would* not *Madame* be proud to get such a rich gentleman away from her rival, Rose Mignon—a man, moreover, who was known in all the theaters?

"Now, to make haste, my dear," rejoined Nana, who perfectly understood the situation, "and tell him he pesters me."

But suddenly there was a reversion of feeling. To-morrow she might want him. Whereupon she laughed, winked once or twice, and with a naughty little gesture cried out,—

"After all's said and done, if I want him, the best way even now is to kick him out of doors."

Zoé seemed much impressed. Struck with a sudden admiration, she gazed at her mistress, and then went and chucked Steiner out of doors without further deliberation.

Meanwhile, Nana waited patiently for a second or two, in order to give her time to sweep the place out, as she phrased it. No one would ever have expected such a siege! She craned her head into the drawing-room, and found it empty. The dining-room was empty too. But as she continued her visitation in a calmer frame of mind, feeling certain that nobody remained behind, she opened the door of a closet and came suddenly upon a very young man. He was sitting on the top of a trunk, holding a huge bouquet on his knees, and looking exceeding quiet and extremely well-behaved.

"Goodness gracious me!" she cried. "There's one of 'em in there even now!"

The very young man had jumped down at sight of her, and was blushing as red as a poppy. He did not know what to do with his bouquet, which he kept shifting from one hand to the other, whilst his looks betrayed the extreme of emotion. His youth, his embarrassment, and the funny figure he cut in his struggles with his flowers, melted Nana's heart, and she burst into a pretty peal of laughter. Well now, the very children were coming, were they? Men were arriving in long clothes. So she gave up all airs and graces, became familiar and maternal, tapped her leg, and asked for fun,—

"You want me to wipe your nose, do you, baby?"

"Yes," replied the lad in a low supplicating tone.

This answer made her merrier than ever. He was seventeen years old, he said. His name was Georges Hugon. He was at the Variétés last night and now he had come to see her.

"These flowers are for me?"

"Yes."

"Then give 'em to me, booby!"

But, as she took the bouquet from him, he sprang upon

her hands and kissed them with all the gluttonous eagerness peculiar to his charming time of life. She had to beat
him to make him leave go. There was a dreadful little drib-
bling customer for you! But as she scolded him, she flushed
rosy-red and began smiling. And with that she sent him
about his business, telling him that he might call again. He
staggered away; he could not find the doors.

Nana went back into her dressing-room, where Francis
made his appearance almost simultaneously in order to dress
her hair for the evening. Seated in front of her mirror, and
bending her head beneath the hairdresser's nimble hands,
she stayed silently meditative. Presently, however, Zoé entered, remarking,—

"There's one of them, *Madame,* who refuses to go."

"Very well, he must be left alone," answered she quietly.

"If that comes to that, they still keep arriving."

"Bah! tell 'em to wait. When they begin to feel too
hungry they'll be off."

Her humor had changed, and she was now delighted to
make people wait about for nothing. A happy thought
struck her as very amusing: she escaped from beneath Francis' hands, and ran and bolted the doors. They might now
crowd in there, as much as they liked: they would probably
refrain from making a hole through the wall. Zoé could
come in and out through the little doorway leading to the
kitchen. However, the electric bell rang more lustily than
ever. Every five minutes a clear lively little ting-ting recurred as regularly as if it had been produced by some well-
adjusted piece of mechanism. And Nana counted these rings
to while the time away withal. But suddenly she remembered something.

"I say, where are my burnt almonds?"

Francis, too, was forgetting about the burnt almonds.
But now he drew a paper bag from one of the pockets of his
frock-coat, and presented it to her with the discreet gesture

of a man who is offering a lady a present. Nevertheless, whenever his accounts came to be settled, he always put the burnt almonds down on his bill. Nana put the bag between her knees, and set to work munching her sweetmeats, turning her head from time to time under the hairdresser's gently-compelling touch.

"The deuce," she murmured, after a silence, "there's a troop for you!"

Thrice, in quick succession, the bell had sounded. Its summonses became fast and furious. There were modest tintinabulations, which seemed to stutter and tremble like a first avowal: there were bold rings which vibrated under some rough touch, and hasty rings which sounded through the house with shivering rapidity. It was a regular peal, as Zoé said, a peal loud enough to upset the neighborhood, seeing that a whole mob of men were jabbing at the ivory button, one after the other. That old joker, Bordenave, had really been far too lavish with her address. Why, the whole of yesterday's house was coming!

"By-the-by, Francis, have you five louis?" said Nana.

He drew back, looked carefully at her head-dress, and then quietly remarked,—

"Five louis, that's according!"

"Ah, you know if you want securities . . ." she continued.

And without finishing her sentence, she indicated the adjoining rooms with a sweeping gesture. Francis lent the five louis. Zoé, during each momentary respite, kept coming in to get *Madame's* things ready. Soon she came to dressing her, whilst the hairdresser lingered with the intention of giving some finishing touches to the head-dress. But the bell kept continually disturbing the lady's maid, who left *Madame* with her stays half-laced and only one shoe on. Despite her long experience, the maid was losing her head. After bringing every nook and corner into requisition, and putting men pretty well everywhere, she had been driven to

stow them away in threes and fours, which was a course of
procedure entirely opposed to her principles. So much the
worse for them if they ate each other up! It would afford
more room! And Nana, sheltering behind her carefully
bolted door, began laughing at them, declaring that she
could hear them pant. They ought to be looking lovely in
there, with their tongues hanging out like a lot of bow-wows
sitting round on their behinds. Yesterday's success was not
yet over, and this pack of men had followed up her scent.

"Provided they don't break anything," she murmured.

She began to feel some anxiety, for she fancied she felt
their hot breath coming through chinks in the door. But Zoé
ushered Labordette in, and the young woman gave a little
shout of relief. He was anxious to tell her about an account
he had settled for her at the Justice of Peace's Court. But
she did not attend, and said,—

"I'll take you along with me. We'll have dinner together,
and afterwards you shall escort me to the Variétés. I don't
go on before half-past nine."

Good old Labordette, how lucky it was he had come! He
was a fellow who never asked for any favors. He was only
the friend of the women, whose little bits of business he arranged for them. Thus, on his way in, he had dismissed the
creditors in the ante-room. Indeed, those good folks really
didn't want to be paid. On the contrary, if they *had* been
pressing for payment, it was only for the sake of complimenting *Madame,* and of personally renewing their offers of
service, after her grand success of yesterday.

"Let's be off, let's be off," said Nana, who was dressed by
now.

But, at that moment, Zoé came in again, shouting:

"I refuse to open the door any more. They're waiting in
a crowd all down the stairs."

A crowd all down the stairs! Francis himself, despite the
English stolidity of manner which he was wont to affect, be-

gan laughing as he put up his combs. Nana, who had already taken Labordette's arm, pushed him into the kitchen, and effected her escape. At last she was delivered from the men, and felt happily conscious that she might now enjoy his society anywhere, without fear of stupid interruptions.

"You shall see me back to my door," said she, as they went down the kitchen stairs. "I shall feel safe, in that case. Just fancy, I want to sleep a whole night quite by myself— yes, a whole night! It's a sort of infatuation, dear boy!"

CHAPTER III

THE Countess Sabine, as it had become customary to call Madame Muffat de Beuville, in order to distinguish her from the Count's mother, who had died the year before, was wont to receive every Tuesday in her house, in the Rue Miromesnil, at the corner of the Rue de Pentièvre. It was a great square building, and the Muffats had lived in it for a hundred years and more. On the side of the street, its frontage seemed to slumber, so lofty was it and dark, so sad and convent-like, with its great outer shutters, which were nearly always closed. And at the back, in a little dark garden, some trees had grown up, and were straining towards the sunlight with such long slender branches that their tips were visible above the roof.

This particular Tuesday, towards ten o'clock in the evening, there were scarcely a dozen people in the drawing-room. When she was only expecting intimate friends, the Countess opened neither the little drawing-room nor the dining-room. One felt more at home on such occasions, and chatted round the fire. The drawing-room was very large and very lofty; its four windows looked out upon the garden, from which, on this rainy evening of the close of April, issued a sensation of damp, despite the great logs burning on the hearth. The sun never shone down into the room; in the daytime it was dimly lit up by a faint greenish light, but at night, when the lamps and the chandelier were burning, it looked merely a serious old chamber with its massive mahogany First Empire furniture, its hangings and chair coverings of yellow velvet, stamped with a large design. Entering it, one was in an atmosphere of cold dignity, of ancient manners, of a vanished age, the air of which seemed devotional.

Opposite the arm-chair, however, in which the Count's mother had died—a square arm-chair of formal design and inhospitable padding, which stood by the hearth-side—the Countess Sabine was seated in a deep and cozy lounge, the red silk upholsteries of which were soft as eider-down. It was the only piece of modern furniture there, a fanciful item introduced amid the prevailing severity, and clashing with it.

"So we shall have the Shah of Persia," the young woman was saying.

They were talking of the crowned heads who were coming to Paris for the Exhibition. Several ladies had formed a circle round the hearth, and Madame du Joncquoy, whose brother, a diplomat, had just fulfilled a mission in the East, was giving some details about the Court of Nazr-ed-Din.

"Are you out of sorts, my dear?" asked Madame Chantereau, the wife of an iron-master, seeing the Countess shivering slightly and growing pale as she did so.

"Oh, no, not at all," replied the latter, smiling. "I felt a little cold. This drawing-room takes so long to warm."

And with that she raised her melancholy eyes, and scanned the walls from floor to ceiling. Her daughter Estelle, a slight, insignificant-looking girl of sixteen, the thankless period of life, quitted the large footstool on which she was sitting, and silently came and propped up one of the logs which had rolled from its place. But Madame de Chezelles, a convent friend of Sabine's, and her junior by five years, exclaimed,—

"Dear me, I would gladly be possessed of a drawing-room such as yours! At any rate, you are able to receive visitors. They only build boxes nowadays. Oh, if I were in your place!"

She ran giddily on, and with lively gestures explained how she would alter the hangings, the seats—everything, in fact. Then, she would give balls to which all Paris should run. Behind her seat, her husband, a magistrate, stood listening with serious air. It was rumored that she deceived him quite openly, but people pardoned her offense, and received her just the same, because, said they, "she's not answerable for her actions."

"Oh, that Léonide!" the Countess Sabine contented herself by murmuring, smiling her faint smile the while.

With a languid movement she eked out the thought that was in her. After having lived there seventeen years, she certainly would not alter her drawing-room now. It would henceforth remain just such as her mother-in-law had wished to preserve it during her lifetime. Then, returning to the subject of conversation,—

"I have been assured," said she, "that we shall also have the King of Prussia and the Emperor of Russia."

"Yes, some very fine fêtes are promised," said Madame du Joncquoy.

The banker Steiner, not long since introduced into this circle by Léonide de Chezelles, who was acquainted with the whole of Parisian society, was sitting chatting on a sofa between two of the windows. He was questioning a Deputy, from whom he was endeavoring with much adroitness to elicit news about a movement on the Stock Exchange of which he had his suspicions, while the Count Muffat, standing in front of them, was silently listening to their talk, looking, as he did so, even grayer than was his wont.

Four or five young men formed another group, near the door, round the Count Xavier de Vandeuvres, who in a low tone was telling them an anecdote. It was doubtless a very risky one, for they were choking with laughter. Companionless in the center of the room, a stout man, a chief clerk at the Ministry of the Interior, sat heavily in an arm-chair, dozing with his eyes open. But when one of the young men appeared to doubt the truth of the anecdote, Vandeuvres raised his voice.

"You are too much of a skeptic, Foucarmont; you'll spoil all your pleasures that way."

And he returned to the ladies with a laugh. Last scion of a great family, of feminine manners and witty tongue, he was at that time running through a fortune with a rage of life and appetite which nothing could appease. His racing stable, which was one of the best known in Paris, cost him a fabulous amount of money; his betting losses at the Imperial Club amounted monthly to an alarming number of pounds, whilst, taking one year with another, his mistresses would be always devouring now a farm, now some acres of arable land or forest, which amounted in fact to quite a respectable slice of his vast estates in Picardy.

"I advise you to call other people skeptics! Why, you don't believe a thing yourself," said Léonide, making shift to find him a little space in which to sit down at her side.

"It's you who spoil your own pleasures."

"Exactly," replied he. "I wish to make others benefit by my experience."

But the company imposed silence on him: he was scandalizing Monsieur Venot. And, the ladies having changed their positions, a little old man of sixty, with bad teeth and a subtle smile, became visible in the depths of an easy-chair. There he sat as comfortably as in his own house, listening to everybody's remarks, and making none himself. With a slight gesture he announced himself by no means scandalized. Vandeuvres had once more assumed his dignified bearing, and added gravely,—

"Monsieur Venot is fully aware that I believe what it is one's duty to believe."

It was an act of faith, and even Léonide appeared satisfied. The young men at the end of the room no longer laughed: the company were old fogeys, and amusement was not to be found there. A cold breath of wind had passed over them, and amid the ensuing silence Steiner's nasal voice became audible. The Deputy's discreet answers were at last driving him to desperation. For a second or two, the Countess Sabine looked at the fire; then she resumed the conversation.

"I saw the King of Prussia at Baden-Baden last year. He's still full of vigor for his age."

"Count Bismarck is to accompany him," said Madame du Joncquoy. "Do you know the Count? I lunched with him at my brother's ages ago, when he was representative of Prussia in Paris. There's a man now whose latest successes I cannot in the least understand."

"But why?" asked Madame Chantereau.

"Good gracious, how am I to explain! He doesn't please me. His appearance is boorish and underbred. Besides, so far as I am concerned, I find him stupid."

With that the whole room spoke of Count Bismarck, and opinions differed considerably. Vandeuvres knew him, and assured the company that he was great in his cups and at play. But when the discussion was at its height, the door was opened, and Hector de la Faloise made his appearance. Fauchery, who followed in his wake, approached the Countess, and bowing,—

"Madame," said he, "I have not forgotten your extremely kind invitation."

She smiled, and made a pretty little speech. The journalist, after bowing to the Count, stood for some moments in the middle of the drawing-room. He only recognized Steiner, and accordingly looked rather out of his element. But Van-

deuvres turned, and came and shook hands with him. And,
forthwith, in his delight at the meeting and with a sudden
desire to be confidential, Fauchery buttonholed him, and said
in a low voice,—

"It's to-morrow. Are you going?"

"Egad, yes."

"At midnight, at her house."

"I know, I know. I'm going with Blanche."

He wanted to escape and return to the ladies in order to
urge yet another reason in Monsieur de Bismarck's favor.
But Fauchery detained him.

"You never will guess whom she has charged me to invite."

And, with a slight nod, he indicated Count Muffat, who
was just then discussing a knotty point in the Budget with
Steiner and the Deputy.

"It's impossible," said Vandeuvres, stupefaction and merriment in his tones.

"My word on it! I had to swear that I would bring him
to her. Indeed, that's one of my reasons for coming here."

Both laughed silently, and Vandeuvres, hurriedly rejoining the circle of ladies, cried out,—

"I declare that on the contrary Monsieur de Bismarck is
exceedingly witty. For instance, one evening he said a charmingly epigrammatic thing in my presence—"

La Faloise meanwhile had heard the few rapid sentences
thus whisperingly interchanged, and he gazed at Fauchery, in
hopes of an explanation which was not vouchsafed him. Of
whom were they talking, and what were they going to do at
midnight to-morrow? He did not leave his cousin's side
again. The latter had gone and seated himself. He was
especially interested by the Countess Sabine. Her name had
often been mentioned in his presence, and he knew that, having been married at the age of seventeen, she must now be
thirty-four, and that since her marriage she had passed a
cloistered existence with her husband and her mother-in-

law. In society, some spoke of her as a woman of religious chastity, whilst others pitied her, and recalled to memory her charming bursts of laughter and the burning glances of her great eyes in the days prior to her imprisonment in this old town house. Fauchery scrutinized her, and yet hesitated. One of his friends, a captain who had recently died in Mexico, had, on the very eve of his departure, made him one of those gross post-prandial confessions, of which even the most prudent among men are occasionally guilty. But of this he only retained a vague recollection; they had dined not wisely but too well that evening; and when he saw the Countess, in her black dress and with her quiet smile, seated in that old-world drawing-room, he certainly had his doubts. A lamp, which had been placed behind her, threw into clear relief her dark, delicate, plump, side face, wherein a certain heaviness in the contours of the mouth alone indicated a species of imperious sensuality.

"What do they want with their Bismarck?" muttered la Faloise, whose constant pretense it was to be bored in good society. "One's ready to kick the bucket here. A pretty idea of yours it was to want to come!"

Fauchery questioned him abruptly.

"Now tell me, does the Countess admit some one to her embraces?"

"Oh, dear, no, no! my dear fellow," he stammered, manifestly taken aback, and quite forgetting his pose. "Where d'you think we are?"

After which he was conscious of a want of up-to-dateness in this outburst of indignation, and throwing himself back on a great sofa, he added,—

"Gad! I say no! but I don't know much about it. There's a little chap out there, Foucarmont they call him, who's to be met with everywhere and at every turn. One's seen faster men than that, though, you bet. However, it doesn't concern me, and indeed all I know is that if the Countess indulges in high jinks, she's still pretty sly about it; for the thing never gets about—nobody talks."

Then, although Fauchery did not take the trouble to question him, he told him all he knew about the Muffats. Amid the conversation of the ladies, which still continued in front of the hearth, they both spoke in subdued tones, and, seeing them there with their white cravats and gloves, one might have supposed them to be discussing, in chosen phraseology, some really serious topic. Old Madame Muffat then, whom la Faloise had been well acquainted with, was an insufferable old lady always hand in glove with the priests. She had the grand manner besides, and an authoritative way of comporting herself which bent everybody to her will. As to Muffat, he was an old man's child; his father, a general, had been created count by Napoleon I., and naturally he had found himself in favor after the 2nd of December. He hadn't much gayety of manner either, but he passed for a very honest man of straightforward intentions and understanding. Add to these a code of old aristocratic ideas, and such a lofty conception of his duties at Court, of his dignities and of his virtues, that he behaved like a God on wheels. It was the Mamma Muffat who had given him this precious education, with its daily visits to the confessional, its complete absence of escapades, and of all that is meant by youth. He was a practicing Christian, and had attacks of faith of such fiery violence that they might be likened to accesses of burning fever. Finally, in order to add a last touch to the picture, la Faloise whispered something in his cousin's ear.

"You don't say so!" said the latter.

"On my word of honor, they swore it was true! He was still like that when he married."

Fauchery chuckled as he looked at the Count, whose face, with its fringe of whiskers and absence of mustaches, seemed to have grown squarer and harder now that he was busy quoting figures to the writhing, struggling Steiner.

"My word, he's got a phiz for it!" murmured Fauchery. "A pretty present he made his wife! Poor little thing, how he must have bored her! She knows nothing about anything, I'll wager!"

Just then the Countess Sabine was saying something to him. But he did not hear her, so amusing and extraordinary did he esteem the Muffats' case. She repeated the question.

"Monsieur Fauchery, have you not published a sketch of Monsieur de Bismarck? You spoke with him once?"

He got up briskly, and approached the circle of ladies, endeavoring to collect himself, and soon with perfect ease of manner finding an answer,—

"Dear me, madam, I assure you I wrote that 'Portrait' with the help of biographies which had been published in Germany. I have never seen Monsieur de Bismarck."

He remained beside the Countess, and, whilst talking with her, continued his meditations. She did not look her age; one would have set her down as being twenty-eight at most, for her eyes above all, which were filled with the dark blue shadow of her long eyelashes, retained the glowing light of youth. Bred in a divided family, so that she used to spend one month with the Marquis de Chouard, another with the Marquise, she had been married very young, urged on doubtless by her father whom she embarrassed after her mother's death. A terrible man was the Marquis, a man about whom strange tales were beginning to be told, and that despite his lofty piety! Fauchery asked if he should have the honor of meeting him. Certainly her father was coming, but only very late; he had so much work on hand! The journalist thought he knew where the old gentleman passed his evenings, and looked grave. But a mole, which he noticed close to her mouth, on the Countess's left cheek, surprised him. Nana had precisely the same mole. It was curious. Tiny hairs curled up on it, only they were golden in Nana's case,

black as jet in this. Ah, well, never mind! This woman
enjoyed nobody's embraces.

"I have always felt a wish to know Queen Augusta," said
she. "They say she is so good, so devout. Do you think
she will accompany the King?"

"It is not thought that she will, madam," replied he.

She had no lovers: the thing was only too apparent. One
had only to look at her there, by the side of that daughter
of hers, sitting so insignificant and constrained on her footstool. That sepulchral drawing-room of hers, which exhaled odors suggestive of being in a church, spoke as plainly
as words could of the iron hand, the austere mode of existence,
that weighed her down. There was nothing suggestive of
her own personality in that ancient abode, black with the
damps of years. It was Muffat who made himself felt there,
who dominated his surroundings with his devotional training, his penances, and his fasts. But the sight of the little
old gentleman with the black teeth and subtle smile, whom he
suddenly discovered in his arm-chair behind the group of
ladies, afforded him a yet more decisive argument. He knew
the personage. It was Théophile Venot, a retired lawyer
who had made a specialty of church cases. He had left off
practice with a handsome fortune, and was now leading a
sufficiently mysterious existence, for he was received everywhere, treated with great deference, and even somewhat
feared, as though he had been the representative of a mighty
force, an occult power, which was felt to be at his back.
Nevertheless, his behavior was very humble. He was church-
warden at the Madeleine Church, and had simply accepted
the post of deputy-mayor at the town house of the Ninth
Arrondissement in order, as he said, to have something to do
in his leisure time. Deuce take it! the Countess was well
guarded; there was nothing to be done in that quarter.

"You're right, it's enough to make one kick the bucket

here," said Fauchery to his cousin, when he had made good his escape from the circle of ladies. "We'll hook it!"

But Steiner, deserted at last by the Count Muffat and the Deputy, came up in a fury. Drops of perspiration stood on his forehead, and he grumbled huskily,—

"Gad! let 'em tell me nothing, if nothing they want to tell me. I shall find people who will talk."

Then he pushed the journalist into a corner, and altering his tone, said in accents of victory,—

"It's to-morrow, eh? I'm of the party, my bully!"

"Indeed!" muttered Fauchery, with some astonishment.

"You didn't know about it. Oh! I had lots of bother to find her at home. Besides, Mignon never would leave me alone."

"But they're to be there, are the Mignons."

"Yes, she told me so. In fact, she did receive my visit, and she invited me. Midnight punctually, after the play."

The banker was beaming. He winked, and added with a peculiar emphasis on the words,—

"You've worked it, eh?"

"Eh, what?" said Fauchery, pretending not to understand him. "She wanted to thank me for my article, so she came and called on me."

"Yes, yes. You fellows are fortunate. You get rewarded. By-the-by, who pays the piper to-morrow?"

The journalist made a slight outward movement with his arms, as though he would intimate that no one had ever been able to find out. But Vandeuvres called to Steiner, who knew Monsieur de Bismarck. Madame du Joncquoy had almost convinced herself of the truth of her suppositions: she concluded with these words:

"He gave me an unpleasant impression: I think his face is evil. But I am quite willing to believe that he has a deal of wit. It would account for his successes."

"Without doubt," said the banker with a faint smile. He was a Jew from Frankfort.

Meanwhile la Faloise at last made bold to question his cousin. He followed him up and got inside his guard:

"There's supper at a woman's to-morrow evening? With which of them, eh?—with which of them?"

Fauchery motioned to him that they were overheard, and must respect the conventions here. The door had just been opened anew, and an old lady had come in, followed by a young man, in whom the journalist recognized the truant schoolboy, perpetrator of the famous and as yet unforgotten *"très chic"* of the *Blonde Venus* first night. This lady's arrival caused a stir among the company. The Countess Sabine had risen briskly from her seat in order to go and greet her, and she had taken both her hands in hers, and addressed her as her "dear Madame Hugon." Seeing that his cousin viewed this little episode with some curiosity, la Faloise sought to arouse his interest, and in a few brief phrases explained the position. Madame Hugon, widow of a notary, lived in retirement at Les Fondettes, an old estate of her family's, in the neighborhood of Orleans, but she also kept up a small establishment in Paris, in a house belonging to her in the Rue de Richelieu, and was now passing some weeks there in order to settle her youngest son, who was reading the law and in his "first year." In old times she had been a dear friend of the Marquise de Chouard, and had assisted at the birth of the Countess, who, prior to her marriage, used to stay at her house for months at a time, and even now was quite familiarly treated by her.

"I have brought Georges to see you," said Madame Hugon to Sabine. "He's grown, I trust."

The young man, with his clear eyes, and the fair curls which suggested a girl dressed up as a boy, bowed easily to the Countess and reminded her of a bout of battledore and shuttlecock they had had together, two years ago, at The Fondettes.

"Philippe is not in Paris?" asked Count Muffat.

"Dear me, no!" replied the old lady. "He is always in garrison at Bourges."

She had seated herself, and began talking with considerable pride of her eldest son, a great big fellow, who, after enlisting in a fit of waywardness, had of late very rapidly attained the rank of lieutenant. All the ladies behaved to her with respectful sympathy, and conversation was resumed in a tone at once more amiable and more refined. Fauchery, at sight of that respectable Madame Hugon, that motherly face lit up with such a kindly smile beneath its broad tresses of white hair, thought how foolish he had been to suspect the Countess Sabine even for an instant.

Nevertheless, the big chair with the red silk upholsteries, in which the Countess sat, had attracted his attention. Its style struck him as crude, not to say fantastically suggestive, in that dim old drawing-room. Certainly, it was not the Count who had inveigled thither that nest of voluptuous idleness. One might have described it as an experiment, marking the birth of an appetite and of an enjoyment. Then he forgot where he was, fell into a brown study, and in thought even harked back to that vague, confidential announcement, imparted to him one evening in the dining-room of a restaurant. Impelled by a sort of sensuous curiosity, he had always wanted an introduction into the Muffats' circle, and, now that his friend was in Mexico through all eternity, who could tell what might happen? "We shall see," he thought. It was a folly doubtless, but the idea kept tormenting him, he felt himself drawn on, and his animal nature aroused. The big chair had a rumpled look—its nether cushions had been tumbled, a fact which now amused him.

"Well, shall we be off?" asked la Faloise, mentally vow-

ing that, once outside, he would find out the name of the
woman with whom people were going to sup.

"All in good time," replied Fauchery.

But he was no longer in any hurry, and excused himself on
the score of the invitation he had been commissioned to give,
and had as yet not found a convenient opportunity to mention. The ladies were chatting about an assumption of the
veil, a very touching ceremony, by which the whole of
Parisian society had for the last three days been greatly
moved. It was the eldest daughter of the Baronne de
Fougeray, who, under stress of an irresistible vocation, had
just entered the Carmelite Convent. Madame Chantereau,
a distant cousin of the Fougerays, told how the baroness had
been obliged to take to her bed the day after the ceremony,
so overdone was she with weeping.

"I had a very good place," declared Léonide. "I found it
interesting."

Nevertheless, Madame Hugon pitied the poor mother.
How sad to lose a daughter in such a way!

"I am accused of being over-religious," said she, in her
quiet frank manner, "but that does not prevent me thinking
the children very cruel who obstinately commit such suicide."

"Yes, it's a terrible thing," murmured the Countess, shivering a little, as became a chilly person, and huddling herself anew in the depths of her big chair in front of the
fire.

Then the ladies fell into a discussion. But their voices
were discreetly attuned, whilst light trills of laughter now
and again interrupted the gravity of their talk. The two
lamps on the chimney-piece, which had shades of rose-
colored lace, cast a feeble light over them, while, on scattered pieces of furniture, there burnt but three other lamps,
so that the great drawing-room remained in soft shadow.

Steiner was getting bored. He was describing to Fauchery
an escapade of that little Madame de Chezelles, whom he

simply referred to as Léonide. "A blackguard woman," said he, lowering his voice behind the ladies' arm-chairs. Fauchery looked at her as she sat quaintly perched, in her voluminous ball-dress of pale blue satin, on the corner of her arm-chair. She looked as slight and impudent as a boy, and he ended by feeling astonished at seeing her there. People comported themselves better at Caroline Héquet's, whose mother had arranged her house on serious principles. Here was a perfect subject for an article. What a strange world was this world of Paris! The most rigid circles found themselves invaded. Evidently that silent Théophile Venot, who contented himself by smiling and shewing his ugly teeth, must have been a legacy from the late Countess. So, too, must have been such ladies of mature age as Madame Chantereau and Madame du Joncquoy, besides four or five old gentlemen, who sat motionless in corners. The Count Muffat attracted to the house a series of functionaries, distinguished by the immaculate personal appearance which was at that time required of the men at the Tuileries. Among others there was the chief clerk, who still sat solitary in the middle of the room, with his closely-shorn cheeks, his vacant glance, and his coat so tight of fit that he could scarce venture to move. Almost all the young men and certain individuals with distinquished aristocratic manners were the Marquis de Chouard's contribution to the circle, he having kept touch with the Legitimist party after making his peace with the Empire on his entrance into the Council of State. There remained Léonide de Chezelles and Steiner, an ugly little knot against which Madame Hugon's elderly and amiable serenity stood out in strange contrast. And Fauchery, having sketched out his article, named this last group "Countess Sabine's little clique."

"On another occasion," continued Steiner in still lower tones, "Léonide got her tenor down to Montauban. She was living in the Château de Beaurecueil, two leagues further off, and she used to come in daily in a carriage and pair in order in visit him at the 'Lion d'Or,' where he had put up. The carriage used to wait at the door, and Léonide would stay hours in the house, while a crowd gathered round and looked at the horses."

There was a pause in the talk, and some solemn moments passed silently by in the lofty room. Two young men were whispering, but they ceased in their turn, and the hushed step of Count Muffat was alone audible as he crossed the floor. The lamps seemed to have paled; the fire was going out; a stern shadow fell athwart the old friends of the house where they sat in the chairs they had occupied there for forty years back. It was as though, in a momentary pause of conversation, the invited guests had become suddenly aware that the Count's mother, in all her glacial stateliness, had returned among them.

But the Countess Sabine had once more resumed,—

"Well, at last the news of it got about. The young man was likely to die, and that would explain the poor child's adoption of the religious life. Besides, they say that Monsieur de Fougeray would never have given his consent to the marriage."

"They say heaps of other things, too," cried Léonide giddily.

She fell a-laughing: she refused to talk. Sabine was won over by this gayety, and put her handkerchief up to her lips. And in the vast and solemn room their laughter sounded a note which struck Fauchery strangely, the note of delicate glass breaking. Assuredly here was the first beginning of the "little rift." Every one began talking again. Madame du Joncquoy demurred; Madame Chantereau knew for certain that a marriage had been projected, but that matters had gone no further; the men even ventured to give their opinions. For some minutes the conversation was a Babel of opinions, in which the divers elements of the circle, whether Bonapart-

ist, or Legitimist, or merely wordly and skeptical, appeared
to jostle one another simultaneously. Estelle had rung to
order wood to be put on the fire; the footman turned up
the lamps; the room seemed to wake from sleep. Fauchery
began smiling, as though once more at his ease.

"Egad, they become the brides of God when they couldn't
be their cousin's," said Vandeuvres between his teeth.

The subject bored him, and he had rejoined Fauchery.

"My dear fellow, have you ever seen a woman who was
really loved become a nun?"

He did not wait for an answer, for he had had enough of
the topic, and in a hushed voice,—

"Tell me," said he, "how many of us will there be to-
morrow? There'll be the Mignons, Steiner, yourself, Blanche
and I: who else?"

"Caroline, I believe, and Simonne, and Gaga without doubt.
One never knows exactly, does one? On such occasions, one
expects the party will number twenty, and you're really
thirty."

Vandeuvres, who was looking at the ladies, passed abruptly
to another subject:

"She must have been very nice-looking, that du Joncquoy
woman, some fifteen years ago. Poor Estelle has grown
lankier than ever. What a nice lath to put into a bed!"

But, interrupting himself, he returned to the subject of
to-morrow's supper.

"What's so tiresome of those shows is that it's always the
same set of women. One wants a novelty. Do try and
invent a new girl. By Jove, happy thought! I'll go and
beseech that stout man to bring the woman he was trotting
about the other evening at the Variétés."

He referred to the chief clerk, sound asleep in the middle
of the drawing-room. Fauchery, afar off, amused himself
by following this delicate negotiation. Vandeuvres had sat
himself down by the stout man, who still looked very sedate.

For some moments they both appeared to be discussing with much propriety the question before the house, which was, "How can one discover the exact state of feeling that urges a young girl to enter into the religious life?" Then the Count returned with the remark,—

"It's impossible. He swears she's straight. She'd refuse; and yet I would have wagered that I once saw her at Laure's."

"Eh, what? You go to Laure's!" murmured Fauchery, with a chuckle. "You venture your reputation in places like that! I was under the impression that it was only we poor devils of outsiders who—"

"Ah, dear boy, one ought to see every side of life."

Then they sneered, and with sparkling eyes they compared notes about the *table d'hôte* in the Rue des Martyrs, where big Laure Piédefer ran a dinner at three francs a head for little women in difficulties. A nice hole, where all the little women used to kiss Laure on the lips! And as the Countess Sabine, who had overheard a stray word or two, turned towards them, they started back, rubbing shoulders in excited merriment. They had not noticed that Georges Hugon was close by, and that he was listening to them, blushing so hotly the while that a rosy flush had spread from his ears to his girlish throat. The infant was full of shame and of ecstasy. From the moment his mother had turned him loose in the room, he had been hovering in the wake of Madame de Chezelles, the only woman present who struck him as being the thing. But after all is said and done, Nana licked her to fits!

"Yesterday evening," Madame Hugon was saying, "Georges took me to the play. Yes, we went to the Variétés, where I certainly had not set foot for the last ten years. That child adores music. As to me, I wasn't in the least amused; but he was so happy! They put extraordinary pieces on the stage nowadays. Besides, music delights me very little, I confess."

"What! you don't love music, madam?" cried Madame du Joncquoy, lifting her eyes to heaven. "Is it possible there should be people who don't love music?"

The exclamation of surprise was general. No one had dropped a single word concerning the performance at the Variétés, at which the good Madame Hugon had not understood any of the allusions. The ladies knew the piece, but said nothing about it, and with that they plunged into the realm of sentiment, and began discussing the masters in a tone of refined and ecstatical admiration. Madame du Joncquoy was not fond of any of them save Weber, while Madame Chantereau stood up for the Italians. The ladies' voices had turned soft and languishing, and in front of the hearth one might have fancied one's self listening, in meditative religious retirement, to the faint, discreet music of a little chapel.

"Now, let's see," murmured Vandeuvres, bringing Fauchery back into the middle of the drawing-room; "notwithstanding it all, we must invent a woman for to-morrow. Shall we ask Steiner about it?"

"Oh, when Steiner's got hold of a woman," said the journalist, "it's because Paris has done with her."

Vandeuvres, however, was searching about on every side.

"Wait a bit," continued he, "the other day I met Foucarmont with a charming blonde. I'll go and tell him to bring her."

And he called to Foucarmont. They exchanged a few words rapidly. There must have been some sort of complication, for both of them, moving carefully forward and stepping over the dresses of the ladies, went off in quest of another young man, with whom they continued the discussion in the embrasure of a window. Fauchery was left to himself, and had just decided to proceed to the hearth, where Madame du Joncquoy was announcing that she never heard Weber played without at the same time seeing lakes, forests, and sunrises over landscapes steeped in dew, when a hand touched his shoulder and a voice behind him remarked,—

"It's not civil of you."

"What d'you mean?" he asked, turning round and recognizing la Faloise.

"Why, about that supper to-morrow. You might easily have got me invited."

Fauchery was at length about to state his reasons, when Vandeuvres came back to tell him,—

"It appears it isn't a girl of Foucarmont's. It's that man's flame out there. She won't be able to come. What a piece of bad luck! But all the same I've pressed Foucarmont into the service, and he's going to try to get Louise from the Palais-Royal."

"Is it not true, Monsieur de Vandeuvres," asked Madame Chantereau, raising her voice, "that Wagner's music was hissed last Sunday?"

"Oh, frightfully, madam," he made answer, coming forward with his usual exquisite politeness.

Then, as they did not detain him, he moved off, and continued whispering in the journalist's ear,—

"I'm going to press some more of them. These young fellows must know some little ladies."

With that he was observed to accost men and to engage them in conversation, in his usual amiable and smiling way, in every corner of the drawing-room. He mixed with the various groups, said something confidential to every one, and walked away again with a sly wink and a secret signal or two. It looked as though he were giving out a watchword in that easy way of his. The news went round, the place of meeting was announced, while the ladies' sentimental dissertations on music served to conceal the small feverish rumor of these recruiting operations.

"No, do not speak of your Germans," Madame Chantereau was saying. "Song is gayety, song is light. Have you heard Patti in the *Barber of Seville?*"

"She was delicious!" murmured Léonide, who strummed none but operatic airs on her piano.

Meanwhile the Countess Sabine had rung. When, on Tuesdays, the number of visitors was small, tea was handed round the drawing-room itself. While directing a footman to clear a round table, the Countess followed the Count de Vandeuvres with her eyes. She still smiled that vague smile which slightly disclosed her white teeth, and, as the Count passed, she questioned him.

"What *are* you plotting, Monsieur de Vandeuvres?"

"What am I plotting, madam?" he answered, quietly, "nothing at all."

"Really! I saw you so busy. Pray, wait, you shall make yourself useful!"

She placed an album in his hands, and asked him to put it on the piano. But he found means to inform Fauchery, in a low whisper, that they would have Tatan Néné, the most finely-developed girl that winter, and Maria Blond, the same who had just made her first appearance at the Folies-Dramatiques. Meanwhile la Faloise stopped him at every step in hopes of receiving an invitation. He ended by offering himself, and Vandeuvres engaged him in the plot at once; only he made him promise to bring Clarisse with him, and when la Faloise pretended to scruple about certain points, he quieted him by the remark,—

"Since I invite you, that's enough!"

Nevertheless, la Faloise would have much liked to know the name of the hostess. But the Countess had recalled Vandeuvres, and was questioning him as to the manner in which the English made tea. He often betook himself to England, where his horses ran. Then, as though he had been inwardly following up quite a laborious train of thought during his remarks, he broke in with the question:

"And the Marquis, by-the-by? Are we not to see him?"

"Oh, certainly you will! My father made me a formal promise that he would come," replied the Countess. "But I'm beginning to be anxious. His duties will have kept him."

Vandeuvres smiled a discreet smile. He too seemed to have his doubts as to the exact nature of the Marquis de Chouard's duties. Indeed, he had been thinking of a pretty woman whom the Marquis occasionally took into the country with him. Perhaps they could get her too.

In the meantime Fauchery decided that the moment had come in which to risk giving Count Muffat his invitation. The evening, in fact, was drawing to a close.

"Are you serious?" asked Vandeuvres, who thought a joke was intended.

"Extremely serious. If I don't execute my commission, she'll tear my eyes out. It's a case of landing her fish, you know."

"Well then, I'll help you, dear boy."

Eleven o'clock struck. Assisted by her daughter, the Countess was pouring out the tea, and as hardly any guests save intimate friends had come, the cups and the platefuls of little cakes were being circulated without ceremony. Even the ladies did not leave their arm-chairs in front of the fire, and sat sipping their tea and nibbling cakes which they held between their finger-tips. From music the talk had declined to purveyors. Boissier was the only person for sweetmeats, and Catherine for ices. Madame Chantereau, however, was all for Latinville. Speech grew more and more indolent, and a sense of lassitude was lulling the room to sleep. Steiner had once more set himself secretly to undermine the Deputy, whom he held in a state of blockade in the corner of a settee. Monsieur Venot, whose teeth must have been ruined by sweet things, was eating little dry cakes, one after the other, with a small nibbling sound suggestive of a mouse, while the chief clerk, his nose in a teacup, seemed never to be going to finish its contents. As to the Countess, she went in a leisurely way from one guest to another, never pressing them, indeed, only pausing a second or two before the gentlemen whom she viewed with an air of dumb interrogation before she smiled and passed on. The great fire had flushed all her face, and she looked as if she were the sister of her daughter, who appeared so withered and ungainly at her side. When she drew near Fauchery, who was chatting with her husband and Vandeuvres, she noticed that they grew suddenly silent: accordingly she did not stop, but handed the cup of tea she was offering to Georges Hugon beyond them.

"It's a lady who desires your company at supper," the journalist gayly continued, addressing Count Muffat.

The last-named, whose face had worn its gray look all the evening, seemed very much surprised. What lady was it?

"Oh, Nana!" said Vandeuvres, by way of forcing the invitation.

The Count became more grave than before. His eyelids trembled just perceptibly, while a look of discomfort, such as headache produces, hovered for a moment athwart his forehead.

"But I'm not acquainted with that lady," he murmured.

"Come, come, you went to her house," remarked Vandeuvres.

"What d'you say? I went to her house? Oh, yes, the other day, in behalf of the Benevolent Association. I had forgotten about it. But, no matter, I am not acquainted with her, and I cannot accept."

He had adopted an icy expression in order to make them understand that this jest did not appear to him to be in good taste. A man of his position did not sit down at the tables of such women as that. Vandeuvres protested: it was to be a supper-party of dramatic and artistic people, and talent excused everything. But without listening further to the arguments urged by Fauchery, who spoke of a dinner where

the Prince of Scots, the son of a queen, had sat down beside
an ex-music-hall singer, the Count only emphasized his refusal. In so doing, he allowed himself, despite his great
politeness, to be guilty of an irritated gesture.

Georges and la Faloise, standing in front of each other
drinking their tea, had overheard the two or three phrases
exchanged in their immediate neighborhood.

"Jove, it's at Nana's then," murmured la Faloise. "I
might have expected as much!"

Georges said nothing, but he was all aflame. His fair
hair was in disorder, his blue eyes shone like tapers, so
fiercely had the vice, which for some days past had surrounded him, inflamed and stirred his blood. At last he was
going to plunge into all that he had dreamt of!

"I don't know the address," la Faloise resumed.

"She lives on a third floor in the Boulevard Haussmann,
between the Rue de l'Arcade and the Rue Pasquier," said
Georges, all in a breath.

And when the other looked at him in much astonishment,
he added, turning very red, and fit to sink into the ground
with embarrassment and conceit,—

"I'm of the party. She invited me this morning."

But there was a great stir in the drawing-room, and Vandeuvres and Fauchery could not continue pressing the Count.
The Marquis de Chouard had just come in, and every one
was anxious to greet him. He had moved painfully forward,
his legs failing under him, and he now stood in the middle
of the room with pallid face and eyes blinking, as though he
had just come out of some dark alley, and were blinded by
the brightness of the lamps.

"I scarcely hoped to see you to-night, father," said the
Countess. "I should have been anxious till the morning."

He looked at her without answering, as a man might who
fails to understand. His nose, which loomed immense on
his shorn face, looked like a swollen pimple, while his lower

lip hung down. Seeing him such a wreck, Madame Hugon, full of kind compassion, said pitying things to him.

"You work too hard. You ought to rest yourself. At our age we ought to leave work to the young people."

"Work! Ah, yes, to be sure, work!" he stammered at last. "Always plenty of work."

He began to pull himself together, straightening up his bent figure, and, passing his hand, as was his wont, over his scant gray hair, of which a few locks strayed behind his ears.

"At what are you working as late as this?" asked Madame du Joncquoy. "I thought you were at the Financial Minister's reception."

But the Countess intervened with,—

"My father had to study the question of a projected law."

"Yes, a projected law," said he; "exactly so, a projected law. I shut myself up for that reason. It refers to work in factories, and I was anxious for a proper observance of the Lord's Day of Rest. It is really shameful that the Government is unwilling to act with vigor in the matter. Churches are growing empty; we are running headlong to ruin."

Vandeuvres had exchanged glances with Fauchery. They both happened to be behind the Marquis, and they were scanning him suspiciously. When Vandeuvres found an opportunity to take him aside, and to speak to him about that good-looking creature he was in the habit of taking down into the country, the old man affected extreme surprise. Perhaps some one had seen him with the Baroness Decker, at whose house, at Viroflay, he sometimes spent a day or so. Vandeuvres's sole vengeance was an abrupt question:

"Tell me, where have you been straying to? Your elbow is covered with cobwebs and plaster."

"My elbow," muttered he, slightly disturbed. "Yes, indeed, it's true. A speck or two. I must have come in for them on my way downstairs from my office."

Several people were taking their departure. It was close

on midnight. Two footmen were noiselessly removing the empty cups and the plates with cakes. In front of the hearth, the ladies had re-formed and, at the same time, narrowed their circle, and were chatting more carelessly than before in the languid atmosphere peculiar to the close of a party. The very room was going to sleep, and slowly creeping shadows were cast by its walls. It was then Fauchery spoke of departure. Yet he once more forgot his intention at sight of the Countess Sabine. She was resting from her cares as hostess, and as she sat in her wonted seat, silent, her eyes fixed on a log which was turning into embers, her face appeared so white and so impassable that doubt again possessed him. In the glow of the fire, the small black hairs on the mole at the corner of her lip became white. It was Nana's very mole, down to the color of the hair. He could not refrain from whispering something about it in Vandeuvres's ear. Gad, it was true, the other had never noticed it before. And both men continued this comparison of Nana and the Countess. They discovered a vague resemblance about the chin and the mouth, but the eyes were not at all like. Then, too, Nana had a good-natured expression, while, with the Countess, it was hard to decide—she might have been a cat, sleeping with claws withdrawn and paws stirred by a scarce perceptible nervous quiver.

"All the same, one could have her," declared Fauchery.

Vandeuvres stripped her at a glance.

"Yes, one could, all the same," said he. "But I think nothing of the thighs, you know. Will you bet she has no thighs?"

He stopped, for Fauchery touched him briskly on the arm, and shewed him Estelle, sitting close to them on her footstool. They had raised their voices without noticing her, and she must have overheard them. Nevertheless, she continued sitting there stiff and motionless, not a hair having lifted on her thin neck, which was that of a girl who had shot up all too quickly. Thereupon they retired three or four paces, and Vandeuvres vowed that the Countess was a very honest woman. Just then voices were raised in front of the hearth. Madame du Joncquoy was saying,—

"I was willing to grant you that Monsieur de Bismarck was perhaps a witty man. Only, if you go as far as to talk of genius—"

The ladies had come round again to their earliest topic of conversation.

"What the deuce! still Monsieur de Bismarck!" muttered Fauchery. "This time I make my escape for good and all."

"Wait a bit," said Vandeuvres, "we must have a definite 'no' from the Count."

The Count Muffat was talking to his father-in-law and a certain serious-looking gentleman. Vandeuvres drew him away and renewed the invitation, backing it up with the information that he was to be at the supper himself. A man might go anywhere; no one could think of suspecting evil where at most there could only be curiosity. The Count listened to these arguments with downcast eyes and expressionless face. Vandeuvres felt him to be hesitating when the Marquis de Chouard approached with a look of interrogation. And when the latter was informed of the question in hand, and Fauchery had invited him in his turn, he looked at his son-in-law furtively. There ensued an embarrassed silence, but both men encouraged one another, and would doubtless have ended by accepting, had not Count Muffat perceived Monsieur Venot's gaze fixed upon him. The little old man was no longer smiling; his face was cadaverous, his eyes bright and keen as steel.

"No," replied the Count directly in so decisive a tone that further insistence became impossible.

Then the Marquis refused with even greater severity of expression. He talked morality. The aristocratic classes ought to set a good example. Fauchery smiled and shook hands with Vandeuvres. He did not wait for him, and took his departure immediately, for he was due at his newspaper office.

"At Nana's at midnight, eh?"

La Faloise retired too. Steiner had made his bow to the Countess. Other men followed them, and the same phrase went round—"At midnight, at Nana's"—as they went to get their overcoats in the ante-room. Georges, who could not leave without his mother, had stationed himself at the door, where he gave the exact address. "Third floor, door on your left." Yet, before going out, Fauchery gave a final glance. Vandeuvres had again resumed his position among the ladies, and was laughing with Léonide de Chezelles. Count Muffat and the Marquis de Chouard were joining in the conversation, whilst the good Madame Hugon was falling asleep open-eyed. Lost among the petticoats, Monsieur Venot was his own small self again, and smiled as of old. Twelve struck slowly in the great solemn room.

"What—what do you mean?" Madame du Joncquoy resumed. "You imagine that Monsieur de Bismarck will make war on us and beat us! Oh, that's unbearable!"

Indeed, they were laughing round Madame Chantereau, who had just repeated an assertion she had heard made in Alsace, where her husband owned a foundry.

"We have the Emperor, fortunately," said Count Muffat, in his grave official way.

It was the last phrase Fauchery was able to catch. He closed the door, after casting one more glance in the direction of the Countess Sabine. She was talking sedately with the chief clerk, and seemed to be interested in that stout individual's conversation. Assuredly, he must have been deceiving himself. There was no "little rift" there at all. It was a pity.

"You're not coming down then?" la Faloise shouted up to him from the entrance-hall.

And out on the pavement, as they separated, they once more repeated,—

"To-morrow, at Nana's."

CHAPTER IV

SINCE morning Zoé had delivered up the flat to a managing man, who had come from Brebant's with a staff of helpers and waiters. Brebant was to supply everything, from the supper, the plates and dishes, the glass, the linen, the flowers, down to the seats and footstools. Nana could not have mustered a dozen napkins out of all her cupboards, and not having had time to get a proper outfit after her new start in life, and scorning to go to the restaurant, she had decided to make the restaurant come to her. It struck her as being more the thing. She wanted to celebrate her great success as an actress with a supper which should set people talking. As her dining-room was too small, the manager had arranged the table in the drawing-room, a table with twenty-five covers, placed somewhat close together.

"Is everything ready?" asked Nana, when she returned at midnight.

"Oh! I don't know," repied Zoé roughly, looking beside herself with worry. "The Lord be thanked, I don't bother about anything. They're making a fearful mess in the kitchen and all over the flat! I've had to fight my battles too. The other two came again. My eye! I did just chuck 'em out!"

She referred of course to her employer's old admirers, the tradesman and the Wallachian, to whom Nana, sure of her future and longing to shed her skin, as she phrased it, had decided to give the go-by.

"There are a couple of leeches for you!" she muttered.

"If they come back, threaten to go to the police."

Then she called Daguenet and Georges, who had remained behind in the ante-room, where they were hanging up their overcoats. They had both met at the stage-door, in the Passage des Panoramas, and she had brought them home with her in a cab. As there was nobody there yet, she shouted to them to come into the dressing-room whilst Zoé was touching up her toilet. Hurriedly and without changing her dress, she had her hair done up, and stuck white roses in her chignon and at her bosom. The little room was littered with the drawing-room furniture, which the workmen had been compelled to roll in there, and it was full of a motley assemblage of round tables, sofas, and arm-chairs, with their legs in air for the most part. Nana was quite ready when her dress caught on a castor and tore upwards. At this she swore furiously; such things only happened to her! Ragingly she took off her dress, a very simple affair of white foulard, of so thin and supple a texture that it clung about her like a long shift. But she put it on again directly, for she could not find another to her taste, and with tears in her eyes declared that she was dressed like a rag-picker. Daguenet and Georges had to patch up the rent with pins, while Zoé once more arranged her hair. All three hurried round her, especially the boy, who knelt on the floor with his hands among her skirts. And at last she calmed down again, when Daguenet assured her it could not be later than a quarter past twelve, seeing that by dint of scamping her words and skipping her lines she had effectually shortened the third act of the *Blonde Venus*.

"The play's still far too good for that crowd of idiots," said she. "Did you see? There were thousands there to-night. Zoé, my girl, you will wait in here. Don't go to bed, I shall want you. By gum, it is time they came. Here's company!"

She ran off, whilst Georges stayed where he was with the skirts of his coat brushing the floor. He blushed, seeing

Daguenet looking at him. Notwithstanding which, they had conceived a tender regard the one for the other. They re-arranged the bows of their cravats in front of the big dressing-glass, and gave each other a mutual dose of the clothes-brush, for they were all white from their close contact with Nana.

"One would think it was sugar," murmured Georges, giggling like a greedy little child.

A footman, hired for the evening, was ushering the guests into the small drawing-room, a narrow slip of a place, in which only four arm-chairs had been left in order the better to pack in the company. From the large drawing-room beyond came a sound as of the moving of plates and silver, while a clear and brilliant ray of light shone from under the door. At her entrance, Nana found Clarisse Besnus, whom la Faloise had brought, already installed in one of the arm-chairs.

"Dear me, you're the first of 'em!" said Nana, who, now that she was successful, treated her familiarly.

"Oh, it's his doing," replied Clarisse. "He's always afraid of not getting anywhere in time. If I'd taken him at his word, I shouldn't have waited to take off my paint and my wig."

The young man, who now saw Nana for the first time, bowed, paid her a compliment, and spoke of his cousin, hiding his agitation behind an exaggeration of politeness. But Nana, neither listening to him, nor recognizing his face, shook hands with him, and then went briskly towards Rose Mignon, with whom she at once assumed a most distinguished manner.

"Ah! how nice of you, my dear madam! I was so anxious to have you here!"

"It's I who am charmed, I assure you," said Rose, with equal amiability.

"Pray sit down. Do you require anything?"

"Thank you, no! Ah, yes, I've left my fan in my pelisse. Steiner, just look in the right-hand pocket."

Steiner and Mignon had come in behind Rose. The banker turned back and reappeared with the fan, while Mignon embraced Nana fraternally, and forced Rose to do so also. Did they not all belong to the same family in the theatrical world? Then he winked as though to encourage Steiner, but the latter was disconcerted by Rose's clear gaze, and contented himself by kissing Nana's hand.

Just then the Count de Vandeuvres made his appearance with Blanche de Sivry. There was an interchange of profound bows, and Nana with the utmost ceremony conducted Blanche to an arm-chair. Meanwhile, Vandeuvres told them laughingly that Fauchery was engaged in a dispute at the foot of the stairs, because the porter had refused to allow Lucy Stewart's carriage to come in at the gate. They could hear Lucy telling the porter he was a dirty blackguard in the ante-room. But when the footman had opened the door, she came forward with her laughing grace of manner, announced her name herself, took both Nana's hands in hers, and told her that she had liked her from the very first, and considered her talent splendid. Nana, puffed up by her novel *rôle* of hostess, thanked her, and was veritably confused. Nevertheless, from the moment of Fauchery's arrival, she appeared preoccupied, and directly she could get near him, she asked him in a low voice,—

"Will he come?"

"No, he did not want to," was the journalist's abrupt reply, for he was taken by surprise, though he had got ready some sort of tale to explain Count Muffat's refusal.

Seeing the young woman's sudden pallor, he became conscious of his folly, and tried to retract his words.

"He was unable to; he is taking the Countess to the ball at the Ministry of the Interior to-night."

"All right," murmured Nana, who suspected him of ill-will, "you'll pay me out for that, my pippin."

She turned on her heel, and so did he; they were angry. Just then, Mignon was pushing Steiner up against Nana, and when Fauchery had left her, he said to her in a low voice, and with the good-natured cynicism of a comrade in arms, who wishes his friend to be happy,—

"He's dying of it, you know, only he's afraid of my wife. Won't you protect him?"

Nana did not appear to understand. She smiled, and looked at Rose, the husband, and the banker, and finally said to the latter,—

"Monsieur Steiner, you will sit next me."

With that there came from the ante-room a sound of laughter and whispering, and a burst of merry chattering voices, which sounded as if a runaway convent were on the premises. And Labordette appeared, towing five women in his rear, his boarding school, as Lucy Stewart cruelly phrased it. There was Gaga, majestic in a blue velvet dress which was too tight for her, and Caroline Héquet, clad as usual in ribbed black silk, trimmed with Chantilly lace. Léa de Horn came next, terribly dressed up, as her wont was, and after her the big Tatan Néné, a good-humored fair girl with the bosom of a wet nurse, at which people laughed, and, finally, little Maria Blond, a young damsel of fifteen, as thin and vicious as a street child, yet on the high road to success owing to her recent first appearance at the Folies. Labordette had brought the whole collection in a single fly, and they were still laughing at the way they had been squeezed with Maria Blond on her knees. But, on entering the room, they pursed up their lips, and all grew very conventional as they shook hands and exchanged salutations. Gaga even affected the infantile, and lisped through excess of genteel deportment. Tatan Néné alone transgressed. They had been telling her as they came along that six absolutely naked

Negroes would serve up Nana's supper, and she now grew
anxious about them, and asked to see them. Labordette
called her a goose, and besought her to be silent.

"And Bordenave?" asked Fauchery.

"Oh! you may imagine how miserable I am," cried Nana;
"he won't be able to join us."

"Yes," said Rose Mignon, "his foot caught in a trap-door,
and he's got a fearful sprain. If only you could hear him
swearing, with his leg tied up and laid out on a chair!"

Thereupon everybody mourned over Bordenave's absence.
No one ever gave a good supper without Bordenave. Ah,
well, they would try and do without him, and they were
already talking about other matters, when a burly voice was
heard,—

"What, eh what? Is that the way they're going to write
my obituary notice?"

There was a shout, and all heads were turned round, for
it was indeed Bordenave. Huge and fiery-faced, he was
standing with his stiff leg in the doorway, leaning for support on Simonne Cabiroche's shoulder. Simonne was for
the time being his mistress. This little creature had had a
certain amount of education, and could play the piano and
talk English. She was a blonde on a tiny, pretty scale, and
so delicately formed that she seemed to bend under Bordenave's rude weight. Yet she was smilingly submissive withal.
He postured there for some moments, for he felt that together they formed a tableau.

"One can't help liking ye, eh?" continued he. "Zounds, I
was afraid I should get bored, and I said to myself,—'Here
goes.'"

But he interrupted himself with an oath.

"Oh, damn!"

Simonne had taken a step too quickly forward, and his
foot had just felt his full weight. He gave her a rough
push, but she, still smiling away, and ducking her pretty

head as some animal might that is afraid of a beating, held him up with all the strength a little plump blonde can command. Amid all these exclamations, there was a rush to his assistance. Nana and Rose Mignon rolled up an arm-chair, into which Bordenave let himself sink, whilst the other women slid a second one under his leg. And with that all the actresses present kissed him—as a matter of course. He kept grumbling and gasping.

"Oh, damn! Oh, damn! Ah, well, the stomach's unhurt, you'll see."

Other guests had arrived by this time, and motion became impossible in the room. The noise of clinking plates and silver had ceased, and now a dispute was heard going on in the big drawing-room, where the voice of the manager grumbled angrily. Nana was growing impatient, for she expected no more invited guests, and wondered why they did not bring in supper. She had just sent Georges to find out what was going on, when, to her great surprise, she noticed the arrival of more guests, both male and female. She did not know them in the least. Whereupon, with some embarrassment, she questioned Bordenave, Mignon, and Labordette about them. They did not know them any more than she did; but when she turned to the Count de Vandeuvres he seemed suddenly to recollect himself. They were the young men he had pressed into her service at Count Muffat's. Nana thanked him. That was capital, capital! Only they would all be terribly crowded, and she begged Labordette to go and have seven more covers set. Scarcely had he left the room than the footman ushered in three new-comers. Nay, this time the thing was becoming ridiculous; one certainly could never take them all in. Nana was beginning to grow angry, and, in her haughtiest manner announced that such conduct was scarcely in good taste. But, seeing two more arrive, she began laughing; it was really too funny. So much the worse. People would have to fit in anyhow! The

company were all on their feet save Gaga, and Rose, and
Bordenave, who alone took up two arm-chairs. There was
a buzz of voices, people talking in low tones, and stifling
slight yawns the while.

"Now what d'you say, my lass," asked Bordenave, "to our
sitting down at table as if nothing had happened? We are
all here, don't you think?"

"Oh, yes, we're all here, I promise you!" she answered
laughingly.

She looked round her, but grew suddenly serious, as though
she were surprised at not finding some one. Doubtless there
was a guest missing whom she did not mention. It was a
case of waiting. But a minute or two later the company
noticed in their midst a tall gentleman with a fine face and
a beautiful white beard. The most astonishing thing about
it was that nobody had seen him come in; indeed, he must
have slipped into the little drawing-room through the bedroom door, which had remained ajar. Silence reigned, broken
only by a sound of whispering. The Count de Vandeuvres
certainly knew who the gentleman was, for they both exchanged a discreet hand-grip; but to the questions which
the women asked him he replied by a smile only. Thereupon
Caroline Héquet wagered in a low voice that it was an
English lord, who was on the eve of returning to London
to be married. She knew him quite well—she had had him.
And this account of the matter went the round of the ladies
present, Maria Blond alone asserting that, for her part, she
recognized a German ambassador. She could prove it, because he often passed the night with one of her friends.
Among the men his measure was taken in a few rapid
phrases. A real swell, to judge by his looks! Perhaps he
would pay for the supper! Most likely. It looked like it.
Bah! provided only the supper was a good one! In the
end the company remained undecided. Nay, they were already beginning to forget the old white-bearded gentleman,

when the manager opened the door of the large drawing-room.

"Supper is on the table, madam."

Nana had already accepted Steiner's proffered arm without noticing a movement on the part of the old gentleman, who started to walk behind her in solitary state. Thus, the march-past could not be organized, and men and women entered anyhow, joking with homely good humor over this absence of ceremony. A long table stretched from one end to the other of the great room, which had been entirely cleared of furniture, and this same table was not long enough, for the plates thereon were touching one another. Four candelabra, with ten candles apiece, lit up the supper, and of these one was gorgeous in silver plate with sheaves of flowers to right and left of it. Everything was luxurious after the restaurant fashion; the china was ornamented with a gold line and lacked the customary monogram, the silver had become worn and tarnished through dint of continual washings, the glass was of the kind that you can complete an odd set of in any cheap emporium.

The scene suggested a premature house-warming in an establishment newly smiled on by Fortune, and as yet lacking the necessary conveniences. There was no central luster, and the candelabra, whose tall tapers had scarcely burnt up properly, cast a pale yellow light among the dishes and stands, on which fruit, cakes, and preserves alternated symmetrically.

"You sit where you like, you know," said Nana. "It's more amusing that way."

She remained standing midway down the side of the table. The old gentleman, whom nobody knew, had placed himself on her right, while she kept Steiner on her left hand. Some guests were already sitting down, when the sound of oaths came from the little drawing-room. It was Bordenave. The company had forgotten him, and he was having all the trouble in the world to raise himself out of his two arm-chairs, for he was howling amain and calling for that cat of a Simonne, who had slipped off with the rest. The women ran in to him, full of pity for his woes, and Bordenave appeared, supported, nay, almost carried, by Caroline, Clarisse, Tatan Néné, and Maria Blond. And there was much to-do over his installation at the table.

"In the middle, facing Nana!" was the cry. "Bordenave in the middle! He'll be our president!"

Thereupon the ladies seated him in the middle. But he needed a second chair for his leg, and two girls lifted it up and stretched it carefully out. It wouldn't matter; he would eat sideways.

"God blast it all!" he grumbled. "We're squashed all the same! Ah, my kittens, papa recommends himself to your tender care!"

He had Rose Mignon on his right and Lucy Stewart on his left hand, and they promised to take good care of him. Everybody was now getting settled. Count de Vandeuvres placed himself between Lucy and Clarisse; Fauchery between Rose Mignon and Caroline Héquet. On the other side of the table, Hector de la Faloise had rushed to get next Gaga, and that despite the calls of Clarisse opposite; while Mignon, who never deserted Steiner, was only separated from him by Blanche, and had Tatan Néné on his left. Then came Labordette, and finally, at the two ends of the table were irregular crowding groups of young men and of women, such as Simonne, Léa de Horn and Maria Blond. It was in this region that Daguenet and Georges foregathered more warmly than ever, whilst smilingly gazing at Nana.

Nevertheless, two people remained standing, and there was much joking about it. The men offered seats on their knees. Clarisse, who could not move her elbows, told Van-deuvres that she counted on him to feed her. And then that Bordenave did just take up space with his chairs! There was a final effort, and at last everybody was seated, but, as Mignon loudly remarked, they were confoundedly like herrings in a barrel.

"Thick asparagus soup *à la Comtesse,* clear soup *à la Deslignac,*" murmured the waiters, carrying about plateful in rear of the guests.

Bordenave was loudly recommending the thick soup, when a shout arose, followed by protests and indignant exclamations. The door had just opened, and three late arrivals, a woman and two men, had just come in. Oh, dear no! there was no space for them! Nana, however, without leaving her chair, began screwing up her eyes in the effort to find out whether she knew them. The woman was Louise Violaine, but she had never seen the men before.

"This gentleman, my dear," said Vandeuvres, "is a friend of mine, a naval officer, Monsieur de Foucarmont by name. I invited him."

Foucarmont bowed, and seemed very much at ease, for he added,—

"And I took leave to bring one of my friends with me."

"Oh, it's quite right, quite right!" said Nana. "Sit down, pray. Let's see, you—Clarisse—push up a little. You're a good deal spread out down there. That's it—where there's a will—"

They crowded more tightly than ever, and Foucarmont and Louise were given a little stretch of table, but the friend had to sit at some distance from his plate, and ate his supper through dint of making a long arm between his neighbors' shoulders. The waiters took away the soup plates, and circulated rissoles of young rabbit with truffles, and "niokys" and powdered cheese. Bordenave agitated the whole table with the announcement that at one moment he had had the idea of bringing with him Prullière, Fontan, and old Bosc. At this Nana looked sedate, and remarked dryly that she would have given them a pretty reception. Had she wanted colleagues, she would certainly have undertaken to ask them herself. No, no, she wouldn't have third-rate play-actors. Old Bosc was always drunk; Prullière was fond of spitting too much, and as to Fontan, he made himself unbearable in society with his loud voice and his stupid doings. Then, you know, third-rate play-actors were always out of place when they found themselves in the society of gentlemen such as those around her.

"Yes, yes, it's true," Mignon declared.

All round the table the gentlemen in question looked un-impeachable in the extreme, what with their evening dress, and their pale features, the natural distinction of which was still further refined by fatigue. The old gentleman was as deliberate in his movements, and wore as subtle a smile, as though he were presiding over a diplomatic congress, and Vaudeuvres, with his exquisite politeness towards the ladies next to him, seemed to be at one of the Countess Muffat's receptions. That very morning Nana had been remarking to her aunt that, in the matter of men, one could not have done better—they were all either well-born or wealthy, in fact quite the thing. And as to the ladies, they were behaving admirably. Some of them, such as Blanche, Léa, and Louise, had come in low dresses, but Gaga's only was per-haps a little too low, the more so because at her age she would have done well not to shew her neck at all. Now that the company were finally settled, the laughter and the light jests began to fail. Georges was under the impression that he had assisted at merrier dinner-parties among the good folks of Orleans. There was scarcely any conversation. The men, not being mutually acquainted, stared at one an-other, while the women sat quite quiet, and it was this which especially surprised Georges. He thought them all smugs—he had been under the impression that everybody would begin kissing at once.

The third course, consisting of a Rhine carp *à la Cham-*

bord and a saddle of venison *à la Anglaise,* was being served, when Blanche remarked aloud,—

"Lucy, my dear, I met your Ollivier on Sunday. How he's grown!"

"Dear me, yes! he's eighteen," replied Lucy. "It doesn't make me feel any younger. He went back to his school yesterday."

Her son Ollivier, whom she was wont to speak of with pride, was a pupil at the Ecole de Marine. Then ensued a conversation about the young people, during which all the ladies waxed very tender. Nana described her own great happiness. Her baby, the little Louis, she said, was now at the house of her aunt, who brought him round to her every morning at eleven o'clock, when she would take him into her bed, where he played with her griffon dog, Lulu. It was enough to make one die of laughing to see them both burying themselves under the clothes at the bottom of the bed. The company had no idea how cunning Louiset had already become.

"Oh! yesterday I did just pass a day!" said Rose Mignon, in her turn. "Just imagine, I went to fetch Charles and Henry at their boarding school; and I had positively to take them to the theater at night. They jumped, they clapped their little hands: 'We shall see mamma act! We shall see mamma act!' Oh! it was a to-do!"

Mignon smiled complaisantly, his eyes moist with paternal tenderness.

"And at the play itself," he continued, "they were so funny! They behaved as seriously as grown men, devoured Rose with their eyes, and asked me why mamma had her legs bare like that."

The whole table began laughing, and Mignon looked radiant, for his pride as a father was flattered. He adored his children, and had but one object in life, which was to increase their fortunes by administering the money, gained by Rose at the theater and elsewhere, with the business-like severity of a faithful steward. When, as first fiddle in the music hall where she used to sing, he had married her, they had been passionately fond of one another. Now, they were good friends. There was an understanding between them: she labored hard to the full extent of her talent and of her beauty; he had given up his violin in order the better to watch over her successes as an actress and as a woman. One could not have found a more homely and united household anywhere!

"What age is your eldest?" asked Vandeuvres.

"Henry's nine," replied Mignon, "but such a big chap for his years!"

Then he chaffed Steiner, who was not fond of children, and with quiet audacity informed him that, were he a father, he would make a less stupid hash of his fortune. Whilst talking, he watched the banker over Blanche's shoulders to see if it was coming off with Nana. But for some minutes, Rose and Fauchery, who were talking very near him, had been getting on his nerves. Was Rose going to waste time over such a folly as that? In that sort of case, by Jove, he blocked the way. And diamond on finger, and with his fine hands in great evidence, he finished discussing a filet of venison.

Elsewhere, the conversation about children continued. La Faloise, rendered very restless by the immediate proximity of Gaga, asked news of her daughter, whom he had had the pleasure of noticing in her company at the Variétés. Lili was quite well, but she was still such a tomboy! He was astonished to learn that Lili was entering on her nineteenth year. Gaga became even more imposing in his eyes, and when he endeavored to find out why she had not brought Lili with her,—

"Oh! no, no, never!" said she stiffly. "Not three months ago she positively insisted on leaving her boarding school. I was thinking of marrying her off at once, but she loves me, so that I had to take her home—oh! so much against my will!"

Her blue eyelids, with their blackened lashes, blinked and wavered, while she spoke of the business of settling her young lady. If, at her time of life, she hadn't laid by a sou, but was still always working to minister to men's pleasures, especially those of very young men, whose grandmother she might well be, it was truly because she considered a good match of far greater importance than mere savings. And with that she leant over la Faloise, who reddened under the huge naked plastered shoulder with which she well nigh crushed him.

"You know," she murmured, "if she fails, it won't be my fault. But they're so strange when they're young!"

There was a considerable bustle round the table, and the waiters became very active. After the third course the *entrées* had made their appearance; they consisted of pullets *à la maréchale,* fillets of sole with shallot sauce, and *escalopes* of Strasbourg *pâté.* The manager, who till then had been having Meursault served, now offered Chambertin and Léoville. Amid the slight hubbub which the change of plates involved, Georges, who was growing momentarily more astonished, asked Daguenet if all the ladies present were similarly provided with children, and the other, who was amused by this question, gave him some further details. Lucy Stewart was the daughter of a man of English origin, who greased the wheels of the trains at the Gare du Nord; she was thirty-nine years old and had the face of a horse, but was adorable withal, and, though consumptive, never died. In fact, she was the smartest woman there, and represented three princes and a duke. Caroline Héquet, born at Bordeaux, daughter of a little clerk long since dead of shame, was lucky enough to be possessed of a mother with a head on her shoulders, who, after having cursed her, had made it up again at the end of a year of reflection, being minded at any rate to save

a fortune for her daughter. The latter was twenty-five years
old, and very passionless, and was held to be one of the finest
women it was possible to enjoy. Her price never varied.
The mother, a model of orderliness, kept the accounts, and
noted down receipts and expenditures with severe precision.
She managed the whole household from some small lodging
two stories above her daughter's, where, moreover, she had
established a workroom for dressmaking and plain sewing.
As to Blanche de Sivry, whose real name was Jacqueline
Bandu, she hailed from a village near Amiens. Magnificent
in person, stupid and untruthful in character, she gave herself out as the grand-daughter of a general, and never owned
to her thirty-two summers. The Russians had a great taste
for her owing to her *embonpoint*. Then Daguenet added a
rapid word or two about the rest. There was Clarisse Besnus,
whom a lady had brought up from Saint-Aubin-sur-Mer
in the capacity of maid, whilst the lady's husband had started
her in quite another line. There was Simonne Cabiroche,
the daughter of a furniture dealer in the Faubourg Saint-
Antoine, who had been educated in a large boarding school
with a view to becoming a governess. Finally, there were
Maria Blond, and Louise Violaine, and Léa de Horn, who
had all shot up to woman's estate on the pavements of Paris,
not to mention Tatan Néné, who had herded cows in Champagne till she was twenty.

Georges listened and looked at these ladies, feeling dizzy
and excited by the coarse recital thus crudely whispered in
his ear, whilst, behind his chair, the waiters kept repeating
in respectful tones,—

"Pullets *à la maréchale:* fillets of sole with *ravigote* sauce."

"My dear fellow," said Daguenet, giving him the benefit of
his experience, "don't take any fish: it'll do you no good at
this time of night. And be content with Léoville: it's less
treacherous."

A heavy warmth floated upward from the candelabras,

from the dishes which were being handed round, from the whole table where thirty-eight human beings were suffocating. And the waiters forgot themselves and ran when crossing the carpet, so that it was spotted with grease. Nevertheless, the supper grew scarce any merrier. The ladies trifled with their meat, left half of it uneaten. Tatan Néné alone partook gluttonously of every dish. At that advanced hour of the night, hunger was of the nervous order only, a mere whimsical craving born of an exasperated stomach.

At Nana's side, the old gentleman refused every dish offered him; he had only taken a spoonful of soup, and he now sat in front of his empty plate gazing silently about. There was some subdued yawning, and occasionally eyelids closed, and faces became haggard and white. It was unutterably slow, as it always was, according to Vandeuvres's dictum. This sort of supper should be served anyhow if it was to be funny, he opined. Otherwise, when elegantly and conventionally done, you might as well feed in good society, where you were not more bored than here. Had it not been for Bordenave, who was still bawling away, everybody would have fallen asleep. That rum old buffer, Bordenave, with his leg duly stretched on its chair, was letting his neighbors, Lucy and Rose, wait on him as though he were a sultan. They were entirely taken up with him, and they helped him and pampered him, and watched over his glass and his plate, and yet that did not prevent his complaining.

"Who's going to cut up my meat for me? I can't, the table's a league away."

Every few seconds Simonne rose, and took up a position behind his back in order to cut his meat and his bread. All the women took a great interest in the things he ate. The waiters were recalled, and he was stuffed to suffocation. Simonne having wiped his mouth for him, whilst Rose and Lucy were changing his plate, her act struck him as very pretty, and, deigning at length to shew contentment,—

"There, there, my daughter," said he, "that's as it should be. Women are made for that!"

There was a slight re-awakening, and conversation became general as they finished discussing some orange sherbet. The hot roast was a fillet with truffles, and the cold roast a galantine of guinea-fowls in jelly. Nana, annoyed by the want of go displayed by her guests, had begun talking with the greatest distinctness.

"You know the Prince of Scots has already had a stage-box reserved so as to see the *Blonde Venus* when he comes to visit the Exhibition."

"I very much hope that all the princes will come and see it," declared Bordenave with his mouth full.

"They are expecting the Shah of Persia next Sunday," said Lucy Stewart.

Whereupon Rose Mignon spoke of the Shah's diamonds. He wore a tunic entirely covered with gems: it was a marvel, a flaming star, it represented millions. And the ladies, with pale faces and eyes glittering with covetousness, craned forward, and ran over the names of the other kings, the other emperors, who were shortly expected. All of them were dreaming of some royal caprice, some night to be paid for by a fortune.

"Now tell me, dear boy," Caroline Héquet asked Vandeuvres, leaning forward as she did so, "how old's the Emperor of Russia?"

"Oh, he's 'present time,'" replied the Count, laughing. "Nothing to be done in that quarter, I warn you."

Nana made pretense of being hurt. The witticism appeared somewhat too stinging, and there was a murmur of protest. But Blanche gave a description of the King of Italy, whom she had once seen at Milan. He was scarcely good-looking, and yet that did not prevent him enjoying all the women. She was put out somewhat when Fauchery assured her that Victor Emmanuel could not come to the Exhibition.

Louise Violaine and Léa favored the Emperor of Austria, and all of a sudden little Maria Blond was heard saying,—

"What an old stick the King of Prussia is! I was at Baden last year, and one was always meeting him about with Count Bismarck."

"Dear me, Bismarck!" Simonne interrupted. "I knew him once, I did. A charming man."

"That's what I was saying yesterday," cried Vandeuvres, "but nobody would believe me."

And, just as at Countess Sabine's, there ensued a long discussion about Bismarck. Vandeuvres repeated the same phrases, and for a moment or two one was again in the Muffats' drawing-room, the only difference being that the ladies were changed. Then, just as last night, they passed on to a discussion of music, after which, Foucarmont having let slip some mention of the assumption of the veil of which Paris was still talking, Nana grew quite interested, and insisted on details about Mademoiselle de Fougeray. Oh, the poor child, fancy her burying herself alive like that! Ah, well, when it was a question of vocation! All round the table the women expressed themselves much touched, and Georges, wearied at hearing these things a second time discussed, was beginning to ask Daguenet about Nana's ways in private life, when the conversation veered fatefully back to Count Bismarck. Tatan Néné bent towards Labordette to ask him privily who this Bismarck might be, for she did not know him. Whereupon Labordette, in cold blood, told her some portentous anecdotes. This Bismarck, said he, was in the habit of eating raw meat, and when he met a woman near his den would carry her off thither on his back; at forty years of age he had already had as many as thirty-two children that way.

"Thirty-two children at forty!" cried Tatan Néné, stupefied and yet convinced. "He must be jolly well worn out for his age."

There was a burst of merriment, and it dawned on her that she was being made game of.

"You sillies! How am I to know if you're joking?"

Gaga, meanwhile, had stopped at the Exhibition. Like all these ladies, she was delightedly preparing for the fray. A good season, provincials and foreigners rushing into Paris! In the long run, perhaps, after the close of the Exhibition, she would, if her business had flourished, be able to retire to a little house at Jouvisy, which she had long had her eye on.

"What's to be done?" said she to la Faloise. "One never gets what one wants! Oh! if only one were still really loved!"

Gaga behaved meltingly because she had felt the young man's knee gently placed against her own. He was blushing hotly, and lisping as elegantly as ever. She weighed him at a glance. Not a very heavy little gentleman, to be sure; but then she wasn't hard to please. La Faloise obtained her address.

"Just look there," murmured Vandeuvres to Clarisse. "I think Gaga's doing you out of your Hector."

"A good riddance, so far as I'm concerned, replied the actress. "That fellow's an idiot. I've already chucked him downstairs three times. You know, I'm disgusted when dirty little boys run after old women."

She broke off, and with a little gesture indicated Blanche, who from the commencement of dinner had remained in a most uncomfortable attitude, sitting up very markedly, with the intention of displaying her shoulders to the old distinguished-looking gentleman three seats beyond her.

"You're being left too," she resumed.

Vandeuvres smiled his thin smile, and made a little movement to signify he did not care. Assuredly, 'twas not he who would ever have prevented poor dear Blanche scoring a success. He was more interested by the spectacle which Steiner was presenting to the table at large. The banker was noted for his sudden flames. That terrible German Jew, who brewed money, whose hands forged millions, was wont to turn imbecile whenever he became enamored of a woman. He wanted them all too! Not one could make her appearance on the stage but he bought her, however expensive she might be. Vast sums were quoted. Twice had his furious appetite for courtesans ruined him. The courtesans, as Vandeuvres used to say, avenged public morality by emptying his money bags. A big operation in the salt works of the Landes had rendered him powerful on 'Change, and so for six weeks past the Mignons had been getting a pretty slice out of those same salt works. But people were beginning to lay wagers that the Mignons would not finish their slice, for Nana was shewing her white teeth. Once again Steiner was in the toils, and so deeply this time that, as he sat by Nana's side, he seemed stunned—he ate without appetite, his lip hung down, his face was mottled. She had only to name a figure. Nevertheless, she did not hurry, but continued playing with him, breathing her merry laughter into his hairy ear, and enjoying the little convulsive movements which kept traversing his heavy face. There would always be time enough to patch all that up if that ninny of a Count Muffat were really to treat her as Joseph did Potiphar's wife.

"Léoville or Chambertin?" murmured a waiter, who came craning forward between Nana and Steiner, just as the latter was addressing her in a low voice.

"Eh? what?" he stammered, losing his head. "Whatever you like—I don't care."

Vandeuvres gently nudged Lucy Stewart, who had a very spiteful tongue and a very fierce invention when once she was set going. That evening Mignon was driving her to exasperation.

"He would gladly be bottle-holder, you know," she remarked to the Count. "He's in hopes of repeating what he did with little Jonquier. You remember: Jonquier was

Rose's man, but he was sweet on big Laure. Now Mignon procured Laure for Jonquier, and then came back arm in arm with him to Rose, as if he were a husband who had been allowed a little peccadillo. But this time the thing's going to fail. Nana doesn't give up the men who are lent her."

"What ails Mignon that he should be looking at his wife in that severe way?" asked Vandeuvres.

He leant forward, and saw Rose growing exceedingly amorous towards Faucbery. This was the explanation of his neighbor's wrath. He resumed laughingly,—

"The devil, are you jealous?"

"Jealous!" said Lucy in a fury. "Good gracious, if Rose is wanting Léon, I give him up willingly—for what he's worth! That's to say, for a bouquet a week, and the rest to match! Look here, my dear boy, these theatrical trollops are all made the same way. Why, Rose cried with rage when she read Léon's article on Nana; I know she did. So now, you understand, she must have an article too, and she's gaining it. As for me, I'm going to chuck Léon downstairs, you'll see!"

She paused to say "Léoville" to the waiter standing behind her with his two bottles, and then resumed in lowered tones,—

"I don't want to shout; it isn't my style. But she's a cocky slut all the same. If I were in her husband's place I should lead her a lovely dance. Oh! she won't be very happy over it. She doesn't know my Faucbery: a dirty gent he is, too, palling up with women like that so as to get on in the world. Oh, a nice lot they are!"

Vandeuvres did his best to calm her down, but Bordenave, deserted by Rose and by Lucy, grew angry, and cried out that they were letting papa perish of hunger and thirst. This produced a fortunate diversion. Yet the supper was flagging; no one was eating now, though platefuls of *cèpes à l'Italienne* and pineapple fritters *à la Pompadour* were being mangled.

The champagne, however, which had been drunk ever since the soup course, was beginning little by little to warm the guests into a state of nervous exaltation. They ended by paying less attention to decorum than before. The women began leaning on their elbows amid the disordered table arrangements, whilst the men, in order to breathe more easily, pushed their chairs back; and soon the black coats appeared buried between the light-colored bodices, and bare shoulders, half turned towards the table, began to gleam as soft as silk. It was too hot, and the glare of the candles above the table grew ever yellower and duller. Now and again, when a woman bent forward, the back of her neck glowed golden under a rain of curls, and the glitter of a diamond clasp lit up a lofty chignon. There was a touch of fire in the passing jests, in the laughing eyes, in the sudden gleam of white teeth, in the reflection of the candelabra, on the surface of a glass of champagne. The company joked at the tops of their voices, gesticulated, asked questions which no one answered, and called to one another across the whole length of the room. But the loudest din was made by the waiters; they fancied themselves at home in the corridors of their parent restaurant; they jostled one another, and served the ices and the dessert to an accompaniment of guttural exclamations.

"My children," shouted Bordenave, "you know we're playing to-morrow. Be careful! not too much champagne!"

"As far as I'm concerned," said Foucarmont, "I've drunk every imaginable kind of wine in all the four quarters of the globe. Extraordinary liquors some of 'em, containing alcohol enough to kill a corpse! Well, and what d'you think? why it never hurt me a bit. I can't make myself drunk. I've tried and I can't."

He was very pale, very calm and collected, and he lolled back in his chair, drinking without cessation.

"Never mind that," murmured Louise Violaine. "Leave

off: you've had enough. It would be a funny business if I
had to look after you the rest of the night."

Such was her state of exaltation that Lucy Stewart's cheeks
were assuming a red consumptive flush, whilst Rose Mignon
with moist eyelids was growing excessively melting. Tatan
Néné, greatly astonished at the thought that she had over-
eaten herself, was laughing vaguely over her own stupidity.
The others, such as Blanche, Caroline, Simonne, and Maria,
were all talking at once, and telling each other about their
private affairs—about a dispute with a coachman, a projected
picnic, and innumerable complex stories of lovers stolen or
restored. Meanwhile, a young man near Georges, having
evinced a desire to kiss Léa de Horn, received a sharp rap,
accompanied by a "Look here, you, let me go!" which was
spoken in a tone of fine indignation; and Georges, who was
now very tipsy and greatly excited by the sight of Nana, hesitated about carrying out a project which he had been gravely
maturing. He had been planning, indeed, to get under the
table on all-fours and to go and crouch at Nana's feet like a
little dog. Nobody would have seen him, and he would have
stayed there in the quietest way. But when, at Léa's urgent
request, Daguenet had told the young man to sit still, Georges
all at once felt grievously chagrined, as though the reproof
had just been leveled at him. Oh, it was all silly, and slow,
and there was nothing worth living for! Daguenet, nevertheless, began chaffing, and obliged him to swallow a big
glassful of water, asking him, at the same time, what he
would do if he were to find himself alone with a woman,
seeing that three glasses of champagne were able to bowl him
over.

"Why, in Havana," resumed Foucarmont, "they make a
spirit with a certain wild berry; you think you're swallowing
fire! Well now, one evening I drank more than a liter of
it, and it didn't hurt me one bit. Better than that, another
time when we were on the coast of Coromandel, some sav-

ages gave us I don't know what sort of a mixture of pepper and vitriol; and that didn't hurt me one bit. I can't make myself drunk."

For some moments past la Faloise's face opposite had excited his displeasure. He began sneering, and giving vent to disagreeable witticisms. La Faloise, whose brain was in a whirl, was behaving very restlessly, and squeezing up against Gaga. But at length he became the victim of anxiety; somebody had just taken his handkerchief, and with drunken obstinacy he demanded it back again, asked his neighbors about it, stooped down in order to look under the chairs and the guests' feet. And when Gaga did her best to quiet him,—

"It's a nuisance," murmured he, "my initials and my coronet are worked in the corner. They may compromise me."

"I say, Monsieur Falamoise, Lamafoise, Mafaloise!" shouted Foucarmont, who thought it exceedingly witty thus to disfigure the young man's name *ad infinitum*.

But la Faloise grew wroth, and talked with a stutter about his ancestry. He threatened to send a water bottle at Foucarmont's head, and Count de Vandeuvres had to interfere in order to assure him that Foucarmont was a great joker. Indeed, everybody was laughing. This did for the already flurried young man, who was very glad to resume his seat, and to begin eating with childlike submissiveness, when, in a loud voice, his cousin ordered him to feed. Gaga had taken him back to her ample side; only from time to time he cast sly and anxious glances at the guests, for he ceased not to search for his handkerchief.

Then Foucarmont, being now in his witty vein, attacked Labordette right at the other end of the table. Louise Violaine strove to make him hold his tongue, for, said she, "when he goes nagging at other people like that, it always ends in mischief for me." He had discovered a witticism which consisted in addressing Labordette as *"Madame,"* and it must have amused him greatly, for he kept on repeating it, while

Labordette tranquilly shrugged his shoulders, and as constantly replied,—

"Pray hold your tongue, my dear fellow, it's stupid."

But as Foucarmont failed to desist, and even became insulting, without his neighbors knowing why, he left off answering him, and appealed to Count Vandeuvres.

"Make your friend hold his tongue, *Monsieur*. I don't wish to become angry."

Foucarmont had twice fought duels, and he was in consequence most politely treated, and admitted into every circle. But there was now a general uprising against him. The table grew merry at his sallies, for they thought him very witty; but that was no reason why the evening should be spoiled. Vandeuvres, whose subtle countenance was darkening visibly, insisted on his restoring Labordette his sex. The other men—Mignon, Steiner, and Bordenave—who were by this time much exalted, also intervened with shouts which drowned his voice. Only the old gentleman, sitting forgotten next to Nana, retained his stately demeanor, and, still smiling in his tired silent way, watched with lack-luster eyes the untoward finish of the dessert.

"What do you say to our taking coffee in here, duckie?" said Bordenave. "We're very comfortable."

Nana did not give an immediate reply. Since the beginning of supper, she had seemed no longer in her own house. All this company had overwhelmed and bewildered her with their shouts to the waiters, the loudness of their voices, and the way in which they put themselves at their ease, just as though they were in a restaurant. Forgetting her *rôle* of hostess, she busied herself exclusively with bulky Steiner, who was verging on apoplexy beside her. She was listening to his proposals, and continually refusing them with shakes of the head, and that temptress's laughter which is peculiar to a voluptuous blonde. The champagne she had been drinking had flushed her a rosy-red; her lips were moist, her eyes sparkled, and the banker's offers rose with every kittenish movement of her shoulders, with every little voluptuous lift and fall of her throat, which occurred when she turned her head. Close by her ear, he kept espying a sweet little satiny corner which drove him crazy. Occasionally Nana was interrupted, and then, remembering her guests, she would try and be pleased as possible in order to shew that she knew how to receive. Towards the end of supper she was very tipsy. It made her miserable to think of it, but champagne had a way of intoxicating her almost directly! Then an exasperating notion struck her. In behaving thus improperly at her table, these ladies were shewing themselves anxious to do her an ugly turn. Oh, yes! she could see it all distinctly. Lucy had given Foucarmont a wink in order to egg him on against Labordette, whilst Rose, Caroline, and the others, were doing all they could to stir up the men. Now there was such a din you couldn't hear your neighbor speak, and so the story would get about that you might allow yourself every kind of liberty when you supped at Nana's. Very well then! they should see! She might be tipsy, if you like, but she was still the smartest and most lady-like woman there.

"Do tell them to serve the coffee here, duckie," resumed Bordenave. "I prefer it here because of my leg."

But Nana had sprung savagely to her feet, after whispering into the astonished ears of Steiner and the old gentleman,—

"It's quite right: it'll teach me to go and invite a dirty lot like that."

Then she pointed to the door of the dining-room, and added at the top of her voice,—

"If you want coffee, it's there, you know."

The company left the table, and crowded towards the dining-room without noticing Nana's indignant outburst. And soon no one was left in the drawing-room save Bordenave, who advanced cautiously, supporting himself against the wall, and cursing away at the confounded women, who chucked papa the moment they were chock-full. The waiters behind him were already busy removing the plates and dishes, in obedience to the loudly-voiced orders of the manager. They rushed to and fro, jostled one another, caused the whole table to vanish, as a pantomime property might at sound of the chief scene-shifter's whistle. The ladies and gentlemen were to return to the drawing-room after drinking their coffee.

"By gum, it's less hot here," said Gaga with a slight shiver as she entered the dining-room.

The window here had remained open. Two lamps illuminated the table, where coffee and liqueurs were set out. There were no chairs, and the guests drank their coffee standing, while the hubbub the waiters were making in the next room grew louder and louder. Nana had disappeared, but nobody fretted about her absence. They did without her excellently well, and everybody helped himself, and rummaged in the drawers of the side-board in search of tea-spoons, which were lacking. Several groups were formed; people separated during supper rejoined each other; and there was an interchange of glances, of meaning laughter, and of phrases which summed up recent situations.

"Ought not Monsieur Fauchery to come and lunch with us one of these days, Auguste?" said Rose Mignon.

Mignon, who was toying with his watch-chain, eyed the journalist for a second or two with his severe glance. Rose was out of her senses. As became a good manager, he would put a stop to such spendthrift courses. In return for a notice well and good, but afterwards decidedly not. Nevertheless, as he was fully aware of his wife's wrong-headedness, and as he made it a rule to wink paternally at a folly now and again, when such was necessary, he answered amiably enough,—

"Certainly, I shall be most happy. Pray come to-morrow, Monsieur Fauchery."

Lucy Stewart heard this invitation given while she was talking with Steiner and Blanche, and, raising her voice, she remarked to the banker,—

"It's a mania they've all of them got. One of them even went so far as to steal my dog. Now, dear boy, am I to blame if you chuck her?"

Rose turned round. She was very pale, and gazed fixedly at Steiner as she sipped her coffee. And then all the concentrated anger she felt at his abandonment of her flamed out in her eyes. She saw more clearly than Mignon; it was stupid in him to have wished to begin the Jonquier ruse a second time—those dodgers never succeeded twice running. Well, so much the worse for him! She would have Fauchery! She had been getting enamored of him since the beginning of supper, and if Mignon was not pleased, it would teach him greater wisdom!

"You are not going to fight?" said Vandeuvres, coming over to Lucy Stewart.

"No, don't you be afraid of that! Only, she must mind and keep quiet, or I let the cat out of the bag!"

Then signing imperiously to Fauchery,—

"I've got your slippers at home, my little man. I'll get them taken to your porter's lodge for you to-morrow."

He wanted to joke about it, but she swept off, looking like a queen. Clarisse, who had propped herself against a wall in order to drink a quiet glass of kirsch, was seen to shrug her shoulders. A pleasant business for a man! Wasn't it true that the moment two women were together in the presence of their lovers their first idea was to do one another out of them? It was a law of nature! As to herself, why, in Heaven's name, if she had wanted to, she would have torn out Gaga's eyes on Hector's account! But la! she despised him. Then, as la Faloise passed by, she contented herself by remarking to him,—

"Listen, my friend, you like 'em well advanced, you do! You don't want 'em ripe, you want 'em mildewed!"

La Faloise seemed much annoyed, and not a little anxious. Seeing Clarisse making game of him, he grew suspicious of her.

"No humbug, I say," he muttered. "You've taken my handkerchief. Well then, give it back!"

"He's dreeing us with that handkerchief of his!" she cried. "Why, you ass, why should I have taken it from you?"

"Why should you?" said he suspiciously, "why, that you may send it to my people and compromise me."

In the meantime, Foucarmont was diligently attacking the liqueurs. He continued to gaze sneeringly at Labordette, who was drinking his coffee in the midst of the ladies. And occasionally he gave vent to fragmentary assertions, as thus: "He's the son of a horse-dealer; some say the illegitimate child of a countess. Never a penny of income, yet always got twenty-five louis in his pocket! Footboy to the ladies of the town! A big lubber, who never goes with any of 'em! Never, never, never!" he repeated, growing furious. "No, by Jove! I must box his ears."

He drained a glass of Chartreuse. The Chartreuse had not the slightest effect upon him; it didn't affect him "even to that extent," and he clicked his thumbnail against the edge of his teeth. But suddenly, just as he was advancing upon Labordette, he grew ashy white and fell down in a heap in front of the side-board. He was dead drunk. Louise Violaine was beside herself. She had been quite right to prophesy that matters would end badly; and now she would have her work cut out for the remainder of the night. Gaga reassured her. She examined the officer with the eye of a woman of experience, and declared that there was nothing much the matter, and that the gentleman would sleep like that for at least a dozen or fifteen hours without any serious consequences. Foucarmont was carried off.

"Well, where's Nana gone to?" asked Vandeuvres.

Yes, she had certainly flown away somewhere on leaving the table. The company suddenly recollected her, and everybody asked for her. Steiner, who for some seconds had been uneasy on her account, asked Vandeuvres about the old gentleman, for he too had disappeared. But the Count reassured him—he had just brought the old gentleman back. He was a stranger, whose name it was useless to mention. Suffice it to say that he was a very rich man, who was quite pleased to pay for suppers! Then, as Nana was once more being forgotten, Vandeuvres saw Daguenet looking out of an open door and beckoning to him. And in the bedroom he found the mistress of the house sitting up, white-lipped and rigid, while Daguenet and Georges stood gazing at her with an alarmed expression.

"What *is* the matter with you?" he asked in some surprise.

She neither answered nor turned her head, and he repeated his question.

"Why, this is what's the matter with me," she cried out at length; "I won't let them make bloody sport of me!"

Thereupon she gave vent to any expression that occurred to her. Yes, oh yes, *she* wasn't a ninny—*she* could see clearly enough. They had been making devilish light of her during supper, and saying all sorts of frightful things, to shew that they thought nothing of her! A pack of sluts, who weren't fit to black her boots! Catch her bothering herself again, just to be badgered for it after! She really didn't know what kept her from chucking all that dirty lot out of the house! And, with this, rage choked her, and her voice broke down in sobs.

"Come, come, my lass, you're drunk," said Vandeuvres, growing familiar. "You must be reasonable."

No, she would give her refusal now; she would stay where she was.

"I am drunk—it's quite likely! But I want people to respect me!"

For a quarter of an hour past, Daguenet and Georges had been vainly beseeching her to return to the drawing-room She was obstinate, however; her guests might do what they liked; she despised them too much to come back amongst them.

No, she never would, never. They might tear her in pieces before she would leave her room!"

"I ought to have had my suspicions," she resumed.

"It's that cat of a Rose who's got the plot up! I'm certain Rose'll have stopped that respectable woman coming, whom I was expecting to-night."

She referred to Madame Robert. Vandeuvres gave her his word of honor that Madame Robert had given a spontaneous refusal. He listened, and he argued with much gravity, for he was well accustomed to similar scenes, and knew how women in such a state ought to be treated. But the moment he tried to take hold of her hands in order to lift her up from her chair and draw her away with him, she struggled free of his clasp, and her wrath redoubled. Now, just look at that! they would never get her to believe that Fauchery had not put the Count Muffat off coming! A regular snake was that Fauchery; an envious sort, a fellow capable of growing mad against a woman and of destroying her whole happiness. For she knew this—the Count had become madly devoted to her! She could have had him!

"Him, my dear, never!" cried Vandeuvres, forgetting himself and laughing aloud.

"Why not?" she asked, looking serious and slightly sobered.

"Because he's thoroughly in the hands of the priests, and if he were only to touch you with the tips of his fingers, he would go and confess it the day after. Now listen to a bit of good advice. Don't let the other man escape you!"

She was silent and thoughtful for a moment or two. Then

she got up, and went and bathed her eyes. Yet, when they wanted to take her into the dining-room, she still shouted "No!" furiously. Vandeuvres left the bedroom, smiling and without further pressing her, and, the moment he was gone, she had an access of melting tenderness, threw herself into Daguenet's arms, and cried out,—

"Ah, my sweetie, there's only you in the world. I love you! *Yes,* I love you from the bottom of my heart! Oh, it would be too nice if we could always live together. My God! how unfortunate women are!"

Then her eye fell upon Georges, who, seeing them kiss, was growing very red, and she kissed him too. Sweetie could not be jealous of a baby! She wanted Paul and Georges always to agree, because it would be so nice for them all three to stay like that, knowing all the time that they loved one another very much. But an extraordinary noise disturbed them: some one was snoring in the room. Whereupon, after some searching, they perceived Bordenave, who, since taking his coffee, must have comfortably installed himself there. He was sleeping on two chairs, his head propped on the edge of the bed, and his leg stretched out in front. Nana thought him so funny with his open mouth and his nose moving with each successive snore, that she was shaken with a mad fit of laughter. She left the room, followed by Daguenet and Georges, crossed the dining-room, entered the drawing-room, her merriment increasing at every step.

"Oh, my dear, you've no idea!" she cried, almost throwing herself into Rose's arms. "Come and see it."

All the women had to follow her. She took their hands coaxingly, and drew them along with her, willy-nilly, accompanying her action with so frank an outburst of mirth that they all of them began laughing on trust. The band vanished, and returned, after standing breathlessly for a second or two round Bordenave's lordly, outstretched form. And then there was a burst of laughter, and when one of them told the rest to be quiet, Bordenave's distant snorings became audible.

It was close on four o'clock. In the dining-room, a card-table had just been set out, at which Vandeuvres, Steiner, Mignon, and Labordette had taken their seats. Behind them Lucy and Caroline stood making bets, whilst Blanche, nodding with sleep and dissatisfied about her night, kept asking Vandeuvres at intervals of five minutes if they weren't going soon. In the drawing-room there was an attempt at dancing. Daguenet was at the piano, or "chest of drawers," as Nana called it. She did not want a "thumper," for Mimi would play as many waltzes and polkas as the company desired. But the dance was languishing, and the ladies were chatting drowsily together in the corners of sofas. Suddenly, however, there was an outburst of noise. A band of eleven young men had arrived and were laughing loudly in the anteroom and crowding to the drawing-room. They had just come from the ball at the Ministry of the Interior, and were in evening dress and wore various unknown orders. Nana was annoyed at this riotous entry, called to the waiters who still remained in the kitchen, and ordered them to throw these individuals out of doors. She vowed that she had never seen any of them before. Fauchery, Labordette, Daguenet, and the rest of the men had all come forward in order to enforce respectful behavior towards their hostess. Big words flew about, arms were outstretched, and for some seconds a general exchange of fisticuffs was imminent. Notwithstanding this, however, a little sickly-looking light-haired man kept insistently repeating,—

"Come, come, Nana, you saw us the other evening at Peters's in the great red saloon! Pray remember you invited us."

The other evening at Peters's? She did not remember it all. To begin with, what evening?

And when the little light-haired man had mentioned the

day, which was Wednesday, she distinctly remembered having supped at Peters's on the Wednesday, but she had given no invitation to any one, she was almost sure of that.

"However, suppose you *have* invited them, my good girl," murmured Labordette, who was beginning to have his doubts. "Perhaps you were a little elevated."

Then Nana fell a-laughing. It was quite possible, she really didn't know. So then, since these gentlemen were on the spot, they had her leave to come in. Everything was quietly arranged, several of the newcomers found friends in the drawing-room, and the scene ended in hand-shakings. The little sickly-looking, light-haired man bore one of the greatest names in France. Furthermore, the eleven announced that others were to follow them, and, in fact, the door opened every few moments, and men in white gloves and official garb presented themselves. They were still coming from the ball at the Ministry. Fauchery jestingly enquired whether the Minister was not coming too, but Nana answered in a huff that the Minister went to the houses of people she didn't care a pin for. What she did not say was, that she was possessed with a hope of seeing Count Muffat enter her room among all that stream of people. He might quite have reconsidered his decision; and so, whilst talking to Rose, she kept a sharp eye on the door.

Five o'clock struck. The dancing had ceased, and the card-players alone persisted in their game. Labordette had vacated his seat, and the women had returned into the drawing-room. The air there was heavy with the somnolence which accompanies a long vigil, and the lamps cast a wavering light, whilst their burnt-out wicks glowed red within their globes. The ladies had reached that vaguely melancholy hour when they felt it necessary to tell each other their histories. Blanche de Sivry spoke of her grandfather, the general, whilst Clarisse invented a romantic story about a Duke seducing her at her uncle's house, whither he used to come for the

boar-hunting. Both women, looking different ways, kept
shrugging their shoulders, and asking themselves how the
deuce the other could tell such woppers! As to Lucy Stewart,
she quietly confessed to her origin, and of her own accord
spoke of her childhood, and of the days when her father, the
wheel-greaser at the Northern Railway Terminus, used to
treat her to an apple puff on Sundays.

"Oh! I must tell you about it!" cried the little Maria
Blond, abruptly. "Opposite to me there lives a gentleman, a
Russian, an awfully rich man! Well, just fancy, yesterday I
received a basket of fruit—oh! it just was a basket! Enormous peaches, grapes as big as that, simply wonderful for the
time of year! And in the middle of them six thousand-franc
notes! It was the Russian's doing. Of course, I sent the
whole thing back again, but I must say my heart ached a
little—when I thought of the fruit!"

The ladies looked at one another and pursed up their lips.
At her age little Maria Blond had a pretty cheek! Besides, to
think that such things should happen to trollops like her!
Infinite was their contempt for her among themselves. It
was Lucy of whom they were particularly jealous, for they
were beside themselves at the thought of her three princes.
Since Lucy had begun taking a daily morning ride in the
Bois, they all had become Amazons, as though a mania
possessed them.

Day was about to dawn, and Nana turned her eyes away
from the door, for she was relinquishing all hope. The company were bored to distraction. Rose Mignon had refused to
sing the "Slipper," and sat huddled up on a sofa, chatting
in a low voice with Fauchery and waiting for Mignon, who
had by now won some fifty louis from Vandeuvres. A fat
gentleman, with a decoration and a serious cast of countenance, had certainly given a recitation, in Alsatian accents,
of "Abraham's Sacrifice," a piece in which the Almighty
says, "By My blasted Name" when He swears, and Isaac

always answers with a "Yes, papa!" Nobody, however, understood what it was all about, and the piece had been voted stupid. People were at their wits' end how to make merry and to finish the night with fitting hilarity. For a moment or two Labordette conceived the idea of denouncing different women in a whisper to la Faloise, who still went prowling round each individual lady, looking to see if she were hiding his handkerchief in her bosom. Soon, as there were still some bottles of champagne on the side-board, the young men again fell to drinking. They shouted to one another; they stirred each other up; but a dreary species of intoxication, which was stupid enough to drive one to despair, began to overcome the company beyond hope of recovery. Then the little fair-haired fellow, the man who bore one of the greatest names in France, and had reached his wits' end and was desperate at the thought that he could not hit upon something really funny, conceived a brilliant notion: he snatched up his bottle of champagne and poured its contents into the piano. His allies were convulsed with laughter.

"La now! why's he putting champagne into the piano?" asked Tatan Néné, in great astonishment as she caught sight of him.

"What, my lass, you don't know why he's doing that?" replied Labordette solemnly. "There's nothing so good as champagne for pianos. It gives 'em tone."

"Ah," murmured Tatan Néné with conviction.

And when the rest began laughing at her, she grew angry. How should she know? They were always confusing her.

Decidedly, the evening was becoming a big failure. The night threatened to end in the unloveliest way. In a corner by themselves, Maria Blond and Léa de Horn had begun squabbling at close quarters, the former accusing the latter of consorting with people of insufficient wealth. They were getting vastly abusive over it, their chief stumbling-block being the good looks of the men in question. Lucy, who was plain, got them to hold their tongues. Good looks were nothing, according to her: good figures were what was wanted. Further off, on a sofa, an attaché had slipped his arm round Simonne's waist, and was trying to kiss her neck; but Simonne, sullen and thoroughly out of sorts, pushed him away at every fresh attempt with cries of "You're pestering me!" and sound slaps of the fan across his face. For the matter of that, not one of the ladies allowed herself to be touched. Did people take them for light women? Gaga, in the mean time, had once more caught la Faloise, and had almost hoisted him upon her knees, whilst Clarisse was disappearing from view between two gentlemen, shaking with nervous laughter as women will when they are tickled. Round about the piano they were still busy with their little game, for they were suffering from a fit of stupid imbecility, which caused each man to jostle his fellow in his frantic desire to empty his bottle into the instrument. It was a simple process and a charming.

"Now then, old boy, drink a glass! Devil take it, he's a thirsty piano! Hi! 'tenshun! here's another bottle! You mustn't lose a drop!"

Nana's back was turned, and she did not see them. Emphatically, she was now falling back on the bulky Steiner, who was seated next to her. So much the worse! It was all on account of that Muffat, who had refused what was offered him. Sitting there in her white foulard dress, which was as light and full of folds as a shift, sitting there with drooped eyelids and cheeks pale with the touch of intoxication from which she was suffering, she offered herself to him with that quiet expression which is peculiar to a good-natured courtesan. The roses in her hair and at her throat had lost their leaves, and their stalks alone remained. Presently, Steiner withdrew his hand quickly from the folds of her skirt, where he had come in contact with the pins that

Georges had stuck there. Some drops of blood appeared on his fingers, and one fell on Nana's dress, and stained it.

"Now, the bargain's struck," said Nana, gravely.

The day was breaking apace. An uncertain glimmer of light, fraught with a poignant melancholy, came stealing through the windows. And with that the guests began to take their departure. It was a most sour and uncomfortable retreat. Caroline Héquet, annoyed at the loss of her night, announced that it was high time to be off unless you were anxious to assist at some pretty scenes. Rose pouted as if her womanly character had been compromised. It was always so with these girls; they didn't know how to behave, and were guilty of disgusting conduct when they made their first appearance in society! And Mignon having cleaned Vandeuvres out completely, the family took their departure. They did not trouble about Steiner, but renewed their invitation for to-morrow to Fauchery. Lucy thereupon refused the journalist's escort home, and sent him back shrilly to his "strolling actress." At this Rose turned round immediately, and hissed out a "Dirty sow" by way of answer. But Mignon, who in feminine quarrels was always paternal, for his experience was a long one, and rendered him superior to them, had already pushed her out of the house, telling her, at the same time, to have done. Lucy came downstairs in solitary state behind them. After which, Gaga had to carry off la Faloise, ill, sobbing like a child, calling after Clarisse, who had long since gone off with her two gentlemen. Simonne, too, had vanished. Indeed, none remained save Tatan, Léa, and Maria, whom Labordette complaisantly took under his charge.

"Oh, but I don't the least bit want to go to bed!" said Nana. "One ought to find something to do."

She looked at the sky through the window-panes. It was a livid sky, and sooty clouds were scudding across it. It was six o'clock in the morning. Over the way, on the opposite

side of the Boulevard Haussmann, the glistening roofs of the
still slumbering houses were sharply outlined against the
twilight sky, whilst, along the deserted roadway, a gang of
street-sweepers passed with a clatter of wooden shoes. As
she viewed Paris thus grimly awakening, she was overcome
by tender girlish feelings, by a yearning for the country, for
idyllic scenes, for things soft and white.

"Now, guess what you're to do," said she, coming back to
Steiner. "You're going to take me to the Bois de Boulogne,
and we'll drink milk there."

She clapped her hands in childish glee. Without waiting
for the banker's reply—he naturally consented, though he
was really rather bored and inclined to think of other things
—she ran off to throw a pelisse over her shoulders. In the
drawing-room there was now no one with Steiner save the
band of young men. These had by this time dropped the
very dregs of their glasses into the piano, and were talking
of going, when one of their number ran in triumphantly. He
held in his hands a last remaining bottle, which he had
brought back with him from the pantry.

"Wait a minute, wait a minute!" he shouted. "Here's a
bottle of Chartreuse; that'll pick him up! And now my
young friends, let's hook it. We're blooming idiots."

In the dressing-room Nana was compelled to wake up Zoé,
who had dozed off on a chair. The gas was still alight, and
Zoé shivered as she helped her mistress on with her hat and
pelisse.

"Well, it's over; I've done what you wanted me to," said
Nana, speaking familiarly to the maid in a sudden burst of
expansive confidence, and much relieved at the thought that
she had at last made her election. "You were quite right;
the banker's as good as another."

The maid was cross, for she was still heavy with sleep.
She grumbled something to the effect that Madame ought to
have come to a decision the first evening. Then, following

her into the bedroom, she asked what she was going to do with "those two," meaning Bordenave, who was snoring away as usual, and Georges, who had slipped in slyly, buried his head in a pillow, and finally falling asleep there, was now breathing as lightly and regularly as a cherub. Nana in reply told her that she was to let them sleep on. But seeing Daguenet come into the room, she again grew tender. He had been watching her from the kitchen, and was looking very wretched.

"Come, my sweetie, be reasonable," said she, taking him in her arms, and kissing him with all sorts of little wheedling caresses. "Nothing's changed; you know that it's sweetie whom I always adore! Eh, dear? I had to do it. Why, I swear to you we shall have even nicer times now. Come to-morrow, and we'll arrange about hours. Now, be quick, kiss and hug me as you love me. Oh! tighter, tighter than that!"

And she escaped, and rejoined Steiner, feeling happy and once more possessed with the idea of drinking milk. In the empty room the Count de Vandeuvres was left alone with the "decorated" man who had recited "Abraham's Sacrifice." Both seemed glued to the card-table; they had lost count of their whereabouts, and never once noticed the broad light of day without, whilst Blanche had made bold to put her feet up on a sofa in order to try and get a little sleep.

"Oh! Blanche is with them!" cried Nana. "We are going to drink milk, dear. Do come; you'll find Vandeuvres here when we return."

Blanche got up lazily. This time the banker's fiery face grew white with annoyance at the idea of having to take that big wench with him too. She was certain to bore him. But the two women had already got him by the arms, and were reiterating,—

"We want them to milk the cow before our eyes, you know."

CHAPTER V

AT the Variétés they were giving the thirty-fourth performance of the *Blonde Venus*. The first act had just finished, and in the green-room, Simonne, dressed as the Little Laundress, was standing in front of a console-table, surmounted by a looking-glass, and situated between the two corner doors which opened obliquely on the end of the dressing-room passage. No one was with her, and she was scrutinizing her face, and rubbing her finger up and down below her eyes, with a view to putting the finishing touches to her make-up. The gas-jets on either side of the mirror flooded her with warm crude light.

"Has he arrived?" asked Prullière, entering the room in his Alpine Admiral's costume, which was set off by a big sword, enormous top-boots, and a vast tuft of plumes.

"Who d'you mean?" said Simonne, taking no notice of him, and laughing into the mirror in order to see how her lips looked.

"The Prince."

"I don't know; I've just come down. Oh, he's certainly due here to-night; he comes every time!"

Prullière had drawn near the hearth opposite the console-table, where a coke fire was blazing, and two more gas-jets were flaring brightly. He lifted his eyes, and looked at the clock and the barometer on his right hand and on his left. They had gilded sphinxes by the way of adornment in the style of the First Empire. Then he stretched himself out in a huge arm-chair with ears, the green velvet of which had been so worn by four generations of comedians that it looked yellow in places, and there he stayed, with moveless limbs and vacant eyes, in that weary and resigned attitude peculiar to actors who are used to long waits before their turn for going on the stage.

Old Bosc, too, had just made his appearance. He came in dragging one foot behind the other, and coughing. He was wrapped in an old box-coat, part of which had slipped from his shoulder in such a way as to uncover the gold-laced cloak of King Dagobert. He put his crown on the piano, and for a moment or two stood moodily stamping his feet. His hands were trembling slightly with the first beginnings of alcoholism, but he looked a sterling old fellow for all that, and a long white beard lent that fiery tippler's face of his a truly venerable appearance. Then, in the silence of the room, while the shower of hail was whipping the panes of the great window that looked out on the court-yard, he shook himself disgustedly.

"What filthy weather!" he growled.

Simonne and Prullière did not move. Four or five pictures —a landscape, a portrait of the actor Vernet—hung yellowing in the hot glare of the gas, and a bust of Potier, one of the bygone glories of the Variétés, stood gazing vacant-eyed from its pedestal. But just then there was a burst of voices outside. It was Fontan, dressed for the second act. He was a young dandy, and his habiliments, even to his gloves, were entirely yellow.

"Now say you don't know!" he shouted, gesticulating. "To-day's my patron saint's day!"

"What?" asked Simonne, coming up smilingly, as though attracted by the huge nose and the vast, comic mouth of the man. "D'you answer to the name of Achille?"

"Exactly so! and I'm going to get 'em to tell Madame Bron to send up champagne after the second act."

For some seconds a bell had been ringing in the distance. The long-drawn sound grew fainter, then louder, and when the bell ceased a shout ran up the stair and down it till it was lost along the passages. "All on the stage for the second act! All on the stage for the second act!" The sound drew near, and a little pale-faced man passed by the green-room

doors, outside each of which he yelled at the top of his shrill
voice, "On the stage for the second act!"

"The deuce, it's champagne!" said Prullière, without appearing to hear the din. "You're prospering!"

"If I were you I should have it in from the café," old
Bosc slowly announced. He was sitting on a bench covered
with green velvet, with his head against the wall.

But Simonne said that it was one's duty to consider
Madame Bron's small perquisites. She clapped her hands
excitedly, and devoured Fontan with her gaze, whilst his
long goat-like visage kept up a continuous twitching of eyes
and nose and mouth.

"Oh, that Fontan!" she murmured. "There's no one like
him, no one like him!"

The two green-room doors stood wide open to the corridor
leading to the wings. And along the yellow wall, which was
brightly lit up by a gas-lamp out of view, passed a string of
rapidly-moving shadows—men in costume, women with
shawls over their scant attire, in a word the whole of the
characters in the second act, who would shortly make their
appearance as masqueraders in the ball at the "Boule Noire."
And at the end of the corridor became audible a shuffling of
feet as these people clattered down the five wooden steps
which led to the stage. As the big Clarisse went running
by, Simonne called to her, but she said she would be back
directly. And indeed she reappeared almost at once, shivering in the thin tunic and scarf which she wore as Iris.

"God bless me!" she said. "It isn't warm, and I've left my
furs in my dressing-room!"

Then as she stood toasting her legs, in their warm rose-
colored tights, in front of the fire-place, she resumed,—

"The Prince has arrived."

"Oh!" cried the rest, with the utmost curiosity.

"Yes, that's why I ran down: I wanted to see. He's in
the first stage-box to the right, the same he was in on Thurs-

day. It's the third time he's been this week, eh? That's Nana; well, she's in luck's way! I was willing to wager he wouldn't come again."

Simonne opened her lips to speak, but her remarks were drowned by a fresh shout, which arose close to the green-room. In the passage the call-boy was yelling at the top of his shrill voice,—"They've knocked!"

"Three times!" said Simonne, when she was again able to speak. "It's getting exciting. You know he won't go to her place; he takes her to his. And it seems that he has to pay for it too!"

"Egad! it's a case of when one 'has to go out,'" muttered Prullière wickedly, and he got up to have a last look at the mirror as became a handsome fellow whom the boxes adored.

"They've knocked! They've knocked!" the call-boy kept repeating, in tones that died gradually away in the distance, as he passed through the various stories and corridors.

Fontan thereupon, knowing how it had all gone off on the first occasion the Prince and Nana met, told the two women the whole story, whilst they in their turn crowded against him and laughed at the tops of their voices whenever he stooped to whisper certain details in their ears. Old Bosc had never budged an inch—he was totally indifferent. That sort of thing no longer interested him now. He was stroking a great tortoise-shell cat, which was lying curled up on the bench. He did so quite beatifically, and ended by taking her in his arms with the tender good-nature becoming a worn-out monarch. The cat arched its back, and then, after a prolonged sniff at the big white beard, the gluey odor of which doubtless disgusted her, she turned, and curling herself up, went to sleep again on the bench beside him. Bosc remained grave and absorbed.

"That's all right, but if I were you I should drink the champagne at the restaurant—it's better there," said he, suddenly addressing Fontan when he had finished his recital.

"The curtain's up!" cried the call-boy, in cracked and long-drawn accents. "The curtain's up! The curtain's up!"

The shout sounded for some moments, during which there had been a noise of rapid footsteps. Through the suddenly-opened door of the passage came a burst of music and a far-off murmur of voices, and then the door shut to again, and you could hear its dull thud as it wedged itself into position once more.

A heavy peaceful atmosphere again pervaded the green-room, as though the place were situated a hundred leagues from the house where crowds were applauding. Simonne and Clarisse were still on the topic of Nana. There was a girl who never hurried herself! Why, yesterday she had again come on too late! But there was a silence; for a tall damsel had just craned her head in at the door, and seeing that she had made a mistake, had departed to the other end of the passage. It was Satin. Wearing a hat and a small veil, for the nonce, she was affecting the manner of a lady about to pay a call.

"A pretty trollop!" muttered Prullière, who had been coming across her for a year past at the "Café des Variétés." And at this Simonne told them how Nana had recognized in Satin an old school-mate, had taken a vast fancy to her, and was now plaguing Bordenave to let her make a first appearance on the stage.

"How d'ye do!" said Fontan, shaking hands with Mignon and Fauchery, who now came into the room.

Old Bosc himself gave them the tips of his fingers, whilst the two women kissed Mignon.

"A good house this evening?" queried Fauchery.

"Oh, a splendid one!" replied Prullière. "You should see 'em gaping!"

"I say, my little dears," remarked Mignon, "it must be your turn!"

Oh, all in good time! They were only at the fourth

scene as yet, but Bosc got up in obedience to instinct as became a rattling old actor who felt that his cue was coming. At that very moment the call-boy was opening the door.

"Monsieur Bosc!" he called, "Mademoiselle Simonne!"

Simonne flung a fur-lined pelisse briskly over her shoulders, and went out. Bosc, without hurrying at all, went and got his crown, which he settled on his brow with a rap. Then, dragging himself unsteadily along in his great coat, he took his departure, grumbling and looking as annoyed as a man who has been rudely disturbed.

"You were very amiable in your last notice," continued Fontan, addressing Fauchery. "Only why do you say that comedians are vain?"

"Yes, my little man, why d'you say that?" shouted Mignon, bringing down his huge hands on the journalist's slender shoulders with such force as almost to double him up.

Prullière and Clarisse refrained from laughing aloud. For some time past, the whole company had been deriving amusement from a comedy which was going on in the wings. Mignon, rendered frantic by his wife's caprice, and annoyed at the thought that this man Fauchery brought nothing but a certain doubtful notoriety to his household, had conceived the idea of revenging himself on the journalist by overwhelming him with tokens of friendship. Every evening, therefore, when he met him behind scenes, he would shower friendly slaps on his back and shoulders, as though fairly carried away by an outburst of tenderness; and Fauchery, who was a frail, small man in comparison to such a giant, was fain to take the raps with a strained smile in order not to quarrel with Rose's husband.

"Ah, ha! my buck, you've insulted Fontan," resumed Mignon, who was doing his best to force the joke. "Stand on guard! One—two—got him right in the middle of his chest!"

He lunged and struck the young man with such force that

the latter grew very pale, and could not speak for some seconds. With a wink Clarisse showed the others where Rose Mignon was standing on the threshold of the green-room. Rose had witnessed the scene, and she marched straight up to the journalist, as though she had failed to notice her husband, and standing on tiptoe, bare-armed and in baby costume, she held her face up to him with a caressing infantine pout.

"Good evening, Baby," said Fauchery, kissing her familiarly.

Thus he indemnified himself. Mignon, however, did not seem to have observed this kiss, for everybody kissed his wife at the theater. But he laughed, and gave the journalist a keen little look. The latter would assuredly have to pay for Rose's bravado.

In the passage the tightly-shutting door opened and closed again, and a tempest of applause was blown as far as the green-room. Simonne came in after her scene.

"Oh! Father Bosc *has* just scored!" she cried. "The Prince was writhing with laughter, and applauded with the rest as though he had been paid to. I say, do you know the big man sitting beside the Prince in the stage-box? A handsome man, with a very sedate expression and splendid whiskers!"

"It's Count Muffat," replied Fauchery. "I know that the Prince, when he was at the Empress's the day before yesterday, invited him to dinner for to-night. He'll have corrupted him afterwards!"

"So that's Count Muffat! We know his father-in-law, eh, Auguste?" said Rose, addressing her remark to Mignon. "'You know the Marquis de Chouard, at whose place I went to sing? Well, he's in the house, too. I noticed him at the back of a box. There's an old boy for you—!"

Prullière, who had just put on his huge plume of feathers, turned round and called her.

"Hi, Rose! let's go now!"

She ran after him, leaving her sentence unfinished. At that moment, Madame Bron, the portress of the theater, passed by the door with an immense bouquet in her arms. Simonne asked cheerfully if it was for her, but the porter-woman did not vouchsafe an answer, and only pointed her chin towards Nana's dressing-room at the end of the passage. Oh, that Nana! they were loading her with flowers! Then, when Madame Bron returned, she handed a letter to Clarisse, who allowed a smothered oath to escape her. That beggar la Faloise again! There was a fellow who wouldn't let her alone! And when she learnt the gentleman in question was waiting for her at the porter's lodge, she shrieked,—

"Tell him I'm coming down after this act. I'm going to catch him one on the face."

Fontan had rushed forward, shouting,—

"Madame Bron, just listen. Please listen, Madame Bron. I want you to send up six bottles of champagne between the acts."

But the call-boy had again made his appearance. He was out of breath, and in a sing-song voice he called out,—

"All to go on the stage! It's your turn, Monsieur Fontan. Make haste, make haste!"

"Yes, yes, I'm going, Father Barillot," replied Fontan in a flurry.

And he ran after Madame Bron, and continued,—

"You understand, eh? Six bottles of champagne, in the green-room, between the acts. It's my patron saint's day, and I'm standing the racket."

Simonne and Clarisse had gone off with a great rustling of skirts. Everybody was swallowed up in the distance, and when the passage-door had banged with its usual hollow sound, a fresh hail shower was heard beating against the windows in the now silent green-room. Barillot, a small, pale-faced ancient, who for thirty years had been a servant

in the theater, had advanced familiarly towards Mignon, and
had presented his open snuff-box to him. This proffer of a
pinch and its acceptance allowed him a minute's rest in his
interminable career up and down stairs, and along the dressing-room passage. He certainly had still to look up Madame
Nana, as he called her; but she was one of those who followed
her own sweet will, and didn't care a pin for penalties. Why,
if she chose to be too late, she was too late! But he stopped
short, and murmured in great surprise,—

"Well I never, she's ready; here she is! She must know
that the Prince is here."

Indeed Nana appeared in the corridor. She was dressed as
a fish-hag: her arms and face were plastered with white paint,
and she had a couple of red dabs under her eyes. Without
entering the green-room, she contented herself by nodding to
Mignon and Fauchery.

"How do? You're all right?"

Only Mignon shook her outstretched hand, and she hied
royally on her way, followed by her dresser, who almost trod
on her heels whilst stooping to adjust the folds of her skirt.
In the rear of the dresser came Satin, closing the procession,
and trying to look quite the lady, though she was already
bored to death.

"And Steiner?" asked Mignon sharply.

"Monsieur Steiner has gone away to the Loiret," said
Barillot, preparing to return to the neighborhood of the stage.
"I expect he's gone to buy a country place in those parts."

"Ah, yes, I know, Nana's country place."

Mignon had grown suddenly serious. Oh, that Steiner!
He had promised Rose a fine house in the old days! Well,
well, it wouldn't do to grow angry with anybody. Here was
a position that would have to be won again. From fire-
place to console-table Mignon paced, sunk in thought yet
still unconquered by circumstances. There was no one in
the green-room now save Fauchery and himself. The

journalist was tired, and had flung himself back into the recesses of the big arm-chair. There he stayed with half-closed eyes, and as quiet as quiet could be, whilst the other glanced down at him as he passed. When they were alone Mignon scorned to slap him at every turn. What good would it have done, since nobody would have enjoyed the spectacle? He was far too disinterested to be personally entertained by the farcical scenes in which he figured as a bantering husband. Glad of this short-lived respite, Fauchery stretched his feet out languidly towards the fire, and let his upturned eyes wander from the barometer to the clock. In the course of his march Mignon planted himself in front of Potier's bust, looked at it without seeming to see it, and then turned back to the window, outside which yawned the darkling gulf of the court-yard. The rain had ceased, and there was now a deep silence in the room, which the fierce heat of the coke fire and the flare of the gas-jets rendered still more oppressive. Not a sound came from the wings: the staircase and the passages were deadly still.

That choking sensation of quiet, which behind the scenes immediately precedes the end of an act, had begun to pervade the empty green-room. Indeed, the place seemed to be drowsing off through very breathlessness, amid that faint murmur which the stage gives forth when the whole troupe are raising the deafening uproar of some grand finale.

"Oh, the cows!" Bordenave suddenly shouted in his hoarse voice.

He had only just come up, and he was already howling complaints about two chorus-girls who had nearly fallen flat on the stage because they were playing the fool together. When his eye lit on Mignon and Fauchery, he called them—he wanted to shew them something. The Prince had just notified a desire to compliment Nana in her dressing-room, during the next interval. But, as he was leading them into the wings, the stage-manager passed.

"Just you fine those hags Fernande and Maria!" cried Bordenave savagely.

Then calming down, and endeavoring to assume the dignified expression worn by "heavy fathers," he wiped his face with his pocket-handkerchief, and added,—

"I am now going to receive his highness."

The curtain fell amid a long-drawn salvo of applause. Then across the twilight stage, which was no longer lit up by the footlights, there followed a disorderly retreat. Actors, and supers, and chorus, made haste to get back to their dressing-rooms, whilst the scene-shifters rapidly changed the scenery. Simonne and Clarisse, however, had remained "at the top," talking together in whispers. On the stage, in an interval between their lines, they had just settled a little matter. Clarisse, after viewing the thing in every light, found she preferred not to see la Faloise, who could never decide to leave her for Gaga, and so Simonne was simply to go and explain that a woman ought not to be palled up to in that fashion! At last she agreed to undertake the mission.

Then Simonne, in her theatrical laundress's attire, but with furs over her shoulders, ran down the greasy steps of the narrow winding stair which led between damp walls to the porter's lodge. This lodge, situated between the actors' staircase and that of the management, was shut in to right and left by large glass partitions, and resembled a huge transparent lantern, in which two gas-jets were flaring.

There was a set of pigeon-holes in the place in which were piled letters and newspapers, whilst on the table various bouquets lay awaiting their recipients in close proximity to neglected heaps of dirty plates and to an old pair of stays, the eyelets of which the portress was busy mending. And in the middle of this untidy, ill-kept store-room sat four fashionable, white-gloved society men. They occupied as many ancient straw-bottomed chairs, and, with an expression at once patient and submissive, kept sharply turning their heads in Madame Bron's direction every time she came down from the theater overhead, for on such occasions she was the bearer of replies. Indeed she had but now handed a note to a young man who had hurried out to open it beneath the gas-light in the vestibule, where he had grown slightly pale on reading the classic phrase—how often had others read it in that very place!—"Impossible to-night, my dearie! I'm booked!" La Faloise sat on one of these chairs, at the back of the room, between the table and the stove. He seemed bent on passing the evening there, and yet he was not quite happy. Indeed he kept tucking up his long legs in his endeavors to escape from a whole litter of black kittens who were gamboling wildly round them, whilst the mother cat sat bolt upright staring at him with yellow eyes.

"Ah, it's you, Mademoiselle Simonne! What can I do for you?" asked the portress.

Simonne begged her to send la Faloise out to her. But Madame Bron was unable to comply with her wishes all at once. Under the stairs in a sort of deep cupboard she kept a little bar, whither the supers were wont to descend for drinks between the acts, and seeing that just at that moment there were five or six tall lubbers there who, still dressed as "Boule Noire" masqueraders, were dying of thirst and in a great hurry, she lost her head a bit. A gas-jet was flaring in the cupboard, within which it was possible to descry a tin-covered table, and some shelves garnished with half-emptied bottles. Whenever the door of this coal-hole was opened, a violent whiff of alcohol mingled with the scent of stale cooking in the lodge, as well as with the penetrating scent of the flowers upon the table.

"Well, now," continued the portress when she had served the supers, "is it the little dark chap out there you want?"

"No, no; don't be silly!" said Simonne. "It's the lanky one by the side of the stove. Your cat's sniffing at his trouser-legs!"

And with that she carried la Faloise off into the lobby, whilst the other gentlemen once more resigned themselves to their fate and to semi-suffocation, and the masqueraders drank on the stairs, and indulged in rough horse-play and guttural drunken jests.

On the stage above Bordenave was wild with the scene-shifters, who seemed never to have done changing scenes. They appeared to be acting of set purpose—the Prince would certainly have some set-piece or other tumbling on his head.

"Up with it! Up with it!" shouted the foreman.

At length the canvas at the back of the stage was raised into position, and the stage was clear. Mignon, who had kept his eye on Fauchery, seized this opportunity in order to start his pummeling matches again. He hugged him in his long arms, and cried,—

"Oh, take care! that mast just missed crushing you!"

And he carried him off, and shook him before setting him down again. In view of the scene-shifters' exaggerated mirth, Fauchery grew white. His lips trembled, and he was ready to flare up in anger, whilst Mignon, shamming good nature, was clapping him on the shoulder with such affection-ate violence as nearly to pulverize him.

"I value your health, I do!" he kept repeating. "Egad! I should be in a pretty pickle if anything serious happened to you!"

But just then a whisper ran through their midst: "The Prince! The Prince!" and everybody turned and looked at the little door which opened out of the main body of the house. At first nothing was visible save Bordenave's round back and beefy neck, which bobbed down and arched up in a series of obsequious obeisances. Then the Prince made his appearance. Largely and strongly built, light of beard and rosy of hue, he was not lacking in the kind of distinction peculiar to a sturdy man of pleasure, the square contours of whose limbs are clearly defined by the irreproachable cut of a frock-coat. Behind him walked Count Muffat and the Marquis de Chouard, but this particular corner of the theater being dark, the group were lost to view amid huge moving shadows.

In order fittingly to address the son of a queen, who would some day occupy a throne, Bordenave had assumed the tone of a man exhibiting a bear in the street. In a voice tremulous with false emotion he kept repeating,—

"If his highness will have the goodness to follow me— would his highness deign to come this way?—His highness will take care!"

The Prince did not hurry in the least. On the contrary, he was greatly interested, and kept pausing in order to look at the scene-shifters' maneuvers. A batten had just been lowered, and the group of gas-lights high up among its iron cross-bars illuminated the stage with a wide beam of light. Muffat, who had never yet been behind scenes at a theater, was even more astonished than the rest. An uneasy feeling of mingled fear and vague repugnance took possession of him. He looked up into the heights above him, where more battens, the gas-jets on which were burning low, gleamed like galaxies of little bluish stars amid a chaos of iron rods, connecting-lines of all sizes, hanging stages, and canvases spread out in space, like huge cloths hung out to dry.

"Lower away!" shouted the foreman, unexpectedly.

And the Prince himself had to warn the Count, for a canvas was descending. They were setting the scenery for the third act, which was the grotto on Mount Etna. Men were busy planting masts in the sockets, whilst others went and took frames, which were leaning against the walls of the stage, and proceeded to lash them with strong cords to the poles already in position. At the back of the stage, with a view to producing the bright rays thrown by Vulcan's glowing forge, a strand had been fixed by a limelight man, who was now lighting various burners under red glasses. The scene was one of confusion, verging to all appearances on absolute chaos, but every little move had been prearranged. Nay, amid all the scurry, the whistle-blower even took a few turns, stepping short as he did so, in order to rest his legs.

"His highness overwhelms me," said Bordenave, still bowing low. "The theater is not large, but we do what we can. Now, if his highness deigns to follow me—"

Count Muffat was already making for the dressing-room passage. The really sharp downward slope of the stage had surprised him disagreeably, and he owed no small part of his present anxiety to a feeling that its boards were moving under his feet. Through the open sockets gas was descried burning in the "dock." Human voices and blasts of air, as from a vault, came up thence, and, looking down into the depths of gloom, one became aware of a whole subterranean existence. But just as the Count was going up the stage, a small incident occurred to stop him. Two little women, dressed for the third act, were chatting by the peep-hole in the curtain. One of them, straining forward, and widening the hole with her fingers in order the better to observe things, was scanning the house beyond.

"I see him," said she sharply. "Oh, what a mug!"

Horrified, Bordenave had much ado not to give her a kick. But the Prince smiled, and looked pleased and excited by the remark. He gazed warmly at the little woman who did not care a button for his highness, and she, on her part, laughed unblushingly. Bordenave, however, persuaded the Prince to follow him. Muffat was beginning to perspire: he had taken his hat off. What inconvenienced him most was the stuffy, dense, overheated air of the place, with its strong haunting smell, a smell peculiar to this part of a theater, and, as such, compact of the reek of gas, of the glue used in the manufacture of the scenery, of dirty dark nooks and corners, and of questionably cleanly chorus-girls. In the passage the air was still more suffocating, and one seemed to

NANA 149

breathe a poisoned atmosphere, which was occasionally relieved by the acid scents of toilet-waters and the perfumes
of various soaps emanating from the dressing-rooms. The
Count lifted his eyes as he passed and glanced up the staircase, for he was well-nigh startled by the keen flood of light
and warmth which flowed down upon his back and shoulders.
High up above him there was a clicking of ewers and basins,
a sound of laughter and of people calling to one another, a
banging of doors, which in their continual opening and shutting allowed an odor of womankind to escape—a musky
scent of oils and essences mingling with the natural pungency
exhaled from human tresses. He did not stop. Nay, he
hastened his walk: he almost ran, his skin tingling with the
breath of that fiery approach to a world he knew nothing of.
"A theater's a curious sight, eh?" said the Marquis de
Chouard, with the enchanted expression of a man who once
more finds himself amid familiar surroundings.
But Bordenave had at length reached Nana's dressing-room
at the end of the passage. He quietly turned the door-
handle; then, cringing again:
"If his highness will have the goodness to enter—"
They heard the cry of a startled woman, and caught sight
of Nana as, stripped to the waist, she slipped behind a curtain,
whilst her dresser, who had been in the act of drying her,
stood towel in air before them.
"Oh, it *is* silly to come in that way!" cried Nana from her
hiding-place. "Don't come in: you see you mustn't come
in!"
Bordenave did not seem to relish this sudden flight.
"Do stay where you were, my dear. Why it doesn't matter," said he. "It's his highness. Come, come, don't be
childish."
And, when she still refused to make her appearance—for
she was startled as yet, though she had begun to laugh—he
added in peevish paternal tones,—

"Good Heavens, these gentlemen know perfectly well what a woman looks like. They won't eat you."

"I'm not so sure of that," said the Prince, wittily.

With that the whole company began laughing in an exaggerated manner in order to pay him proper court.

"An exquisitely witty speech—an altogether Parisian speech," as Bordenave remarked.

Nana vouchsafed no further reply, but the curtain began moving. Doubtless she was making up her mind. Then Count Muffat, with glowing cheeks, began to take stock of the dressing-room. It was a square room with a very low ceiling, and it was entirely hung with a light-colored Havana stuff. A curtain of the same material depended from a copper rod, and formed a sort of recess at the end of the room, whilst two large windows opened on the court-yard of the theater, and were faced, at a distance of three yards at most, by a leprous-looking wall, against which the panes cast squares of yellow light amid the surrounding darkness. A large dressing-glass faced a white marble toilet-table, which was garnished with a disorderly array of flasks and glass boxes, containing oils, essences, and powders. The Count went up to the dressing-glass and discovered that he was looking very flushed, and had small drops of perspiration on his forehead. He dropped his eyes, and came and took up a position in front of the toilet-table, where the basin, full of soapy water, the small scattered ivory toilet utensils, and the damp sponges, appeared for some moments to absorb his attention. The feeling of dizziness, which he had experienced when he first visited Nana in the Boulevard Haussmann, once more overcame him. He felt the thick carpet soften under foot, and the gas-jets burning by the dressing-table and by the glass seemed to shoot whistling flames about his temples. For one moment, being afraid of fainting away under the influence of those feminine odors which he now reëncountered intensified by the heat under the low-pitched ceiling, he sat down on the edge of a softly-padded divan between the two windows. But he got up again almost directly, and, returning to the dressing-table, seemed to gaze with vacant eyes into space, for he was thinking of a bouquet of tuberoses which had once faded in his bedroom, and had nearly killed him in their death. When tuberoses are turning brown, they have a human smell.

"Make haste!" Bordenave whispered, putting his head in behind the curtain.

The Prince, however, was listening complaisantly to the Marquis de Chouard, who had taken up a hare's-foot on the dressing-table and had begun explaining the way grease paint is put on. In a corner of the room, Satin, with her pure virginal face, was scanning the gentlemen keenly, whilst the dresser, Madame Jules by name, was getting ready Venus's tights and tunic. Madame Jules was a woman of no age. She had the parchment skin and changeless features peculiar to old maids whom no one ever knew in their younger years. She had indeed shrivelled up in the burning atmosphere of the dressing-rooms and amid the most famous thighs and bosoms in all Paris. She wore everlastingly a faded black dress, and on her flat and sexless chest a perfect forest of pins clustered above the spot where her heart should have been.

"I beg your pardon, gentlemen," said Nana, drawing aside the curtain, "but you took me by surprise."

They all turned round. She had not clothed herself at all, had in fact only buttoned on a little pair of linen stays which half revealed her bosom. When the gentlemen had put her to flight, she had scarcely begun undressing, and was rapidly taking off her fish-wife's costume. Through the opening in her drawers behind, a corner of her shift was even now visible. There she stood, bare-armed, bare-shouldered, bare-breasted, in all the adorable glory of her youth and plump fair beauty,

but she still held the curtain with one hand, as though ready
to draw it to again upon the slightest provocation.

"Yes, you took me by surprise! I never shall dare—" she
stammered in pretty mock confusion, while rosy blushes
crossed her neck and shoulders, and smiles of embarrassment
played about her lips.

"Oh, don't apologize," cried Bordenave, "since these gentlemen approve of your good looks!"

But she still tried the hesitating, innocent, girlish game, and,
shivering as though some one were tickling her, she continued:

"His highness does me too great an honor. I beg his highness will excuse my receiving him thus—"

"It is I who am importunate," said the Prince, "but,
Madam, I could not resist the desire of complimenting you."

Thereupon, in order to reach her dressing-table, she walked
very quietly, and just as she was, through the midst of the
gentlemen, who made way for her to pass.

She had strongly-marked hips, which filled her drawers out
roundly, whilst, with swelling bosom, she still continued bowing, and smiling her delicate little smile. Suddenly she
seemed to recognize Count Muffat, and she extended her
hand to him as an old friend. Then she scolded him for not
having come to her supper-party. His highness deigned to
chaff Muffat about this, and the latter stammered and
thrilled again at the thought that, for one second, he had
held in his own feverish clasp a little fresh and perfumed
hand. The Count had dined excellently at the Prince's, who
indeed was a heroic eater and drinker. Both of them were
even a little intoxicated, but they behaved very creditably.
To hide the commotion within him, Muffat could only remark about the heat.

"Good Heavens, how hot it is here!" said he. "How do
you manage to live in such a temperature, madam?"

And conversation was about to ensue on this topic, when

noisy voices were heard at the dressing-room door. Bordenave drew back the slide over a grated peep-hole of the kind
used in convents. Fontan was outside with Prullière and Bosc,
and all three had bottles under their arms and their hands
full of glasses. He began knocking, and shouting out that
it was his patron saint's day, and that he was standing champagne round. Nana consulted the Prince with a glance.
Eh! oh, dear yes! His highness did not want to be in any
one's way; he would be only too happy! But without waiting for permission, Fontan came in, repeating in baby accents,—

"Me not a cad, me pay for champagne!"

Then, all of a sudden, he became aware of the Prince's
presence, of which he had been totally ignorant. He stopped
short, and assuming an air of farcical solemnity, announced,—

"King Dagobert is in the corridor, and is desirous of drinking the health of his royal highness."

The Prince having made answer with a smile, Fontan's
sally was voted charming. But the dressing-room was too
small to accommodate everybody, and it became necessary to
crowd up anyhow, Satin and Madame Jules standing back
against the curtain at the end, and the men clustering closely
round the half-naked Nana. The three actors still had on
the costumes they had been wearing in the second act, and
whilst Prullière took off his Alpine Admiral's cocked hat, the
huge plume of which would have knocked the ceiling, Bosc,
in his purple cloak and tinware crown, steadied himself on his
tipsy old legs and greeted the Prince as became a monarch
receiving the son of a powerful neighbor. The glasses were
filled, and the company began clinking them together.

"I drink to Your Highness!" said ancient Bosc, royally.

"To the Army!" added Prullière.

"To Venus!" cried Fontan.

The Prince complaisantly poised his glass, waited quietly,
bowed thrice, and murmured,—

"Madam! Admiral! your Majesty!"

Then he drank it off. Count Muffat and the Marquis de Chouard had followed his example. There was no more jesting now—the company were at Court. Actual life was prolonged in the life of the theater, and a sort of solemn farce was enacted under the hot flare of the gas. Nana, quite forgetting that she was in her drawers, and that a corner of her shift stuck out behind, became the great lady, the Queen of Love, in act to open her most private palace chambers to State dignitaries. In every sentence she used the words "royal highness," and bowing with the utmost conviction, treated the masqueraders, Bosc and Prullière, as if the one were a sovereign and the other his attendant minister. And no one dreamt of smiling at this strange contrast, this real prince, this heir to a throne, drinking a petty actor's champagne, and taking his ease amid a carnival of gods, a masquerade of royalty, in the society of dressers and courtesans, shabby players and showmen of venal beauty. Bordenave was simply ravished by the dramatic aspects of the scene, and began dreaming of the receipts which would have accrued had his highness only consented thus to appear in the second act of the *Blonde Venus*.

"I say, shall we have our little women down?" cried he, becoming familiar.

Nana would not hear of it. But, notwithstanding this, she was giving way herself. Fontan attracted her with his comic make-up. She brushed against him, and eyeing him as a woman in the family-way might do when she fancies some unpleasant kind of food, she suddenly became extremely familiar:

"Now then, fill up again, ye great brute!"

Fontan charged the glasses afresh, and the company drank, repeating the same toasts.

"To His Highness!"

"To the Army!"

"To Venus!"

But with that Nana made a sign and obtained silence. She raised her glass, and cried,—

"No, no! to Fontan! It's Fontan's day; to Fontan! to Fontan!"

Then they clinked glasses a third time, and drank Fontan with all the honors. The Prince, who had noticed the young woman devoring the actor with her eyes, saluted him with a "Monsieur Fontan, I drink to your success!" This he said with his customary lofty courtesy.

But meanwhile the tail of his highness's frock-coat was sweeping the marble of the dressing-table. The place, indeed, was like an alcove, or narrow bath-room, full as it was of the stream of hot water and sponges, and of the strong scent of essences which mingled with the tartish intoxicating fumes of the champagne. The Prince and Count Muffat, between whom Nana was wedged, had to lift up their hands so as not to brush against her hips or her breast with every little movement. And there stood Madame Jules, waiting, cool and rigid as ever, whilst Satin, marveling in the depths of her vicious soul to see a prince and two gentlemen in black coats going after a naked woman in the society of dressed-up actors, secretly concluded that fashionable people were not so very particular after all.

But Father Barillot's tinkling bell approached along the passage. At the door of the dressing-room he stood amazed when he caught sight of the three actors still clad in the costumes which they had worn in the second act.

"Gentlemen, gentlemen," he stammered, "do please make haste. They've just rung the bell in the public foyer."

"Bah! the public will have to wait," said Bordenave placidly.

However, as the bottles were now empty the comedians went upstairs to dress after yet another interchange of civilities. Bosc having dipped his beard in the champagne

had taken it off, and under his venerable disguise the drunk-
ard had suddenly reappeared. His was the haggard em-
purpled face of the old actor who has taken to drink. At
the foot of the stairs he was heard remarking to Fontan in
his boozy voice,—

"I pulverized him, eh?"

He was alluding to the Prince.

In Nana's dressing-room none now remained save his highness, the count, and the marquis. Bordenave had withdrawn with Barillot, whom he advised not to knock without first letting madam know.

"You will excuse me, gentlemen?" asked Nana, again setting to work to make up her arms and face, of which
she was now particularly careful owing to her nude appearance in the third act.

The Prince seated himself by the Marquis de Chouard
on the divan, and Count Muffat alone remained standing.
In that suffocating heat, the two glasses of champagne they
had drunk had increased their intoxication. Satin, when
she saw the gentlemen thus closeting themselves with her
friend, had deemed it discreet to vanish behind the curtain,
where she sat waiting on a trunk, much annoyed at being
compelled to remain motionless, whilst Madame Jules came
and went quietly without word or look.

"You sang your numbers marvellously," said the Prince.

And with that they began a conversation, but their sentences were short and their pauses frequent. Nana indeed
was not always able to reply. After rubbing cold cream over
her arms and face with the palm of her hand, she laid
on the grease paint with the corner of a towel. For one
second only she ceased looking in the glass, and smilingly
stole a glance at the Prince.

"His highness is spoiling me," she murmured, without putting down the grease paint.

Her task was a complicated one, and the Marquis de

Chouard followed it with an expression of devout enjoyment. He spoke in his turn.

"Could not the band accompany you more softly?" said he. "It drowns your voice, and that's an unpardonable crime."

This time Nana did not turn round. She had taken up the hare's-foot, and was lightly manipulating it. All her attention was concentrated on this action, and she bent forward over her toilet-table so very far that the white round contour of her drawers and the little patch of chemise stood out with the unwonted tension. But she was anxious to prove that she appreciated the old man's compliment, and therefore made a little swinging movement with her hips.

Silence reigned. Madame Jules had noticed a tear in the right leg of her drawers. She took a pin from over her heart, and for a second or so knelt on the ground, busily at work about Nana's leg, whilst the young woman, without seeming to notice her presence, applied the rice-powder, taking extreme pains, as she did so, to avoid putting any on the upper part of her cheeks. But when the Prince remarked that if she were to come and sing in London all England would want to applaud her, she laughed amiably, and turned round for a moment, with her left cheek looking very white, amid a perfect cloud of powder. Then she became suddenly serious; for she had come to the operation of rouging. And, with her face once more close to the mirror, she dipped her finger in a jar, and began applying the rouge below her eyes, and gently spreading it back towards her temples. The gentlemen maintained a respectful silence.

Count Muffat, indeed, had not yet opened his lips. He was thinking perforce of his own youth. The bedroom of his childish days had been quite cold, and later, when he had reached the age of sixteen, and would give his mother a good-night kiss every evening, he used to carry the icy feeling of the embrace into the world of dreams. One day, in passing a half-open door, he had caught sight of a maid-servant washing herself; and that was the solitary recollection which had in any way troubled his peace of mind from the days of puberty till the time of marriage. Afterwards, he had found his wife strictly obedient to her conjugal duties, but had himself felt a species of religious dislike to them. He had grown to man's estate, and was now ageing, in ignorance of the flesh, in the humble observance of rigid devotional practices, and in obedience to a rule of life full of precepts and moral laws. And now, suddenly, he was dropped down in this actress's dressing-room, in the presence of this undraped courtesan. He, who had never seen the Countess Muffat putting on her garters, was witnessing, amid that wild disarray of jars and basins, and that strong sweet perfume, the intimate details of a woman's toilet. His whole being was in turmoil; he was terrified by the stealthy, all-pervading influence which for some time past Nana's presence had been exercising over him, and he recalled to mind the pious accounts of diabolic possession which had amused his early years. He was a believer in the devil, and, in a con-fused kind of way, Nana was he; with her laughter, and her bosom, and her hips, which seemed swollen with many vices. But he promised himself that he would be strong—nay, he would know how to defend himself.

"Well, then, it's agreed," said the Prince, lounging quite comfortably on the divan. "You will come to London next year, and we shall receive you so cordially that you will never return to France again. Ah, my dear Count, you don't value your pretty women enough. We shall take them all from you!"

"That won't make much odds to him," murmured the Marquis de Chouard wickedly, for he occasionally said a risky thing among friends. "The Count is virtue itself."

Hearing his virtue mentioned, Nana looked at him so comically that Muffat felt a keen twinge of annoyance. But directly afterwards he was surprised and angry with himself. Why, in the presence of this courtesan, should the idea of being virtuous embarrass him? He could have struck her. But in attempting to take up a brush, Nana had just let it drop on the ground, and as she stooped to pick it up he rushed forward. Their breath mingled for one moment, and the loosened tresses of Venus flowed over his hands. But remorse mingled with his enjoyment, a kind of enjoyment, moreover, peculiar to good Catholics, whom the fear of hell torments in the midst of their sin.

At this moment Father Barillot's voice was heard outside the door.

"May I give the knocks, madam? The house is growing impatient."

"All in good time," answered Nana, quietly.

She had dipped her paint-brush in a pot of kohl, and, with the point of her nose close to the glass, and her left eye closed, she passed it delicately along between her eyelashes. Muffat stood behind her, looking on. He saw her reflection in the mirror, with her rounded shoulders and her bosom half hidden by a rosy shadow. And despite all his endeavors he could not turn away his gaze from that face so merry with dimples and so worn with desire, which the closed eye rendered more seductive. When she shut her right eye and passed the brush along it, he understood that he belonged to her.

"They are stamping their feet, madam," the call-boy once more cried. "They'll end by smashing the seats. May I give the knocks?"

"Oh, bother!" said Nana, impatiently. "Knock away: I don't care! If I'm not ready, well! they'll have to wait for me!"

She grew calm again, and turning to the gentlemen, added with a smile,—

"It's true: we've only got a minute left for our talk."

Her face and arms were now finished, and with her fingers
she put two large dabs of carmine on her lips. Count Muffat
felt more excited than ever. He was ravished by the perverse
transformation wrought by powders and paints, and filled by
a lawless yearning for those young painted charms, for the
too red mouth and the too white face, and the exaggerated
eyes, ringed round with black, and burning and dying for
very love. Meanwhile, Nana went behind the curtain for a
second or two in order to take off her drawers and slip on
Venus's tights. After which, with tranquil immodesty, she
came out and undid her little linen stays, and held out her
arms to Madame Jules, who drew the short-sleeved tunic over
them.

"Make haste; they're growing angry!" she muttered.

The Prince with half-closed eyes marked the swelling lines
of her bosom with an air of connoisseurship, whilst the Marquis de Chouard wagged his head involuntarily. Muffat
gazed at the carpet in order not to see any more. At length,
Venus, with only her gauze veil over her shoulders, was ready
to go on the stage. Madame Jules, with vacant, unconcerned
eyes and an expression suggestive of a little elderly wooden
doll, still kept circling round her. With brisk movements
she took pins out of the inexhaustible pin-cushion over her
heart, and pinned up Venus's tunic, but as she ran over all
those plump nude charms with her shrivelled hands, nothing
was suggested to her. She was as one whom her sex does not
concern.

"There!" said the young woman, taking a final look at
herself in the mirror.

Bordenave was back again. He was anxious, and said the
third act had begun.

"Very well! I'm coming," replied Nana. "Here's a pretty
fuss! Why, it's usually I that waits for the others."

The gentlemen left the dressing-room, but they did not
say good-by, for the Prince had expressed a desire to assist

behind the scenes at the performance of the third act. Left
alone, Nana seemed greatly surprised, and looked round her
in all directions.

"Where can she be?" she queried.

She was searching for Satin. When she had found her
again, waiting on her trunk behind the curtain, Satin quietly
replied,—

"Certainly, I didn't want to be in your way with all those
men there!"

And she added further that she was going now. But Nana
held her back. What a silly girl she was! Now that Bordenave had agreed to take her on! Why, the bargain was to
be struck after the play was over! Satin hesitated. There
were too many bothers; she was out of her element! Nevertheless, she stayed.

As the Prince was coming down the little wooden staircase, a strange sound of smothered oaths and stamping
scuffling feet became audible on the other side of the theater.
The actors waiting for their cues were being scared by quite
a serious episode. For some seconds past, Mignon had been
renewing his jokes and smothering Fauchery with caresses.
He had at last invented a little game of a novel kind, and
had begun flicking the other's nose, in order, as he phrased it,
to keep the flies off him. This kind of game naturally diverted the actors to any extent.

But success had suddenly thrown Mignon off his balance.
He had launched forth into extravagant courses, and had
given the journalist a box on the ear, an actual, a vigorous
box on the ear. This time he had gone too far: in the
presence of so many spectators, it was impossible for Fauchery
to pocket such a blow with laughing equanimity. Whereupon the two men had desisted from their farce, had sprung
at one another's throats, their faces livid with hate, and were
now rolling over and over behind a set of side-lights, pound-
ing away at each other as though they weren't breakable.

"Monsieur Bordenave, Monsieur Bordenave!" said the stage-manager, coming up in a terrible flutter.

Bordenave made his excuses to the Prince, and followed him. When he recognized Fauchery and Mignon in the men on the floor, he gave vent to an expression of annoyance. They had chosen a nice time, certainly, with his highness on the other side of the scenery, and all that houseful of people who might have overheard the row! To make matters worse, Rose Mignon arrived out of breath at the very moment she was due on the stage. Vulcan, indeed, was giving her the cue, but Rose stood rooted to the ground, marveling at sight of her husband and her lover as they lay wallowing at her feet, strangling one another, kicking, tearing their hair out, and whitening their coats with dust. They barred the way. A scene-shifter had even stopped Fauchery's hat just when the devilish thing was going to bound onto the stage in the middle of the struggle. Meanwhile Vulcan, who had been gagging away to amuse the audience, gave Rose her cue a second time. But she stood motionless, still gazing at the two men.

"Oh, don't look at *them!*" Bordenave furiously whispered to her. "Go on the stage, go on, do! It's no business of yours! Why, you're missing your cue!"

And with a push from the manager, Rose stepped over the prostrate bodies, and found herself in the flare of the footlights and in the presence of the audience. She had quite failed to understand why they were fighting on the floor behind her. Trembling from head to foot and with a humming in her ears, she came down to the footlights, Diana's sweet amorous smile on her lips, and attacked the opening lines of her duet with so feeling a voice that the public gave her a veritable ovation.

Behind the scenery she could hear the dull thuds caused by the two men. They had rolled down to the wings, but fortunately the music covered the noise made by their feet as they kicked against them.

"By God!" yelled Bordenave in exasperation, when at last he had succeeded in separating them, "why couldn't you fight at home? You know as well as I do that I don't like this sort of thing. You, Mignon, you'll do me the pleasure of staying over here on the prompt side, and you, Fauchery, if you leave the O.P. side, I'll chuck you out of the theater. You understand, eh?—prompt side and O.P. side, or I forbid Rose to bring you here at all."

When he returned to the Prince's presence, the latter asked what was the matter.

"Oh, nothing at all," murmured he quietly.

Nana was standing wrapped in furs, talking to these gentlemen, whilst awaiting her cue. As Count Muffat was coming up in order to peep between two of the wings at the stage, he understood from a sign made him by the stage-manager that he was to step softly. Drowsy warmth was streaming down from the flies, and in the wings, which were lit by vivid patches of light, only a few people remained talking in low voices, or making off on tip-toe. The gas-man was at his post amid an intricate arrangement of cocks; a fireman, leaning against the side-lights, was craning forward, trying to catch a glimpse of things; whilst, on his seat, high up, the curtain-man was watching with resigned expression, careless of the play, constantly on the alert for the bell to ring him to his duty among the ropes. And amid the close air, and the shuffling of feet, and the sound of whispering, the voices of the actors on the stage sounded strange, deadened, surprisingly discordant. Further off, again, above the confused noises of the band, a vast breathing sound was audible. It was the breath of the house, which sometimes swelled up till it burst in vague rumors, in laughter, in applause. Though invisible, the presence of the public could be felt, even in the silences.

"There's something open," said Nana, sharply, and with that she tightened the folds of her fur cloak. "Do look, Barillot. I bet they've just opened a window. Why, one might catch one's death of cold here!"

Barillot swore that he had closed every window himself, but suggested that possibly there were broken panes about. The actors were always complaining of draughts. Through the heavy warmth of that gas-lit region blasts of cold air were constantly passing—it was a regular influenza-trap, as Fontan phrased it.

"I should like to see *you* in a low-cut dress," continued Nana, growing annoyed.

"Hush!" murmured Bordenave.

On the stage Rose rendered a phrase in her duet so cleverly that the stalls burst into universal applause. Nana was silent at this, and her face grew grave. Meanwhile the Count was venturing down a passage when Barillot stopped him and said he would make a discovery there. Indeed he obtained an oblique back-view of the scenery, and of the wings which had been strengthened, as it were, by a thick layer of old posters. Then he caught sight of a corner of the stage, of the Etna cave hollowed out in a silver mine, and of Vulcan's forge in the background. Battens, lowered from above, lit up a sparkling substance which had been laid on with large dabs of the brush. Side-lights, with red glasses and blue, were so placed as to produce the appearance of a fiery brazier, whilst, on the floor of the stage, in the far background, long lines of gas-light had been laid down in order to throw a wall of dark rocks into sharp relief. Hard by, on a gentle "practicable" incline, amid little points of light resembling the illumination-lamps scattered about in the grass on the night of a public holiday, old Madame Drouard, who played Juno, was sitting dazed and sleepy, waiting for her cue.

Presently there was a commotion, for Simonne, whilst listening to a story Clarisse was telling her, cried out,—

"My! It's the Tricon!"

It was indeed the Tricon, wearing the same old curls and looking as like a litigious great lady as ever.

When she saw Nana, she went straight up to her.

"No," said the latter after some rapid phrases had been exchanged, "not now."

The old lady looked grave. Just then Prullière passed by and shook hands with her, whilst two little chorus-girls stood gazing at her with looks of deep emotion. For a moment she seemed to hesitate. Then she beckoned to Simonne, and the rapid exchange of sentences began again.

"Yes," said Simonne at last. "In half an hour."

But as she was going upstairs again to her dressing-room, Madame Bron, who was once more going the rounds with letters, presented one to her. Bordenave lowered his voice, and furiously reproached the portress for having allowed the Tricon to come in. That woman! And on such an evening of all others! It made him so angry because his highness was there! Madame Bron, who had been thirty years in the theater, replied quite sourly. How was she to know? she asked. The Tricon did business with all the ladies—Monsieur de Directeur had met her a score of times without making remarks. And whilst Bordenave was muttering oaths, the Tricon stood quietly by, scrutinizing the Prince as became a woman who weighs a man at a glance. A smile lit up her yellow face. Presently she paced slowly off through the crowd of deeply-deferential little women.

"Immediately, eh?" she queried, turning round again to Simonne.

Simonne seemed much worried. The letter was from a young man to whom she had engaged herself for that evening. She gave Madame Bron a scribbled note, in which were the words, "Impossible to-night, darling—I'm booked." But she was still apprehensive—the young man might possibly wait for her in spite of everything. As she was not playing in the third act, she had a mind to be off at once, and accordingly begged Clarisse to go and see if the man were there. Clarisse was only due on the stage towards the end of the act, and so she went downstairs, whilst Simonne ran up for a minute to their common dressing-room.

In Madame Bron's drinking-bar downstairs a super, who was charged with the part of Pluto, was drinking in solitude, amid the folds of a great red robe diapered with golden flames. The little business plied by the good portress must have been progressing finely, for the cellar-like hole under the stairs was wet with emptied heel-taps and water. Clarisse picked up the tunic of Iris, which was dragging over the greasy steps behind her, but she halted prudently at the turn in the stairs, and was content simply to crane forward and peer into the lodge. She certainly had been quick to scent things out! Just fancy! that idiot la Faloise was still there, sitting on the same old chair between the table and the stove! He had made pretense of sneaking off in front of Simonne, and had returned after her departure. For the matter of that, the lodge was still full of gentlemen, who sat there gloved, elegant, submissive, and patient as ever. They were all waiting, and viewing each other gravely as they waited. On the table there were now only some dirty plates, Madame Bron having recently distributed the last of the bouquets. A single fallen rose was withering on the floor in the neighborhood of the black cat, who had lain down and curled herself up, whilst the kittens ran wild races and danced fierce gallops among the gentlemen's legs. Clarisse was momentarily inclined to turn la Faloise out. The idiot wasn't fond of animals, and that put the finishing touch to him! He was busy drawing in his legs because the cat was there, and he didn't want to touch her.

"He'll nip you: take care!" said Pluto, who was a joker, as he went upstairs, wiping his mouth with the back of his hand.

After that, Clarisse gave up the idea of hauling la Faloise

over the coals. She had seen Madame Bron giving the letter to Simonne's young man, and he had gone out to read it under the gas-light in the lobby. "Impossible to-night, darling—I'm booked." And with that he had peaceably departed, as one who was doubtless used to the formula. He at any rate knew how to conduct himself! Not so the others, the fellows who sat there doggedly, on Madame Bron's battered straw-bottomed chairs, in the great glazed lantern, where the heat was enough to roast you, and there was an unpleasant odor. What a lot of men it must have held! Clarisse went upstairs again in disgust, crossed over behind scenes, and nimbly mounted three flights of steps which led to the dressing-rooms, in order to bring Simonne her reply.

Downstairs, the Prince had withdrawn from the rest and stood talking to Nana. He never left her; he stood brooding over her through half-shut eyelids. Nana did not look at him, but smiling nodded "yes." Suddenly, however, Count Muffat obeyed an overmastering impulse, and leaving Bordenave, who was explaining to him the working of the rollers and windlasses, he came up in order to interrupt their confabulations. Nana lifted her eyes, and smiled at him as she smiled at his highness. But she kept her ears open notwithstanding, for she was waiting for her cue.

"The third act is the shortest, I believe," the Prince began saying, for the Count's presence embarrassed him.

She did not answer: her whole expression altered: she was suddenly intent on her business. With a rapid movement of the shoulders, she had let her furs slip from her, and Madame Jules, standing behind, had caught them in her arms. And then, after passing her two hands to her hair as though to make it fast, she went on the stage in all her nudity.

"Hush, hush!" whispered Bordenave.

The Count and the Prince had been taken by surprise. There was profound silence, and then a deep sigh and the far-off murmur of a multitude became audible. Every evening when Venus entered in her god-like nakedness the same effect was produced. Then Muffat was seized with a desire to see; he put his eye to a peep-hole. Above and beyond the glowing arc formed by the footlights the dark body of the house seemed full of ruddy vapor, and against this neutral-tinted background, where row upon row of faces struck a pale, uncertain note, Nana stood forth white and vast, so that the boxes from the balcony to the flies were blotted from view. He saw her from behind—noted her swelling hips, her outstretched arms, whilst down on the floor, on the same level as her feet, the prompter's head—an old man's head with a humble, honest face—stood on the edge of the stage looking as though it had been severed from the body. At certain points in her opening number an undulating movement seemed to run from her neck to her waist, and to die out in the trailing border of her tunic. When amid a tempest of applause she had sung her last note, she bowed, and the gauze floated forth round about her limbs, and her hair swept over her waist as she bent sharply backwards. And seeing her thus as, with bending form and with exaggerated hips, she came backing towards the Count's peep-hole, he stood upright again, and his face was very white. The stage had disappeared, and he now saw only the reverse side of the scenery with its display of old posters pasted up in every direction. On the practicable slope, among the lines of gas-jets, the whole of Olympus had rejoined the dozing Madame Drouard. They were waiting for the close of the act. Bosc and Fontan sat on the floor with their knees drawn up to their chins, and Prullière stretched himself and yawned before going on. Everybody was worn out; their eyes were red, and they were longing to go home to sleep.

Just then Fauchery, who had been prowling about on the O.P. side ever since Bordenave had forbidden him the other, came and buttonholed the Count in order to keep himself in countenance, and offered, at the same time, to shew him the dressing-rooms. An increasing sense of languor had left Muffat without any power of resistance, and after looking round for the Marquis de Chouard, who had disappeared, he ended by following the journalist. He experienced a mingled feeling of relief and anxiety as he left the wings whence he had been listening to Nana's songs.

Fauchery had already preceded him up the staircase, which was closed on the first and second floors by low paneled doors. It was one of those stairways which you find in miserable tenements. Count Muffat had seen many such during his rounds as member of the Benevolent Organization. It was bare and dilapidated: there was a wash of yellow paint on its walls, its steps had been worn by the incessant passage of feet, and its iron balustrade had grown smooth under the friction of many hands. On a level with the floor, on every stair-head, there was a low window which resembled a deep square vent-hole, whilst in lanterns fastened to the walls flaring gas-jets crudely illuminated the surrounding squalor, and gave out a glowing heat, which, as it mounted up the narrow stair-well, grew ever more intense.

When he reached the foot of the stairs, the Count once more felt that hot breath upon his neck and shoulders. As of old it was laden with the odor of women, wafted amid floods of light and sound, from the dressing-rooms above; and now, with every upward step he took, the musky scent of powders and the tart perfume of toilet vinegars heated and bewildered him more and more. On the first floor two corridors ran backward, branching sharply off and presenting a set of doors to view which were painted yellow and num-bered with great white numerals in such a way as to suggest a hotel with a bad reputation. The tiles on the floor had been many of them unbedded, and the old house, being in a state of subsidence, they stuck up like hummocks. The Count dashed recklessly forward, glanced through a half-open door,

and saw a very dirty room, which resembled a barber's shop
in a poor part of the town. It was furnished with two
chairs, a mirror, and a small table containing a drawer which
had been blackened by the grease from brushes and combs.
A great perspiring fellow, with smoking shoulders, was
changing his linen there, whilst in a similar room, next door,
a woman was drawing on her gloves preparatory to departure.
Her hair was damp and out of curl, as though she had just had
a bath. But Fauchery began calling the Count, and the latter
was rushing up without delay, when a furious "damn!" burst
from the corridor on the right. Mathilde, a little drab of a
miss, had just broken her wash-hand basin, the soapy water
from which was flowing out to the stair-head. A dressing-
room door banged noisily. Two women in their stays skipped
across the passage, and another, with the hem of her shift in
her mouth, appeared and immediately vanished from view.
Then followed a sound of laughter, a dispute, the snatch of a
song, which was suddenly broken off short. All along the
passage, naked gleams, sudden visions of white skin and wan
underlinen, were observable through chinks in doorways.
Two girls were making very merry, shewing each other their
birth-marks. One of them, a very young girl, almost a
child, had drawn her skirts up over her knees in order to sew
up a rent in her drawers, and the dressers, catching sight of
the two men, drew some curtains half to, for decency's sake.
The wild stampede which follows the end of a play had already begun, the grand removal of white paint and rouge, the
reassumption amid clouds of rice-powder of ordinary attire.
The strange animal scent came in whiffs of redoubled intensity through the lines of banging doors. On the third
story, Muffat abandoned himself to the feeling of intoxication which was overpowering him. For the chorus-girls'
dressing-room was there, and you saw a crowd of twenty
women, and a wild display of soaps and flasks of lavender
water. The place resembled the common room in a slum

lodging-house. As he passed by he heard fierce sounds of washing behind a closed door, and a perfect storm raging in a wash-hand basin. And, as he was mounting up to the topmost story of all, curiosity led him to risk one more little peep through an open loop-hole. The room was empty, and, under the flare of the gas, a solitary chamber pot stood forgotten among a heap of petticoats trailing on the floor. This room afforded him his ultimate impression. Upstairs, on the fourth floor, he was well-nigh suffocated. All the scents, all the blasts of heat, had found their goal there. The yellow ceiling looked as if it had been baked, and a lamp burned amid fumes of russet-colored fog. For some seconds he leant upon the iron balustrade, which felt warm and damp, and well-nigh human to the touch. And he shut his eyes, and drew a long breath, and drank in the sexual atmosphere of the place. Hitherto he had been utterly ignorant of it, but now it beat full in his face.

"Do come here," shouted Fauchery, who had vanished some moments ago. "You're being asked for."

At the end of the corridor was the dressing-room belonging to Clarisse and Simonne. It was a long, ill-built room under the roof, with a garret ceiling and sloping walls. The light penetrated to it from two deep-set openings high up in the wall, but at that hour of the night the dressing-room was lit by flaring gas. It was papered with a paper at seven sous a roll, with a pattern of roses twining over green trellis-work. Two boards, placed near one another and covered with oil-cloth, did duty for dressing-tables. They were black with spilt water, and underneath them was a fine medley of dinted zinc jugs, slop-pails, and coarse yellow earthenware crocks. There was an array of fancy articles in the room—a battered, soiled, and well-worn array of chipped basins, of toothless combs, of all those manifold untidy trifles, which, in their hurry and carelessness, two women will leave scattered about when they undress and wash together amid purely temporary

surroundings, the dirty aspect of which has ceased to concern them.

"Do come here," Fauchery repeated, with the good-
humored familiarity which men adopt among their fallen
sisters, "Clarisse is wanting to kiss you."

Muffat entered the room at last. But what was his surprise when he found the Marquis de Chouard snugly en-
sconced on a chair between the two dressing-tables. The
Marquis had withdrawn thither some time ago. He was
spreading his feet apart because a pail was leaking and letting
a whitish flood spread over the floor. He was visibly much
at his ease, as became a man who knew all the snug corners,
and had grown quite merry in the close dressing-room, where
people might have been bathing, and amid those quietly im-
modest feminine surroundings which the uncleanness of the
little place rendered at once natural and poignant.

"D'you go with the old boy?" Simonne asked Clarisse, in a
whisper.

"Rather!" replied the latter, aloud.

The dresser, a very ugly and extremely familiar young girl,
who was helping Simonne into her coat, positively writhed
with laughter. The three pushed each other, and babbled
little phrases which redoubled their merriment.

"Come, Clarisse, kiss the gentleman," said Fauchery.
"You know, he's got the rhino."

And turning to the Count,—

"You'll see, she's very nice! She's going to kiss you!"

But Clarisse was disgusted by the men. She spoke in
violent terms of the dirty lot waiting at the porter's lodge
down below. Besides, she was in a hurry to go downstairs
again—they were making her miss her last scene. Then, as
Fauchery blocked up the doorway, she gave Muffat a couple
of kisses on the whiskers, remarking as she did so,—

"It's not for you at any rate! It's for that nuisance
Fauchery!"

And with that she darted off, and the Count remained
much embarrassed in his father-in-law's presence. The blood
had rushed to his face. In Nana's dressing-room, amid all
the luxury of hangings and mirrors, he had not experienced
the sharp physical sensation which the shameful wretchedness
of that sorry garret excited within him, redolent as it was
of these two girls' self-abandonment. Meanwhile the Marquis had hurried in the rear of Simonne, who was making
off at the top of her pace; and he kept whispering in her ear,
whilst she shook her head in token of refusal. Fauchery followed them laughing. And with that the Count found himself alone with the dresser, who was washing out the basins.
Accordingly, he took his departure too, his legs almost failing
under him. Once more he put up flights of half-dressed
women, and caused doors to bang, as he advanced. But amid
the disorderly disbanded troops of girls to be found on each
of the four stories, he was only distinctly aware of a cat, a
great tortoise-shell cat, which went gliding upstairs through
the oven-like place, where the air was poisoned with musk,
rubbing its back against the banisters, and keeping its tail exceedingly erect.

"Yes, to be sure!" said a woman, hoarsely. "I thought
they'd keep us back to-night! What a niusance they are
with their calls!"

The end had come, the curtain had just fallen. There was
a veritable stampede on the staircase—its walls rang with exclamations, and every one was in a savage hurry to dress and
be off. As Count Muffat came down the last step or two, he
saw. Nana and the Prince passing slowly along the passage.
The young woman halted, and lowered her voice as she said
with a smile,—

"All right then—by-an-by!"

The Prince returned to the stage, where Bordenave was
awaiting him. And, left alone with Nana, Muffat gave way
to an impulse of anger and desire. He ran up behind her,

and as she was on the point of entering her dressing-room, imprinted a rough kiss on her neck, among little golden hairs curling low down between her shoulders. It was as though he had returned the kiss that had been given him upstairs. Nana was in a fury—she lifted her hand, but when she recognized the Count, she smiled.

"Oh, you frightened me!" said she simply.

And her smile was adorable in its embarrassment and submissiveness, as though she had despaired of this kiss and were happy to have received it. But she could do nothing for him either that evening or the day after. It was a case of waiting. Nay, even if it had been in her power she would still have let herself be desired. Her glance said as much. At length she continued,—

"I'm a landowner, you know. Yes, I'm buying a country house near Orleans, in a part of the world to which you sometimes betake yourself. Baby told me you did—little Georges Hugon, I mean. You know him? So come and see me down there."

The Count was a shy man, and the thought of his roughness had frightened him—he was ashamed of what he had done, and he bowed ceremoniously, promising, at the same time, to take advantage of her invitation. Then he walked off as one who dreams.

He was rejoining the Prince when, passing in front of the foyer, he heard Satin screaming out,—

"Oh, the dirty old thing! Just you bloody well leave me alone!"

It was the Marquis de Chouard, who was tumbling down over Satin. The girl had decidedly had enough of the fashionable world! Nana had certainly introduced her to Bordenave, but the necessity of standing with sealed lips, for fear of allowing some awkward phrase to escape her, had been too much for her feelings, and now she was anxious to regain her freedom, the more so as she had run against an old flame of hers in the wings. This was the super, to whom the task of impersonating Pluto had been entrusted, a pastry-cook, who had already treated her to a whole week of love and flagellation. She was waiting for him, much irritated at the things the Marquis was saying to her as though she were one of those theatrical ladies! And so at last she assumed a highly respectable expression, and jerked out this phrase:

"My husband's coming! You'll see."

Meanwhile, the worn-looking artistes were dropping off one after the other, in their outdoor coats. Groups of men and women were coming down the little winding staircase, and the outlines of battered hats and worn-out shawls were visible in the shadows. They looked colorless and unlovely as became poor play-actors who have got rid of their paint. On the stage, where the side-lights and battens were being extinguished, the Prince was listening to an anecdote Bordenave was telling him. He was waiting for Nana, and when at length she made her appearance, the stage was dark, and the fireman on duty was finishing his round, lantern in hand. Bordenave, in order to save his highness going about by the Passage des Panoramas, had made them open the corridor which led from the porter's lodge to the entrance-hall of the theater. Along this narrow alley little women were racing pell-mell, for they were delighted to escape from the men who were waiting for them in the other passage. They went jostling and elbowing along, casting apprehensive glances behind them, and only breathing freely when they got outside. Fontan, Bosc, and Prullière, on the other hand, retired at a leisurely pace, joking at the figure cut by the serious, paying admirers who were striding up and down the Galerie des Variétés at a time when the little dears were escaping along the boulevard with the men of their hearts. But Clarisse was especially sly. She had her suspicions about la Faloise, and, as a matter of fact, he was still in his place, in the lodge, among the gentlemen obstinately waiting on

Madame Bron's chairs. They all stretched forward, and, with that, she passed brazenly by, in the wake of a friend. The gentlemen were blinking in bewilderment over the wild whirl of petticoats eddying at the foot of the narrow stairs. It made them desperate to think they had waited so long only to see them all flying away like this without being able to recognize a single one. The litter of little black cats were sleeping on the oil-cloth nestled against their mother's belly, and the latter was stretching her paws out in a state of beatitude, whilst the big tortoise-shell cat sat at the other end of the table, her tail stretched out behind her, and her yellow eyes solemnly following the flight of the women.

"If his highness will be good enough to come this way," said Bordenave, at the bottom of the stairs, and he pointed to the passage.

Some chorus-girls were still crowding along it. The Prince began following Nana, whilst Muffat and the Marquis walked behind.

It was a long narrow passage lying between the theater and the house next door, a kind of contracted by-lane, which had been covered with a sloping glass roof. Damp oozed from the walls, and the footfall sounded as hollow on the tiled floor as in an underground vault. It was crowded with the kind of rubbish usually found in a garret. There was a work-bench on which the porter was wont to plane such parts of the scenery as required it, besides a pile of wooden barriers which at night were placed at the doors of the theater for the purpose of regulating the incoming stream of people. Nana had to pick up her dress as she passed a hydrant, which, through having been carelessly turned off, was flooding the tiles underfoot. In the entrance-hall the company bowed and said good-by. And when Bordenave was alone, he summed up his opinion of the Prince in a shrug of eminently philosophic disdain.

"He's a bit of a duffer all the same," said he to Fauchery,

without entering on further explanations; and with that Rose Mignon carried the journalist off with her husband in order to effect a reconciliation between them at home.

Muffat was left alone on the sidewalk. His highness had handed Nana quietly into his carriage, and the Marquis had slipped off after Satin and her super. In his excitement he was content to follow this vicious pair in vague hopes of some stray favor being granted him. Then, with brain on fire, Muffat decided to walk home. The struggle within him had wholly ceased. The ideas and beliefs of the last forty years were being drowned in a flood of new life. Whilst he was passing along the boulevards, the roll of the last carriages deafened him with the name of Nana: the gas-lights set nude limbs dancing before his eyes—the nude limbs, the lithe arms, the white shoulders of Nana. And he felt that he was hers utterly: he would have abjured everything, sold everything, to possess her for a single hour that very night. Youth, a lustful puberty of early manhood, was stirring within him at last, flaming up suddenly in the chaste heart of the Catholic and amid the dignified traditions of middle age.

CHAPTER VI

COUNT MUFFAT, accompanied by his wife and daughter, had arrived over-night at The Fondettes, where Madame Hugon, who was staying there with only her son Georges, had invited them to come and spend a week. The house, which had been built at the end of the eighteenth century, stood in the middle of a huge square enclosure. It was perfectly unadorned, but the garden possessed magnificent shady trees, and a chain of tanks fed by running spring water. It stood at the side of the road which leads from Orleans to Paris, and with its rich verdure and high-embowered trees broke the monotony of that flat countryside, where fields stretched to the horizon's verge.

At eleven o'clock, when the second lunch-bell had called the whole household together, Madame Hugon, smiling in her kindly maternal way, gave Sabine two great kisses, one on each cheek, and said as she did so,—

"You know it's my custom in the country. Oh, seeing you here makes me feel twenty years younger. Did you sleep well in your old room?"

Then, without waiting for her reply, she turned to Estelle:

"And this little one, has she had a nap too? Give me a kiss, my child."

They had taken their seats in the vast dining-room, the windows of which looked out on the park. But they only occupied one end of the long table, where they sat somewhat crowded together for company's sake. Sabine, in high good spirits, dwelt on various childish memories which had been stirred up within her—memories of months passed at The Fondettes, of long walks, of a tumble into one of the tanks on a summer evening, of an old romance of chivalry discovered by her on the top of a cupboard and read, during the winter, before fires made of vine-branches. And Georges, who had not seen the Countess for some months, thought there was something curious about her. Her face seemed changed somehow, whilst, on the other hand, that stick of an Estelle seemed more insignificant, and dumb, and awkward than ever.

Whilst such simple fare as cutlets and boiled eggs was being discussed by the company, Madame Hugon, as became a good housekeeper, launched out into complaints. The butchers, she said, were becoming impossible. She bought everything at Orleans, and yet they never brought her the pieces she asked for. Yet, alas! if her guests had nothing worth eating, it was their own fault: they had come too late in the season.

"There's no sense in it," said she. "I've been expecting you since June, and now we're half through September. You see, it doesn't look pretty."

And with a movement, she pointed to the trees on the grass outside, the leaves of which were beginning to turn yellow. The day was covered, and the distance was hidden by a bluish haze, which was fraught with a sweet and melancholy peacefulness.

"Oh, I'm expecting company," she continued. "We shall be gayer then! The first to come will be two gentlemen whom Georges has invited—Monsieur Fauchery and Monsieur Daguenet: you know them, do you not? Then we shall have Monsieur de Vandeuvres, who has promised me a visit these five years past. This time, perhaps, he'll make up his mind!"

"Oh, well and good!" said the Countess, laughing; "if we only can get Monsieur de Vandeuvres! But he's too much engaged."

"And Philippe?" queried Muffat.

"Philippe has asked for a furlough," replied the old lady; "but without doubt you won't be at The Fondettes any longer when he arrives."

The coffee was served. Paris was now the subject of conversation, and Steiner's name was mentioned, at which Madame Hugon gave a little cry.

"Let me see," said she, "Monsieur Steiner is that stout man I met at your house one evening. He's a banker, is he not? Now there's a detestable man for you! Why, he's gone and bought an actress an estate, about a league from here, over Gumières way, beyond the Choue. The whole countryside's scandalized. Did you know about that, my friend?"

"I knew nothing about it," replied Muffat. "Ah, then, Steiner's bought a country place in the neighborhood!"

Hearing his mother broach the subject, Georges looked into his coffee-cup, but, in his astonishment at the Count's

answer, he glanced up at him and stared. Why was he
lying so glibly? The Count, on his side, noticed the young
fellow's movement, and gave him a suspicious glance. Madame Hugon continued to go into details: the country place
was called La Mignotte. In order to get there one had to
go up the bank of the Choue as far as Gumières in order to
cross the bridge; otherwise one got one's feet wet and ran
the risk of a ducking.

"And what is the actress's name?" asked the Countess.

"Oh, I wasn't told," murmured the old lady. "Georges,
you were there the morning the gardener spoke to us
about it."

Georges appeared to rack his brains. Muffat waited, twirling a teaspoon between his fingers. Then the Countess addressed her husband:

"Isn't Monsieur Steiner with that singer at the Variétés,
that Nana?"

"Nana, that's the name! A horrible woman!" cried Madame Hugon, with growing annoyance. "And they are expecting her at The Mignotte. I've heard all about it from
the gardener. Didn't the gardener say they were expecting
her this evening, Georges?"

The Count gave a little start of astonishment, but Georges
replied with much vivacity,—

"Oh, mother, the gardener spoke without knowing anything about it. Directly afterwards, the coachman said just
the opposite. Nobody's expected at The Mignotte before the
day after to-morrow."

He tried hard to assume a natural expression, whilst he
slyly watched the effect of his remarks on the Count. The
latter was twirling his spoon again as though reassured. The
Countess, her eyes fixed dreamily on the blue distances of
the park, seemed to have lost all interest in the conversation.
The shadow of a smile on her lips, she seemed to be following up a secret thought which had been suddenly awakened

within her. Estelle, on the other hand, sitting stiffly on her chair, had heard all that had been said about Nana, but her white virginal face had not betrayed a trace of emotion.

"Dear me, dear me! I've got no right to grow angry," murmured Madame Hugon, after a pause, and with a return to her old good humor, she added,—"Everybody's got a right to live. If we meet this said lady on the road, we shall not bow to her—that's all!"

And as they got up from table she once more gently upbraided the Countess Sabine for having been so long in coming to her that year. But the Countess defended herself, and threw the blame of the delays upon her husband's shoulders. Twice on the eve of departure, when all the trunks were locked, he counter-ordered their journey on the plea of urgent business. Then he had suddenly decided to start just when the trip seemed shelved. Thereupon the old lady told them how Georges in the same way had twice announced his arrival without arriving, and had finally cropped up at The Fondettes the day before yesterday, when she was no longer expecting him. They had come down into the garden, and the two men, walking beside the ladies, were listening to them in consequential silence.

"Never mind," said Madame Hugon, kissing her son's sunny locks, "Zizi is a very good boy to come and bury himself in the country with his mother. He's a dear Zizi not to forget me!"

In the afternoon she expressed some anxiety for Georges, directly after leaving the table had complained of a heavy feeling in his head, and now seemed in for an atrocious sick headache. Towards four o'clock he said he would go upstairs to bed: it was the only remedy. After sleeping till to-morrow morning he would be perfectly himself again. His mother was bent on putting him to bed herself, but, as she left the room, he ran and locked the door, explaining that he was shutting himself in so that no one should come

and disturb him. Then caressingly he shouted "Good night
till to-morrow, little mother!" and promised to take a nap.
But he did not go to bed again, and with flushed cheeks and
bright eyes noiselessly put on his clothes. Then he sat on a
chair and waited. When the dinner-bell rang, he listened
for Count Muffat, who was on his way to the dining-room,
and ten minutes later, when he was certain that no one would
see him, he slipped from the window to the ground with the
assistance of a rain-pipe. His bedroom was situated on the
first floor, and looked out upon the rear of the house. He
threw himself among some bushes, and got out of the park,
and then galloped across the fields with empty stomach and
heart beating with excitement. Night was closing in, and
a small fine rain was beginning to fall.

It was the very evening that Nana was due at The Mignotte. Ever since, in the preceding May, Steiner had bought
her this country house, she had from time to time been so
filled with the desire of taking possession, that she had wept
hot tears about; but on each of these occasions Bordenave
had refused to give her even the shortest leave, and had de-
ferred her holiday till September on the plea that he did not
intend putting an under-study in her place, even for one
evening, now that the Exhibition was on. Towards the close
of August he spoke of October. Nana was furious, and declared that she would be at The Mignotte in the middle of
September. Nay, in order to dare Bordenave, she even invited a crowd of guests in his very presence. One afternoon,
in her rooms, as Muffat, whose advances she still adroitly resisted, was beseeching her with tremulous emotion to yield
to his entreaties, she at length promised to be kind, but not
in Paris; and to him, too, she named the middle of September. Then, on the twelfth, she was seized by a desire to be
off forthwith, with Zoé as her sole companion. It might
be that Bordenave had got wind of her intentions, and was
about to discover some means of detaining her. She was

delighted at the notion of putting him in a fix, and she sent
him a doctor's certificate. When once the idea had entered
her head of being the first to get to The Mignotte, and of
living there two days without anybody knowing anything
about it, she rushed Zoé through the operation of packing,
and finally pushed her into a cab, where, in a sudden burst
of extreme contrition, she kissed her and begged her pardon.
It was only when they got to the station refreshment-room
that she thought of writing Steiner of her movements. She
begged him to wait till the day after to-morrow before rejoining her, if he wanted to find her quite bright and fresh.
And then, suddenly conceiving another project, she wrote a
second letter, in which she besought her aunt to bring little
Louis to her at once. It would do baby so much good! And
how happy they would be together in the shade of the trees!
In the railway carriage between Paris and Orleans she spoke
of nothing else; her eyes were full of tears, she had an unexpected attack of maternal tenderness, and mingled together
flowers, birds, and child in her every sentence.

La Mignotte was more than three leagues away from the
station, and Nana lost a good hour over the hire of a carriage, a huge dilapidated calash, which rumbled slowly along
to an accompaniment of rattling old iron. She had at once
taken possession of the coachman, a little taciturn old man,
whom she overwhelmed with questions. Had he often passed
by La Mignotte? It was behind this hill, then? There ought
to be lots of trees there, eh? And the house, could one see
it at a distance? The little old man answered with a succession of grunts. Down in the calash Nana was almost dancing
with impatience, whilst Zoé, in her annoyance at having left
Paris in such a hurry, sat stiffly sulking beside her. The horse
suddenly stopped short, and the young woman thought they
had reached their destination. She put her head out of the
carriage-door, and asked,—

"Are we there, eh?"

By way of answer the driver whipped up his horse, which was in the act of painfully climbing a hill. Nana gazed ecstatically at the vast plain beneath the gray sky where great clouds were banked up.

"Oh, do look, Zoé! There's greenery! Now, is that all wheat? Good Lord, how pretty it is!"

"One can quite see that *Madame* doesn't come from the country," was the servant's prim and tardy rejoinder. "As for me, I knew the country only too well, when I was with my dentist. He had a house at Bougival. No, it's cold, too, this evening. It's damp in these parts."

They were driving under the shadow of a wood, and Nana sniffed up the scent of the leaves as a young dog might. All of a sudden, at a turn of the road, she caught sight of the corner of a house among the trees. Perhaps it was there! And with that she began a conversation with the driver, who continued shaking his head by way of saying no. Then, as they drove down the other side of the hill, he contented himself by holding out his whip and muttering,—" 'Tis down there."

She got up, and stretched herself almost bodily out of the carriage-door.

"Where is it? Where is it?" she cried, with pale cheeks, but as yet she saw nothing.

At last she caught sight of a bit of wall. And then followed a succession of little cries and jumps, the ecstatic behavior of a woman overcome by a new and vivid sensation.

"I see it! I see it, Zoé! Look out at the other side. Oh, there's a terrace, with brick ornaments on the roof! And there's a hothouse down there! But the place is immense— oh, how happy I am! Do look, Zoé! Now, do look!"

The carriage had by this time pulled up before the park gates. A side-door was opened, and the gardener, a tall dry fellow, made his appearance, cap in hand. Nana made an effort to regain her dignity, for the driver seemed now to be suppressing a laugh behind his dry, speechless lips. She refrained from setting off at a run, and listened to the gardener, who was a very talkative fellow. He begged *Madame* to excuse the disorder in which she found everything, seeing that he had only received *Madame's* letter that very morning. But, despite all his efforts, she flew off at a tangent, and walked so quickly that Zoé could scarcely follow her. At the end of the avenue she paused for a moment, in order to take the house in at a glance. It was a great pavilion-like building in the Italian manner, and it was flanked by a smaller construction, which a rich Englishman, after two years' residence in Naples had caused to be erected and had forthwith become disgusted with.

"I'll take *Madame* over the house," said the gardener.

But she had outrun him entirely, and she shouted back that he was not to put himself out, and that she would go over the house by herself. She preferred doing that, she said. And, without removing her hat, she dashed into the different rooms, calling to Zoé as she did so, shouting her impressions from one end of each corridor to the other, and filling the empty house, which for long months had been uninhabited, with exclamations and bursts of laughter. In the first place, there was the hall. It was a little damp, but that didn't matter; one wasn't going to sleep in it. Then came the drawing-room, quite the thing the drawing-room, with its windows opening on the lawn. Only the red upholsteries there were hideous: she would alter all that. As to the dining-room—well, it was a lovely dining-room, eh? What big blow-outs you might give in Paris if you had a dining-room as large as that! As she was going upstairs to the first floor it occurred to her that she had not seen the kitchen, and she went down again and indulged in ecstatic exclamations. Zoé ought to admire the beautiful dimensions of the sink and the width of the hearth, where you might have roasted a sheep! When she had gone upstairs again,

her bedroom especially enchanted her. It had been hung
with delicate rose-colored Louis XVI cretonne by an Orleans
upholsterer. Dear me, yes! one ought to sleep jolly sound
in such a room as that: why, it was a real best bedroom!
Then came four or five guest chambers, and then some splendid garrets, which would be extremely convenient for trunks
and boxes. Zoé looked very gruff, and cast a frigid glance
into each of the rooms as she lingered in *Madame's* wake.
She saw Nana disappearing up the steep garret ladder, and
said, "Thanks, I haven't the least wish to break my legs."
But the sound of a voice reached her from far away; indeed,
it seemed to come whistling down a chimney.

"Zoé, Zoé, where are you? Come up, do! You've no idea!
It's like fairyland!"

Zoé went up grumbling. On the roof she found her mistress leaning against the brick-work balustrade, and gazing
at the valley which spread out into the silence. The horizon
was immeasurably wide, but it was now covered by masses
of gray vapor, and a fierce wind was driving fine rain before
it. Nana had to hold her hat on with both hands to keep
it from being blown away, whilst her petticoats streamed out
behind her, flapping like a flag.

"Not if I know it!" said Zoé, drawing her head in at once.
"*Madame* will be blown away. What beastly weather!"

Madame did not hear what she said. With her head over
the balustrade she was gazing at the grounds beneath. They
consisted of seven or eight acres of land, enclosed within a
wall. Then the view of the kitchen garden entirely engrossed
her attention. She darted back, jostling the lady's maid at
the top of the stairs, and bursting out,—

"It's full of cabbages! Oh, such woppers! And lettuces,
and sorrel, and onions, and everything! Come along, make
haste!"

The rain was falling more heavily now, and she opened
her white silk sunshade, and ran down the garden walks.

"*Madame* will catch cold," cried Zoé, who had stayed quietly behind under the awning over the garden-door.

But *Madame* wanted to see things, and at each new discovery there was a burst of wonderment.

"Zoé, here's spinach! Do come. Oh! look at the artichokes! They are funny. So they grow in the ground, do they? Now, what can that be? I don't know it. Do come, Zoé, perhaps you know."

The lady's maid never budged an inch. *Madame* must really be raving mad. For now the rain was coming down in torrents, and the little white silk sunshade was already dark with it. Nor did it shelter *Madame,* whose skirts were wringing wet. But that didn't put her out in the smallest degree, and in the pouring rain she visited the kitchen garden and the orchard, stopping in front of every fruit tree, and bending over every bed of vegetables. Then she ran and looked down the well, and lifted up a frame to see what was underneath it, and was lost in the contemplation of a huge pumpkin. She wanted to go along every single garden walk, and to take immediate possession of all the things she had been wont to dream of in the old days, when she was a slipshod work-girl on the Paris pavements. The rain redoubled, but she never heeded it, and was only miserable at the thought that the daylight was fading. She could not see clearly now, and touched things with her fingers to find out what they were. Suddenly, in the twilight, she caught sight of a bed of strawberries, and all that was childish in her awoke.

"Strawberries! strawberries! There are some here: I can feel them! A plate, Zoé! Come and pick strawberries."

And, dropping her sunshade, Nana crouched down in the mire under the full force of the downpour. With drenched hands she began gathering the fruit among the leaves. But Zoé in the mean time brought no plate, and when the young woman rose to her feet again she was frightened. She thought she had seen a shadow close to her.

"It's some beast!" she screamed.

But she stood rooted to the path in utter amazement. It was a man, and she recognized him.

"Gracious me, it's Baby! What *are* you doing there, Baby?"

" 'Gad, I've come—that's all!" replied Georges.

Her head swam.

"You knew I'd come through the gardener telling you? Oh, that poor child! Why, he's soaking!"

"Oh, I'll explain that to you! The rain caught me on my way here, and then, as I didn't wish to go up stream as far as Gumières, I crossed the Choue, and fell into a blessed hole."

Nana forgot the strawberries forthwith. She was trembling and full of pity. That poor dear Zizi in a hole full of water! And she drew him with her in the direction of the house, and spoke of making up a roaring fire.

"You know," he murmured, stopping her among the shadows, "I was in hiding, because I was afraid of being scolded, like in Paris, when I come and see you and you're not expecting me."

She made no reply, but burst out laughing, and gave him a kiss on the forehead. Up till to-day she had always treated him like a naughty urchin, never taking his declarations seriously, and amusing herself at his expense as though he were a little man of no consequence whatever. There was much ado to install him in the house. She absolutely insisted on the fire being lit in her bedroom, as being the most comfortable place for his reception. Georges had not surprised Zoé, who was used to all kinds of encounters; but the gardener, who brought the wood upstairs, was greatly nonplused at sight of this dripping gentleman to whom he was certain he had not opened the front door. He was, however, dismissed, as he was no longer wanted.

A lamp lit up the room, and the fire burnt with a great bright flame.

"He'll never get dry, and he'll catch cold," said Nana, seeing Georges beginning to shiver.

And there were no men's trousers in her house! She was on the point of calling the gardener back, when an idea struck her. Zoé, who was unpacking the trunks in the dressing-room, brought her mistress a change of underwear, consisting of a shift and some petticoats, with a dressing-jacket.

"Oh, that's first rate!" cried the young woman. "Zizi can put 'em all on. You're not angry with me, eh? When your clothes are dry, you can put them on again, and then off with you, as fast as fast can be, so as not to have a scolding from your mamma. Make haste! I'm going to change my things too, in the dressing-room."

Ten minutes afterward, when she reappeared in a tea-gown, she clasped her hands in a perfect ecstasy.

"Oh, the darling! How sweet he looks dressed like a little woman!"

He had simply slipped on a long night-gown with an insertion front, a pair of worked drawers, and the dressing-jacket, which was a long cambric garment trimmed with lace. Thus attired, and with his delicate young arms shewing, and his bright damp hair falling almost to his shoulders, he looked just like a girl.

"Why, he's as slim as I am!" said Nana, putting her arm round his waist. "Zoé, just come here and see how it suits him. It's made for him, eh?—all except the bodice part, which is too large. He hasn't got as much as I have, poor dear Zizi!"

"Oh, to be sure, I'm a bit wanting there," murmured Georges, with a smile.

All three grew very merry about it. Nana had set to work buttoning the dressing-jacket from top to bottom, so as to make him quite decent. Then she turned him round as though he were a doll, gave him little thumps, made the skirt stand well out behind. After which she asked him questions. Was he comfortable? Did he feel warm? Zounds, yes, he was comfortable! Nothing fitted more closely and warmly than a woman's shift: had he been able, he would always have worn one. He moved round and about therein, delighted with the fine linen and the soft touch of that unmanly garment, in the folds of which he thought he discovered some of Nana's own warm life.

Meanwhile, Zoé had taken the soaked clothes down to the kitchen in order to dry them as quickly as possible in front of a vine-branch fire. Then Georges, as he lounged in an easy chair, ventured to make a confession.

"I say, are you going to feed this evening? I'm dying of hunger. I haven't dined."

Nana was vexed. The great silly thing to go sloping off from mamma's with an empty stomach, just to chuck himself into a hole full of water! But she was as hungry as a hunter, too. They certainly must feed! Only they would have to eat what they could get. Whereupon a round table was rolled up in front of the fire, and the queerest of dinners was improvised thereon. Zoé ran down to the gardener's, he having cooked a mess of cabbage soup in case *Madame* should not dine at Orleans before her arrival. *Madame*, indeed, had forgotten to tell him what he was to get ready in the letter she had sent him. Fortunately the cellar was well furnished. Accordingly they had cabbage soup, followed by a piece of bacon. Then Nana rummaged in her hand-bag, and found quite a heap of provisions which she had taken the precaution of stuffing into it. There was a Strasbourg *pâté*, for instance, and a bag of sweetmeats, and some oranges. So they both ate away like ogres, and, whilst they satisfied their healthy young appetites, treated one another with easy good fellowship. Nana kept calling Georges "dear old girl," a form of address which struck her as at

once tender and familiar. At dessert, in order not to give
Zoé any more trouble, they used the same spoon turn and
turn about, whilst demolishing a pot of preserve they had
discovered at the top of a cupboard.

"Oh, you dear old girl!" said Nana, pushing back the
round table, "I haven't made such a good dinner these ten
years past!"

Yet it was growing late, and she wanted to send her boy
off for fear he should be suspected of all sorts of things.
But he kept declaring that he had plenty of time to spare.
For the matter of that his clothes were not drying well, and
Zoé averred that it would take an hour longer at least; and,
as she was dropping with sleep after the fatigues of the journey, they sent her off to bed. After which they were alone
in the silent house.

It was a very charming evening. The fire was dying out
amid glowing embers, and in the great blue room, where Zoé
had made up the bed before going upstairs, the air felt a
little oppressive. Nana, overcome by the heavy warmth, got
up to open the window for a few minutes, and, as she did
so, she uttered a little cry.

"Great heavens, how beautiful it is! Look, dear old girl!"
Georges had come up, and as though the window-bar had
not been sufficiently wide, he put his arm round Nana's
waist, and rested his head against her shoulder. The weather
had undergone a brisk change: the skies were clearing, and
a full moon lit up the country with its golden disc of light.
A sovran quiet reigned over the valley. It seemed wider and
larger as it opened on the immense distances of the plain,
where the trees loomed like little shadowy islands amid a
shining and waveless lake. And Nana grew tender-hearted,
felt herself a child again. Most surely she had dreamed of
nights like this at an epoch which she could not recall. Since
leaving the train, every object of sensation—the wide countryside, the green things with their pungent scents, the house,

the vegetables—had stirred her to such a degree that now
it seemed to her as if she had left Paris twenty years ago.
Yesterday's existence was far, far away, and she was full of
sensations of which she had no previous experience. Georges,
meanwhile, was giving her neck little coaxing kisses, and this
again added to her sweet unrest. With hesitating hand she
pushed him from her, as though he were a child whose affectionate advances are fatiguing, and once more she told him
that he ought to take his departure. He did not gainsay
her. All in good time—he would go all in good time!

But a bird raised its song, and again was silent. It was a
robin, in an elder tree, below the window.

"Wait one moment," whispered Georges; "the lamp's
frightening him; I'll put it out."

And when he came back and took her waist again, he
added—

"We'll relight it in a minute."

Then as she listened to the robin, and the boy pressed
against her side, Nana remembered. Ah, yes, it was in novels
that she had got to know all this! In other days she would
have given her heart to have a full moon, and robins, and a
lad dying of love for her. Great God! she could have cried,
so good and charming did it all seem to her! Beyond a doubt
she had been born to live honestly! So she pushed Georges
away again, and he grew yet bolder.

"No, let me be: I don't care about it. It would be very
wicked at your age. Now listen—I'll always be your
mamma."

A sudden feeling of shame overcame her. She was blushing exceedingly, and yet not a soul could see her. The room
behind them was full of black night, whilst the country
stretched before them in silence and lifeless solitude. Never
had she known such a sense of shame before. Little by little,
she felt her power of resistance ebbing away, and that despite
her embarrassed efforts to the contrary. That disguise of his,

that woman's shift and that dressing-jacket, set her laughing
again. It was as though a girl-friend were teasing her.

"Oh, it's not right, it's not right!" she stammered, after
a last effort.

And with that, in face of the lovely night, she sank like
a young virgin into the arms of this mere child. The house
slept.

Next morning, at The Fondettes, when the bell rang for
lunch, the dining-room table was no longer too big for the
company. Fauchery and Daguenet had been driven up together in one carriage, and after them another had arrived
with the Count de Vandeuvres, who had followed by the
next train. Georges was the last to come downstairs. He
was looking a little pale, and his eyes were sunken, but, in
answer to questions, he said that he was much better, though
he was still somewhat shaken by the violence of the attack.
Madame Hugon looked into his eyes with an anxious smile,
and adjusted his hair, which had been carelessly combed that
morning, but he drew back as though embarrassed by this
tender little action. During the meal she chaffed Vandeuvres
very pleasantly, and declared that she had expected him for
five years past.

"Well, here you are at last! How have you managed it?"

Vandeuvres took her remarks with equal pleasantry. He
told her that he had lost a fabulous sum of money at the
club yesterday, and thereupon had come away with the intention of ending up in the country.

" 'Pon my word, yes, if only you can find me an heiress
in these rustic parts! There must be delightful women here-
abouts."

The old lady rendered equal thanks to Daguenet and Fauchery for having been so good as to accept her son's invitation, and then, to her great and joyful surprise, she saw the
Marquis de Chouard enter the room. A third carriage had
brought him.

"Dear me, you've made this your trysting-place to-day!"
cried she. "You've passed word round! But what's happening? For years I've never succeeded in bringing you all
together, and now you all drop in at once. Oh, I certainly
don't complain."

Another place was laid. Fauchery found himself next the
Countess Sabine, whose liveliness and gayety surprised him
when he remembered her drooping languid state in the austere Rue Miromesnil drawing-room. Daguenet, on the other
hand, who was seated on Estelle's left, seemed slightly put
out by his propinquity to that tall silent girl. The angularity
of her elbows was disagreeable to him. Muffat and Chouard
had exchanged a sly glance, whilst Vandeuvres continued
joking about his coming marriage.

"Talking of ladies," Madame Hugon ended by saying, "I
have a new neighbor whom you probably know."

And she mentioned Nana. Vaudeuvres affected the live-
liest astonishment.

"Well, that is strange! Nana's property near here!"

Fauchery and Daguenet indulged in a similar demonstra-
tion, whilst the Marquis de Chouard discussed the breast of
a chicken without appearing to comprehend their meaning.
Not one of the men had smiled.

"Certainly," continued the old lady, "and the person in
question arrived at The Mignotte yesterday evening, as I was
saying she would. I got my information from the gardener
this morning."

At these words the gentlemen could not conceal their very
real surprise. They all looked up. Eh? what? Nana had
come down! But they were only expecting her next day:
they were privately under the impression that they would
arrive before her! Georges alone sat looking at his glass with
drooped eyelids and a tired expression. Ever since the beginning of lunch, he had seemed to be sleeping with open
eyes and a vague smile on his lips.

"Are you still in pain, my Zizi?" asked his mother, who had been gazing at him throughout the meal.

He started, and blushed as he said that he was very well now, but the worn-out insatiate expression of a girl who has danced too much did not fade from his face.

"What's the matter with your neck?" resumed Madame Hugon, in an alarmed tone. "It's all red."

He was embarrassed, and stammered. He did not know— he had nothing the matter with his neck. Then, drawing his shirt-collar up,—

"Ah, yes, some insect stung me there!"

The Marquis de Chouard had cast a sidelong glance at the little red place. Muffat, too, looked at Georges. The company was finishing lunch, and planning various excursions. Fauchery was growing increasingly excited with the Countess Sabine's laughter. As he was passing her a dish of fruit, their hands touched, and for one second she looked at him with eyes so full of dark meaning that he once more thought of the secret, which had been communicated to him one evening after an uproarious dinner. Then, too, she was no longer the same woman. Something was more pronounced than of old, and her gray foulard gown, which fitted loosely over her shoulders, added a touch of license to her delicate, high-strung elegance.

When they rose from the table, Daguenet remained behind with Fauchery in order to impart to him the following crude witticism about Estelle: "A nice broomstick that to shove into a man's hands!" Nevertheless, he grew serious when the journalist told him the amount she was worth in the way of dowry.

"Four hundred thousand francs."

"And the mother?" queried Fauchery. "She's all right, eh?"

"Oh! *she'll* work the oracle! But it's no go, my dear man!"

"Bah! How are we to know? We must wait and see."

It was impossible to go out that day, for the rain was still falling in heavy showers. Georges had made haste to disappear from the scene, and had double-locked his door. These gentlemen avoided mutual explanations, though they were none of them deceived as to the reasons which had brought them together. Vandeuvres, who had had a very bad time at play, had really conceived the notion of lying fallow for a season, and he was counting on Nana's presence in the neighborhood as a safeguard against excessive boredom. Fauchery had taken advantage of the holidays granted him by Rose, who just then was extremely busy. He was thinking of discussing a second notice with Nana, in case country air should render them reciprocally affectionate. Daguenet, who had been just a little sulky with her since Steiner had come upon the scene, was dreaming of resuming the old connection, or at least of snatching some delightful opportunities, if occasion offered. As to the Marquis de Chouard, he was watching for times and seasons. But, among all those men who were busy following in the tracks of Venus —a Venus with the rouge scarce washed from her cheeks— Muffat was at once the most ardent and the most tortured by the novel sensations of desire and fear and anger warring in his anguished members. A formal promise had been made him; Nana was awaiting him. Why, then, had she taken her departure two days sooner than was expected?

He resolved to betake himself to The Mignotte after dinner that same evening.

At night, as the Count was leaving the park, Georges fled forth after him. He left him to follow the road to Gumières, crossed the Choue, rushed into Nana's presence, breathless, furious, and with tears in his eyes. Ah, yes, he understood everything! That old fellow, now on his way to her, was coming to keep an appointment! Nana was dumbfounded by this ebullition of jealousy; and, greatly moved by the way things were turning out, she took him in her arms, and comforted him to the best of her ability. Oh, no, he was quite beside the mark; she was expecting no one. If the gentleman came it would not be her fault. What a great ninny that Zizi was to be taking on so about nothing at all! By her child's soul she swore she loved nobody except her own Georges. And with that she kissed him, and wiped away his tears.

"Now just listen! You'll see that it's all for your sake," she went on, when he had grown somewhat calmer. "Steiner has arrived—he's up above there now. You know, duckie, I can't turn *him* out of doors."

"Yes, I know, I'm not talking of *him*," whispered the boy.

"Very well then, I've stuck him into the room at the end. I said I was out of sorts. He's unpacking his trunk. Since nobody's seen you, be quick and run up, and hide in my room, and wait for me."

Georges sprang at her and threw his arms round her neck. It was true after all! She loved him a little! So they would put the lamp out as they did yesterday, and be in the dark till daytime! Then, as the front-door bell sounded, he quietly slipped away. Upstairs, in the bedroom, he at once took off his shoes so as not to make any noise, and straightway crouched down behind a curtain and waited soberly.

Nana welcomed Count Muffat, who, though still shaken with passion, was now somewhat embarrassed. She had pledged her word to him, and would even have liked to keep it since he struck her as a serious, practicable lover. But truly, who could have foreseen all that happened yesterday? There was the voyage, and the house she had never set eyes on before, and the arrival of the drenched little lover! How sweet it had all seemed to her, and how delightful it would be to continue in it! So much the worse for the gentleman! For three months past she had been keeping him dangling after her whilst she affected conventionality in order the

further to inflame him. Well, well! he would have to continue dangling, and if he didn't like that he could go! She
would sooner have thrown up everything than have played
false to Georges.

The Count had seated himself with all the ceremonious
politeness becoming a country caller. Only his hands were
trembling slightly. Lust, which Nana's skillful tactics daily
exasperated, had at last wrought terrible havoc in that san-
guine, uncontaminated nature. The grave man, the chamberlain who was wont to tread the state apartments at the
Tuileries with slow and dignified step, was now nightly
driven to plunge his teeth into his bolster, whilst, with sobs
of exasperation, he pictured to himself a sensual shape which
never changed. But this time he was determined to make
an end of the torture. Coming along the highroad, in the
deep quiet of the gloaming, he had meditated a fierce course
of action. And the moment he had finished his opening
remarks he tried to take hold of Nana with both hands.

"No, no! take care!" she said, simply. She was not vexed;
nay, she even smiled.

He caught her again, clenching his teeth as he did so.
Then, as she struggled to get free, he coarsely and crudely
reminded her that he had come to stay the night. Though
much embarrassed at this, Nana did not cease to smile. She
took his hands, and spoke very familiarly in order to soften
her refusal.

"Come now, darling, do be quiet! Honor bright, I can't:
Steiner's upstairs."

But he was beside himself. Never yet had she seen a man
in such a state. She grew frightened, and put her hand over
his mouth in order to stifle his cries. Then, in lowered tones,
she besought him to be quiet and to let her alone. Steiner
was coming downstairs. Things were getting stupid, to be
sure! When Steiner entered the room, he heard Nana remarking,—

"I adore the country."

She was lounging comfortably back in her deep easy chair, and she turned round and interrupted herself.

"It's Monsieur le Comte Muffat, darling. He saw a light here while he was strolling past, and he came in to bid us welcome."

The two men clasped hands. Muffat, with his face in shadow, stood silent for a moment or two. Steiner seemed sulky. Then they chatted about Paris: business there was at a standstill; abominable things had been happening on 'Change. When a quarter of an hour had elapsed, Muffat took his departure, and, as the young woman was seeing him to the door, he tried, without success, to make an assignation for the following night. Steiner went up to bed almost directly afterwards, grumbling, as he did so, at the everlasting little ailments that seemed to afflict the genus courtesan. The two old boys had been packed off at last! When she was able to rejoin him, Nana found Georges still hiding exemplarily behind the curtain. The room was dark. He pulled her down on to the floor, as she sat near him, and together they began playfully rolling on the ground, stopping now and again, and smothering their laughter with kisses whenever they struck their bare feet against some piece of furniture. Far away, on the road to Gumières, Count Muffat walked slowly home, and, hat in hand, bathed his burning forehead in the freshness and silence of the night.

During the days that followed, Nana found life adorable. In the lad's arms she was once more a girl of fifteen, and under the caressing influence of this renewed childhood, love's white flower once more blossomed forth in a nature which had grown hackneyed and disgusted in the service of the other sex. She would experience sudden fits of shame, sudden vivid emotions which left her trembling. She wanted to laugh and to cry, and she was beset by nervous maidenly feelings, mingled with warm desires that made her blush

again. Never yet had she felt anything comparable to this.
The country filled her with tender thoughts. As a little girl
she had long wished to dwell in a meadow, tending a goat,
because one day, on the talus of the fortifications, she had
seen a goat bleating at the end of its tether. Now, this estate,
this stretch of land belonging to her, simply swelled her heart
to bursting, so utterly had her old ambition been surpassed.
Once again she tasted the novel sensations experienced by
chits of girls, and at night, when she went upstairs, dizzy
with her day in the open air, and intoxicated by the scent
of green leaves, and rejoined her Zizi behind the curtain, she
fancied herself a school-girl enjoying a holiday escapade. It
was an amour, she thought, with a young cousin, to whom
she was going to be married. And so she trembled at the
slightest noise, and dread lest parents should hear her, whilst
making the delicious experiments and suffering the voluptuous terrors attendant on a girl's first slip from the path of
virtue.

Nana in those days was subject to the fancies a sentimental
girl will indulge in. She would gaze at the moon for hours.
One night she had a mind to go down into the garden with
Georges, when all the household was asleep. When there,
they strolled under the trees, their arms round each other's
waists, and finally went and laid down in the grass, where
the dew soaked them through and through. On another
occasion, after a long silence up in the bedroom, she fell sobbing on the lad's neck, declaring in broken accents that she
was afraid of dying. She would often croon a favorite ballad
of Madame Lerat's, which was full of flowers and birds. The
song would melt her to tears, and she would break off in
order to clasp Georges in a passionate embrace, and to extract
from him vows of undying affection. In short she was extremely silly, as she herself would admit when they both became jolly good fellows again, and sat up smoking cigarettes

on the edge of the bed, dangling their bare legs over it the while, and tapping their heels against its wooden side.

But what utterly melted the young woman's heart was Louiset's arrival. She had an access of maternal affection which was as violent as a mad fit. She would carry off her boy into the sunshine outside to watch him kicking about; she would dress him like a little prince and roll with him in the grass. The moment he arrived she decided that he was to sleep near her, in the room next hers, where Madame Lerat, whom the country greatly affected, used to begin snoring the moment her head touched the pillow. Louiset did not hurt Zizi's position in the least. On the contrary, Nana said that she had now two children, and she treated them with the same wayward tenderness. At night, more than ten times running, she would leave Zizi to go and see if Louiset were breathing properly, but on her return she would re-embrace her Zizi, and lavish on him the caresses that had been destined for the child. She played at being mamma, whilst he wickedly enjoyed being dandled in the arms of the great wench and allowed himself to be rocked to and fro like a baby that is being sent to sleep. It was all so delightful, and Nana was so charmed with her present existence, that she seriously proposed to him never to leave the country. They would send all the other people away, and he, she, and the child would live alone. And with that they would make a thousand plans till day-break, and never once hear Madame Lerat as she snored vigorously after the fatigues of a day spent in picking country flowers.

This charming existence lasted nearly a week. Count Muffat used to come every evening, and go away again with disordered face and burning hands. One evening he was not even received, as Steiner had been obliged to run up to Paris. He was told that *Madame* was not well. Nana grew daily more disgusted at the notion of deceiving Georges. He was such an innocent lad, and he had such faith in her! She would have looked on herself as the lowest of the low had she played him false. Besides, it would have sickened her to do so! Zoé, who took her part in this affair in mute disdain, believed that *Madame* was growing senseless.

On the sixth day a band of visitors suddenly blundered into Nana's idyl. She had, indeed, invited a whole swarm of people under the belief that none of them would come. And so, one fine afternoon, she was vastly astonished and annoyed to see an omnibus full of people pulling up outside the gate of La Mignotte.

"It's us!" cried Mignon, getting down first from the conveyance, and extracting then his sons, Henri and Charles.

Labordette thereupon appeared, and began handing out an interminable file of ladies—Lucy Stewart, Caroline Héquet, Tatan Néné, Maria Blond. Nana was in hopes that they would end there, when la Faloise sprang from the step in order to receive Gaga and her daughter Amélie in his trembling arms. That brought the number up to eleven people. Their installation proved a laborious undertaking. There were five spare rooms at The Mignotte, one of which was already occupied by Madame Lerat and Louiset. The largest was devoted to the Gaga and la Faloise establishment, and it was decided that Amélie should sleep on a truckle bed in the dressing-room at the side. Mignon and his two sons had the third room, Labordette the fourth. There thus remained one room, which was transformed into a dormitory with four beds in it, for Lucy, Caroline, Tatan and Maria. As to Steiner, he would sleep on the divan in the drawing-room. At the end of an hour, when every one was duly settled, Nana, who had begun by being furious, grew enchanted at the thought of playing hostess on a grand scale. The ladies complimented her on The Mignotte. "It's a stunning property, my dear!" And then too they brought her quite a whiff of Parisian air, and talking all together with bursts of laughter, and exclamations, and emphatic little gestures, they gave her all the petty gossip of the week just past. By-the-by, and how about Bordenave? What had he said about her prank? Oh, nothing much! After bawling about having her brought back by the police, he had simply put somebody else in her place at night. Little Violaine was the under-study, and she had even obtained a very pretty success as the Blonde Venus. Which piece of news made Nana rather serious.

It was only four o'clock in the afternoon, and there was some talk of taking a stroll round.

"Oh, I haven't told you," said Nana, "I was just off to get up potatoes when you arrived."

Thereupon they all wanted to go and dig potatoes without even changing their dresses first. It was quite a party. The gardener and two helpers were already in the potato field at the end of the grounds. The ladies knelt down, and began fumbling in the mold with their be-ringed fingers, shouting gayly whenever they discovered a potato of exceptional size. It struck them as so amusing! But Tatan Néné was in a state of triumph! So many were the potatoes she had gathered in her youth, that she forgot herself entirely, and gave the others much good advice, treating them like geese the while. The gentlemen toiled less strenuously. Mignon looked every inch the good citizen and father, and made his stay in the country an occasion for completing his boys' education. Indeed, he spoke to them of Parmentier!

Dinner that evening was wildly hilarious. The company ate ravenously. Nana, in a state of great elevation, had a warm disagreement with her butler, an individual who had been in service at the bishop's palace in Orleans. The ladies smoked over their coffee. An ear-splitting noise of merry-making issued from the open windows, and died out far away under the serene evening sky, whilst peasants, belated in the lanes, turned and looked at the flaring rooms.

"It's most tiresome that you're going back the day after

to-morrow," said Nana. "But never mind, we'll get up an excursion all the same!"

They decided to go on the morrow, Sunday, and visit the ruins of the old Abbey of Chamont, which were some seven kilomètres distant. Five carriages would come out from Orleans, take up the company after lunch, and bring them back to dinner at The Mignotte at about seven. It would be delightful.

That evening, as his wont was, Count Muffat mounted the hill to ring at the outer gate. But the brightly-lit windows and the shouts of laughter astonished him. When, however, he recognized Mignon's voice, he understood it all, and went off, raging at this new obstacle, driven to extremities, bent on some violent act. Georges passed through a little door, of which he had the key, slipped along the staircase walls, and went quietly up into Nana's room. Only he had to wait for her till past midnight. She appeared at last in a high state of intoxication, and more maternal even than on the previous nights. Whenever she had drunk anything she became so amorous as to be absurd. Accordingly, she now insisted on his accompanying her to the Abbaye de Chamont. But he stood out against this; he was afraid of being seen: if he were to be seen driving with her, there would be an atrocious scandal. But she burst into tears, and evinced the noisy despair of a slighted woman. And he thereupon consoled her, and formally promised to be one of the party.

"So you do love me very much," she blurted out. "Say you love me very much. Oh, my darling old bear, if I were to die, would you feel it very much? Confess!"

At The Fondettes, the near neighborhood of Nana had utterly disorganized the party. Every morning, during lunch, good Madame Hugon returned to the subject despite herself, told her guests the news the gardener had brought her, and gave evidence of the absorbing curiosity with which notorious courtesans are able to inspire even the worthiest old ladies. Tolerant though she was, she was revolted and maddened by a vague presentiment of coming ill, which frightened her in the evenings as thoroughly as if a wild beast had escaped from a menagerie and were known to be lurking in the countryside.

She began trying to pick a little quarrel with her guests, whom she each and all accused of prowling round The Mignotte. Count Vandeuvres had been seen laughing on the high road with a golden-haired lady; but he defended himself against the accusation, he denied that it was Nana, the fact being that Lucy had been with him and had told him how she had just turned her third prince out of doors. The Marquis de Chouard used also to go out every day, but his excuse was doctor's orders. Towards Daguenet and Fauchery Madame Hugon behaved unjustly too. The former especially never left The Fondettes, for he had given up the idea of renewing the old connection, and was busy paying the most respectful attentions to Estelle. Fauchery also stayed with the Muffat ladies. On one occasion only he had met Mignon with an armful of flowers, putting his sons through a course of botanical instruction in a by-path. The two men had shaken hands, and given each other the news about Rose. She was perfectly well and happy: they had both received a letter from her that morning, in which she besought them to profit by the fresh country air for some days longer. Among all her guests the old lady spared only Count Muffat and Georges. The Count, who said he had serious business in Orleans, could certainly not be running after the bad woman, and as to Georges, the poor child was at last causing her grave anxiety, seeing that every evening he was seized with atrocious sick headaches which kept him to his bed in broad daylight.

Meanwhile, Fauchery had become the Countess Sabine's faithful attendant in the absence, during each afternoon, of

Count Muffat. Whenever they went to the end of the park, he carried her camp-stool and her sunshade. Besides, he amused her with the original witticisms peculiar to a second-rate journalist, and in so doing he prompted her to one of those sudden intimacies which are allowable in the country. She had apparently consented to it from the first, for she had grown quite a girl again in the society of a young man whose noisy humor seemed unlikely to compromise her. But now and again, when for a second or two they found themselves alone behind the shrubs, their eyes would meet, they would pause amid their laughter, grow suddenly serious, and view one another darkly, as though they had fathomed and divined their inmost hearts.

On Friday a fresh place had to be laid at lunch-time. Monsieur Théophile Venot, whom Madame Hugon remembered to have invited at the Muffats' last winter, had just arrived. He sat stooping humbly forward, and behaved with much good nature, as became a man of no account, nor did he seem to notice the anxious deference with which he was treated. When he had succeeded in getting the company to forget his presence, he sat nibbling small lumps of sugar during dessert, looking sharply up at Daguenet as the latter handed Estelle strawberries, and listening to Fauchery, who was making the Countess very merry over one of his anecdotes. Whenever any one looked at *him*, he smiled in his quiet way. When the guests rose from table, he took the Count's arm, and drew him into the park. He was known to have exercised great influence over the latter ever since the death of his mother. Indeed, singular stories were told about the kind of dominion which the ex-lawyer enjoyed in that household. Fauchery, whom his arrival doubtless embarrassed, began explaining to Georges and Daguenet the origin of the man's wealth. It was a big lawsuit, with the management of which the Jesuits had entrusted him in days gone by. In his opinion, the worthy man was a terrible fellow, despite his gentle plump face, and at this time of day had his finger in all the intrigues of the priesthood. The two young men had begun joking at this, for they thought the little old gentleman had an idiotic expression. The idea of an unknown Venot, a gigantic Venot, acting for the whole body of the clergy, struck them in the light of a comical invention. But they were silenced when, still leaning on the old man's arm, Count Muffat reappeared with blanched cheeks and eyes reddened as if by recent weeping.

"I bet they've been chatting about hell," muttered Fauchery, in a bantering tone.

The Countess Sabine overheard the remark. She turned her head slowly, and their eyes met in that long gaze with which they were accustomed to sound one another prudently before venturing once for all.

After the breakfast it was the guests' custom to betake themselves to a little flower-garden on a terrace overlooking the plain. This Sunday afternoon was exquisitely mild. There had been signs of rain towards ten in the morning, but the sky, without ceasing to be covered, had, as it were, melted into milky fog, which now hung like a cloud of luminous dust in the golden sunlight. Soon Madame Hugon proposed that they should step down through a little doorway below the terrace, and take a walk on foot in the direction of Gumières and as far as the Choue. She was fond of walking, and, considering her threescore years, was very active. Besides, all her guests declared that there was no need to drive. So, in a somewhat straggling order, they reached the wooden bridge over the river. Fauchery and Daguenet headed the column with the Muffat ladies, and were followed by the Count and the Marquis, walking on either side of Madame Hugon, whilst Vandeuvres, looking fashionable and out of his element on the high road, marched in the rear, smoking a cigar. Monsieur Venot, now slackening, now hastening his pace, passed smilingly from group to group, as though bent on losing no scrap of conversation.

"To think of poor dear Georges at Orleans!" said Madame Hugon. "He was anxious to consult old Doctor Tavernier, who never goes out now, on the subject of his sick head-aches. Yes, you were not up, as he went off before seven o'clock. But it'll be a change for him all the same."

She broke off, exclaiming,—

"Why, what's making them stop on the bridge?"

The fact was the ladies, and Fauchery and Daguenet, were standing stock-still on the crown of the bridge. They seemed to be hesitating as though some obstacle or other rendered them uneasy, and yet the way lay clear before them.

"Go on!" cried the Count.

They never moved, and seemed to be watching the approach of something, which the rest had not yet observed. Indeed the road wound considerably, and was bordered by a thick screen of poplar trees. Nevertheless, a dull sound began to grow momentarily louder, and soon there was a noise of wheels, mingled with shouts of laughter and the cracking of whips. Then, suddenly, five carriages came into view, driving one behind the other. They were crowded to bursting, and bright with a galaxy of white, blue, and pink costumes.

"What is it?" said Madame Hugon, in some surprise.

Then her instinct told her, and she felt indignant at such an untoward invasion of her road.

"Oh, that woman!" she murmured. "Walk on, pray walk on. Don't appear to notice—"

But it was too late. The five carriages, which were taking Nana and her circle to the ruins of Chamont, rolled on to the narrow wooden bridge. Fauchery, Daguenet, and the Muffat ladies were forced to step backward, whilst Madame Hugon and the others had also to stop in Indian file, along the roadside. It was a superb ride-past! The laughter in the carriages had ceased, and faces were turned with an expression of curiosity. The rival parties took stock of each other amid a silence broken only by the measured trot of the horses. In the first carriage, Maria Blond and Tatan Néné were lolling backwards like a pair of duchesses, their skirts swelling forth over the wheels, and as they passed they cast disdainful glances at the honest women who were walking afoot. Then came Gaga, filling up a whole seat, and half smothering la Faloise beside her, so that little but his small anxious face was visible. Next followed Caroline Héquet with Labordette, Lucy Stewart with Mignon and his boys, and at the close of all Nana in a victoria with Steiner, and on a bracket-seat in front of her, that poor darling Zizi, with his knees jammed against her own.

"It's the last of them, isn't it?" the Countess placidly asked Fauchery, pretending, at the same time, not to recognize Nana.

The wheel of the victoria came near grazing her, but she did not step back. The two women had exchanged a deeply significant glance. It was, in fact, one of those momentary scrutinies which are at once complete and definite. As to the men, they behaved unexceptionably. Fauchery and Daguenet looked icy, and recognized no one. The Marquis, more nervous than they, and afraid of some farcical ebullition on the part of the ladies, had plucked a blade of grass and was rolling it between his fingers. Only Vandeuvres, who had stayed somewhat apart from the rest of the company, winked imperceptibly at Lucy, who smiled at him as she passed.

"Be careful!" Monsieur Venot had whispered, as he stood behind Count Muffat.

The latter in extreme agitation gazed after this illusive vision of Nana, whilst his wife turned slowly round and scrutinized him. Then he cast his eyes on the ground as though to escape the sound of galloping hoofs which were sweeping away both his senses and his heart. He could have cried aloud in his agony, for, seeing Georges among Nana's skirts, he understood it all now. A mere child! He was broken-hearted at the thought that she should have preferred a mere child to him! Steiner was his equal, but that child—!

Madame Hugon, in the mean time, had not at once recognized Georges. Crossing the bridge, he was fain to jump into the river, but Nana's knees restrained him. Then white as a sheet, and icy cold, he sat rigidly up in his place, and looked at no one. It was just possible no one would notice him.

"Oh, my God!" said the old lady, suddenly, "Georges is with her!"

The carriages had passed quite through the uncomfortable crowd of people who recognized and yet gave no sign of recognition. The short critical encounter seemed to have been going on for ages. And now the wheels whirled away the carriage-loads of girls more gayly than ever. Towards the fair open country they went, amid the buffetings of the fresh air of heaven. Bright-colored fabrics fluttered in the wind, and the merry laughter burst forth anew, as the voyagers began jesting and glancing back at the respectable folk halting with looks of annoyance at the roadside. Turning round, Nana could see the walking party hesitating, and then returning the way they had come, without crossing the bridge. Madame Hugon was leaning silently on Count Muffat's arm, and so sad was her look that no one dared comfort her.

"I say, did you see Fauchery, dear?" Nana shouted to Lucy, who was leaning out of the carriage in front. "What a brute he was! He shall pay out for that. And Paul, too, a fellow I've been so kind to! Not a sign! They're polite, *I'm* sure!"

And with that she gave Steiner a terrible dressing, he having ventured to suggest that the gentlemen's attitude had been quite as it should be. So then, they weren't even worth a bow? The first blackguard that came by might insult them? Thanks! He was the right sort, too, he was! It couldn't be better! One ought always to bow to a woman. "Who's the tall one?" asked Lucy at random, shouting through the noise of the wheels.

"It's the Countess Muffat," answered Steiner.

"There now! I suspected as much," said Nana. "Now, my dear fellow, it's all very well her being a Countess, for she's no better than she should be. Yes, yes, she's no better than she should be. You know I've got an eye for such things, I have! And now I know your Countess as well as if I had been at the making of her! I'll bet you that she's the mistress of that viper Fauchery! I tell you she's his mistress! Between women, you guess that sort of thing at once!"

Steiner shrugged his shoulders. Since the previous day his irritation had been hourly increasing. He had received letters which necessitated his leaving the following morning, added to which he did not much appreciate coming down to the country in order to sleep on the drawing-room divan.

"And this poor baby boy!" Nana continued, melting suddenly at sight of Georges's pale face, as he still sat rigid and breathless in front of her.

"D'you think mamma recognized me?" he stammered at last.

"Oh, most surely she did! Why, she cried out! But it's my fault. He didn't want to come with us: I forced him to. Now listen, Zizi, would you like me to write to your mamma? She looks such a kind, decent sort of lady! I'll tell her that I never saw you before, and that it was Steiner who brought you with him for the first time to-day."

"No, no, don't write," said Georges, in great anxiety. "I'll explain it all myself. Besides, if they bother me about it, I shan't go home again."

But he continued plunged in thought, racking his brains for excuses against his return home in the evening. The five carriages were rolling through a flat country, along an interminable straight road bordered by fine trees. The country was bathed in a silvery gray atmosphere. The ladies still continued shouting remarks from carriage to carriage behind the backs of the drivers, who chuckled over their extraordinary fares. Occasionally one of them would rise to her feet to look at the landscape, and, supporting herself on a neighbor's shoulder, would grow extremely excited till a sudden jolt brought her down to the seat again. Caroline Héquet, in the mean time, was having a warm discussion with Labordette. Both of them were agreed that Nana would be selling her country house before three months were out, and Caroline was urging Labordette to buy it back for her for as little as it was likely to fetch. In front of them, la Faloise, who was very amorous, and could not get at Gaga's apoplectic neck, was imprinting kisses on her spine, through her dress, the strained fabric of which was nigh splitting, whilst Amélie, perching stiffly on the bracket-seat, was bidding them be quiet, for she was horrified to be sitting idly by watching her mother being kissed. In the next carriage, Mignon, in order to astonish Lucy, was making his sons recite a fable by La Fontaine. Henri was prodigious at this exercise: he could spout you one without pause or hesitation. But Maria Blond, at the head of the procession, was beginning to feel extremely bored. She was tired of hoaxing that blockhead of a Tatan Néné with a story to the effect that the Parisian dairywomen were wont to fabricate eggs with a mixture of paste and saffron. The distance was too great: were they never going to get to their destination? And the question was transmitted from carriage to carriage, and finally reached Nana, who, after questioning her driver, got up and shouted,—

"We've not got a quarter of an hour more to go. You see that church behind the trees down there."

Then she continued,—

"Do you know, it appears the owner of the Château de

Chamont is an old lady of Napoleon's time? Oh, *she* was a merry one! At least, so Joseph told me, and he heard it from the servants at the bishop's palace. There's no one like it nowadays, and for the matter of that, she's become goody-goody."

"What's her name?" asked Lucy.

"Madame d'Anglars."

"Irma d'Anglars, I knew her!" cried Gaga.

Admiring exclamations burst from the line of carriages, and were borne down the wind, as the horses quickened their trot. Heads were stretched out in Gaga's direction; Maria Blond and Tatan Néné turned round and knelt on the seat, while they leant over the carriage-hood; and the air was full of questions and cutting remarks, tempered by a certain obscure admiration. Gaga had known her! The idea filled them all with respect for that far-off past.

"Dear me, I was young then," continued Gaga. "But never mind, I remember it all: I saw her pass. They said she was disgusting in her own house, but, driving in her carriage, she *was* just smart! And the stunning tales about her! Dirty doings and money flung about like one o'clock! I don't wonder at all that she's got a fine place. Why she used to clean out a man's pockets as soon as look at him. Irma d'Anglars still in the land of the living! Why, my little pets, she must be near ninety."

At this the ladies became suddenly serious. Ninety years old! The deuce, there wasn't one of them, as Lucy loudly declared, who would live to that age. They were all done for. Besides, Nana said she didn't want to make old bones; it wouldn't be amusing. They were drawing near their destination, and the conversation was interrupted by the cracking of whips as the drivers put their horses to their best paces. Yet, amid all the noise, Lucy continued talking, and, suddenly changing the subject, urged Nana to come to town with them all to-morrow. The Exhibition was soon to close,

and the ladies must really return to Paris, where the season
was surpassing their expectations. But Nana was obstinate.
She loathed Paris; she wouldn't set foot there yet!

"Eh, darling, we'll stay?" said she, giving Georges's knees
a squeeze, as though Steiner were of no account.

The carriages had pulled up abruptly, and, in some surprise, the company got out on some waste ground at the bottom of a small hill. With his whip one of the drivers had
to point them out the ruins of the old Abbey of Chamont,
where they lay hidden among trees. It was a great sell! The
ladies voted them silly. Why, they were only a heap of old
stones, with briers growing over them, and part of a tumble-
down tower. It really wasn't worth coming a couple of
leagues to see that! Then the driver pointed out to them
the country-seat, the park of which stretched away from
the Abbey, and he advised them to take a little path and
follow the walls surrounding it. They would thus make the
tour of the place, whilst the carriages would go and await
them in the village square. It was a delightful walk, and
the company agreed to the proposition.

"Lord love me, Irma knows how to take care of herself!"
said Gaga, halting before a gate at the corner of the park
wall abutting on the high road.

All of them stood silently gazing at the enormous bush
which stopped up the gateway. Then, following the little
path, they skirted the park wall, looking up from time to
time to admire the trees, whose lofty branches stretched out
over them and formed a dense vault of greenery. After three
minutes or so they found themselves in front of a second gate.
Through this a wide lawn was visible, over which two venerable oaks cast dark masses of shadow. Three minutes further
on yet another gate afforded them an extensive view of a
great avenue, a perfect corridor of shadow, at the end of
which a bright spot of sunlight gleamed like a star. They
stood in silent, wondering admiration, and then, little by

little, exclamations burst from their lips. They had been trying hard to joke about it all, with a touch of envy at heart, but this decidedly and immeasurably impressed them. What a genius that Irma was! A sight like this gave you a rattling notion of the woman! The trees stretched away and away, and there were endlessly recurrent patches of ivy along the wall, with glimpses of lofty roofs, and screens of poplars interspersed with dense masses of elms and aspens. Was there no end to it, then? The ladies would have liked to catch sight of the mansion-house, for they were weary of circling on and on, weary of seeing nothing but leafy recesses through every opening they came to. They took the rails of the gate in their hands, and pressed their faces against the iron-work. And thus excluded and isolated, a feeling of respect began to overcome them, as they thought of the castle lost to view in surrounding immensity. Soon, being quite unused to walking, they grew tired. And the wall did not leave off; at every turn of the small deserted path the same range of gray stones stretched ahead of them. Some of them began to despair of ever getting to the end of it, and began talking of returning. But the more their long walk fatigued them, the more respectful they became, for at each successive step they were increasingly impressed by the tranquil, lordly dignity of the domain.

"It's getting silly, this is!" said Caroline Héquet, grinding her teeth.

Nana silenced her with a shrug. For some moments past she had been rather pale and extremely serious, and had not spoken a single word. Suddenly the path gave a final turn, the wall ended, and as they came out on the village square, the mansion-house stood before them, on the further side of its grand outer court. All stopped to admire the proud sweep of the wide steps, the twenty frontage windows, the arrangement of the three wings, which were built of brick framed by courses of stone. Henri IV. had erewhile inhabited this historic mansion, and his room, with its great bed hung with Genoa velvet, was still preserved there. Breathless with admiration, Nana gave a little childish sigh.

"Great God!" she whispered very quietly to herself.

But the party were deeply moved when Gaga suddenly announced that Irma herself was standing yonder, in front of the church. She recognized her perfectly. She was as upright as of old, the hoary campaigner, and that despite her age, and she still had those eyes which flashed when she moved in that proud way of hers! Vespers were just over, and, for a second or two, *Madame* stood in the church porch. She was dressed in a dark brown silk, and looked very simple and very tall, her venerable face reminding one of some old marquise who had survived the horrors of the Great Revolution. In her right hand a huge Book of Hours shone in the sunlight, and very slowly, she crossed the square, followed some fifteen paces off by a footman in livery. The church was emptying, and all the inhabitants of Chamont bowed before her with extreme respect. An old man even kissed her hand, and a woman wanted to fall on her knees. Truly this was a potent queen, full of years and honors. She mounted her flight of steps, and vanished from view.

"That's what one attains to when one has methodical habits!" said Mignon, with an air of conviction, looking at his sons and improving the occasion.

Then everybody said his say. Labordette thought her extraordinarily well preserved. Maria Blond let slip a foul expression, and vexed Lucy, who declared that one ought to honor gray hairs. All the women, to sum up, agreed that she was a perfect marvel. Then the company got into their conveyances again. From Chamont all the way to La Mignotte Nana remained silent. She had twice turned round to look back at the house, and now, lulled by the sound of the wheels, she forgot that Steiner was at her side and that Georges was in front of her. A vision had come up out of the twilight, and the great lady seemed still to be sweeping by with all the majesty of a potent queen, full of years and of honors.

That evening Georges re-entered The Fondettes in time for dinner. Nana, who had grown increasingly absent-minded and singular in point of manner, had sent him to ask his mamma's forgiveness. It was his plain duty, she remarked severely, growing suddenly solicitous for the decencies of family life. She even made him swear not to return for the night; she was tired, and, in shewing proper obedience, he was doing no more than his duty. Much bored by this moral discourse, Georges appeared in his mother's presence with heavy heart and downcast head.

Fortunately for him, his brother Philippe, a great merry devil of a military man, had arrived during the day, a fact which greatly curtailed the scene he was dreading. Madame Hugon was content to look at him with eyes full of tears, whilst Philippe, who had been put in possession of the facts, threatened to go and drag him home by the scruff of the neck if ever he went back into that woman's society. Somewhat comforted, Georges began slyly planning how to make his escape towards two o'clock next day in order to arrange about future meetings with Nana.

Nevertheless, at dinner-time, the house party at The Fondettes seemed not a little embarrassed. Vandeuvres had given notice of departure, for he was anxious to take Lucy back to Paris with him. He was amused at the idea of carrying off this girl whom he had known for ten years, yet never desired. The Marquis de Chouard bent over his plate, and meditated on Gaga's young lady. He could well remember dandling Lili on his knee. What a way children had of shooting up! This little thing was becoming extremely plump! But Count Muffat especially was silent and absorbed. His cheeks glowed, and he had given Georges one long look. Dinner over, he went upstairs, intending to shut himself in his bedroom, his

pretext being a slight feverish attack. Monsieur Venot had
rushed after him, and upstairs, in the bedroom, a scene ensued.
The Count threw himself upon the bed, and strove to stifle a
fit of nervous sobbing in the folds of the pillow, whilst Monsieur Venot, in a soft voice, called him brother, and advised
him to implore Heaven for mercy. But he heard nothing:
there was a rattle in his throat. Suddenly he sprang off the
bed, and stammered:

"I am going there. I can't resist any longer."

"Very well," said the old man, "I go with you."

As they left the house, two shadows were vanishing into
the dark depths of a garden walk, for every evening now
Fauchery and the Countess Sabine left Daguenet to help Estelle make tea. Once on the high road the Count walked so
rapidly that his companion had to run in order to follow him.
Though utterly out of breath, the latter never ceased shower-
ing on him the most conclusive arguments against the temp-
tations of the flesh. But the other never opened his mouth as
he hurried away into the night. Arrived in front of The
Mignotte, he said simply,—

"I can't resist any longer. Go!"

"God's will be done, then!" muttered Monsieur Venot.
"He uses every method to assure His final triumph. Your sin
will become His weapon."

At The Mignotte there was much wrangling during the
evening meal. Nina had found a letter from Bordenave
awaiting her, in which he advised rest, just as though he were
anxious to be rid of her. Little Violaine, he said, was being
encored twice nightly. But when Mignon continued urging
her to come away with them on the morrow, Nana grew exasperated, and declared that she did not intend taking advice
from anybody. In other ways, too, her behavior at table
was ridiculously stuck-up. Madame Lerat having made
some sharp little speech or other, she loudly announced that,
God willing, she wasn't going to let any one—no, not even

her own aunt—make improper remarks in her presence.
After which, she dreed her guests with honorable sentiments.
She seemed to be suffering from a fit of stupid right-minded-
ness, and she treated them all to projects of religious education for Louiset and to a complete scheme of regeneration
for herself. When the company began laughing, she gave
vent to profound opinions, nodding her head like a grocer's
wife who knows what she is saying. Nothing but Order
could lead to Fortune! And, so far as she was concerned,
she had no wish to die like a beggar! She set the ladies' teeth
on edge. They burst out in protest. Could any one have
been converting Nana? No, it was impossible! But she sat
quite still, and with absent looks once more plunged into
dreamland, where the vision of an extremely-wealthy and
greatly-courted Nana rose up before her.

The household were going upstairs to bed when Muffat put
in an appearance. It was Labordette who caught sight of
him in the garden. He understood it all at once, and did
him a service, for he got Steiner out of the way, and, taking
his hand, led him along the dark corridor as far as Nana's
bedroom. In affairs of this kind, Labordette was wont to
display the most perfect tact and cleverness. Indeed he
seemed delighted to be making other people happy. Nana
shewed no surprise: she was only somewhat annoyed by the
excessive heat of Muffat's pursuit. Life was a serious affair,
was it not? Love was too silly: it led to nothing. Besides,
she had her scruples in view of Zizi's tender age. Indeed, she
had scarcely behaved quite fairly towards him. Dear me,
yes, she was choosing the proper course again in taking up
with an old fellow.

"Zoé," said she to the lady's maid, who was enchanted at
the thought of leaving the country, "pack the trunks when
you get up to-morrow. We are going back to Paris."

And she went to bed with Muffat, but experienced no
pleasure.

CHAPTER VII

ONE December evening, three months afterwards, Count
Muffat was strolling in the Passage des Panoramas.
The evening was very mild, and owing to a passing shower
the passage had just become crowded with people. There
was a perfect mob of them, and they thronged slowly and
laboriously along between the shops on either side. Under
the windows, white with reflected light, the pavement was
violently illuminated. A perfect stream of brilliancy emanated from white globes, red lanterns, blue transparencies, lines
of gas-jets, gigantic watches and fans, outlined in flame and
burning in the open. And the motley displays in the shops,
the gold ornaments of the jewelers, the glass ornaments of
the confectioners, the light-colored silks of the modistes,
seemed to shine again in the crude light of the reflectors
behind the clear plate-glass windows; whilst, among the
bright-colored disorderly array of shop-signs, a huge purple
glove loomed in the distance, like a bleeding hand which had
been severed from an arm and fastened to a yellow cuff.

Count Muffat had slowly returned as far as the boulevard.
He glanced out at the roadway, and then came sauntering
back along the shop-windows. The damp and heated atmosphere filled the narrow passage with a slight luminous
mist. Along the flagstones, which had been wetted by the
drip-drip of umbrellas, the footsteps of the crowd rang continually, but there was no sound of voices. Passers-by el-
bowed him at every turn, and cast enquiring looks at his
silent face, which the gaslight rendered pale. And to escape
these curious manifestations the Count posted himself in front
of a stationer's, where with profound attention he contemplated an array of paper-weights in the form of glass bowls
containing floating landscapes and flowers.

He was conscious of nothing: he was thinking of Nana.

Why had she lied to him again? That morning she had written and told him not to trouble about her in the evening, her excuse being that Louiset was ill, and that she was going to pass the night at her aunt's in order to nurse him. But he had felt suspicious, and had called at her house, where he learnt from the porter that *Madame* had just gone off to her theater. He was astonished at this, for she was not playing in the new piece. Why then should she have told him this falsehood, and what could she be doing at the Variétés that evening? Hustled by a passer-by, the Count unconsciously left the paper-weights, and found himself in front of a glass case full of toys, where he grew absorbed over an array of pocket-books and cigar-cases, all of which had the same blue swallow stamped on one corner. Nana was most certainly not the same woman! In the early days after his return from the country, she used to drive him wild with delight, as with pussy-cat caresses she kissed him all round his face and whiskers, and vowed that he was her own dear pet and the only little man she adored. He was no longer afraid of Georges, whom his mother kept down at The Fondettes. There was only fat Steiner to reckon with, and he believed he was really ousting him, but he did not dare provoke an explanation on his score. He knew he was once more in an extraordinary financial scrape, and on the verge of being declared bankrupt on 'Change, so much so that he was clinging fiercely to the shareholders in the Landes Salt Pits, and striving to sweat a final subscription out of them. Whenever he met him at Nana's, she would explain, reasonably enough, that she did not wish to turn him out of doors like a dog, after all he had spent on her. Besides, for the last three months, he had been living in such a whirl of sensual excitement, that, beyond the need of possessing her, he had felt no very distinct impressions. His was a tardy awakening of the fleshly instinct, a childish greed of enjoyment, which left no room for either vanity or jealousy. Only one definite feeling could affect him now, and that was Nana's decreasing kindness. She no longer kissed him on the beard! It made him anxious; and as became a man quite ignorant of womankind, he began asking himself what possible cause of offense he could have given her. Besides. he was under the impression that he was satisfying all her desires. And so he harked back again and again to the letter he had received that morning with its tissue of falsehoods, invented for the extremely simple purpose of passing an evening at her own theater. The crowd had pushed him forward again, and he had crossed the passage and was puzzling his brain in front of the entrance to a restaurant, his eyes fixed on some plucked larks and on a huge salmon laid out inside the window.

At length he seemed to tear himself away from this spectacle. He shook himself, looked up, and noticed that it was close on nine o'clock. Nana would soon be coming out, and he would make her tell the truth. And with that he walked on, and recalled to memory the evenings he once passed in that region in the days when he used to meet her at the door of the theater.

He knew all the shops, and in the gas-laden air he recognized their different scents, such, for instance, as the strong savour of Russia leather, the perfume of vanilla emanating from a chocolate-dealer's basement, the savor of musk blown in whiffs from the open doors of the perfumers. But he did not dare linger under the gaze of the pale shop-women, who looked placidly at him as though they knew him by sight. For one instant he seemed to be studying the line of little round windows above the shops, as though he had never noticed them before among the medley of signs. Then, once again, he went up to the boulevard, and stood still a minute or two. A fine rain was now falling, and the cold feel of it on his hands calmed him. He thought of his wife who was staying in a country house near Mâcon, where her friend Madame de Chezelles had been ailing a good deal since the autumn.

The carriages in the roadway were rolling through a stream
of mud. The country, he thought, must be detestable in
such vile weather. But suddenly he became anxious and re-
entered the hot, close passage, down which he strode among
the strolling people. A thought had struck him: if Nana
were suspicious of his presence there, she would be off along
the Galerie Montmartre.

After that, the Count kept a sharp look-out at the very
door of the theater, though he did not like this passage-end,
where he was afraid of being recognized. It was at the corner
between the Galerie des Variétés and the Galerie Saint-Marc,
an equivocal corner full of obscure little shops. Of these
last one was a shoemaker's, where customers never seemed to
enter. Then there were two or three upholsterers', deep in
dust, and a smoky, sleepy reading-room and library, the
shaded lamps in which cast a green and slumbrous light all
the evening through. There was never any one in this corner
save well-dressed, patient gentlemen, who prowled about the
wreckage peculiar to a stage-door, where drunken scene-
shifters and ragged chorus-girls congregate. In front of the
theater, a single gas-jet, in a ground-glass globe, lit up the
doorway. For a moment or two Muffat thought of questioning Madame Bron; then he grew afraid lest Nana should
get wind of his presence and escape by way of the boulevard.
So he went on the march again, and determined to wait till
he was turned out at the closing of the gates, an event which
had happened on two previous occasions. The thought of returning home to his solitary bed simply wrung his heart with
anguish. Every time that golden-haired girls and men in
dirty linen came out and stared at him, he returned to his
post in front of the reading-room, where, looking in between
two advertisements posted on a window-pane, he was always
greeted by the same sight. It was a little old man, sitting
stiff and solitary at the vast table, and holding a green newspaper in his green hands under the green light of one of the

lamps. But shortly before ten o'clock, another gentleman, a
tall, good-looking, fair man, with well-fitting gloves, was
also walking up and down in front of the stage-door. Thereupon, at each successive turn, the pair treated each other to
a suspicious sidelong glance. The Count walked to the corner
of the two galleries, which was adorned with a high mirror,
and when he saw himself therein, looking grave and elegant,
he was both ashamed and nervous.

Ten o'clock struck, and suddenly it occurred to Muffat that
it would be very easy to find out whether Nana were in her
dressing-room or not. He went up the three steps, crossed
the little yellow-painted lobby, and slipped into the court by
a door which simply shut with a latch. At that hour of the
night, the narrow damp well of a court, with its pestiferous
water-closets, its fountain, its back view of the kitchen stove,
and the collection of plants with which the portress used
to litter the place, was drenched in dark mist; but the two
walls, rising pierced with windows on either hand, were flaming with light, since the property room and the firemen's office were situated on the ground floor, with the managerial
bureau on the left, and on the right and upstairs the dressing-
rooms of the company. The mouths of furnaces seemed to
be opening on the outer darkness from top to bottom of this
well. The Count had at once marked the light in the windows of the dressing-room on the first floor; and, as a man
who is comforted and happy, he forgot where he was, and
stood gazing upward amid the foul mud and faint decaying
smell peculiar to the premises of this antiquated Parisian
building. Big drops were dripping from a broken water-
spout, and a ray of gaslight slipped from Madame Bron's
window, and cast a yellow glare over a patch of moss-clad
pavement, over the base of a wall which had been rotted by
water from a sink, over a whole cornerful of nameless filth
amid which old pails and broken crocks lay in fine confusion

round a spindling tree, growing mildewed in its pot. A window-fastening creaked, and the Count fled.

Nana was certainly going to come down. He returned to his post in front of the reading-room; among its slumbering shadows, which seemed only broken by the glimmer of a night-light, the little old man still sat motionless, his side-face sharply outlined against his newspaper. Then Muffat walked again, and this time took a more prolonged turn, and, crossing the large gallery, followed the Galerie des Variétés as far as that of Feydeau. The last-mentioned was cold and deserted, and buried in melancholy shadow. He returned from it, passed by the theater, turned the corner of the Galerie Saint-Marc, and ventured as far as the Galerie Montmartre, where a sugar-chopping machine in front of a grocer's interested him a while. But when he was taking his third turn, he was seized with such dread lest Nana should escape behind his back that he lost all self-respect. Thereupon he stationed himself beside the fair gentleman, in front of the very theater. Both exchanged a glance of fraternal humility, with which was mingled a touch of distrust, for it was possible they might yet turn out to be rivals. Some scene-shifters, who came out smoking their pipes between the acts, brushed rudely against them, but neither one nor the other ventured to complain. Three big wenches with untidy hair and dirty gowns appeared on the doorstep. They were munching apples and spitting out the cores, but the two men bowed their heads, and patiently braved their impudent looks and rough speeches, though they were hustled, and as it were soiled, by these trollops, who amused themselves by pushing each other down upon them.

At that very moment Nana descended the three steps. She grew very pale when she noticed Muffat.

"Oh, it's you!" she stammered.

The sniggering extra ladies were quite frightened when they recognized her, and they formed in line, and stood up looking as stiff and serious as servants whom their mistress has caught behaving badly. The tall fair gentleman had moved away; he was at once reassured and sad at heart.

"Well, give me your arm," Nana continued impatiently.

They walked quietly off. The Count had been getting ready to question her, and now found nothing to say.

It was she who in rapid tones told a story to the effect that she had been at her aunt's as late as eight o'clock, when, seeing Louiset very much better, she had conceived the idea of going down to the theater for a few minutes.

"On some important business?" he queried.

"Yes, a new piece," she replied, after some slight hesitation. "They wanted my advice."

He knew that she was not speaking the truth, but the warm touch of her arm, as it leant firmly on his own, left him powerless. He felt neither anger nor rancor after his long, long wait: his one thought was to keep her where she was now that he had got hold of her. To-morrow, and not before, he would try and find out what she had come to her dressing-room after. But Nana still appeared to hesitate: she was manifestly a prey to the sort of secret anguish that besets people when they are trying to regain lost ground and to initiate a plan of action. Accordingly, as they turned the corner of the Galerie des Variétés, she stopped in front of the show in a fan-seller's window.

"I say, that's pretty," she whispered; "I mean that mother-of-pearl mount with the feathers."

Then, indifferently,—

"So you're seeing me home?"

"Of course," said he, with some surprise, "since your child's better."

She was sorry she had told him that story. Perhaps Louiset was passing through another crisis! She talked of returning to the Batignolles. But when he offered to accompany her she did not insist on going. For a second or two she was possessed with the kind of white-hot fury which a woman experiences when she feels herself entrapped and must nevertheless behave prettily. But in the end she grew resigned, and determined to gain time. If only she could get rid of the Count towards midnight, everything would happen as she wished.

"Yes, it's true, you're a bachelor to-night," she murmured. "Your wife doesn't return till to-morrow, eh?"

"Yes," replied Muffat. It embarrassed him somewhat to hear her talking familiarly about the Countess.

But she pressed him further, asking at what time the train was due, and wanting to know whether he were going to the station to meet her. She had begun to walk more slowly than ever, as though the shops interested her very much.

"Now do look!" said she, pausing anew before a jeweler's window, "what a funny bracelet!"

She adored the Passage des Panoramas. The tinsel of the *article de Paris*, the false jewelry, the gilded zinc, the cardboard made to look like leather, had been the passion of her early youth. It remained, and when she passed the shop-windows she could not tear herself away from them. It was the same with her to-day as when she was a ragged, slouching child, who fell into reveries in front of the chocolate-maker's sweet-stuff shows, or stood listening to a musical box in a neighboring shop, or fell into supreme ecstasies over cheap, vulgarly-designed knick-knacks, such as nutshell work-boxes, rag-pickers' baskets for holding toothpicks, Vendôme Columns and Luxor Obelisks on which thermometers were mounted. But that evening she was too much agitated, and looked at things without seeing them. When all was said and done, it bored her to think she was not free. An obscure revolt raged within her, and amid it all she felt a wild desire to do something foolish. It was a great thing gained, forsooth, to be mistress of men of position! She had been devouring the Prince's substance, and Steiner's, too, with her childish caprices, and yet she had no notion where her money went. Even, at this time of day, her flat in the Boulevard Haussmann was not entirely furnished. The drawing-room alone was finished, and with its red satin upholsteries and excess of ornamentation and furniture it struck a decidedly false note. Her creditors, moreover, would now take to tormenting her more than ever before whenever she had no money in hand, a fact which caused her constant surprise, seeing that she was wont to quote herself as a model of economy. For a month past that thief Steiner had been scarcely able to pay up his thousand francs on the occasions when she threatened to kick him out of doors in case he failed to bring them. As to Muffat, he was an idiot: he had no notion as to what it was usual to give, and she could not therefore grow angry with him on the score of miserliness. Oh, how gladly she would have turned all these folks off, had she not repeated to herself, a score of times daily, a whole string of economical maxims!

One ought to be sensible, Zoé kept saying every morning, and Nana herself was constantly haunted by the queenly vision seen at Chamont. It had now become an almost religious memory with her, and through dint of being ceaselessly recalled it grew even more grandiose. And for these reasons, though trembling with repressed indignation, she now hung submissively on the Count's arm as they went from window to window among the fast-diminishing crowd. The pavement was drying outside, and a cool wind blew along the gallery, swept the close hot air up beneath the glass that imprisoned it, and shook the colored lanterns, and the lines of gas-jets, and the giant fan which was flaring away like a set piece in an illumination. At the door of the restaurant a waiter was putting out the gas, while the motionless attendants in the empty glaring shops looked as though they had dropped off to sleep with their eyes open.

"Oh, what a duck!" continued Nana, retracing her steps

as far as the last of the shops in order to go into ecstasies over a porcelain greyhound, standing with raised fore paw in front of a nest hidden among roses.

At length they quitted the passage, but she refused the offer of a cab. It was very pleasant out, she said; besides, they were in no hurry, and it would be charming to return home on foot. When they were in front of the Café Anglais she had a sudden longing to eat oysters. Indeed, she said that owing to Louiset's illness she had tasted nothing since morning. Muffat dared not oppose her. Yet, as he did not in those days wish to be seen about with her, he asked for a private supper-room, and hurried to it along the corridors. She followed him with the air of a woman familiar with the house, and they were on the point of entering a private room, the door of which a waiter held open, when from a neighboring saloon, whence issued a perfect tempest of shouts and laughter, a man rapidly emerged. It was Daguenet.

"By Jove, it's Nana!" cried he.

The Count had briskly disappeared into the private room, leaving the door ajar behind him. But Daguenet winked behind his round shoulders, and added in chaffing tones,—

"The deuce, but you're doing nicely! You catch 'em in the Tuileries nowadays!"

Nana smiled and laid a finger on her lips to beg him to be silent. She could see he was very much exalted, and yet she was glad to have met him, for she still felt tenderly towards him, and that despite the nasty way he had cut her when in the company of fashionable ladies.

"What are you doing now?" she asked amicably.

"Becoming respectable. Yes, indeed, I'm thinking of getting married."

She shrugged her shoulders with a pitying air. But he jokingly continued to the effect that to be only just gaining enough on 'Change to buy ladies bouquets could scarcely be called an income, provided you wanted to look respectable

too! His three hundred thousand francs had only lasted him
eighteen months! He wanted to be practical, and he was
going to marry a girl with a huge dowry, and end off as a
préfet, like his father before him! Nana still smiled in-
credulously. She nodded in the direction of the saloon:
"Who are you with in there?"

"Oh! a whole gang," said he, forgetting all about his
projects under the influence of returning intoxication. "Just
think! Léa is telling us about her trip in Egypt. Oh, it's
screaming! There's a bathing story—"

And he told the story, while Nana lingered complaisantly.
They had ended by leaning up against the wall in the corridor, facing one another. Gas-jets were flaring under the
low ceiling, and a vague smell of cookery hung about the
folds of the hangings. Now and again, in order to hear
each other's voices, when the din in the saloon became louder
than ever, they had to lean well forward. Every few seconds, however, a waiter with an armful of dishes found his
passage barred, and disturbed them. But they did not cease
their talk for that; on the contrary, they stood close up to
the walls, and, amid the uproar of the supper-party and the
jostlings of the waiters, chatted as quietly as if they were
by their own firesides.

"Just look at that," whispered the young man, pointing to
the door of the private room, through which Muffat had
vanished.

Both looked. The door was quivering slightly; a breath of
air seemed to be disturbing it, and at last, very, very slowly,
and without the least sound, it was shut-to. They exchanged
a silent chuckle. The Count must be looking charmingly
happy, all alone in there!

"By-the-by," she asked, "have you read Fauchery's article
about me?"

"Yes, 'The Golden Fly,'" replied Daguenet; "I didn't
mention it to you, as I was afraid of paining you."

"Paining me—why? His article's a very long one."

She was flattered to think that the *Figaro* should concern itself about her person. But failing the explanations of her hairdresser Francis, who had brought her the paper, she would not have understood that it was she who was in question. Daguenet scrutinized her slyly, sneering in his chaffing way. Well, well, since she was pleased, everybody else ought to be.

"By your leave!" shouted a waiter, holding a dish of iced cheese in both hands, as he separated them.

Nana had stepped towards the little saloon, where Muffat was waiting.

"Well, good-by!" continued Daguenet. "Go and find your cuckold again."

But she halted afresh.

"Why d'you call him cuckold?"

"Because he is a cuckold, by Jove!"

She came and leaned against the wall again; she was profoundly interested.

"Ah!" said she, simply.

"What, d'you mean to say you didn't know that? Why, my dear girl, his wife's Fauchery's mistress. It probably began in the country. Some time ago, when I was coming here, Fauchery left me, and I suspect he's got an assignation with her at his place to-night. They've made up a story about a journey, I fancy."

Overcome with surprise, Nana remained voiceless.

"I suspected it," said she at last, slapping her leg. "I guessed it by merely looking at her on the high road that day. To think of its being possible for an honest woman to deceive her husband, and with that blackguard Fauchery too! He'll teach her some pretty things!"

"Oh, it isn't her trial trip," muttered Daguenet, wickedly. "Perhaps she knows as much about it as he does."

At this Nana gave vent to an indignant exclamation.

"Indeed she does! What a nice world! It's too foul!"

"By your leave!" shouted a waiter, laden with bottles, as he separated them.

Daguenet drew her forward again, and held her hand for a second or two. He adopted his crystalline tone of voice, the voice with notes as sweet as those of a harmonica, which had gained him his success among the ladies of Nana's type.

"Good-by, darling! You know I love you always."

She disengaged her hand from his, and while a thunder of shouts and bravos, which made the door in the saloon tremble again, almost drowned her words, she smiling remarked,—

"It's over between us, stupid! But that doesn't matter. Do come up one of these days, and we'll have a chat."

Then she became serious again, and in the outraged tones of a respectable woman,—

"So he's a cuckold, is he?" she cried. "Well, that *is* a nuisance, dear boy. They've always sickened me, cuckolds have."

When at length she went into the private room she noticed that Muffat was sitting resignedly on a narrow divan with pale face and twitching hands. He did not reproach her at all, and she, greatly moved, was divided between feelings of pity and of contempt. The poor man! To think of his being so unworthily cheated by a vile wife! She had a good mind to throw her arms round his neck and comfort him. But it was only fair all the same! He was a fool with women, and this would teach him a lesson! Nevertheless, pity overcame her. She did not get rid of him as she had determined to do after the oysters had been discussed. They scarcely stayed a quarter of an hour in the Café Anglais, and together they went into the house in the Boulevard Haussmann. It was then eleven. Before midnight she would easily have discovered some means of getting rid of him kindly.

In the ante-room, however, she took the precaution of giving Zoé an order.

"You'll look out for him, and you'll tell him not to make a noise if the other man's still with me."

"But where shall I put him, *Madame?*"

"Keep him in the kitchen. It's more safe."

In the room inside, Muffat was already taking off his overcoat. A big fire was burning on the hearth. It was the same room as of old, with its rose-wood furniture and its hangings and chair coverings of figured damask with the large blue flowers on a gray background. On two occasions Nana had though of having it re-done, the first in black velvet, the second in white satin, with bows; but directly Steiner consented, she demanded the money that these changes would cost simply with a view to pillaging him. She had, indeed, only indulged in a tiger-skin rug for the hearth and a cut-glass hanging-lamp.

"I'm not sleepy: I'm not going to bed," said she, the moment they were shut in together.

The Count obeyed her submissively as became a man no longer afraid of being seen. His one care now was to avoid vexing her.

"As you will," he murmured.

Nevertheless, he took his boots off, too, before seating himself in front of the fire. One of Nana's pleasures consisted in undressing herself in front of the mirror on her wardrobe door, which reflected her whole height. She would let everything slip off her in turn, and then would stand perfectly naked, and gaze and gaze in complete oblivion of all around her. Passion for her own body, ecstasy over her satin skin and the supple contours of her shape, would keep her serious, attentive, and absorbed in the love of herself. The hair-dresser frequently found her standing thus, and would enter without her once turning to look at him. Muffat used to grow angry then, but he only succeeded in astonishing her. What was coming over the man? She was doing it to please herself, not other people.

That particular evening, she wanted to have a better view of herself, and she lit the six candles attached to the frame of the mirror. But while letting her shift slip down, she paused. She had been preoccupied for some moments past, and a question was on her lips.

"You haven't read the *Figaro* article, have you? The paper's on the table."

Daguenet's laugh had recurred to her recollection, and she was harassed by a doubt. If that Fauchery had slandered her, she would be revenged.

"They say that it's about me," she continued, affecting indifference. "What's your notion, eh, darling?"

And letting go her shift, and waiting till Muffat should have done reading, she stood naked. Muffat was reading slowly Fauchery's article, entitled "The Golden Fly," describing the life of a harlot, descended from four or five generations of drunkards, and tainted in her blood by a cumulative inheritance of misery and drink, which in her case has taken the form of a nervous exaggeration of the sexual instinct. She has shot up to womanhood in the slums and on the pavements of Paris and tall, handsome, and as superbly grown as a dung-hill plant, she avenges the beggars and outcasts of whom she is the ultimate product. With her the rottenness that is allowed to ferment among the populace is carried upwards and rots the aristocracy. She becomes a blind power of nature, a leaven of destruction, and unwittingly she corrupts and disorganizes all Paris, churning it between her snow-white thighs as milk is monthly churned by housewives. And it was at the end of this article that the comparison with a fly occurred, a fly of sunny hue, which has flown up out of the dung, a fly which sucks in death on the carrion tolerated by the roadside, and then buzzing, dancing, and glittering like a precious stone, enters the windows of palaces and poisons the men within by merely settling on them in her flight.

Muffat lifted his head; his eyes stared fixedly; he gazed at the fire.

"Well?" asked Nana.

But he did not answer. It seemed as though he wanted to read the article again. A cold shivering feeling was creeping from his scalp to his shoulders. This article had been written anyhow. The phrases were wildly extravagant, the unexpected epigrams and quaint collocations of words went beyond all bounds. Yet, notwithstanding this, he was struck by what he had read, for it had rudely awakened within him much that for months past he had not cared to think about.

He looked up. Nana had grown absorbed in her ecstatic self-contemplation. She was bending her neck and was looking attentively in the mirror at a little brown mark above her right haunch. She was touching it with the tip of her finger, and by dint of bending backward was making it stand out more clearly than ever. Situated where it was, it doubtless struck her as both quaint and pretty. After that she studied other parts of her body with an amused expression, and much of the vicious curiosity of a child. The sight of herself always astonished her, and she would look as surprised and ecstatic as a young girl who has discovered her puberty. Slowly, slowly she spread out her arms in order to give full value to her figure, which suggested the torso of a plump Venus. She bent herself this way and that, and examined herself before and behind, stopping to look at the side-view of her bosom and at the sweeping contours of her thighs. And she ended with a strange amusement, which consisted of swinging to right and left, her knees apart, and her body swaying from the waist with the perpetual jogging, twitching movements peculiar to an Oriental dancer in the *danse du ventre*.

Muffat sat looking at her. She frightened him. The newspaper had dropped from his hand. For a moment he saw her as she was, and he despised himself. Yes, it was just that;

she had corrupted his life, he already felt himself tainted to his very marrow by impurities hitherto undreamt of. Everything was now destined to rot within him, and in the twinkling of an eye he understood what this evil entailed. He saw the ruin brought about by this kind of "leaven"— himself poisoned, his family destroyed, a bit of the social fabric cracking and crumbling. And, unable to take his eyes from the sight, he sat looking fixedly at her, striving to inspire himself with loathing for her nakedness.

Nana no longer moved. With an arm behind her neck, one hand clasped in the other, and her elbows far apart, she was throwing back her head, so that he could see a fore-shortened reflection of her half-closed eyes, her parted lips, her face clothed with amorous laughter. Her masses of yellow hair were unknotted behind, and they covered her back with the fell of a lioness.

Bending back thus, she displayed her solid Amazonian waist and firm bosom, where strong muscles moved under the satin texture of the skin. A delicate line, to which the shoulder and the thigh added their slight undulations, ran from one of her elbows to her foot, and Muffat's eyes followed this tender profile, and marked how the outlines of the fair flesh vanished in golden gleams, and how its rounded contours shone like silk in the candle-light. He thought of his old dread of Woman, of the Beast of the Scriptures, at once lewd and wild. Nana was all covered with fine hair, a russet down made her body velvety; whilst the Beast was apparent in the almost equine development of her flanks, in the fleshy exuberances and deep hollows of her body, which lent her sex the mystery and suggestiveness lurking in their shadows. She was, indeed, that Golden Creature, blind as brute force, whose very odor ruined the world. Muffat gazed and gazed as a man possessed, till, at last, when he had shut his eyes in order to escape it, the Brute reappeared in the darkness of the brain, larger, more terrible, more suggestive in its attitude. Now, he understood, it would remain before his eyes, in his very flesh, forever.

But Nana was gathering herself together. A little thrill of tenderness seemed to have traversed her members. Her eyes were moist; she tried, as it were, to make herself small, as though she could feel herself better thus. Then she threw her head and bosom back, and melting, as it were, in one great bodily caress, she rubbed her cheeks coaxingly first against one shoulder then against the other. Her lustful mouth breathed desire over her limbs. She put out her lips, kissed herself long and long in the neighborhood of her armpit, and laughed at the other Nana who, also, was kissing herself in the mirror.

Then Muffat gave a long sigh. This solitary pleasure exasperated him. Suddenly all his resolutions were swept away as though by a mighty wind. In a fit of brutal passion he caught Nana to his breast and threw her down on the carpet.

"Leave me alone!" she cried. "You're hurting me!"

He was conscious of his undoing; he recognized in her stupidity, vileness, and falsehood, and he longed to possess her, poisoned though she was.

"Oh, you're a fool!" said she savagely, when he let her get up.

Nevertheless, she grew calm. He would go now. She slipped on a night-gown, trimmed with lace, and came and sat down on the floor in front of the fire. It was her favorite position. When she again questioned him about Fauchery's article, Muffat replied vaguely, for he wanted to avoid a scene. Besides, she declared that she had found a weak spot in Fauchery. And with that she relapsed into a long silence, and reflected on how to dismiss the Count. She would have liked to do it in an agreeable way, for she was still a good-natured wench, and it bored her to cause others pain, especially in the present instance where the man was a cuckold.

The mere thought of his being that had ended by rousing her sympathies!

"So you expect your wife to-morrow morning?" said she at last.

Muffat had stretched himself in an arm-chair. He looked drowsy, and his limbs were tired. He gave a sign of assent. Nana sat gazing seriously at him, with a dull tumult in her brain. Propped on one leg, among her slightly-rumpled laces, she was holding one of her bare feet between her hands, and was turning it mechanically about and about.

"Have you been married long?" she asked.

"Nineteen years," replied the Count.

"Ah! And is your wife amiable? Do you get on comfortably together?"

He was silent. Then, with some embarrassment,—

"You know I've begged you never to talk of those matters."

"Dear me, why's that?" she cried, beginning to grow vexed directly. "I'm sure I won't eat your wife if I *do* talk about her. Dear boy, why every woman's worth—"

But she stopped for fear of saying too much. She contented herself by assuming a superior expression, since she considered herself extremely kind. The poor fellow, he needed delicate handling! Besides, she had been struck by a laughable notion, and she smiled as she looked him carefully over.

"I say," she continued, "I haven't told you the story about you that Fauchery's circulating. There's a viper, if you like! I don't bear him any ill-will, because his article may be all right, but he's a regular viper all the same."

And laughing more gayly than ever, she let go her foot, and, crawling along the floor, came and propped herself against the Count's knees.

"Now just fancy, he swears you were still like a babe

when you married your wife. You were still like that, eh? Is it true, eh?"

Her eyes pressed for an answer, and she raised her hands to his shoulders, and began shaking him in order to extract the desired confession.

"Without doubt," he at last made answer gravely.

Thereupon she again sank down at his feet. She was shaking with uproarious laughter, and she stuttered, and dealt him little slaps.

"No, it's too funny! There's no one like you; you're a marvel. But, my poor pet, you must just have been stupid! When a man doesn't know, oh, it is so comical! Good heavens, I should have liked to have seen you! And it came off well, did it? Now tell me something about it! Oh, do, do tell me!"

She overwhelmed him with questions, forgetting nothing, and requiring the veriest details. And she laughed such sudden merry peals, which doubled her up with mirth, and her chemise slipped and got turned down to such an extent, and her skin looked so golden in the light of the big fire that, little by little, the Count described to her his bridal night. He no longer felt at all awkward. He himself began to be amused at last as he spoke. Only he kept choosing his phrases, for he still had a certain sense of modesty. The young woman, now thoroughly interested, asked him about the Countess. According to his account she had a marvelous figure, but was a regular iceberg for all that.

"Oh! get along with you!" he muttered, indolently. "You have no cause to be jealous."

Nana had ceased laughing, and she now resumed her former position, and, with her back to the fire, brought her knees up under her chin with her clasped hands. Then, in a serious tone, she declared,—

"It doesn't pay, dear boy, to look like a ninny with one's wife the first night."

"Why?" queried the astonished Count.

"Because," she replied, slowly, assuming a doctorial expression.

And with that she looked as if she were delivering a lecture, and shook her head at him. In the end, however, she condescended to explain herself more lucidly.

"Well, look here! I know how it all happens. Yes, dearie, women don't like a man to be foolish. They don't say anything, because there's such a thing as modesty, you know, but you may be sure they think about it for a jolly long time to come. And sooner or later, when a man's been an ignoramus, they go and make other arrangements. That's it, my pet."

He did not seem to understand. Whereupon she grew more definite still. She became maternal, and taught him his lesson out of sheer goodness of heart, as a friend might do. Since she had discovered him to be a cuckold, the information had weighed on her spirits; she was madly anxious to discuss his position with him.

"Good heavens! I'm talking of things that don't concern me. I've said what I have because everybody ought to be happy. We're having a chat, eh? Well, then, you're to answer me as straight as you can."

But she stopped to change her position, for she was burning herself.

"It's jolly hot, eh? My back's roasted. Wait a second, I'll cook my tummy a bit. That's what's good for the aches!"

And when she had turned round with her breast to the fire, and her feet tucked under her,—

"Let me see," she said, "you don't sleep with your wife any longer?"

"No, I swear to you I don't," said Muffat, dreading a scene.

"And you believe she's really a stick?"

He bowed his head in the affirmative.

"And that's why you love me? Answer me! I shan't be angry."

He repeated the same movement.

"Very well then," she concluded. "I suspected as much! Oh! the poor pet. Do you know my aunt Lerat? When she comes, get her to tell you the story about the fruiterer who lives opposite her. Just fancy that man— Damn it, how hot this fire is! I must turn round. I'm going to roast my left side now."

And as she presented her side to the blaze, a droll idea struck her, and like a good-tempered thing, she made fun of herself, for she was delighted to see that she was looking so plump and pink in the light of the coal fire.

"I look like a goose, eh? Yes, that's it! I'm a goose on the spit, and I'm turning, turning, and cooking in my own juice, eh?"

And she was once more indulging in a merry fit of laughter, when a sound of voices and slamming doors became audible. Muffat was surprised, and he questioned her with a look. She grew serious, and an anxious expression came over her face. It must be Zoé's cat, a cursed beast that broke everything. It was half-past twelve o'clock. How long was she going to bother herself in her cuckold's behalf? Now that the other man had come, she ought to get him out of the way, and that quickly.

"What were you saying?" asked the Count complaisantly, for he was charmed to see her so kind to him.

But in her desire to be rid of him, she suddenly changed her mood, became brutal, and did not take care what she was saying.

"Oh, yes! the fruiterer and his wife. Well, my dear fellow, they never once touched one another! Not the least bit! She was very keen on it, you understand, but he, the ninny, didn't know it. He was so green that he thought her a stick, and so he went elsewhere, and took up with streetwalkers, who treated him to all sorts of nastiness, whilst she, on her part, made up for it beautifully with fellows who were a lot slyer than her green-horn of a husband. And things always turn out that way through people not understanding one another. I know it, I do!"

Muffat was growing pale. At last he was beginning to understand her allusions, and he wanted to make her keep silence. But she was in full swing.

"No, hold your tongue, will you? If you weren't brutes you would be as nice with your wives as you are with us, and if your wives weren't geese they would take as much pains to keep you as we do to get you. That's the way to behave. Yes, my duck, you can put that in your pipe and smoke it."

"Do not talk of honest women," said he, in a hard voice. "You do not know them."

At that Nana rose to her knees.

"I don't know them! Why, they aren't even clean, your honest women aren't! They aren't even clean! I defy you to find me one who would dare show herself as I am doing. Oh, you make me laugh with your honest women! Don't drive me to it; don't oblige me to tell you things I may regret afterwards."

The Count, by way of answer, mumbled something insulting. Nana became quite pale in her turn. For some seconds she looked at him without speaking. Then, in her decisive way,—

"What would you do if your wife were deceiving you?"

He made a threatening gesture.

"Well, and if I were to?"

"Oh! you," he muttered, with a shrug of his shoulders.

Nana was certainly not spiteful. Since the beginning of the conversation, she had been strongly tempted to throw his cuckold's reputation in his teeth, but she had resisted. She would have liked to confess him quietly on the subject, but he had begun to exasperate her at last. The matter ought to stop now.

"Well, then, my dearie," continued she, "I don't know what you're getting at with me. For two hours past you've been worrying my life out. No do just go and find your wife, for she's at it with Fauchery. Yes, it's quite correct; they're in the Rue Taitbout, at the corner of the Rue de Provençe. You see, I'm giving you the address."

Then, triumphantly, as she saw Muffat stagger to his feet like an ox under the hammer,—

"If honest women must meddle in our affairs and take our sweethearts from us—! Oh, you bet they're a nice lot, those honest women!"

But she was unable to proceed. With a terrible push he had cast her full length on the floor, and lifting his heel he seemed on the point of crushing in her head in order to silence her. For the twinkling of an eye she felt sickening dread. Blinded with rage he had begun beating about the room like a maniac. Then his choking silence and the struggle with which he was shaken melted her to tears. She felt a mortal regret, and rolling herself up in front of the fire so as to roast her right side, she undertook the task of comforting him.

"I take my oath, darling, I thought you knew it all. Otherwise I shouldn't have spoken, you may be sure. But perhaps it isn't true. I don't say anything for certain. I've been told it, and people are talking about it; but what does that prove? Oh, get along! you're very silly to grow riled about it. If I were a man I shouldn't care a rush for the women! All the women are alike, you see, high or low; they're all rowdy and the rest of it."

In a fit of self-abnegation she was severe on womankind, for she wished thus to lessen the cruelty of her blow. But he did not listen to her or hear what she said. With fumbling movements he had put on his boots and his overcoat.

For a moment longer he raved round, and then, in a final outburst, finding himself near the door, he rushed from the room. Nana was very much annoyed.

"Well, well! A prosperous trip to you!" she continued aloud, though she was now alone. "He's polite, too, that fellow is, when he's spoken to! And I had to defend myself at that! Well, I was the first to get back my temper, and I made plenty of excuses, I'm thinking! Besides, he had been getting on my nerves!"

Nevertheless, she was not happy, and sat scratching her legs with both hands. Then she took high ground:

"Tut, tut, it isn't my fault if he is a cuckold!"

And toasted on every side, and as hot as a roast bird, she went and buried herself under the bedclothes, after ringing for Zoé to usher in the other man, who was waiting in the kitchen.

Once outside, Muffat began walking at a furious pace. A fresh shower had just fallen, and he kept slipping on the greasy pavement. When he looked mechanically up into the sky, he saw ragged, soot-colored clouds scudding in front of the moon. At this hour of the night passers-by were becoming few and far between in the Boulevard Haussmann. He skirted the enclosures round the opera-house in his search for darkness, and, as he went along, he kept mumbling inconsequent phrases. That girl had been lying. She had invented her story out of sheer stupidity and cruelty. He ought to have crushed her head when he had it under his heel. After all was said and done, the business was too shameful. Never would he see her, never would he touch her again, or, if he did, he would be miserably weak. And with that he breathed hard, as though he were free once more. Oh, that naked, cruel monster, roasting away like any goose, and slavering over everything that he had respected for forty years back. The moon had come out, and the empty street was bathed in white light. He felt afraid, and he burst into a great fit of sobbing, for he had grown suddenly hopeless and maddened, as though he had sunk into a fathomless void.

"My God!" he stuttered out. "It's finished! There's nothing left now!"

Along the boulevards belated people were hurrying. He tried hard to be calm, and as the story told him by that courtesan kept recurring to his burning consciousness, he wanted to reason the matter out. The Countess was coming up from Madame de Chezelles's country house to-morrow morning. Yet nothing, in fact, could have prevented her from returning to Paris the night before, and passing it with that man. He now began recalling to mind certain details of their stay at The Fondettes. One evening, for instance, he had surprised Sabine in the shade of some trees, when she was so much agitated as to be unable to answer his questions. The man had been present; why should she not be with him now? The more he thought about it the more possible the whole story became, and he ended by thinking it natural and even inevitable. Whilst he was in his shirt-sleeves in the house of a harlot, his wife was undressing in her lover's room. Nothing could be simpler or more logical! Reasoning in this way he forced himself to keep cool. He felt as if there were a great downward movement in the direction of fleshly madness, a movement which, as it grew, was overcoming the whole world round about him. Warm images pursued him in imagination. A naked Nana suddenly evoked a naked Sabine. At this vision, which seemed to bring them together in shameless relationship, and under the influence of the same lusts, he literally stumbled, and in the road a cab nearly ran over him. Some women who had come out of a café jostled him amid loud laughter. Then a fit of weeping once more overcame him, despite all his efforts to the contrary, and, not wishing to shed tears in the presence of others, he plunged into a dark and empty street. It was the Rue Rossini, and along its silent length he wept like a child.

"It's over with us," said he in hollow tones. "There's nothing left us now, nothing left us now!"

He wept so violently that he had to lean up against a door as he buried his face in his wet hands. A noise of footsteps drove him away. He felt a shame and a fear which made him fly before people's faces with the restless step of a bird of darkness. When passers-by met him on the pavement he did his best to look and walk in a leisurely way, for he fancied they were reading his secret in the very swing of his shoulders. He had followed the Rue de la Grange Batelière as far as the Rue du Faubourg Montmartre, where the brilliant lamplight surprised him, and he retraced his steps. For nearly an hour he traversed the district thus, choosing always the darkest corners. Doubtless there was some goal whither his steps were patiently, instinctively, leading him through a labyrinth of endless turnings. At length he lifted his eyes up at a street-corner. He had reached his destination, the point where the Rue Taitbout and the Rue de la Provençe met. He had taken an hour, amid his painful mental sufferings to arrive at a place he could have reached in five minutes. One morning, a month ago, he remembered going up to Fauchery's rooms to thank him for a notice of a ball at the Tuileries, in which the journalist had mentioned him. The flat was between the ground floor and the first story, and had a row of small square windows which were half-hidden by the colossal signboard belonging to a shop. The last window on the left was bisected by a brilliant band of lamplight coming from between the half-closed curtains. And he remained, absorbed and expectant, with his gaze fixed on this shining streak.

The moon had disappeared in an inky sky, whence an icy drizzle was falling. Two o'clock struck at the Trinité. The Rue de Provençe and the Rue Taitbout lay in shadow,

bestarred at intervals by bright splashes of light from the
gas-lamps, which in the distance were merged in yellow
mist. Muffat did not move from where he was standing.
That was the room. He remembered it now: it had hangings of red "andrinople," and a Louis XIII. bed stood at one
end of it. The lamp must be standing on the chimney-piece
to the right. Without doubt they had gone to bed, for no
shadows passed across the window, and the bright streak
gleamed as motionless as the light of a night-lamp. With his
eyes still uplifted, he began forming a plan; he would ring
the bell, go upstairs despite the porter's remonstrances, break
the doors in with a push of his shoulder, and fall upon them
in the very bed without giving them time to unlace their
arms. For one moment the thought that he had no weapon
upon him gave him pause, but directly afterwards he decided
to throttle them. He returned to the consideration of his
project, and he perfected it, whilst waiting for some sign,
some indication, which should bring certainty with it.

Had a woman's shadow only shewn itself at that moment,
he would have rung. But the thought that perhaps he was
deceiving himself froze him. How could he be certain?
Doubts began to return. His wife could not be with that
man. It was monstrous and impossible. Nevertheless he
stayed where he was, and was gradually overcome by a species
of torpor which merged into sheer feebleness, whilst he waited
long and long, and the fixity of his gaze induced hallucina-
tions.

A shower was falling. Two policemen were approaching,
and he was forced to leave the doorway where he had taken
shelter. When these were lost to view in the Rue de Provençe, he returned to his post, wet and shivering. The luminous streak still traversed the window, and this time he was
going away for good when a shadow crossed it. It moved so
quickly, that he thought he had deceived himself. But first
one and then another black thing followed quickly after it,

and there was a regular commotion in the room. Riveted
anew to the pavement, he experienced an intolerable burning sensation in his inside as he waited to find out the meaning of it all. Outlines of arms and legs flitted after one
another; and an enormous hand traveled about with the silhouette of a water-jug. He distinguished nothing clearly,
but he thought he recognized a woman's head-dress. And he
disputed the point with himself; it might well have been
Sabine's hair, only the neck did not seem sufficiently slim.
At that hour of the night he had lost the power of recognition and of action. In this terribly agony of uncertainty,
his inside caused him such acute suffering that he pressed
against the door in order to calm himself, shivering like a
man in rags as he did so. Then seeing that, despite everything, he could not turn his eyes away from the window, his
anger changed into a fit of moralizing. He fancied himself a
Deputy; he was haranguing an assembly, loudly denouncing debauchery, prophesying national ruin. And he recon-
structed Fauchery's article on the poisoned fly, and he came
before the house and declared that morals such as these, which
could only be paralleled in the days of the later Roman Empire, rendered society an impossibility: that did him good.
But the shadows had meanwhile disappeared. Doubtless they
had gone to bed again, and, still, watching, he continued
waiting where he was.

Three o'clock struck, then four, but he could not take his
departure. When showers fell, he buried himself in a corner of the doorway, his legs splashed with wet. Nobody
passed by now, and occasionally his eyes would close, as
though scorched by the streak of light, which he kept watching obstinately, fixedly, with idiotic persistence. On two
subsequent occasions the shadows flitted about, repeating the
same gestures and agitating the silhouette of the same gigantic jug; and twice quiet was re-established, and the night-
lamp again glowed discreetly out. These shadows only in-

creased his uncertainty. Then, too, a sudden idea soothed
his brain, whilst it postponed the decisive moment. After
all, he had only to wait for the woman when she left the
house. He could quite easily recognize Sabine. Nothing
could be simpler, and there would be no scandal, and he
would be sure of things one way or the other. It was only
necessary to stay where he was. Among all the confused
feelings which had been agitating him, he now merely felt a
dull need of certain knowledge. But sheer weariness and
vacancy began lulling him to sleep under his doorway, and
by way of distraction he tried to reckon up how long he
would have to wait. Sabine was to be at the station towards
nine o'clock; that meant about four hours and a half more.
He was very patient; he would even have been content not
to move again; and he found a certain charm in fancying
that his night-vigil would last through eternity.

Suddenly the streak of light was gone. This extremely
simple event was to him an unforeseen catastrophe, at once
troublesome and disagreeable. Evidently they had just put
the lamp out, and were going to sleep. It was reasonable
enough at that hour, but he was irritated thereat, for now
the darkened window ceased to interest him. He watched it
for a quarter of an hour longer, and then grew tired, and
leaving the doorway took a turn upon the pavement. Until
five o'clock he walked to and fro looking upwards from time
to time. The window seemed a dead thing, and now and
then he asked himself if he had not dreamed that shadows
had been dancing up there behind the panes. An intolerable
sense of fatigue weighed him down, a dull heavy feeling,
under the influence of which he forgot what he was waiting
for at that particular street-corner. He kept stumbling on
the pavement, and starting into wakefulness with the icy
shudder of a man who does not know where he is. Nothing
seemed to justify the painful anxiety he was inflicting on
himself. Since those people were asleep—well then, let

them sleep! What good could it do mixing in their affairs? It was very dark; no one would ever know anything about this night's doings. And with that every sentiment within him, down to curiosity itself, took flight before the longing to have done with it all and to find relief somewhere. The cold was increasing, and the street was becoming insufferable. Twice he walked away and slowly returned, dragging one foot behind the other, only to walk further away next time. It was all over; nothing was left him now, and so he went down the whole length of the boulevard and did not return.

His was a melancholy progress through the streets. He walked slowly, never changing his pace, and simply keeping along the walls of the houses.

His boot-heels re-echoed, and he saw nothing but his shadow moving at his side. As he neared each successive gas-light it grew taller, and immediately afterwards diminished. But this lulled him and occupied him mechanically. He never knew afterwards where he had been; it seemed as if he had dragged himself round and round in a circle for hours. One reminiscence only was very distinctly retained by him. Without his being able to explain how it came about he found himself with his face pressed closed against the gate at the end of the Passage des Panoramas and his two hands grasping the bars. He did not shake them, but his whole heart swelling with emotion, he simply tried to look into the passage. But he could make nothing out clearly, for shadows flooded the whole length of the deserted gallery, and the wind, blowing hard down the Rue Saint-Marc, puffed in his face with the damp breath of a cellar. For a time he tried doggedly to see into the place, and then, awakening from his dream, he was filled with astonishment, and asked himself what he could possibly be seeking for at that hour and in that position, for he had pressed against the railings so fiercely that they had left their mark on his face. Then he went on tramp once more. He was hopeless, and his heart was full of infinite sorrow, for he felt, amid all those shadows, that he was evermore betrayed and alone.

Day broke at last. It was the murky dawn that follows winter nights, and looks so melancholy from muddy Paris pavements. Muffat had returned into the wide streets, which were then in course of construction on either side of the New Opera House. Soaked by the rain and cut up by cartwheels, the chalky soil had become a lake of liquid mire. But he never looked to see where he was stepping, and walked on and on, slipping and regaining his footing as he went. The awakening of Paris, with its gangs of sweepers and early workmen trooping to their destinations, added to his troubles as day brightened. People stared at him in surprise, as he went by with scared look, and soaked hat, and muddy clothes. For a long while he sought refuge against palings and among scaffoldings, his desolate brain haunted by the single remaining thought that he was very miserable.

Then he thought of God. The sudden idea of Divine help, of superhuman consolation, surprised him, as though it were something unforeseen and extraordinary. The image of Monsieur Venot was evoked thereby, and he saw his little plump face and ruined teeth. Assuredly Monsieur Venot, whom for months he had been avoiding and thereby rendering miserable, would be delighted were he to go and knock at his door and fall weeping into his arms. In the old days God had been always so merciful towards him. At the least sorrow, the slightest obstacle on the path of life, he had been wont to enter a church, where, kneeling down, he would humble his littleness in the presence of Omnipotence. And he had been used to go forth thence, fortified by prayer, fully prepared to give up the good things of this world, possessed by the single yearning for eternal salvation. But at present he only practiced by fits and starts, when the terror of hell came upon him. All kinds of weak inclinations had over-

come him, and the thought of Nana disturbed his devotions.
And now the thought of God astonished him. Why had he
not thought of God before, in the hour of that terrible agony
when his feeble humanity was breaking up in ruin?

Meanwhile, with slow and painful steps, he sought for a
church. But he had lost his bearings; the early hour had
changed the face of the streets. Soon, however, as he turned
the corner of the Rue de la Chaussée-d'Antin, he noticed a
tower looming vaguely in the fog at the end of the Trinité
Church. The white statues, overlooking the bare garden,
seemed like so many chilly Venuses among the yellow foliage
of a park. Under the porch he stood and panted a little, for
the ascent of the wide steps had tired him. Then he went in.
The church was very cold, for its heating-apparatus had been
fireless since the previous evening, and its lofty vaulted aisles
were full of a fine damp vapor which had come filtering
through the windows. The aisles were deep in shadow; not a
soul was in the church, and the only sound audible, amid
the unlovely darkness, was that made by the old shoes of
some verger or other, who was dragging himself about in
sulky semi-wakefulness. Muffat, however, after knocking
forlornly against an untidy collection of chairs, sank on his
knees with bursting heart, and propped himself against the
rails in front of a little chapel, close by a font. He clasped
his hands, and began searching within himself for suitable
prayers, whilst his whole being yearned towards a transport.
But only his lips kept stammering empty words; his heart
and brain were far away, and with them he returned to the
outer world, and began his long unresting march through the
streets, as though lashed forward by implacable necessity.
And he kept repeating, "O my God, come to my assistance!
O my God, abandon not Thy creature, who delivers himself
up to Thy justice! O my God, I adore Thee: Thou wilt not
leave me to perish under the buffetings of mine enemies!"
Nothing answered: the shadows and the cold weighed upon

him, and the noise of the old shoes continued in the distance, and prevented him praying. Nothing indeed save that tiresome noise was audible in the deserted church, where the matutinal sweeping was unknown before the early masses had somewhat warmed the air of the place. After that he rose to his feet with the help of a chair, his knees cracking under him as he did so. God was not yet there. And why should he weep in Monsieur Venot's arms? The man could do nothing.

And then, mechanically, he returned to Nana's house. Outside he slipped, and he felt the tears welling to his eyes again, but he was not angry with his lot—he was only feeble and ill. Yes, he was too tired, the rain had wetted him too much, he was nipped with cold, but the idea of going back to his great dark house in the Rue Miromesnil froze his heart. The house-door at Nana's was not open as yet, and he had to wait till the porter made his appearance. He smiled as he went upstairs, for he already felt penetrated by the soft warmth of that cosy retreat, where he would be able to stretch his limbs and go to sleep.

When Zoé opened the door to him, she gave a start of most uneasy astonishment. *Madame* had been taken ill with an atrocious sick headache, and she hadn't closed her eyes all night. Still, she could quite go and see whether *Madame* had gone to sleep for good. And with that she slipped into the bedroom, whilst he sank back into one of the arm-chairs in the drawing-room. But almost at that very moment Nana appeared. She had just jumped out of bed, and had scarce had time to slip on a petticoat. Her feet were bare, her hair in wild disorder, her night-gown all crumpled.

"What! you here again!" she cried, with a red flush on her cheeks.

Up she rushed, stung by sudden indignation, in order herself to thrust him out of doors. But when she saw him in

such sorry plight—nay, so utterly done for, she felt infinite
pity.

"Well, you are a pretty sight, my poor fellow!" she continued more gently. "But what's the matter? You've
spotted them, eh? And it's given you the hump?"

He did not answer: he looked like a broken-down animal.
Nevertheless, she came to the conclusion that he still lacked
proofs, and, to hearten him up, she said—

"You see now I was on the wrong tack. Your wife's an
honest woman, on my word of honor! And now, my little
friend, you must go home to bed. You want it badly."

He did not stir.

"Now then, be off! I can't keep you here. But perhaps
you won't presume to stay at such a time as this?"

"Yes, let's go to bed," he stammered.

She repressed a violent gesture, for her patience was de-
serting her. Was the man going crazy?

"Come, be off!" she repeated.

"No."

But she flared up in exasperation, in utter rebellion.

"It's sickening! Don't you understand I'm jolly tired of
your company? Go and find your wife, who's making a
cuckold of you. Yes, she's making a cuckold of you. I say
so—yes, I do now. There, you've got the sack! Will you
leave me, or will you not?"

Muffat's eyes filled with tears. He clasped his hands together.

"Oh, let's go to bed!"

At this Nana suddenly lost all control over herself, and
was choked by nervous sobs. She was being taken advantage
of, when all was said and done! What had these stories to
do with her? She certainly had used all manner of delicate
methods in order to teach him his lesson gently. And now
he was for making her pay the damages! No, thank you!
She was kind-hearted, but not to that extent!

"The devil, but I've had enough of this!" she swore, bringing her fist down on the furniture. "Yes, yes, I wanted to be faithful—it was all I could do to be that! Yet, if I spoke the word, I could be rich to-morrow, my dear fellow!"

He looked up in surprise. Never once had he thought of the monetary question. If she only expressed a desire, he would realize it at once; his whole fortune was at her service.

"No, it's too late now," she replied, furiously. "I like men who give without being asked. No, if you were to offer me a million for a single interview, I should say no! It's over between us: I've got other fish to fry there! So be off, or I shan't answer for the consequences. I shall do something dreadful."

She advanced threateningly towards him, and whilst she was raving as became a good courtesan, who, though driven to desperation, was yet firmly convinced of her rights and her superiority over tiresome, honest folk, the door opened suddenly, and Steiner presented himself. That proved the finishing touch. She shrieked aloud:

"Well, I never! Here's the other one!"

Bewildered by her piercing outcry, Steiner stopped short. Muffat's unexpected presence annoyed him, for he feared an explanation and had been doing his best to avoid it these three months past. With blinking eyes, he stood first on one leg, then on the other, looking embarrassed the while, and avoiding the Count's gaze. He was out of breath, and as became a man who had rushed across Paris with good news only to find himself involved in unforeseen trouble, his face was flushed and distorted.

"Que veux-tu, toi?" asked Nana, roughly, using the second person singular in open mockery of the Count.

"What—what do I—?" he stammered. "I've got it for you—you know what."

"Eh?"

He hesitated. The day before yesterday she had given him

to understand that, if he could not find her a thousand francs to pay a bill with, she would not receive him any more. For two days he had been loafing about the town in quest of the money, and had at last made the sum up that very morning.

"The thousand francs!" he ended by declaring, as he drew an envelope from his pocket.

Nana had not remembered.

"The thousand francs!" she cried. "D'you think I'm begging alms? Now, look here, that's what I value your thousand francs at!"

And, snatching the envelope, she threw it full in his face. As became a prudent Hebrew, he picked it up slowly and painfully, and then looked at the young woman with a dull expression of face. Muffat and he exchanged a despairing glance, whilst she put her arms akimbo in order to shout more loudly than before.

"Come now, will you soon have done insulting me? I'm glad you've come too, dear boy, because now you see the clearance'll be quite complete. Now then, gee up! Out you go!"

Then, as they did not hurry in the least, for they were parlayzed,—

"D'you mean to say I'm acting like a fool, eh? It's likely enough! But you've bored me too much! And, hang it all! I've had enough of swelldom! If I die of what I'm doing— well, it's my fancy!"

They sought to calm her; they begged her to listen to reason.

"Now, then, once, twice, thrice!— Won't you go? Very well! Look there! I've got company."

And with a brisk movement she flung wide the bedroom door. Whereupon, in the middle of the tumbled bed, the two men caught sight of Fontan. He had not expected to be shewn off in this situation; nevertheless, he took things very easily, for he was used to sudden surprises on the stage.

Indeed, after the first shock, he even hit upon a grimace cal-
culated to tide him honorably over his difficulty: he "turned
rabbit," as he phrased it, and stuck out his lips, and wrinkled
up his nose, so as completely to transform the lower half of
his face. His base, satyr-like head seemed to exude inconti-
nence. It was this man Fontan, then, whom Nana had been
to fetch at the Variétés every day for a week past, for she was
smitten with that fierce sort of passion which the grimacing
ugliness of a low comedian is wont to inspire in the genus
courtesan.

"There!" said she, pointing him out with tragic gesture.

Muffat, who hitherto had pocketed everything, rebelled
at this affront.

"Bitch!" he stammered.

But Nana, who was once more in the bedroom, came back
in order to have the last word.

"How am I a bitch? What about your wife?"

And she was off, and slamming the door with a bang she
noisily pushed to the bolt. Left alone, the two men gazed at
one another in silence. Zoé had just come into the room, but
she did not drive them out. Nay, she spoke to them in the
most sensible manner. As became a woman with a head on
her shoulders, she decided that *Madame's* conduct was rather
too much of a good thing. But she defended her none the
less: this union with the play actor couldn't last: the madness
must be allowed to pass off! The two men retired without
uttering a sound. On the pavement outside they shook hands
silently, as though swayed by a mutual sense of fraternity.
Then they turned their backs on one another, and went
crawling off in opposite directions.

When at last Muffat entered his town house in the Rue
Miromesnil, his wife was just arriving. The two met on
the great staircase, whose walls exhaled an icy chill. They
lifted up their eyes and beheld one another. The Count still
wore his muddy clothes, and his pale, bewildered face be-

trayed the prodigal returning from his debauch. The Countess looked as though she were utterly fagged out by a night in the train. She was dropping with sleep, her hair had been brushed anyhow, and her eyes were deeply sunken.

CHAPTER VIII

WE are in a little set of lodgings on the fourth floor in the Rue Véron at Montmartre. Nana and Fontan have invited a few friends to cut their Twelfth-Night cake with them. They are giving their house-warming, though they have been only three days settled.

They had no fixed intention of keeping house together, but the whole thing had come about suddenly in the first glow of the honeymoon. After her grand blow-up, when she had turned the Count and the banker so vigorously out of doors, Nana felt the world crumbling about her feet. She estimated the situation at a glance; the creditors would swoop down on her ante-room, would mix themselves up with her love affairs, and threaten to sell her little all unless she continued to act sensibly. Then, too, there would be no end of disputes and carking anxieties if she attempted to save her furniture from their clutches. And so she preferred giving up everything. Besides the flat in the Boulevard Haussmann was plaguing her to death. It was so stupid with its great gilded rooms! In her access of tenderness for Fontan, she began dreaming of a pretty little bright chamber. Indeed, she returned to the old ideals of the florist days, when her highest ambition was to have a rose-wood cupboard with a plate-glass door, and a bed hung with blue "reps." In the course of two days she sold what she could smuggle out of the house in the way of knick-knacks and jewelry, and then disappeared, taking with her ten thousand francs, and never even warning the porter's wife. It was a plunge into the dark, a merry spree; never a trace was left behind. In this way she would prevent the men from coming dangling after her. Fontan was very nice. He did not say No to anything, but just let her do as she liked. Nay, he even displayed an admirable spirit of comradeship. He had, on his part, nearly seven thousand francs, and, despite the fact that people accused him of stinginess, he consented to add them to the young woman's ten thousand. The sum struck them as a solid foundation on which to begin housekeeping. And so they started away, drawing from their common hoard, in order to hire and furnish the two rooms in the Rue Véron, and sharing everything together like old friends. In the early days it was really delicious.

On Twelfth Night Madame Lerat and Louiset were the first to arrive. As Fontan had not yet come home, the old lady ventured to give expression to her fears, for she trembled to see her niece renouncing the chance of wealth.

"Oh, aunt, I love him so dearly!" cried Nana, pressing her hands to her heart with the prettiest of gestures.

This phrase produced an extraordinary effect on Madame Lerat, and tears came into her eyes.

"That's true," said she with an air of conviction. "Love before all things!"

And with that she went into raptures over the prettiness of the rooms. Nana took her to see the bedroom, the parlor, and the very kitchen. Gracious goodness, it wasn't a vast place, but then they had painted it afresh, and put up new wall-papers. Besides, the sun shone merrily into it during the daytime.

Thereupon Madame Lerat detained the young woman in the bedroom, whilst Louiset installed himself behind the charwoman in the kitchen in order to watch a chicken being roasted. If, said Madame Lerat, she permitted herself to say what was in her mind, it was because Zoé had just been at her house. Zoé had stayed courageously in the breach, because she was devoted to her mistress. *Madame* would pay her later on: she was in no anxiety about that! And amid the break-up of the Boulevard Haussmann establishment, it was she who shewed the creditors a bold front; it was she who conducted a dignified retreat, saving what she could from the wreck, and telling every one that her mistress was traveling. She never once gave them her address. Nay, through fear of being followed, she even deprived herself of the pleasure of calling on *Madame*. Nevertheless, that same morning she had run round to Madame Lerat's because matters were taking a new turn. The evening before, creditors in the persons of the upholsterer, the charcoal merchant, and the laundress, had put in an appearance, and had offered to give *Madame* an extension of time. Nay, they had even proposed to advance *Madame* a very considerable amount, if only *Madame* would return to her flat and conduct herself like a sensible person. The aunt repeated Zoé's words. Without doubt there was a gentleman behind it all.

"I'll never consent!" declared Nana, in great disgust. "Ah, they're a pretty lot, those trademen! Do they think I'm to be sold so that they can get their bills paid? Why, look here, I'd rather die of hunger than deceive Fontan."

"That's what I said," averred Madame Lerat. "My niece," said I, "is too noble-hearted!"

Nana, however, was much vexed to learn that La Mignotte was being sold, and that Labordette was buying it for Caroline Héquet at an absurdly low price. It made her angry with that clique. Oh, they were a regular cheap lot, in spite of their airs and graces! Yes, by Jove, she was worth more than the whole lot of them!

"They can have their little joke out," she concluded, "but money will never give them true happiness! Besides, you know, aunt, I don't even know now whether all that set are alive or not: I'm much too happy."

At that very moment Madame Maloir entered, wearing

one of those hats of which she alone understood the shape.
It was delightful meeting again. Madame Maloir explained
that magnificence frightened her, and that *now,* from time
to time, she would come back for her game of bézique. A
second visit was paid to the different rooms in the lodgings,
and in the kitchen Nana talked of economy in the presence
of the charwoman, who was basting the fowl, and said that
a servant would have cost too much, and that she was herself desirous of looking after things. Louiset was gazing
beatifically at the roasting process.

But presently there was a loud outburst of voices. Fontan
had come in with Bosc and Prullière, and the company could
now sit down to table. The soup had been already served
when Nana for the third time shewed off the lodgings.

"Ah, dear children, how comfortable you are here!" Bosc
kept repeating, simply for the sake of pleasing the chums
who were standing the dinner. At bottom, the subject of
the "nook," as he called it, nowise touched him.

In the bedroom he harped still more vigorously on the
amiable note. Ordinarily he was wont to treat women like
cattle, and the idea of a man bothering himself about one of
the dirty brutes excited within him the only angry feelings
of which, in his comprehensive, drunken disdain of the universe, he was still capable.

"Ah, ha! the villains," continued he, with a wink, "they've
done this on the sly. Well, you were certainly right. It will
be charming, and, by Heaven, we'll come and see you!"

But when Louiset arrived on the scene, astride upon a
broomstick, Prullière chuckled spitefully and remarked,—
"Well, I never! You've got a baby already?"

This struck everybody as very droll, and Madame Lerat
and Madame Maloir shook with laughter. Nana, far from
being vexed, laughed tenderly, and said that unfortunately
this was not the case. She would very much have liked it,
both for the little one's sake and for her own, but perhaps

one would arrive all the same. Fontan, in his *rôle* of honest
citizen, took Louiset in his arms, and began playing with
him and lisping.

"Never mind! It loves its daddy! Call me 'papa,' you
little blackguard!"

"Papa, papa!" stammered the child.

The company overwhelmed him with caresses, but Bosc
was bored, and talked of sitting down to table. That was
the only serious business in life. Nana asked her guests' permission to put Louiset's chair next her own. The dinner
was very merry, but Bosc suffered from the near neighborhood of the child, from whom he had to defend his plate.
Madame Lerat bored him too. She was in a melting mood,
and kept whispering to him all sorts of mysterious things
about gentlemen of the first fashion who were still running
after Nana. Twice he had to push away her knee, for she
was positively invading him in her gushing, tearful mood.
Prullière behaved with great incivility towards Madame Maloir, and did not once help her to anything. He was entirely taken up with Nana, and looked annoyed at seeing
her with Fontan. Besides, the turtle-doves were kissing so
excessively as to be becoming positive bores. Contrary to all
known rules they had elected to sit side by side.

"Devil take it! Why don't you eat? You've got plenty
of time ahead of you!" Bosc kept repeating with his mouth
full. "Wait till we are gone!"

But Nana could not restrain herself. She was in a perfect ecstasy of love. Her face was as full of blushes as an
innocent young girl's, and her looks and her laughter seemed
to overflow with tenderness. Gazing on Fontan, she overwhelmed him with pet names—"my doggie! my old bear!
my kitten!"— and, whenever he passed her the water or the
salt she bent forward and kissed him at random on lips, eyes,
nose, or ear. Then, if she met with reproof, she would return to the attack with the cleverest maneuvers, and with

infinite submissiveness, and the supple cunning of a beaten cat, would catch hold of his hand, when no one was looking, in order to kiss it again. It seemed she must be touching something belonging to him. As to Fontan, he gave himself airs, and let himself be adored with the utmost condescension. His great nose sniffed with entirely sensual content: his goat face, with its quaint monstrous ugliness, positively glowed in the sunlight of devoted adoration lavished upon him by that superb woman, who was so fair and so plump of limb. Occasionally he gave a kiss in return, as became a man who is having all the enjoyment, and is yet willing to behave prettily.

"Well, you're growing maddening!" cried Prullière. "Get away from her, you fellow there!"

And he dismissed Fontan, and changed covers, in order to take his place at Nana's side. The company shouted and applauded at this, and gave vent to some stiffish epigrammatic witticisms. Fontan counterfeited despair, and assumed the quaint expression of Vulcan crying for Venus. Straightway Prullière became very gallant, but Nana, whose foot he was groping for under the table, caught him a slap to make him keep quiet. No, no, she was certainly not going to become his mistress. A month ago she had begun to take a fancy to him because of his good looks, but now she detested him. If he pinched her again under pretense of picking up her napkin, she would throw her glass in his face!

Nevertheless the evening passed off well. The company had naturally begun talking about the Variétés. Wasn't that cad of a Bordenave going to go off the hooks after all? His nasty diseases kept reappearing, and causing him such suffering that you couldn't come within six yards of him nowadays. The day before, during rehearsal, he had been incessantly yelling at Simonne. There was a fellow whom the theatrical people wouldn't shed many tears over. Nana announced that if he were to ask her to take another part she

would jolly well send him to the right-about. Moreover, she
began talking of leaving the stage: the theater was not to
compare with her home. Fontan, who was not in the present
piece nor in that which was then being rehearsed, also talked
big about the joy of being entirely at liberty and of passing
his evenings, with his feet on the fender, in the society of his
little pet. And at this the rest exclaimed delightedly, treating their entertainers as lucky people and pretending to envy
their felicity.

The Twelfth-Night cake had been cut and handed round.
The bean had fallen to the lot of Madame Lerat, who popped
it into Bosc's glass. Whereupon there were shouts of "The
King drinks! The King drinks!" Nana took advantage of
this outburst of merriment, and went and put her arms
round Fontan's neck again, kissing him and whispering in his
ear. But Prullière, laughing angrily as became a pretty man,
declared that they were not playing the game. Louiset,
meanwhile, slept soundly on two chairs. It was nearing one
o'clock when the company separated, shouting *Au revoir* as
they went downstairs.

For three weeks the existence of the pair of lovers was
really charming. Nana fancied she was returning to those
early days when her first silk dress had caused her infinite
delight. She went out little, and affected a life of solitude
and simplicity. One morning early, when she had gone
down to buy fish *in propria persona* in the La Rochefoucauld
Market, she was vastly surprised to meet her old hairdresser
Francis, face to face. His get-up was as scrupulously careful
as ever: he wore the finest linen and his frock-coat was beyond reproach; in fact, Nana felt ashamed that he should
see her in the street with a dressing-jacket, and disordered
hair, and down-at-heel shoes. But he had the tact, if possible,
to intensify his politeness towards her. He did not permit
himself a single inquiry, and affected to believe that *Madame*
was at present on her travels. Ah, but *Madame* had ren-

dered many persons unhappy when she decided to travel! All the world had suffered loss. The young woman, however, ended by asking him questions, for a sudden fit of curiosity had made her forget her previous embarrassment. Seeing that the crowd was jostling them, she pushed him into a doorway, and, still holding her little basket in one hand, stood chatting in front of him. What were people saying about her high jinks? Good heavens! the ladies to whom he went said this, and that, and all sorts of things. In fact, she had made a great noise, and was enjoying a real boom. And Steiner? Monsieur Steiner was in a very bad way—would make an ugly finish, if he couldn't hit on some new commercial operation. And Daguenet? Oh, *he* was getting on swimmingly. Monsieur Daguenet was settling down. Nana, under the exciting influence of various recollections, was just opening her mouth with a view to a further examination, when she felt it would be awkward to utter Muffat's name. Thereupon Francis smiled, and spoke instead of her. As to Monsieur le Comte, it was all a great pity, so sad had been his sufferings since *Madame's* departure.

He had been like a soul in pain—you might have met him wherever *Madame* was likely to be found. At last Monsieur Mignon had come across him, and had taken him home to his own place. This piece of news caused Nana to laugh a good deal. But her laughter was not of the easiest kind.

"Ah, he's with Rose now," said she. "Well, then, you must know, Francis, I've done with him! Oh, the canting thing! Its learnt some pretty habits—can't even go fasting for a week now! And to think that he used to swear he wouldn't have any woman after me!"

She was raging inwardly.

"My leavings, if you please!" she continued. "A pretty Johnnie for Rose to go and treat herself to! Oh, I understand it all now: she wanted to have her revenge because I got that brute of a Steiner away from her. Ain't it sly to get a man to come to her when I've chucked him out of doors?"

"Monsieur Mignon doesn't tell that tale," said the hairdresser. "According to his account, it was Monsieur le Comte who chucked you out. Yes, and in a pretty disgusting way too—with a kick on the bottom!"

Nana became suddenly very pale.

"Eh, what?" she cried, "with a kick on my bottom? He's going too far, he is! Look here, my little friend, it was I who threw him downstairs, the cuckold, for he is a cuckold, I must inform you. His countess is making him one with every man she meets—yes, even with that good-for-nothing of a Fauchery. And that Mignon, who goes loafing about the pavement in behalf of his harridan of a wife, whom nobody wants because she's so lean! What a foul lot! What a foul lot!"

She was choking, and she paused for breath.

"Oh, that's what they say, is it? Very well, my little Francis, I'll go and look 'em up, I will. Shall you and I go to them at once? Yes, I'll go, and we'll see whether they will have the cheek to go telling about kicks on the bottom. Kicks! I never took one from anybody! And nobody's ever going to strike me—d'ye see?—for I'd smash the man who laid a finger on me!"

Nevertheless, the storm subsided at last. After all, they might jolly well say what they liked! She looked upon them as so much filth underfoot! It would have soiled her to bother about people like that. She had a conscience of her own, she had! And Francis, seeing her thus giving herself away, what with her housewife's costume and all, became familiar, and, at parting, made so bold as to give her some good advice. It was wrong of her to be sacrificing everything for the sake of an infatuation: such infatuations ruined existence. She listened to him with bowed head, whilst he spoke to her with a pained expression, as became a connoisseur who could not bear to see so fine a girl making such a hash of things.

"Well, that's my affair," she said at last. "Thanks all the same, dear boy."

She shook his hand, which despite his perfect dress, was always a little greasy, and then went off to buy her fish. During the day, that story about the kick on the bottom occupied her thoughts. She even spoke about it to Fontan, and again posed as a sturdy woman who was not going to stand the slightest flick from anybody. Fontan, as became a philosophic spirit, declared that all men of fashion were beasts whom it was one's duty to despise. And from that moment forth Nana was full of very real disdain.

That same evening they went to the Bouffes-Parisiens Theatre to see a little woman of Fontan's acquaintance make her *début* in a part of some ten lines. It was close on one o'clock when they once more trudged up the heights of Montmartre. They had purchased a cake, a "Moka," in the Rue de la Chaussée-d'-Antin; and they ate it in bed, seeing that the night was not warm and it was not worth while lighting a fire. Sitting up, side by side, with the bed-clothes pulled up in front, and the pillows piled up behind, they supped and talked about the little woman. Nana thought her plain and lacking in style. Fontan, lying on his stomach, passed up the pieces of cake, which had been put between the candle and the matches on the edge of the night-table. But they ended by quarreling.

"Oh, just to think of it!" cried Nana. "She's got eyes like gimlet holes, and her hair's the color of tow."

"Hold your tongue, do!" said Fontan. "She has a superb head of hair and such fire in her looks! It's lovely the way you women always tear each other to pieces!"

He looked annoyed.

"Come now, we've had enough of it!" he said at last, in

savage tones. "You know I don't like being bored. Let's
go to sleep, or things'll take a nasty turn."

And he blew out the candle, but Nana was furious, and
went on talking. She was not going to be spoken to in that
voice—she was accustomed to being treated with respect!
As he did not vouchsafe any further answer, she was silenced,
but she could not go to sleep, and lay tossing to and fro.

"Great God! have you done moving about?" cried he suddenly, giving a brisk jump upwards.

"It isn't my fault if there are crumbs in the bed," said she
curtly.

In fact, there were crumbs in the bed. She felt them down
to her middle, she was everywhere devoured by them. One
single crumb was scorching her, and making her scratch herself till she bled. Besides, when one eats a cake, isn't it usual
to shake out the bed-clothes afterwards? Fontan, white with
rage, had relit the candle, and they both got up, and barefooted and in their night-dresses, they turned down the
clothes and swept up the crumbs on the sheet with their
hands. Fontan went to bed again shivering, and told her
to go to the devil when she advised him to wipe the soles
of his feet carefully. And in the end she came back to her
old position, but scarce had she stretched herself out than she
danced again. There were fresh crumbs in the bed!

"By Jove, it was sure to happen!" she cried. "You've
brought them back again under your feet. I can't go on like
this! No, I tell you, I can't go on like this!"

And with that she was on the point of stepping over him
in order to jump out of bed again, when Fontan in his longing for sleep grew desperate, and dealt her a ringing box on
the ear. The blow was so smart that Nana suddenly found
herself lying down again with her head on the pillow.

She lay half stunned.

"Oh!" she ejaculated simply, sighing a child's big sigh.

For a second or two he threatened her with a second slap,

asking her at the same time if she meant to move again.
Then he put out the light, settled himself squarely on his
back, and in a trice was snoring. But she buried her face in
the pillow and began sobbing quietly to herself. It was cowardly of him to take advantage of his superior strength! She
had experienced very real terror all the same, so terrible had
that quaint mask of Fontan's become. And her anger began
dwindling down as though the blow had calmed her. She
began to feel respect towards him, and accordingly squeezed
herself against the wall in order to leave him as much room
as possible. She even ended by going to sleep, her cheek
tingling, her eyes full of tears, and feeling so deliciously
depressed, and wearied, and submissive, that she no longer
noticed the crumbs. When she woke up in the morning she
was holding Fontan in her naked arms and pressing him
tightly against her breast. He would never begin it again,
eh? Never again? She loved him too dearly. Why, it was
even nice to be beaten if he struck the blow!

After that night a new life began. For a mere trifle—a
yes, a no—Fontan would deal her a blow. She grew accustomed to it, and pocketed everything. Sometimes she shed
tears and threatened him, but he would pin her up against
the wall and talk of strangling her, which had the effect
of rendering her extremely obedient. As often as not, she
sank down on a chair, and sobbed for five minutes on end.
But afterwards, she would forget all about it, grow very
merry, fill the little lodgings with the sound of song, and
laughter, and the rapid rustle of skirts. The worst of it
was that Fontan was now in the habit of disappearing for
the whole day and never returning home before midnight,
for he was going to cafés and meeting his old friends again.
Nana bore with everything. She was tremulous and caressing, her only fear being that she might never see him again
if she reproached him. But on certain days, when she had
neither Madame Maloir, nor her aunt and Louiset with her,

she grew mortally dull. Thus, one Sunday, when she was
bargaining for some pigeons at the La Rochefoucauld Market,
she was delighted to meet Satin, who, in her turn, was
busy purchasing a bunch of radishes. Since the evening
when the Prince had drunk Fontan's champagne, they had
lost sight of one another.

"What? It's you! D'you live in our parts?" said Satin,
astounded at seeing her in the street at that hour of the
morning, and in slippers too. "Oh, my poor dear girl, you're
really ruined then!"

Nana knitted her brows as a sign that she was to hold her
tongue, for they were surrounded by other women who wore
dressing-gowns, and were without linen, whilst their di-
sheveled tresses were white with fluff. In the morning, when
the man picked up overnight had been newly dismissed, all
the courtesans of the quarter were wont to come marketing here, their eyes heavy with sleep, their feet in old down-
at-heel shoes, and themselves full of the weariness and ill-
humor entailed by a night of boredom. From the four con-
verging streets they came down into the market, looking
still rather young in some cases, and very pale and charming
in their utter unconstraint, in others, hideous and old, with
bloated faces and peeling skin. The latter did not the least
mind being seen thus outside working hours, and not one of
them deigned to smile when the passers-by on the side-walk
turned round to look at them. Indeed they were all very
full of business, and wore a disdainful expression as became
good housewives for whom men had ceased to exist. Just
as Satin, for instance, was paying for her bunch of radishes,
a young man, who might have been a shop-boy going late to
his work, threw her a passing greeting:

"Good morning, duckie."

She straightened herself up at once, and with the dignified
manner becoming an offended queen, remarked,—

"What's up with that swine there?"

Then she fancied she recognized him. Three days ago, towards midnight, as she was coming back alone from the boulevards, she had talked to him at the corner of the Rue Labruyère for nearly half an hour, with a view to persuading him to come home with her. But this recollection only angered her the more.

"Fancy, they're brutes enough to shout things to you in broad daylight!" she continued. "When one's out on business, one ought to be respectfully treated, eh?"

Nana had ended by buying her pigeons, although she certainly had her doubts of their freshness. After which Satin wanted to shew her where she lived in the Rue Rochefoucauld close by. And the moment they were alone, Nana told her of her passion for Fontan. Arrived in front of the house, the girl stopped, with her bundle of radishes under her arm, and listened eagerly to a final detail which the other imparted to her. Nana fibbed away, and vowed that it was she who had turned Count Muffat out of doors with a perfect hail of kicks on the posterior.

"Oh, how smart!" Satin repeated; "how very smart! Kicks, eh? And he never said a word, did he? What a blooming coward! I wish I'd been there to see his ugly mug! My dear girl, you were quite right. A pin for the coin! When *I'm* on with a mash, I starve for it! You'll come and see me, eh? You promise? It's the left-hand door. Knock three knocks, for there's a whole heap of damned squints about."

After that, whenever Nana grew too weary of life, she went down and saw Satin. She was always sure of finding her, for the girl never went out before six in the evening. Satin occupied a couple of rooms, which a chemist had furnished for her in order to save her from the clutches of the police; but in little more than a twelvemonth she had broken the furniture, knocked in the chairs, dirtied the curtains, and that in a manner so furiously filthy and untidy, that the lodgings seemed as though inhabited by a pack of mad cats. On the mornings when she grew disgusted with herself, and thought about cleaning up a bit, chair-rails and strips of curtain would come off in her hands during her struggle with superincumbent dirt. On such days the place was fouler than ever, and it was impossible to enter it owing to the things which had fallen down across the doorway. At length she ended by leaving her house severely alone. When the lamp was lit, the cupboard with plate-glass doors, the clock, and what remained of the curtains, still served to impose on the men. Besides, for six months past, her landlord had been threatening to evict her. Well then, for whom should she be keeping the furniture nice? For him more than any one else, perhaps! And so, whenever she got up in a merry mood, she would shout "Gee up!" and give the sides of the cupboard and the chest of drawers such a tremendous kick that they cracked again.

Nana nearly always found her in bed. Even on the days when Satin went out to do her marketing, she felt so tired on her return upstairs that she flung herself down on the bed and went to sleep again. During the day she dragged herself about, and dozed off on chairs. Indeed, she did not emerge from this languid condition till the evening drew on, and the gas was lit outside. Nana felt very comfortable at Satin's, sitting doing nothing on the untidy bed, whilst basins stood about on the floor at her feet, and petticoats which had been bemired last night hung over the backs of arm-chairs and stained them with mud. They had long gossips together, and were endlessly confidential, whilst Satin lay on her stomach in her night-gown, waving her legs above her head, and smoking cigarettes as she listened. Sometimes, on such afternoons as they had troubles to retail, they treated themselves to absinthe in order, as they termed it, "to forget." Satin did not go downstairs or put on a petticoat, but simply went and leant over the banisters, and shouted her order to the portress's little girl, a chit of ten, who when she brought up the absinthe in a glass would look furtively at the lady's bare legs. Every conversation led up to one subject—the beastliness of the men. Nana was overpowering on the subject of Fontan. She could not say a dozen words without lapsing into endless repetitions of his sayings and his doings. But Satin, like a good-natured girl, would listen unwearyingly to everlasting accounts of how Nana had watched for him at the window, how they had fallen out over a burnt dish of hash, and how they had made it up in bed after hours of silent sulking. In her desire to be always talking about these things, Nana had got to tell of every slap that he dealt her. Last week he had given her a swollen eye; nay, the night before he had given her such a box on the ear as to throw her across the night-table, and all because he could not find his slippers. And the other woman did not evince any astonishment, but blew out cigarette smoke, and only paused a moment to remark that, for her part, she always ducked under, which sent the gentleman pretty nearly sprawling. Both of them settled down with a will to these anecdotes about blows: they grew supremely happy and excited over these same idiotic doings, about which they told one another a hundred times or more, whilst they gave themselves up to the soft and pleasing sense of weariness which was sure to follow the drubbings they talked of. It was the delight of rediscussing Fontan's blows, and of explaining his works and his ways, down to the very manner in which he took off his boots, which brought Nana back daily to Satin's place. The latter, moreover, used to end by growing sympathetic in her turn, and would cite even more violent cases, as, for instance, that of a pastrycook, who had left her for dead on the floor. Yet she loved him, spite of it all! Then came the days on which Nana cried, and declared that things could not go on as they were doing. Satin would escort her back to her own door, and would linger an hour out in the street to see that he did not murder her. And the next day the two women would rejoice over the reconciliation the whole afternoon through. Yet, though they did not say so, they preferred the days when thrashings were, so to speak, in the air, for then their comfortable indignation was all the stronger.

They became inseparable. Yet, Satin never went to Nana's, Fontan having announced that he would have no trollops in his house. They used to go out together, and thus it was that Satin one day took her friend to see another woman. This woman turned out to be that very Madame Robert who had interested Nana, and inspired her with a certain respect, ever since she had refused to come to her supper. Madame Robert lived in the Rue Mosnier, a silent new street in the Quartier de l'Europe, where there were no shops, and the handsome houses, with their small limited flats, were peopled by ladies. It was five o'clock, and along the silent pavements, in the quiet aristocratic shelter of the tall white houses, were drawn up the broughams of Stock Exchange people and merchants, whilst men walked hastily about, looking up at the windows, where women in dressing-jackets seemed to be awaiting them. At first Nana refused to go up, remarking with some constraint that she had not the pleasure of the lady's acquaintance. But Satin would take no refusal. She was only desirous of paying a civil call, for Madame Robert, whom she had met in a restaurant the day before, had made herself extremely agreeable, and had got her to promise to come and see her. And at last Nana consented. At the top of the stairs a little drowsy maid informed them that *Madame* had not come home yet, but she ushered them into the drawing-room notwithstanding, and left them there.

"The deuce, it's a smart show!" whispered Satin. It was a stiff, middle-class room, hung with dark-colored fabrics, and suggested the conventional taste of a Parisian shopkeeper who has retired on his fortune. Nana was struck, and did her best to make merry about it. But Satin shewed annoyance, and spoke up for Madame Robert's strict adherence to the proprieties. She was always to be met with in the society of elderly, grave-looking men, on whose arms she leaned. At present, she had a retired chocolate-seller in tow, a serious soul. Whenever he came to see her he was so charmed by the solid, handsome way in which the house was arranged, that he had himself announced and addressed its mistress as "dear child."

"Look! here she is!" continued Satin, pointing to a photograph which stood in front of the clock. Nana scrutinized the portrait for a second or so. It represented a very dark brunette, with a longish face and lips pursed up in a discreet smile. "A thoroughly fashionable lady," one might have said of the likeness, "but one who is rather more reserved than the rest."

"It's strange," murmured Nana at length, "but I've certainly seen that face somewhere. Where I don't remember. But it can't have been in a pretty place—oh, no, I'm sure it wasn't in a pretty place."

And turning towards her friend, she added, "So she's made you promise to come and see her? What does she want with you?"

"What does she want with me? 'Gad! to talk, I expect— to be with me a bit. It's her politeness."

Nana looked steadily at Satin: "Tut, tut," she said softly. After all, it didn't matter to her! Yet, seeing that the lady was keeping them waiting, she declared that she would not stay longer, and accordingly they both took their departure.

The next day Fontan informed Nana that he was not coming home to dinner, and she went down early to find Satin, with a view to treating her at a restaurant. The choice of the restaurant involved infinite debate. Satin proposed various brewery bars, which Nana thought detestable,

and at last persuaded her to dine at Laure's. This was a
table d' hôte in the Rue des Martyrs, where the dinner cost
three francs.

Tired of waiting for the dinner-hour and not knowing
what to do out in the street, the pair went up to Laure's
twenty minutes too early. The three dining-rooms there
were still empty, and they sat down at a table, in the very
saloon where Laure Piédefer was enthroned on a high bench
behind a bar. This Laure was a lady of some fifty summers, whose swelling contours were tightly laced by belts
and corsets. Women kept entering in quick procession, and
each, in passing, craned upward so as to overtop the saucers
raised on the counter, and kissed Laure on the mouth with
tender familiarity, whilst the monstrous creature tried, with
tears in her eyes, to divide her attentions among them in such
a way as to make no one jealous. On the other hand, the
servant, who waited on the ladies, was a tall, lean woman.
She seemed wasted with disease, and her eyes were ringed
with dark lines and glowed with somber fire. Very rapidly
the three saloons filled up. There were some hundred customers, and they had seated themselves wherever they could
find vacant places. The majority were nearing the age of
forty: their flesh was puffy, and so bloated by vice as almost to hide the outlines of their flaccid mouths. But amid
all these gross bosoms and figures, some slim, pretty girls
were observable. These still wore a modest expression, despite their impudent gestures, for they were only beginners
in their art, who had started life in the ball-rooms of the
slums, and had been brought to Laure's by some customer
or other. Here the tribe of bloated women, excited by the
sweet scent of their youth, jostled one another, and, whilst
treating them to dainties, formed a perfect court round
them, much as old amorous bachelors might have done. As
to the men, they were not numerous. There were ten or
fifteen of them at the outside, and, if we except four tall

fellows who had come to see the sight, and were cracking jokes and taking things easy, they behaved humbly enough amid this whelming flood of petticoats.

"I say, their stew's very good, ain't it?" said Satin.

Nana nodded with much satisfaction. It was the old substantial dinner you get in a country hotel, and consisted of *vol-au-vent à la financière*, fowls boiled in rice, beans with a sauce, and vanille creams, iced and flavored with burnt sugar. The ladies made an especial onslaught on the boiled fowl and rice: their stays seemed about to burst, they wiped their lips with slow luxurious movements. At first Nana had been afraid of meeting old friends, who might have asked her silly questions; but she grew calm at last, for she recognized no one she knew among that extremely motley throng, where faded dresses and lamentable hats contrasted strangely with handsome costumes, the wearers of which fraternized in vice with their shabbier neighbors. She was momentarily interested, however, at the sight of a young man, with short curly hair and insolent face, who kept a whole tableful of vastly fat women breathlessly attentive to his slightest caprice. But when the young man began to laugh, his bosom swelled.

"Good lack, it's a woman!"

She let a little cry escape as she spoke, and Satin, who was stuffing herself with boiled fowl, lifted up her head and whispered,—

"Oh, yes! I know her. A smart lot, eh? They do just fight for her."

Nana pouted disgustingly. She could not understand the thing as yet. Nevertheless, she remarked, in her sensible tone, that there was no disputing about tastes or colors, for you never could tell what you yourself might one day have a liking for. So she ate her cream with an air of philosophy, though she was perfectly well aware that Satin with her great blue virginal eyes was throwing the neighboring tables into a state of great excitement. There was one woman in particular, a powerful fair-haired person who sat close to her and made herself extremely agreeable. She seemed all aglow with affection, and pushed towards the girl so eagerly that Nana was on the point of interfering.

But at that very moment a woman who was entering the room gave her a shock of surprise. Indeed, she had recognized Madame Robert. The latter, looking as was her wont like a pretty brown mouse, nodded familiarly to the tall, lean serving-maid, and came and leant upon Laure's counter. Then both women exchanged a long kiss. Nana thought such an attention on the part of a woman so distinguished-looking very amusing, the more so because Madame Robert had quite altered her usual modest expression. On the contrary, her eye roved about the saloon as she kept up a whispered conversation. Laure had resumed her seat, and once more settled herself down with all the majesty of an old image of Vice, whose face has been worn and polished by the kisses of the faithful. Above the range of loaded plates she sat enthroned in all the opulence which an hotel-keeper enjoys after forty years of activity, and as she sat there she swayed her bloated following of large women, in comparison with the biggest of whom she seemed monstrous.

But Madame Robert had caught sight of Satin, and leaving Laure she ran up and behaved charmingly, telling her how much she regretted not having been at home the day before. When Satin, however, who was ravished at this treatment, insisted on finding room for her at the table, she vowed she had already dined. She had simply come up to look about her. As she stood talking behind her new friend's chair, she leant lightly on her shoulders, and in a smiling, coaxing manner remarked,—

"Now, when shall I see you? If you were free—"

Nana unluckily failed to hear more. The conversation vexed her, and she was dying to tell this honest lady a few home truths. But the sight of a troop of new arrivals paralyzed her. It was composed of smart, fashionably-dressed women, who were wearing their diamonds. Under the influence of perverse impulse, they had made up a party to come to Laure's—whom, by-the-by, they all treated with great familiarity—to eat the three-franc dinner, whilst flashing their jewels of great price in the jealous and astonished eyes of poor bedraggled prostitutes. The moment they entered, talking and laughing in their shrill clear tones, and seeming to bring sunshine with them from the outside world, Nana turned her head rapidly away. Much to her annoyance, she had recognized Lucy Stewart and Maria Blond amongst them, and for nearly five minutes, during which the ladies chatted with Laure before passing into the saloon beyond, she kept her head down, and seemed deeply occupied in rolling bread pills on the cloth in front of her. But, when at length she was able to look round, what was her astonishment to observe the chair next to hers vacant! Satin had vanished.

"Gracious, where can she be?" she loudly ejaculated.

The sturdy fair woman, who had been overwhelming Satin with civil attentions, laughed ill-temperedly, and when Nana, whom the laugh irritated, looked threatening, she remarked in a soft drawling way,—

"It's certainly not me that's done you this turn; it's the other one!"

Thereupon, Nana understood that they would most likely make game of her, and so said nothing more. She even kept her seat for some moments, as she did not wish to shew how angry she felt. She could hear Lucy Stewart laughing at the end of the next saloon, where she was treating a whole tableful of little women, who had come from the public balls at Montmartre and la Chapelle. It was very hot; the servant was carrying away piles of dirty plates with a strong scent of boiled fowl and rice, whilst the four gentlemen had

ended by regaling quite half a dozen couples with capital
wine in the hope of making them tipsy and hearing some
pretty stiffish things. What at present most exasperated
Nana was the thought of paying for Satin's dinner. There
was a wench for you, who allowed herself to be amused,
and then made off with never a thank-you in company with
the first petticoat that came by! Without doubt it was only
a matter of three francs, but she felt it was hard lines all
the same—her way of doing it was too disgusting. Nevertheless she paid up, throwing the six francs at Laure, whom
at the moment she despised more than the mud in the street.
In the Rue des Martyrs Nana felt her bitterness increasing.
She was certainly not going to run after Satin! It was a
nice filthy business for one to be poking one's nose into!
But her evening was spoilt, and she walked slowly up again
towards Montmartre, raging against Madame Robert in particular. Gracious goodness, that woman had a fine cheek to
go playing the lady—yes, the lady in the dust-bin! She
now felt sure she had met her at the "Papillon," a wretched
public-house ball in the Rue des Poissonniers, where men conquered her scruples for thirty sous. And to think a thing
like that got hold of important functionaries with her modest looks! And to think she refused suppers to which one
did her the honor of inviting her, because forsooth she was
playing the virtuous game! Oh, yes, she'd get virtued! It
was always those conceited prudes who went the most fearful
lengths in low corners nobody knew anything about.

Revolving these matters, Nana at length reached her home
in the Rue Véron, and was taken aback on observing a light
in the window. Fontan had come home in a sulk, for he
too had been deserted by the friend who had been dining
with him. He listened coldly to her explanations, whilst
she trembled lest he should strike her. It scared her to find
him at home, seeing that she had not expected him before
one in the morning, and she told him a fib, and confessed

that she had certainly spent six francs, but in Madame Maloir's society. He was not ruffled, however, and he handed her a letter, which, though addressed to her, he had quietly opened. It was a letter from Georges, who was still a prisoner at The Fondettes, and comforted himself weekly with the composition of glowing pages. Nana loved to be written to, especially when the letters were full of grand, lover-like expressions, with a sprinkling of vows. She used to read them to everybody. Fontan was familiar with the style employed by Georges, and appreciated it. But that evening she was so afraid of a scene that she affected complete indifference, skimming through the letter with a sulky expression and flinging it aside as soon as read. Fontan had begun beating a tattoo on a window-pane: the thought of going to bed so early bored him, and yet he did not know how to employ his evening. He turned briskly round:

"Suppose we answer that young vagabond at once," said he.

It was the custom for him to write the letters in reply. He was wont to vie with the other in point of style. Then, too, he used to be delighted when Nana, grown enthusiastic after the letter had been read over aloud, would kiss him with the announcement that nobody but he could "say things like that." Thus their latent affections would be stirred, and they would end with mutual adoration.

"As you will," she replied. "I'll make tea, and we'll go to bed after."

Thereupon Fontan installed himself at the table, on which pen, ink, and paper were at the same time grandly displayed. He curved his arm: he drew a long face.

"My Heart's Own," he began aloud.

And, for more than an hour he applied himself to his task, polishing here, weighing a phrase there, whilst he sat with his head between his hands, and laughed inwardly whenever he hit upon a peculiarly tender expression. Nana had already consumed two cups of tea in silence, when at last he read out the letter in the level voice, and with the two or three emphatic gestures, peculiar to such performances on the stage. It was five pages long, and he spoke therein of "the delicious hours passed at The Mignotte, those hours of which the memory lingered like subtle perfume." He vowed "eternal fidelity to that springtide of Love," and ended by declaring that his sole wish was to "recommence that happy time, if, indeed, happiness can recommence."

"I say that out of politeness, y'know," he explained. "The moment it becomes laughable—eh, what! I think she's felt it, she has!"

He glowed with triumph. But Nana was unskillful: she still suspected an outbreak, and now was mistaken enough not to fling her arms round his neck in a burst of admiration. She thought the letter a respectable performance, nothing more. Thereupon he was much annoyed. If his letter did not please her, she might write another! And so, instead of bursting out in lover-like speeches and exchanging kisses, as their wont was, they sat coldly facing one another at the table. Nevertheless, she poured him out a cup of tea.

"Here's a filthy mess," he cried, after dipping his lips in the mixture. "You've put salt in it, you have!"

Nana was unlucky enough to shrug her shoulders, and at that he grew furious.

"Ah, ha! things are taking a wrong turn to-night!"

And with that the quarrel began. It was only ten by the clock, and this was a way of killing time. So he lashed himself into a rage, and threw in Nana's teeth a whole string of insults and all kinds of accusations, which followed one another so closely that she had no time to defend herself. She was dirty, she was stupid, she had knocked about in all sorts of low places! After that, he waxed frantic over the money question. Did he spend six francs when he dined out? No, somebody was treating him to a dinner; otherwise he would have eaten his ordinary meal at home. And to think of spending them on that old procuress of a Maloir, a jade he would chuck out of the house to-morrow! Yes, by Jingo! they would get into a nice mess if he and she were to go throwing six francs out of window every day!

"Now, to begin with, I want your accounts," he shouted. "Let's see; hand over the money! Now, where do we stand?"

All his sordid avaricious instincts came to the surface. Nana was cowed and scared, and she made haste to fetch their remaining cash out of the desk, and to bring it him. Up to that time the key had lain on this common treasury, from which they had drawn as freely as they wished.

"How's this?" said he, when he had counted up the money, "there are scarcely seven thousand francs remaining out of seventeen thousand, and we've only been together three months. The thing's impossible."

He rushed forward, gave the desk a savage shake, and brought the drawer forward in order to ransack it in the light of the lamp. But it actually contained only six thousand eight hundred and odd francs. Thereupon the tempest burst forth.

"Ten thousand francs in three months!" he yelled. "By God! what have you done with it all? Eh? Answer! It all goes to your jade of an aunt, eh? Or you're keeping men, that's plain! Will you answer?"

"Oh, well! if you must get in a rage!" said Nana. "Why, the calculation's easily made! You haven't allowed for the furniture; besides, I've had to buy linen. Money goes quickly when one's settling in a new place."

But while requiring explanations he refused to listen to them.

"Yes, it goes a deal too quickly!" he rejoined more calmly. "And look here, little girl, I've had enough of this mutual housekeeping. You know those seven thousand francs are mine. Yes, and as I've got 'em, I shall keep 'em! Hang it, the moment you become wasteful I get anxious not to be ruined. To each man his own."

And he pocketed the money in a lordly way, whilst Nana gazed at him dumbfounded. He continued speaking complaisantly,—

"You must understand I'm not such a fool as to keep aunts and likewise children who don't belong to me. You were pleased to spend your own money—well, that's your affair! But my money—no, that's sacred! When in future you cook a leg of mutton, I'll pay for half of it. We'll settle up to-night—there!"

Straightway Nana rebelled. She could not help shouting,—

"Come, I say, it's you who've run through my ten thousand francs. It's a dirty trick, I tell you!"

But he did not stop to discuss matters further, for he dealt her a random box on the ear across the table, remarking as he did so,—

"Let's have that again!"

She let him have it again, despite his blow. Whereupon he fell upon her, and kicked and cuffed her heartily. Soon he had reduced her to such a state that she ended, as her wont was, by undressing and going to bed in a flood of tears.

He was out of breath, and was going to bed in his turn, when he noticed the letter he had written to Georges lying on the table. Whereupon he folded it up carefully, and, turning towards the bed, remarked in threatening accents,—

"It's very well written, and I'm going to post it myself, because I don't like women's fancies. Now don't go moaning any more; it puts my teeth on edge."

Nana, who was crying and gasping, thereupon held her breath. When he was in bed she choked with emotion, and threw herself upon his breast with a wild burst of sobs. Their scuffles always ended thus, for she trembled at the thought of losing him, and, like a coward, wanted always to feel that he belonged entirely to her, despite everything.

Twice he pushed her magnificently away, but the warm embrace of this woman, who was begging for mercy with great tearful eyes as some faithful brute might do, finally aroused desire. And he became royally condescending, without, however, lowering his dignity before any of her advances. In fact, he let himself be caressed and taken by force, as became a man whose forgiveness is worth the trouble of winning. Then he was seized with anxiety, fearing that Nana was playing a part with a view to regaining possession of the treasury key. The light had been extinguished when he felt it necessary to reaffirm his will and pleasure.

"You must know, my girl, that this is really very serious, and that I keep the money."

Nana, who was falling asleep with her arms round his neck, uttered a sublime sentiment.

"Yes, you need fear nothing! I'll work for both of us!"

But from that evening onwards, their life in common became more and more difficult. From one week's end to the other the noise of slaps filled the air, and resembled the ticking of a clock by which they regulated their existence. Through dint of being much beaten, Nana became as pliable as fine linen; her skin grew delicate, and pink and white, and so soft to the touch and clear to the view that she may be said to have grown more good-looking than ever. Prullière, moreover, began running after her like a madman, coming in when Fontan was away, and pushing her into corners in order to snatch an embrace. But she used to struggle out of his grasp, full of indignation, and blushing with shame. It disgusted her to think of him wanting to deceive a friend. Prullière would thereupon begin sneering with a wrathful expression. Why, she was growing jolly stupid nowadays! How could she take up with such an ape? For indeed Fontan was a regular ape, with that great swingeing nose of his. Oh, he had an ugly mug! Besides, the man knocked her about too!

"It's possible: I like him as he is," she one day made answer, in the quiet voice peculiar to a woman who confesses to an abominable taste.

Bosc contented himself by dining with them as often as possible. He shrugged his shoulders behind Prullière's back —a pretty fellow to be sure, but a frivolous! Bosc had on more than one occasion assisted at domestic scenes, and at dessert, when Fontan slapped Nana, he went on chewing solemnly, for the thing struck him as being quite in the course of nature. In order to give some return for his dinner, he used always to go into ecstasies over their happiness. He declared himself a philosopher, who had given up everything, glory included. At times Prullière and Fontan lolled back in their chairs, losing count of time in front of the empty table, whilst with theatrical gestures and intonation they discussed their former successes till two in the morning. But he would sit by, lost in thought, finishing the brandy bottle in silence, and only occasionally emitting a little contemptuous sniff. Where was Talma's tradition? Nowhere. Very well, let them leave him jolly well alone! It was too stupid to go on as they were doing!

One evening he found Nana in tears. She took off her dressing-jacket in order to shew him her back and her arms, which were black and blue. He looked at her skin without being tempted to abuse the opportunity, as that ass of a Prullière would have been. Then, sententiously,—

"My dear girl, where there are women there are sure to be ructions. It was Napoleon who said that, I think. Wash yourself with salt water. Salt water's the very thing for those little knocks. Tut, tut, you'll get others as bad, but don't complain so long as no bones are broken. I'm inviting myself to dinner, you know; I've spotted a leg of mutton."

But Madame Lerat had less philosophy. Every time Nana shewed her a fresh bruise on the white skin she screamed aloud. They were killing her niece: things couldn't go on as they were doing. As a matter of fact, Fontan had turned Madame Lerat out of doors, and had declared that he would not have her at his house in the future, and ever since that day, when he returned home and she happened to be there, she had to make off through the kitchen, which was a horrible humiliation to her. Accordingly, she never ceased inveighing against that brutal individual. She especially blamed his ill-breeding, pursing up her lips, as she did so, like a highly respectable lady, whom nobody could possibly remonstrate with on the subject of good manners.

"Oh, you notice it at once," she used to tell Nana; "he hasn't the barest notion of the very smallest proprieties. His mother must have been common! Don't deny it—the thing's obvious! I don't speak on my own account, though a person of my years has a right to respectful treatment: but *you*— how do *you* manage to put up with his bad manners? For, though I don't want to flatter myself, I've always taught you how to behave, and, among our own people you always enjoyed the best possible advice. We were all very well-bred in our family, weren't we now?"

Nana used never to protest, but would listen with bowed head.

"Then, too," continued the aunt, "you've only known perfect gentlemen hitherto. We were talking of that very topic with Zoé, at my place, yesterday evening. She can't understand it any more than I can. 'How is it,' said she, 'that *Madame*, who used to have that perfect gentleman, Monsieur le Comte, at her beck and call'—for between you and me it seems you drove him silly—'how is it that *Madame* lets herself be made into mince-meat by that clown of a fellow?' I remarked at the time that you might put up with the beatings, but that I would never have allowed him to be lacking in proper respect. In fact, there isn't a word to be said for him. I wouldn't have his portrait in my room even! And you ruin yourself for such a bird as that; yes, you ruin

yourself, my darling; you toil and you moil, when there are
so many others, and such rich men too, some of them even
connected with the Government! Ah, well, it's not I who
ought to be telling you this, of course! But, all the same,
when next he tries any of his dirty tricks on, I should cut
him short with a 'Monsieur, what d'you take me for?' You
know how to say it in that grand way of yours! It would
downright cripple him."

Thereupon Nana burst into sobs, and stammered out,—

"Oh, aunt, I love him!"

The fact of the matter was that Madame Lerat was beginning to feel anxious at the painful way her niece doled out
the sparse occasional francs, destined to pay for little Louis's
board and lodging. Doubtless she was willing to make
sacrifices, and to keep the child by her whatever might
happen, whilst waiting for more prosperous times, but the
thought that Fontan was preventing her, and the brat, and
its mother, from swimming in a sea of gold, made her so
savage that she was ready to deny the very existence of true
love. Accordingly she ended up with the following severe
remarks:

"Now listen, some fine day when he's taken the skin off
your back, you'll come and knock at my door, and I'll open it
to you."

Soon, money began to engross Nana's whole attention.
Fontan had caused the seven thousand francs to vanish away.
Without doubt they were quite safe: indeed, she would never
have dared ask him questions about them, for she was wont
to be blushingly diffident with that bird, as Madame Lerat
called him. She trembled lest he should think her capable
of quarreling with him about halfpence. He had certainly
promised to subscribe towards their common household expenses, and in the early days he had given out three francs
every morning. But he was as exacting as a boarder: he
wanted everything for his three francs—butter, meat, early

fruit and early vegetables—and if she ventured to make an observation, if she hinted that you could not have everything in the market for three francs, he flew into a temper and treated her as a useless, wasteful woman, a confounded donkey, whom the tradespeople were robbing. Moreover, he was always ready to threaten that he would take lodgings somewhere else. At the end of a month, on certain mornings, he had forgotten to deposit the three francs on the chest of drawers, and she had ventured to ask for them in a timid roundabout way. Whereupon there had been such bitter disputes, and he had seized every pretext to render her life so miserable, that she had found it best no longer to count upon him. Whenever, however, he had omitted to leave behind the three one-franc pieces, and found a dinner awaiting him all the same, he grew as merry as a sand-boy, kissed Nana gallantly, and waltzed with the chairs. And she was so charmed by this conduct that she at length got to hope that nothing would be found on the chest of drawers, despite the difficulty she experienced in making both ends meet. One day she even returned him his three francs, telling him a tale to the effect that she still had yesterday's money. As he had given her nothing then, he hesitated for some moments, as though he dreaded a lecture. But she gazed at him with her loving eyes, and hugged him in such utter self-surrender, that he pocketed the money again with that little convulsive twitch of the fingers peculiar to a miser when he regains possession of that which has been well-nigh lost. From that day forth he never troubled himself about money again, nor enquired whence it came. But when there were potatoes on the table he looked intoxicated with delight, and would laugh and smack his lips before her turkeys and legs of mutton, though of course this did not prevent his dealing Nana sundry sharp smacks, as though to keep his hand in, amid all his happiness.

Nana had indeed found means to provide for all needs,

and the place on certain days overflowed with good things. Twice a week regularly, Bosc had indigestion. One evening as Madame Lerat was withdrawing from the scene in high dudgeon because she had noticed a copious dinner she was not destined to eat in process of preparation, she could not prevent herself asking brutally who paid for it all. Nana was taken by surprise: she grew foolish, and began crying.

"Ah! that's a pretty business," said the aunt, who had divined her meaning.

Nana had resigned herself to it for the sake of enjoying peace in her own home. Then, too, the Tricon was to blame. She had come across her in the Rue de Laval, one fine day when Fontan had gone out raging about a dish of cod. She had accordingly consented to the proposals made her by the Tricon, who happened just then to be in a difficulty. As Fontan never came in before six o'clock, she made arrangements for her afternoons, and used to bring back forty francs, sixty francs, sometimes more. She might have made it a matter of ten and fifteen louis had she been able to maintain her former position, but, as matters stood, she was very glad thus to earn enough to keep the pot boiling. At night she used to forget all her sorrows, when Bosc sat there bursting with dinner, and Fontan leant on his elbows, and with an expression of lofty superiority becoming a man who is loved for his own sake, allowed her to kiss him on the eyelids.

In due course Nana's very adoration of her darling, her dear old duck, which was all the more passionately blind seeing that now she paid for everything, plunged her back into the muddiest depths of her calling. She roamed the streets, and loitered on the pavement in quest of a five-franc piece, just as when she was a slipshod baggage years ago. One Sunday, at the La Rochefoucauld Market, she had made her peace with Satin, after having flown at her with furious reproaches about Madame Robert. But Satin had been content to answer that, when one didn't like a thing, there was no reason why one should want to disgust others with it. And Nana, who was by way of being wide-minded, had accepted the philosophic view that you never can tell where your tastes will lead you, and had forgiven her. Her curiosity was even excited, and she began questioning her about obscure vices, and was astounded to be adding to her information at her time of life and with her knowledge. She burst out laughing and gave vent to various expressions of surprise. It struck her as so queer, and yet she was a little shocked by it, for she was really quite the Philistine outside the pale of her own habits. So she went back to Laure's and fed there when Fontan was dining out. She derived much amusement from the stories, and the amours, and the jealousies, which inflamed the female customers without hindering their appetites in the slightest degree. Nevertheless, she still was not quite in it, as she herself phrased it. The vast Laure, meltingly maternal as ever, used often to invite her to pass a day or two at her Asnières Villa, a country house containing seven spare bedrooms. But she used to refuse: she was afraid. Satin, however, swore she was mistaken about it, for that gentlemen from Paris swung you in swings, and played *tonneau* with you, and so she promised to come at some future time, when it would be possible for her to leave town.

At that time Nana was much tormented by circumstances, and not at all festively inclined. She needed money, and when the Tricon did not want her, which too often happened, she had no notion where to bestow her charms. Then began a series of wild descents upon the Parisian pavement, plunges into the baser sort of vice, whose votaries prowl in muddy by-streets under the restless flicker of gas-lamps. Nana went back to the public-house balls in the suburbs, where she had kicked up her heels in the early ill-shod days. She revisited the dark corners on the outer boulevards, where, when she was fifteen years old, men used to hug her, whilst her father was looking for her in order to give her a hiding. Both the women would speed along, visiting all the ball-rooms and restaurants in a quarter, and climbing innumerable staircases, which were wet with spittle and spilt beer, or they would stroll quietly about, going up streets and planting themselves in front of carriage-gates. Satin, who had served her apprenticeship in the Quartier Latin, used to take Nana to Bullier's and the public-houses in the Boulevard Saint-Michel. But the vacations were drawing on, and the "Quarter" looked too starved. Eventually they always returned to the principal boulevards, for it was there they ran the best chance of getting what they wanted. From the heights of Montmartre to the Observatory plateau, they scoured the whole town in the way we have been describing. They were out on rainy evenings, when their boots got worn down, and on hot evenings when their linen clung to their skins. There were long periods of waiting and endless periods of walking; there were jostlings and disputes, and the nameless brutal caresses of the stray passer-by who was taken by them to some miserable furnished room, and came swearing down the greasy stairs afterwards.

The summer was drawing to a close, a stormy summer of burning nights. The pair used to start out together after dinner towards nine o'clock. On the pavements of the Rue Notre Dame de la Lorette two long files of women scudded along with tucked-up skirts and bent heads, keeping close to the shops, but never once glancing at the displays in the shop-windows, as they hurried busily down towards the boulevards. This was the hungry exodus from the Quartier Breda which took place nightly when the street lamps had just been lit. Nana and Satin used to skirt the church and then march off along the Rue le Peletier. When they were some hundred yards from the Café Riche, and had fairly reached their scene of operations, they would shake out the skirts of their dresses which up till that moment they had been holding carefully up, and begin sweeping the pavements, regardless of dust. With much swaying of the hips they strolled delicately along, slackening their pace when they crossed the bright light thrown from one of the great cafés. With shoulders thrown back, shrill and noisy laughter, and many backward glances at the men who turned to look at them, they marched about and were completely in their element. In the shadow of night, their artificially whitened faces, their rouged lips, and their darkened eyelids became as charming and suggestive as if the inmates of a make-believe trumpery Oriental bazaar had been sent forth into the open street. Till eleven at night they sauntered gayly along among the rudely-jostling crowds, contenting themselves with an occasional "dirty ass!" hurled after the clumsy people whose boot-heels had torn a flounce or two from their dresses. Little familiar salutations would pass between them and the café waiters, and at times they would stop and chat in front of a small table and accept of drinks, which they consumed with much deliberation, as became people not sorry to sit down for a bit whilst waiting for the theaters to empty. But, as night advanced, if they had not made one or two trips in the direction of the Rue la Rochefoucauld, they became abject strumpets, and their hunt for men grew more ferocious than ever. Beneath the trees, in the darkening and fast-emptying boulevards, fierce bargainings took place, accompanied by oaths and blows. Respectable family parties—fathers, mothers, and daughters—who were used to such scenes, would pass quietly by the while, without quickening their pace. Afterwards, when they had walked from the Opera to the Gymnase some half score times, and, in the deepening night, men were rapidly dropping off homewards for good and all, Nana and Satin kept to the side-walk in the Rue du Faubourg Montmartre. There, up till two o'clock in the morning, restaurants, bars, and ham-and-beef shops

were brightly lit up, whilst a noisy mob of women hung
obstinately round the doors of the cafés. This suburb was
the only corner of night Paris which was still alight and
still alive, the only market still open to nocturnal bargains.
These last were openly struck between group and group, and
from one end of the street to the other, just as in the wide
and open corridor of a disorderly house. On such evenings
as the pair came home, without having had any success, they
used to wrangle together. The Rue Notre Dame de la
Lorette stretched dark and deserted in front of them. Here
and there the crawling shadow of a woman was discernible;
for the quarter was going home, and going home late, and
poor creatures, exasperated at a night of fruitless loitering,
were unwilling to give up the chase, and would still stand
disputing in hoarse voices with any strayed reveler they
could catch at the corner of the Rue Breda or the Rue Fontaine.

Nevertheless, some windfalls came in their way now and
then, in the shape of louis picked up in the society of elegent
gentlemen, who slipped their decorations into their pockets
as they went upstairs with them. Satin had an especially
keen scent for these. On rainy evenings, when the dripping
city exhaled an unpleasant odor suggestive of a great untidy
bed, she knew that the soft weather and the fetid reek of
the town's holes and corners were sure to send the men mad.
And so she watched the best dressed among them, for she
knew by their pale eyes what their state was. On such
nights it was as though a fit of fleshly madness were passing
over Paris. The girl was rather nervous certainly, for the
most modish gentlemen were always the most obscene. All
the varnish would crack off a man, and the brute beast would
shew itself, exacting, monstrous in lust, a past master in
corruption. But besides being nervous, that trollop of a
Satin was lacking in respect. She would blurt out awful
things in front of dignified gentlemen in carriages, and assure

them that their coachmen were better bred than they, because
they behaved respectfuly towards the women and did not
half kill them with their diabolical tricks and suggestions.
The way in which smart people sprawled head over heels
into all the cesspools of vice still caused Nana some surprise,
for she had a few prejudices remaining, though Satin was
rapidly destroying them.

"Well, then," she used to say, when talking seriously about
the matter, "there's no such thing as virtue left, is there?"

From one end of the social ladder to the other everybody
was on the loose! Good gracious! some nice things ought
to be going on in Paris between nine o'clock in the evening
and three in the morning! And with that she began making
very merry and declaring that, if one could only have looked
into every room, one would have seen some funny sights—
the little people going it head over ears, and a good lot of
swells, too, playing the swine rather harder than the rest.
Oh, she was finishing her education!

One evening when she came to call for Satin she recognized the Marquis de Chouard. He was coming downstairs
with quaking legs—his face was ashen white and he leant
heavily on the banisters. She pretended to be blowing her
nose. Upstairs she found Satin amid indescribable filth.
No household work had been done for a week, her bed was
disgusting, and ewers and basins were standing about in all
directions. Nana expressed surprise at her knowing the
Marquis. Oh, yes, she knew him! He had jolly well bored
her confectioner and her when they were together. At
present, he used to come back now and then, but he nearly
bothered her life out, going sniffing into all the dirty corners—yes, even into her slippers!

"Yes, dear girl, my slippers! Oh! he's the dirtiest old
beast, always wanting one to do things!"

The sincerity of these low debauches rendered Nana
especially uneasy, Seeing the courtesans around her slowly

dying of it every day, she recalled to mind the comedy of
pleasure she had taken part in when she was in the heydey
of success. Moreover, Satin inspired her with an awful fear
of the police. She was full of anecdotes about them. Formerly she had been the mistress of a plain-clothes man—
had consented to this in order to be left in peace, and on
two occasions he had prevented her from being put "on the
lists." But, at present, she was in a great fright, for, if she
were to be nabbed again, there was a clear case against her.
You had only to listen to her! For the sake of perquisites,
the police used to take up as many women as possible. They
laid hold of everybody, and quieted you with a slap if you
shouted, for they were sure of being defended in their actions
and rewarded, even when they had taken a virtuous girl
amongst the rest. In the summer they would swoop upon
the boulevard in parties of twelve or fifteen, surrounding a
whole long reach of side-walk and fishing up as many as
thirty women in an evening. Satin, however, knew the
likely places, and the moment she saw a plain-clothes man
heaving in sight she took to her heels, while the long lines
of women on the pavements scattered in consternation and
fled through the surrounding crowd. The dread of the law
and of the magistracy was such that certain women would
stand as though paralyzed in the doorways of the cafés, whilst
the raid was sweeping the avenue without. But Satin was
even more afraid of being denounced; for her pastrycook
had proved blackguard enough to threaten to sell her when
she had left him. Yes, that was a fake by which men lived
on their mistresses! Then, too, there were the dirty women
who delivered you up out of sheer treachery, if you were
prettier than they! Nana listened to these recitals, and felt
her terrors growing upon her. She had always trembled
before the Law, that unknown power, that form of revenge
practiced by men able and willing to crush her in the certain
absence of all defenders. Saint-Lazare she pictured as a

grave, a dark hole, in which they buried live women after they had cut off their hair. She admitted that it was only necessary to leave Fontan and seek powerful protectors. But as matters stood, it was in vain that Satin talked to her of certain lists of women's names, which it was the duty of the plain-clothes men to consult, and of certain photographs accompanying the lists, the originals of which were on no account to be touched. The reassurance did not make her tremble the less, and she still saw herself hustled and dragged along, and finally subjected to the official medical inspection. The thought of the official arm-chair filled her with shame and anguish, for had she not bade it defiance a score of times?

Now it so happened that, one evening towards the close of September, as she was walking with Satin in the Boulevard Poissonnière, the latter suddenly began tearing along at a terrible pace. And when Nana asked her what she meant thereby,—

"It's the plain-clothes men!" whispered Satin. "Off with you! Off with you!"

A wild stampede took place amid the surging crowd. Skirts streamed out behind, and were torn. There were blows and shrieks. A woman fell down. The crowd of by-standers stood hilariously watching this rough police raid, whilst the plain-clothes men rapidly narrowed their circle. Meanwhile, Nana had lost Satin. Her legs were failing her, and she would have been taken up for a certainty, had not a man caught her by the arm and led her away in front of the angry police. It was Prullière, and he had just recognized her. Without saying a word, he turned down the Rue Rougemont with her. It was just then quite deserted, and she was able to regain breath there, but at first her faintness and exhaustion were such that he had to support her. She did not even thank him.

"Look here," said he, "you must recover a bit. Come up
to my rooms."

He lodged in the Rue Bergère close by. But she straightened herself up at once.

"No, I don't want to."

Thereupon he waxed coarse, and rejoined,—

"Why don't you want to, eh? Why, everybody visits my
rooms."

"Because I don't."

In her opinion that explained everything. She was too
fond of Fontan to betray him with one of his friends. The
other people ceased to count the moment there was no pleasure
in the business, and necessity compelled her to it. In view
of her idiotic obstinacy, Prullière, as became a pretty fellow
whose vanity had been wounded, did a cowardly thing.

"Very well, do as you like!" he cried. "Only I don't side
with you, my dear. You must get out of the scrape by yourself."

And with that he left her. Terrors got hold of her again,
and scurrying past shops and turning white whenever a man
drew nigh, she fetched an immense compass before reaching
Montmartre.

On the morrow, whilst still suffering from the shock of
last night's terrors, Nana went to her aunt's, and, at the foot
of a small empty street in the Batignolles, found herself face
to face with Labordette. At first they both appeared embarrassed, for with his usual complaisance he was busy on a
secret errand. Nevertheless, he was the first to regain his
self-possession and to announce himself fortunate in meeting
her. Yes, certainly, everybody was still wondering at Nana's
total eclipse. People were asking for her, and old friends
were pining. And with that he grew quite paternal, and
ended by sermonizing.

"Frankly speaking, between you and me, my dear, the

thing's getting stupid. One can understand a mash, but to go to that extent, to be trampled on like that, and to get nothing but knocks! Are you playing up for the 'Virtue Prizes' then?"

She listened to him with an embarrassed expression. But when he told her about Rose, who was triumphantly enjoying her conquest of Count Muffat, a flame came into her eyes.

"Oh! if I wanted to——" she muttered.

As became an obliging friend, he at once offered to act as intercessor. But she refused his help, and he thereupon attacked her in an opposite quarter.

He informed her that Bordenave was busy mounting a play of Fauchery's, containing a splendid part for her.

"What! a play with a part!" she cried in amazement. "But he's in it, and he's told me nothing about it!"

She did not mention Fontan by name. However, she grew calm again directly, and declared that she would never go on the stage again. Labordette doubtless remained unconvinced, for he continued with smiling insistence.

"You know you need fear nothing with me. I get your Muffat ready for you, and you go on the stage again, and I bring him to you like a little dog!"

"No!" cried she, decisively.

And she left him. Her heroic conduct made her tenderly pitiful towards herself. No blackguard of a man would ever have sacrificed himself like that without trumpeting the fact abroad. Nevertheless, she was struck by one thing: Labordette had given her exactly the same advice as Francis had given her. That evening, when Fontan came home, she questioned him about Fauchery's piece. The former had been back at the Variétés for two months past. Why, then, had he not told her about the part?

"What part?" said he, in his ill-humored tone. "The grand lady's part, maybe? The deuce, you believe you've got talent then! Why, such a part would utterly do for you, my girl! You're meant for comic business—there's no denying it!"

She was dreadfully wounded. All that evening he kept chaffing her, calling her Mademoiselle Mars. But the harder he hit, the more bravely she suffered, for she derived a certain bitter satisfaction from this heroic devotion of hers, which rendered her very great and very loving in her own eyes. Ever since she had gone with other men in order to supply his wants, her love for him had increased, and the fatigues and disgusts encountered outside only added to the flame. He was fast becoming a sort of pet vice for which she paid, a necessity of existence it was impossible to do without, seeing that blows only stimulated her desires. He, on his part, seeing what a good tame thing she had become, ended by abusing his privileges. She was getting on his nerves, and he began to conceive so fierce a loathing for her that he forgot to keep count of his real interests. When Bosc made his customary remarks to him, he cried out in exasperation, for which there was no apparent cause, that he had had enough of her and of her good dinners, and that he would shortly chuck her out of doors if only for the sake of making another woman a present of his seven thousand francs. Indeed, that was how their liaison ended.

One evening Nana came in towards eleven o'clock, and found the door bolted. She tapped once—there was no answer; twice—still no answer. Meanwhile, she saw light under the door, and Fontan inside did not trouble to move. She rapped again unwearyingly; she called him, and began to get annoyed. At length Fontan's voice became audible; he spoke slowly and rather unctuously, and uttered but this one word:

"*Merde!*"

She beat on the door with her fists.

"*Merde!*"

She banged hard enough to smash in the woodwork.
"Merde!"

And for upwards of a quarter of an hour the same foul
expression buffeted her, answering like a jeering echo to
every blow wherewith she shook the door. At length, seeing
that she was not growing tired, he opened sharply, planted
himself on the threshold, folded his arms, and said in the
same cold, brutal voice,—

"By God! have you done yet? What d'you want? Are
you going to let us sleep in peace, eh? You can quite see I've
got company to-night."

He was certainly not alone, for Nana perceived the little
woman from the Bouffes, with the untidy tow hair and the
gimlet-hole eyes, standing enjoying herself in her shift among
the furniture she had paid for. But Fontan stepped out on
the landing. He looked terrible, and he spread out and
crooked his great fingers as if they were pincers.

"Hook it, or I'll strangle you!"

Thereupon Nana burst into a nervous fit of sobbing. She
was frightened, and she made off. This time it was she that
was being kicked out of doors. And in her fury the thought
of Muffat suddenly occurred to her. Ah, to be sure, Fontan
of all men ought never to have done her such a turn!

When she was out in the street, her first thought was to
go and sleep with Satin, provided the girl had no one with
her. She met her in front of her house, for she, too, had
been turned out of doors by her landlord. He had just had
a padlock affixed to her door—quite illegally, of course, seeing that she had her own furniture. She swore, and talked
of having him up before the commissary of police. In the
mean time, as midnight was striking, they had to begin thinking of finding a bed. And Satin, deeming it unwise to let
the plain-clothes men into her secrets, ended by taking Nana
to a woman who kept a little hotel in the Rue Laval. Here
they were assigned a narrow room on the first floor, the

window of which opened on the court-yard. Satin re-marked,—

"I should gladly have gone to Madame Robert's. There's always a corner there for me. But with you it's out of the question. She's getting absurdly jealous; she beat me the other night."

When they had shut themselves in, Nana, who had not yet relieved her feelings, burst into tears and again recounted Fontan's dirty behavior. Satin listened complaisantly, com-forted her, grew even more angry than she in denunciation of the male sex.

"Oh, the pigs, the pigs! Look here, we'll have nothing more to do with them!"

Then she helped Nana to undress with all the small busy attentions becoming a humble little friend. She kept saying coaxingly,—

"Let's go to bed as fast as we can, pet. We shall be better off there! Oh, how silly you are to get crusty about things! I tell you they're dirty brutes. Don't think any more about 'em. I—I love you very much. Don't cry, and oblige your own little darling girl."

And, once in bed, she forthwith took Nana in her arms, and soothed and comforted her. She refused to hear Fon-tan's name mentioned again, and each time it recurred to her friend's lips, she stopped it with a kiss. Her lips pouted in pretty indignation, her hair lay loose about her, and her face glowed with tenderness and childlike beauty. Little by little her soft embrace compelled Nana to dry her tears. She was touched, and replied to Satin's caresses. When two o'clock struck the candle was still burning, and a sound of soft smothered laughter and lovers' talk was audible in the room.

But suddenly a loud noise came up from the lower floors of the hotel, and Satin, with next to nothing on, got up and listened intently.

"The police!" said she, growing very pale.

"Oh, blast our bad luck! We're bloody well done for!"

Often and often had she told stories about the raids on hotels made by the plain-clothes men. But that particular night neither of them had suspected anything when they took shelter in the Rue Laval. At the sound of the word "police," Nana lost her head. She jumped out of bed, and ran across the room with the scared look of a mad woman about to jump out of the window. Luckily, however, the little courtyard was roofed with glass, which was covered with an iron-wire grating at the level of the girls' bedroom. At sight of this, she ceased to hesitate; she stepped over the window prop, and with her chemise flying and her legs bared to the night air, she vanished in the gloom.

"Stop! stop!" said Satin in a great fright. "You'll kill yourself."

Then, as they began hammering at the door, she shut the window like a good-natured girl, and threw her friend's clothes down into a cupboard. She was already resigned to her fate, and comforted herself with the thought that after all if she were to be put on the official list, she would no longer be so "beastly frightened" as of yore. So she pretended to be heavy with sleep. She yawned, she palavered, and ended by opening the door to a tall burly fellow with an unkempt beard, who said to her,—

"Shew your hands! You've got no needle-pricks on them: you don't work. Now then, dress!"

"But I'm not a dressmaker, I'm a burnisher," Satin brazenly declared.

Nevertheless, she dressed with much docility, knowing that argument was out of the question. Cries were ringing through the hotel, a girl was clinging to doorposts, and refusing to budge an inch. Another girl, in bed with a lover, who was answering for her legality, was acting the honest woman who had been grossly insulted, and spoke of bringing an action against the Prefect of Police. For close on an hour there was a noise of heavy shoes on the stairs, of fists ham mering on doors, of shrill disputes terminating in sobs, of pet- ticoats rustling along the walls, of all the sounds, in fact, at- tendant of the sudden awakening and scared departure of a flock of women, as they were roughly packed off by three plain-clothes men, headed by a little oily-mannered, fair- haired commissary of police. After they had gone, the hotel relapsed into deep silence.

Nobody had betrayed her; Nana was saved. Shivering and half dead with fear, she came groping back into the room. Her bare feet were cut and bleeding, for they had been torn by the grating. For a long while she remained sitting on the edge of the bed, listening and listening. Towards morning, however, she went to sleep again, and at eight o'clock, when she woke up, she escaped from the hotel and ran to her aunt's. When Madame Lerat, who happened just then to be drinking her morning coffee with Zoé, beheld her bedraggled plight and haggard face, she took note of the hour, and at once understood the state of the case.

"It's come to it, eh?" she cried. "I certainly told you that he would take the skin off your back one of these days. Well, well, come in; you'll always find a kind welcome here."

Zoé had risen from her chair, and was muttering with re- spectful familiarity,—

"*Madame* is restored to us at last. I was waiting for *Madame*."

But Madame Lerat insisted on Nana's going and kissing Louiset at once, because, said she, the child took delight in his mother's nice ways. Louiset, a sickly child with poor blood, was still asleep, and when Nana bent over his white scrofulous face, the memory of all she had undergone during the last few months brought a choking lump into her throat.

"Oh! my poor little one, my poor little one!" she gasped, bursting into a final fit of sobbing.

CHAPTER IX

THE *Petite Duchesse* was being rehearsed at the Variétés. The first act had just been carefully gone through, and the second was about to begin. Seated in old arm-chairs in the front of the stage, Fauchery and Bordenave were discussing various points, whilst the prompter, Father Cossard, a little hump-backed man, perched on a straw-bottomed chair, was turning over the pages of the manuscript, a pencil between his lips.

"Well, what are they waiting for?" cried Bordenave on a sudden, tapping the floor savagely with his heavy cane. "Barillot, why don't they begin?"

"It's Monsieur Bosc that has disappeared," replied Barillot, who was acting as second stage manager.

Then there arose a tempest, and everybody shouted for Bosc, whilst Bordenave swore.

"Always the same thing, by God! It's all very well ringing for 'em: they're always where they've no business to be. And then they grumble when they're kept till after four o'clock."

But Bosc just then came in with supreme tranquillity.

"Eh? What? What do they want me for? Oh, it's my turn! You ought to have said so. All right! Simonne gives the cue: 'Here are the guests,' and I come in—which way must I come in?"

"Through the door, of course," cried Fauchery in great exasperation.

"Yes, but where is the door?"

At this, Bordenave fell upon Barillot, and once more set to work swearing and hammering the boards with his cane.

"By God! I said a chair was to be put there to stand for the door, and every day we have to get it done again. Barillot? Where's Barillot? Another of 'em! Why, they're all going!"

Nevertheless, Barillot came and planted the chair down in person, mutely weathering the storm as he did so. And the rehearsal began again. Simonne, in her hat and furs, began moving about like a maid-servant busy arranging furniture. She paused to say,—

"I'm not warm, you know, so I keep my hands in my muff."

Then, changing her voice, she greeted Bosc with a little cry:

"La, it's *Monsieur le Comte*. You're the first to come, *Monsieur le Comte*, and *Madame* will be delighted."

Bosc had muddy trousers and a huge yellow overcoat, round the collar of which a tremendous comforter was wound. On his head he wore an old hat, and he kept his hands in his pockets. He did not act, but dragged himself along, remarking in a hollow voice,—

"Don't disturb your mistress, Isabelle; I want to take her by surprise."

The rehearsal took its course. Bordenave knitted his brows. He had slipped down low in his arm-chair, and was listening with an air of fatigue. Fauchery was nervous, and kept shifting about in his seat. Every few minutes he itched with the desire to interrupt, but he restrained himself. He heard a whispering in the dark and empty house behind him.

"Is she there?" he asked, leaning over towards Bordenave.

The latter nodded affirmatively. Before accepting the part of Géraldine which he was offering her, Nana had been anxious to see the piece, for she hesitated to play a courtesan's part a second time. She, in fact, aspired to an honest woman's part. Accordingly she was hiding in the shadows of a corner box in company with Labordette, who was managing matters for her with Bordenave. Fauchery glanced in her direction, and then once more set himself to follow the rehearsal.

Only the front of the stage was lit up. A flaring gas-burner on a support, which was fed by a pipe from the foot-lights, burnt in front of a reflector, and cast its full bright-ness over the immediate foreground. It looked like a big yellow eye glaring through the surrounding semi-obscurity, where it flamed in a doubtful, melancholy way. Cossard was holding up his manuscript against the slender stem of this arrangement. He wanted to see more clearly, and in the flood of light his hump was sharply outlined. As to Bordenave and Fauchery, they were already drowned in shadow. It was only in the heart of this enormous structure, on a few square yards of stage, that a faint glow suggested the light cast by some lantern nailed up in a railway station. It made the actors look like eccentric phantoms, and set their shadows dancing after them. The remainder of the stage was full of mist, and suggested a house in process of being pulled down, a church nave in utter ruin. It was littered with ladders, with set-pieces, and with scenery, of which the faded painting suggested heaped-up rubbish. Hanging high in air, the scenes had the appearance of great ragged clouts suspended from the rafters of some vast old-clothes shop, whilst above these again a ray of bright sunlight fell from a window and clove the shadow round the flies with a bar of gold.

Meanwhile actors were chatting at the back of the stage, whilst awaiting their cues. Little by little they had raised their voices.

"Confound it, will you be silent?" howled Bordenave, raging up and down in his chair. "I can't hear a word. Go outside, if you want to talk: *we* are at work. Barillot, if there's any more talking, I clap on fines all round!"

They were silent for a second or two. They were sitting in a little group on a bench and some rustic chairs in the corner of a scenic garden, which was standing ready to be put in position as it would be used in the opening act the same evening. In the middle of this group Fontan and Prullière were listening to Rose Mignon, to whom the manager of the Folies-Dramatique Theatre had been making magnificent offers. But a voice was heard shouting,—

"The Duchess! Saint-Firmin! The Duchess and Saint-Firmin are wanted!"

Only when the call was repeated did Prullière remember that he was Saint-Firmin! Rose, who was playing the Duchesse Hélène, was already waiting to go on with him, whilst old Bosc slowly returned to his seat, dragging one foot after the other over the sonorous and deserted boards. Clarisse offered him a place on the bench beside her.

"What's he bawling like that for?" said she, in allusion to Bordenave. "Things will be getting rosy soon! A piece can't be put on nowadays without its getting on his nerves."

Bosc shrugged his shoulders; he was above such storms. Fontan whispered,—

"He's afraid of a fiasco. The piece strikes me as idiotic."

Then he turned to Clarisse, and again referred to what Rose had been telling them:

"D'you believe in the offers of the Folies people, eh? Three hundred francs an evening for a hundred nights! Why not a country-house into the bargain? If his wife were to be given three hundred francs, Mignon would chuck my friend Bordenave, and do it jolly sharp too!"

Clarisse was a believer in the three hundred francs. That man Fontan was always picking holes in his friends' successes! Just then Simonne interrupted her. She was shivering with cold. Indeed, they were all buttoned up to the ears and had comforters on, and they looked up at the ray of sunlight, which shone brightly above them, but did not penetrate the cold gloom of the theater. In the streets outside there was a frost under a November sky.

"And there's no fire in the green-room!" said Simonne.

"It's disgusting; he *is* just becoming a skinflint! I want to be off; I don't want to get seedy."

"Silence, I say!" Bordenave once more thundered.

Then, for a minute or so, a confused murmur alone was audible as the actors went on repeating their parts. There was scarcely any appropriate action, and they spoke in even tones so as not to tire themselves. Nevertheless, when they did emphasize a particular shade of meaning, they cast a glance at the house, which lay before them like a yawning gulf. It was suffused with vague ambient shadow, which resembled the fine dust floating pent in some high windowless loft. The deserted house, whose sole illumination was the twilight radiance of the stage, seemed to slumber in melancholy and mysterious effacement. Near the ceiling dense night smothered the frescoes, whilst from the several tiers of stage-boxes on either hand huge widths of gray canvas stretched down to protect the neighboring hangings. In fact there was no end to these coverings; bands of canvas had been thrown over the velvet-covered ledges in front of the various galleries which they shrouded thickly. Their pale hue stained the surrounding shadows, and of the general decorations of the house only the dark recesses of the boxes were distinguishable. These served to outline the framework of the several stories, where the seats were so many stains of red velvet turned black. The chandelier had been let down as far as it would go, and it so filled the region of the stalls with its pendants as to suggest a flitting, and to set one thinking that the public had started on a journey from which they would never return.

Just about then, Rose, as the little Duchess who has been misled into the society of a courtesan, came to the footlights, lifted up her hands and pouted adorably at the dark and empty theater, which was as sad as a house of mourning.

"Good Heavens, what queer people!" said she, emphasizing the phrase, and confident that it would have its effect.

Far back in the corner box, in which she was hiding, Nana
sat enveloped in a great shawl. She was listening to the play,
and devouring Rose with her eyes. Turning towards
Labordette, she asked him in a low tone,—

"You are sure he'll come?"

"Quite sure. Without doubt, he'll come with Mignon,
so as to have an excuse for coming. As soon as he makes his
appearance, you'll go up into Mathilde's dressing-room, and
I'll bring him to you there."

They were talking of Count Muffat. Labordette had arranged this interview with him on neutral ground. He had
had a serious talk with Bordenave, whose affairs had been
gravely damaged by two successive failures. Accordingly
Bordenave had hastened to lend him his theater and to offer
Nana a part, for he was anxious to win the Count's favor,
and hoped to be able to borrow from him.

"And this part of Géraldine, what d'you think of it?"
continued Labordette.

But Nana sat motionless, and vouchsafed no reply. After
the first act, in which the author shewed how the Duc de
Beaurivage played his wife false with the blonde Géraldine,
a comic-opera celebrity, the second act witnessed the Duchess
Hélène's arrival at the house of the actress on the occasion of
a masked ball being given by the latter. The Duchess has
come to find out by what magical process ladies of that sort
conquer and retain their husbands' affections. A cousin, the
handsome Oscar de Saint-Firmin, introduces her, and hopes
to be able to debauch her. And her first lesson causes her
great surprise, for she hears Géraldine swearing like a hod-
man at the Duke, who suffers with most ecstatic submissiveness. The episode causes her to cry out, "Dear me, if
that's the way one ought to talk to the men!" Géraldine
had scarce any other scene in the act save this one. As to
the Duchess, she was very soon punished for her curiosity
for an old buck, the Baron de Tardiveau, took her for a

courtesan and became very gallant, whilst, on her other side, Beaurivage sat on a lounging chair and made his peace with Géraldine by dint of kisses and caresses. As this last lady's part had not yet been assigned to any one, Father Cossard had got up to read it, and he was now figuring away in Bosc's arms and emphasizing it despite himself. At this point, whilst the rehearsal was dragging monotonously on, Fauchery suddenly jumped from his chair. He had restrained himself up to that moment, but now his nerves got the better of him.

"That's not it!" he cried.

The actors paused awkwardly enough, whilst Fontan sneered, and asked in his most contemptuous voice,—

"Eh? What's not it? Who's not doing it right?"

"Nobody is! You're quite wrong, quite wrong!" continued Fauchery, and, gesticulating wildly, he came striding over the stage, and began himself to act the scene.

"Now look here, you Fontan, do please comprehend the way Tardiveau gets packed off. You must lean forward like this in order to catch hold of the Duchess. And then you, Rose, must change your position like that, but not too soon—only when you hear the kiss."

He broke off, and in the heat of explanation shouted to Cossard,—

"Géraldine, give the kiss! Loudly, so that it may be heard!"

Father Cossard turned towards Bosc, and smacked his lips vigorously.

"Good! That's the kiss," said Fauchery triumphantly. "Once more, let's have it once more. Now you see, Rose, I've had time to move, and then I give a little cry—so: 'Oh, she's given him a kiss.' But, before I do that, Tardiveau must go up the stage. D'you hear, Fontan, you go up. Come, let's try it again, all together."

The actors continued the scene again, but Fontan played

his part with such an ill grace that they made no sort of
progress. Twice Fauchery had to repeat his explanation, each
time acting it out with more warmth than before. The
actors listened to him with melancholy faces, gazed momentarily at one another as though he had asked them to walk
on their heads, and then awkwardly essayed the passage only
to pull up short directly afterwards, looking as stiff as pup-
pets whose strings have just been snapped.

"No, it beats me; I can't understand it," said Fontan at
length, speaking in the insolent manner peculiar to him.

Bordenave had never once opened his lips. He had slipped
quite down in his arm-chair, so that only the top of his hat
was now visible in the doubtful flicker of the gas-light on the
stand. His cane had fallen from his grasp, and lay slant-
wise across his waistcoat. Indeed he seemed to be asleep.
But suddenly he sat bolt upright.

"It's idiotic, my boy," he announced quietly to Fauchery.

"What d'you mean? Idiotic!" cried the author, growing
very pale. "It's you that are the idiot, my dear boy!"

Bordenave began to get angry at once. He repeated the
word "idiotic," and, seeking a more forcible expression, hit
upon "imbecile" and "damned foolish." The public would
hiss, and the act would never be finished! And when Fauchery, without indeed being very deeply wounded by these
big phrases, which always recurred when a new piece was
being put on, grew savage and called the other a brute, Bordenave went beyond all bounds, brandished his cane in the
air, snorted like a bull, and shouted,—

"Good God! why the hell can't you shut up? We've lost
a quarter of an hour over this folly. Yes, folly! There's
no sense in it. And it's so simple, after all's said and done!
You, Fontan, mustn't move. You, Rose, must make your
little movement; just that, no more, d'ye see? And then you
come down. Now, then let's get it done this journey. Give
the kiss, Cossard."

Then ensued confusion. The scene went no better than before. Bordenave, in his turn, shewed them how to act it about as gracefully as an elephant might have done, whilst Fauchery sneered and shrugged pityingly. After that Fontan put his word in, and even Bosc made so bold as to give advice. Rose, thoroughly tired out, had ended by sitting down on the chair which indicated the door. No one knew where they had got to, and by way of finish to it all Simonne made a premature entry, under the impression that her cue had been given her, and arrived amid the confusion. This so enraged Bordenave that he whirled his stick round in a terrific manner, and caught her a sounding thwack to the rearward. At rehearsal he used frequently to drub his former mistress. Simonne ran away, and this furious outcry followed her:

"Take that, and, by God! if I'm annoyed again I shut the whole shop up at once!"

Fauchery pushed his hat down over his forehead, and pretended to be going to leave the theater. But he stopped at the top of the stage, and came down again when he saw Bordenave perspiringly resuming his seat. Then he too took up his old position in the other arm-chair. For some seconds they sat motionlessly side by side, whilst oppressive silence reigned in the shadowy house. The actors waited for nearly two minutes. They were all heavy with exhaustion, and felt as though they had performed an overwhelming task.

"Well, let's go on," said Bordenave at last. He spoke in his usual voice, and was perfectly calm.

"Yes, let's go on," Fauchery repeated. "We'll arrange the scene to-morrow."

And with that they dragged on again, and rehearsed their parts with as much listlessness and as fine an indifference as ever. During the dispute between manager and author, Fontan and the rest had been taking things very comfortably on the rustic bench and seats at the back of the stage, where they had been chuckling, grumbling, and saying fiercely cutting things. But when Simonne came back, still smarting from her blow and choking with sobs, they grew melodramatic and declared that had they been in her place they would have strangled the swine. She began wiping her eyes and nodding approval. It was all over between them, she said. She was leaving him, especially as Steiner had offered to give her a grand start in life only the day before. Clarisse was much astonished at this, for the banker was quite ruined; but Prullière began laughing and reminded them of the neat manner in which that confounded Israelite had puffed himself alongside of Rose, in order to get his Landes Saltworks afloat on 'Change. Just at that time he was airing a new project, namely, a tunnel under the Bosphorus. Simonne listened with the greatest interest to this fresh piece of information.

As to Clarisse, she had been raging for a week past. Just fancy, that beast la Faloise, whom she had succeeded in chucking into Gaga's venerable embrace, was coming into the fortune of a very rich uncle! It was just her luck; she had always been destined to make things cosy for other people. Then, too, that pig Bordenave had once more given her a mere scrap of a part, a paltry fifty lines, just as if she could not have played Géraldine! She was yearning for the *rôle*, and hoping that Nana would refuse it.

"Well, and what about me?" said Prullière, with much bitterness. "I haven't got more than two hundred lines. I wanted to give the part up. It's too bad to make me play that fellow Saint-Firmin: why it's a regular failure! And then what a style it's written in, my dears! It'll fall dead flat, you may be sure."

But just then Simonne, who had been chatting with Father Barillot, came back breathless, and announced,—

"By-the-by, talking of Nana, she's in the house."

"Where, where?" asked Clarisse briskly, getting up to look for her.

The news spread at once, and everyone craned forward. The rehearsal was, as it were, momentarily interrupted. But Bordenave emerged from his quiescent condition, shouting,—

"What's up, eh? Finish the act, I say. And be quiet out there: it's unbearable!"

Nana was still following the piece from the corner box. Twice Labordette shewed an inclination to chat, but she grew impatient and nudged him to make him keep silent. The second act was drawing to a close, when two shadows loomed at the back of the theater. They were creeping softly down, avoiding all noise, and Nana recognized Mignon and Count Muffat. They came forward and silently shook hands with Bordenave.

"Ah, there they are," she murmured with a sigh of relief.

Rose Mignon delivered the last sentences of the act. Thereupon Bordenave said that it was necessary to go through the second again before beginning the third. With that he left off attending to the rehearsal, and greeted the Count with looks of exaggerated politeness, whilst Fauchery pretended to be entirely engrossed with his actors, who now grouped themselves round him. Mignon stood whistling carelessly, with his hands behind his back and his eyes fixed complacently on his wife, who seemed rather nervous.

"Well, shall we go upstairs?" Labordette asked Nana. "I'll install you in the dressing-room, and come down again and fetch him."

Nana forthwith left the corner box. She had to grope her way along the passage outside the stalls, but Bordenave guessed where she was as she passed along in the dark, and caught her up at the end of the corridor passing behind the scenes, a narrow tunnel where the gas burnt day and night. Here, in order to bluff her into a bargain, he plunged into a discussion of the courtesan's part.

"What a part it is, eh? What a wicked little part! It's made for you. Come and rehearse to-morrow."

Nana was frigid. She wanted to know what the third act was like.

"Oh! it's superb, the third act is! The Duchess plays the courtesan in her own house, and this disgusts Beaurivage, and makes him amend his way. Then there's an awfully funny *quid pro quo,* when Tardiveau arrives and is under the impression that he's at an opera dancer's house."

"And what does Géraldine do in it all?" interrupted Nana.

"Géraldine?" repeated Bordenave, in some embarrassment. "She has a scene, not a very long one, but a great success. It's made for you, I assure you! Will you sign?"

She looked steadily at him, and at length made answer,— "We'll see about that, all in good time."

And she rejoined Labordette, who was waiting for her on the stairs. Everybody in the theater had recognized her, and there was now much whispering, especially between Prullière, who was scandalized at her return, and Clarisse, who was very desirous of the part. As to Fontan, he looked coldly on, pretending unconcern, for he did not think it becoming to round on a woman he had loved. Deep down in his heart, though, his old love had turned to hate, and he nursed the fiercest rancor against her in return for the constant devotion, the personal beauty, the life in common, of which his perverse and monstrous tastes had made him tire.

In the mean time, when Labordette reappeared and went up to the Count, Rose Mignon, whose suspicions Nana's presence had excited, understood it all forthwith. Muffat was bothering her to death, but she was beside herself at the thought of being left like this. She broke the silence which she usually maintained on such subjects in her husband's society, and said bluntly,—

"You see what's going on? My word, if she tries the Steiner trick on again, I'll tear her eyes out!"

Tranquilly and haughtily, Mignon shrugged his shoulders, as became a man from whom nothing could be hidden.

"Do be quiet," he muttered. "Do me the favor of being quiet, won't you?"

He knew what to rely on now. He had drained his Muffat dry, and he knew that at a sign from Nana he was ready to lie down and be a carpet under her feet. There is no fighting against passions such as that. Accordingly, as he knew what men were, he thought of nothing but how to turn the situation to the best possible account.

It would be necessary to wait on the course of events. And he waited on them.

"Rose, it's your turn!" shouted Bordenave. "The second act's being begun again."

"Off with you, then," continued Mignon, "and let me arrange matters."

Then he began bantering, despite all his troubles, and was pleased to congratulate Fauchery on his piece. A very strong piece! Only why was his great lady so chaste? It wasn't natural! With that he sneered, and asked who had sat for the portrait of the Duke of Beaurivage, Géraldine's worn-out *roué*. Fauchery smiled—he was far from annoyed. But Bordenave glanced in Muffat's direction, and looked vexed, and Mignon was struck at this and became serious again.

"Let's begin, for God's sake!" yelled the manager. "Now then, Barillot? Eh? What? Isn't Bosc there? Is he bloody well making game of me now?"

Bosc, however, made his appearance quietly enough, and the rehearsal began again just as Labordette was taking the Count away with him. The latter was tremulous at the thought of seeing Nana once more. After the rupture had taken place between them, there had been a great void in his life. He was idle, and fancied himself about to suffer through the sudden change his habits had undergone, and accordingly

he had let them take him to see Rose. Besides, his brain had
been in such a whirl that he had striven to forget everything,
and had strenuously kept from seeking out Nana whilst
avoiding an explanation with the Countess. He thought,
indeed, that he owed his dignity such a measure of forget-
fulness. But mysterious forces were at work within, and
Nana began slowly to reconquer him. First came thoughts
of her, then fleshly cravings, and finally a new set of exclusive, tender, well-nigh paternal feelings.

The abominable events attendant on their last interview
were gradually effacing themselves. He no longer saw Fontan, he no longer heard the stinging taunt about his wife's
adultery with which Nana cast him out of doors. These
things were as words whose memory vanishes. Yet, deep
down in his heart, there was a poignant smart which wrung
him with such increasing pain that it nigh choked him.
Childish ideas would occur to him; he imagined that she
would never have betrayed him if he had really loved her,
and he blamed himself for this. His anguish was becoming
unbearable; he was really very wretched. His was the pain
of an old wound, rather than the blind present desire which
puts up with everything for the sake of immediate possession.
He felt a jealous passion for the woman, and was haunted by
longings for her and her alone, her hair, her mouth, her body.
When he remembered the sound of her voice, a shiver ran
through him; he longed for her as a miser might have done,
with refinements of desire beggaring description. He was
in fact so dolorously possessed by his passion, that when
Labordette had begun to broach the subject of an assignation,
he had thrown himself into his arms in obedience to irresistible impulse. Directly afterwards he had, of course, been
ashamed of an act of self-abandonment which could not but
seem very ridiculous in a man of his position; but Labordette
was one who knew when to see and when not to see things,
and he gave a further proof of his tact when he left the

Count at the foot of the stairs, and without effort let slip only these simple words:

"The right-hand passage on the second floor. The door's not shut."

Muffat was alone in that silent corner of the house. As he passed before the players' waiting-room, he had peeped through the open doors and noticed the utter dilapidation of the vast chamber, which looked shamefully stained and worn in broad daylight. But what surprised him most, as he emerged from the darkness and confusion of the stage, was the pure clear light and deep quiet at present pervading the lofty staircase, which one evening, when he had seen it before, had been bathed in gas-fumes and loud with the footsteps of women scampering over the different floors. He felt that the dressing-rooms were empty, the corridors deserted; not a soul was there; not a sound broke the stillness; whilst, through the square windows on the level of the stairs, the pale November sunlight filtered and cast yellow patches of light, full of dancing dust, amid the dead, peaceful air which seemed to descend from the regions above.

He was glad of this calm and this silence, and he went slowly up, trying to regain breath as he went, for his heart was thumping, and he was afraid lest he might behave childishly and give way to sighs and tears. Accordingly, on the first-floor landing, he leant up against a wall—for he was sure of not being observed—and pressed his handkerchief to his mouth, and gazed at the warped steps, the iron balustrade bright with the friction of many hands, the scraped paint on the walls—all the squalor, in fact, which that house of tolerance so crudely displayed at the pale afternoon hour when courtesans are asleep. When he reached the second floor he had to step over a big yellow cat, which was lying curled up on a step. With half-closed eyes this cat was keeping solitary watch over the house, where the close and now

frozen odors which the women nightly left behind them had
rendered him somnolent.

In the right-hand corridor, the door of the dressing-room
had indeed not been closed entirely. Nana was waiting.
That little Mathilde, a drab of a young girl, kept her dressing-room in a filthy state. Chipped jugs stood about anyhow; the dressing-table was greasy, and there was a chair
covered with red stains, which looked as if some one had bled
over the straw. The paper pasted on walls and ceiling was
splashed from top to bottom with spots of soapy water, and
this smelt so disagreeably of lavender scent turned sour that
Nana opened the window, and for some moments stayed
leaning on the sill, breathing the fresh air, and craning forward to catch sight of Madame Bron underneath. She could
hear her broom wildly at work on the mildewed pantiles of
the narrow court, which was buried in shadow. A canary,
whose cage hung on a shutter, was trilling away piercingly.
The sound of carriages in the boulevard and neighboring
streets was no longer audible, and the quiet and the wide
expanse of sleeping sunlight suggested the country. Looking
further afield, her eye fell on the small buildings and glass
roofs of the galleries in the Passage, and beyond these, on the
tall houses in the Rue Vivienne, the backs of which rose silent
and apparently deserted over against her. There was a succession of terrace-roofs close by, and on one of these a
photographer had perched a big cage-like construction of
blue glass. It was all very gay, and Nana was becoming
absorbed in contemplation, when it struck her some one had
knocked at the door.

She turned round and shouted,—

"Come in!"

At sight of the Count she shut the window, for it was not
warm, and there was no need for the eavesdropping Madame
Bron to listen. The pair gazed at one another gravely.
Then, as the Count still kept standing stiffly in front of her,

looking ready to choke with emotion, she burst out laughing, and said,—

"Well! So you're here again, you silly big beast!"

The tumult going on within him was so great that he seemed a man frozen to ice. He addressed Nana as "madam," and esteemed himself happy to see her again. Thereupon, she became more familiar than ever, in order to bounce matters through.

"Don't do it in the dignified way! You wanted to see me, didn't you? But you didn't intend us to stand looking at one another like a couple of chinaware dogs. We've both been in the wrong— Oh, I certainly forgive you!"

And herewith they agreed not to talk of that affair again, Muffat nodding his assent as Nana spoke. He was calmer now, but as yet could find nothing to say, though a thousand things rose tumultuously to his lips. Surprised at his apparent coldness, she began acting a part with much vigor.

"Come," she continued with a faint smile; "you're a sensible man! Now that we've made our peace, let's shake hands and be good friends in future."

"What? Good friends?" he murmured in sudden anxiety.

"Yes; it's idiotic, perhaps, but I should like you to think well of me. We've had our little explanation out, and if we meet again we shan't at any rate look like a pair of boobies."

He tried to interrupt her with a movement of the hand.

"Let me finish! There's not a man, you understand, able to accuse me of doing him a blackguardly turn: well, and it struck me as horrid to begin in your case. We all have our sense of honor, dear boy."

"But that's not my meaning!" he shouted violently. "Sit down—listen to me!"

And as though he were afraid of seeing her take her departure, he pushed her down on the solitary chair in the room. Then he paced about in growing agitation. The little dressing-room was airless and full of sunlight, and no sound from

the outside world disturbed its pleasant, peaceful, dampish
atmosphere. In the pauses of conversation the shrillings of
the canary were alone audible, and suggested the distant
piping of a flute.

"Listen," said he, planting himself in front of her, "I've
come to possess myself of you again. Yes, I want to begin
again. You know that well, then why do you talk to me as
you do? Answer me; tell me you consent."

Her head was bent, and she was scratching the blood-red
straw of the seat underneath her. Seeing him so anxious,
she did not hurry to answer. But at last she lifted up her
face. It had assumed a grave expression, and into the beautiful eyes she had succeeded in infusing a look of sadness.

"Oh, it's impossible, little man. Never, never, will I
live with you again."

"Why?" he stuttered, and his face seemed contracted in
unspeakable suffering.

"Why? Hang it all, because—! It's impossible, that's
about it. I don't want to."

He looked ardently at her for some seconds longer. Then
his legs curved under him, and he fell on the floor. In a
bored voice she added this simple advice:

"Ah, don't be a baby!"

But he was one already. Dropping at her feet, he had put
his arms round her waist, and was hugging her closely, pressing his face hard against her knees. When he felt her thus—
when he once more divined the presence of her velvety limbs
beneath the thin fabric of her dress, he was suddenly convulsed, and trembled, as it were, with fever, whilst madly,
savagely, he pressed his face against her knees as though he
had been anxious to force through her flesh. The old chair
creaked, and beneath the low ceiling, where the air was
pungent with stale perfumes, smothered sobs of desire were
audible.

"Well, and after?" Nana began saying, letting him do as

he would. "All this doesn't help you a bit, seeing that the thing's impossible. Good God, what a child you are!"

His energy subsided, but he still stayed on the floor, nor did he relax his hold of her, as he said in a broken voice,—

"Do at least listen to what I came to offer you. I've already seen a town house close to the Parc Monceau—I would gladly realize your smallest wish—in order to have you all to myself, I would give my whole fortune. Yes, that would be my only condition, that I should have you all to myself! Do you understand? And if you were to consent to be mine only, oh, then I should want you to be the loveliest, the richest woman on earth. I should give you carriages, and diamonds, and dresses!"

At each successive offer Nana shook her head proudly. Then seeing that he still continued them, that he even spoke of settling money on her—for he was at loss what to lay at her feet—she apparently lost patience.

"Come, come, have you done bargaining with me? I'm a good sort, and I don't mind giving in to you for a minute or two, as your feelings are making you so ill; but I've had enough of it now, haven't I? So let me get up. You're tiring me."

She extricated herself from his clasp, and once on her feet,—

"No, no, no!" said she. "I don't want to!"

With that he gathered himself up painfully, and feebly dropped into a chair, in which he leant back with his face in his hands. Nana began pacing up and down in her turn. For a second or two she looked at the stained wall-paper, the greasy toilet-table, the whole dirty little room as it basked in the pale sunlight. Then she paused in front of the Count, and spoke with quiet directness.

"It's strange, how rich men fancy they can have everything for their money. Well, and if I don't want to consent—what then? I don't care a pin for your presents! You might give

me Paris, and yet I should say no! always no! Look here,
it's scarcely clean in this room, yet I should think it very
nice if I wanted to live in it with you. But one's fit to kick
the bucket in your palaces, if one isn't in love. Ah, as to
money, my poor pet, I can lay my hands on that if I want to,
but I tell you, I trample on it, I spit on it!"

And with that she assumed a disgusted expression. Then
she became sentimental, and added in a melancholy tone,—

"I know of something worth more than money. Oh, if
only some one were to give me what I long for!"

He slowly lifted his head, and there was a gleam of hope in
his eyes.

"Oh, you can't give it me," she continued; "it doesn't
depend on you, and that's the reason I'm talking to you about
it. Yes, we're having a chat, so I may as well mention to
you that I should like to play the part of the respectable
woman in that show of theirs."

"What respectable woman?" he muttered in astonishment.

"Why, their Duchess Hélène! If they think I'm going to
play Géraldine, a part with nothing in it, a scene, and nothing
besides—if they think that! Besides, that isn't the reason.
The fact is I've had enough of courtesans. Why there's no
end to 'em. They'll be fancying I've got 'em on the brain,
to be sure they will! Besides, when all's said and done, it's
annoying, for I can quite see they seem to think me uneducated. Well, my boy, they're jolly well in the dark about
it, I can tell you! When I want to be a perfect lady, why
then I am a swell, and no mistake! Just look at this."

And she withdrew as far as the window, and then came
swelling back, with the mincing gait and circumspect air of a
portly hen that fears to dirty her claws. As to Muffat, he
followed her movements with eyes still wet with tears. He
was stupefied by this sudden transition from anguish to
comedy. She walked about for a moment or two in order
the more thoroughly to shew off her paces, and as she walked

she smiled subtly, closed her eyes demurely, and managed her skirts with great dexterity. Then she posted herself in front of him again.

"I guess I've hit it, eh?"

"Oh, thoroughly," he stammered with a broken voice and a troubled expression.

"I tell you I've got hold of the honest woman! I've tried at my own place. Nobody's got my little knack of looking like a duchess who don't care a damn for the men. Did you notice it when I passed in front of you? Why, the thing's in my blood! Besides, I want to play the part of an honest woman. I dream about it day and night—I'm miserable about it. I must have the part, d'you hear!"

And with that she grew serious, speaking in a hard voice and looking deeply moved, for she was really tortured by her stupid, tiresome wish. Muffat, still smarting from her late refusals, sat on without appearing to grasp her meaning. There was a silence, during which the very flies abstained from buzzing through the quiet, empty place.

"Now look here," she resumed bluntly, "you're to get them to give me the part."

He was dumfounded, and with a despairing gesture,—

"Oh, it's impossible! You yourself were saying just now that it didn't depend on me."

She interrupted him with a shrug of the shoulders.

"You'll just go down, and you'll tell Bordenave you want the part. Now don't be such a silly! Bordenave wants money—well, you'll lend him some, since you can afford to make ducks and drakes of it."

And as he still struggled to refuse her, she grew angry.

"Very well, I understand; you're afraid of making Rose angry. I didn't mention the woman when you were crying down on the floor—I should have had too much to say about it all. Yes, to be sure, when one has sworn to love a woman for ever, one doesn't usually take up with the first creature

that comes by directly after. Oh, that's where the shoe
pinches, I remember! Well, dear boy, there's nothing very
savory in the Mignons' leavings! Oughtn't you to have
broken it off with that dirty lot, before coming and squirm-
ing on my knees?"

He protested vaguely, and at last was able to get out a
phrase.

"Oh, I don't care a jot for Rose; I'll give her up at once."

Nana seemed satisfied on this point. She continued,—

"Well then, what's bothering you? Bordenave's master
here. You'll tell me there's Fauchery after Bordenave—"

She had sunk her voice, for she was coming to the delicate
part of the matter. Muffat sat silent, his eyes fixed on the
ground. He had remained voluntarily ignorant of Fauchery's assiduous attentions to the Countess, and time had
lulled his suspicions, and set him hoping that he had been
deceiving himself during that fearful night passed in a doorway of the Rue Taitbout. But he still felt a dull angry
repugnance to the man.

"Well, what then? Fauchery isn't the devil!" Nana repeated, feeling her way cautiously and trying to find out how
matters stood between husband and lover. "One can get
over his soft side. I promise you he's a good sort at bottom!
So it's a bargain, eh? You'll tell him that it's for my sake?"

The idea of taking such a step disgusted the Count.

"No, no! Never!" he cried.

She paused, and this sentence was on the verge of utterance:

"Fauchery can refuse you nothing."

But she felt that by way of argument it was rather too
much of a good thing. So she only smiled a queer smile
which spoke as plainly as words. Muffat had raised his eyes
to her, and now once more lowered them, looking pale and
full of embarrassment.

"Ah, you're not good-natured," she muttered at last.

"I cannot," said he, with a voice and a look of the utmost anguish. "I'll do whatever you like, but not that, dear love! Oh, I beg you not to insist on that!"

Thereupon she wasted no more time in discussion, but took his head between her small hands, pushed it back a little, bent down, and glued her mouth to his in a long long kiss. He shivered violently; he trembled beneath her touch; his eyes were closed, and he was beside himself. She lifted him to his feet.

"Go," said she simply.

He walked off, making towards the door. But as he passed out she took him in her arms again, became meek and coaxing, lifted her face to his, and rubbed her cheek against his waistcoat, much as a cat might have done.

"Where's the fine house?" she whispered in laughing embarrassment, like a little girl who returns to the pleasant things she has previously refused.

"In the Avenue de Villiers."

"And there are carriages there?"

"Yes."

"Lace? Diamonds?"

"Yes."

"Oh, how good you are, my old pet! You know it was all jealousy just now! And this time I solemnly promise you it won't be like the first, for now you understand what's due to a woman. You give all, don't you? Well, then, I don't want anybody but you! Why, look here, there's some more for you! There, and there, *and* there!"

When she had pushed him from the room, after firing his blood with a rain of kisses on hands and on face, she panted awhile. Good Heavens! what an unpleasant smell there was in that slut Mathilde's dressing-room! It was warm, if you will, with the tranquil warmth peculiar to rooms in the South when the winter sun shines into them, but really it smelt far too strong of stale lavender water, not to mention other less cleanly things! She opened the window, and again leaning on the window-still began watching the glass roof of the passage below in order to kill time.

Muffat went staggering downstairs. His head was swimming. What should he say? How should he broach the matter, which, moreover, did not concern him? He heard sounds of quarreling as he reached the stage. The second act was being finished, and Prullière was beside himself with wrath, owing to an attempt on Fauchery's part to cut short one of his speeches.

"Cut it all out then," he was shouting. "I should prefer that! Just fancy I haven't two hundred lines, and they're still cutting me down. No, by Jove, I've had enough of it: I give the part up."

He took a little crumpled manuscript book out of his pocket, and fingered its leaves feverishly as though he were just about to throw it on Cossard's lap. His pale face was convulsed by outraged vanity; his lips were drawn and thin, his eyes flamed; he was quite unable to conceal the struggle that was going on inside him. To think that he, Prullière, the idol of the public, should play a part of only two hundred lines!

"Why not make me bring in letters on a tray?" he continued bitterly.

"Come, come, Prullière, behave decently," said Bordenave, who was anxious to treat him tenderly because of his influence over the boxes. "Don't begin making a fuss. We'll find some points. Eh, Fauchery, you'll add some points? In the third act it would even be possible to lengthen a scene out."

"Well, then, I want the last speech of all," the comedian declared. "I certainly deserve to have it."

Fauchery's silence seemed to give consent, and Prullière, still greatly agitated, and discontented despite everything, put his part back into his pocket. Bosc and Fontan had appeared profoundly indifferent during the course of this explanation. Let each man fight for his own hand, they reflected; the present dispute had nothing to do with them; they had no interest therein! All the actors clustered round Fauchery, and began questioning him and fishing for praise, whilst Mignon listened to the last of Prullière's complaints without, however, losing sight of Count Muffat, whose return he had been on the watch for.

Entering in the half light, the Count had paused at the back of the stage, for he hesitated to interrupt the quarrel. But Bordenave caught sight of him, and ran forward.

"Aren't they a pretty lot?" he muttered. "You can have no idea what I've got to undergo with that lot, Monsieur le Comte. Each man's vainer than his neighbor, and they're wretched players all the same, a scabby lot, always mixed up in some dirty business or other! Oh, they'd be delighted if I were to come to smash. But I beg pardon—I'm getting beside myself."

He ceased speaking, and silence reigned, whilst Muffat sought how to broach his announcement gently. But he failed, and, in order to get out of his difficulty the more quickly, ended by an abrupt announcement:

"Nana wants the Duchess's part."

Bordenave gave a start, and shouted,—

"Come now, it's sheer madness!"

Then looking at the Count, and finding him so pale and so shaken, he was calm at once.

"Devil take it!" he said simply.

And with that there ensued a fresh silence. At bottom he didn't care a pin about it. That great thing Nana playing the Duchess might possibly prove amusing! Besides, now that this had happened, he had Muffat well in his grasp. Accordingly, he was not long in coming to a decision, and so he turned round and called out,—

"Fauchery!"

The Count had been on the point of stopping him. But Fauchery did not hear him, for he had been pinned against the curtain by Fontan, and was being compelled to listen patiently to the comedian's reading of the part of Tardiveau. Fontan imagined Tardiveau to be a native of Marseilles with a dialect; and he imitated the dialect. He was repeating whole speeches. Was that right? Was this the thing? Apparently he was only submitting ideas to Fauchery of which he was himself uncertain, but as the author seemed cold and raised various objections, he grew angry at once.

Oh, very well, the moment the spirit of the part escaped him, it would be better for all concerned that he shouldn't act it at all!

"Fauchery!" shouted Bordenave once more.

Thereupon the young man ran off, delighted to escape from the actor, who was wounded not a little by his prompt retreat.

"Don't let's stay here," continued Bordenave. "Come this way, gentlemen."

In order to escape from curious listeners, he led them into the property-room, behind the scenes, whilst Mignon watched their disappearance in some surprise. They went down a few steps, and entered a square room, whose two windows opened upon the court-yard. A faint light stole through the dirty panes, and hung wanly under the low ceiling. In pigeon-holes and shelves which filled the whole place up lay a collection of the most varied kind of *bric-à-brac*. Indeed it suggested an old clothes' shop in the Rue de Lappe in process of selling off, so indescribable was the hotch-potch of plates, gilt paste-board cups, old red umbrellas, Italian jars, clocks in all styles, platters and ink-pots, firearms and squirts, which lay chipped and broken, and in unrecognizable heaps, under a layer of dust an inch deep. An unendurable odor of old iron, rags, and damp cardboard, emanated from the various piles, where the *débris* of forgotten dramas had been collecting for half a century.

"Come in," Bordenave repeated. "We shall be alone at any rate."

The Count was extremely embarrassed, and he contrived to let the manager risk his proposal for him. Fauchery was astonished.

"Eh? What?" he asked.

"Just this," said Bordenave finally. "An idea has occurred to us. Now whatever you do, don't jump! It's most serious. What do you think of Nana for the Duchess's part?"

The author was bewildered; then he burst out with,—

"Ah, no, no! You're joking, aren't you? People would laugh far too much."

"Well, and it's a point gained already if they do laugh! Just reflect, my dear boy. The idea pleases Monsieur le Comte very much."

In order to keep himself in countenance Muffat had just picked out of the dust on a neighboring shelf an object which he did not seem to recognize. It was an egg-cup, and its stem had been mended with plaster. He kept hold of it unconsciously, and came forward muttering,—

"Yes, yes, it would be capital."

Fauchery turned towards him with a brisk, impatient gesture. The Count had nothing to do with his piece, and he said decisively,—

"Never! Let Nana play the courtesan as much as she likes, but a lady— No, by Jove!"

"You are mistaken, I assure you," rejoined the Count, growing bolder. "This very minute she has been playing the part of a pure woman for my benefit."

"Where?" queried Fauchery, with growing surprise.

"Upstair in a dressing-room. Yes, she has indeed, and with such distinction! She's got a way of glancing at you as she goes by you—something like this, you know!"

And, egg-cup in hand, he endeavored to imitate Nana, quite forgetting his dignity in his frantic desire to convince the others. Fauchery gazed at him in a state of stupefaction. He understood it all now, and his anger had ceased. The Count felt that he was looking at him, mockingly and pityingly, and he paused with a slight blush on his face.

"'Egad, it's quite possible!" muttered the author complaisantly. "Perhaps she would do very well, only the part's been assigned. We can't take it away from Rose."

"Oh, if that's all the trouble," said Bordenave, "I'll undertake to arrange matters."

But presently, seeing them both against him, and guessing that Bordenave had some secret interest at stake, the young man thought to avoid acquiescence by redoubling the violence of his refusal. The consultation was on the verge of being broken up.

"Oh, dear! No, no! Even if the part were unassigned, I should never give it her! There, is that plain? Do let me alone: I have no wish to ruin my play!"

He lapsed into silent embarrassment. Bordenave deeming himself *de trop*, went away, but the Count remained with bowed head. He raised it with an effort, and said in a breaking voice,—

"Supposing, my dear fellow, I were to ask this of you as a favor?"

"I cannot, I cannot," Fauchery kept repeating as he writhed to get free.

Muffat's voice became harder.

"I pray and beseech you for it! I want it!"

And with that he fixed his eyes on him. The young man read menaces in that darkling gaze, and suddenly gave way with a splutter of confused phrases:

"Do what you like—I don't care a pin about it. Yes, yes, you're abusing your power, but you'll see, you'll see!"

At this the embarrassment of both increased. Fauchery

was leaning up against a set of shelves, and was tapping nervously on the ground with his foot. Muffat seemed busy
examining the egg-cup, which he was still turning round
and about.

"It's an egg-cup," Bordenave obligingly came and remarked.

"Yes, to be sure! it's an egg-cup," the Count repeated.

"Excuse me, you're covered with dust," continued the
manager, putting the thing back on a shelf. "If one had
to dust every day, there'd be no end to it, you understand.
But it's hardly clean here—a filthy mess, eh? Yet, you may
believe me or not, when I tell you there's money in it. Now
look, just look at all that!"

He walked Muffat round in front of the pigeon-holes and
shelves, and in the greenish light which filtered through the
court-yard, told him the names of different properties, for
he was anxious to interest him in his marine-stores inven-
tory, as he jocosely termed it.

Presently, when they had returned into Fauchery's neighborhood, he said carelessly enough,—

"Listen, since we're all of one mind, we'll finish the matter
at once. Here's Mignon, just when he's wanted."

For some little time past Mignon had been prowling in the
adjoining passage, and the very moment Bordenave began
talking of a modification of their agreement he burst into
wrathful protest. It was infamous—they wanted to spoil
his wife's career—he'd go to law about it! Bordenave meanwhile was extremely calm and full of reasons. He did not
think the part worthy of Rose, and he preferred to reserve
her for an operetta, which was to be put on after the *Little
Duchess*. But when her husband still continued shouting,
he suddenly offered to cancel their arrangement in view of
the offers which the Folies-Dramatiques had been making the
singer. At this Mignon was momentarily put out, so without denying the truth of these offers he loudly professed a

vast disdain for money. His wife, he said, had been engaged
to play the Duchesse Hélène, and she would play the part
even if he, Mignon, were to be ruined over it. His dignity,
his honor, were at stake! Starting from this basis, the discussion grew interminable. The manager, however, always returned to the following argument: since the Folies had offered
Rose three hundred francs a night during a hundred performances, and since she only made a hundred and fifty with
him, she would be the gainer by fifteen thousand francs the
moment he let her depart. The husband, on his part, did
not desert the artist's position. What would people say if
they saw his wife deprived of her part? Why, that she was
not equal to it; that it had been deemed necessary to find a
substitute for her! And this would do great harm to Rose's
reputation as an artist; nay, it would diminish it. Oh, no,
no! Glory before gain! Then without a word of warning
he pointed out a possible arrangement: Rose, according to
the terms of her agreement, was pledged to pay a forfeit of
ten thousand francs in case she gave up the part. Very well,
then, let them give her ten thousand francs, and she would
go to the Folies-Dramatiques. Bordenave was utterly dumfounded, whilst Mignon, who had never once taken his eyes
off the Count, tranquilly awaited results.

"Then everything can be settled," murmured Muffat in
tones of relief; "we can come to an understanding."

"The deuce, no! that would be too stupid!" cried Bordenave, mastered by his commercial instincts. "Ten thousand francs to let Rose go! Why, people would make game
of me!"

But the Count, with a multiplicity of nods, bade him accept. He hesitated, and at last with much grumbling and
infinite regret over the ten thousand francs, which, by-
the-by, were not destined to come out of his own pocket,
he bluntly continued,—

"After all, I consent. At any rate I shall have you off my hands."

For a quarter of an hour past Fontan had been listening in the court-yard. Such had been his curiosity that he had come down and posted himself there; but, the moment he understood the state of the case, he went upstairs again and enjoyed the treat of telling Rose. Dear me! they were just haggling in her behalf! He dinned his words into her ears; she ran off to the property-room. They were silent as she entered. She looked at the four men. Muffat hung his head; Fauchery answered her questioning glance with a despairing shrug of the shoulders; as to Mignon, he was busy discussing the terms of the agreement with Bordenave.

"What's up?" she demanded curtly.

"Nothing," said her husband. "Bordenave here is giving ten thousand francs in order to get you to give up your part."

She grew tremulous with anger, and very pale, and she clenched her little fists. For some moments she stared at him; her whole nature in revolt. Ordinarily, in matters of business, she was wont to trust everything obediently to her husband, leaving him to sign agreements with managers and lovers. Now she could but cry,—

"Oh, come, you're too base for anything!"

The words fell like a lash. Then she sped away, and Mignon, in utter astonishment, ran after her. What next? Was she going mad? He began explaining to her in low tones that ten thousand francs from one party, and fifteen thousand from the other, came to twenty-five thousand. A splendid deal! Muffat was getting rid of her in every sense of the word; it was a pretty trick to have plucked him of this last feather! But Rose in her anger vouchsafed no answer. Whereupon Mignon in disdain left her to her feminine spite, and turning to Bordenave, who was once more on the stage with Fauchery and Muffat, said,—

"We'll sign to-morrow morning. Have the money in readiness."

At this moment Nana, to whom Labordette had brought the news, came down to the stage in triumph. She was quite the honest woman now, and wore a most distinguished expression, in order to overwhelm her friends and prove to the idiots that when she chose she could give them all points in the matter of smartness. But she nearly got into trouble, for at the sight of her Rose darted forward, choking with rage and stuttering,—

"Yes, you, I'll pay you out! Things can't go on like this, d'you understand!"

Nana forgot herself in face of this brisk attack, and was going to put her arms akimbo and give her what for. But she controlled herself, and looking like a marquise who is afraid of treading on an orange peel, fluted in still more silvery tones.

"Eh, what?" said she. "You're mad, my dear!"

And with that she continued in her graceful affectation, whilst Rose took her departure, followed by Mignon, who now refused to recognize her. Clarisse was enraptured, having just obtained the part of Géraldine from Bordenave. Fauchery, on the other hand, was gloomy: he shifted from one foot to the other: he could not decide whether to leave the theater or no. His piece was bedeviled, and he was seeking how best to save it. But Nana came up, took him by both hands, and drawing him towards her, asked whether he thought her so very atrocious after all. She wasn't going to eat his play—not she! Then she made him laugh, and gave him to understand that ne would be foolish to be angry with her in view of his relationship to the Muffats. If, said she, her memory failed her she would take her lines from the prompter. The house, too, would be packed in such a way as to ensure applause. Besides, he was mistaken about her, and he would soon see how she would rattle through her part.

By-and-by it was arranged that the author should make a few changes in the *rôle* of the Duchess so as to extend that of Prullière. The last-named personage was enraptured. Indeed, amid all the joy which Nana now quite naturally diffused, Fontan alone remained unmoved. In the middle of the yellow lamp-light, against which the sharp outline of his goat-like profile shone out with great distinctness, he stood shewing off his figure and affecting the pose of one who has been cruelly abandoned. Nana went quietly up and shook hands with him.

"How are you getting on?"

"Oh! pretty fairly. And how are you?"

"Very well, thank you."

That was all. They seemed to have only parted at the doors of the theater the day before. Meanwhile, the players were waiting about, but Bordenave said that the third act would not be rehearsed. And so it chanced that old Bosc went grumbling away at the proper time, whereas usually the company were needlessly detained and lost whole afternoons in consequence. Every one went off. Down on the pavement they were blinded by the broad daylight, and stood blinking their eyes in a dazed sort of way, as became people who had passed three hours squabbling with tight-strung nerves in the depths of a cellar. The Count, with racked limbs and vacant brain, got into a conveyance with Nana, whilst Labordette took Fauchery off and comforted him.

A month later the first night of the *Petite Duchesse* proved supremely disastrous to Nana. She was atrociously bad, and displayed such pretensions towards high comedy that the public grew mirthful. They did not hiss—they were too amused. From a stage-box Rose Mignon kept greeting her rival's successive entrances with a shrill laugh, which set the whole house off. It was the beginning of her revenge. Accordingly, when at night Nana, greatly chagrined, found herself alone with Muffat, she said furiously,—

"What a conspiracy, eh? It's all owing to jealousy. Oh! if they only knew how I despise 'em! What do I want them for nowadays? Look here! I'll bet a hundred louis that I'll bring all those who made fun to-day and make 'em lick the ground at my feet! Yes, I'll fine-lady your Paris for you, I will!"

CHAPTER X

THEREUPON Nana became a smart woman, mistress of all that is foolish and filthy in man, marquise in the ranks of her calling. It was a sudden but decisive start, a plunge into the garish day of gallant notoriety and mad expenditure, and that dare-devil wastefulness peculiar to beauty. She at once became queen among the most expensive of her kind. Her photographs were displayed in shop-windows, and she was mentioned in the papers. When she drove in her carriage along the boulevards, the people would turn and tell one another who that was, with all the unction of a nation saluting its sovereign, whilst the object of their adoration lolled easily back in her diaphanous dresses, and smiled gayly under the rain of little golden curls which ran riot above the blue of her made-up eyes and the red of her painted lips. And the wonder of wonders was that the great creature, who was so awkward on the stage, so very absurd the moment she sought to act the chaste woman, was able without effort to assume the *rôle* of an enchantress in the outer world. Her movements were lithe as a serpent's, and the studied and yet seemingly involuntary carelessness with which she dressed was really exquisite in its elegance. There was a nervous distinction in all she did which suggested a well-born Persian cat; she was an aristocrat in vice, and proudly and rebelliously trampled upon a prostrate Paris like a sovereign whom none dare disobey. She set the fashion, and great ladies imitated her.

Nana's fine house was situated at the corner of the Rue Cardinet, in the Avenue de Villiers. The avenue was part of the luxurious quarter at that time springing up in the vague district which had once been the Plaine Monceau. The house had been built by a young painter, who was intoxicated by a first success, and had been perforce resold almost as soon as it was habitable. It was in the palatial Renaissance manner, and had fantastic interior arrangements which consisted of modern conveniences framed in a setting of somewhat artificial originality. Count Muffat had bought the house ready furnished, and full of hosts of beautiful objects—lovely Eastern hangings, old credences, huge chairs of the Louis XIII. epoch. And thus Nana had come into artistic surroundings of the choicest kind and of the most extravagantly various dates. But since the studio, which occupied the central portion of the house, could not be of any use to her, she had upset existing arrangements, establishing a small drawing-room on the first floor, next to her bedroom and dressing-room, and leaving a conservatory, a large drawing-room, and a dining-room, to look after themselves underneath. She astonished the architect with her ideas, for, as became a Parisian work-girl who understands the elegancies of life by instinct, she had suddenly developed a very pretty taste for every species of luxurious refinement. Indeed she did not spoil her house overmuch; nay, she even added to the richness of the furniture, save here and there, where certain traces of tender foolishness and vulgar magnificence betrayed the ex-flower-seller who had been wont to dream in front of shop-windows in the arcades.

A carpet was spread on the steps beneath the great awning over the front door in the court, and the moment you entered the hall you were greeted by a perfume as of violets and a soft warm atmosphere which thick hangings helped to produce. A window, whose yellow and rose-colored panes suggested the warm pallor of human flesh, gave light to the wide staircase, at the foot of which a Negro in carved wood held out a silver tray full of visiting cards, and four white marble women, with bosoms displayed, raised lamps in their uplifted hands. Bronzes and Chinese vases full of flowers, divans covered with old Persian rugs, arm-chairs upholstered in old tapestry, furnished the entrance-hall, adorned the stair-heads, and gave the first-floor landing the appearance of an ante-room. Here men's overcoats and hats were always in evidence, and there were thick hangings which deadened every sound. It seemed a place apart: on entering it you might have fancied yourself in a chapel, whose very air was thrilling with devotion, whose very silence and seclusion were fraught with mystery.

Nana only opened the large and somewhat too-sumptuous Louis XVI. drawing-room on those gala nights when she received society from the Tuileries or strangers of distinction. Ordinarily, she only came downstairs at meal-times, and she would feel rather lost on such days as she lunched by herself in the lofty dining-room, with its Gobelins tapestry, and its monumental sideboard, adorned with old porcelain and mar- velous pieces of ancient plate. She used to go upstairs again as quickly as possible, for her home was on the first floor, in the three rooms, the bed, dressing, and small drawing-room above described. Twice already she had done the bed-cham- ber up anew; on the first occasion in mauve satin, on the second in blue silk under lace. But she had not been satisfied with this; it had struck her as "no-howish," and she was still unsuccessfully seeking for new colors and designs. On the elaborately-upholstered bed, which was as low as a sofa, there were twenty thousand francs' worth of *point de Venise* lace. The furniture was lacquered blue and white under designs in silver filigree; and everywhere lay such numbers of white bearskins that they hid the carpet. This was a luxurious caprice on Nana's part, she having never been able to break herself of the habit of sitting on the floor to take her stockings off. Next door to the bedroom the little saloon was full of an amusing medley of exquisitely artistic objects. Against the hangings of pale rose-colored silk—a faded Turkish rose-color, embroidered with gold thread—a whole world of them stood sharply outlined. They were from every land and in every possible style. There were Italian cabinets, Spanish and Portuguese coffers, models of Chinese pagodas, a Japanese screen of precious workmanship, besides china, bronzes, embroidered silks, hangings of the finest needlework. Armchairs wide as beds, and sofas deep as alcoves, suggested voluptuous idleness and the somnolent life of the seraglio. The prevailing tone of the room was old gold, blended with green and red, and nothing it contained too forcibly indicated the presence of the courtesan save the luxuriousness of the seats. Only two "biscuit" statuettes, a woman in her shift hunting for fleas, and another with nothing at all on walking on her hands and waving her feet in the air, sufficed to sully the room with a note of stupid originality.

Through a door, which was nearly always ajar, the dressing-room was visible. It was all in marble and glass, with a white bath, silver jugs and basins, and crystal and ivory appointments. A drawn curtain filled the place with a clear twilight, which seemed to slumber in the warm scent of violets, that suggestive perfume peculiar to Nana wherewith the whole house from the roof to the very court-yard was penetrated.

The furnishing of the house was a most important undertaking. Nana certainly had Zoé with her, that girl so devoted to her fortunes. For months she had been tranquilly awaiting this abrupt new departure as became a woman who was certain of her powers of prescience, and now she was triumphant; she was mistress of the house, and was putting by a round sum whilst serving *Madame* as honestly as possible. But a solitary lady's maid was no longer sufficient. A butler, a coachman, a porter, and a cook were wanted. Besides, it was necessary to fill the stables. It was then that Labordette made himself most useful. He undertook to perform all sorts of errands which bored the Count; he made a comfortable job of the purchase of horses, he visited the coach-builders, he guided the young woman in her choice of things. She was to be met with at the shops, leaning on his arm. Labordette even got in the servants—Charles, a great tall coachman, who had been in service with the Duc de Corbreuse; Julien, a little, smiling, much-becurled butler; and a married couple, of whom the wife, Victorine, became cook, whilst the husband, François, was taken on as porter and footman. The last mentioned in powder and breeches wore Nana's livery, which was a sky-blue one adorned with silver lace, and he received visitors in the hall. The whole thing was princely in the correctness of its style.

At the end of two months the house was set going. The cost had been more than three hundred thousand francs. There were eight horses in the stables, and five carriages in the coach-houses, and of these five one was a landau with silver embellishments, which for the moment occupied the attention of all Paris. And, amid this great wealth, Nana began settling down, and making her nest. After the third representation of the *Petite Duchesse* she had quitted the theater, leaving Bordenave to struggle on against a bankruptcy which, despite the Count's money, was imminent. Nevertheless, she was still bitter about her failure. It added to that other bitterness, the lesson Fontan had given her, a shameful lesson for which she held all men responsible. Accordingly, she now declared herself very firm, and quite proof against sudden infatuations, but thoughts of vengeance took no hold of her volatile brain. What did maintain a hold on it, in the hours when she was not indignant, was an ever-wakeful lust of expenditure, added to a natural contempt for the man who paid, and to a perpetual passion for consumption and waste, which took pride in the ruin of her lovers.

At starting, Nana put the Count on a proper footing, and clearly mapped out the conditions of their relationship. The Count gave twelve thousand francs monthly, presents excepted, and demanded nothing in return save absolute fidelity. She swore fidelity, but insisted also on being treated with the utmost consideration, on enjoying complete liberty as mistress of the house, and on having her every wish respected. For instance, she was to receive her friends every day, and he was to come only at stated times. In a word, he was to repose a blind confidence in her in everything. And when he was seized with jealous anxiety, and hesitated to grant what she wanted, she stood on her dignity, and threatened to give him back all he had given, or even swore by little Louiset to perform what she promised. This was to suffice him. There was no love where mutual esteem was wanting. At the end of the first month Muffat respected her.

But she desired and obtained still more. Soon she began to influence him as became a good-natured courtesan. When he came to her in a moody condition she cheered him up, confessed him, and then gave him good advice. Little by little she interested herself in the annoyances of his home life, in his wife, in his daughter, in his love affairs and financial difficulties; she was very sensible, very fair, and right-minded. On one occasion only did she let anger get the better of her, and that was when he confided to her that doubtless Daguenet was going to ask for his daughter Estelle in marriage. When the Count began making himself notorious, Daguenet had thought it a wise move to break off with Nana. He had treated her like a base hussy, and had sworn to snatch his future father-in-law out of the creature's clutches. In return, Nana abused her old Mimi in a charming fashion. He was a renegade who had devoured his fortune in the company of vile women; he had no moral sense. True, he did not let

them pay him money, but he profited by that of others, and
only repaid them at rare intervals with a bouquet or a dinner.
And when the Count seemed inclined to find excuses for
these failings she bluntly informed him that Daguenet had
enjoyed her favors, and she added disgusting particulars.
Muffat had grown ashen-pale. There was no question of the
young man now. This would teach him to be lacking in
gratitude!

Meanwhile, the house had not been entirely furnished,
when, one evening after she had lavished the most energetic
promises of fidelity on Muffat, Nana kept the Count Xavier
de Vandeuvres for the night. For the last fortnight he had
been paying her assiduous court, visiting her and sending
presents of flowers, and now she gave way not so much out
of sudden infatuation as to prove that she was a free woman.
The idea of gain followed later, when, the day after, Vandeuvres helped her to pay a bill which she did not wish to
mention to the other man. From Vandeuvres she would certainly derive from eight to ten thousand francs a month, and
this would prove very useful as pocket-money. In those days
he was finishing the last of his fortune in an access of burning, feverish folly. His horses and Lucy had devoured three
of his farms, and at one gulp Nana was going to swallow his
last château, near Amiens. He seemed in a hurry to sweep
everything away, down to the ruins of the old tower, built
by a Vandeuvres under Philip Augustus. He was mad for
ruin, and thought it a great thing to leave the last golden
bezants of his coat-of-arms in the grasp of this courtesan,
whom the world of Paris desired. He, too, accepted Nana's
conditions, leaving her entire freedom of action and claim-
ing her caresses only on certain days. He was not even
naïvely impassioned enough to require her to make vows.
Muffat suspected nothing. As to Vandeuvres, he knew
things would take place for a certainty, but he never made
the least allusion to them, and pretended total ignorance,

whilst his lips wore the subtle smile of the skeptical man of pleasure, who does not seek the impossible provided he can have his day and that Paris is aware of it.

From that time forth Nana's house was really properly appointed. The staff of servants was complete in the stable, in the kitchen, and in my lady's chamber. Zoé organized everything, and passed successfully through the most unforeseen difficulties. The household moved as easily as the scenery in a theater, and was regulated like a grand administrative concern. Indeed, it worked with such precision that during the early months there were no jars and no derangements. *Madame*, however, pained Zoé extremely with her imprudent acts, her sudden fits of unwisdom, her mad bravado. Still the lady's maid grew gradually lenient, for she had noticed that she made increased profits in seasons of wanton waste when *Madame* had committed a folly which must be made up for. It was then that the presents began raining on her, and she fished up many a louis out of the troubled waters.

One morning when Muffat had not yet left the bedroom, Zoé ushered a gentleman into the dressing-room, where Nana was changing her underwear. He was trembling violently.

"Good gracious! It's Zizi!" said the young woman, in great astonishment.

It was indeed Georges. But when he saw her in her shift, with her golden hair over her bare shoulders, he threw his arms round her neck and round her waist, and kissed her in all directions. She began struggling to get free, for she was frightened, and in smothered tones she stammered,—

"Do leave off! He's there! Oh, it's silly of you! And you, Zoé, are you out of your senses? Take him away, and keep him downstairs: I'll try and come down."

Zoé had to push him in front of her. When Nana was able to rejoin them in the drawing-room downstairs, she scolded them both, and Zoé pursed up her lips, and took her

departure with a vexed expression, remarking that she had
only been anxious to give *Madame* a pleasure. Georges was
so glad to see Nana again, and gazed at her with such delight, that his fine eyes began filling with tears. The miserable days were over now; his mother believed him to have
grown reasonable, and had allowed him to leave The Fondettes. Accordingly, the moment he had reached the terminus, he had got a conveyance in order the more quickly
to come and kiss his sweet darling. He spoke of living at
her side in future, as he used to do down in the country,
when he waited for her barefooted in the bedroom at The
Mignotte. And as he told her about himself, he let his fingers
creep forward, for he longed to touch her after that cruel
year of separation. Then he got possession of her hands,
felt about in the wide sleeves of her dressing-jacket, traveled
up as far as her shoulders.

"You still love your baby?" he asked, in his child-voice.

"Oh, I certainly love him!" answered Nana, briskly getting out of his clutches; "but you come popping in without
warning. You know, my little man, I'm not my own mistress; you must be good!"

Georges, when he got out of his cab, had been so dizzy
with the feeling that his long desire was at last about to be
satisfied, that he had not even noticed what sort of house
he was entering. But now he became conscious of a change
in the things around him. He examined the sumptuous dining-room, with its lofty decorated ceiling, its Gobelins hangings, its buffet blazing with plate.

"Yes, yes!" he remarked sadly.

And with that she made him understand that he was never
to come in the mornings, but between four and six in the
afternoon, if he cared to. That was her reception-time.
Then, as he looked at her with suppliant questioning eyes
and craved no boon at all, she, in her turn, kissed him on
the forehead in the most amiable way.

"Be very good," she whispered. "I'll do all I can."

But the truth was that this remark now meant nothing. She thought Georges very nice, and would have liked him as a companion, but as nothing else. Nevertheless, when he arrived daily at four o'clock, he seemed so wretched, that she was often fain to be as compliant as of old, and would hide him in cupboards, and constantly allow him to pick up the crumbs from Beauty's table. He hardly ever left the house now, and became as much one of its inmates as the little dog Bijou. Together they nestled among mistress's skirts and enjoyed a little of her at a time, even when she was with another man, whilst doles of sugar and stray caresses not seldom fell to their share in her hours of loneliness and boredom.

Doubtless Madame Hugon found out that the lad had again returned to that wicked woman's arms, for she hurried up to Paris, and came and sought aid from her other son, the Lieutenant Philippe, who was then in garrison at Vincennes. Georges, who was hiding from his elder brother, was seized with despairing apprehension, for he feared the latter might adopt violent tactics, and as his tenderness for Nana was so nervously expansive that he could not keep anything from her, he soon began talking of nothing but his big brother, a great strong fellow who was capable of all kinds of things.

"You know," he explained, "mamma won't come to you whilst she can send my brother. Oh, she'll certainly send Philippe to fetch me."

The first time he said this Nana was deeply wounded. She said frigidly,—

"Gracious me, I should like to see him come! For all that he's a lieutenant in the army, François will chuck him out in double-quick time!"

Soon, as the lad kept returning to the subject of his brother, she ended by taking a certain interest in Philippe,

and in a week's time she knew him from head to foot—
knew him as very tall and very strong, and merry and somewhat rough. She learnt intimate details, too, and found out
that he had hair on his arms and a birthmark on his shoulder. So thoroughly did she learn her lesson that one day,
when she was full of the image of the man who was to be
turned out of doors by her orders, she cried out,—

"I say, Zizi, your brother's not coming. He's a base de-
serter!"

The next day, when Georges and Nana were alone together, François came upstairs to ask whether *Madame* would
receive Lieutenant Philippe Hugon. Georges grew extremely
white, and murmured,—

"I suspected it; mamma was talking about it this morning."

And he besought the young woman to send down word
that she could not see visitors. But she was already on her
feet, and seemed all aflame as she said,—

"Why should I not see him? He would think me afraid.
Dear me, we'll have a good laugh! Just leave the gentleman
in the drawing-room for a quarter of an hour, François;
afterwards bring him up to me."

She did not sit down again, but began pacing feverishly to
and fro between the fire-place and a Venetian mirror hanging above an Italian chest. And each time she reached the
latter she glanced at the glass and tried the effect of a smile,
whilst Georges sat nervously on a sofa, trembling at the
thought of the coming scene. As she walked up and down
she kept jerking out such little phrases as,—

"It will calm the fellow down if he has to wait a quarter
of an hour. Besides, if he thinks he's calling on a Tottie,
the drawing-room will stun him! Yes, yes, have a good look
at everything, my fine fellow! It isn't imitation, and it'll
teach you to respect the lady who owns it. Respect's what

men need to feel! The quarter of an hour's gone by, eh?
No? Only ten minutes? Oh! we've got plenty of time."

She did not stay where she was, however. At the end of
the quarter of an hour she sent Georges away, after making
him solemnly promise not to listen at the door, as such conduct would scarcely look proper in case the servants saw him.
As he went into her bedroom, Zizi ventured, in a choking
sort of way to remark,—

"It's my brother, you know—"

"Don't you fear," she said, with much dignity; "if he's
polite, I'll be polite!"

François ushered in Philippe Hugon, who wore morning
dress. Georges began crossing on tiptoe on the other side
of the room, for he was anxious to obey the young woman.
But the sound of voices retained him, and he hesitated in
such anguish of mind that his knees gave way under him.
He began imagining that a dread catastrophe would befall,
that blows would be struck, that something abominable would
happen, which would make Nana everlastingly odious to him.
And so he could not withstand the temptation to come back
and put his ear against the door. He heard very ill, for the
thick *portières* deadened every sound; but he managed to
catch certain words spoken by Philippe, stern phrases in
which such terms as "mere child," "family," "honor," were
distinctly audible. He was so anxious about his darling's
possible answers that his heart beat violently and filled his
head with a confused buzzing noise. She was sure to give
vent to a "Dirty blackguard!" or to a "Leave me bloody
well alone! I'm in my own house!" But nothing happened
—not a breath came from her direction. Nana seemed dead
in there! Soon even his brother's voice grew gentler, and
he could not make it out at all, when a strange murmuring
sound finally stupefied him. Nana was sobbing! For a moment or two he was the prey of contending feelings, and

knew not whether to run away or to fall upon Philippe. But just then Zoé came into the room, and he withdrew from the door, ashamed at being thus surprised.

She began quietly to put some linen away in a cupboard, whilst he stood mute and motionless, pressing his forehead against a winodw-pane. He was tortured by uncertainty. After a short silence the woman asked,—

"It's your brother that's with *Madame?*"

"Yes," replied the lad, in a choking voice.

There was a fresh silence.

"And it makes you anxious, doesn't it, Monsieur Georges?"

"Yes," he rejoined in the same painful, suffering tone.

Zoé was in no hurry. She folded up some lace, and said slowly,—

"You're wrong: *Madame* will manage it all."

And then the conversation ended: they said not another word. Still she did not leave the room. A long quarter of an hour passed, and she turned round again without seeming to notice the look of exasperation overspreading the lad's face, which was already white with the effects of uncertainty and constraint. He was casting sidelong glances in the direction of the drawing-room.

Maybe Nana was still crying. The other must have grown savage and have dealt her blows. Thus, when Zoé finally took her departure, he ran to the door, and once more pressed his ear against it. He was thunderstruck; his head swam, for he heard a brisk outburst of gayety, tender whispering voices, and the smothered giggles of a woman who is being tickled. Besides, almost directly afterwards, Nana conducted Philippe to the head of the stairs, and there was an exchange of cordial and familiar phrases.

When Georges again ventured into the drawing-room the young woman was standing before the mirror, looking at herself.

"Well?" he asked in utter bewilderment.

"Well, what?" said she, without turning round. Then, negligently,—

"What did you mean? He's very nice, is your brother!"

"So it's all right, is it?"

"Oh, certainly it's all right! Goodness me, what's over you? One would have thought we were going to fight!"

Georges still failed to understand.

"I thought I heard—that is, you didn't cry?" he stammered out.

"Me cry!" she exclaimed, looking fixedly at him. "Why, you're dreaming! What makes you think I cried?"

Thereupon the lad was treated to a distressing scene for having disobeyed and played Paul Pry behind the door. She sulked, and he returned with coaxing submissiveness to the old subject, for he wished to know all about it.

"And my brother, then?"

"Your brother saw where he was at once. You know I might have been a Tottie, in which case his interference would have been accounted for by your age and the family honor! Oh, yes, I understand those kinds of feelings! But a single glance was enough for him, and he behaved like a well-bred man at once. So don't be anxious any longer, it's all over—he's gone to quiet your mamma!"

And she went on laughingly,—

"For that matter, you'll see your brother here. I've invited him, and he's going to return."

"Oh, he's going to return," said the lad, growing white. He added nothing, and they ceased talking of Philippe. She began dressing to go out, and he watched her with his great sad eyes. Doubtless he was very glad that matters had got settled, for he would have preferred death to a rupture of their connection, but deep down in his heart there was a silent anguish, a profound sense of pain, which he had no experience of and dared not talk about. How Philippe quieted their mother's fears he never knew, but three days later she returned to The Fondettes, apparently satisfied. On the evening of her return, at Nana's house, he trembled when François announced the lieutenant, but the latter jested gayly, and treated him like a young rascal, whose escapade he had favored as something not likely to have any consequences. The lad's heart was sore within him, he scarcely dared move, and blushed girlishly at the least word that was spoken to him. He had not lived much in Philippe's society, he was ten years his junior, and he feared him as he would a father, from whom stories about women are concealed. Accordingly, he experienced an uneasy sense of shame when he saw him so free in Nana's company, and heard him laugh uproariously as became a man who was plunging into a life of pleasure with the gusto born of magnificent health. Nevertheless, when his brother shortly began to present himself every day, Georges ended by getting somewhat used to it all. Nana was radiant.

This her latest installation had been involving all the riotous waste attendant on the life of gallantry; and now her housewarming was being defiantly celebrated in a grand mansion positively overflowing with males and with furniture.

One afternoon when the Hugons were there, Count Muffat arrived out of hours. But when Zoé told him that *Madame* was with friends, he refused to come in and took his departure discreetly, as became a gallant gentleman. When he made his appearance again in the evening, Nana received him with the frigid indignation of a grossly-affronted woman.

"Sir," said she, "I have given you no cause why you should insult me. You must understand this: when I am at home to visitors, I beg you to make your appearance just like other people."

The Count simply gaped in astonishment. "But my dear—?" he endeavored to explain.

"Perhaps it was because I had visitors! Yes, there were men here, but what d'you suppose I was doing with those men? You only advertise a woman's affairs when you act the discreet lover, and I don't want to be advertised, I don't!"

He obtained his pardon with difficulty, but at bottom he was enchanted. It was with scenes such as these that she kept him in unquestioning and docile submission. She had long since succeeded in imposing Georges on him as a young vagabond who, she declared, amused her. She made him dine with Philippe, and the Count behaved with great amiability. When they rose from table, he took the young man on one side, and asked news of his mother. From that time forth the young Hugons, Vandeuvres, and Muffat were openly about the house, and shook hands as guests and intimates might have done. It was a more convenient arrangement than the previous one. Muffat alone still abstained discreetly from too frequent visits, thus adhering to the ceremonious policy of an ordinary strange caller. At night when Nana was sitting on her bearskins drawing off her stockings, he would talk amicably about the other three gentlemen, and lay especial stress on Philippe, who was loyalty itself.

"It's very true; they're nice," Nana would say, as she lingered on the floor to change her shift. "Only, you know, they see what I am. One word about it, and I should chuck 'em all out of doors for you!"

Nevertheless, despite her luxurious life and her group of courtiers, Nana was nearly bored to death. She had men for every minute of the night, and money overflowed even among the brushes and combs in the drawers of her dressing-table. But all this had ceased to satisfy her; she felt that there was a void somewhere or other, an empty place provocative of yawns. Her life dragged on devoid of occupation, and successive days only brought back the same monotonous hours. To-morrow had ceased to be; she lived like a bird: sure of her food, and ready to perch and roost on any branch which she came to. This certainty of food and drink left her lolling effortless for whole days, lulled her to sleep in conventual idleness and submission as though she were the prisoner of her trade. Never going out except to drive, she was losing her walking powers. She reverted to low childish tastes, would kiss Bijou from morning to night and kill time with stupid pleasures, whilst waiting for the man whose caresses she tolerated with an appearance of complaisant lassitude. Amid this species of self-abandonment she now took no thought about anything save her personal beauty; her sole care was to look after herself, to wash and to perfume her limbs, as became one who was proud of being able to undress at any moment and in face of anybody without having to blush for her imperfections.

At ten in the morning Nana would get up. Bijou, the Scotch griffon dog, used to lick her face and wake her, and then would ensue a game of play lasting some five minutes, during which the dog would race about over her arms and legs, and cause Count Muffat much distress. Bijou was the first little male he had ever been jealous of. It was not at all proper, he thought, that an animal should go poking its nose under the bed-clothes like that! After this Nana would proceed to her dressing-room, where she took a bath. Towards eleven o'clock, François would come and do up her hair before beginning the elaborate manipulations of the afternoon.

At breakfast, as she hated feeding alone, she nearly always had Madame Maloir at table with her. This lady would arrive from unknown regions in the morning, wearing her extravagantly quaint hats, and would return at night to that mysterious existence of hers, about which no one ever troubled. But the hardest to bear were the two or three hours between lunch and the toilet. On ordinary occasions she proposed a game of bézique to her old friend, on others she would read the *Figaro*, in which the theatrical echoes and the fashionable news interested her. Sometimes she even opened a book, for she fancied herself in literary matters. Her toilet kept her till close on five o'clock, and then only she would wake from her day-long drowse, and drive out or receive a whole mob of men at her own house. She would often dine abroad, and always go to bed very late, only to rise again on the morrow with the same languor as before, and to begin another day differing in nothing from its predecessor.

The great distraction was to go to the Batignolles and see her little Louis at her aunt's. For a fortnight at a time she forgot all about him, and then would follow an access of maternal love, and she would hurry off on foot with all the modesty and tenderness becoming a good mother. On such occasions she would be the bearer of snuff for her aunt and of oranges and biscuits for the child, the kind of presents one takes to a hospital. Or again she would drive up in her landau on her return from the Bois, decked in costumes, the resplendence of which greatly excited the dwellers in the solitary street. Since her niece's magnificent elevation, Madame Lerat had been puffed up with vanity. She rarely presented herself in the Avenue Villiers, for she was pleased to remark that it wasn't her place to do so, but she enjoyed triumphs in her own street. She was delighted when the young woman arrived in dresses that had cost four or five thousand francs, and would be occupied during the whole of the next day in shewing off her presents and in citing prices which quite stupefied the neighbors. As often as not, Nana kept Sunday free for the sake of "her family"; and on such occasions, if Muffat invited her, she would refuse with the smile of a good little shopwoman. It was impossible, she would answer; she was dining at her aunt's, she was going to see baby. Moreover, that poor little man Louiset was always ill. He was almost three years old, growing quite a great boy! But he had had an eczema on the back of his neck, and now concretions were forming in his ears, which pointed, it was feared, to decay of the bones of the skull. When she saw how pale he looked, with his spoilt blood and his flabby flesh all out in yellow patches, she would become serious, but her principal feeling would be one of astonishment. What could be the matter with the little love that he should grow so weakly? She, his mother, was so strong and well!

On the days when her child did not engross attention, Nana would again sink back into the noisy monotony of her existence, with its drives in the Bois, first nights at the theater, dinners and suppers at the Maison-d'Or or the Café Anglais, not to mention all the places of public resort, all the spectacles to which crowds rushed—Mabille, the reviews, the races. But whatever happened she still felt that stupid, idle void, which caused her, as it were, to suffer internal cramps. Despite the incessant infatuations that possessed her heart, she would stretch out her arms with a gesture of immense weariness the moment she was left alone. Solitude rendered her low spirited at once, for it brought her face to face with the emptiness and boredom within her. Extremely gay by nature and profession, she became dismal in solitude, and would sum up her life in the following ejaculation, which recurred incessantly between her yawns:

"Oh, how the men bother me!"

One afternoon, as she was returning home from a concert, Nana, on the sidewalk in the Rue Montmartre, noticed a woman trotting along in down-at-heels boots, dirty petticoats, and a hat utterly ruined by the rain. She recognized her suddenly.

"Stop, Charles!" she shouted to the coachman, and began calling: "Satin, Satin!"

Passers-by turned their heads, the whole street stared. Satin had drawn near, and was still further soiling herself against the carriage wheels.

"Do get in, my dear girl," said Nana tranquilly, disdaining the onlookers.

And with that she picked her up and carried her off, though she was in disgusting contrast to her light blue landau and her dress of pearl-gray silk, trimmed with Chantilly, whilst the street smiled at the coachman's loftily dignified demeanor.

From that day forth Nana had a passion to occupy her thoughts. Satin became her vicious foible. Washed and dressed, and duly installed in the house in the Avenue de Villiers, during three days the girl talked of Saint-Lazare, and the annoyances the sisters had caused her, and how those dirty police people had put her down on the official list. Nana grew indignant, and comforted her, and vowed she would get her name taken off, even though she herself should have to go and find out the Minister of the Interior. Meanwhile, there was no sort of hurry: nobody would come and search for her at Nana's—that was certain. And thereupon the two women began to pass tender afternoons together, making numberless endearing little speeches, and mingling their kisses with laughter. The same little sport, which the arrival of the plain-clothes men had interrupted in the Rue de Laval, was beginning again in a jocular sort of spirit. One fine evening, however, it became serious, and Nana, who had been so disgusted at Laure's, now understood what it meant. She was upset and enraged by it, the more so because Satin disappeared on the morning of the fourth day. No one had seen her go out. She had, indeed, slipped away in her new dress, seized by a longing for air, full of sentimental regret for her old street existence.

That day there was such a terrible storm in the house that all the servants hung their heads in sheepish silence. Nana had come near beating François for not throwing himself across the door through which Satin escaped. She did her best, however, to control herself, and talked of Satin as a dirty swine. Oh, it would teach her to pick filthy things like that out of the gutter!

When *Madame* shut herself up in her room in the afternoon, Zoé heard her sobbing. In the evening she suddenly

asked for her carriage and had herself driven to Laure's. It
had occurred to her that she would find Satin at the *table
d'hôte* in the Rue des Martyrs. She was not going there for
the sake of seeing her again, but in order to catch her one in
the face! As a matter of fact, Satin was dining at a little
table with Madame Robert. Seeing Nana, she began to laugh;
but the former, though wounded to the quick, did not make
a scene. On the contrary, she was very sweet and very compliant. She paid for champagne, made five or six tablefuls
tipsy, and then carried off Satin when Madame Robert was
in the closets. Not till they were in the carriage did she make
a mordant attack on her, threatening to kill her if she did it
again.

After that day, the same little business began again continually. On twenty different occasions, Nana, tragically
furious as only a jilted woman can be, ran off in pursuit of
this sluttish creature, whose flights were prompted by the
boredom she suffered amid the comforts of her new home.
Nana began to talk of boxing Madame Robert's ears; one
day she even meditated a duel: there was one woman too
many, she said.

In these latter times, whenever she dined at Laure's, she
donned her diamonds, and occasionally brought with her
Louise Violaine, Maria Blond, and Tatan Néné, all of them
ablaze with finery; and whilst the sordid feast was progressing
in the three saloons, and the yellow gaslight flared overhead,
these four resplendent ladies would demean themselves with
a vengeance, for it was their delight to dazzle the little local
courtesans and to carry them off when dinner was over. On
days such as these, Laure, sleek and tight-laced as ever, would
kiss every one with an air of expanded maternity. Yet notwithstanding all these circumstances, Satin's blue eyes and
pure virginal face remained as calm as heretofore; torn,
beaten, and pestered by the two women, she would simply
remark that it was a funny business, and they would have

done far better to make it up at once. It did no good to
slap her; she couldn't cut herself in two, however much she
wanted to be nice to everybody. It was Nana who finally
carried her off in triumph, so assiduously had she loaded Satin
with kindnesses and presents. In order to be revenged, however, Madame Robert wrote abominable, anonymous letters
to her rival's lovers.

For some time past Count Muffat had appeared suspicious,
and one morning, with considerable show of feeling, he laid
before Nana an anonymous letter, where, in the very first
sentences, she read that she was accused of deceiving the
Count with Vandeuvres and the young Hugons.

"It's false! It's false!" she loudly exclaimed in accents of
extraordinary candour.

"You swear?" asked Muffat, already willing to be comforted.

"I'll swear by whatever you like—yes! by the head of my
child!"

But the letter was long. Soon her connection with Satin
was described in the broadest and most ignoble terms. When
she had done reading, she smiled.

"Now I know who it comes from," she remarked simply.

And, as Muffat wanted her denial to the charges therein
contained, she resumed quietly enough,—

"That's a matter which doesn't concern you, dear old pet.
How can it hurt you?"

She did not deny anything. He used some horrified expressions. Thereupon she shrugged her shoulders. Where
had he been all this time? Why it was done everywhere!
And she mentioned her friends, and swore that fashionable
ladies went in for it. In fact, to hear her speak, nothing
could be commoner or more natural. But a lie was a lie, and
so, a moment ago, he had seen how angry she grew in the
matter of Vandeuvres and the young Hugons! Oh, if that
had been true, he would have been justified in throttling

her! But what was the good of lying to him about a matter of no consequence? And with that she repeated her previous expression:

"Come now, how can it hurt you?"

Then, as the scene still continued, she closed it with a rough speech:

"Besides, dear boy, if the thing doesn't suit you, it's very simple: the house-door's open! There now you must take me as you find me!"

He hung his head, for the young woman's vows of fidelity made him happy at bottom. She, however, now knew her power over him, and ceased to consider his feelings. And from that time forth Satin was openly installed in the house, on the same footing as the gentlemen. Vandeuvres had not needed anonymous letters in order to understand how matters stood, and accordingly he joked and tried to pick jealous quarrels with Satin. Philippe and Georges, on their parts, treated her like a jolly good fellow, shaking hands with her, and cracking the riskiest jokes imaginable.

Nana had an adventure one evening when this slut of a girl had given her the go-by, and she had gone to dine in the Rue des Martyrs without being able to catch her. Whilst she was dining by herself, Daguenet had appeared on the scene, for, although he had reformed, he still occasionally dropped in, under the influence of his old vicious inclinations. He hoped of course that no one would meet him in these black recesses, dedicated to the town's lowest depravity. Accordingly even Nana's presence seemed to embarrass him at the outset. But he was not the man to run away, and coming forward with a smile, he asked if *Madame* would be so kind as to allow him to dine at her table. Noticing his jocular tone, Nana assumed her magnificently frigid demeanor, and icily replied:

"Sit down where you please, sir. We are in a public place."

Thus begun, the conversation proved amusing. But, at

dessert, Nana, bored and burning for a triumph, put her elbows on the table, and began in the old familiar way:.

"Well, what about your marriage, my lad? Is it getting on all right?"

"Not much," Daguenet averred.

As a matter of fact, just when he was about to venture on his request at the Muffats', he had met with such a cold reception from the Count that he had prudently refrained. The business struck him as a failure. Nana fixed her clear eyes on him: she was sitting leaning her chin on her hand, and there was an ironical curve about her lips.

"Oh, yes! I'm a baggage," she resumed slowly. "Oh, yes, the future father-in-law will have to be dragged from between my claws! Dear me, dear me, for a fellow with *nous*, you're jolly stupid! What! d'you mean to say you're going to tell your tales to a man who adores me and tells me everything! Now just listen: you shall marry if I wish it, my little man!"

For a minute or two, he had felt the truth of this, and now he began scheming out a method of submission. Nevertheless, he still talked jokingly, not wishing the matter to grow serious, and, after he had put on his gloves, he demanded the hand of Mlle. Estelle de Beuville in the strict regulation manner. Nana ended by laughing, as though she had been tickled. Oh, that Mimi! it was impossible to bear him a grudge! Daguenet's great successes with ladies of her class were due to the sweetness of his voice, a voice of such musical purity and pliancy as to have won him among courtesans the sobriquet of "Velvet-Mouth." Every woman would give way to him when he lulled her with his sonorous caresses. He knew this power, and rocked Nana to sleep with endless words, telling her all kinds of idiotic anecdotes. When they left the *table d'hôte*, she was blushing rosy-red; she trembled as she hung on his arm; he had reconquered her. As it was very fine, she sent her carriage away, and walked with him as far as his own place, where she went upstairs with him naturally enough. Two hours later, as she was dressing again, she said,—

"So, you hold to this marriage of yours, Mimi?"

"Egad," he muttered; "it's the best thing I could possibly do after all! You know I'm stony broke."

She summoned him to button her boots, and after a pause,—

"Good heavens! I've no objection. I'll shove you on! She's as dry as a lath is that little thing, but since it suits your game—oh! I'm agreeable: I'll run the thing through for you."

Then, with bosom still uncovered, she began laughing:

"Only, what will you give me?"

He had caught her in his arms and was kissing her on the shoulders in a perfect access of gratitude, whilst she quivered with excitement and struggled merrily, and threw herself backwards in her efforts to be free.

"Oh! I know," she cried, excited by the contest. "Listen to what I want in the way of commission. On your wedding day, you shall make me a present of your innocence. Before your wife, d'you understand?"

"That's it! That's it!" said he, laughing even louder than Nana.

The bargain amused them—they thought the whole business very good indeed.

Now, as it happened, there was a dinner at Nana's next day. For the matter of that, it was the customary Thursday dinner, and Muffat, Vandeuvres, the young Hugons, and Satin were present. The Count arrived early. He stood in need of eighty thousand francs wherewith to free the young woman from two or three debts and to give her a set of sapphires she was dying to possess. As he had already seriously lessened his capital, he was in search of a lender, for he did not dare to sell another property. With the advice of Nana

herself, he had addressed himself to Labordette, but the latter, deeming it too heavy an undertaking, had mentioned it
to the hairdresser Francis, who willingly busied himself in
such affairs in order to oblige his lady clients. The Count
put himself into the hands of these gentlemen, but expressed
a formal desire not to appear in the matter; and they both
undertook to keep in hand the bill for a hundred thousand
francs which he was to sign, excusing themselves at the same
time for charging a matter of twenty thousand francs interest, and loudly denouncing the blackguard usurers, to
whom, they declared, it had been necessary to have recourse.
When Muffat had himself announced, Francis was putting the
last touches to Nana's coiffure. Labordette also was sitting
familiarly in the dressing-room as became a friend of no consequence. Seeing the Count, he discreetly placed a thick
bundle of bank-notes among the powders and pomades, and
the bill was signed on the marble-topped dressing-table.
Nana was anxious to keep Labordette to dinner, but he declined—he was taking a rich foreigner about Paris. Muffat,
however, led him aside, and begged him to go to Becker, the
jeweler, and bring him back thence the set of sapphires,
which he wanted to present the young woman by way of surprise that very evening. Labordette willingly undertook the
commission, and half an hour later Julien handed the jewel-
case mysteriously to the Count.

During dinner-time Nana was nervous. The sight of the
eighty thousand francs had excited her. To think all that
money was to go to tradespeople! It was a disgusting
thought. After soup had been served she grew sentimental,
and in the splendid dining-room, glittering with plate and
glass, she talked of the bliss of poverty. The men were in
evening dress, Nana in a gown of white embroidered satin,
whilst Satin made a more modest appearance in black silk,
with a simple gold heart at her throat, which was a present
from her kind friend. Julien and François waited behind

the guests, and were assisted in this by Zoé. All three looked most dignified.

"It's certain I had far greater fun when I hadn't a cent!" Nana repeated.

She had placed Muffat on her right hand and Vandeuvres on her left, but she scarcely looked at them so taken up was she with Satin, who sat in state between Philippe and Georges on the opposite side of the table.

"Eh, duckie?" she kept saying at every turn. "How we did use to laugh, in those days, when we went to Mother Josse's school in the Rue Polonceau!"

When the roast was being served the two women plunged into a world of reminiscences. They used to have regular chattering fits of this kind when a sudden desire to stir the muddy depths of their childhood would possess them. These fits always occurred when men were present: it was as though they had given way to a burning desire to treat them to the dunghill on which they had grown to woman's estate. The gentlemen paled visibly and looked embarrassed. The young Hugons did their best to laugh, whilst Vandeuvres nervously toyed with his beard, and Muffat redoubled his gravity.

"You remember Victor?" said Nana. "There was a wicked little fellow for you! Why, he used to take the little girls into cellars!"

"I remember him perfectly," replied Satin. "I recollect the big court-yard at your place very well. There was a portress there with a broom!"

"Mother Boche: she's dead."

"And I can still picture your shop. Your mother was a great fatty. One evening when we were playing your father came in drunk. Oh, so drunk!"

At this point Vandeuvres tried to intercept the ladies' reminiscences and to effect a diversion.

"I say, my dear, I should be very glad to have some more truffles. They're simply perfect. Yesterday I had some at

the house of the Duc de Corbreuse, which did not come up
to them at all."

"The truffles, Julien!" said Nana roughly.

Then returning to the subject:

"By Jove, yes, dad hadn't any sense! And then what a
smash there was! You should have seen it—down, down,
down we went, starving away all the time. I can tell you I've
had to bear pretty well everything, and it's a miracle I didn't
kick the bucket over it, like daddy and mammy."

This time Muffat, who was playing with his knife in a
state of infinite exasperation, made so bold as to intervene.

"What you're telling us isn't very cheerful."

"Eh, what? Not cheerful!" cried she, with a withering
glance. "I believe you, it isn't cheerful! Somebody had to
earn a living for us, dear boy. Oh, yes, you know, I'm the
right sort; I don't mince matters. Mammy was a laundress;
daddy used to get drunk, and he died of it! There! if it
doesn't suit you—if you're ashamed of my family—"

They all protested. What was she after now? They had
every sort of respect for her family! But she went on:

"If you're ashamed of my family, you'll please leave me,
because I'm not one of those women who deny their father
and mother. You must take me and them together, d'you
understand?"

They took her as required; they accepted the dad, the
mammy, the past; in fact, whatever she chose. With their
eyes fixed on the table-cloth, the four now sat shrinking and
insignificant, whilst Nana, in a transport of omnipotence,
trampled on them in the old muddy boots worn long since
in the Rue Goutte-d'Or. She was determined not to lay
down the cudgels just yet. It was all very fine to bring her
fortunes, to build her palaces, she would never leave off re-
gretting the time when she munched apples! Oh, what bosh
that stupid thing money was! It was made for the tradespeople! Finally her outburst ended in a sentimentally-ex-

pressed desire for a simple, open-hearted existence, to be passed in an atmosphere of universal benevolence.

When she got to this point she noticed Julien waiting idly by.

"Well, what's the matter? Hand the champagne, then!" said she. "Why d'you stand staring at me like a goose?"

During this scene the servants had never once smiled. They apparently heard nothing, and the more their mistress let herself down, the more majestic they became. Julien set to work to pour out the champagne, and did so without mishap, but François, who was handing round the fruit, was so unfortunate as to tilt the fruit-dish too low, and the apples, the pears, and the grapes rolled on the table.

"You bloody clumsy lot!" cried Nana.

The footman was mistaken enough to try and explain that the fruit had not been firmly piled up. Zoé had disarranged it by taking out some oranges.

"Then it's Zoé that's the goose!" said Nana.

"*Madame—,*" murmured the lady's maid in an injured tone.

Straightway *Madame* rose to her feet, and in a sharp voice, and with royally-authoritative gesture,—

"We've had enough of this, haven't we? Leave the room all of you! We don't want you any longer!"

This summary procedure calmed her down, and she was forthwith all sweetness and amiability. The dessert proved charming, and the gentlemen grew quite merry waiting on themselves. But Satin, having peeled a pear, came and ate it behind her darling, leaning on her shoulder the while, and whispering sundry little remarks in her ear, at which they both laughed very loudly. By-and-by she wanted to share her last piece of pear with Nana, and presented it to her between her teeth. Whereupon there was a great nibbling of lips, and the pear was finished amid kisses. At this there was a burst of comic protest from the gentlemen, Philippe shouting to them to take it easy, and Vandeuvres asking if one ought to leave the room. Georges, meanwhile, had come and put his arm round Satin's waist, and had brought her back to her seat.

"How silly of you!" said Nana; "you're making her blush, the poor darling duck. Never mind, dear girl, let them chaff. It's our own little private affair."

And turning to Muffat, who was watching them with his serious expression,—

"Isn't it, my friend?"

"Yes, certainly," he murmured with a slow nod of approval. He no longer protested now. And so, amid that company of gentlemen with the great names and the old upright traditions, the two women sat face to face, exchanging tender glances, conquering, reigning, in tranquil defiance of the laws of sex, in open contempt for the male portion of the community. The gentlemen burst into applause.

The company went upstairs to take coffee in the little drawing-room, where a couple of lamps cast a soft glow over the rosy hangings and the lacquer and old gold of the knickknacks. At that hour of the evening the light played discreetly over coffers, bronzes, and china, lighting up silver or ivory inlaid work, bringing into view the polished contours of a carved stick, and gleaming over a panel with glossy silky reflections. The fire, which had been burning since the afternoon, was dying out in glowing embers. It was very warm—the air behind the curtains and hangings was languid with warmth. The room was full of Nana's intimate existence: a pair of gloves, a fallen handkerchief, an open book, lay scattered about, and their owner seemed present in careless attire with that well-known odor of violets, and that species of untidiness which became her in her character of good-natured courtesan, and had such a charming effect among all those rich surroundings. The very arm-chairs, which were as wide as beds, and the sofas, which were as deep as alcoves, invited to slumber oblivious of the flight of time, and to tender whispers in shadowy corners.

Satin went and lolled back in the depths of a sofa near the fire-place. She had lit a cigarette; but Vandeuvres began amusing himself by pretending to be ferociously jealous. Nay, he even threatened to send her his seconds if she still persisted in keeping Nana from her duty. Philippe and Georges joined him, and teased her and badgered her so mercilessly that at last she shouted out,—

"Darling! Darling! Do make 'em keep quiet! They're still after me!"

"Now then, let her be," said Nana seriously. "I won't have her tormented, you know that quite well. And you, my pet, why d'you always go mixing yourself up with them when they've got so little sense?"

Satin, blushing all over and putting out her tongue, went into the dressing-room, through the widely-open door of which you caught a glimpse of pale marbles gleaming in the milky light of a gas-flame in a globe of rough glass. After that Nana talked to the four men as charmingly as hostess could. During the day she had read a novel, which was at that time making a good deal of noise. It was the history of a courtesan; and Nana was very indignant, declaring the whole thing to be untrue, and expressing angry dislike to that kind of monstrous literature which pretends to paint from nature. "Just as though one could describe everything," she said. Just as though a novel ought not to be written so that the reader may while away an hour pleasantly! In the matter of books and of plays Nana had very decided opinions: she wanted tender and noble productions, things that would set her dreaming and would elevate her soul. Then allusion being made in the course of conversation to the troubles agitating Paris, the incendiary articles in the papers, the incipient popular disturbances which followed the calls to arms nightly raised at public meetings, she waxed wroth with the Republicans. What on earth did those dirty people who never washed really want? Were folks not happy? Had not the Emperor done everything for the People? A nice filthy lot of People! She knew 'em, she could talk about 'em, and, quite forgetting the respect which at dinner she had just been insisting should be paid to her humble circle in the Rue de la Goutte-d'Or, she began blackguarding her own class with all the terror and disgust peculiar to a woman who had risen successfully above it. That very afternoon she had read in the *Figaro* an account of the proceedings at a public meeting which had verged on the comic. Owing to the slang words that had been used, and to the piggish behavior of a drunken man who had got himself chucked, she was laughing at those proceedings still.

"Oh, those drunkards!" said she with a disgusted air. "No, look you here, their Republic would be a great misfortune for everybody! Oh, may God preserve us the Emperor as long as possible!"

"God will hear your prayer, my dear," Muffat replied gravely. "To be sure, the Emperor stands firm."

He liked her to express such excellent views. Both, indeed, understood one another in political matters. Vandeuvres and Captain Hugon likewise indulged in endless jokes against the "cads," the quarrelsome set who scuttled off the moment they clapped eyes on a bayonet. But Georges that evening remained pale and somber.

"What can be the matter with that baby?" asked Nana, noticing his troubled appearance.

"With me? Nothing—I am listening," he mutterd.

But he was really suffering. On rising from table, he had heard Philippe joking with the young woman, and now it was Philippe, and not himself, who sat beside her. His heart, he knew not why, swelled to bursting. He could not bear to see them so close together; such vile thoughts oppressed him that shame mingled with his anguish. He who laughed at Satin, who had accepted Steiner, and Muffat, and all the rest, felt outraged and murderous at the thought that Philippe might some day touch that woman.

"Here, take Bijou," said she, to comfort him, and she passed him the little dog which had gone to sleep on her dress.

And with that Georges grew happy again, for with the beast still warm from her lap in his arms, he held, as it were, part of her.

Allusion had been made to a considerable loss which Vandeuvres had last night sustained at the Imperial Club. Muffat, who did not play, expressed great astonishment, but Vandeuvres smilingly alluded to his imminent ruin, about which Paris was already talking. The kind of death you chose did not much matter, he averred; the great thing was to die handsomely. For some time past, Nana had noticed that he was nervous, and had a sharp downward droop of the mouth, and fitful gleam in the depths of his clear eyes. But he retained his haughty aristocratic manner, and the delicate elegance of his impoverished race; and as yet these strange manifestations were only, so to speak, momentary fits of vertigo overcoming a brain already sapped by play and by debauchery. One night, as he lay beside her, he had frightened her with a dreadful story. He had told her he contemplated shutting himself up in his stable and setting fire to himself and his horses at such time as he should have devoured all his substance. His only hope at that period was a horse, Lusignan by name, which he was training for the Prix de Paris. He was living on this horse, which was the sole stay of his shaken credit, and, whenever Nana grew exacting, he would put her off till June and to the probability of Lusignan's winning.

"Bah! he may very likely lose," said she merrily, "since he's going to clear them all out at the races."

By way of reply he contented himself by smiling a thin mysterious smile. Then, carelessly,—

"By-the-by, I've taken the liberty of giving your name to my outsider, the filly. Nana, Nana—that sounds well. You're not vexed?"

"Vexed, why?" said she, in a state of inward ecstasy.

The conversation continued, and some mention was made of an execution shortly to take place. The young woman said she was burning to go to it, when Satin appeared at the dressing-room door, and called her in tones of entreaty. She got up at once, and left the gentlemen lolling lazily about, whilst they finished their cigars and discussed the grave question as to how far a murderer subject to chronic alcoholism is responsible for his act. In the dressing-room Zoé sat helpless on a chair, crying her heart out, whilst Satin vainly endeavored to console her.

"What's the matter?" said Nana, in surprise.

"Oh, darling, do speak to her!" said Satin. "I've been trying to make her listen to reason for the last twenty minutes. She's crying because you called her a goose."

"Yes, *Madame*, it's very hard—very hard," stuttered Zoé, choked by a fresh fit of sobbing.

This sad sight melted the young woman's heart at once. She spoke kindly, and when the other woman still refused to grow calm, she sank down in front of her, and took her round the waist with truly cordial familiarity:

"But, you silly, I said 'goose' just as I might have said anything else. How shall I explain? I was in a passion—it was wrong of me: now calm down."

"I who love *Madame* so," stuttered Zoé; "after all I've done for *Madame*."

Thereupon Nana kissed the lady's maid, and, wishing to shew her she wasn't vexed, gave her a dress she had worn three times. Their quarrels always ended up in the giving of presents! Zoé plugged her handkerchief into her eyes. She carried the dress off over her arm, and added, before leaving, that they were very sadly in the kitchen, and that Julien and François had been unable to eat, so entirely had *Madame's* anger taken away their appetites. Thereupon *Madame* sent them a louis as a pledge of reconciliation. She suffered too much if people around her were sorrowful.

Nana was returning to the drawing-room, happy in the thought that she had patched up a disagreement, which was rendering her quietly apprehensive of the morrow, when Satin came and whispered vehemently in her ear. She was full of complaint, threatened to be off if those men still went on teasing her, and kept insisting that her darling should turn them all out of doors for that night, at any rate. It would be a lesson to them. And then it would be so nice to be alone, both of them! Nana, with a return of anxiety, declared it to be impossible. Thereupon, the other shouted at her like a violent child, and tried hard to overrule her.

"I wish it, d'you see? Send 'em away, or I'm off!"

And she went back into the drawing-room, stretched herself out in the recesses of a divan, which stood in the background near the window, and lay waiting, silent and deathlike, with her great eyes fixed upon Nana.

The gentlemen were deciding against the new criminological theories. Granted that lovely invention of irresponsibility in certain pathological cases and criminals ceased to exist, and sick people alone remained. The young woman, expressing approval with an occasional nod, was busy considering how best to dismiss the Count. The others would soon be going, but he would assuredly prove obstinate. In fact, when Philippe got up to withdraw, Georges followed him at once —he seemed only anxious not to leave his brother behind. Vandeuvres lingered some minutes longer, feeling his way, as it were, and waiting to find out if, by any chance, some important business would oblige Muffat to cede him his place. Soon, however, when he saw the Count deliberately taking up his quarters for the night, he desisted from his purpose, and said good-by as became a man of tact. But, on his way to the door, he noticed Satin staring fixedly at Nana, as usual. Doubtless he understood what this meant, for he seemed amused, and came and shook hands with her.

"We're not angry, eh?" he whispered. "Pray pardon me. You're the nicer attraction of the two, on my honor!"

Satin deigned no reply. Nor did she take her eyes off Nana and the Count, who were now alone. Muffat, ceasing to be ceremonious, had come to sit beside the young woman. He took her fingers, and began kissing them. Whereupon, Nana, seeking to change the current of his thoughts, asked him if his daughter Estelle were better. The previous night he had been complaining of the child's melancholy behavior —he could not even spend a day happily at his own house, with his wife always out and his daughter icily silent.

In family matters of this kind Nana was always full of good advice, and when Muffat abandoned all his usual self-control under the influence of mental and physical relaxation, and once more launched out into his former plaints, she remembered the promise she had made.

"Suppose you were to marry her?" said she. And with that she ventured to talk of Daguenet. At the mere mention of the name the Count was filled with disgust. "Never," said he, after what she had told him!

She pretended great surprise and then burst out laughing and put her arm round his neck.

"Oh, the jealous man! To think of it! Just argue it out a little. Why, they slandered me to you—I was furious. At present I should be ever so sorry if—"

But over Muffat's shoulder she met Satin's gaze. And she left him anxiously, and in a grave voice continued,—

"This marriage must come off, my friend; I don't want to prevent your daughter's happiness. The young man's most charming; you could not possibly find a better sort."

And she launched into extraordinary praise of Daguenet. The Count had again taken her hands; he no longer refused now; he would see about it, he said; they would talk the matter over. By-and-by, when he spoke of going to bed, she sank her voice and excused herself. It was impossible; she was not well. If he loved her at all he would not insist! Nevertheless, he was obstinate; he refused to go away, and she was beginning to give in when she met Satin's eyes once more. Then she grew inflexible. No, the thing was out of the question! The Count, deeply moved and with a look of suffering, had risen and was going in quest of his hat. But in the doorway he remembered the set of sapphires; he could feel the case in his pocket. He had been wanting to hide it at the bottom of the bed, so that, when she entered it before him, she should feel it against her legs. Since dinner-time he had been meditating this little surprise like a school-boy, and now, in trouble and anguish of heart at being thus dismissed, he gave her the case without further ceremony.

"What is it?" she queried. "Sapphires? dear me! Oh, yes, it's that set. How sweet you are! But I say, my darling, d'you believe it's the same one? In the shop-window it made a much greater show."

That was all the thanks he got, and she let him go away. He noticed Satin stretched out silent and expectant, and with that he gazed at both women, and without further insistence submitted to his fate and went downstairs. The hall door had not yet closed when Satin caught Nana round the waist, and danced and sang. Then she ran to the window.

"Oh, just look at the figure he cuts down in the street!" The two women leant upon the wrought-iron window-rail in the shadow of the curtains. One o'clock struck. The Avenue de Villiers was deserted, and its double file of gas-lamps stretched away into the darkness of the damp March night, through which great gusts of wind kept sweeping, laden with

rain. There were vague stretches of land on either side of
the road, which looked like gulfs of shadow, whilst scaffoldings round mansions in process of construction loomed upward under the dark sky. They laughed uncontrollably as
they watched Muffat's rounded back and glistening shadow
disappearing along the wet sidewalk into the glacial desolate
plains of new Paris. But Nana silenced Satin.

"Take care: there are the police!"

Thereupon they smothered their laughter, and gazed in
secret fear at two dark figures walking with measured tread
on the opposite side of the Avenue. Amid all her luxurious
surroundings, amid all the royal splendors of the woman
whom all must obey, Nana still stood in horror of the police,
and did not like to hear them mentioned any oftener than
death. She felt distinctly unwell when a policeman looked
up at her house. One never knew what such people might
do! They might easily take them for loose women if they
heard them laughing at that hour of the night. Satin, with
a little shudder, had squeezed herself up against Nana.
Nevertheless, the pair stayed where they were, and were soon
interested in the approach of a lantern, the light of which
danced over the puddles in the road. It was an old rag-
picker woman who was busy raking in the gutters. Satin
recognized her.

"Dear me," she exclaimed, "it's Queen Pomaré with her
wickerwork shawl!"

And while a gust of wind lashed the fine rain in their faces,
she told her beloved the story of Queen Pomaré. Oh! she
had been a splendid girl once upon a time: all Paris had talked
of her beauty. And such devilish go, and such cheek! Why,
she led the men about like dogs, and great people stood
blubbering on her stairs! Now, she was in the habit of
getting tipsy, and the women round about would make her
drink absinthe for the sake of a laugh, after which the street-

boys would throw stones at her and chase her. In fact, it
was a regular smash-up: the queen had tumbled into the
mud! Nana listened, feeling cold all over.

"You shall see," added Satin.

She whistled a man's whistle, and the rag-picker, who was
then below the window, lifted her head and shewed herself
by the yellow flare of her lantern. Framed among rags, a
perfect bundle of them, a face looked out from under a tat-
tered kerchief—a blue seamed face with a toothless cavernous
mouth, and fiery bruises where the eyes should be. And
Nana, seeing the frightful old woman, the wanton drowned
in drink, had a sudden fit of recollection, and saw far back
amid the shadows of consciousness the vision of Chamont,—
Irma d'Anglars, the old harlot crowned with years and honors,
ascending the steps in front of her château amid abjectly rev-
erential villagers. Then, as Satin whistled again, making
game of the old hag, who could not see her—

"Do leave off, there are the police!" she murmured in
changed tones. "In with us, quick, my pet!"

The measured steps were returning, and they shut the
window. Turning round again, shivering, and with the
damp of night on her hair, Nana was momentarily astounded
at sight of her drawing-room. It seemed as though she had
forgotten it, and were entering an unknown chamber. So
warm, so full of perfume was the air she encountered, that
she experienced a sense of delightd surprise. The heaped-up
wealth of the place, the old-world furniture, the fabrics of
silk and gold, the ivory, the bronzes, were slumbering in the
rosy light of the lamps, whilst from the whole of the silent
house a rich feeling of great luxury ascended, the luxury of
the solemn reception-rooms, of the comfortable ample dining-
room, of the vast retired staircase, with their soft carpets and
seats. Her individuality, with its longing for domination
and enjoyment, and its desire to possess everything that she
might destroy everything, was suddenly increased. Never

before had she felt so profoundly the puissance of her sex. She gazed slowly round, and remarked with an expression of grave philosophy,—

"Ah, well, all the same, one's jolly well right to profit by things when one's young!"

But now Satin was rolling on the bearskins in the bed-room, and calling her.

"Oh, do come! do come!"

Nana undressed in the dressing-room, and, in order to be quicker about it, she took her thick fell of blonde hair in both hands, and began shaking it above the silver wash-hand basin, whilst a downward hail of long hair-pins rang a little chime on the shining metal.

CHAPTER XI

ONE Sunday, the race for the Grand Prix de Paris was being run in the Bois de Boulogne beneath skies ren-dered sultry by the first heats of June. The sun, that morn-ing, had risen amid a mist of dun-colored dust, but towards eleven o'clock, just when the carriages were reaching the Longchamps course, a southerly wind had swept away the clouds, long streamers of gray vapor were disappearing across the sky, and gaps shewing an intense blue beyond were spread-ing from one end of the horizon to the other. In the bright bursts of sunlight which alternated with the clouds, the whole scene shone again, from the field which was gradually filling with a crowd of carriages, horsemen and pedestrians, to the still vacant course, where the judge's box stood, together with the "posts," and the masts for signalling numbers, and thence on to the five symmetrical stands of brick-work and timber, rising gallery upon gallery in the middle of the weigh-ing-enclosure opposite. Beyond these, bathed in the light of noon, lay the vast level plain, bordered with little trees, and shut in to the westward by the wooded heights of Saint-Cloud and Suresnes, which, in their turn, were dominated by the severe outlines of Mont-Valérien.

Nana, as excited as if the Grand Prix were going to make her fortune, wanted to take up a position by the railing next the winning post. She had arrived very early—she was in fact one of the first to come—in a landau adorned with silver, and drawn, *à la* Daumont, by four splendid white horses. This landau was a present from Count Muffat. When she had made her appearance at the entrance to the field, with two postillions jogging blithely on the near horses, and two footmen perching motionless behind the carriage, the people had rushed to look as though a queen were passing. She sported the blue and white colors of the Vandeuvres stable, and her dress was remarkable. It consisted of a little blue silk bodice and tunic, which fitted closely to the body and bulged out enormously behind her waist, thereby bringing her lower limbs into bold relief in such a manner as to be extremely noticeable in that epoch of voluminous skirts. Then there was a white satin dress with white satin sleeves, and a sash worn crosswise over the shoulders, the whole ornamented with silver guipure which shone in the sun. In addition to this, in order to be still more like a jockey, she had stuck a blue toque with a white feather jauntily upon her chignon, the fair tresses from which flowed down beyond her shoulders and resembled an enormous russet pigtail.

Twelve struck. The public would have to wait more than three hours for the Grand Prix to be run. When the landau had drawn up beside the barriers, Nana settled herself comfortably down as though she were in her own house. A whim had prompted her to bring Bijou and Louiset with her, and the dog crouched among her skirts, shivering with cold despite the heat of the day, whilst, amid a bedizenment of ribbons and laces, the child's poor little face looked waxen and dumb and white in the open air. Meanwhile the young woman, without troubling about the people near her, talked at the top of her voice with Georges and Philippe Hugon, who were seated opposite on the front seat among such a mountain of bouquets of white roses and blue myosotis that they were buried up to their shoulders.

"Well, then," she was saying, "as he bored me to death, I shewed him the door. And now it's two days that he's been sulking."

She was talking of Muffat, but she took care not to confess to the young men the real reason for this first quarrel, which was that one evening he had found a man's hat in her bedroom. She had indeed brought home a passer-by out of sheer ennui—a silly infatuation.

"You have no idea how funny he is," she continued, growing merry over the particulars she was giving. "He's a regular bigot at bottom, so he says his prayers every evening. Yes, he does. He's under the impression I notice nothing because I go to bed first so as not to be in his way; but I watch him out of the corner of my eye. Oh! he jaws away, and then he crosses himself, when he turns round to step over me and get to the inside of the bed."

"Jove; it's sly," muttered Philippe. "That's what happens before, but afterwards, what then?"

She laughed merrily.

"Yes, just so, before and after! When I'm going to sleep I hear him jawing away again. But the biggest bore of all is that we can't argue about anything now without his growing 'pi.' I've always been religious. Yes, chaff as much as you like, that won't prevent me believing what I do believe! Only he's too much of a nuisance: he blubbers, he talks about remorse. The day before yesterday, for instance, he had a regular fit of it after our usual row, and I wasn't the least bit reassured when all was over."

But she broke off, crying out,—

"Just look at the Mignons arriving. Dear me, they've

brought the children! Oh, how those little chaps are dressed up!"

The Mignons were in a landau of severe hue: there was something substantially luxurious about their turn-out, suggesting rich retired tradespeople. Rose was in a gray silk gown, trimmed with red knots and with puffs; she was smiling happily at the joyous behaviour of Henri and Charles, who sat on the front seat, looking awkward in their ill-fitting collegians' tunics. But, when the landau had drawn up by the rails, and she perceived Nana sitting in triumph among her bouquets, with her four horses, and her liveries, she pursed up her lips, sat bolt upright, and turned her head away. Mignon, on the other hand, looking the picture of freshness and gayety, waved her a salutation. He made it a matter of principle to keep out of feminine disagreements.

"By-the-by," Nana resumed, "d'you know a little old man who's very clean and neat and has bad teeth—a Monsieur Venot? He came to see me this morning."

"Monsieur Venot," said Georges, in great astonishment, "it's impossible! Why, the man's a Jesuit!"

"Precisely; I spotted that. Oh, you have no idea what our conversation was like! It was just funny! He spoke to me about the Count, about his divided house, and begged me to restore a family its happiness. He was very polite, and very smiling for the matter of that. Then I answered to the effect that I wanted nothing better, and I undertook to reconcile the Count and his wife. You know it's not humbug. I should be delighted to see them all happy again, the poor things! Besides it would be a relief to me, for there are days —yes, there are days when he bores me to death."

The weariness of the last months escaped her in this heart-felt outburst. Moreover, the Count appeared to be in big money difficulties; he was anxious, and it seemed likely that the bill which Labordette had put his name to would not be met.

"Dear me, the Countess is down yonder," said Georges, letting his gaze wander over the stands.

"Where, where?" cried Nana. "What eyes that baby's got! Hold my sunshade, Philippe."

But with a quick forward dart Georges had outstripped his brother. It enchanted him to be holding the blue silk sunshade with its silver fringe. Nana was scanning the scene through a huge pair of field-glasses.

"Ah, yes! I see her," said she at length. "In the right-hand stand, near a pillar, eh? She's in mauve, and her daughter in white by her side. Dear me, there's Daguenet going to bow to them."

Thereupon, Philippe talked of Daguenet's approaching marriage with that lath of an Estelle. It was a settled matter—the banns were being published. At first the Countess had opposed it, but the Count, they said, had insisted. Nana smiled.

"I know, I know," she murmured. "So much the better for Paul. He's a nice boy—he deserves it."

And leaning towards Louiset,—

"You're enjoying yourself, eh? What a grave face!"

The child never smiled. With a very old expression he was gazing at all those crowds, as though the sight of them filled him with melancholy reflections. Bijou, chased from the skirts of the young woman, who was moving about a great deal, had come to nestle shivering against the little fellow.

Meanwhile, the field was filling up. Carriages, a compact, interminable file of them, were continually arriving through the Porte de la Cascade. There were big omnibuses such as the *Pauline*, which had started from the Boulevard des Italiens, freighted with its fifty passengers, and was now going to draw up to the right of the stands. Then, there were dogcarts, victorias, landaus, all superbly well turned out, mingled with lamentable cabs, which jolted along behind sorry old hacks, and four-in-hands, sending along their four horses, and mail-coaches, where the masters sat on the seats above and left the servants to take care of the hampers of champagne inside, and "spiders," the immense wheels of which were a flash of glittering steel, and light tandems, which looked as delicately formed as the works of a clock and slipped along amid a peal of little bells. Every few seconds an equestrian rode by, and a swarm of people on foot rushed in a scared way among the carriages. On the green, the far-off rolling sound which issued from the avenues in the Bois died out suddenly in dull rustlings, and now nothing was audible save the hubbub of the ever-increasing crowds, and cries, and calls, and the crackings of whips in the open. When the sun, amidst bursts of wind, reappeared at the edge of a cloud, a long ray of golden light ran across the field, lit up the harness and the varnished coach-panels, and touched the ladies' dresses with fire, whilst, amid the dusty radiance, the coachmen, high up on their boxes, flamed beside their great whips.

Labordette was getting out of an open carriage where Gaga, Clarisse, and Blanche de Sivry had kept a place for him. As he was hurrying to cross the course and enter the weighing-enclosure, Nana got Georges to call him. Then when he came up,—

"What's the betting on me?" she asked, laughingly.

She referred to the filly, Nana, the Nana who had let herself be shamefully beaten in the race for the Prix de Diane, and had not even been placed in April and May last when she ran for the Prix des Cars and the Grande Poule des Produits, both of which had been gained by Lusignan, the other horse in the Vandeuvres stable. Lusignan had all at once become prime favorite, and since yesterday he had been currently taken at two to one.

"Always fifty to one against," replied Labordette.

"The deuce! I'm not worth much," rejoined Nana, amused

by the jest. "I don't back myself, then; no, by Jingo! I don't put a single louis on myself."

Labordette went off again in a great hurry, but she recalled him. She wanted some advice. Since he kept in touch with the world of trainers and jockeys, he had special information about various stables. His prognostications had come true a score of times already, and people called him the "King of Tipsters."

"Let's see, what horses ought I to choose?" said the young woman. "What's the betting on the Englishman?"

"Spirit? three to one against. Valerio II. the same. As to the others, they're laying twenty-five to one against Cosinus, forty to one against Hazard, thirty to one against Boum, thirty-five to one against Pichenette, ten to one against Frangipane."

"No, I don't bet on the Englishman, I don't. I'm a patriot. Perhaps Valerio II. would do, eh? The Duc de Corbreuse was beaming a little while ago. Well, no, after all! Fifty louis on Lusignan, what do you say to that?"

Labordette looked at her with a singular expression. She leant forward and asked him questions in a low voice, for she was aware that Vandeuvres commissioned him to arrange matters with the bookmakers so as to be able to bet the more easily. Supposing him to have got to know something, he might quite well tell it her. But without entering into explanations Labordette persuaded her to trust to his sagacity. He would put on her fifty louis for her as he might think best, and she would not repent of his arrangement.

"All the horses you like!" she cried gayly, letting him take his departure; "but no 'Nana'; she's a jade!"

There was a burst of uproarious laughter in the carriage. The young men thought her sally very amusing, whilst Louiset in his ignorance lifted his pale eyes to his mother's face, for her loud exclamations surprised him. However, there was no escape for Labordette as yet. Rose Mignon had made a

sign to him, and was now giving him her commands, whilst
he wrote figures in a note-book. Then Clarisse and Gaga
called him back, in order to change their bets; for they had
heard things said in the crowd, and now they didn't want to
have anything more to do with Valerio II. and were choosing
Lusignan. He wrote down their wishes with an impassible
expression, and at length managed to escape. He might be
seen disappearing between two of the stands on the other
side of the course.

Carriages were still arriving. They were by this time
drawn up five rows deep, and a dense mass of them spread
along the barriers, chequered by the light coats of white
horses. Beyond them, other carriages stood about in compara-
tive isolation, looking as though they had stuck fast in the
grass. Wheels and harness were here, there, and everywhere,
according as the conveyances to which they belonged were
side by side, at an angle, across and across, or head to head.
Over such spaces of turf as still remained unoccupied cavaliers
kept trotting, and black groups of pedestrians moved continually. The scene resembled the field where a fair is being
held, and above it all, amid the confused motley of the crowd,
the drinking-booths raised their gray canvas roofs, which
gleamed white in the sunshine. But a veritable tumult, a
mob, an eddy of hats surged round the several bookmakers,
who stood in open carriages, gesticulating like itinerant den-
tists, while their odds were pasted up on tall boards beside
them.

"All the same, it's stupid not to know on what horse one's
betting," Nana was remarking. "I really must risk some louis
in person."

She had stood up to select a bookmaker with a decent expression of face, but forgot what she wanted on perceiving
a perfect crowd of her acquaintance. Besides the Mignons,
besides Gaga, Clarisse, and Blanche, there were present, to the
right and left, behind and in the middle of the mass of car-

riages now hemming in her landau, the following ladies: Tatan Néné and Maria Blond in a victoria, Caroline Héquet with her mother and two gentlemen in an open carriage, Louise Violaine quite alone, driving a little basket-chaise, decked with orange and green ribbons, the colors of the Méchain stables, and finally, Léa de Horn on the lofty seat of a mail-coach, where a band of young men were making a great din. Further off, in a *huit ressorts* of aristocratic appearance, Lucy Stewart, in a very simple black silk dress, sat, looking distinguished beside a tall young man in the uniform of a naval cadet. But what most astounded Nana was the arrival of Simonne in a tandem, which Steiner was driving, whilst a footman sat motionless, with folded arms, behind them. She looked dazzling in white satin, striped with yellow, and was covered with diamonds from waist to hat. The banker, on his part, was handling a tremendous whip, and sending along his two horses, which were harnessed tandemwise, the leader being a little warm-colored chestnut, with a mouse-like trot, the shaft horse a big brown bay, a stepper, with a fine action.

"Deuce take it!" said Nana. "So that thief Steiner has cleared the Bourse again, has he? I say, isn't Simonne a swell! It's too much of a good thing, he'll get into the clutches of the law!"

Nevertheless, she exchanged greetings at a distance. Indeed, she kept waving her hand, and smiling, turning round and forgetting no one in her desire to be seen by everybody. At the same time she continued chatting.

"It's her son Lucy's got in tow! He's charming in his uniform. That's why she's looking so grand, of course! You know she's afraid of him, and that she passes herself off as an actress. Poor young man, I pity him all the same! He seems quite unsuspicious."

"Bah," muttered Philippe, laughing, "she'll be able to find him an heiress in the country when she likes."

Nana was silent, for she had just noticed the Tricon amid the thick of the carriages. Having arrived in a cab, whence she could not see anything, the Tricon had quietly mounted the coach-box. And there, straightening up her tall figure, with her noble face enshrined in its long curls, she dominated the crowd, as though enthroned amid her feminine subjects. All the latter smiled discreetly at her, whilst she, in her superiority, pretended not to know them. She wasn't there for business purposes: she was watching the races for the love of the thing, as became a frantic gambler with a passion for horseflesh.

"Dear me, there's that idiot la Faloise!" said Georges, suddenly.

It was a surprise to them all. Nana did not recognize her la Faloise, for since he had come into his inheritance he had grown extraordinarily up to date. He wore a low collar, and was clad in a cloth of delicate hue, which fitted close to his meager shoulders. His hair was in little *bandeaux*, and he affected a weary kind of swagger, a soft tone of voice, and slang words and phrases which he did not take the trouble to finish.

"But he's quite the thing!" declared Nana, in perfect enchantment.

Gaga and Clarisse had called la Faloise, and were throwing themselves at him in their efforts to regain his allegiance, but he left them immediately, rolling off in a chaffing, disdainful manner. Nana dazzled him. He rushed up to her and stood on the carriage-step, and when she twitted him about Gaga he murmured,—

"Oh, dear no! We've seen the last of the old lot! Mustn't play her off on me any more. And then, you know, it's you now, Juliet mine!"

He had put his hand to his heart. Nana laughed a good deal at this exceedingly sudden out-of-doors declaration. She continued,—

"I say, that's not what I'm after. You're making me forget that I want to lay wagers. Georges, you see that bookmaker down there, a great red-faced man with curly hair. He's got a dirty blackguard expression which I like. You're to go and choose—Oh! I say, what can one choose?"

"I'm not a patriotic soul—oh, dear no!" la Faloise blurted out. "I'm all for the Englishman. It will be ripping if the Englishman gains! The French may go to Jericho!"

Nana was scandalized. Presently the merits of the several horses began to be discussed, and la Faloise, wishing to be thought very much in the swim, spoke of them all as sorry jades. Frangipane, Baron Verdier's horse, was by The Truth out of Lenore. A big bay horse he was, who would certainly have stood a chance if they hadn't let him get foundered during training. As to Valerio II., from the Corbreuse stable, he wasn't ready yet; he'd had the colic in April. Oh, yes! they were keeping that dark, but he was sure of it, on his honor! In the end he advised Nana to choose Hazard, the most defective of the lot, a horse nobody would have anything to do with. Hazard, by jingo—such superb lines, and such an action! That horse was going to astonish the people.

"No," said Nana, "I'm going to put ten louis on Lusignan and five on Boum."

La Faloise burst forth at once:

"But, my dear girl, Boum's all rot! Don't choose him! Gasc himself is chucking up backing his own horse. And your Lusignan—never! Why, it's all humbug! By Lamb and Princess—just think! By Lamb and Princess—no, by Jove! All too short in the legs!"

He was choking. Philippe pointed out that, notwithstanding this, Lusignan had won the Prix des Cars and the Grande Poule des Produits. But the other ran on again. What did that prove? Nothing at all. On the contrary, one ought to distrust him. And besides, Gresham rode Lusignan; well then, let them jolly well dry up! Gresham had bad luck: he would never get to the post.

And, from one end of the field to the other, the discussion raging in Nana's landau seemed to spread and increase. Voices were raised in a scream; the passion for gambling filled the air, set faces glowing, and arms waving excitedly, whilst the bookmakers, perched on their conveyances, shouted odds and jotted down amounts right furiously. Yet these were only the small fry of the betting world; the big bets were made in the weighing-enclosure. Here, then, raged the keen contest of people with light purses, who risked their five-franc pieces and displayed infinite covetousness for the sake of a possible gain of a few louis. In a word, the battle would be between Spirit and Lusignan. Englishmen, plainly recognizable as such, were strolling about among the various groups. They were quite at home, their faces were fiery with excitement, they were already triumphant. Bramah, a horse belonging to Lord Reading, had gained the Grand Prix the previous year, and this had been a defeat over which hearts were still bleeding. This year it would be terrible if France were beaten anew. Accordingly, all the ladies were wild with national pride. The Vandeuvres stable became the rampart of our honor, and Lusignan was pushed, and defended, and applauded exceedingly. Gaga, Blanche, Caroline, and the rest betted on Lusignan. Lucy Stewart abstained from this on account of her son, but it was bruited abroad that Rose Mignon had commissioned Labordette to risk two hundred louis for her. The Tricon, as she sat alone next her driver, waited till the last moment. Very cool indeed amid all these disputes, very far above the ever-increasing uproar in which horses' names kept recurring, and lively Parisian phrases mingled with guttural English exclamations, she sat listening, and taking notes majestically.

"And Nana?" said Georges. "Does no one want her?"

Indeed, nobody was asking for the filly; she was not even

being mentioned. The outsider of the Vandeuvres's stud was swamped by Lusignan's popularity. But la Faloise flung his arms up, crying,—

"I've an inspiration. I'll bet a louis on Nana."

"Bravo! I bet a couple," said Georges.

"And I three," added Philippe.

And they mounted up and up, bidding against one another good-humoredly, and naming prices as though they had been haggling over Nana at an auction. La Faloise said he would cover her with gold. Besides, everybody was to be made to back her; they would go and pick up backers. But as the three young men were darting off to propagandize, Nana shouted after them,—

"You know I don't want to have anything to do with her; I don't for the world! Georges, ten louis on Lusignan and five on Valerio II."

Meanwhile they had started fairly off, and she watched them gayly as they slipped between wheels, ducked under horses' heads, and scoured the whole field. The moment they recognized any one in a carriage they rushed up and urged Nana's claims. And there were great bursts of laughter among the crowd when sometimes they turned back triumphantly signaling amounts with their fingers, whilst the young woman stood and waved her sunshade. Nevertheless, they made poor enough work of it. Some men let themselves be persuaded; Steiner, for instance, ventured three louis, for the sight of Nana stirred him. But the women refused pointblank. Thanks," said they, "to lose for a certainty!" Besides, they were in no hurry to work for the benefit of a dirty wench who was overwhelming them all with her four white horses, her postillions, and her outrageous assumption of side. Gaga and Clarisse looked exceedingly prim, and asked la Faloise whether he was jolly well making fun of them. When Georges boldly presented himself before the Mignons' carriage, Rose turned her head away in the most marked manner and did not answer him. One must be a pretty foul sort to let one's name be given to a horse! Mignon, on the contrary, followed the young man's movements with a look of amusement, and declared that the women always brought luck.

"Well?" queried Nana, when the young men returned after a prolonged visit to the bookmakers.

"The odds are forty to one against you," said la Faloise.

"What's that? Forty to one!" she cried astounded. "They were fifty to one against me. What's happened?"

Labordette had just then reappeared. The course was being cleared, and the pealing of a bell announced the first race. Amid the expectant murmur of the bystanders, she questioned him about this sudden rise in her value. But he replied evasively; doubtless a demand for her had arisen. She had to content herself with this explanation. Moreover, Labordette announced with a preoccupied expression that Vandeuvres was coming, if he could get away.

The race was ending unnoticed, people were all waiting for the Grand Prix to be run—when a storm burst over the Hippodrome. For some minutes past the sun had disappeared, and a wan twilight had darkened over the multitude. Then the wind rose, and there ensued a sudden deluge. Huge drops, perfect sheets of water, fell. There was a momentary confusion, and people shouted, and joked, and swore, whilst those on foot scampered madly off to find refuge under the canvas of the drinking-booths. In the carriages the women did their best to shelter themselves, grasping their sunshades with both hands, whilst the bewildered footmen ran to the hoods. But the shower was already nearly over, and the sun began shining brilliantly through escaping clouds of fine rain. A blue cleft opened in the stormy mass, which was blown off over the Bois, and the skies seemed to smile again and to set the women laughing in a reassured manner, whilst, amid the snorting of horses and the disarray and agitation of the

drenched multitude that was shaking itself dry, a broad flush
of golden light lit up the field, still dripping and glittering
with crystal drops.

"Oh, that poor dear Louiset!" said Nana. "Are you very
drenched, my darling?"

The little thing silently allowed his hands to be wiped.
The young woman had taken out her handkerchief. Then
she dabbed it over Bijou, who was trembling more violently
than ever. It would not matter in the least; there were a
few drops on the white satin of her dress, but she didn't care
a pin for them. The bouquets, refreshed by the rain, glowed
like snow, and she smelt one ecstatically, drenching her lips
in it as though it were wet with dew.

Meanwhile, the burst of rain had suddenly filled the stands.
Nana looked at them through her field-glasses. At that distance you could only distinguish a compact, confused mass
of people, heaped up, as it were, on the ascending ranges of
steps, a dark background relieved by light dots which were
human faces. The sunlight filtered in through openings near
the roof at each end of the stand, and detached and illumined
portions of the seated multitude, where the ladies' dresses
seemed to lose their distinguishing colors. But Nana was
especially amused by the ladies whom the shower had driven
from the rows of chairs, ranged on the sand at the base of
the stands. As courtesans were absolutely forbidden to enter
the enclosure, she began making exceedingly bitter remarks
about all the fashionable women therein assembled. She
thought them fearfully dressed up, and such guys!

There was a rumor that the Empress was entering the little
central stand, a pavilion built like a chalet, with a wide balcony furnished with red arm-chairs.

"Why, there he is!" said Georges. "I didn't think he was
on duty this week."

The stiff and solemn form of the Count Muffat had appeared behind the Empress. Thereupon the young men

jested, and were sorry that Satin wasn't there to go and dig him in the ribs. But Nana's field-glass focused the head of the Prince of Scots in the imperial stand.

"Gracious, it's Charles!" she cried.

She thought him stouter than formerly. In eighteen months he had broadened, and with that she entered into particulars. Oh, yes, he was a big, solidly-built fellow!

All round her, in the ladies' carriages, they were whispering that the Count had given her up. It was quite a long story. Since he had been making himself noticeable, the Tuileries had grown scandalized at the Chamberlain's conduct. Whereupon, in order to retain his position, he had recently broken it off with Nana. La Faloise bluntly reported this account of matters to the young woman, and addressing her as his Juliet, again offered himself. But she laughed merrily, and remarked,—

"It's idiotic! you don't know him; I've only to say 'Come here,' for him to chuck up everything."

For some seconds past she had been examining the Countess Sabine and Estelle. Daguenet was still at their side. Fauchery had just arrived, and was disturbing the people round in his desire to make his bow to them. He, too, stayed smilingly beside them. After that Nana pointed with disdainful action at the stands, and continued,—

"Then, you know, those people don't fetch me any longer now! I know 'em too well. You should see 'em behind scenes. No more honor! It's all up with honor! Filth below stairs, filth above stairs, filth everywhere. That's why I won't be bothered about 'em!"

And with a comprehensive gesture she took in everybody, from the grooms leading the horses on to the course, to the sovereign lady busy chatting with Charles, a prince and a dirty fellow to boot.

"Bravo, Nana! Awfully smart, Nana!" cried la Faloise, enthusiastically.

The tolling of a bell was lost in the wind; the races continued. The Prix d'Ispahan had just been run for and Berlingot, a horse belonging to the Méchain stable, had won. Nana recalled Labordette in order to obtain news of the hundred louis, but he burst out laughing, and refused to let her know the horses he had chosen for her, so as not to disturb the luck, as he phrased it. Her money was well placed; she would see that all in good time. And when she confessed her bets to him, and told him how she had put ten louis on Lusignan, and five on Valerio II., he shrugged his shoulders, as who should say that women did stupid things whatever happened. His action surprised her; she was quite at sea.

Just then the field grew more animated than before. Open-air lunches were arranged in the interval before the Grand Prix. There was much eating and more drinking in all directions, on the grass, on the high seats of the four-in-hands and mail-coaches, in the victorias, the broughams, the landaus. There was a universal spread of cold viands, and a fine disorderly display of champagne baskets which footmen kept handing down out of the coach-boots. Corks came out with feeble pops, which the wind drowned. There was an interchange of jests, and the sound of breaking glasses imparted a note of discord to the high-strung gayety of the scene. Gaga and Clarisse, together with Blanche, were making a serious repast, for they were eating sandwiches on the carriage-rug with which they had been covering their knees. Louise Violaine had got down from her basket-carriage, and had joined Caroline Héquet. On the turf, at their feet, some gentlemen had instituted a drinking-bar, whither Tatan, Maria, Simonne, and the rest came to refresh themselves, whilst high in air and close at hand bottles were being emptied on Léa de Horn's mail-coach, and, with infinite bravado and gesticulation, a whole band were making themselves tipsy in the sunshine, above the heads of the crowd. Soon, however, there was an especially large crowd by Nana's landau.

She had risen to her feet, and had set herself to pour out glasses of champagne for the men who came to pay her their respects. François, one of the footmen, was passing up the bottles, whilst la Faloise, trying hard to imitate a coster's accents, kept pattering away:

" 'Ere y'are, given away, given away! There's some for everybody!"

"Do be still, dear boy," Nana ended by saying. "We look like a set of tumblers."

She thought him very droll, and was greatly entertained. At one moment she conceived the idea of sending Georges with a glass of champagne to Rose Mignon, who was affecting temperance. Henri and Charles were bored to distraction; they would have been glad of some champagne, the poor little fellows. But Georges drank the glassful, for he feared an argument. Then Nana remembered Louiset, who was sitting forgotten behind her. Maybe he was thirsty, and she forced him to take a drop or two of wine, which made him cough dreadfully.

" 'Ere y'are, 'ere y'are, gemmen!" la Faloise riterated. "It don't cost two sous: it don't cost one. We give it away."

But Nana broke in with an exclamation,—

"Gracious, there's Bordenave down there! Call him. Oh, run, please, please do!"

It was indeed Bordenave. He was strolling about with his hands behind his back, wearing a hat that looked rusty in the sunlight, and a greasy frock-coat that was glossy at the seams. It was Bordenave shattered by bankruptcy, yet furious despite all reverses, a Bordenave who flaunted his misery among all the fine folks with the hardihood becoming a man ever ready to take Dame Fortune by storm.

"The deuce, how smart we are!" said he, when Nana extended her hand to him like the good-natured wench she was.

Presently, after emptying a glass of champagne, he gave vent to the following profoundly regretful phrase:

"Ah! if only I were a woman! But, by God, that's nothing! Would you like to go on the stage again? I've a notion: I'll hire the Gaîté, and we'll gobble up Paris between us. You certainly owe it me, eh?"

And he lingered grumbling beside her, though glad to see her again; for, said he, that confounded Nana was balm to his feelings. Yes, it was balm to them merely to exist in her presence! She was his daughter: she was blood of his blood!

The circle increased, for now la Faloise was filling glasses, and Georges and Philippe were picking up friends. A stealthy impulse was gradually bringing in the whole field. Nana would fling every one a laughing smile or an amusing phrase. The groups of tipplers were drawing near, and all the champagne scattered over the place was moving in her direction. Soon there was only one noisy crowd, and that was round her landau, where she queened it among outstretched glasses, her yellow hair floating on the breeze, and her snowy face bathed in the sunshine. Then, by way of finishing touch, and to make the other women, who were mad at her triumph, simply perish of envy, she lifted a brimming glass on high, and assumed her old pose as Venus Victrix.

But somebody touched her shoulder, and she was surprised, on turning round, to see Mignon on the seat. She vanished from view an instant, and sat herself down beside him, for he had come to communicate a matter of importance. Mignon had everywhere declared that it was ridiculous of his wife to bear Nana a grudge: he thought her attitude stupid and useless.

"Look here, my dear," he whispered. "Be careful: don't madden Rose too much. You understand, I think it best to warn you. Yes, she's got a weapon in store, and, as she's never forgiven you the *Petite Duchesse* business—"

"A weapon," said Nana; "what's that blooming well got to do with me?"

"Just listen: it's a letter she must have found in Fauchery's pocket, a letter written to that screw Fauchery by the Countess Muffat. And by Jove! it's clear the whole story's in it. Well, then, Rose wants to send the letter to the Count so as to be revenged on him and on you."

"What the deuce has that got to do with me?" Nana repeated. "It's a funny business. So the whole story about Fauchery's in it! Very well, so much the better: the woman has been exasperating me! We shall have a good laugh!"

"No, I don't wish it," Mignon briskly rejoined. "There'll be a pretty scandal! Besides, we've got nothing to gain."

He paused, fearing lest he should say too much, whilst she loudly averred that she was most certainly not going to get a chaste woman into trouble.

But when he still insisted on his refusal, she looked steadily at him. Doubtless he was afraid of seeing Fauchery again introduced into his family in case he broke with the Countess. Whilst avenging her own wrongs, Rose was anxious for that to happen, since she still felt a kindness towards the journalist. And Nana waxed meditative, and thought of Monsieur Venot's call, and a plan began to take shape in her brain, whilst Mignon was doing his best to talk her over.

"Let's suppose that Rose sends the letter, eh? There's food for scandal: you're mixed up in the business, and people say you're the cause of it all. Then, to begin with, the Count separates from his wife."

"Why should he?" said she. "On the contrary—"

She broke off, in her turn. There was no need for her to think aloud. So, in order to be rid of Mignon, she looked as though she entered into his view of the case, and when he advised her to give Rose some proof of her submission— to pay her a short visit on the race-course, for instance, where everybody would see her—she replied that she would see about it, that she would think the matter over.

A commotion caused her to stand up again. On the course the horses were coming in amid a sudden blast of wind. The prize given by the City of Paris had just been run for, and Cornemuse had gained it. Now the Grand Prix was about to be run, and the fever of the crowd increased and they were tortured by anxiety, and stamped and swayed as though they wanted to make the minutes fly faster. At this ultimate moment the betting world was surprised and startled by the continued shortening of the odds against Nana, the outsider of the Vandeuvres stables. Gentlemen kept returning every few moments with a new quotation: the betting was thirty to one against Nana; it was twenty-five to one against Nana, then twenty to one, then fifteen to one. No one could understand it. A filly beaten on all the race-courses! a filly which that same morning no single sportsman would take at fifty to one against! What did this sudden madness betoken? Some laughed at it, and spoke of the pretty doing awaiting the duffers who were being taken in by the joke. Others looked serious and uneasy, and sniffed out something ugly under it all. Perhaps there was a "deal" in the offing. Allusion was made to well-known stories about the robberies which are winked at on race-courses, but on this occasion the great name of Vandeuvres put a stop to all such accusations, and the skeptics in the end prevailed when they prophesied that Nana would come in last of all.

"Who's riding Nana?" queried la Faloise.

Just then the real Nana reappeared, whereat the gentleman lent his question an indecent meaning, and burst into an uproarious fit of laughter. Nana bowed.

"Price is up," she replied.

And with that the discussion began again. Price was an English celebrity. Why had Vandeuvres got this jockey to come over, seeing that Gresham ordinarily rode Nana? Besides, they were astonished to see him confiding Lusignan to this man Gresham, who according to la Faloise never got a place. But all these remarks were swallowed up in jokes, contradictions, and an extraordinarily noisy confusion of opinions. In order to kill time the company once more set themselves to drain bottles of champagne. Presently a whisper ran round, and the different groups opened outwards. It was Vandeuvres. Nana affected vexation.

"Dear me, you're a nice fellow to come at this time of day! Why, I'm burning to see the enclosure."

"Well, come along then," said he; "there's still time. You'll take a stroll round with me. I just happen to have a permit for a lady about me."

And he led her off on his arm, whilst she enjoyed the jealous glances with which Lucy, Caroline, and the others followed her. The young Hugons and la Faloise remained in the landau behind her retreating figure, and continued to do the honors of her champagne. She shouted to them that she would return immediately.

But Vandeuvres caught sight of Labordette and called him, and there was an interchange of brief sentences.

"You've scraped everything up?"

"Yes."

"To what amount?"

"Fifteen hundred louis—pretty well all over the place."

As Nana was visibly listening, and that with much curiosity, they held their tongues. Vandeuvres was very nervous, and he had those same clear eyes, shot with little flames, which so frightened her the night he spoke of burning himself and his horses together. As they crossed over the course, she spoke low and familiarly.

"I say, do explain this to me. Why are the odds on your filly changing?"

He trembled, and this sentence escaped him:

"Ah, they're talking, are they? What a set those betting

men are! When I've got the favorite, they all throw themselves upon him, and there's no chance for me. After that,
when an outsider's asked for, they give tongue, and yell as
though they were being skinned."

"You ought to tell me what's going to happen—I've made
my bets," she rejoined. "Has Nana a chance?"

A sudden, unreasonable burst of anger overpowered him.
"Won't you deuced well let me be, eh? Every horse has
a chance. The odds are shortening, because, by Jove! people
have taken the horse. Who, I don't know. I should prefer
leaving you if you must needs badger me with your idiotic
questions."

Such a tone was not germane either to his temperament
or his habits, and Nana was rather surprised than wounded.
Besides, he was ashamed of himself directly afterwards, and
when she begged him in a dry voice to behave politely, he
apologized. For some time past he had suffered from such
sudden changes of temper. No one in the Paris of pleasure
or of society was ignorant of the fact that he was playing
his last trump-card to-day. If his horses did not win, if,
moreover, they lost him the considerable sums wagered upon
them, it would mean utter disaster and collapse for him, and
the bulwark of his credit and the lofty appearance which,
though undermined, he still kept up, would come ruining
noisily down. Moreover, no one was ignorant of the fact
that Nana was the devouring siren who had finished him
off, who had been the last to attack his crumbling fortunes
and to sweep up what remained of them. Stories were told
of wild whims and fancies, of gold scattered to the four
winds, of a visit to Baden-Baden, where she had not left
him enough to pay the hotel bill, of a handful of diamonds
cast on the fire during an evening of drunkenness in order
to see whether they would burn like coal. Little by little
her great limbs and her coarse, plebeian way of laughing
had gained complete mastery over this elegant degenerate

son of an ancient race. At that time he was risking his all,
for he had been so utterly overpowered by his taste for ordure
and stupidity as to have even lost the vigor of his skepticism.
A week before Nana had made him promise her a château
on the Norman coast between Havre and Trouville, and now
he was staking the very foundations of his honor on the ful-
fillment of his word. Only she was getting on his nerves, and
he could have beaten her, so stupid did he feel her to be.

The man at the gate, not daring to stop the woman hanging on the Count's arm, had allowed them to enter the
enclosure. Nana, greatly puffed up at the thought that at
last she was setting foot on the forbidden ground, put on her
best behavior, and walked slowly by the ladies seated at the
foot of the stands. On ten rows of chairs the toilets were
densely massed, and in the blithe open air their bright colors
mingled harmoniously. Chairs were scattered about, and, as
people met one another, friendly circles were formed, just
as though the company had been sitting under the trees in a
public garden. Children had been allowed to go free, and
were running from group to group, whilst, overhead, the
stands rose tier above crowded tier, and the light-colored
dresses therein faded into the delicate shadows of the
timber-work. Nana stared at all these ladies. She stared
steadily and markedly at the Countess Sabine. After which,
as she was passing in front of the imperial stand, the sight of
Muffat, looming in all his official stiffness by the side of the
Empress, made her very merry.

"Oh, how silly he looks!" said she at the top of her voice
to Vandeuvres.

She was anxious to pay everything a visit. This small
park-like region, with its green lawns and groups of trees,
rather charmed her than otherwise. A vendor of ices had
set up a large buffet near the entrance-gates, and beneath a
rustic thatched roof a dense throng of people were shouting
and gesticulating. This was the Ring. Close by were some

empty stalls, and Nana was disappointed at discovering only
a gendarme's horse there. Then there was the paddock, a
small course some hundred mètres in circumference, where a
stable-help was walking about Valerio II. in his horse-cloths.
And oh, what a lot of men on the graveled side-walks, all
of them with their tickets forming an orange-colored patch
in their button-holes! And what a continual parade of
people in the open galleries of the grand stands! The scene
interested her for a moment or two, but truly it was not
worth while getting the spleen because they didn't admit you
inside here.

Daguenet and Fauchery passed by and bowed to her. She
made them a sign, and they had to come up. Thereupon she
made hay of the weighing-in enclosure. But she broke off
abruptly:

"Dear me, there's the Marquis de Chouard! How old
he's growing! That old man's killing himself! Is he still
as mad about it as ever?"

Thereupon Daguenet described the old man's last brilliant
stroke. The story dated from the day before yesterday, and
no one knew it as yet. After dangling about for months, he
had bought her daughter Amélie from Gaga for thirty thousand francs, they said.

"Good gracious! that's a nice business!" cried Nana in
disgust. "Go in for the regular thing, please! But now
that I come to think of it, that must be Lili down there on
the grass, with a lady in a brougham. I recognized the face.
The old boy will have brought her out."

Vandeuvres was not listening—he was impatient and
longed to get rid of her. But Fauchery having remarked at
parting that if she had not seen the bookmakers she had seen
nothing, the Count was obliged to take her to them in spite
of his obvious repugnance. And she was perfectly happy at
once; that truly was a curious sight, she said!

Amid lawns bordered by young horse-chestnut trees, there

was a round open enclosure, where, forming a vast circle under the shadow of the tender green leaves, a dense line of bookmakers was waiting for betting men, as though they had been hucksters at a fair. In order to overtop and command the surrounding crowd, they had taken up positions on wooden benches, and they were advertising their prices on the trees beside them. They had an ever-vigilant glance, and they booked wagers in answer to a single sign, a mere wink, so rapidly, that certain curious onlookers watched them open-mouthed, without being able to understand it all. Confusion reigned; prices were shouted, and any unexpected change in a quotation was received with something like tumult. Occasionally scouts entered the place at a run, and redoubled the uproar as they stopped at the entrance to the rotunda and, at the tops of their voices, announced departures and arrivals. In this place, where the gambling fever was pulsing in the sunshine, such announcements were sure to raise a prolonged muttering sound.

"They *are* funny!" murmured Nana, greatly entertained. "Their features look as if they had been put on the wrong way. Just you see that big fellow there; I shouldn't care to meet him all alone in the middle of a wood."

But Vandeuvres pointed her out a bookmaker, once a shopman in a fancy repository, who had made three million francs in two years. He was slight of build, delicate, and fair, and people all round him treated him with great respect. They smiled when they addressed him, whilst others took up positions close by in order to catch a glimpse of him.

They were at length leaving the ring, when Vandeuvres nodded slightly to another bookmaker, who thereupon ventured to call him. It was one of his former coachmen, an enormous fellow with the shoulders of an ox, and a high color. Now that he was trying his fortunes at race-meetings, on the strength of some mysteriously-obtained capital, the Count was doing his utmost to push him, confiding to him his secret bets, and treating him on all occasions as a servant to whom one shews one's true character. Yet, despite this protection, the man had in rapid succession lost very heavy sums, and to-day he too was playing his last card. There was blood in his eyes; he looked fit to drop with apoplexy.

"Well, Maréchal," queried the Count in the lowest of voices, "to what amount have you laid odds?"

"To five thousand louis, Monsieur le Comte," replied the bookmaker, likewise lowering his voice. "A pretty job, eh? I'll confess to you that I've increased the odds; I've made it three to one."

Vandeuvres looked very much put out.

"No, no, I don't want you to do that: put it at two to one again directly. I shan't tell you any more, Maréchal."

"Oh, how can it hurt, Monsieur le Comte, at this time o' day?" rejoined the other, with the humble smile befitting an accomplice. "I had to attract the people so as to lay your two thousand louis."

At this Vandeuvres silenced him. But as he was going off, Maréchal remembered something, and was sorry he had not questioned him about the shortening of the odds on the filly. It would be a nice business for him if the filly stood a chance, seeing that he had just laid fifty to one about her in two hundreds.

Nana, though she did not understand a word of what the Count was whispering, dared not, however, ask for new explanations. He seemed more nervous than before, and abruptly handed her over to Labordette, whom they came upon in front of the weighing-in room.

"You'll take her back," said he. "I've got something on hand. Au revoir!"

And he entered the room, which was narrow and low-pitched, and half filled with a great pair of scales. It was like a waiting-room in a suburban station, and Nana was again hugely disillusioned, for she had been picturing to herself something on a very vast scale, a monumental machine, in fact, for weighing horses. Dear me, they only weighed the jockeys! Then it wasn't worth while making such a fuss with their weighing! In the scale, a jockey with an idiotic expression was waiting, harness on knee, till a stout man in a frock-coat should have done verifying his weight. At the door, a stable-help was holding a horse, Cosinus, round which a silent and deeply-interested throng was clustering.

The course was about to be cleared. Labordette hurried Nana, but retraced his steps in order to shew her a little man talking with Vandeuvres at some distance from the rest.

"Dear me, there's Price!" said he.

"Ah, yes! the man who's mounting me," she murmured laughingly.

And she declared him to be exquisitely ugly. All jockeys struck her as looking idiotic, doubtless, said she, because they were prevented from growing bigger. This particular jockey was a man of forty, and with his long, thin, deeply furrowed, hard, dead countenance, he looked like an old shriveled-up child. His body was knotty, and so reduced in size that his blue jacket with its white sleeves looked as if it had been thrown over a lay figure.

"No," she resumed as she walked away, "he would never make me very happy, you know."

A mob of people were still crowding the course, the turf of which had been wetted and trampled on, till it had grown black. In front of the two telegraphs, which hung very high up on their cast-iron pillars, the crowd were jostling together, with upturned faces, uproariously greeting the numbers of the different horses as an electric wire in connection with the weighing-room made them appear. Gentlemen were pointing at programs: Pichenette had been scratched by his owner, and this caused some noise. However, Nana did not do more than cross over the course on Labordette's arm. The bell hanging on the flag-staff was ringing persistently to warn people to leave the course.

"Ah! my little dears," said she, as she got up into her landau again, "their enclosure's all humbug!"

She was welcomed with acclamation; people around her clapped their hands:

"Bravo Nana! Nana's ours again!"

What idiots they were, to be sure! Did they think she was the sort to cut old friends? She had come back just at the auspicious moment. Now then, 'tenshun! The race was beginning! And the champagne was accordingly forgotten, and every one left off drinking.

But Nana was astonished to find Gaga in her carriage, sitting with Bijou and Louiset on her knees. Gaga had indeed decided on this course of action in order to be near la Faloise, but she told Nana that she had been anxious to kiss baby. She adored children.

"By-the-by, what about Lili?" asked Nana. "That's certainly she over there, in that old fellow's brougham. They've just told me something very nice!"

Gaga had adopted a lachrymose expression.

"My dear, it's made me ill," said she dolorously. "Yesterday I had to keep my bed, I cried so, and to-day I didn't think I should be able to come. You know what my opinions were, don't you? I didn't desire that kind of thing at all. I had her educated in a convent with a view to a good marriage. And, then, to think of the strict advice she had, and the constant watching! Well, my dear, it was she who wished it. We had such a scene—tears—disagreeable speeches! It even got to such a point that I caught her a box on the ear. She was too much bored by existence, she said; she wanted to get out of it. By-and-by, when she began to say, ' 'Tisn't you, after all, who've got the right to prevent me,' I said to her: 'You're a miserable wretch: you're bringing dishonor upon us: begone!' and it was done. I con-

sented to arrange about it. But my last hope's blooming
well blasted, and oh, I used to dream about such nice things!"

The noise of a quarrel caused them to rise. It was Georges,
in the act of defending Vandeuvres against certain vague
rumors which were circulating among the various groups.

"Why should you say that he's laying off his own horse?"
the young man was exclaiming. "Yesterday, in the Salon
des Courses, he took the odds on Lusignan for a thousand
louis."

"Yes, I was there," said Philippe in affirmation of this.
"And he didn't put a single louis on Nana. If the betting's
ten to one against Nana, he's got nothing to win there. It's
absurd to imagine people are so calculating. Where would
his interest come in?"

Labordette was listening with a quiet expression. Shrugging his shoulders, he said,—

"Oh, leave them alone; they must have their say. The
Count has again laid at least as much as five hundred louis
on Lusignan, and if he's wanted Nana to run to a hundred
louis, it's because an owner ought always to look as if he
believes in his horses."

"Oh, bosh! What the deuce does that matter to us?"
shouted la Faloise, with a wave of his arms. "Spirit's going
to win! Down with France—bravo England!"

A long shiver ran through the crowd, whilst a fresh peal
from the bell announced the arrival of the horses upon the
race-course. At this, Nana got up and stood on one of the
seats of her carriage so as to obtain a better view, and in so
doing she trampled the bouquets of roses and myosotis underfoot. With a sweeping glance she took in the wide, vast
horizon. At this last feverish moment the course was empty,
and closed by gray barriers, between the posts of which stood
a line of policemen. The strip of grass, which lay muddy in
front of her, grew brighter as it stretched away, and turned
into a tender green carpet in the distance. In the middle

landscape, as she lowered her eyes, she saw the field swarming with vast numbers of people, some on tip-toe, others
perched on carriages, and all heaving and jostling in sudden
passionate excitement.

Horses were neighing, tent-canvases flapped, whilst eques-
trians urged their hacks forward amid a crowd of pedestrians
rushing to get places along the barriers. When Nana turned
in the direction of the stands on the other side, the faces
seemed diminished, and the dense masses of heads were only
a confused and motley array, filling gangways, steps, and ter-
races, and looming in deep, dark, serried lines against the sky.
And beyond these again, she overlooked the plain surrounding the course. Behind the ivy-clad mill to the right, meadows, dotted over with great patches of umbrageous wood,
stretched away into the distance; whilst opposite to her, as
far as the Seine flowing at the foot of a hill, the avenues
of the Park intersected one another, filled at that moment
with long motionless files of waiting carriages; and, in the
direction of Boulogne, on the left, the landscape widened
anew, and opened out towards the blue distances of Meudon
through an avenue of paulownias, whose rosy, leafless tops
were one stain of brilliant lake color. People were still arriving, and a long procession of human ants kept coming along
the narrow ribbon of road which crossed the distance, whilst,
very far away, on the Paris side, the non-paying public, herd-
ing like sheep among the woods, loomed in a moving line of
little dark spots under the trees on the skirts of the Bois.

Suddenly a cheering influence warmed the hundred thousand souls who covered this part of the plain like insects
swarming madly under the vast expanse of heaven. The
sun, which had been hidden for about a quarter of an hour,
made his appearance again, and shone out amid a perfect
sea of light. And everything flamed afresh: the women's
sunshades turned into countless golden targes above the
heads of the crowd. The sun was applauded, saluted with

bursts of laughter. And people stretched their arms out as though to brush apart the clouds.

Meanwhile, a solitary police officer advanced down the middle of the deserted race-course, whilst higher up, on the left, a man appeared with a red flag in his hand.

"It's the starter, the Baron de Mauriac," said Labordette in reply to a question from Nana. All round the young woman exclamations were bursting from the men who were pressing to her very carriage-step. They kept up a disconnected conversation, jerking out phrases under the immediate influence of passing impressions. Indeed, Philippe and Georges, Bordenave and la Faloise, could not be quiet.

"Don't shove! Let me see! Ah, the judge is getting into his box. D'you say it's Monsieur de Souvigny? You must have good eyesight—eh? to be able to tell what half a head is out of a fakement like that! Do hold your tongue—the banner's going up. Here they are—'tenshun! Cosinus is the first!"

A red and yellow banner was flapping in mid-air, at the top of a mast. The horses came on the course one by one, they were led by stable-boys, and the jockeys were sitting idle-handed in the saddles, the sunlight making them look light bright dabs of color. After Cosinus appeared Hazard and Boum. Presently a murmur of approval greeted Spirit, a magnificent big brown bay, the harsh citron-color and black of whose jockey were cheerlessly Britannic. Valerio II. scored a success as he came in; he was small and very lively, and his colors were soft green bordered with pink. The two Vandeuvres' horses were slow to make their appearance, but at last, in Frangipane's rear, the blue and white shewed themselves. But Lusignan, a very dark bay, of irreproachable shape, was almost forgotten amid the astonishment caused by Nana. People had not seen her looking like this before, for now the sudden sunlight was dyeing the chestnut filly the brilliant color of a girl's red-gold hair.

She was shining in the light like a new gold coin; her chest was deep, her head and neck tapered lightly from the delicate, high-strung line of her long back.

"Gracious, she's got my hair!" cried Nana in an ecstasy. "You bet you know I'm proud of it!"

The men clambered up on the landau, and Bordenave narrowly escaped putting his foot on Louiset, whom his mother had forgotten. He took him up with an outburst of paternal grumbling, and hoisted him on his shoulder, muttering at the same time:

"The poor little brat, he must be in it too! Wait a bit, I'll shew you mamma. Eh? Look at mummy out there."

And, as Bijou was scratching his legs, he took charge of him too, whilst Nana, rejoicing in the brute that bore her name, glanced round at the other women to see how they took it. They were all raging madly. Just then, on the summit of her cab, the Tricon, who had not moved till that moment, began waving her hand and giving a bookmaker her orders above the heads of the crowd. Her instinct had at last prompted her; she was backing Nana.

La Faloise meanwhile was making an insufferable noise. He was getting wild over Frangipane.

"I've an inspiration," he kept shouting. "Just look at Frangipane. What an action, eh? I back Frangipane at eight to one. Who'll take me?"

"Do keep quiet now," said Labordette at last. "You'll be sorry for it, if you do."

"Frangipane's a screw," Philippe declared. "He's been utterly blown upon already. You'll see the canter."

The horses had gone up to the right, and they now started for the preliminary canter, passing in loose order before the stands. Thereupon there was a passionate fresh burst of talk, and people all spoke at once.

"Lusignan's too long in the back, but he's very fit. Not a cent, I tell you, on Valerio II.; he's nervous—gallops with

his head up—it's a bad sign. Jove! Burne's riding Spirit.
I tell you he's got no shoulders. A well-made shoulder—
that's the whole secret. No, decidedly, Spirit's too quiet.
Now listen, Nana, I saw her after the Grande Poule des
Produits, and she was dripping, and draggled, and her sides
were trembling like one o'clock. I lay twenty louis she
isn't placed! Oh, shut up! He's boring us with his Frangipane. There's no time to make a bet now; there, they're
off!"

Almost in tears, la Faloise was struggling to find a bookmaker. He had to be reasoned with. Every one craned forward, but the first go-off was bad; the starter, who looked in
the distance like a slim dash of blackness, not having lowered
his flag. The horses came back to their places after galloping a moment or two. There were two more false starts.
At length the starter got the horses together and sent them
away with such address as to elicit shouts of applause.

"Splendid! No, it was mere chance! Never mind—it's
done it!"

The outcries were smothered by the anxiety which tortured
every breast. The betting stopped now, and the game was
being played on the vast course itself. Silence reigned at the
outset as though every one were holding his breath. White
faces and trembling forms were stretched forward in all
directions. At first Hazard and Cosinus made the running
at the head of the rest; Valerio II. followed close by, and the
field came on in a confused mass behind. When they passed
in front of the stands, thundering over the ground in their
course like a sudden storm-wind, the mass was already some
fourteen lengths in extent. Frangipane was last, and Nana
was slightly behind Lusignan and Spirit.

"Egad!" muttered Labordette, "how the Englishman is
pulling it off out there!"

The whole carriage-load again burst out with phrases and
exclamations. Every one rose on tiptoe and followed the

bright splashes of color, which were the jockeys as they rushed through the sunlight.

At the rise Valerio II. took the lead, whilst Cosinus and Hazard lost ground, and Lusignan and Spirit were running neck to neck with Nana still behind them.

"By jingo, the Englishman's gained! it's palpable!" said Bordenave. "Lusignan's in difficulties, and Valerio II. can't stay."

"Well, it will be a pretty biz if the Englishman wins!" cried Philippe, in an access of patriotic grief.

A feeling of anguish was beginning to choke all that crowded multitude. Another defeat! And with that a strange ardent prayer, which was almost religious, went up for Lusignan, whilst people heaped abuse on Spirit and his dismal mute of a jockey. Among the crowd scattered over the grass the wind of excitement put up whole groups of people and set their boot-soles flashing in air as they ran. Horsemen crossed the green at a furious gallop. And Nana, who was slowly revolving on her own axis, saw beneath her a surging waste of beasts and men, a sea of heads swayed and stirred, all round the course, by the whirlwind of the race, which clove the horizon with the bright lightning flash of the jockeys. She had been following their movement from behind, whilst the cruppers sped away and the legs seemed to grow longer as they raced, and then diminished till they looked slender as strands of hair. Now the horses were running at the end of the course, and she caught a side view of them looking minute and delicate of outline against the green distances of the Bois. Then, suddenly, they vanished behind a great clump of trees growing in the middle of the Hippodrome.

"Don't talk about it!" cried Georges, who was still full of hope. "It isn't over yet. The Englishman's touched."

But la Faloise was again seized with contempt for his country, and grew positively outrageous in his applause of

Spirit. Bravo! That was right! France needed it! Spirit first and Frangipane second—that would be a nasty one for his native land! He exasperated Labordette, who threatened seriously to throw him off the carriage.

"Let's see how many minutes they'll be about it," said Bordenave peaceably, for, though holding up Louiset, he had taken out his watch.

One after the other the horses reappeared from behind the clump of trees. There was stupefaction: a long murmur arose among the crowd. Valerio II. was still leading, but Spirit was gaining on him, and behind him Lusignan had slackened, whilst another horse was taking his place. People could not make this out all at once: they were confused about the colors. Then there was a burst of exclamations.

"But it's Nana! Nana? Get along! I tell you Lusignan hasn't budged. Dear me, yes, it's Nana. You can certainly recognize her by her golden color. D'you see her now? She's blazing away. Bravo Nana! What a ripper she is! Bah, it doesn't matter a bit: she's making the running for Lusignan!"

For some seconds this was everybody's opinion. But little by little, the filly kept gaining and gaining, spurting hard all the while. Thereupon a vast wave of feeling passed over the crowd, and the tail of horses in the rear ceased to interest. A supreme struggle was beginning between Spirit, Nana, Lusignan, and Valerio II. They were pointed out: people estimated what ground they had gained or lost in disconnected, gasping phrases. And Nana, who had mounted up on the coach-box, as though some power had lifted her thither, stood white and trembling, and so deeply moved as not to be able to speak. At her side Labordette smiled as of old.

"The Englishman's in trouble, eh?" said Philippe joyously. "He's going badly."

"In any case, it's all up with Lusignan," shouted la Faloise.

"Valerio II. is coming forward. Look, there they are all four together."

The same phrase was in every mouth.

"What a rush, my dears! By God, what a rush!"

The squad of horses was now passing in front of them like a flash of lightning. Their approach was perceptible— the breath of it was as a distant muttering, which increased at every second. The whole crowd had thrown themselves impetuously against the barriers, and a deep clamor issued from innumerable chests before the advance of the horses, and drew nearer and nearer like the sound of a foaming tide. It was the last fierce outburst of colossal partisanship—a hundred thousand spectators were possessed by a single passion, burning with the same gambler's lust, as they gazed after the beasts, whose galloping feet were sweeping millions with them. The crowd pushed and crushed—fists were clenched, people gaped, open-mouthed; every man was fighting for himself, every man with voice and gesture was madly speeding the horse of his choice. And the cry of all this multitude, a wild beast's cry despite the garb of civilization, grew ever more distinct,—

"Here they come! Here they come! Here they come!"

But Nana was still gaining ground, and now Valerio II. was distanced, and she was heading the race, with Spirit two or three necks behind. The rolling thunder of voices had increased. They were coming in; a storm of oaths greeted them from the landau.

"Gee up, Lusignan, you great coward! The Englishman's stunning! Do it again, old boy, do it again! Oh, that Valerio! it's sickening! Oh, the carcass! My ten louis damned well lost! Nana's the only one! Bravo, Nana! Bravo!"

And without being aware of it Nana, upon her seat, had begun jerking her hips and waist as though she were racing herself. She kept striking her side—she fancied it was a help to the filly. With each stroke she sighed with fatigue, and said in low anguished tones,—

"Go it, go it, go it!"

Then a splendid sight was witnessed. Price, rising in his stirrups and brandishing his whip, flogged Nana with an arm of iron. The old shriveled-up child, with his long, hard, dead face, seemed to breathe flame. And in a fit of furious audacity and triumphant will, he put his heart into the filly, held her up, lifted her forward drenched in foam, with eyes of blood. The whole rush of horses passed with a roar of thunder: it took away people's breaths; it swept the air with it, whilst the judge sat frigidly waiting, his eye adjusted to its task. Then there was an immense reëchoing burst of acclamation. With a supreme effort, Price had just flung Nana past the post, thus beating Spirit by a head.

There was an uproar as of a rising tide. "Nana! Nana! Nana!" The cry rolled up and swelled with the violence of a tempest, till, little by little, it filled the distance, the depths of the Bois as far as Mont Valérien, the meadows of Long-champs and the Plaine de Boulogne. In all parts of the field the wildest enthusiasm declared itself. "Vive Nana! Vive la France! Down with England!" The women waved their sunshades; men leapt and spun round, vociferating as they did so, whilst others with shouts of nervous laughter threw their hats in the air. And from the other side of the course, the enclosure made answer, the people on the stands were stirred, though nothing was distinctly visible save a tremulous motion of the air, as though an invisible flame were burning in a brazier above the living mass of gesticulating arms, and little, wildly-moving faces, where the eyes and gaping mouths looked like black dots. The noise did not cease, but swelled up and recommenced in the recesses of far-away avenues and among the people encamped under the trees, till it spread on and on and attained its climax in the imperial stand, where the Empress herself had applauded.

"Nana! Nana! Nana!" The cry rose heavenward in the glorious sunlight, whose golden rain beat fiercely on the dizzy heads of the multitude.

Then Nana, looming large on the seat of her landau, fancied that it was she whom they were applauding. For a moment or two she had stood devoid of motion, stupefied by her triumph, gazing at the course as it was invaded by so dense a flood of people that the turf became invisible beneath the sea of black hats. By-and-by, when this crowd had become somewhat less disorderly, and a lane had been formed as far as the exit, and Nana was again applauded as she went off with Price hanging lifelessly and vacantly over her neck, she smacked her thigh energetically, lost all self-possession, triumphed in crude phrases:

"Oh, by God, it's me, it's me! Oh, by God, what luck!"

And, scarce knowing how to give expression to her overwhelming joy, she hugged and kissed Louiset, whom she now discovered high in air on Bordenave's shoulder.

"Three minutes and fourteen seconds," said the latter as he put his watch back in his pocket.

Nana kept hearing her name; the whole plain was echoing it back to her. Her people were applauding her whilst she towered above them in the sunlight, in the splendor of her starry hair, and white and sky-blue dress. Labordette, as he made off, had just announced to her a gain of two thousand louis, for he had put her fifty on Nana, at forty to one. But the money stirred her less than this unforseen victory, the fame of which made her Queen of Paris. All the other ladies were losers. With a raging movement Rose Mignon had snapped her sunshade; and Caroline Héquet, and Clarisse, and Simonne—nay, Lucy Stewart herself, despite the presence of her son, were swearing low in their exasperation at that great wench's luck, whilst the Tricon, who had made the sign of the cross at both start and finish, straightened up her tall form above them, went into an ecstasy over her intuition, and damned Nana admiringly as became an experienced matron.

Meanwhile, round the landau the crush of men increased. The band of Nana's immediate followers had made a fierce uproar, and now Georges, choking with emotion, continued shouting all by himself in breaking tones. As the champagne had given out, Philippe, taking the footmen with him, had run to the wine-bars. Nana's court was growing and growing, and her present triumph caused many loiterers to join her. Indeed, that movement which had made her carriage a center of attraction to the whole field was now ending in an apotheosis, and Queen Venus was enthroned amid suddenly-maddened subjects. Bordenave, behind her, was muttering oaths, for he yearned to her as a father. Steiner himself had been reconquered—he had deserted Simonne and had hoisted himself up on one of Nana's carriage-steps. When the champagne had arrived, when she lifted her brimming glass, such applause burst forth, and "Nana! Nana! Nana!" was so loudly repeated, that the crowd looked round in astonishment for the filly, nor could any tell whether it was the horse or the woman that filled all hearts.

Whilst this was going on, Mignon came hastening up in defiance of Rose's terrible frown. That confounded girl simply maddened him, and he wanted to kiss her. Then, after imprinting a paternal salute on both her cheeks,—

"What bothers me," said he, "is that now Rose is certainly going to send the letter. She's raging, too, fearfully."

"So much the better! It'll do my business for me!" Nana let slip.

But noting his utter astonishment, she hastily continued,—
"No, no, what am I saying? Indeed, I don't rightly know what I'm saying now! I'm drunk."

And drunk indeed, drunk with joy, drunk with sunshine, she still raised her glass on high and applauded herself.

"To Nana! To Nana!" she cried, amid a redoubled up-

roar of laughter and bravos, which little by little overspread
the whole Hippodrome.

The races were ending, and the Prix Vaublanc was run
for. Carriages began driving off one by one. Meanwhile,
amid much disputing, the name of Vandeuvres was again
mentioned. It was quite evident now: for two years past
Vandeuvres had been preparing his final stroke, and had
accordingly told Gresham to hold Nana in, whilst he had
only brought Lusignan forward in order to make play for
the filly. The losers were vexed, the winners shrugged their
shoulders. After all, wasn't the thing permissible? An
owner was free to run his stud in his own way. Many others
had done as he had! In fact the majority thought Vandeuvres had displayed great skill in raking in all he could
get about Nana through the agency of friends, a course of
action which explained the sudden shortening of the odds.
People spoke of his having laid two thousand louis on the
horse, which, supposing the odds to be thirty to one against,
gave him twelve hundred thousand francs, an amount so
vast as to inspire respect and to excuse everything.

But other rumors of a very serious nature were being
whispered about: they issued in the first instance from the
enclosure, and the men who returned thence were full of
exact particulars. Voices were raised, an atrocious scandal
began to be openly canvassed. That poor fellow Vandeuvres
was done for; he had spoilt his splendid hit with a piece
of flat stupidity, an idiotic robbery, for he had commissioned Maréchal, a shady bookmaker, to lay two thousand
louis on his account against Lusignan, in order thereby to
get back his thousand and odd openly wagered louis. It was
a miserable business, and it proved to be the last rift necessary to the utter break-up of his fortune. The bookmaker
being thus warned that the favorite would not win, had
realized some sixty thousand francs over the horse. Only
Labordette, for lack of exact and detailed instructions, had

just then gone to him to put two hundred louis on Nana, which the bookmaker, in his ignorance of the stroke actually intended, was still quoting at fifty to one against. Cleared of one hundred thousand francs over the filly, and a loser to the tune of forty thousand, Maréchal, who felt the world crumbling under his feet, had suddenly divined the situation when he saw the Count and Labordette talking together in front of the enclosure, just after the race was over. Furious, as became an ex-coachman of the Count's, and brutally frank as only a cheated man can be, he had just made a frightful scene in public, had told the whole story in atrocious terms, and had thrown every one into angry excitement. It was further stated that the stewards were about to meet.

Nana, whom Philippe and Georges were whisperingly putting in possession of the facts, gave vent to a series of reflections, and yet ceased not to laugh and drink. After all it was quite likely; she remembered such things, and then that Maréchal had a dirty, hangdog look. Nevertheless, she was still rather doubtful when Labordette appeared. He was very white.

"Well?" she asked in a low voice.

"Bloody well smashed up!" he replied simply.

And he shrugged his shoulders. That Vandeuvres was a mere child! She made a bored little gesture.

That evening at the Bal Mabille Nana obtained a colossal success. When, towards ten o'clock, she made her appearance, the uproar was already formidable. That classic night of madness had brought together all that was young and pleasure-loving, and now this smart world was wallowing in the coarseness and imbecility of the servants' hall. There was a fierce crush under the festoons of gas-lamps, and men in evening coats and women in outrageous low-necked old toilets, which they did not mind soiling, were howling and surging to and fro under the maddening influence of a vast drunken fit. At a distance of thirty paces the brass instruments of the orchestra were inaudible. Nobody was dancing. Stupid witticisms, repeated no one knew why, were going the round of the various groups. People were straining after wit without succeeding in being funny. Seven women, imprisoned in the cloak-room, were crying to be set free. A shallot had been found, put up to auction, and knocked down at two louis. Just then Nana arrived, still wearing her blue-and-white race-course costume, and amid a thunder of applause the shallot was presented to her. People caught hold of her in her own despite, and three gentlemen bore her triumphantly into the garden, across ruined grass-plats and ravaged masses of greenery. As the band-stand presented an obstacle to her advance, it was taken by storm, and chairs and music-stands were smashed. A paternal police organized the disorder.

It was only on Tuesday that Nana recovered from the excitements of victory. That morning, she was chatting with Madame Lerat, the old lady having come in to bring her news of Louiset, whom the open air had upset. A long story, which was occupying the attention of all Paris, interested her beyond measure. Vandeuvres, after being warned off all race-courses and posted at the Cercle Imperial on the very evening after the disaster had set fire to his stable on the morrow, and had burnt himself and his horses to death.

"He certainly told me he was going to," the young woman kept saying. "That man was a regular maniac! Oh, how they did frighten me when they told me about it yesterday evening! You see he might easily have murdered me some fine night. And besides, oughtn't he to have given me a hint about his horse? I should at any rate have made my fortune! He said to Labordette that if I knew about the matter I would immediately inform my hairdresser and a whole lot of other men. How polite, eh? Oh, dear no, I certainly can't grieve much for him."

After some reflection, she had grown very angry. Just then Labordette came in; he had seen about her bets, and was now the bearer of some forty thousand francs. This only added to her bad temper, for she ought to have gained a million. Labordette, who during the whole of this episode had been pretending entire innocence, abandoned Vandeuvres in decisive terms. Those old families, he opined, were worn out, and apt to make a stupid ending.

"Oh, dear no!" said Nana; "it isn't stupid to burn one's self in one's stable as he did. For my part, I think he made a dashing finish; but oh, you know, I'm not defending that story about him and Maréchal. It's too silly. Just to think that Blanche has had the cheek to want to lay the blame of it on me! I said to her: 'Did I tell him to steal?' Don't you think one can ask a man for money without urging him to commit crime? If he had said to me, 'I've got nothing left,' I should have said to him, 'All right, let's part.' And the matter wouldn't have gone further."

"Just so," said the aunt gravely. "When men are obstinate about a thing, so much the worse for them!"

"But as to the merry little finish up, oh, that was awfully smart!" continued Nana. "It appears to have been terrible enough to give you the shudders! He sent everybody away, and boxed himself up in the place with a lot of petroleum. And it blazed! you should have seen it! Just think, a great big affair, almost all made of wood, and stuffed with hay and straw! The flames simply towered up, and the finest part of the business was that the horses didn't want to be roasted. They could be heard plunging, throwing themselves against the doors, crying aloud just like human beings. Yes, people haven't got rid of the horror of it yet."

Labordette let a low, incredulous whistle escape him. For his part he did not believe in the death of Vandeuvres. Somebody had sworn he had seen him escaping through a window. He had set fire to his stable in a fit of aberration,

but when it had begun to grow too warm it must have
sobered him. A man so besotted about the women and so
utterly worn out could not possibly die so pluckily.

Nana listened in her disillusionment, and could only remark:

"Oh! the poor wretch, it was so beautiful!"

CHAPTER XII

TOWARDS one in the morning, in the great bed of the
Venice point draperies, Nana and the Count lay still
awake. He had returned to her that evening after a three
days' sulking fit. The room, which was dimly illumined by a
lamp, seemed to slumber amid a warm, damp odor of love,
whilst the furniture, with its white lacquer and silver in-
crustations, loomed vague and wan through the gloom. A
curtain had been drawn to, so that the bed lay flooded with
shadow. A sigh became audible; then a kiss broke the silence,
and Nana, slipping off the coverlet, sat for a moment or two,
bare-legged, on the edge of the bed. The Count let his
head fall back on the pillow, and remained in darkness.

"Dearest, you believe in the good God, don't you?" she
queried after some moments' reflection. Her face was serious; she had been overcome by pious terrors on quitting her
lover's arms.

Since morning, indeed, she had been complaining of feeling uncomfortable, and all her stupid notions, as she phrased
it, notions about death and hell, were secretly torturing her.
From time to time she had nights such as these, during which
childish fears and atrocious fancies would thrill her with
waking nightmares. She continued,—

"I say, d'you think I shall go to heaven?"

And with that she shivered, whilst the Count, in his surprise at her putting such singular questions at such a moment,

felt his old religious remorse returning upon him. Then, with her chemise slipping from her shoulders and her hair unpinned, she again threw herself upon his breast, sobbing and clinging to him as she did so.

"I'm afraid of dying! I'm afraid of dying!" He had all the trouble in the world to disengage himself. Indeed, he was himself afraid of giving in to the sudden madness of this woman clinging to his body in her dread of the Invisible. Such dread is contagious, and he reasoned with her. Her conduct was perfect—she had only to conduct herself well in order one day to merit pardon. But she shook her head. Doubtless she was doing no one any harm; nay, she was even in the constant habit of wearing a medal of the Virgin, which she shewed to him as it hung by a red thread between her breasts. Only it had been foreordained that all unmarried women who held conversation with men would go to hell. Scraps of her catechism recurred to her remembrance. Ah! if one only knew for certain; but, alas! one was sure of nothing; nobody ever brought back any information; and then, truly, it would be stupid to bother one's self about things if the priests were talking foolishness all the time. Nevertheless, she religiously kissed her medal, which was still warm from contact with her skin, as though by way of charm against death, the idea of which filled her with icy horror. Muffat was obliged to accompany her into the dressing-room, for she shook at the idea of being alone there one moment, even though she had left the door open. When he had lain down again she still roamed about the room, visiting its several corners, and starting and shivering at the slightest noise. A mirror stopped her, and as of old she lapsed into oblivious contemplation of her nakedness. But the sight of her breast, her waist, and her thighs only doubled her terror, and she ended by feeling with both hands very slowly over the bones of her face.

"You're ugly when you're dead," said she in deliberate tones.

And she pressed her cheeks, enlarging her eyes and pushing down her jaw, in order to see how she would look. Thus disfigured she turned towards the Count:

"Do look! my head'll be quite small, it will!"

At this he grew vexed.

"You're mad; come to bed!"

He fancied he saw her in a grave, emaciated by a century of sleep, and he joined his hands and stammered a prayer. It was some time ago that the religious sense had reconquered him, and now his daily access of faith had again assumed the apoplectic intensity which was wont to leave him well-nigh stunned. The joints of his fingers used to crack, and he would repeat without cease these words only: "My God, my God, my God!" It was the cry of his impotence, the cry of that sin against which, though his damnation was certain, he felt powerless to strive. When Nana returned, she found him hidden beneath the bed-clothes; he was haggard, he had dug his nails into his bosom, and his eyes stared upward as though in search of heaven. And with that she started to weep again. Then they both embraced, and their teeth chattered they knew not why, as the same imbecile obsession overmastered them. They had already passed a similar night, but on this occasion, the thing was utterly idiotic, as Nana declared when she ceased to be frightened. She suspected something, and this caused her to question the Count in a prudent sort of way. It might be that Rose Mignon had sent the famous letter! But that was not the case; it was sheer fright, nothing more, for he was still ignorant whether he was a cuckold or no.

Two days later, after a fresh disappearance, Muffat presented himself in the morning, a time of day at which he never came. He was livid; his eyes were red, and his whole man still shaken by a great internal struggle. But Zoé, being scared herself, did not notice his troubled state. She had run to meet him, and now began crying,—

"Oh, *Monsieur*, do come in! *Madame* nearly died yesterday evening!"

And, when he asked for particulars,—

"Something it's impossible to believe has happened—a miscarriage, *Monsieur*."

Nana had been in the family way for the past three months. For long she had simply thought herself out of sorts, and Doctor Boutarel had himself been in doubt. But when afterwards he made her a decisive announcement, she felt so bored thereby that she did all she possibly could to disguise her condition. Her nervous terrors, her dark humors, sprang to some extent from this unfortunate state of things, the secret of which she kept very shamefacedly, as became a courtesan-mother who is obliged to conceal her plight. The thing struck her as a ridiculous accident, which made her appear small in her own eyes, and would, had it been known, have led people to chaff her.

"A poor joke, eh?" said she. "Bad luck, too, certainly."

She was necessarily very sharp-set when she thought her last hour had come. There was no end to her surprise, too; her sexual economy seemed to her to have got out of order, it produced children, then, even when one did not want them, and when one employed it for quite other purposes! Nature drove her to exasperation; this appearance of serious motherhood in a career of pleasure, this gift of life amid all the deaths she was spreading around, exasperated her. Why could one not dispose of one's self as fancy dictated, without all this fuss? And whence had this brat come? She could not even suggest a father. Ah, dear heaven! the man who made him would have a splendid notion had he kept him in his own hands, for nobody asked for him, he was in everybody's way, and he would certainly not have much happiness in life!

Meanwhile Zoé described the catastrophe.

"*Madame* was seized with colic towards four o'clock. When she didn't come back out of the dressing-room, I went in, and found her lying stretched on the floor in a faint. Yes, *Monsieur,* on the floor, in a pool of blood, as though she had been murdered. Then I understood, you see. I was furious; Madame might quite well have confided her trouble to me. At it happened, Monsieur Georges was there, and he helped me to lift her up, and directly a miscarriage was mentioned he felt ill in his turn! Oh, it's true I've had the hump since yesterday!"

In fact the house seemed utterly upset. All the servants were galloping upstairs, downstairs, and through the rooms. Georges had passed the night on an arm-chair in the drawing-room. It was he who had announced the news to *Madame's* friends at that hour of the evening when *Madame* was in the habit of receiving. He had still been very pale, and he had told his story very feelingly and as though stupefied. Steiner, la Faloise, Philippe, and others besides, had presented themselves, and, at the end of the lad's first phrase, they burst into exclamations. The thing was impossible! It must be a farce! After which they grew serious, and gazed with an embarrassed expression at her bedroom-door. They shook their heads: it was no laughing matter.

Till midnight a dozen gentlemen had stood talking in low voices in front of the fire-place. All were friends, all were deeply exercised by the same idea of paternity. They seemed to be mutually excusing themselves, and they looked as confused as if they had done something clumsy. Eventually, however, they put a bold face on the matter. It had nothing to do with them: the fault was hers! What a stunner that Nana was, eh? One would never have believed her capable of such a fake! And with that they departed one by one, walking on tip-toe as though in a chamber of death where you cannot laugh.

"Come up all the same, *Monsieur*," said Zoé to Muffat. "*Madame* is much better, and will see you. We are expecting the doctor, who promised to come back this morning."

The lady's maid had persuaded Georges to go back home to sleep, and upstairs in the drawing-room only Satin remained. She lay stretched on a divan, smoking a cigarette, and scanning the ceiling. Amid the household scare which had followed the accident, she had been white with rage, had shrugged her shoulders violently, and had made ferocious remarks. Accordingly, when Zoé was passing in front of her and telling Monsieur that poor dear *Madame* had suffered a great deal,—

"That's right; it'll teach him!" said Satin curtly.

They turned round in surprise, but she had not moved a muscle; her eyes were still turned towards the ceiling, and her cigarette was still wedged tightly between her lips.

"Dear me, you're charming, you are!" said Zoé.

But Satin sat up, looked savagely at the Count, and once more hurled her remark at him.

"That's right; it'll teach him!"

And she lay down again, and blew forth a thin jet of smoke, as though she had no interest in present events and were resolved not to meddle in any of them. No, it was all too silly!

Zoé, however, introduced Muffat into the bedroom, where a scent of ether lingered amid warm heavy silence, scarce broken by the dull roll of occasional carriages in the Avenue de Villiers. Nana, looking very white on her pillow, was lying awake with wide-open, meditative eyes. She smiled when she saw the Count, but did not move.

"Ah, dear pet!" she slowly murmured; "I really thought I should never see you again."

Then, as he leant forward to kiss her on the hair, she grew tender towards him, and spoke frankly about the child, as though he were its father.

"I never dared tell you, I felt so happy about it! Oh, I used to dream about it; I should have liked to be worthy of you! And now there's nothing left. Ah well, perhaps that's best. I don't want to bring a stumbling-block into your life."

Astounded by this story of paternity, he began stammering vague phrases. He had taken a chair, and had sat down by the bed, leaning one arm on the coverlet. Then the young woman noticed his wild expression, the blood reddening his eyes, the fever that set his lips aquiver.

"What's the matter, then?" she asked. "You're ill, too."

"No," he answered with extreme difficulty.

She gazed at him with a profound expression. Then she signed to Zoé to retire, for the latter was lingering round arranging the medicine bottles. And when they were alone she drew him down to her and again asked,—

"What's the matter with you, darling? The tears are ready to burst from your eyes—I can see that quite well. Well, now, speak out; you've come to tell me something."

"No, no, I swear I haven't," he blurted out. But he was choking with suffering, and this sick-room, into which he had suddenly entered unawares, so worked on his feelings that he burst out sobbing, and buried his face in the bed-clothes to smother the violence of his grief. Nana understood. Rose Mignon had most assuredly decided to send the letter. She let him weep for some moments, and he was shaken by convulsions so fierce that the bed trembled under her. At length, in accents of motherly compassion, she queried,—

"You've had bothers at your home?"

He nodded affirmatively. She paused anew, and then very low,—

"Then you know all?"

He nodded assent. And a heavy silence fell over the chamber of suffering. The night before, on his return from a party given by the Empress, he had received the letter

Sabine had written her lover. After an atrocious night passed in the meditation of vengeance, he had gone out in the morning in order to resist a longing which prompted him to kill his wife. Outside, under a sudden sweet influence of a fine June morning, he had lost the thread of his thoughts, and had come to Nana's as he always came at terrible moments in his life. There only he gave way to his misery, for he felt a cowardly joy at the thought that she would console him.

"Now look here, be calm!" the young woman continued, becoming at the same time extremely kind. "I've known it a long time, but it was certainly not I that would have opened your eyes. You remember you had your doubts last year, but then things arranged themselves owing to my prudence. In fact, you wanted proofs. The deuce you've got one to-day, and I know it's hard lines. Nevertheless, you must look at the matter quietly: you're not dishonored because it's happened."

He had left off weeping. A sense of shame restrained him from saying what he wanted to, although he had long ago slipped into the most intimate confessions about his household. She had to encourage him. Dear me, she was a woman; she could understand everything. When in a dull voice he exclaimed,—

"You're ill. What's the good of tiring you? It was stupid of me to have come. I'm going—"

"No," she answered briskly enough. "Stay! Perhaps I shall be able to give you some good advice. Only don't make me talk too much: the medical man's forbidden it."

He had ended by rising, and he was now walking up and down the room. Then she questioned him.

"Now what are you going to do?"

"I'm going to box the man's ears—by heavens, yes!"

She pursed up her lips disapprovingly.

"That's not very wise. And about your wife?"

"I shall go to law: I've proofs."

"Not at all wise, my dear boy. It's stupid even. You know I shall never let you do that!"

And in her feeble voice she shewed him decisively how useless and scandalous a duel and a trial would be. He would be a nine days' newspaper sensation—his whole existence would be at stake, his peace of mind, his high situation at Court, the honor of his name, and all for what? That he might have the laughers against him.

"What will it matter?" cried he. "I shall have had my revenge."

"My pet," said she, "in a business of that kind one never has one's revenge if one doesn't take it directly."

He paused and stammered. He was certainly no poltroon, but he felt that she was right. An uneasy feeling was growing momentarily stronger within him, a poor shameful feeling which softened his anger now that it was at its hottest. Moreover, in her frank desire to tell him everything, she dealt him a fresh blow.

"And d'you want to know what's annoying you, dearest? Why, that you are deceiving your wife yourself. You don't sleep away from home for nothing, eh? Your wife must have her suspicions. Well, then, how can you blame her? She'll tell you that you've set her the example, and that'll shut you up. There, now, that's why you're stamping about here instead of being at home murdering both of 'em."

Muffat had again sunk down on the chair; he was overwhelmed by these home thrusts. She broke off and took breath, and then in a low voice,—

"Oh, I'm a wreck! Do help me to sit up a bit. I keep slipping down, and my head's too low."

When he had helped her she sighed and felt more comfortable. And with that she harked back to the subject. What a pretty sight a divorce suit would be! Couldn't he imagine the advocate of the Countess amusing Paris with his remarks about Nana? Everything would have come out—her fiasco at the Variétés, her house, her manner of life. Oh, dear no! she had no wish for all that amount of advertising. Some dirty women might, perhaps, have driven him to it for the sake of getting a thundering big advertisement, but she—she desired his happiness before all else. She had drawn him down towards her, and, after passing her arm round his neck, was nursing his head close to hers, on the edge of the pillow. And with that she whispered softly:

"Listen, my pet, you shall make it up with your wife."

But he rebelled at this. It could never be! His heart was nigh breaking at the thought: it was too shameful. Nevertheless, she kept tenderly insisting.

"You shall make it up with your wife. Come, come, you don't want to hear all the world saying that I've tempted you away from your home? I should have too vile a reputation! What would people think of me? Only swear that you'll always love me, because the moment you go with another woman—"

Tears choked her utterance, and he intervened with kisses, and said,—

"You're beside yourself: it's impossible!"

"Yes, yes," she rejoined, "you must. But I'll be reasonable. After all, she's your wife, and it isn't as if you were to play me false with the first comer."

And she continued in this strain, giving him the most excellent advice. She even spoke of God, and the Count thought he was listening to Monsieur Venot, when that old gentleman endeavored to sermonize him out of the grasp of sin. Nana, however, did not speak of breaking it off entirely: she preached indulgent good nature, and suggested that, as became a dear nice old fellow, he should divide his attentions between his wife and his mistress, so that they would all enjoy a quiet life, devoid of any kind of annoyance, something, in fact, in the nature of a happy slumber amid the inevitable miseries of existence. Their life would be nowise changed: he would still be the little man of her heart. Only he would come to her a bit less often and would give the Countess the nights not passed with her. She had got to the end of her strength, and left off speaking under her breath.

"After that, I shall feel I've done a good action, and you'll love me all the more."

Silence reigned. She had closed her eyes, and lay wan upon her pillow. The Count was patiently listening to her, not wishing her to tire herself. A whole minute went by before she reopened her eyes, and murmured,—

"Besides, how about the money? Where would you get the money from, if you must grow angry and go to law? Labordette came for the bill yesterday. As for me, I'm out of everything; I have nothing to put on now."

Then she shut her eyes again, and looked like one dead. A shadow of deep anguish had passed over Muffat's brow. Under the present stroke, he had since yesterday forgotten the money troubles, from which he knew not how to escape. Despite formal promises to the contrary, the bill for a hundred thousand francs had been put in circulation after being once renewed, and Labordette, pretending to be very miserable about it, threw all the blame on Francis, declaring that he would never again mix himself up in such a matter with an uneducated man. It was necessary to pay, for the Count would never have allowed his signature to be protested. Then, in addition to Nana's novel demands, his home expenses were extraordinarily confused. On their return from The Fondettes, the Countess had suddenly manifested a taste for luxury, a longing for worldly pleasures, which was devouring their fortune. Her ruinous caprices began to be talked about. Their whole household management was altered, and five hundred thousand francs were squandered in utterly transforming the old house in the Rue Miromesnil. Then there were extravagantly magnificent gowns, and large sums disappeared, squandered, or perhaps given away, without her ever dreaming of accounting for them. Twice Muffat ventured to mention this, for he was anxious to know how the money went; but on these occasions she had smiled and gazed at him with so singular an expression that he dared not interrogate her further for fear of a too unmistakable answer. If he were taking Daguenet as son-in-law as a gift from Nana it was chiefly with the hope of being able to reduce Estelle's dower to two hundred thousand francs and of then being free to make any arrangements he chose about the remainder with a young man who was still rejoicing in this unexpected match.

Nevertheless for the last week, under the immediate necessity of finding Labordette's hundred thousand francs, Muffat had been able to hit on but one expedient, from which he recoiled. This was that he should sell the Bordes, a magnificent property, valued at half a million, which an uncle had recently left the Countess. However, her signature was necessary, and she herself, according to the terms of the deed, could not alienate the property without the Count's authorization. The day before he had indeed resolved to talk to his wife about this signature. And now everything was ruined; at such a moment he would never accept of such a compromise. This reflection added bitterness to the frightful disgrace of the adultery. He fully understood what Nana was asking for, since in that evergrowing self-abandonment which prompted him to put her in possession of all his secrets, he had complained to her of his position, and had confided to her the tiresome difficulty he was in with regard to the signature of the Countess.

Nana, however, did not seem to insist. She did not open her eyes again; and seeing her so pale, he grew frightened and made her inhale a little ether. She gave a sigh, and, without mentioning Daguenet, asked him some questions.

"When is the marriage?"

"We sign the contract on Tuesday in five days' time," he replied.

Then, still keeping her eyelids closed as though she were speaking from the darkness and silence of her brain,—

"Well, then, pet, see to what you've got to do. As far as I'm concerned, I want everybody to be happy and comfortable."

He took her hand and soothed her. Yes, he would see about it; the important thing now was for her to rest. And the revolt within him ceased, for this warm and slumbrous sick-room, with its all-pervading scent of ether, had ended by lulling him into a mere longing for happiness and peace. All his manhood, erewhile maddened by wrong, had departed out of him in the neighborhood of that warm bed and that suffering woman, whom he was nursing under the influence of her feverish heat and of remembered delights. He leant over her and pressed her in a close embrace, whilst, despite her unmoved features, her lips wore a delicate victorious smile. But the Docteur Boutarel made his appearance.

"Well, and how's this dear child?" said he familiarly to Muffat, whom he treated as her husband. "The deuce but we've made her talk!"

The Doctor was a good-looking man, and still young. He had a superb practice among the gay world, and being very merry by nature, and ready to laugh and joke in the friendliest way with the *demi-monde* ladies, with whom, however, he never went further, he charged very high fees and got them paid with the greatest punctuality. Moreover, he would put himself out to visit them on the most trivial occasions, and Nana, who was always trembling at the fear of death, would send and fetch him two or three times a week,

and would anxiously confide to him little infantile ills which
he would cure to an accompaniment of amusing gossip and
hare-brained anecdotes. The ladies all adored him. But this
time the little ill was serious.

Muffat withdrew deeply moved. Seeing his poor Nana so
very weak, his sole feeling was now one of tenderness. As
he was leaving the room she motioned him back, and gave
him her forehead to kiss. In a low voice, and with a play-
fully-threatening look, she said,—

"You know what I've allowed you to do. Go back to
your wife, or it's all over and I shall grow angry!"

The Countess Sabine had been anxious that her daughter's
wedding contract should be signed on a Tuesday in order
that the renovated house, where the paint was still scarcely
dry, might be reopened with a grand entertainment. Five
hundred invitations had been issued to people in all kinds
of sets. On the morning of the great day the upholsterers
were still nailing up hangings, and towards nine at night,
just when the lusters were going to be lit, the architect, accompanied by the eager and interested Countess, was given
his final orders.

It was one of those spring festivities which have a delicate
charm of their own. Owing to the warmth of the June
nights it had become possible to open the two doors of the
great drawing-room and to extend the dancing floor to the
sanded paths of the garden. When the first guests arrived
and were welcomed at the door by the Count and the Countess, they were positively dazzled. One had only to recall
to mind the drawing-room of the past, through which flitted
the icy, ghostly presence of the Countess Muffat, that antique
room full of an atmosphere of religious austerity, with its
massive First Empire mahogany furniture, its yellow velvet
hangings, its moldy ceiling through which the damp had
soaked. Now from the very threshold of the entrance-hall,
mosaics set off with gold were glittering under the lights of

lofty candelabras, whilst the marble staircase unfurled, as it were, a delicately chiseled balustrade. Then, too, the drawing-room looked splendid; it was hung with Genoa velvet, and a huge decorative design by Boucher covered the ceiling, a design for which the architect had paid a hundred thousand francs at the sale of the Château de Dampierre. The lusters and the crystal ornaments lit up a luxurious display of mirrors and precious furniture. It seemed as though Sabine's long chair, that solitary red silk chair, whose soft contours were so marked in the old days, had grown and spread till it filled the whole great house with voluptuous idleness and a sense of tense enjoyment not less fierce and hot than a fire which has been long in burning up.

People were already dancing. The band, which had been located in the garden, in front of one of the open windows, was playing a waltz, the supple rhythm of which came softly into the house through the intervening night air. And the garden seemed to spread away and away, bathed in transparent shadow and lit by Venetian lamps, whilst in a purple tent, pitched on the edge of a lawn, a table for refreshments had been established. The waltz, which was none other than the quaint vulgar one in the *Blonde Venus*, with its laughing, blackguard lilt, penetrated the old hotel with sonorous waves of sound, and sent a feverish thrill along its walls. It was as though some fleshly wind had come up out of the common street and were sweeping the relics of a vanished epoch out of the proud old dwelling, bearing away the Muffats' past, the age of honor and religious faith which had long slumbered beneath the lofty ceilings.

Meanwhile, near the hearth, in their accustomed places, the old friends of the Count's mother were taking refuge. They felt out of their element—they were dazzled and they formed a little group amid the slowly-invading mob. Madame du Joncquoy, unable to recognize the various rooms, had come in through the dining-saloon. Madame Chantereau was gazing with a stupefied expression at the garden, which struck her as immense. Presently there was a sound of low voices, and the corner gave vent to all sorts of bitter reflections.

"I declare," murmured Madame Chantereau, "just fancy if the Countess were to return to life. Why, can you not imagine her coming in among all these crowds of people! And then there's all this gilding, and this uproar! It's scandalous!"

"Sabine's out of her senses," replied Madame du Joncquoy. "Did you see her at the door? Look, you can catch sight of her here; she's wearing all her diamonds."

For a moment or two they stood up in order to take a distant view of the Count and Countess. Sabine was in a white dress, trimmed with marvelous English point lace. She was triumphant in beauty; she looked young and gay, and there was a touch of intoxication in her continual smile. Beside her stood Muffat, looking aged and a little pale, but he too was smiling in his calm and worthy fashion.

"And just to think that he was once master," continued Madame Chantereau, "and that not a single rout seat would have come in without his permission! Ah well, she's changed all that; it's her house now. D'you remember when she did not want to do her drawing-room up again? She's done up the entire house."

But the ladies grew silent, for Madame de Chezelles was entering the room, followed by a band of young men. She was going into ecstasies, and marking her approval with a succession of little exclamations.

"Oh, it's delicious, exquisite! What taste!" And she shouted back to her followers:

"Didn't I say so? There's nothing equal to these old places when one takes them in hand. They become dazzling! It's quite in the grand seventeenth century style. Well, *now* she can receive."

The two old ladies had again sat down, and with lowered tones began talking about the marriage, which was causing astonishment to a good many people. Estelle had just passed by them. She was in a pink silk gown, and was as pale, flat, silent, and virginal as ever. She had accepted Daguenet very quietly; and now evinced neither joy nor sadness, for she was still as cold and white as on those winter evenings when she used to put logs on the fire. This whole fête given in her honor, these lights and flowers and tunes, left her quite unmoved.

"An adventurer," Madame du Joncquoy was saying. "For my part I've never seen him."

"Take care, here he is," whispered Madame Chantereau.

Daguenet, who had caught sight of Madame Hugon and her sons, had eagerly offered her his arm. He laughed and was effusively affectionate towards her, as though she had had a hand in his sudden good fortune.

"Thank you," said she, sitting down near the fire-place. "You see it's my old corner."

"You know him?" queried Madame du Joncquoy, when Daguenet had gone.

"Certainly I do—a charming young man. Georges is very fond of him. Oh, they're a most respected family."

And the good lady defended him against the mute hostility which was apparent to her. His father, held in high esteem by Louis-Philippe, had been a *préfêt* up to the time of his death. The son had been a little dissipated, perhaps; they said he was ruined; but, in any case, one of his uncles, who was a great landowner, was bound to leave him his fortune. The ladies, however, shook their heads, whilst Madame Hugon, herself somewhat embarrassed, kept harking back to the extreme respectability of his family. She was very much fatigued, and complained of her feet. For some months she had been occupying her house in the Rue Richelieu, having, as she said, a whole lot of things on hand. A look of sorrow overshadowed her smiling, motherly face.

"Never mind," Madame Chantereau concluded, "Estelle could have aimed at something much better."

There was a flourish. A quadrille was about to begin, and the crowd flowed back to the sides of the drawing-room in order to leave the floor clear. Bright dresses flitted by and mingled together amid the dark evening coats, whilst the intense light set jewels flashing, and white plumes quivering, and lilacs and roses gleaming and flowering amid the sea of many heads. It was already very warm, and a penetrating perfume was exhaled from light tulles and crumpled silks and satins, from which bare shoulders glimmered white, whilst the orchestra played its lively airs. Through open doors ranges of seated ladies were visible in the background of adjoining rooms: they flashed a discreet smile, their eyes glowed, and they made pretty mouths as the breath of their fans caressed their faces. And guests still kept arriving, and a footman announced their names, whilst gentlemen advanced slowly amid the surrounding groups, striving to find places for ladies, who hung with difficulty on their arms, and stretching forward in quest of some far-off vacant arm-chair. The house kept filling, and crinolined skirts got jammed together with a little rustling sound. There were corners where an amalgam of laces, bunches, and puffs would completely bar the way, whilst all the other ladies stood waiting, politely resigned and imperturbably graceful, as became people who were made to take part in these dazzling crushes. Meanwhile, across the garden, couples, who had been glad to escape from the close air of the great drawing-room, were wandering away under the roseate gleam of the Venetian lamps, and shadowy dresses kept flitting along the edge of the lawn, as though in rhythmic time to the music of the quadrille, which sounded sweet and distant behind the trees.

Steiner had just met with Foucarmont and la Faloise, who

were drinking a glass of champagne in front of the buffet.

"It's beastly smart," said la Faloise as he took a survey of the purple tent, which was supported by gilded lances. "You might fancy yourself at the Ginger-bread Fair. That's it, eh?—the Ginger-bread Fair!"

In these days he continually affected a bantering tone, posing as the young man who has abused every mortal thing and now finds nothing worth taking seriously.

"How surprised poor Vandeuvres would be if he were to come back," murmured Foucarmont. "You remember how he simply nearly died of boredom in front of the fire in there. Egad, it was no laughing matter."

"Vandeuvres—oh, let him be. He's a gone coon!" la Faloise disdainfully rejoined. "He jolly well choused himself, he did, if he thought he could make us sit up with his roast meat story! Not a soul mentions it now. Blotted out, done for, buried—that's what's the matter with Vandeuvres! Here's to the next man!"

Then, as Steiner shook hands with him,—

"You know Nana's just arrived. Oh, my boys, it was a state entry! It was too brilliant for anything! First of all she kissed the Countess. Then, when the children came up, she gave them her blessing, and said to Daguenet,—'Listen, Paul, if you go running after the girls, you'll have to answer for it to me.' What, d'you mean to say you didn't see that? Oh, it *was* smart! A success, if you like!"

The other two listened to him open-mouthed, and at last burst out laughing. He was enchanted, and thought himself in his best vein.

"You thought it had really happened, eh? Confound it, since Nana's made the match! Anyway, she's one of the family."

The young Hugons were passing, and Philippe silenced him. And with that they chatted about the marriage from the male point of view. Georges was vexed with la Faloise

for telling an anecdote. Certainly, Nana had fubbed off on
Muffat one of her old flames as son-in-law; only it was not
true that she had been to bed with Daguenet as lately as
yesterday. Foucarmont made bold to shrug his shoulders.
Could any one ever tell when Nana was in bed with any
one? But Georges grew excited, and answered with an "I
can tell, sir!" which set them all laughing. In a word, as
Steiner put it, it was all a very funny kettle of fish!

The buffet was gradually invaded by the crowd, and still
keeping together they vacated their positions there. La
Faloise stared brazenly at the women as though he believed
himself to be Mabille. At the end of a garden walk the
little band was surprised to find Monsieur Venot busily con-
ferring with Daguenet, and with that they indulged in some
facile pleasantries which made them very merry. He was
confessing him, giving him advice about the bridal night!
Presently they returned in front of one of the drawing-room
doors, within which a polka was sending the couples whirling to and fro till they seemed to leave a wake behind them
among the crowd of men who remained standing about.
In the slight puffs of air which came from outside, the tapers
flared up brilliantly, and when a dress floated by in time to
the rat-tat of the measure, a little gust of wind cooled the
sparkling heat which streamed down from the lusters.

"Egad, they're not cold in there!" muttered la Faloise.

They blinked after emerging from the mysterious shadows
of the garden. Then they pointed out to one another the
Marquis de Chouard where he stood apart, his tall figure
towering above the bare shoulders which surrounded him.
His face was pale and very stern, and beneath its crown of
scant white hair it wore an expression of lofty dignity. Scandalized by Count Muffat's conduct, he had publicly broken
off all intercourse with him, and was by way of never again
setting foot in the house. If he had consented to put in an
appearance that evening it was because his granddaughter

had begged him to. But he disapproved of her marriage, and had inveighed indignantly against the way in which the governing classes were being disorganized by the shameful compromises engendered by modern debauchery.

"Ah! it's the end of all things," Madame du Joncquoy whispered in Madame Chantereau's ear as she sat near the fire-place. "That bad woman has bewitched the unfortunate man. And to think we once knew him such a true believer, such a noble-hearted gentleman!"

"It appears he is ruining himself," continued Madame Chantereau. "My husband has had a bill of his in his hands. At present he's living in that house in the Avenue de Villiers; all Paris is talking about it. Good heavens! I don't make excuses for Sabine, but you must admit that he gives her infinite cause of complaint, and, dear me, if she throws money out of the window, too—"

"She does not only throw money," interrupted the other. "In fact, between them, there's no knowing where they'll stop; they'll end in the mire, my dear."

But just then a soft voice interrupted them. It was Monsieur Venot and he had come and seated himself behind them, as though anxious to disappear from view. Bending forward he murmured,—

"Why despair? God manifests Himself when all seems lost."

He was assisting peacefully at the downfall of the house which he erewhile governed. Since his stay at The Fondettes, he had been allowing the madness to increase, for he was very clearly aware of his own powerlessness. He had, indeed, accepted the whole position—the Count's wild passion for Nana, Fauchery's presence, even Estelle's marriage with Daguenet. What did these things matter? He even became more supple and mysterious, for he nursed a hope of being able to gain the same mastery over the young as over the disunited couple, and he knew that great disorders lead to great conversions. Providence would have its opportunity.

"Our friend," he continued in a low voice, "is always animated by the best religious sentiments. He has given me the sweetest proofs of this."

"Well," said Madame du Joncquoy, "he ought first to have made it up with his wife."

"Doubtless. At this moment I have hopes that the reconciliation will be shortly effected."

Whereupon the two old ladies questioned him.

But he grew very humble again. "Heaven," he said, "must be left to act." His whole desire in bringing the Count and the Countess together again was to avoid a public scandal, for religion tolerated many faults when the proprieties were respected.

"In fact," resumed Madame du Joncquoy, "you ought to have prevented this union with an adventurer."

The little old gentleman assumed an expression of profound astonishment.

"You deceive yourself. Monsieur Daguenet is a young man of the greatest merit. I am acquainted with his thoughts; he is anxious to live down the errors of his youth. Estelle will bring him back to the path of virtue, be sure of that."

"Oh, Estelle!" Madame Chantereau murmured disdainfully. "I believe the dear young thing to be incapable of willing anything; she is so insignificant!"

This opinion caused Monsieur Venot to smile. However, he went into no explanations about the young bride, and shutting his eyes, as though to avoid seeming to take any further interest in the matter, he once more lost himself in his corner behind the petticoats. Madame Hugon, though weary and absent-minded, had caught some phrases of the conversation, and she now intervened, and summed up in her tolerant way by remarking to the Marquis de Chouard, who just then bowed to her,—

"These ladies are too severe. Existence is so bitter for every one of us! Ought we not to forgive others much, my friend, if we wish to merit forgiveness ourselves?"

For some seconds the Marquis appeared embarrassed, for he was afraid of allusions. But the good lady wore so sad a smile that he recovered almost at once, and remarked,—

"No; there is no forgiveness for certain faults. It is by reason of this kind of accommodating spirit that a society sinks into the abyss of ruin."

The ball had grown still more animated. A fresh quadrille was imparting a slight swaying motion to the drawing-room floor, as though the old dwelling had been shaken by the impulse of the dance. Now and again, amid the wan confusion of heads, a woman's face with shining eyes and parted lips stood sharply out, as it was whirled away by the dance, the light of the lusters gleaming on the white skin. Madame du Joncquoy declared that the present proceedings were senseless. It was madness to crowd five hundred people into a room which would scarcely contain two hundred. In fact, why not sign for the wedding contract on the Place du Carrousel? This was the outcome of the new code of manners, said Madame Chantereau. In old times these solemnities took place in the bosom of the family; but to-day one must have a mob of people, the whole street must be allowed to enter quite freely, and there must be a great crush, or else the evening seems a chilly affair. People now advertised their luxury and introduced the mere foam on the wave of Parisian society into their houses, and accordingly it was only too natural if illicit proceedings such as they had been discussing afterwards polluted the hearth. The ladies complained that they could not recognize more than fifty people. Where did all this crowd spring from? Young girls with

low necks were making a great display of their shoulders.
A woman had a golden dagger stuck in her chignon, whilst
a bodice thickly embroidered with jet beads clothed her in
what looked like a coat of mail. People's eyes kept following
another lady smilingly, so singularly marked were her clinging skirts. All the luxuriant splendor of the departing winter was there—the over-tolerant world of pleasure, the
scratch gathering a hostess can get together after a first introduction, the sort of society in fact, in which great names and
great shames jostle together in the same fierce quest of enjoyment. The heat was increasing, and amid the over-
crowded rooms the quadrille unrolled the cadenced symmetry
of its figures.

"Very smart—the Countess!" la Faloise continued at the
garden door. "She's ten years younger than her daughter.
By-the-by, Foucarmont, you must decide on a point. Vandeuvres once betted that she had no thighs."

This affectation of cynicism bored the other gentlemen, and
Foucarmont contented himself by saying,—

"Ask your cousin, dear boy. Here he is."

"Jove, it's a happy thought!" cried la Faloise. "I bet ten
louis she has thighs."

Fauchery did indeed come up. As became a constant in-
mate of the house, he had gone round by the dining-room in
order to avoid the crowded doors. Rose had taken him up
again at the beginning of the winter, and he was now divid-
ing himself between the singer and the Countess, but he was
extremely fatigued, and did not know how to get rid of one
of them. Sabine flattered his vanity, but Rose amused him
more than she. Besides, the passion Rose felt was a real one:
her tenderness for him was marked by a conjugal fidelity
which drove Mignon to despair.

"Listen, we want some information," said la Falois, as he
squeezed his cousin's arm. "You see that lady in white silk."

Ever since his inheritance had given him a kind of insolent

dash of manner, he had affected to chaff Fauchery, for he had an old grudge to satisfy, and wanted to be revenged for much bygone raillery, dating from the days when he was just fresh from his native province.

"Yes, that lady with the lace."

The journalist stood on tiptoe, for as yet he did not understand.

"The Countess?" he said at last.

"Exactly, my good friend. I've bet ten louis—now, has she thighs?"

And he fell a-laughing, for he was delighted to have succeeded in snubbing a fellow who had once come heavily down on him for asking whether the Countess slept with any one. But Fauchery, without shewing the very slightest astonishment, looked fixedly at him.

"Get along, you idiot!" he said finally, as he shrugged his shoulders.

Then he shook hands with the other gentlemen, whilst la Faloise, in his discomfiture, felt rather uncertain whether he had said something funny. The men chatted. Since the races the banker and Foucarmont had formed part of the set in the Avenue de Villiers. Nana was going on much better, and every evening the Count came and asked how she did. Meanwhile, Fauchery, though he listened, seemed preoccupied; for, during a quarrel that morning, Rose had roundly confessed to the sending of the letter. Oh, yes, he might present himself at his great lady's house: he would be well received! After long hesitation, he had come despite of everything—out of sheer courage. But la Faloise's imbecile pleasantry had upset him in spite of his apparent tranquillity.

"What's the matter?" asked Philippe. "You seem in trouble."

"I do? Not at all. I've been working: that's why I came so late."

Then coldly, in one of those heroic moods which, although

unnoticed, are wont to solve the vulgar tragedies of existence,—

"All the same, I haven't made my bow to our hosts. One must be civil."

He even ventured on a joke, for he turned to la Faloise, and said,—

"Eh, you idiot?"

And with that he pushed his way through the crowd. The valet's full voice was no longer shouting out names, but, close to the door, the Count and Countess were still talking, for they were detained by ladies coming in. At length he joined them, whilst the gentlemen who were still on the garden steps stood on tiptoe so as to watch the scene. Nana, they thought, must have been chattering.

"The Count hasn't noticed him," muttered Georges. "Look out! He's turning round: there, it's done!"

The band had again taken up the waltz in the *Blonde Venus*. Fauchery had begun by bowing to the Countess, who was still smiling in ecstatic serenity. After which he had stood motionless a moment, waiting very calmly behind the Count's back. That evening the Count's deportment was one of lofty gravity: he held his head high, as became the official and the great dignitary. And when at last he lowered his gaze in the direction of the journalist, he seemed still further to emphasize the majesty of his attitude. For some seconds the two men looked at one another. It was Fauchery who first stretched out his hand. Muffat gave him his. Their hands remained clasped, and the Countess Sabine with downcast eyes stood smiling before them, whilst the waltz continually beat out its mocking vagabond rhythm.

"But the thing's going on wheels!" said Steiner.

"Are their hands glued together?" asked Foucarmont, surprised at this prolonged clasp. A memory he could not forget brought a faint glow to Fauchery's pale cheeks, and in his mind's eye he saw the property-room bathed in greenish

twilight and filled with dusty *bric-à-brac*. And Muffat was
there, egg-cup in hand, making a clever use of his suspicions. At this moment Muffat was no longer suspicious,
and the last vestige of his dignity was crumbling in ruin.
Fauchery's fears were assuaged, and when he saw the frank
gayety of the Countess he was seized with a desire to laugh.
The thing struck him as comic.

"Ah, ha, here she is at last!" cried la Faloise, who did not
abandon a jest when he thought it a good one. "D'you see
Nana coming in over there?"

"Hold your tongue, do, you idiot!" muttered Philippe.

"But I tell you it is Nana! They're playing her waltz
for her, by Jove! She's making her entry. And she takes
part in the reconciliation, the devil she does! What? You
don't see her! She's squeezing all three of 'em to her heart—
my cousin Fauchery, my lady cousin, and her husband, and
she's calling 'em her dear kitties. Oh, those family scenes
give me a turn!"

Estelle had come up, and Fauchery complimented her whilst
she stood stiffly up in her rose-colored dress, gazing at him
with the astonished look of a silent child, and constantly
glancing aside at her father and mother. Daguenet, too, exchanged a hearty shake of the hand with the journalist. Together they made up a smiling group, whilst Monsieur Venot
came gliding in behind them. He gloated over them with a
beatified expression, and seemed to envelop them in his pious
sweetness, for he rejoiced in these last instances of self-abandonment which were preparing the means of grace.

But the waltz still beat out its swinging, laughing, voluptuous measure; it was like a shrill continuation of the life of
pleasure which was beating against the old house like a rising
tide. The band blew louder trills from their little flutes;
their violins sent forth more swooning notes. Beneath the
Genoa velvet hangings, the gilding and the paintings, the
lusters exhaled a living heat and a great glow of sunlight,

whilst the crowd of guests, multiplied in the surrounding mirrors, seemed to grow and increase as the murmur of many voices rose ever louder. The couples who whirled round the drawing-room, arm about waist, amid the smiles of the seated ladies, still further accentuated the quaking of the floors. In the garden a dull fiery glow fell from the Venetian lanterns, and threw a distant reflection of flame over the dark shadows moving in search of a breath of air about the walks at its further end. And this trembling of walls, and this red glow of light, seemed to betoken a great ultimate conflagration in which the fabric of an ancient honor was cracking and burning on every side. The shy early beginnings of gayety, of which Fauchery one April evening had heard the vocal expression in the sound of breaking glass, had little by little grown bolder, wilder, till they had burst forth in this festival. Now the rift was growing; it was crannying the house, and announcing approaching downfall. Among drunkards in the slums it is black misery, an empty cupboard, which put an end to ruined families; it is the madness of drink which empties the wretched beds. Here the waltz-tune was sounding the knell of an old race amid the suddenly-ignited ruins of accumulated wealth, whilst Nana, although unseen, stretched her lithe limbs above the dancers' heads, and sent corruption through their caste, drenching the hot air with the ferment of her exhalations and the vagabond lilt of the music.

On the evening after the celebration of the church marriage Count Muffat made his appearance in his wife's bedroom, where he had not entered for the last two years. At first, in her great surprise, the Countess drew back from him. But she was still smiling the intoxicated smile, which she now always wore. He began stammering in extreme embarrassment; whereupon she gave him a short moral lecture. However, neither of them risked a decisive explanation. It was religion, they pretended, which required this process of mutual forgiveness, and they agreed by a tacit understanding to retain their freedom. Before going to bed, seeing that the Countess still appeared to hesitate, they had a business conversation, and the Count was the first to speak of selling the Bordes. She consented at once. They both stood in great want of money, and they would share and share alike. This completed the reconciliation, and Muffat, remorseful though he was, felt veritably relieved.

That very day, as Nana was dozing towards two in the afternoon, Zoé made so bold as to knock at her bedroom door. The curtains were drawn to, and a hot breath of wind kept blowing through a window into the fresh twilight stillness within. During these last days the young woman had been getting up and about again, but she was still somewhat weak. She opened her eyes, and asked,—

"Who is it?"

Zoé was about to reply, but Daguenet pushed by her, and announced himself in person. Nana forthwith propped herself up on her pillow, and, dismissing the lady's maid,—

"What! is that you?" she cried. "On the day of your marriage? What can be the matter?"

Taken aback by the darkness, he stood still in the middle of the room. However, he grew used to it, and came forward at last. He was in evening dress, and wore a white cravat and gloves.

"Yes, to be sure, it's me!" he said. "You don't remember?"

No, she remembered nothing, and in his chaffing way he had to offer himself frankly to her.

"Come now, here's your commission. I've brought you the handsel of my innocence!"

And with that, as he was now by the bedside, she caught him in her bare arms, and shook with merry laughter, and almost cried, she thought it so pretty of him.

"Oh, that Mimi, how funny he is! He's thought of it

after all! And to think I didn't remember it any longer! So you've slipped off: you're just out of church. Yes, certainly, you've got a scent of incense about you. But kiss me, kiss me! Oh, harder than that, Mimi dear! Bah! perhaps it's for the last time."

In the dim room, where a vague odor of ether still lingered, their tender laughter died away suddenly. The heavy, warm breeze swelled the window-curtains, and children's voices were audible in the Avenue without. Then the lateness of the hour tore them asunder and set them joking again. Daguenet took his departure with his wife directly after the breakfast.

CHAPTER XIII

TOWARDS the end of September Count Muffat, who was to dine at Nana's that evening, came at nightfall to inform her of a summons to the Tuileries. The lamps in the house had not been lit yet, and the servants were laughing uproariously in the kitchen regions, as he softly mounted the stairs where the tall windows gleamed in warm shadow. The door of the drawing-room upstairs opened noiselessly. A faint pink glow was dying out on the ceiling of the room, and the red hangings, the deep divans, the lacquered furniture, with their medley of embroidered fabrics, and bronzes and china, were already sleeping under a slowly-creeping flood of shadows, which drowned nooks and corners, and blotted out the gleam of ivory and the glint of gold. And there in the darkness, on the white surface of a wide outspread petticoat, which alone remained clearly visible, he saw Nana lying stretched in the arms of Georges. Denial in any shape or form was impossible. He gave a choking cry and stood gaping at them.

Nana had bounded up, and now she pushed him into the bedroom in order to give the lad time to escape.

"Come in," she murmured, with reeling senses, "I'll explain."

She was exasperated at being thus surprised. Never before had she given way like this in her own house, in her own drawing-room, when the doors were open. It was a long story: Georges and she had had a disagreement: he had been mad with jealousy of Philippe, and he had sobbed so bitterly on her bosom that she had yielded to him, not knowing how else to calm him, and really very full of pity for him at heart. And, on this solitary occasion, when she had been stupid enough to forget herself thus with a little rascal, who could not even now bring her bouquets of violets, so short did his mother keep him—on this solitary occasion, the Count turned up and came straight down on them. 'Gad, she had very bad luck! That was what one got if one was a good-natured wench!

Meanwhile in the bedroom, into which she had pushed Muffat, the darkness was complete. Whereupon, after some groping, she rang furiously and asked for a lamp. It was Julien's fault, too! If there had been a lamp in the drawing-room, the whole affair would not have happened. It was the stupid nightfall which had got the better of her heart.

"I beseech you to be reasonable, my pet," said she, when Zoé had brought in the lights.

The Count, with his hands on his knees, was sitting gazing at the floor. He was stupefied by what he had just seen. He did not cry out in anger. He only trembled, as though overtaken by some horror which was freezing him. This dumb misery touched the young woman, and she tried to comfort him.

"Well, yes, I've done wrong. It's very bad what I did. You see I'm sorry for my fault. It makes me grieve very much because it annoys you. Come now, be nice, too, and forgive me."

She had crouched down at his feet, and was striving to

catch his eye with a look of tender submission. She was fain
to know whether he was very vexed with her. Presently, as
he gave a long sigh and seemed to recover himself, she grew
more coaxing, and with grave kindness of manner added a
final reason:

"You see, dearie, you must try and understand how it is:
I can't refuse it to my poor friends."

The Count consented to give way, and only insisted that
Georges should be dismissed once for all. But all his illu-
sions had vanished, and he no longer believed in her sworn
fidelity. Next day Nana would deceive him anew, and he
only remained her miserable possessor in obedience to a cowardly necessity and to terror at the thought of living without her.

This was the epoch in her existence when Nana flared upon
Paris with redoubled splendor. She loomed larger than heretofore on the horizon of vice, and swayed the town with her
impudently flaunted splendor, and that contempt of money,
which made her openly squander fortunes. Her house had
become a sort of glowing smithy, where her continual desires were the flames, and the slightest breath from her lips
changed gold into fine ashes, which the wind hourly swept
away. Never had eye beheld such a rage of expenditure.
The great house seemed to have been built over a gulf, in
which men—their worldly possessions, their fortunes, their
very names—were swallowed up without leaving even a handful of dust behind them. This courtesan, who had the tastes
of a parrot, and gobbled up radishes and burned almonds,
and pecked at the meat upon her plate, had monthly table-
bills amounting to five thousand francs. The wildest waste
went on in the kitchen: the place, metaphorically speaking,
was one great river, which stove in cask upon cask of wine
and swept great bills with it, swollen by three or four successive manipulators. Victorine and François reigned supreme in the kitchen, whither they invited friends. In ad-

dition to these, there was quite a little tribe of cousins, who were cockered up in their own homes with cold meats and strong soup. Julien made the tradespeople give him commissions, and the glaziers never put up a pane of glass at a cost of a franc and a half but he had a franc put down to himself. Charles devoured the horses' oats, and doubled the amount of their provender, re-selling at the back door what came in at the carriage-gate; whilst, amid the general pillage, the sack of the town after the storm, Zoé, by dint of cleverness, succeeded in saving appearances, and covering the thefts of all in order the better to slur over and make good her own. But the household waste was worse than the household dishonesty. Yesterday's food was thrown into the gutter, and the collection of provisions in the house was such that the servants grew disgusted with it. The glass was all sticky with sugar, and the gas-burners flared and flared till the rooms seemed ready to explode. Then, too, there were instances of negligence and mischief and sheer accident—of everything, in fact, which can hasten the ruin of a house devoured by so many mouths. Upstairs, in *Madame's* quarters, destruction raged more fiercely still. Dresses, which cost ten thousand francs and had been twice worn, were sold by Zoé: jewels vanished as though they had crumbled deep down in their drawers; stupid purchases were made; every novelty of the day was brought, and left to lie forgotten in some corner the morning after, or swept up by rag-pickers in the street. She could not see any very expensive object without wanting to possess it, and so she constantly surrounded herself with the wrecks of bouquets, and costly knick-knacks, and was the happier the more her passing fancy cost. Nothing remained intact in her hands, she broke everything; and this object withered, and that grew dirty, in the clasp of her lithe white fingers. A perfect heap of nameless *débris*, of twisted shreds and muddy rags, followed her and marked her passage. Then, amid this utter

squandering of pocket-money, cropped up a question about
the big bills and their settlement. Twenty thousand francs
were due to the *modiste,* thirty thousand to the linen-draper,
twelve thousand to the boot-maker. Her stable devoured
fifty thousand for her, and in six months she ran up a bill
of a hundred and twenty thousand francs at her ladies'
tailor. Though she had not enlarged her scheme of expenditure, which Labordette reckoned at four hundred thousand
francs on an average, she ran up that same year to a million.
She was herself stupefied by the amount, and was unable to
tell whither such a sum could have gone. Heaps upon heaps
of men, barrowsful of gold, failed to stop up the hole, which,
amid this ruinous luxury, continually gaped under the floor
of her house.

Meanwhile Nana had cherished her latest caprice. Once
more exercised by the notion that her room needed re-doing,
she fancied she had hit on something at last. The room should
be done in velvet of the color of tea-roses, with silver buttons, and golden cords, tassels and fringes, and the hangings should be caught up to the ceiling after the manner of
a tent. This arrangement ought to be both rich and tender,
she thought, and would form a splendid background to her
blonde *vermeil*-tinted skin. However, the bedroom was only
designed to serve as a setting to the bed, which was to be a
dazzling affair, a prodigy. Nana meditated a bed such as
had never before existed; it was to be a throne, an altar,
whither Paris was to come in order to adore her sovran
nudity. It was to be all in gold and silver beaten-work—
it should suggest a great piece of jewelry with its golden
roses climbing on a trellis-work of silver. On the head-
board a band of Loves should peep forth laughing from amid
the flowers as though they were watching the voluptuous
dalliance within the shadow of the bed-curtains. Nana had
applied to Labordette who had brought two goldsmiths to
see her. They were already busy with the designs. The

bed would cost fifty thousand francs, and Muffat was to give
it her as a New Year's present.

What most astonished the young woman was that she was
endlessly short of money amid a river of gold, the tide of
which almost enveloped her. On certain days she was at her
wit's end for want of ridiculously small sums—sums of only
a few louis. She was driven to borrow from Zoé, or she
scraped up cash as well as she could on her own account.
But before resignedly adopting extreme measures, she tried
her friends, and in a joking sort of way got the men to give
her all they had about them, even down to their coppers.
For the last three months she had been emptying Philippe's
pockets especially, and now, on days of passionate enjoyment,
he never came away but he left his purse behind him. Soon
she grew bolder, and asked him for loans of two hundred
francs, three hundred francs—never more than that—
wherewith to pay the interest of bills or to stave off outrageous debts. And Philippe, who in July had been appointed paymaster to his regiment, would bring the money the
day after, apologizing at the same time for not being rich,
seeing that good mamma Hugon now treated her sons with
singular financial severity. At the close of three months
these little oft-renewed loans mounted up to a sum of ten
thousand francs. The captain still laughed his hearty sounding laugh, but he was growing visibly thinner, and sometimes he seemed absent-minded, and a shade of suffering
would pass over his face. But one look from Nana's eyes
would transfigure him in a sort of sensual ecstasy. She had
a very coaxing way with him and would intoxicate him with
furtive kisses, and yield herself to him in sudden fits of self-
abandonment, which tied him to her apron-strings the moment he was able to escape from his military duties.

One evening, Nana having announced that her name too
was Thérèse, and that her fête-day was the fifteenth of October, the gentlemen all sent her presents. Captain Philippe

brought his himself; it was an old comfit-dish in Dresden china, and it had a gold mount. He found her alone in her dressing-room. She had just emerged from the bath, had nothing on save a great red and white flannel bathing-wrap, and was very busy examining her presents, which were ranged on a table. She had already broken a rock-crystal flask in her attempts to un-stopper it.

"Oh, you're too nice!" said she. "What is it? Let's have a peep! What a baby you are to spend your pennies in little fakements like that!"

She scolded him, seeing that he was not rich, but at heart she was delighted to see him spending his whole substance for her. Indeed, this was the only proof of love which had power to touch her. Meanwhile, she was fiddling away at the comfit-dish, opening it and shutting it, in her desire to see how it was made.

"Take care," he murmured, "it's brittle."

But she shrugged her shoulders. Did he think her as clumsy as a street-porter? And all of a sudden the hinge came off between her fingers and the lid fell and was broken. She was stupefied, and remained gazing at the fragments, as she cried,—

"Oh, it's smashed!"

Then she burst out laughing. The fragments lying on the floor tickled her fancy. Her merriment was of the nervous kind, the stupid spiteful laughter of a child who delights in destruction. Philippe had a little fit of disgust, for the wretched girl did not know what anguish this curio had cost him. Seeing him thoroughly upset, she tried to contain herself.

"Gracious me, it isn't my fault! It was cracked; those old things barely hold together. Besides, it was the cover! Didn't you see the bound it gave?"

And she once more burst into uproarious mirth.

But, though he made an effort to the contrary, tears appeared in the young man's eyes and with that she flung her arms tenderly round his neck.

"How silly you are! You know I love you all the same. If one never broke anything the tradesmen would never sell anything. All that sort of thing's made to be broken. Now look at this fan; it's only held together with glue!"

She had snatched up a fan and was dragging at the blades so that the silk was torn in two. This seemed to excite her, and in order to shew that she scorned the other presents, the moment she had ruined his, she treated herself to a general massacre, rapping each successive object and proving clearly that not one was solid in that she had broken them all. There was a lurid glow in her vacant eyes, and her lips, slightly drawn back, displayed her white teeth. Soon, when everything was in fragments, she laughed cheerily again, and with flushed cheeks beat on the table with the flat of her hands, lisping like a naughty little girl:

"All over! Got no more! Got no more!"

Then Philippe was overcome by the same mad excitement, and pushing her down he merrily kissed her bosom. She abandoned herself to him, and clung to his shoulders with such gleeful energy that she could not remember having enjoyed herself so much for an age past. Without letting go of him she said caressingly,—

"I say, dearie, you ought certainly to bring me ten louis to-morrow. It's a bore, but there's the baker's bill worrying me awfully."

He had grown pale. Then, imprinting a final kiss on her forehead, he said simply,—

"I'll try."

Silence reigned. She was dressing, and he stood pressing his forehead against the window-panes. A minute passed, and he returned to her and deliberately continued,—

"Nana, you ought to marry me."

This notion straightway so tickled the young woman that she was unable to finish tying on her petticoats.

"My poor pet, you're ill! D'you offer me your hand because I ask you for ten louis? No, never! I'm too fond of you. Good gracious, what a silly question!"

And, as Zoé entered in order to put her boots on, they ceased talking of the matter. The lady's maid had at once espied the presents lying broken in pieces on the table. She asked if she should put those things away, and *Madame* having bidden her get rid of them, she carried the whole collection off in the folds of her dress. In the kitchen, a sorting-out process began, and *Madame's débris* were shared among the servants.

That day Georges had slipped into the house despite Nana's orders to the contrary. François had certainly seen him pass, but the servants had now got to laugh among themselves at their good lady's embarrassing situations. He had just slipped as far as the little drawing-room, when his brother's voice stopped him, and, as one powerless to tear himself from the door, he overheard everything that went on within, the kisses, the offer of marriage. A feeling of horror froze him, and he went away in a state bordering on imbecility, feeling as though there were a great void in his brain. It was only in his own room, above his mother's flat, in the Rue Richelieu, that his heart broke in a storm of furious sobs. This time there could be no doubt about the state of things; a horrible picture of Nana in Philippe's arms kept rising before his mind's eye. It struck him in the light of an incest. When he fancied himself calm again, the remembrance of it all would return, and in fresh access of raging jealousy he would throw himself on the bed, biting the coverlet, shouting infamous accusations which maddened him the more. Thus the day passed. In order to stay shut up in his room, he spoke of having a sick headache. But the night proved more terrible still; a murder-fever shook him amid continual night-mares. Had his brother lived in the house, he would have gone and killed him with the stab of a knife. When day returned he tried to reason things out. It was he who ought to die, and he determined to throw himself out of the window when an omnibus was passing. Nevertheless, he went out towards ten o'clock, and traversed Paris, wandered up and down on the bridges, and at the last moment felt an unconquerable desire to see Nana once more. With one word, perhaps, she would save him. And three o'clock was striking when he entered the house in the Avenue de Villiers.

Towards noon a frightful piece of news had simply crushed Madame Hugon. Philippe had been in prison since the evening of the previous day, accused of having stolen twelve thousand francs from the chest of his regiment. For the last three months he had been withdrawing small sums there-from in the hope of being able to repay them, whilst he had covered the deficit with false money. Thanks to the negli-gence of the administrative committee, this fraud had been constantly successful. The old lady, humbled utterly by her child's crime, had at once cried out in anger against Nana. She knew Philippe's connection with her, and her melancholy had been the result of this miserable state of things, which kept her in Paris in constant dread of some final catastrophe. But she had never looked forward to such shame as this, and now she blamed herself for refusing him money, as though such refusal had made her accessory to his act. She sank down on an arm-chair; her legs were seized with paraly-sis, and she felt herself to be useless, incapable of action, and destined to stay where she was till she died. But the sudden thought of Georges comforted her. Georges was still left her; he would be able to act, perhaps to save them. There-upon, without seeking aid of any one else—for she wished to keep these matters shrouded in the bosom of her family—she dragged herself up to the next story, her mind possessed

by the idea that she still had some one to love about her. But
upstairs she found an empty room. The porter told her that
Monsieur Georges had gone out at an early hour. The room
was haunted by the ghost of yet another calamity; the bed
with its gnawed bed-clothes bore witness to some one's anguish, and a chair, which lay amid a heap of clothes on the
ground, looked like something dead. Georges must be at
that woman's house; and so, with dry eyes and feet that had
regained their strength, Madame Hugon went downstairs.
She wanted her sons; she was starting to reclaim them.

Since morning Nana had been much worried. First of
all it was the baker, who at nine o'clock had turned up bill
in hand. It was a wretched story. He had supplied her
with bread to the amount of a hundred and thirty-three
francs, and, despite her royal housekeeping, she could not
pay it. In his irritation at being put off, he had presented
himself a score of times since the day he had refused further
credit, and the servants were now espousing his cause. François kept saying that *Madame* would never pay him unless
he made a fine scene; Charles talked of going upstairs, too,
in order to get an old unpaid straw bill settled, whilst Victorine advised them to wait till some gentleman was with
her, when they would get the money out of her by suddenly asking for it in the middle of conversation. The
kitchen was in a savage mood—the tradesmen were all kept
posted in the course events were taking, and there were gossiping consultations, lasting three or four hours on a stretch,
during which *Madame* was stripped, plucked, and talked over
with the wrathful eagerness peculiar to an idle, over-pros-
perous servants' hall. Julien, the house-steward, alone pretended to defend his mistress. She was quite the thing, whatever they might say! And when the others accused him of
sleeping with her, he laughed fatuously, thereby driving the
cook to distraction, for she would have liked to be a man
in order to "spit on such women's backsides," so utterly

would they have disgusted her. François, without informing *Madame* of it, had wickedly posted the baker in the hall,
and when she came downstairs at lunch-time, she found herself face to face with him. Taking the bill, she told him to
return towards three o'clock, whereupon, with many foul
expressions, he departed, vowing that he would have things
properly settled and get his money by hook or by crook.

Nana made a very bad lunch, for the scene had annoyed
her. Next time the man would have to be definitely got rid
of. A dozen times she had put his money aside for him, but
it had as constantly melted away, sometimes in the purchase
of flowers, at others in the shape of a subscription got up
for the benefit of an old *gendarme*. Besides, she was counting on Philippe, and was astonished not to see him make
his appearance with his two hundred francs. It was regular
bad luck, seeing that the day before yesterday she had again
given Satin an outfit, a perfect trousseau this time, some
twelve hundred francs' worth of dresses and linen, and now
she had not a louis remaining.

Towards two o'clock, when Nana was beginning to be
anxious, Labordette presented himself. He brought with
him the designs for the bed, and this caused a diversion, a
joyful interlude which made the young woman forget all her
troubles. She clapped her hands and danced about. After
which, her heart bursting with curiosity, she leant over a
table in the drawing-room, and examined the designs, which
Labordette proceeded to explain to her.

"You see," said he, "this is the body of the bed. In the
middle here, there's a bunch of roses in full bloom, and then
comes a garland of buds and flowers. The leaves are to be
in yellow and the roses in red gold. And here's the grand
design for the bed's-head; Cupids dancing in a ring on a silver trellis-work."

But Nana interrupted him, for she was beside herself with
ecstasy.

"Oh, how funny that little one is, that one in the corner, with his behind in the air! Isn't he now? And what a sly laugh! They've all got such dirty wicked eyes! You know, dear boy, I shall never dare play any silly tricks before *them!*"

Her pride was flattered beyond measure. The goldsmiths had declared that no queen anywhere slept in such a bed. However, a difficulty presented itself. Labordette showed her two designs for the foot-board, one of which reproduced the pattern on the sides, whilst the other, a subject by itself, represented Night wrapped in her veil, and discovered by a faun in all her splendid nudity. He added that, if she chose this last subject, the goldsmiths intended making Night in her own likeness. This idea, the taste of which was rather risky, made her grow white with pleasure, and she pictured herself as a silver statuette symbolic of the warm voluptuous delights of darkness.

"Of course you will only sit for the head and shoulders," said Labordette.

She looked quietly at him.

"Why? The moment a work of art's in question, I don't mind the sculptor that takes my likeness a blooming bit!"

Of course it must be understood that she was choosing the subject. But at this he interposed.

"Wait a moment; it's six thousand francs extra."

"It's all the same to me, by Jove!" cried she, bursting into a laugh. "Hasn't my little rough got the rhino?"

Nowadays among her intimates, she always spoke thus of Count Muffat, and the gentlemen had ceased to inquire after him otherwise.

"Did you see your little rough last night?" they used to say.

"Dear me, I expected to find the little rough here!"

It was a simple familiarity enough, which nevertheless she did not as yet venture on in his presence.

Labordette began rolling up the designs as he gave the

final explanations. The goldsmiths, he said, were undertaking to deliver the bed in two months' time, towards the 25th of December, and next week a sculptor would come to make a model for the Night. As she accompanied him to the door, Nana remembered the baker, and briskly inquired:

"By-the-by, you wouldn't be having ten louis about you?"

Labordette made it a solemn rule, which stood him in good stead, never to lend women money. He used always to make the same reply.

"No, my girl, I'm short. But would you like me to go to your little rough?"

She refused; it was useless. Two days before she had succeeded in getting five thousand francs out of the Count. However, she soon regretted her discreet conduct, for the moment Labordette had gone the baker reappeared, though it was barely half-past two and with many loud oaths roughly settled himself on a bench in the hall. The young woman listened to him from the first floor. She was pale, and it caused her especial pain to hear the servants' secret rejoicings swelling up louder and louder till they even reached her ears. Down in the kitchen they were dying of laughter. The coachman was staring across from the other side of the court, François was crossing the hall without any apparent reason. Then he hurried off to report progress, after sneering knowingly at the baker. They didn't care a damn for *Madame:* the walls were echoing to their laughter, and she felt that she was deserted on all hands and despised by the servants' hall, the inmates of which were watching her every movement and literally bespattering her with the filthiest of chaff. Thereupon she abandoned the intention of borrowing the hundred and thirty-three francs from Zoé; she already owed the maid money, and she was too proud to risk a refusal now. Such a burst of feeling stirred her that she went back into her room, loudly remarking,—

"Come, come, my girl, don't count on any one but yourself. Your body's your own property, and it's better to make use of it than to let yourself be insulted."

And without even summoning Zoé she dressed herself with feverish haste in order to run round to the Tricon's. In hours of great embarrassment this was her last resource. Much sought after and constantly solicited by the old lady, she would refuse or resign herself according to her needs; and on these increasingly frequent occasions when both ends would not meet in her royally-conducted establishment, she was sure to find twenty-five louis awaiting her at the other's house. She used to betake herself to the Tricon's with the ease born of use, just as the poor go to the pawn-shop.

But as she left her own chamber Nana came suddenly upon Georges, standing in the middle of the drawing-room. Not noticing his waxen pallor and the somber fire in his wide eyes, she gave a sigh of relief.

"Ah! you've come from your brother."

"No," said the lad, growing yet paler.

At this she gave a despairing shrug. What did he want? Why was he barring her way? She was in a hurry—yes, she was. Then, returning to where he stood,—

"You've no money, have you?"

"No."

"That's true. How silly of me! Never a stiver; not even their omnibus fares. Mamma doesn't wish it! Oh, what a set of men!"

And she escaped. But he held her back; he wanted to speak to her. She was fairly under way, and again declared she had no time, but he stopped her with a word.

"Listen; I know you're going to marry my brother."

Gracious! the thing was too funny! And she let herself down into a chair in order to laugh at her ease.

"Yes," continued the lad, "and I don't wish it. It's I you're going to marry. That's why I've come."

"Eh, what? You too?" she cried. "Why it's a family

disease, is it? No, never! What a fancy, to be sure! Have I ever asked you to do anything so nasty? Neither one nor t'other of you! No, never!"

The lad's face brightened. Perhaps he had been deceiving himself! He continued:

"Then swear to me that you don't go to bed with my brother."

"Oh, you're beginning to bore me now!" said Nana, who had risen with renewed impatience. "It's amusing for a little while, but when I tell you I'm in a hurry—! I go to bed with your brother if it pleases me. Are you keeping me—are you paymaster here, that you insist on my making a report? Yes, I go to bed with your brother."

He had caught hold of her arm, and squeezed it hard enough to break it, as he stuttered:

"Don't say that! Don't say that!"

With a slight blow she disengaged herself from his grasp. "He's maltreating me now! Here's a young ruffian for you! My chicken, you'll leave this jolly sharp. I used to keep you about out of niceness. Yes, I did! You may stare! Did you think I was going to be your mammy till I died? I've got better things to do than to bring up brats."

He listened to her stark with anguish, yet in utter submission. Her every word cut him to the heart so sharply that he felt he should die. She did not so much as notice his suffering, and continued delightedly to revenge herself on him for the annoyances of the morning.

"It's like your brother; he's another pretty Johnny, he is! He promised me two hundred francs. Oh, dear me; yes, I can wait for 'em. It isn't his money I care for! I've not got enough to pay for hair oil. Yes, he's leaving me in a jolly fix! Look here, d'you want to know how matters stand? Here goes, then: it's all owing to your brother that I'm going out to earn twenty-five louis with another man."

At these words his head spun, and he barred her egress.

He cried, he besought her not to go, clasping his hands to-gether, and blurting out:

"Oh, no! oh, no!"

"I want to, I do," said she. "Have you the money?"

No, he had not got the money. He would have given his life to have the money! Never before had he felt so miser-able, so useless, so very childish. All his wretched being was shaken with weeping, and gave proof of such heavy suffer-ing that at last she noticed it and grew kind. She pushed him away softly.

"Come, my pet, let me pass: I must. Be reasonable. You're a baby boy, and it was very nice for a week, but nowa-days I must look after my own affairs. Just think it over a bit. Now, your brother's a man: what I'm saying doesn't apply to him. Oh, please do me a favor; it's no good telling him all this. He needn't know where I'm going. I always let out too much when I'm in a rage."

She began laughing. Then taking him in her arms, and kissing him on the forehead,—

"Good-by, baby," she said; "it's over, quite over between us, d'you understand. And now I'm off!"

And she left him, and he stood in the middle of the draw-ing-room. Her last words rang like the knell of a tocsin in his ears: "It's over, quite over!" and he thought the ground was opening beneath his feet. There was a void in his brain, from which the man awaiting Nana had disap-peared. Philippe alone remained there in the young woman's bare embrace, for ever and ever. She did not deny it: she loved him, since she wanted to spare him the pain of her in-fidelity. It was over, quite over. He breathed heavily, and gazed round the room, suffocating beneath a crushing weight. Memories kept recurring to him one after the other—mem-ories of merry nights at The Mignotte, of amorous hours during which he had fancied himself her child, of pleasures stolen in this very room. And now these things would never,

never recur! He was too small, he had not grown up quickly enough; Philippe was supplanting him because he was a bearded man. So then, this was the end; he could not go on living. His vicious passion had become transformed into an infinite tenderness, a sensual adoration, in which his whole being was merged. Then, too, how was he to forget it all if his brother remained—his brother, blood of his blood, a second self, whose enjoyment drove him mad with jealousy? It was the end of all things; he wanted to die.

All the doors remained open, as the servants noisily scattered over the house, after seeing *Madame* make her exit on foot. Downstairs, on the bench in the hall, the baker was laughing with Charles and François. Zoé came running across the drawing-room and seemed surprised at sight of Georges. She asked him if he were waiting for *Madame*. Yes, he was waiting for her; he had forgotten to give her an answer to a question. And when he was alone, he set to work and searched. Finding nothing else to suit his purpose, he took up in the dressing-room a pair of very sharply-pointed scissors, with which Nana had a mania for ceaselessly trimming herself either by polishing her skin or cutting off little hairs. Then for a whole hour he waited patiently, his hand in his pocket, and his fingers tightly clasped round the scissors.

"Here's *Madame*," said Zoé returning. She must have espied her through the bedroom window.

There was a sound of people racing through the house, and laughter died away, and doors were shut. Georges heard Nana paying the baker, and speaking in the curtest way. Then she came upstairs.

"What, you're here still!" said she as she noticed him. "Ah, ha! we're going to grow angry, my good man!"

He followed her as she walked towards her bedroom.

"Nana, will you marry me?"

She shrugged her shoulders. It was too stupid: she refused

to answer any more, and conceived the idea of slamming the door in his face.

"Nana, will you marry me?"

She slammed the door. He opened it with one hand, whilst he brought the other and the scissors out of his pocket. And, with one great stab, he simply buried them in his breast.

Nana, meanwhile, had felt conscious that something dreadful would happen, and she had turned round. When she saw him stab himself she was seized with indignation.

"Oh, what a fool he is! what a fool! And with my scissors! Will you leave off, you naughty little rogue? Oh, my God! Oh, my God!"

She was scared. Sinking on his knees, the boy had just given himself a second stab, which sent him down at full length on the carpet. He blocked the threshold of the bedroom. With that Nana lost her head utterly, and screamed with all her might, for she dared not step over his body, which shut her in and prevented her from running to seek assistance.

"Zoé! Zoé! Come at once. Make him leave off. It's getting stupid—a child like that! He's killing himself now! And in my place too! Did you ever see the like of it!"

He was frightening her. He was all white, and his eyes were shut. There was scarcely any bleeding—only a little blood, a tiny stain which was oozing down into his waistcoat. She was making up her mind to step over the body, when an apparition sent her starting back. An old lady was advancing through the drawing-room door, which remained wide open opposite. And in her terror she recognized Madame Hugon, but could not explain her presence. Still wearing her gloves and hat, Nana kept edging backwards, and her terror grew so great that she sought to defend herself, and in a shaky voice,—

"*Madame,*" cried she, "it isn't I, I swear to you it isn't.

He wanted to marry me, and I said no, and he's killed himself!"

Slowly Madame Hugon drew near—she was in black, and her face shewed pale under her white hair. In the carriage, as she drove thither, the thought of Georges had vanished, and that of Philippe's misdoing had again taken complete possession of her. It might be that this woman could afford explanations to the judges which would touch them, and so she conceived the project of begging her to bear witness in her son's favor. Downstairs, the doors of the house stood open, but as she mounted to the first floor her sick feet failed her, and she was hesitating as to which way to go when suddenly horror-stricken cries directed her. Then, upstairs, she found a man lying on the floor with blood-stained shirt. It was Georges—it was her other child.

Nana, in idiotic tones, kept saying,—

"He wanted to marry me, and I said no, and he's killed himself."

Uttering no cry, Madame Hugon stooped down. Yes, it was the other one, it was Georges. The one was brought to dishonor, the other murdered! It caused her no surprise, for her whole life was ruined. Kneeling on the carpet, utterly forgetting where she was, noticing no one else, she gazed fixedly at her boy's face, and listened with her hand on his heart. Then she gave a feeble sigh—she had felt the heart beating. And with that she lifted her head and scrutinized the room and the woman, and seemed to remember. A fire glowed forth in her vacant eyes, and she looked so great and terrible in her silence that Nana trembled as she continued to defend herself above the body that divided them.

"I swear it, *Madame*! If his brother were here, he could explain it to you."

"His brother has robbed—he is in prison," said the mother, in a hard voice.

Nana felt a choking sensation. Why, what was the reason of it all? The other had turned thief now! They were mad in that family! She ceased struggling in self-defense: she seemed no longer mistress in her own house, and allowed Madame Hugon to give what orders she liked. The servants had at last hurried up, and the old lady insisted on their carrying the fainting Georges down to her carriage. She preferred killing him rather than letting him remain in that house. With an air of stupefaction Nana watched the retreating servants as they supported poor dear Zizi by his legs and shoulders. The mother walked behind them in a state of collapse; she supported herself against the furniture; she felt as if all she held dear had vanished in the void. On the landing a sob escaped her: she turned, and twice ejaculated,—

"Oh, but you've done us infinite harm! You've done us infinite harm!"

That was all. In her stupefaction Nana had sat down: she still wore her gloves and her hat. The house once more lapsed into heavy silence; the carriage had driven away; and she sat motionless, not knowing what to do next, her head swimming after all she had gone through. A quarter of an hour later, Count Muffat found her thus, but at sight of him she relieved her feelings in an overflowing current of talk. She told him all about the sad incident, repeated the same details twenty times over, picked up the blood-stained scissors in order to imitate Zizi's gesture when he stabbed himself. And above all she nursed the idea of proving her own innocence.

"Look you here, dearie, is it my fault? If you were the judge, would you condemn me? I certainly didn't tell Philippe to meddle with the till any more than I urged that wretched boy to kill himself. I've been most unfortunate throughout it all. They come and do stupid things in my place, they make me miserable, they treat me like a hussy."

And she burst into tears. A fit of nervous expansiveness

rendered her soft and doleful, and her immense distress melted her utterly.

"And you, too, look as if you weren't satisfied. Now do just ask Zoé if I'm at all mixed up in it. Zoé, do speak: explain to *Monsieur*—"

The lady's maid, having brought a towel and a basin of water out of the dressing-room, had for some moments past been rubbing the carpet in order to remove the blood-stains before they dried.

"Oh, *Monsieur*," she declared, "*Madame* is utterly miserable!"

Muffat was still stupefied: the tragedy had frozen him, and his imagination was full of the mother weeping for her sons. He knew her greatness of heart, and pictured her in her widow's weeds, withering solitarily away at The Fondettes. But Nana grew ever more despondent, for now the memory of Zizi, lying stretched on the floor, with a red hole in his shirt, almost drove her senseless.

"He used to be such a darling, so sweet and caressing. Oh, you know, my pet—I'm sorry if it vexes you—I loved that baby! I can't help saying so: the words must out. Besides, now it ought not to hurt you at all. He's gone. You've got what you wanted: you're quite certain never to surprise us again."

And this last reflection tortured her with such regret that he ended by turning comforter. Well, well, said he, she ought to be brave; she was quite right, it wasn't her fault! But she checked her lamentations of her own accord in order to say,—

"Listen, you must run round and bring me news of him. At once! I wish it!"

He took his hat and went to get news of Georges. When he returned, after some three-quarters of an hour, he saw Nana leaning anxiously out of a window; and he shouted up to her from the pavement that the lad was not dead, and that they even hoped to bring him through. At this she immediately exchanged grief for excess of joy, and began to sing, and dance, and vote existence delightful. Zoé, meanwhile, was still dissatisfied with her washing. She kept looking at the stain, and every time she passed it she repeated,—

"You know, it's not gone yet, *Madame*."

As a matter of fact, the pale red stain kept reappearing on one of the white roses in the carpet pattern. It was as though, on the very threshold of the room, a splash of blood were barring the doorway.

"Bah!" said the joyous Nana, "that'll be rubbed out under people's feet."

After the following day, Count Muffat had likewise forgotten the incident. For a moment or two, when in the cab which drove him to the Rue Richelieu, he had busily sworn never to return to that woman's house. Heaven was warning him; the misfortunes of Philippe and Georges were, he opined, prophetic of his proper ruin. But neither the sight of Madame Hugon in tears, nor that of the boy burning with fever, had been strong enough to make him keep his vow, and the short-lived horror of the situation had only left behind it a sense of secret delight at the thought that he was now well quit of a rival, the charm of whose youth had always exasperated him. His passion had by this time grown exclusive; it was, indeed, the passion of a man who has had no youth. He loved Nana as one who yearned to be her sole possessor, to listen to her, to touch her, to be breathed on by her. His was now a super-sensual tenderness, verging on pure sentiment; it was an anxious affection, and as such was jealous of the past, and apt at times to dream of a day of redemption and pardon received, when both should kneel before God the Father. Every day, religion kept regaining its influence over him. He again became a practicing Christian; he confessed himself and communicated, whilst a ceaseless struggle raged within him, and remorse redoubled the joys of sin and of repentance. Afterwards, when his director gave him leave to spend his passion, he had made a habit of this daily perdition, and would redeem the same by ecstasies of faith, which were full of pious humility. Very naïvely he offered Heaven, by way of expiatory anguish, the abominable torment from which he was suffering. This torment grew and increased, and he would climb his Calvary with the deep and solemn feelings of a believer, though steeped in a harlot's fierce sensuality. That which made his agony most poignant was this woman's continued faithlessness. He could not share her with others, nor did he understand her imbecile caprices. Undying, unchanging love was what he wished for. However, she had sworn, and he paid her as having done so. But he felt that she was untruthful, incapable of common fidelity, apt to yield to friends, to stray passers-by, like a good-natured animal, born to live minus a shift.

One morning when he saw Foucarmont emerging from her bedroom at an unusual hour, he made a scene about it. But, in her weariness of his jealousy, she grew angry directly. On several occasions ere that she had behaved rather prettily. Thus the evening when he surprised her with Georges she was the first to regain her temper and to confess herself in the wrong. She had loaded him with caresses and dosed him with soft speeches in order to make him swallow the business. But he had ended by boring her to death with his obstinate refusal to understand the feminine nature, and now she was brutal.

"Very well, yes! I've slept with Foucarmont. What then? That's flattened you out a bit, my little rough, hasn't it?"

It was the first time she had thrown "my little rough" in his teeth. The frank directness of her avowal took his breath away; and when he began clenching his fists, she marched up to him, and looked him full in the face.

"We've had enough of this, eh? If it doesn't suit you, you'll do me the pleasure of leaving the house. I don't want you to go yelling in my place. Just you get it into your noodle that I mean to be quite free. When a man pleases me I go to bed with him. Yes, I do—that's my way! And you must make up your mind directly. Yes or no! If it's no, out you may walk!"

She had gone and opened the door, but he did not leave. That was her way now of binding him more closely to her. For no reason whatever, at the slightest approach to a quarrel, she would tell him he might stop or go, as he liked; and she would accompany her permission with a flood of odious reflections. She said she could always find better than he; she had only too many from whom to choose; men in any quantity could be picked up in the street, and men a good deal smarter too, whose blood boiled in their veins. At this he would hang his head, and wait for those gentler moods when she wanted money. She would then become affectionate, and he would forget it all, one night of tender dalliance making up for the tortures of a whole week. His reconciliation with his wife had rendered his home unbearable. Fauchery, having again fallen under Rose's dominion, the Countess was running madly after other loves. She was entering on the forties, that restless, feverish time in the life of women, and ever hysterically nervous, she now filled her mansion with the maddening whirl of her fashionable life. Estelle, since her marriage, had seen nothing of her father: the undeveloped, insignificant girl had suddenly become a woman of iron will, so imperious withal that Daguenet trembled in her presence. In these days he accompanied her to mass: he was converted, and he raged against his father-in-law for ruining them with a courtesan. Monsieur Venot alone still remained kindly inclined towards the Count, for he was biding his time. He had even succeeded in getting into Nana's immediate circle. In fact he frequented both houses, where you encountered his continual smile behind doors. So Muffat, wretched at home, driven out by ennui and shame, still preferred to live in the Avenue de Villiers, even though he was abused there.

Soon there was but one question between Nana and the Count, and that was "money." One day, after having formally promised her ten thousand francs, he had dared keep his appointment empty-handed. For two days past she had been surfeiting him with love, and such a breach of faith, such a waste of caresses, made her ragingly abusive. She was white with fury.

"So you've not got the money, eh? Then go back where you came from, my little rough, and look sharp about it! There's a bloody fool for you! He wanted to kiss me again! Mark my words—no money, no nothing!"

He explained matters; he would be sure to have the money the day after to-morrow. But she interrupted him violently.

"And my bills! They'll sell me up while *Monsieur's* playing the fool. Now then, look at yourself. D'ye think I love you for your figure? A man with a mug like yours has to pay the women who are kind enough to put up with him. By God, if you don't bring me that ten thousand francs to-night, you shan't even have the tip of my little finger to suck. I mean it! I shall send you back to your wife!"

At night he brought the ten thousand francs. Nana put up her lips, and he took a long kiss which consoled him for the whole day of anguish. What annoyed the young woman was to have him continually tied to her apron strings. She complained to Monsieur Venot, begging him to take her little rough off to the Countess. Was their reconciliation good for nothing, then? She was sorry she had mixed herself up in it, since, despite everything, he was always at her heels. On the days when, out of anger, she forgot her own interest, she swore to play him such a dirty trick that he would never again be able to set foot in her place. But when

she slapped her leg and yelled at him, she might quite as well
have spat in his face too: he would still have stayed and even
thanked her. Then the rows about money matters kept continually recurring. She demanded money savagely; she
rowed him over wretched little amounts; she was odiously
stingy with every minute of her time; she kept fiercely informing him that she slept with him for his money, not for
any other reasons, and that she did not enjoy it a bit; that, in
fact, she loved another and was awfully unfortunate in need-
ing an idiot of his sort! They did not even want him at
Court now, and there was some talk of requiring him to send
in his resignation. The Empress had said,—"He is too disgusting." It was true enough. So Nana repeated the phrase
by way of closure to all their quarrels.

"Look here! You disgust me!"
Nowadays she no longer minded her p's and q's; she had
regained the most perfect freedom.

Every day she did her round of the lake, beginning ac-
quaintanceships which ended elsewhere. Here was the happy
hunting ground *par excellence*, where courtesans of the first
water spread their nets in open daylight, and flaunted themselves amid the tolerating smiles and brilliant luxury of Paris.
Duchesses pointed her out to one another with a passing look
—rich shopkeepers' wives copied the fashion of her hats.
Sometimes her landau, in its haste to get by, stopped a file of
puissant turn-outs, wherein sat plutocrats able to buy up all
Europe, or cabinet ministers with plump fingers tight-pressed
to the throat of France. She belonged to this Bois society, occupied a prominent place in it, was known in every capital,
and asked about by every foreigner. The splendors of this
crowd were enhanced by the madness of her profligacy as
though it were the very crown, the darling passion, of the
nation. Then there were unions of a night, continual passages
of desire, which she lost count of the morning after, and these
sent her touring through the grand restaurants, and on fine

days, as often as not, to "Madrid." The staffs of all the embassies visited her, and she, Lucy Stewart, Caroline Héquet, and Maria Blond would dine in the society of gentlemen who murdered the French language and paid to be amused, engaging them by the evening with orders to be funny, and yet proving so *blasés* and so worn-out that they never even touched them. This the ladies called "going on a spree," and they would return home happy at having been despised, and would finish the night in the arms of the lovers of their choice.

When she did not actually throw the men at his head, Count Muffat pretended not to know about all this. However, he suffered not a little from the lesser indignities of their daily life. The mansion in the Avenue de Villiers was becoming a hell, a house full of mad people, in which every hour of the day wild disorders led to hateful complications. Nana even fought with her servants. One moment she would be very nice with Charles, the coachman. When she stopped at a restaurant she would send him out beer by the waiter, and would talk with him from the inside of her carriage when he slanged the cabbies at a block in the traffic, for then he struck her as funny, and cheered her up. Then, the next moment, she called him a fool for no earthly reason. She was always squabbling over the straw, the bran, or the oats; in spite of her love for animals she thought her horses ate too much. Accordingly, one day, when she was settling up, she accused the man of robbing her. At this Charles got in a rage and called her a whore right out; his horses, he said, were distinctly better than she was, for they did not sleep with everybody. She answered him in the same strain, and the Count had to separate them and give the coachman the sack. This was the beginning of a rebellion among the servants. When her diamonds had been stolen, Victorine and François left. Julien himself disappeared; and the tale ran that the master had given him a big bribe, and had begged

him to go, because he slept with the mistress. Every week
there were new faces in the servants' hall. Never was there
such a mess; the house was like a passage down which the
scum of the registry offices galloped, destroying everything in
their path. Zoé alone kept her place; she always looked clean,
and her only anxiety was how to organize this riot until she
had got enough together to set up on her own account in ful-
fillment of a plan she had been hatching for some time past.

These, again, were only the anxieties he could own to.
The Count put up with the stupidity of Madame Maloir,
playing bézique with her in spite of her musty smell. He
put up with Madame Lerat and her encumbrances, with
Louiset and the mournful complaints peculiar to a child who
is being eaten up with the rottenness inherited from some
unknown father. But he spent hours worse than these. One
evening he had heard Nana angrily telling her maid that a
man pretending to be rich had just swindled her—a handsome man calling himself an American, and owning gold
mines in his own country, a beast who had gone off while
she was asleep without giving her a copper, and had even taken
a packet of cigarette papers with him. The Count had turned
very pale, and had gone downstairs again on tip-toe so as not
to hear more. But later he had to hear all. Nana having been
smitten with a baritone in a music-hall and having been
thrown over by him, wanted to commit suicide during a fit
of sentimental melancholia. She swallowed a glass of water,
in which she had soaked a box of matches. This made her
terribly sick, but did not kill her. The Count had to nurse
her, and to listen to the whole story of her passion, her tearful protests, and her oaths never to take to any man again.
In her contempt for those swine, as she called them, she
could not, however, keep her heart free, for she always had
some sweetheart round her, and her exhausted body inclined
to incomprehensible fancies and perverse tastes. As Zoé des-
ignedly relaxed her efforts, the service of the house had got

to such a pitch that Muffat did not dare to push open a door,
to pull a curtain, or to unclose a cupboard. The bells did not
ring; men lounged about everywhere, and at every moment
knocked up against one another. He had now to cough
before entering a room, having almost caught the girl hanging round Francis' neck one evening that he had just gone
out of the dressing-room for two minutes to tell the coachman to put the horses to, whilst her hairdresser was finishing
her hair. She gave herself up suddenly behind his back; she
took her pleasure in every corner, quickly, with the first man
she met. Whether she was in her chemise or in full dress did
not matter. She would come back to the Count red all
over, happy at having cheated him. As for him, he was
plagued to death; it was an abominable infliction!

In his jealous anguish the unhappy man was comparatively
at peace when he left Nana and Satin alone together. He
would have willingly urged her on to this vice, to keep the
men off her. But all was spoilt in this direction, too. Nana
deceived Satin as she deceived the Count, going mad over
some monstrous fancy or other, and picking up girls at the
street corners. Coming back in her carriage, she would suddenly be taken with a little slut that she saw on the pavement; her senses would be captivated; her imagination excited. She would take the little slut in with her, pay her,
and send her away again. Then, disguised as a man, she would
go to infamous houses, and look on at scenes of debauch
to while away hours of boredom. And Satin, angry at
being thrown over every moment, would turn the house
topsy-turvy with the most awful scenes. She had at last acquired a complete ascendancy over Nana, who now respected
her. Muffat even thought of an alliance between them.
When he dared not say anything, he let Satin loose. Twice she
had compelled her darling to take up with him again; whilst
he shewed himself obliging, and effaced himself in her favor
at the least sign. But this good understanding lasted no time,

for Satin, too, was a little cracked. On certain days she would very nearly go mad, and would smash everything, wearing herself out in tempests of love and anger, but pretty all the time. Zoé must have excited her, for the maid took her into corners as if she wanted to tell her about her great design of which she as yet spoke to no one.

At times, however, Count Muffat was still singularly revolted. He who had tolerated Satin for months, who had at last shut his eyes to the unknown herd of men that scampered so quickly through Nana's bedroom, became terribly enraged at being deceived by one of his own set, or even by an acquaintance. When she confessed her relations with Foucarmont, he suffered so acutely, he thought the treachery of the young man so base, that he wished to insult him and fight a duel. As he did not know where to find seconds for such an affair, he went to Labordette. The latter, astonished, could not help laughing.

"A duel about Nana? But, my dear sir, all Paris would be laughing at you. Men do not fight for Nana; it would be ridiculous."

The Count grew very pale, and made a violent gesture.

"Then I shall slap his face in the open street."

For an hour Labordette had to argue with him. A blow would make the affair odious; that evening every one would know the real reason of the meeting; it would be in all the papers. And Labordette always finished with the same expression:

"It is impossible; it would be ridiculous."

Each time Muffat heard these words they seemed sharp and keen as a stab. He could not even fight for the woman he loved; people would have burst out laughing. Never before had he felt more bitterly the misery of his love, the contrast between his heavy heart and the absurdity of this life of pleasure in which it was now lost. This was his last rebellion; he allowed Labordette to convince him, and he was present

afterwards at the procession of his friends, who lived there as
if at home.

Nana in a few months finished them up greedily, one after
the other. The growing needs, entailed by her luxurious
way of life, only added fuel to her desires, and she finished a
man up at one mouthful. First she had Foucarmont, who
did not last a fortnight. He was thinking of leaving the
Navy, having saved about thirty thousand francs, in his ten
years of service, which he wished to invest in the United
States. His instincts, which were prudential, even miserly,
were conquered; he gave her everything, even his signature to
notes of hand, which pledged his future. When Nana had
done with him he was penniless. But then she proved very
kind, she advised him to return to his ship. What was the
good of getting angry? Since he had no money, their relations were no longer possible. He ought to understand
that, and to be reasonable. A ruined man fell from her
hands like a ripe fruit, to rot on the ground by himself.

Then Nana took up with Steiner, without disgust but
without love. She called him a dirty Jew; she seemed to
be paying back an old grudge, of which she had no distinct
recollection. He was fat; he was stupid, and she got him
down and took two bites at a time in order the quicker to do
for this Prussian. As for him, he had thrown Simonne over.
His Bosphorus scheme was getting shaky, and Nana hastened
the downfall by wild expenses. For a month he struggled
on, doing miracles of finance. He filled Europe with posters,
advertisements, and prospectuses of a colossal scheme, and obtained money from the most distant climes. All these savings, the pounds of speculators, and the pence of the poor,
were swallowed up in the Avenue de Villiers. Again he was
partner in an iron works in Alsace; where, in a small provincial town, workmen, blackened with coal dust and soaked
with sweat, day and night strained their sinews and heard
their bones crack to satisfy Nana's pleasures. Like a huge

fire, she devoured all the fruits of stock-exchange swindling and the profits of labor. This time she did for Steiner; she brought him to the ground, sucked him dry to the core, left him so cleaned out that he was unable to invent a new roguery. When his bank failed, he stammered and trembled at the idea of prosecution. His bankruptcy had just been published, and the simple mention of money flurried him, and threw him into a childish embarrassment. And this was he who had played with millions. One evening, at Nana's, he began to cry and asked her for a loan of a hundred francs wherewith to pay his maid-servant. And Nana, much affected and amused at the end of this terrible old man, who had squeezed Paris for twenty years, brought it to him and said,—

"I say, I'm giving it you because it seems so funny! But, listen to me, my boy, you are too old for me to keep. You must find something else to do."

Then Nana started on la Faloise at once. He had for some time been longing for the honor of being ruined by her in order to put the finishing stroke on his smartness. He needed a woman to launch him properly; it was the one thing still lacking. In two months all Paris would be talking of him, and he would see his name in the papers. Six weeks were enough. His inheritance was in landed estate, houses, fields, woods and farms. He had to sell all, one after the other, as quickly as he could. At every mouthful Nana swallowed an acre. The foliage trembling in the sunshine, the wide fields of ripe grain, the vineyards so golden in September, the tall grass in which the cows stood knee-deep, all passed through her hands as if engulfed by an abyss. Even fishing rights, a stone quarry, and three mills disappeared. Nana passed over them like an invading army, or one of those swarms of locusts whose flight scours a whole province. The ground was burnt up where her little foot had rested. Farm by farm, field by field, she ate up the man's patrimony very prettily and quite inattentively, just as she would have eaten

a box of sweetmeats flung into her lap between meal-times.
There was no harm in it all; they were only sweets! But at
last, one evening, there only remained a single little wood.
She swallowed it up disdainfully, as it was hardly worth the
trouble of opening one's mouth for. La Faloise laughed
idiotically and sucked the top of his stick. His debts were
crushing him, he was not worth a hundred francs a year, and
he saw that he would be compelled to go back into the country
and live with his maniacal uncle. But that did not matter;
he had achieved smartness; the *Figaro* had printed his name
twice. And with his meager neck sticking up between the
turn-down points of his collar, and his figure squeezed into
all too short a coat, he would swagger about, uttering his
parrot-like exclamations and affecting a solemn listlessness
suggestive of an emotionless marionette. He so annoyed Nana
that she ended by beating him.

Meanwhile Fauchery had returned; his cousin having
brought him. Poor Fauchery had now set up housekeeping.
After having thrown over the Countess, he had fallen into
Rose's hands, and she treated him as a lawful wife would
have done. Mignon was simply *Madame's* major-domo. Installed as master of the house, the journalist lied to Rose, and
took all sorts of precautions when he deceived her. He was
as scrupulous as a good husband, for he really wanted to
settle down at last. Nana's triumph consisted in possessing
and in ruining a newspaper that he had started with a friend's
capital. She did not proclaim her triumph; on the contrary,
she delighted in treating him as a man who had to be circumspect; and when she spoke of Rose it was as "poor Rose." The
newspaper kept her in flowers for two months. She took all
the provincial subscriptions; in fact she took everything, from
the column of news and gossip down to the dramatic notes.
Then, the editorial staff having been turned topsy-turvy and
the management completely disorganized, she satisfied a fanciful caprice and had a winter garden constructed in a corner

of her house: that carried off all the type. But then it was no joke after all! When, in his delight at the whole business, Mignon came to see if he could not saddle Fauchery on her altogether, she asked him if he took her for a fool. A penniless fellow living by his articles and his plays—not if she knew it! That sort of foolishness might be all very well for a clever woman like her poor dear Rose! She grew distrustful: she feared some treachery on Mignon's part, for he was quite capable of peaching to his wife, and so she gave Fauchery his *congé* as he now only paid her in fame.

But she always recollected him kindly. They had both enjoyed themselves so much at the expense of that fool of a la Faloise! They would never have thought of seeing each other again if the delight of fooling such a perfect idiot had not egged them on! It seemed an awfully good joke to kiss each other under his very nose. They cut a regular dash with his coin; they would send him off full speed to the other end of Paris in order to be alone, and then, when he came back, they would crack jokes and make allusions he could not understand. One day, urged by the journalist, she bet that she would smack his face, and that she did the very same evening, and went on to harder blows, for she thought it a good joke, and was glad of the opportunity of shewing how cowardly men were. She called him her "slap-jack," and would tell him to come and have his smack! The smacks made her hands red, for as yet she was not up to the trick. La Faloise laughed in his idiotic, languid way, though his eyes were full of tears. He was delighted at such familiarity; he thought it simply stunning.

One night when he had received sundry cuffs, and was greatly excited,—

"Now, d'you know," said he, "you ought to marry me. We should be as jolly as grigs together, eh?"

This was no empty suggestion. Seized with a desire to astonish Paris, he had been slyly projecting this marriage.

"Nana's husband! Wouldn't that sound smart, eh?" Rather a stunning apotheosis that! But Nana gave him a fine snubbing.

"Me marry you! Lovely! If such an idea had been tormenting me, I should have found a husband a long time ago! And he'd have been a man worth twenty of you, my pippin! I've had a heap of proposals. Why look here, just reckon 'em up with me: Philippe, Georges, Foucarmont, Steiner—that makes four, without counting the others you don't know. It's a chorus they all sing. I can't be nice but they forthwith begin yelling, 'Will you marry me? Will you marry me?'"

She lashed herself up, and then burst out in fine indignation.

"Oh, dear no! I don't want to! D'you think I'm built that way? Just look at me a bit! Why, I shouldn't be Nana any longer if I fastened a man on behind! And, besides, it's too foul."

And she spat and hiccoughed with disgust, as though she had seen all the dirt in the world spread out beneath her.

One evening la Faloise vanished, and a week later it became known that he was in the country with an uncle whose mania was botany. He was pasting his specimens for him, and stood a chance of marrying a very plain pious cousin. Nana shed no tears for him. She simply said to the Count,—

"Eh, little rough, another rival less! You're chortling to-day. But he was becoming serious! He wanted to marry me."

He waxed pale, and she flung her arms round his neck and hung there laughing, whilst she emphasized every little cruel speech with a caress.

"You can't marry Nana! Isn't that what's fetching you, eh? When they're all bothering me with their marriages, you're raging in your corner. It isn't possible; you must wait till your wife kicks the bucket. Oh! if she were only

to do that, how you'd come rushing round! How you'd
fling yourself on the ground and make your offer with all
the grand accompaniments—sighs, and tears, and vows!
Wouldn't it be nice, darling, eh?"

Her voice had become soft, and she was chaffing him in a
ferociously wheedling manner. He was deeply moved, and
began blushing as he paid her back her kisses. Then she
cried,—

"By God! to think I should have guessed! He's thought
about it; he's waiting for his wife to go off the hooks! Well,
well, that's the finishing touch! Why, he's even a bigger
rascal than the others!"

Muffat had resigned himself to "the others." Nowadays
he was trusting to the last relics of his personal dignity in
order to remain *"Monsieur"* among the servants and intimates of the house, the man, in fact, who because he gave
most was the official lover. And his passion grew fiercer.
He kept his position because he paid for it, buying even
smiles at a high price. He was even robbed, and he never
got his money's worth; but a disease seemed to be gnawing
his vitals from which he could not prevent himself suffering.
Whenever he entered Nana's bedroom he was simply content
to open the windows for a second or two, in order to get rid
of the odors the others left behind them, the essential smells
of fair-haired men and dark, the smoke of cigars, of which the
pungency choked him. This bedroom was becoming a
veritable thoroughfare, so continually were boots wiped on
its threshold. Yet never a man among them was stopped by
the blood-stain barring the door. Zoé was still preoccupied
by this stain; it was a simple mania with her, for she was a
clean girl, and it horrified her to see it always there. Despite
of everything, her eyes would wander in its direction, and
she now never entered *Madame's* room without remarking,—

"It's strange that don't go. All the same, plenty of folk
come in this way."

Nana kept receiving the best news from Georges, who was by that time already convalescent in his mother's keeping at The Fondettes, and she used always to make the same reply.

"Oh, hang it, time's all that's wanted. It's apt to grow paler as feet cross it."

As a matter of fact, each of the gentlemen, whether Foucarmont, Steiner, la Faloise, or Fauchery, had borne away some of it on their boot-soles. And Muffat, whom the bloodstain preoccupied as much as it did Zoé, kept studying it in his own despite, as though in its gradual rosy disappearance he would read the number of men that passed. He secretly dreaded it, and always stepped over it out of a vivid fear of crushing some live thing, some naked limb lying on the floor.

But in the bedroom within he would grow dizzy and intoxicated, and would forget everything—the mob of men which constantly crossed it, the sign of mourning which barred its door. Outside, in the open air of the street, he would weep occasionally out of sheer shame and disgust, and would vow never to enter the room again. And, the moment the portière had closed behind him, he was under the old influence once more, and felt his whole being melting in the damp warm air of the place, felt his flesh penetrated by a perfume, felt himself overborne by a voluptuous yearning for self-annihilation. Pious, and habituated to ecstatic experiences in sumptuous chapels, he there re-encountered precisely the same mystical sensations as when he knelt under some painted window, and gave way to the intoxication of organ music and incense. Woman swayed him as jealously and despotically as the God of wrath, terrifying him, granting him moments of delight, which were like spasms in their keenness, in return for hours filled with frightful, tormenting visions of hell and eternal tortures. In Nana's presence, as in church, the same stammering accents were his, the same prayers and the same fits of despair—nay, the same paroxysms of humility peculiar to an accursed creature, who is crushed down in the mire from whence he has sprung. His fleshly desires, his spiritual needs, were confounded together, and seemed to spring from the obscure depths of his being, and to bear but one blossom on the tree of his existence. He abandoned himself to the power of love and of faith, those twin levers which move the world. And despite all the struggles of his reason, this bedroom of Nana's always filled him with madness, and he would sink shuddering under the almighty dominion of sex, just as he would swoon before the vast unknown of Heaven.

Then, when she felt how humble he was, Nana grew tyrannously triumphant. The rage for debasing things was inborn in her. It did not suffice her to destroy them, she must soil them too. Her delicate hands left abominable traces, and themselves decomposed whatever they had broken. And he in his imbecile condition lent himself to this sort of sport, for he was possessed by vaguely-remembered stories of saints who were devoured by vermin, and in turn devoured their own excrements. When once she had him fast in her room, and the doors were shut, she treated herself to a man's infamy. At first they joked together, and she would deal him light blows, and impose quaint tasks on him, making him lisp like a child, and repeat tags of sentences.

"Say as I do:—'tonfound it! Ickle man dam vell don't tare about it!'"

He would prove so docile as to reproduce her very accent.

"—tonfound it! Ickle man dam vell don't tare about it!"

Or again she would play bear, walking on all fours on her rugs, when she had only her chemise on, and turning round with a growl as though she wanted to eat him. She would even nibble his calves for the fun of the thing. Then, getting up again,—

"It's your turn now, try it a bit. I bet you don't play bear like me."

It was still charming enough. As bear she amused him with her white skin and her fell of ruddy hair. He used to laugh, and go down on all fours too, and growl, and bite her calves, whilst she ran from him with an affectation of terror.

"Are we beasts, eh?" she would end by saying. "You've no notion how ugly you are, my pet! Just think if they were to see you like that at the Tuileries!"

But ere long these little games were spoilt. It was not cruelty in her case, for she was still a good-natured girl; it was as though a passing wind of madness were blowing ever more strongly in the shut-up bedroom. A storm of lust disordered their brains, plunged them into the delirious imaginations of the flesh. The old pious terrors of their sleepless nights were now transforming themselves into a thirst for bestiality, a furious longing to walk on all fours, to growl and to bite. One day, when he was playing bear, she pushed him so roughly that he fell against a piece of furniture, and when she saw the lump on his forehead she burst into involuntary laughter. After that, her experiments on la Faloise having whetted her appetite, she treated him like an animal, thrashing him and chasing him to an accompaniment of kicks.

"Gee up! Gee up! You're a horse. Hoi! gee up! Won't you hurry up, you dirty screw!"

At other times he was a dog. She would throw her scented handkerchief to the far end of the room, and he had to run and pick it up with his teeth, dragging himself along on hands and knees.

"Fetch it, Cæsar! Look here, I'll give you what for if you don't look sharp! Well done, Cæsar! Good dog! Nice old fellow! Now behave pretty!"

And he loved his abasement, and delighted in being a brute beast. He longed to sink still further, and would cry,—

"Hit harder. On, on! I'm wild! Hit away!"

She was seized with a whim, and insisted on his coming to her one night clad in his magnificent Chamberlain's cos-

tume. Then how she did laugh and make fun of him when
she had him there in all his glory, with the sword, and the
cocked hat, and the white breeches, and the full-bottomed
coat of red cloth laced with gold, and the symbolic key hanging on its left-hand skirt. This key made her especially
merry, and urged her to a wildly fanciful and extremely
filthy discussion of it. Laughing without cease, and carried
away by her irreverence for pomp and by the joy of debasing him in the official dignity of his costume, she shook him,
pinched him, shouted, "Oh, get along with ye, Chamberlain!" and ended by an accompaniment of swinging kicks
behind. Oh, those kicks. How heartily she rained them on
the Tuileries, and the majesty of the Imperial Court, thron-
ing on high above an abject and trembling people. That's
what she thought of society! That was her revenge! It was
an affair of unconscious hereditary spite; it had come to her
in her blood. Then, when once the Chamberlain was undressed and his coat lay spread on the ground, she shrieked,
"Jump!" and he jumped; she shrieked, "Spit!" and he spat.
With a shriek she bade him walk on the gold, on the eagles,
on the decorations, and he walked on them. Hi tiddly hi ti!
Nothing was left; everything was going to pieces. She
smashed a Chamberlain just as she smashed a flask or a com-
fit-box, and she made filth of him, reduced him to a heap
of mud at a street-corner.

Meanwhile, the goldsmiths had failed to keep their promise,
and the bed was not delivered till one day about the middle
of January. Muffat was just then in Normandy, whither he
had gone to sell a last stray shred of property, but Nana demanded four thousand francs forthwith. He was not due in
Paris till the day after to-morrow, but when his business was
once finished, he hastened his return, and without even paying
a flying visit in the Rue Miromesnil, came direct to the Avenue de Villiers. Ten o'clock was striking. As he had a key
of a little door opening on the Rue Cardinet, he went up un-

hindered. In the drawing-room upstairs, Zoé, who was polishing the bronzes, stood dumfounded at sight of him, and not
knowing how to stop him she began with much circumlocu-
tion informing him that Monsieur Venot, looking utterly
beside himself, had been searching for him since yesterday,
and that he had already come twice to beg her to send
Monsieur to his house, if *Monsieur* arrived at *Madame's* before
going home. Muffat listened to her without in the least understanding the meaning of her recital; then he noticed her
agitation, and was seized by a sudden fit of jealousy of which
he no longer believed himself capable. He threw himself
against the bedroom door, for he heard the sound of laughter
within. The door gave, its two flaps flew asunder, whilst
Zoé withdrew, shrugging her shoulders. So much the worse
for *Madame!* As *Madame* was bidding good-by to her wits,
she might arrange matters for herself.

And, on the threshold, Muffat uttered a cry at the sight
that was presented to his view.

"My God! My God!"

The renovated bedroom was resplendent in all its royal
luxury. Silver buttons gleamed like bright stars on the tea-
rose velvet of the hangings. These last were of that pink
flesh tint which the skies assume on fine evenings, when Venus
lights her fires on the horizon against the clear back-ground
of fading daylight. The golden cords and tassels hanging in
corners, and the gold lace-work surrounding the panels, were
like little flames or ruddy strands of loosened hair, and they
half covered the wide nakedness of the room whilst they emphasized its pale voluptuous tone. Then, over against him,
there was the gold and silver bed, which shone in all the fresh
splendor of its chiselled workmanship, a throne this of sufficient extent for Nana to display the out-stretched glory
of her naked limbs, an altar of Byzantine sumptuousness,
worthy of the almighty puissance of Nana's sex, which at
this very hour lay nudely displayed there in the religious im-

modesty befitting an idol of all men's worship. And close by, beneath the snowy reflections of her bosom, and amid the triumph of the goddess, lay wallowing a shameful decrepit thing, a comic and lamentable ruin, the Marquis de Chouard in his night-shirt.

The Count had clasped his hands together and, shaken by a paroxysmal shuddering, he kept crying,—

"My God! My God!"

It was for the Marquis de Chouard, then, that the golden roses flourished on the side-panels, those bunches of golden roses blooming among the golden leaves; it was for him that the Cupids leaned forth with amorous roguish laughter from their tumbling ring on the silver trellis-work. And it was for him that the faun at his feet discovered the nymph sleeping, tired with dalliance, the figure of Night copied down to the exaggerated thighs—which caused her to be recognizable of all—from Nana's renowned nudity. Cast there like the rag of something human, which has been spoilt and dissolved by sixty years of debauchery, he suggested the charnel-house amid the glory of the woman's dazzling contours. Seeing the door open, he had risen up, smitten with sudden terror as became an infirm old man. This last night of passion had rendered him imbecile; he was entering on his second childhood; and, his speech failing him, he remained in an attitude of flight, half-paralyzed, stammering, shivering, his night-shirt half up his skeleton shape, and one leg outside the clothes, a livid leg, covered with gray hair. Despite her vexation, Nana could not keep from laughing.

"Do lie down! Stuff yourself into the bed," said she, pulling him back and burying him under the coverlet, as though he were some filthy thing she could not shew any one.

Then she sprang up to shut the door again. She was decidedly never lucky with her little rough. He was always coming when least wanted. And why had he gone to fetch money in Normandy? The old man had brought her the

four thousand francs, and she had let him have his will of
her. She pushed back the two flaps of the door and shouted,—

"So much the worse for you! It's your fault. Is that the
way to come into a room? I've had enough of this sort of
thing. Ta ta!"

Muffat remained standing before the closed door, thunderstruck by what he had just seen. His shuddering fit increased. It mounted from his feet to his heart and brain.
Then, like a tree shaken by a mighty wind, he swayed to and
fro, and dropped on his knees, all his muscles giving way
under him. And with hands despairingly outstretched he
stammered,—

"This is more than I can bear, my God! more than I can
bear!"

He had accepted every situation but he could do so no
longer. He had come to the end of his strength, and was
plunged in the dark void where man and his reason are together overthrown. In an extravagant access of faith he
raised his hands ever higher and higher, searching for heaven
—calling on God.

"Oh, no, I do not desire it! Oh, come to me, my God!
Succour me; nay, let me die sooner! Oh, no, not that man,
my God! It is over: take me, carry me away, that I may not
see, that I may not feel any longer! Oh, I belong to you,
my God! Our Father which art in heaven—"

And, burning with faith, he continued his supplication,
and an ardent prayer escaped from his lips. But some one
touched him on the shoulder. He lifted his eyes; it was
Monsieur Venot. He was surprised to find him praying
before that closed door. Then, as though God Himself had
responded to his appeal, the Count flung his arms round the
little old gentleman's neck. At last he could weep, and he
burst out sobbing, and repeated,—

"My brother, my brother."

All his suffering humanity found comfort in that cry. He

drenched Monsieur Venot's face with tears; he kissed him, uttering fragmentary ejaculations.

"Oh, my brother, how I am suffering! You only are left me, my brother. Take me away for ever—oh, for mercy's sake, take me away!"

Then Monsieur Venot pressed him to his bosom, and called him "brother" also. But he had a fresh blow in store for him. Since yesterday he had been searching for him in order to inform him that the Countess Sabine, in a supreme fit of moral aberration, had but now taken flight with the manager of one of the departments in a large fancy emporium. It was a fearful scandal, and all Paris was already talking about it. Seeing him under the influence of such religious exaltation, Venot felt the opportunity to be favorable, and at once told him of the meanly tragic shipwreck of his house. The Count was not touched thereby. His wife had gone? That meant nothing to him; they would see what would happen later on. And again he was seized with anguish, and gazing with a look of terror at the door, the walls, the ceiling, he continued pouring forth his single supplication:

"Take me away! I cannot bear it any longer! take me away!"

Monsieur Venot took him away as though he had been a child. From that day forth Muffat belonged to him entirely; he again became strictly attentive to the duties of religion; his life was utterly blasted. He had resigned his position as Chamberlain out of respect for the outraged modesty of the Tuileries, and soon Estelle, his daughter, brought an action against him for the recovery of a sum of sixty thousand francs, a legacy left her by an aunt to which she ought to have succeeded at the time of her marriage. Ruined, and living narrowly on the remains of his great fortune, he let himself be gradually devoured by the Countess, who ate up the husks Nana had rejected. Sabine was indeed ruined by the example of promiscuity set her by her husband's inter-

course with the wanton. She was prone to every excess, and
proved the ultimate ruin and destruction of his very hearth.
After sundry adventures she had returned home, and he had
taken her back in a spirit of Christian resignation and forgiveness. She haunted him as his living disgrace, but he
grew more and more indifferent, and at last ceased suffering
from these distresses. Heaven took him out of his wife's
hands in order to restore him to the arms of God, and so the
voluptuous pleasures he had enjoyed with Nana were prolonged in religious ecstasies, accompanied by the old stammering utterances, the old prayers and despairs, the old fits
of humility which befit an accursed creature who is crushed
beneath the mire whence he sprang. In the recesses of
churches, his knees chilled by the pavement, he would once
more experience the delights of the past, and his muscles
would twitch, and his brain would whirl deliciously, and the
satisfaction of the obscure necessities of his existence would
be the same as of old.

On the evening of the final rupture Mignon presented
himself at the house in the Avenue de Villiers. He was growing accustomed to Fauchery, and was beginning at last to
find the presence of his wife's husband infinitely advanta-
geous to him. He would leave all the little household cares
to the journalist, and would trust him in the active super-
intendence of all their affairs. Nay, he devoted the money
gained by his dramatic successes to the daily expenditure of
the family, and as, on his part, Fauchery behaved sensibly,
avoiding ridiculous jealousy, and proving not less pliant than
Mignon himself whenever Rose found her opportunity, the
mutual understanding between the two men constantly im-
proved. In fact they were happy in a partnership which
was so fertile in all kinds of amenities, and they settled down
side by side, and adopted a family arrangement which no
longer proved a stumbling-block. The whole thing was conducted according to rule; it suited admirably; and each man

vied with the other in his efforts for the common happiness.
That very evening Mignon had come by Fauchery's advice
to see if he could not steal Nana's lady's maid from her, the
journalist having formed a high opinion of the woman's
extraordinary intelligence. Rose was in despair; for a month
past she had been falling into the hands of inexperienced
girls who were causing her continual embarrassment. When
Zoé received him at the door he forthwith pushed her into
the dining-room. But at his opening sentence she smiled.
The thing was impossible, she said, for she was leaving *Madame* and establishing herself on her own account. And she
added with an expression of discreet vanity that she was daily
receiving offers, that the ladies were fighting for her, and
that Madame Blanche would give a pile of gold to have her
back.

Zoé was taking the Tricon's establishment. It was an old
project and had been long brooded over. It was her ambition to make her fortune thereby, and she was investing all
her savings in it. She was full of great ideas, and meditated
increasing the business, and hiring a house, and combining
all the delights within its walls. It was with this in view
that she had tried to entice Satin, a little pig at that moment
dying in hospital, so terribly had she done for herself.

Mignon still insisted with his offer, and spoke of the risks
run in the commercial life, but Zoé, without entering into
explanations about the exact nature of her establishment,
smiled a pinched smile, as though she had just put a sweet-
meat in her mouth, and was content to remark,—

"Oh, luxuries always pay. You see I've been with others
quite long enough, and now I want others to be with me."

And a fierce look set her lip curling. At last she would
be *"Madame,"* and, for the sake of earning a few louis, all
those women, whose slops she had emptied during the last
fifteen years, would prostrate themselves before her.

Mignon wished to be announced, and Zoé left him for a

moment, after remarking that *Madame* had passed a miserable day. He had only been at the house once before, and he did not know it at all. The dining-room with its Gobelins tapestry, its sideboard, and its plate, filled him with astonishment. He opened the doors familiarly, and visited the drawing-room, and the winter garden, returning thence into the hall. This overwhelming luxury, this gilded furniture, these silks and velvets, gradually filled him with such a feeling of admiration that it set his heart beating. When Zoé came down to fetch him, she offered to show him the other rooms, the dressing-room, that is to say, and the bedroom. In the latter, Mignon's feelings overcame him, he was carried away by them; they filled him with tender enthusiasm.

That damned Nana was simply stupefying him, and yet he thought he knew a thing or two. Amid the downfall of the house, and the servants' wild wasteful race to destruction, massed-up riches still filled every gaping hole and overtopped every ruined wall. And Mignon, as he viewed this lordly monument of wealth, began recalling to mind the various great works he had seen. Near Marseilles they had shown him an aqueduct, the stone arches of which bestrode an abyss, a Cyclopean work which cost millions of money and ten years of intense labor. At Cherbourg he had seen the new harbor, with its enormous works, where hundreds of men sweated in the sun, whilst cranes filled the sea with huge squares of rock, and built up a wall where a workman now and again remained crushed into bloody pulp. But all that now struck him as insignificant. Nana excited him far more. Viewing the fruit of her labors, he once more experienced the feelings of respect that had overcome him one festal evening in a sugar refiner's château. This château had been erected for the refiner, and its palatial proportions and royal splendor had been paid for by a single material—sugar. It was with something quite different, with a little laughable folly, a little delicate nudity—it was with this shameful trifle, which is so powerful as to move the universe, that she alone, without workmen, without the inventions of engineers, had shaken Paris to its foundations, and had built up a fortune on the bodies of dead men.

"Oh, by God, what an implement!"

Mignon let the words escape him in his ecstasy, for he felt a return of personal gratitude.

Nana had gradually lapsed into a most mournful condition. To begin with, the meeting of the Marquis and the Count had given her a severe fit of feverish nervousness, which verged at times on laughter. Then the thought of this old man going away half dead in a cab, and of her poor rough, whom she would never set eyes on again, now that she had driven him so wild, brought on what looked like the beginnings of melancholia. After that, she grew vexed to hear about Satin's illness. The girl had disappeared about a fortnight ago, and was now ready to die at Lariboisière, to such a damnable state had Madame Robert reduced her. When she ordered the horses to be put to in order that she might have a last sight of this vile little wretch, Zoé had just quietly given her a week's notice. The announcement drove her to desperation at once! it seemed to her she was losing a member of her own family. Great heavens! what was to become of her when left alone? And she besought Zoé to stay, and the latter, much flattered by *Madame's* despair, ended by kissing her to shew that she was not going away in anger. No, she had positively to go: the heart could have no voice in matters of business.

But that day was one of annoyances. Nana was thoroughly disgusted, and gave up the idea of going out. She was dragging herself wearily about the little drawing-room, when Labordette came up to tell her of a splendid chance of buying magnificent lace, and in the course of his remarks casually let slip the information that Georges was dead. The announcement froze her.

"Zizi dead!" cried she.

And, involuntarily, her eyes sought the pink stain on the carpet, but it had vanished at last: passing footsteps had worn it away. Meanwhile, Labordette entered into particulars. It was not exactly known how he died. Some spoke of a wound reopening, others of suicide. The lad had plunged, said they, into a tank at The Fondettes. Nana kept repeating:

"Dead! dead!"

She had been choking with grief since morning, and now she burst out sobbing, and thus sought relief. Hers was an infinite sorrow: it overwhelmed her with its depth and immensity. Labordette wanted to comfort her as touching Georges, but she silenced him with a gesture, and blurted out,—

"It isn't only he; it's everything, everything. I'm very wretched. Oh, yes, I know! They'll again be saying I'm a hussy. To think of the mother mourning down there, and of the poor man who was groaning in front of my door this morning, and of all the other people that are now ruined after running through all they had with me! That's it; punish Nana; punish the beastly thing! Oh, I've got a broad back! I can hear them as if I were actually there! 'That dirty wench who lies with everybody, and cleans out some, and drives others to death, and causes a whole heap of people pain!'"

She was obliged to pause, for tears choked her utterance, and in her anguish she flung herself athwart a divan, and buried her face in a cushion. The miseries she felt to be around her, miseries of which she was the cause, overwhelmed her with a warm continuous stream of self-pitying tears; and her voice failed as she uttered a little girl's broken plaint:

"Oh, I'm wretched! Oh, I'm wretched! I can't go on like this: it's choking me. It's too hard to be misunderstood, and to see them all siding against you because they're the stronger. However, when you've got nothing to reproach yourself with, and your conscience is clear, why then I say, 'I won't have it! I won't have it!' "

In her anger she began rebelling against circumstances, and getting up, she dried her eyes, and walked about in much agitation.

"I won't have it! They can say what they like, but it's not my fault! Am I a bad lot, eh? I give away all I've got; I wouldn't crush a fly! It's they who are bad! Yes, it's they! *I* never wanted to be horrid to them. And they came dangling after me, and to-day they're kicking the bucket, and begging, and going to ruin on purpose."

Then she paused in front of Labordette, and tapped his shoulders.

"Look here," said she, "you were there all along, now speak the truth: did I urge them on? Weren't there always a dozen of 'em squabbling who could invent the dirtiest trick? They used to disgust me, they did! I did all I knew not to copy them: I was afraid to. Look here, I'll give you a single instance: they all wanted to marry me! A pretty notion, eh? Yes, dear boy, I could have been countess or baroness a dozen times over, and more, if I'd consented. Well now, I refused, because I was reasonable. Oh, yes, I saved 'em some crimes and other foul acts! They'd have stolen, murdered, killed father and mother. I had only to say one word, and I didn't say it. You see what I've got for it to-day. There's Daguenet, for instance. I married that chap off! I made a position for the beggarly fellow, after keeping him gratis for weeks! And I met him yesterday, and he looks the other way! Oh, get along, you swine! I'm less dirty than you!"

She had begun pacing about again, and now she brought her fist violently down on a round table.

"By God, it isn't fair! Society's all wrong. They come down on the women when it's the men who want you to do things. Yes, I can tell you this now: when I used to go with them—see? I didn't enjoy it, no, I didn't enjoy it one bit. It bored me, on my honor. Well then, I ask you whether I've got anything to do with it! Yes, they bored me to death! If it hadn't been for them and what they made of me, dear boy, I should be in a convent saying my prayers to the good God, for I've always had my share of religion. Dash it, after all if they have dropped their money and their lives over it, what do I care? It's their fault. I've had nothing to do with it!"

"Certainly not," said Labordette with conviction.

Zoé ushered in Mignon, and Nana received him smilingly. She had cried a good deal, but it was all over now. Still glowing with enthusiasm, he complimented her on her installation; but she let him see that she had had enough of her mansion, and that now she had other projects, and would sell everything up one of these days. Then, as he excused himself for calling on the ground that he had come about a benefit performance in aid of old Bosc, who was tied to his arm-chair by paralysis, she expressed extreme pity, and took two boxes. Meanwhile Zoé announced that the carriage was waiting for *Madame,* and she asked for her hat, and as she tied the strings told them about poor dear Satin's mishap, adding,—

"I'm going to the hospital. Nobody ever loved me as she did. Oh, they're quite right when they accuse the men of heartlessness! Who knows; perhaps I shan't see her alive. Never mind, I shall ask to see her: I want to give her a kiss."

Labordette and Mignon smiled, and, as Nana was no longer melancholy, she smiled too. Those two fellows didn't count; they could enter into her feelings. And they both stood and admired her in silent abstraction, whilst she finished buttoning her gloves. She alone kept her feet amid the heaped-up .

riches of her mansion, while a whole generation of men lay stricken down before her. Like those antique monsters whose redoubtable domains were covered with skeletons, she rested her feet on human skulls. She was ringed round with catastrophes. There was the furious immolation of Vandeuvres; the melancholy state of Foucarmont, who was lost in the China seas; the smash-up of Steiner, who now had to live like an honest man; the satisfied idiocy of la Faloise; and the tragic shipwreck of the Muffats. Finally, there was the white corpse of Georges, over which Philippe was now watching, for he had come out of prison but yesterday. She had finished her labor of ruin and death. The fly that had flown up from the ordure of the slums, bringing with it the leaven of social rottenness, had poisoned all these men by merely alighting on them. It was well done—it was just. She had avenged the beggars and the wastrels from whose caste she issued. And whilst, metaphorically speaking, her sex rose in a halo of glory and beamed over prostrate victims like a mounting sun shining brightly over a field of carnage, the actual woman remained as unconscious as a splendid animal, and in her ignorance of her mission was the good-natured courtesan to the last. She was still big, she was still plump, her health was excellent, her spirits capital. But this went for nothing now, for her house struck her as ridiculous. It was too small; it was full of furniture which got in her way. It was a wretched business, and the long and the short of the matter was she would have to make a fresh start. In fact she was meditating something much better, and so she went off to kiss Satin for the last time. She was in all her finery, and looked clean, and solid, and as brand-new as if she had never seen service before.

CHAPTER XIV

NANA suddenly disappeared. It was a fresh plunge, an escapade, a flight into barbarous regions. Before her departure she had treated herself to a new sensation: she had held a sale, and had made a clean sweep of everything—house, furniture, jewelry, nay, even dresses and linen. Prices were cited—the five days' sale produced more than six hundred thousand francs. For the last time Paris had seen her in a fairy piece. It was called *Mélusine*, and it played at the Théâtre de la Gaîté, which the penniless Bordenave had taken out of sheer audacity. Here she again found herself in company with Prullière and Fontan. Her part was simply spectacular, but it was the great attraction of the piece, consisting, as it did, of three *poses plastiques*, each of which represented the same dumb and puissant fairy. Then one fine morning, amid his grand success, when Bordenave, who was mad after advertisement, kept firing the Parisian imagination with colossal posters, it became known that she must have started for Cairo the previous day. She had simply had a few words with her manager. Something had been said which did not please her; the whole thing was the caprice of a woman who is too rich to let herself be annoyed. Besides, she had indulged an old infatuation, for she had long meditated visiting the Turks.

Months passed—she began to be forgotten. When her name was mentioned, among the ladies and gentlemen we wot of, the strangest stories were told, and everybody gave the most contradictory and at the same time prodigious information. She had made a conquest of the Viceroy, she was reigning, in the recesses of a palace, over two hundred slaves whose heads she now and then cut off for the sake of a little amusement. No, not at all! She had ruined herself with a great big nigger! A filthy passion this, which had

left her wallowing without a chemise to her back in the
crapulous debauchery of Cairo. A fortnight later, much
astonishment was produced when some one swore to having
met her in Russia. A legend began to be formed, she was
the mistress of a prince, and her diamonds were mentioned.
All the women were soon acquainted with them from the
current descriptions, but nobody could cite the precise source
of all this information. There were finger-rings, earrings,
bracelets, a rivière of phenomenal width, a queenly diadem,
surmounted by a central brilliant the size of one's thumb.
In the retirement of those far-away countries she began to
gleam forth as mysteriously as a gem-laden idol. People now
mentioned her without laughing, for they were full of meditative respect for this fortune acquired among the barbarians.

One evening in July, towards eight o'clock, Lucy, whilst
getting out of her carriage in the Rue du Faubourg-Saint-
Honoré, noticed Caroline Héquet, who had come out on foot
to order something at a neighboring tradesman's. Lucy
called her, and at once burst out with,—

"Have you dined? Are you disengaged? Oh! then come
with me, my dear. Nana's back."

The other got in at once, and Lucy continued,—

"And you know, my dear, she may be dead while we're
gossiping."

"Dead! What an idea!" cried Caroline, in stupefaction.
"And where is she? And what's it of?"

"At the Grand Hôtel, of small-pox. Oh! it's a long
story!"

Lucy had bidden her coachman drive fast, and, whilst the
horses trotted rapidly along the Rue Royale and the Boulevards, she told what had happened to Nana in jerky breathless sentences.

"You can't imagine it. Nana plumps down out of Russia.
I don't know why—some dispute with her prince. She leaves
her traps at the station; she lands at her aunt's—you remem-

ber the old thing. Well, and then she finds her baby dying of small-pox. The baby dies next day, and she has a row with the aunt about some money she ought to have sent, of which the other one has never seen a sou. Seems the child died of that: in fact, it was neglected and badly cared for. Very well; Nana slopes; goes to a hotel, then meets Mignon just as she was thinking of her traps. She has all sorts of queer feelings, shivers, wants to be sick, and Mignon takes her back to her place, and promises to look after her affairs. Isn't it odd, eh? Doesn't it all happen pat? But this is the best part of the story: Rose finds out about Nana's illness, and gets indignant at the idea of her being alone in furnished apartments. So she rushes off, crying, to look after her. You remember how they used to detest one another—like regular furies! Well then, my dear, Rose has had Nana transported to the Grand Hôtel, so that she should at any rate die in a smart place, and now she's already passed three nights there and is free to die of it after. It's Labordette who told me all about it. Accordingly, I wanted to see for myself—"

"Yes, yes," interrupted Caroline, in great excitement. "We'll go up to her."

They had arrived at their destination. On the boulevard the coachman had had to rein in his horses amid a block of carriages and people on foot. During the day the Corps Législatif had voted for war; and now a crowd was streaming down all the streets, flowing along all the pavements, invading the middle of the roadway. Beyond the Madeleine the sun had set behind a blood-red cloud, which cast a reflection as of a great fire and set the lofty windows flaming. Twilight was falling, and the hour was oppressively melancholy, for now the avenues were darkening away into the distance, but were not as yet dotted over by the bright sparks of the gas-lamps. And, among the marching crowds, distant voices swelled and grew ever louder, and eyes gleamed from pale faces, whilst a great spreading wind of anguish and stupor set every head whirling.

"Here's Mignon," said Lucy. "He'll give us news."

Mignon was standing under the vast porch of the Grand Hôtel. He looked nervous, and was gazing at the crowd. After Lucy's first few questions, he grew impatient and cried out,—

"How should I know! These last two days I haven't been able to tear Rose away from up there. It's getting stupid, when all's said, for her to be risking her life like that! She'll be charming, if she gets over it, with holes in her face! It'll suit us to a T!"

The idea that Rose might lose her beauty was exasperating him. He was giving up Nana in the most downright fashion, and he could not in the least understand these stupid feminine devotions. But Fauchery was crossing the boulevard, and he too came up anxiously and asked for news. The two men egged each other on. They addressed one another familiarly in these days.

"Always the same business, my sonny," declared Mignon. "You ought to go upstairs; you would force her to follow you."

"Come now, you're kind, you are!" said the journalist. "Why don't you go upstairs yourself?"

Then, as Lucy began asking for Nana's number, they besought her to make Rose come down; otherwise, they would end by getting angry.

Nevertheless, Lucy and Caroline did not go up at once. They had caught sight of Fontan, strolling about with his hands in his pockets, and greatly amused by the quaint expressions of the mob. When he became aware that Nana was lying ill upstairs, he affected sentiment and remarked,—

"The poor girl! I'll go and shake her by the hand. What's the matter with her, eh?"

"Small-pox," replied Mignon.

The actor had already taken a step or two in the direction of the court but he came back, and simply murmured with a shiver,—

"Oh, damn it!"

The small-pox was no joke. Fontan had been near having it when he was five years old, whilst Mignon gave them an account of one of his nieces who had died of it. As to Fauchery, he could speak of it from personal experience, for he still bore marks of it in the shape of three little lumps at the base of his nose, which he shewed them. And when Mignon again egged him on to the ascent, on the pretext that you never had it twice, he violently combated this theory, and with infinite abuse of the doctors instanced various cases. But Lucy and Caroline interrupted them, for the growing multitude filled them with astonishment.

"Just look! Just look what a lot of people!" The night was deepening, and in the distance, the gas-lamps were being lit one by one. Meanwhile, interested spectators became visible at windows, whilst, under the trees, the human flood grew every minute more dense, till it ran in one enormous stream from the Madeleine to the Bastille. Carriages rolled slowly along. A roaring sound went up from this compact and as yet inarticulate mass. Each member of it had come out impelled by the desire to form a crowd, and was now trampling along, steeping himself in the pervading fever. But a great movement caused the mob to flow asunder. Among the jostling, scattering groups, a band of men in workmen's caps and white blouses had come in sight, uttering a rhythmical cry which suggested the beat of hammers upon an anvil.

"To Ber-lin! To Ber-lin! To Ber-lin!" And the crowd stared in gloomy distrust, yet felt themselves already possessed and inspired by heroic imaginings, as though a military band were passing.

"Oh, yes, go and get your throats cut!" muttered Mignon, overcome by an access of philosophy.

But Fontan thought it very fine indeed, and spoke of enlisting. When the enemy was on the frontier, all citizens ought to rise up in defense of the fatherland! And with that he assumed an attitude suggestive of Bonaparte at Austerlitz.

"Look here, are you coming up with us?" Lucy asked him.

"Oh, dear no! to catch something horrid?" said he.

On a bench, in front of the Grand Hôtel, a man sat hiding his face in a handkerchief. On arriving Fauchery had indicated him to Mignon with a wink of the eye. Well, he was still there; yes, he was always there. And the journalist detained the two women also in order to point him out to them. When the man lifted his head they recognized him, and an exclamation escaped them. It was the Count Muffat, and he was giving an upward glance at one of the windows.

"You know he's been waiting there since this morning," Mignon informed them. "I saw him at six o'clock, and he hasn't moved since. Directly Labordette spoke about it he came there with his handkerchief up to his face. Every half hour he comes dragging himself to where we're standing to ask if the person upstairs is doing better, and then he goes back and sits down. Hang it, that room isn't healthy! It's all very well being fond of people, but one doesn't want to kick the bucket."

The Count sat with uplifted eyes, and did not seem conscious of what was going on around him. Doubtless he was ignorant of the declaration of war, and he neither felt nor saw the crowd.

"Look, here he comes!" said Fauchery. "Now you'll see."

The Count had, in fact, quitted his bench and was entering the lofty porch. But the porter, who was getting to know his face at last did not give him time to put his question. He said sharply,—

"She's dead, *Monsieur*, this very minute."

Nana dead! It was a blow to them all. Without a word
Muffat had gone back to the bench, his face still buried in
his handkerchief. The others burst into exclamations, but
they were cut short, for a fresh band passed by howling, "*À
Berlin! à Berlin! à Berlin!*" Nana dead! Hang it, and such
a fine girl too! Mignon sighed and looked relieved, for at
last Rose would come down. A chill fell on the company.
Fontan, meditating a tragic *rôle*, had assumed a look of woe,
and was drawing down the corners of his mouth, and rolling
his eyes askance, whilst Fauchery chewed his cigar nervously,
for despite his cheap journalistic chaff he was really touched.
Nevertheless, the two women continued to give vent to their
feelings of surprise. The last time Lucy had seen her was
at the Gaîté; Blanche, too, had seen her in *Mélusine*. Oh,
how stunning it was, my dear, when she appeared in the
depths of the crystal grot! The gentlemen remembered the
occasion perfectly. Fontan had played the Prince Cocorico.
And, their memories once stirred up, they launched into interminable particulars. How ripping she looked with that
rich coloring of hers in the crystal grot? Didn't she, now?
She didn't say a word: the authors had even deprived her of
a line or two, because it was superfluous. No, never a word!
It was grander that way, and she drove her public wild by
simply shewing herself. You wouldn't find another body
like hers! Such shoulders as she had, and such legs, and such
a figure! Strange that she should be dead! You know,
above her tights, she had nothing on but a golden girdle
which hardly concealed her behind and in front. All round
her, the grotto, which was entirely of glass, shone like day.
Cascades of diamonds were flowing down, strings of brilliant
pearls glistened among the stalactites in the vault overhead,
and amid the transparent atmosphere and flowing fountain
water, which was crossed by a wide ray of electric light, she
gleamed like the sun with that flame-like skin and hair of

hers. Paris would always picture her thus—would see her shining high up among crystal glass like the good God Himself. No, it was too stupid to let herself die under such conditions! She must be looking pretty by this time, in that room up there!

"And what a lot of pleasures bloody well wasted!" said Mignon in melancholy tones, as became a man who did not like to see good and useful things lost.

He sounded Lucy and Caroline in order to find out if they were going up after all. Of course they were going up; their curiosity had increased. Just then Blanche arrived, out of breath and much exasperated at the way the crowds were blocking the pavement, and when she heard the news there was a fresh outburst of exclamations, and with a great rustling of skirts the ladies moved towards the staircase. Mignon followed them, crying out,—

"Tell Rose that I'm waiting for her. She'll come at once, eh?"

"They do not exactly know whether the contagion is to be feared at the beginning or near the end," Fontan was explaining to Fauchery. "A medical I know was assuring me that the hours immediately following death are particularly dangerous. There are miasmatic exhalations then. Ah! but I do regret this sudden ending; I should have been so glad to shake hands with her for the last time."

"What good would it do you now?" said the journalist.

"Yes, what good?" the two others repeated.

The crowd was still on the increase. In the bright light thrown from shop-windows and beneath the wavering glare of the gas, two living streams were distinguishable as they flowed along the pavement, innumerable hats apparently drifting on their surface. At that hour the popular fever was gaining ground rapidly, and people were flinging themselves in the wake of the bands of men in blouses. A constant forward movement seemed to sweep the roadway, and

the cry kept recurring; obstinately, abruptly, there rang
from thousands of throats,—

"*À Berlin! À Berlin! À Berlin!*"

The room on the fourth floor upstairs cost twelve francs
a day, since Rose had wanted something decent and yet not
luxurious, for sumptuousness is not necessary when one is
suffering. Hung with Louis XIII. cretonne, which was
adorned with a pattern of large flowers, the room was furnished with the mahogany commonly found in hotels. On
the floor there was a red carpet variegated with black foliage.
Heavy silence reigned save for an occasional whispering sound
caused by voices in the corridor.

"I assure you we're lost. The waiter told us to turn to
the right. What a barrack of a house!"

"Wait a bit: we must have a look. Room No. 401, Room
No. 401!"

"Oh, it's this way: 405, 403. We ought to be there. Ah,
at last, 401! This way! Hush now, hush!"

The voices were silent. Then there was a slight coughing, and a moment or so of mental preparation. Then the
door opened slowly, and Lucy entered, followed by Caroline
and Blanche. But they stopped directly; there were already
five women in the room; Gaga was lying back in the solitary
arm-chair, which was a red velvet Voltaire. In front of the
fire-place, Simonne and Clarisse were standing talking to Léa
de Horn, who was seated, whilst, by the bed, to the left of
the door, Rose Mignon, perched on the edge of a chest, sat
gazing fixedly at the body where it lay hidden in the shadow
of the curtains. All the others had their hats and gloves on,
and looked as if they were paying a call: she alone sat there
with bare hands and untidy hair, and cheeks rendered pale
by three nights of watching. She felt stupid in the face of
this sudden death, and her eyes were swollen with weeping. A shaded lamp, standing on the corner of the chest of
drawers, threw a bright flood of light over Gaga.

"What a sad misfortune, is it not?" whispered Lucy, as she shook hands with Rose. "We wanted to bid her good-by."

And she turned round, and tried to catch sight of her, but the lamp was too far off, and she did not dare bring it nearer. On the bed lay stretched a gray mass, but only the ruddy chignon was distinguishable and a pale blotch which might be the face. Lucy added:

"I never saw her since that time at the Gaîté, when she was at the end of the grotto."

At this Rose awoke from her stupor, and smiled as she said:

"Ah, she's changed, she's changed."

Then she once more lapsed into contemplation, and neither moved nor spoke. Perhaps they would be able to look at her presently! And with that the three women joined the others in front of the fire-place. Simonne and Clarisse were discussing the dead woman's diamonds in low tones. Well, did they really exist—those diamonds? Nobody had seen them; it must be a bit of humbug. But Léa de Horn knew some one who knew all about them. Oh, they were monster stones! Besides, they weren't all; she had brought back lots of other precious property from Russia—embroidered stuffs, for instance, valuable knick-knacks, a gold dinner service, nay, even furniture. "Yes, my dear, fifty-two boxes, enormous cases some of them, three truck-loads of them!" They were all lying at the station. "Wasn't it hard lines, eh?—to die without even having time to unpack one's traps." Then, she had a lot of tin besides—something like a million! Lucy asked who was going to inherit it all. Oh, distant relations—the aunt, without doubt! It would be a pretty surprise for that old body. She knew nothing about it yet, for the sick woman had obstinately refused to let them warn her, for she still owed her a grudge over her little boy's death. Thereupon, they were all moved to pity about the little boy, and they remembered seeing him at the races. Oh, it was a wretchedly sickly baby; it looked so old and so sad. In fact, it was one of those poor brats who never asked to be born!

"He's happier under the ground," said Blanche.

"Bah, and so's she!" added Caroline. "Life isn't so funny!"

In that gloomy room melancholy ideas began to take possession of their imaginations. They felt frightened. It was silly to stand talking so long, but a longing to see her kept them rooted to the spot. It was very hot—the lamp-glass threw a round moon-like patch of light upon the ceiling, but the rest of the room was drowned in steamy darkness. Under the bed, a deep plate, full of phenol, exhaled an insipid smell. And, every few moments, tiny gusts of wind swelled the window-curtains. The window opened on the boulevard, whence rose a dull roaring sound.

"Did she suffer much?" asked Lucy, who was absorbed in contemplation of the clock, the design of which represented the Three Graces as nude young women, smiling like opera-dancers.

Gaga seemed to wake up,—

"My word, yes! I was present when she died. I promise you it was not at all pleasant to see. Why, she was taken with a shuddering fit—"

But she was unable to proceed with her explanation for a cry arose outside,—

"À Berlin! À Berlin! À Berlin!"

And Lucy, who felt suffocated, flung wide the window, and leant upon the sill. It was pleasant there; the air came fresh from the starry sky. Opposite her the windows were all aglow with light and the gas sent dancing reflections over the gilt lettering of the shop-signs.

Beneath these, again, a most amusing scene presented itself. The streams of people were discernible rolling torrent-wise along the sidewalks, and in the roadway, where there was a confused procession of carriages. Everywhere there were vast moving shadows in which lanterns and lamp-posts gleamed like sparks. But the band which now came roaring by carried torches, and a red glow streamed down from the direction of the Madeleine, crossed the mob like a trail of fire, and spread out over the heads in the distance like the vivid reflection of a burning house. Lucy called Blanche and Caroline, forgetting where she was, and shouting,—

"Do come! You get a capital view from this window!"

They all three leant out, greatly interested. The trees got in their way, and occasionally the torches disappeared under the foliage. They tried to catch a glimpse of the men of their own party below, but a protruding balcony hid the door, and they could only make out Count Muffat, who looked like a dark parcel thrown down on the bench where he sat. He was still burying his face in his handkerchief. A carriage had stopped in front, and yet another woman hurried up, in whom Lucy recognized Maria Blond. She was not alone: a stout man got down after her.

"It's that thief of a Steiner," said Caroline. "How is it they haven't sent him back to Cologne yet? I want to see how he looks when he comes in."

They turned round, but when, after the lapse of ten minutes, Maria Blond appeared, she was alone. She had twice mistaken the staircase. And when Lucy, in some astonishment, questioned her,—

"What he!" said she. "My dear, don't you go fancying that he'll come upstairs! It's a great wonder he's escorted me as far as the door. There are nearly a dozen of them smoking cigars.

As a matter of fact, all the gentlemen were meeting downstairs. They had come strolling thither in order to have a look at the boulevards, and they hailed one another and commented loudly on that poor girl's death. Then they began discussing politics and strategy. Bordenave, Daguenet, Labordette, Prullière and others besides, had swollen the

group, and now they were all listening to Fontan, who was
explaining his plan for taking Berlin within a week.

Meanwhile, Maria Blond was touched as she stood by the
bedside, and murmured, as the others had done before her,—

"Poor pet! the last time I saw her was in the grotto at the
Gaîté."

"Ah, she's changed, she's changed!" Rose Mignon repeated with a smile of gloomiest dejection.

Two more women arrived. These were Tatan Néné and
Louise Violaine. They had been wandering about the Grand
Hôtel for twenty minutes past, bandied from waiter to waiter,
and had ascended and descended more than thirty flights of
stairs, amid a perfect stampede of travelers who were hurrying to leave Paris amid the panic caused by the war and the
excitement on the boulevards. Accordingly they just dropped
down on chairs when they came in, for they were too tired
to think about the dead. At that moment a loud noise came
from the room next door where people were pushing trunks
about and striking against furniture to an accompaniment
of strident outlandish syllables. It was a young Austrian
couple, and Gaga told how during her agony the neighbors
had played a game of catch as catch can, and how, as only an
unused door divided the two rooms, they had heard them
laughing and kissing when one or the other was caught.

"Come, it's time we were off," said Clarisse. "We shan't
bring her to life again. Are you coming, Simonne?"

They all looked at the bed out of the corners of their
eyes, but they did not budge an inch. Nevertheless, they
began getting ready, and gave their skirts various little pats.
Lucy was again leaning out of window. She was alone now,
and a sorrowful feeling began little by little to overpower
her, as though an intense wave of melancholy had mounted
up from the howling mob. Torches still kept passing, shaking out clouds of sparks, and far away in the distance the
various bands stretched into the shadows, surging unquietly

to and fro like flocks being driven to the slaughter-house at night. A dizzy feeling emanated from these confused masses as the human flood rolled them along,—a dizzy feeling, a sense of terror, and all the pity of the massacres to come. The people were going wild; their voices broke; they were drunk with a fever of excitement which sent them rushing towards the unknown "out there" beyond the dark wall of the horizon.

"*À Berlin! À Berlin! À Berlin!*"

Lucy turned round. She leant her back against the window, and her face was very pale.

"Good God! what's to become of us?"

The ladies shook their heads. They were serious, and very anxious about the turn events were taking.

"For my part," said Caroline Héquet in her decisive way, "I start for London the day after to-morrow. Mamma's already over there getting a house ready for me. I'm certainly not going to let myself be massacred in Paris."

Her mother, as became a prudent woman, had invested all her daughter's money in foreign lands. One never knows how a war may end! But Maria Blond grew vexed at this. She was a patriot, and spoke of following the army.

"There's a coward for you! Yes, if they wanted me, I should put on man's clothes just to have a good shot at those pigs of Prussians! And if we all die after? What of that? Our wretched skins aren't so valuable!"

Blanche de Sivry was exasperated.

"Please don't speak ill of the Prussians! They are just like other men, and they're not always running after the women, like your Frenchmen. They've just expelled the little Prussian who was with me. He was an awfully rich fellow and so gentle: he couldn't have hurt a soul. It's disgraceful: I'm ruined by it. And, you know you mustn't say a word, or I go and find him out in Germany!"

After that, whilst the two were at loggerheads, Gaga began murmuring in dolorous tones,—

"It's all over with me; my luck's always bad. It's only a week ago that I finished paying for my little house at Juvisy. Ah, God knows what trouble it cost me! I had to go to Lili for help! And now here's the war declared, and the Prussians'll come, and they'll burn everything. How am I to begin again at my time of life, I should like to know?"

"Bah!" said Clarisse, "I don't care a damn about it. I shall always find what I want."

"Certainly you will," added Simonne. "It'll be a joke. Perhaps, after all, it'll be good biz."

And her smile hinted what she thought. Tatan Néné and Louise Violaine were of her opinion. The former told them that she had enjoyed the most roaring jolly good times with soldiers. Oh! they were good fellows, and would have done any mortal thing for the girls. But as the ladies had raised their voices unduly, Rose Mignon, still sitting on the chest by the bed, silenced them with a softly-whispered "Hush!" They stood quite still at this, and glanced obliquely towards the dead woman, as though this request for silence had emanated from the very shadows of the curtains. In the heavy peaceful stillness which ensued, a void, deathly stillness which made them conscious of the stiff dead body lying stretched close by them, the cries of the mob burst forth,—

"À Berlin! À Berlin! À Berlin!"

But soon they forgot. Léa de Horn, who had a political *salon* where former ministers of Louis-Philippe were wont to indulge in delicate epigrams, shrugged her shoulders and continued the conversation in a low tone:

"What a mistake this war is! What a bloodthirsty piece of stupidity!"

At this Lucy forthwith took up the cudgels for the Empire. She had been the mistress of a Prince of the Imperial

House, and its defense became a point of family honor with her.

"Do leave them alone, my dear. We couldn't let ourselves be further insulted! Why, this war concerns the honor of France. Oh, you know, I don't say that because of the Prince. He *was* just mean! Just imagine, at night, when he was going to bed, he hid his gold in his boots, and when we played at bézique he used beans, because one day I pounced down on the stakes for fun. But that doesn't prevent my being fair. The Emperor was right."

Léa shook her head with an air of superiority, as became a woman who was repeating the opinions of important personages. Then, raising her voice,—

"This is the end of all things. They're out of their minds at the Tuileries. France ought to have driven them out yesterday. Don't you see?"

They all violently interrupted her. What was up with her? Was she mad about the Emperor? Were people not happy? Was business doing badly? Paris would never enjoy itself so thoroughly again.

Gaga was beside herself: she woke up and was very indignant.

"Be quiet! It's idiotic! You don't know what you're saying. I—I've seen Louis-Philippe's reign: it was full of beggars and misers, my dear. And then came 'Forty-eight!' Oh, it was a pretty disgusting business was their Republic! After 'February,' I was simply dying of starvation—yes, I, Gaga. Oh, if only you'd been through it all, you would go down on your knees before the Emperor, for he's been a father to us; yes, a father to us."

She had to be soothed, but continued with pious fervor:

"O my God, do Thy best to give the Emperor the victory. Preserve the Empire to us!"

They all repeated this aspiration, and Blanche confessed that she burnt candles for the Emperor. Caroline had been smitten by him, and for two whole months had walked where he was likely to pass, but had failed to attract his attention. And with that the others burst forth into furious denunciations of the Republicans, and talked of exterminating them on the frontiers, so that Napoleon III., after having beaten the enemy, might reign peacefully amid universal enjoyment.

"That dirty Bismarck—there's another cad for you!" Maria Blond remarked.

"To think that I should have known him!" cried Simonne. "If only I could have foreseen, I'm the one that would have put some poison in his glass."

But Blanche, on whose heart the expulsion of her Prussian still weighed, ventured to defend Bismarck. Perhaps he wasn't such a bad sort. To every man his trade!

"You know," she added, "he adores women."

"What the hell has that got to do with us?" said Clarisse. "We don't want to cuddle him, eh?"

"There's always too many men of that sort!" declared Louise Violaine, gravely. "It's better to do without 'em than to mix one's self up with such monsters!"

And the discussion continued, and they stripped Bismarck, and, in her Bonapartist zeal, each of them gave him a sounding kick, whilst Tatan Néné kept saying,—

"Bismarck! Why they've simply driven me crazy with the chap! Oh, I hate him! *I* didn't know that there Bismarck! One can't know everybody."

"Never mind," said Léa de Horn, by way of conclusion, "that Bismarck will give us a jolly good thrashing."

But she could not continue. The ladies were all down on her at once. Eh, what? A thrashing? It was Bismarck they were going to escort home, with blows from the butt-ends of their muskets. What was this bad Frenchwoman going to say next!

"Hush," whispered Rose, for so much noise hurt her.

The cold influence of the corpse once more overcame them,

and they all paused together. They were embarrassed; the dead woman was before them again, a dull thread of coming ill possessed them. On the boulevard the cry was passing, hoarse and wild,—

"*À Berlin ! À Berlin! À Berlin!*"

Presently, when they were making up their minds to go, a voice was heard calling from the passage,—

"Rose! Rose!"

Gaga opened the door in astonishment, and disappeared for a moment. When she returned,—

"My dear," said she, "it's Fauchery. He's out there at the end of the corridor. He won't come any further, and he's beside himself because you still stay near that body."

Mignon had at last succeeded in urging the journalist upstairs. Lucy, who was still at the window, leant out, and caught sight of the gentlemen out on the pavement. They were looking up, making energetic signals to her. Mignon was shaking his fists in exasperation, and Steiner, Fontan, Bordenave, and the rest were stretching out their arms with looks of anxious reproach, whilst Daguenet simply stood smoking a cigar, with his hands behind his back, so as not to compromise himself.

"It's true, dear," said Lucy, leaving the window open, "I promised to make you come down. They're all calling us now."

Rose slowly and painfully left the chest.

"I'm coming down, I'm coming down," she whispered. "It's very certain she no longer needs me. They're going to send in a Sister of Mercy."

And she turned round searching for her hat and shawl. Mechanically she filled a basin of water on the toilet-table, and whilst washing her hands and face, continued,—

"I don't know! It's been a great blow to me. We used scarcely to be nice to one another. Ah, well! you see I'm quite silly over it now. Oh! I've got all sorts of strange ideas

—I want to die myself—I feel the end of the world's coming. Yes, I need air."

The corpse was beginning to poison the atmosphere of the room. And after long heedlessness there ensued a panic.

"Let's be off, let's be off, my little pets!" Gaga kept saying. "It isn't wholesome here."

They went briskly out, casting a last glance at the bed as they passed it. But whilst Lucy, Blanche, and Caroline still remained behind, Rose gave a final look round, for she wanted to leave the room in order. She drew a curtain across the window, and then it occurred to her that the lamp was not the proper thing, and that a taper should take its place. So she lit one of the copper candelabra on the chimney-piece and placed it on the night-table beside the corpse. A brilliant light suddenly illumined the dead woman's face. The women were horror-struck. They shuddered and escaped.

"Ah, she's changed, she's changed!" murmured Rose Mignon, who was the last to remain.

She went away; she shut the door. Nana was left alone, with upturned face in the light cast by the candle. She was fruit of the charnel-house, a heap of matter and blood, a shovelful of corrupted flesh thrown down on the pillow. The pustules had invaded the whole of the face, so that each touched its neighbor. Fading and sunken, they had assumed the grayish hue of mud, and on that formless pulp, where the features had ceased to be traceable, they already resembled some decaying damp from the grave. One eye, the left eye, had completely foundered among bubbling purulence, and the other, which remained half open, looked like a deep black ruinous hole. The nose was still suppurating. Quite a reddish crust was peeling from one of the cheeks, and invading the mouth, which it distorted into a horrible grin. And over this loathsome and grotesque mask of death, the hair, the beautiful hair, still blazed like sunlight and flowed downwards in rippling gold. Venus was rotting.

It seemed as though the poison she had assimilated in the gutters, and on the carrion tolerated by the roadside, the leaven with which she had poisoned a whole people, had but now remounted to her face and turned it to corruption.

The room was empty. A great despairing breath came up from the boulevard, and swelled the curtain.

"*À Berlin! À Berlin! À Berlin!*"

THE END

HARPER'S MODERN CLASSICS

WITH INTRODUCTION BY

Austen, PRIDE AND PREJUDICE . . . . *Louis Kronenberger*
Bennett, THE OLD WIVES' TALE . . . . *J. B. Priestley*
Brontë, C., JANE EYRE . . . . *Alice Green Fredman*
Brontë, E., WUTHERING HEIGHTS . . . . *Bruce McCullough*
Butler, THE WAY OF ALL FLESH . . . . . *William York Tindall*
Conrad, THE NIGGER OF THE NARCISSUS . . . *Morton Dauwen Zabel*
Crane, THE RED BADGE OF COURAGE and OTHER STORIES *Daniel G. Hoffman*
Dostoevsky, CRIME AND PUNISHMENT . . . . *Avrahm Yarmolinsky*
Doyle, ADVENTURES OF SHERLOCK HOLMES . . . . *John Baker Opdycke*
Flaubert, MADAME BOVARY . . . . *Caroline Gordon*
Franklin, AUTOBIOGRAPHY OF BENJAMIN FRANKLIN . . *Verner W. Crane*
Garland, MAIN-TRAVELLED ROADS . . . . . *B. R. McElderry, Jr.*
Hardy, FAR FROM THE MADDING CROWD . . . . . . *W. T. Brewster*
Hardy, JUDE THE OBSCURE . . . . *Carl J. Weber*
Hardy, THE MAYOR OF CASTERBRIDGE . . . . *J. F. A. Pyre*
Hardy, THE RETURN OF THE NATIVE . . . . *Warner Taylor*
Hardy, TESS OF THE D'URBERVILLES . . . . . *Albert J. Guérard*
Hawthorne, THE SCARLET LETTER . . . . *Newton Arvin*
Hudson, GREEN MANSIONS . . . . *Louise Bogan*
Huxley, ANTIC HAY and THE GIOCONDA SMILE . . . *Charles J. Rolo*
Huxley, BRAVE NEW WORLD . . . . *Charles J. Rolo*
Huxley, POINT COUNTER POINT . . . . *Harold H. Watts*
James, THE AMBASSADORS . . . . *John C. Gerber*
James, WASHINGTON SQUARE and DAISY MILLER . . . . *Oscar Cargill*
Lawrence, SONS AND LOVERS . . . . *Mark Schorer*
Melville, MOBY DICK . . . . *Clifton Fadiman*
Millay, SECOND APRIL and THE BUCK IN THE SNOW . *William Rose Benét*
Paine, THE BOYS' LIFE OF MARK TWAIN . . . . . *Walter Barnes*
Pyle, MEN OF IRON . . . . *Eleanor Tourison*
Robinson, THE MIND IN THE MAKING . . . . *Stuart Chase*
Rölvaag, GIANTS IN THE EARTH . . . . *V. L. Parrington*
Sinclair, THE JUNGLE . . . . *John Fischer*
Steinbeck, THE GRAPES OF WRATH . . . . *Charles Poore*
Swift, GULLIVER'S TRAVELS . . . . *George Sherburn*
Tarkington, SEVENTEEN . . . . *Mabel Dodge Holmes*
Tarkington, THE TURMOIL . . . . *Elizabeth W. Baker*
Thackeray, HENRY ESMOND . . . . *Lionel Stevenson*
Thoreau, WALDEN . . . . *Joseph Wood Krutch*
Turgenev, FATHERS AND SONS . . . . *Delmore Schwartz*
Twain, THE ADVENTURES OF HUCKLEBERRY FINN . . . *Dixon Wecter*
Twain, THE ADVENTURES OF TOM SAWYER . . . . . *Max J. Herzberg*
Twain, LIFE ON THE MISSISSIPPI . . . . *Dixon Wecter*
Twain, THE PRINCE AND THE PAUPER . . . . . . *Barry and Bruner*
Wescott, THE GRANDMOTHERS . . . . *Fred B. Millett*
White, ONE MAN'S MEAT . . . . *Morris Bishop*
Whitman, LEAVES OF GRASS . . . . *Oscar Cargill*
Wilder, THE IDES OF MARCH . . . . *Brooks Atkinson*
Wolfe, YOU CAN'T GO HOME AGAIN . . . . . . *Edward C. Aswell*
Wright, NATIVE SON . . . . *William A. Owens*
Zola, NANA . . . . *John C. Lapp*